SelectEditions

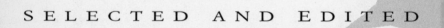

SELECTED AND EDITED

SelectEditions

BY READER'S DIGEST

VOLUME 6 2000
THE READER'S DIGEST ASSOCIATION, INC.
PLEASANTVILLE, NEW YORK

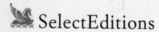 SelectEditions

Editor-in-Chief: Tanis H. Erdmann
Deputy Editor: Laura E. Kelly

Volume Editor: Mark Poirier

Editors: Dana Adkins, Maxine Bartow, Thomas Froncek,
Tatiana Ivanow, Eva C. Jaunzems, Marilyn J. Knowlton,
Paula Marchese, Joseph P. McGrath, James J. Menick,
Angela H. Plowden-Wardlaw, Amy M. Reilly

Art Director: Robin Arzt
Art Associate: Janine L. Megna

RIGHTS AND PERMISSIONS
Director: Alfredo G. Santana
Associate Director: Lisa Garrett-Smith
Assistant Manager: Carol Weiss Staudter

INTERNATIONAL EDITIONS
Executive Editor: Gary Q. Arpin
Senior Editor: Bonnie Grande

CONTENTS

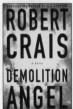

BEFORE I SAY GOOD-BYE

MARY HIGGINS CLARK

The truth—that's all Nell wants. Her peace of mind and her future are at stake. But every step she takes draws her deeper into a sinister game of smoke and mirrors.

Prologue

FIFTEEN-YEAR-OLD Nell MacDermott turned and began the swim back to shore. Her body tingled with youthful exhilaration as she looked about, taking in the glorious combination of the sun in the cloudless sky; the light, fresh breeze; the salty, foaming whitecaps breaking around her. She had been in Maui only an hour but already had decided that she liked it better than the Caribbean, which for the past several years was where her grandfather had taken the family for their annual post-Christmas vacation.

Actually, "family" seemed something of an exaggeration. This was the fourth year that their family had consisted of just her grandfather and herself. It had been five years ago when Cornelius MacDermott, legendary Congressman from New York, had been called off the floor of the House of Representatives to be given the news that his son and daughter-in-law, both anthropologists on an expedition in the Brazilian jungle, had died in the crash of their small chartered plane.

He immediately had rushed to New York to pick up Nell at school. It was news that she had to hear from him. He arrived to find his granddaughter in the nurse's office, weeping.

"When we were coming in from recess this morning, I suddenly felt that Dad and Mommy were with me and that they had come to say good-bye," she told him as he held her. "I didn't actually see them, but I felt Mom kiss me, and then Dad ran his fingers through my hair."

Later that day Nell and the housekeeper who took care of her when her parents were away had moved into the brownstone on East Seventy-ninth Street, the place where her grandfather had been born and where her father had been raised.

Nell flashed briefly on these memories as she began her swim back to shore and to her grandfather, who was sitting in a beach chair under an umbrella, having reluctantly acquiesced to her plea for one quick swim before they unpacked.

"Don't go out too far," he had cautioned as he opened his book. "It's six o'clock, and the lifeguard is leaving."

Even from a good distance out, Nell could see that he was still absorbed in his reading. She knew, though, that it wouldn't last much longer; he'd soon realize he was hungry. Okay, she thought as she picked up her stroke, let's make waves.

Suddenly Nell felt disoriented, as if she were turned around. *What was happening?* The shore disappeared as she felt herself being yanked from side to side, then pulled under. Stunned, she opened her mouth to call for help but immediately found herself swallowing salty water and gasping for breath.

Riptide! She had overheard two bellmen talking about it. There'd been a riptide on the other side of the island, and two guys had drowned because they fought against the pull instead of letting themselves get carried beyond it.

Still, Nell's arms flailed. It was impossible not to resist as she felt herself being pulled under the churning waves, down, down, and away from shore. I can't let myself get carried out! she thought in a flash of panic. I can't! If I go out, I'll never get back in. She managed to orient herself long enough to glimpse the candy-striped umbrella.

"Help me!" she said feebly, her effort to scream ending when the salty water filled her mouth, gagging her. In desperation she flipped onto her back and let her arms go limp. Moments later she was struggling again, resisting the horrifying feeling of her body being rushed out away from any hope of help.

I don't want to die! she kept saying to herself. I don't want to die! "Help me!" she said again, then began to sob.

And then, just as suddenly as it had begun, it was over. The invisible foamy chains abruptly released her. She had been tossed beyond the riptide.

Don't get back into it, she told herself. Swim around it.

But she was too tired. She was too far out. She looked at the distant shore. She would never make it. The water felt warm, like a blanket. She was getting sleepy.

Swim, Nell. You can make it!

It was her mother's voice, imploring her to fight.

Nell, get moving!

The urgent command from her father stung her senses. With blind obedience Nell swam straight out, then began to make a wide circle around the area of the riptide. Every breath was a sob, every movement an impossible struggle, but she persevered.

Agonizing minutes later, nearing exhaustion, she managed to dive into a swelling wave that grabbed her and rushed her toward shore, tossing her onto the hard, wet sand.

Firm hands lifted her to her feet. "I was just coming to call you in," Cornelius MacDermott said sharply. "No more swimming today, young lady. They're putting up the red flag. They say there are riptides nearby."

Trembling violently, Nell only nodded.

His face creased with concern, MacDermott pulled off his terry-cloth robe and wrapped it around her. "You're chilled, Nell. You shouldn't have stayed in so long."

"Thank you, Grandpa. I'm fine." Nell knew better than to tell her beloved no-nonsense grandfather what had happened, and she especially did not want him to know that once again she had had one of those experiences of being in communication with her parents, experiences that this most pragmatic of men brusquely dismissed as youthful fantasy.

One

NELL set off at a brisk pace on the walk from her apartment on Park Avenue and Seventy-third Street to her grandfather's office on Seventy-second and York. From the curt summons she had received, she knew that the situation with Bob Gorman must have come to a head. She was not looking forward to the meeting.

Deep in thought, she was oblivious to the admiring glances that occasionally came her way. A tall woman, with the slim, strong body of an athlete, she had short chestnut-colored hair that was now forming into humidity-caused ringlets, midnight-blue eyes, and a generous mouth. While growing up, and frequently attending public events with her grandfather, Nell's rueful observation was that when the media described her, the word used was usually "attractive."

"To me attractive is like having a guy say, 'She's not much to look at, but what a personality!' It's the kiss of death. Just once I want to be described as 'stunning,' " she had complained.

Typically, her grandfather's comment had been, "For God's sake don't be so silly. Be grateful you've got a head on your shoulders and know how to use it."

AT EIGHTY-TWO Cornelius MacDermott had lost little of the vigor that had made him one of the nation's most prominent Congressmen. Elected at thirty to represent the midtown Manhattan district where he had been raised, he stayed in that spot for fifty years, resisting all arguments to run for the Senate. On his eightieth birthday he had chosen not to run again.

Retirement for Mac meant opening a consulting office and making sure that New York City and State stayed in his party's political fold. An endorsement from him was a virtual laying on of hands for neophyte campaigners. Recognized everywhere, he could not walk down the street without being showered with affectionate and respectful greetings.

Occasionally he grumbled to Nell, "Can't set foot outside my door without making sure I'm camera-ready."

To which she replied, "You'd have a heart attack if people ignored you, and you know it."

When she reached his office today, Nell waved to the receptionist and walked back to her grandfather's suite. "The mood?" she asked Liz Hanley, his longtime secretary.

Liz, a handsome sixty-year-old with dark brown hair and a no-nonsense expression, raised her eyes to heaven.

"Oh, boy, that bad," Nell said, sighing. She tapped on the door of the private office as she let herself in. "Top of the day, Congressman."

"You're late, Nell," Cornelius MacDermott barked as he spun his desk chair around to face her.

"Not according to my watch. Three on the dot."

"I thought I told you to get here *by* three."

"I had a column to turn in. Now, how about showing me the winning smile that melts the voters' hearts?"

"Today I haven't got one. Sit down." MacDermott indicated the couch beneath the corner window that offered panoramic views of his longtime congressional district. Nell called it his fiefdom.

Settled on the couch, she looked at him anxiously. There was an unfamiliar weariness clouding his blue eyes. Even his famous shock of white hair appeared thinner. As she watched, he shrugged his shoulders as though trying to dislodge an invisible burden. With sinking heart Nell thought for the first time in her memory that her grandfather looked his age.

"Nell, we've got a crisis, and you've got to solve it. After being nominated for a second term, that weasel Bob Gorman's been offered a sweetheart deal to head up a new Internet company. He'll serve out his term till the election but says he can't live on a Congressman's salary."

She waited. Last week's rumors about Gorman's not running for a second term had obviously been confirmed.

"Nell, there's only one person who can keep that seat in the party." MacDermott frowned. "You should have done it two years ago when I retired, and you know it." He paused. "It's in your blood. You wanted to do it from the start, but Adam talked you out of it. Don't let that happen again."

"Mac, please don't start on Adam."

"I'm not starting on anyone, Nell. I'm telling you that I know you, and you're a political animal. I've been grooming you for my job since you were a teenager. I wasn't thrilled when you married Adam Cauliff, but don't forget, I helped him to get his start in New York at a fine architectural firm." Mac's lips tightened. "It didn't make me look good when, after less than three years, Adam walked out on them, taking their chief assistant, and opened his own operation. All right, maybe that's good business. But from the outset Adam knew my plans for you—and your plans for yourself. What made him change his mind?"

"Mac, I enjoy being a columnist. I get mighty good feedback."

"You write a darn good column. I grant you that. But it's not enough for you, and you know it."

"Look, my reluctance now isn't that Adam asked me to give up the idea of running. We both want children. You know that. He suggested that I wait until after that happens. In ten years I'll only be forty-two. That would be a good age to start elective office."

"Nell, in ten years the parade will have passed you by. Events move too fast to wait. Admit it. You're aching to throw your hat in the ring." Mac leaned forward. "Seize the moment. If you don't, you'll regret it. When Gorman confirms that he isn't running, there'll be a scramble for the nomination. I want the committee to consider candidates behind you from the get-go."

"When is the get-go?" she asked cautiously.

"At the annual dinner, on the thirtieth. You and Adam will be there. Gorman will get teary-eyed and say that while this was a difficult decision to make, something has made it much easier. Then he's going to dry his eyes, point to you, and bellow that *you,* Cornelia MacDermott Cauliff, are going to run for the seat. It will be Cornelia replacing Cornelius. The wave of the third millennium." Mac smiled broadly. "Nell, it'll bring the house down."

With a pang of regret Nell remembered that two years ago, when Bob Gorman ran for Mac's seat, she had had a wild sense of impatience, a compulsion to be there, a need to see herself in his place. Mac was right. She was a political animal. If she didn't get into the arena now, it *could* be too late.

"What's Adam's problem, Nell? He didn't used to pull this stuff on you."

"I know."

"Is anything wrong between you two?"

"No." She managed a dismissive smile. How long had it been going on? she wondered. At what point had Adam become distracted, even remote? At first her concerned questions had been brushed off lightly. Now she detected an edge of anger. Only recently she had told him point-blank that if there was a serious problem with their relationship, then she deserved to hear about it.

"Where *is* Adam?" her grandfather asked.

"He's in Philadelphia, speaking at a seminar for architects and interior designers. He'll be back tomorrow."

"I want him at the dinner, standing by your side, applauding your decision. Okay?"

"I don't know how much applauding he'll do," she said.

When she and Adam were first married, he'd been enthusiastic over the idea that she would continue to act as Mac's confidential assistant. But that had changed when her grandfather announced his retirement.

"Nell, we now have a chance for a life that doesn't revolve around the almighty Cornelius MacDermott," Adam had said. "I'm sick of your being at his beck and call. If you campaign for his seat, he won't give you the chance to breathe, unless he's exhaling for you." His voice was pleading. "You've never known anything except politics. The *Journal* wants you to do a regular column, and you might like the freedom. Sit it out, Nell."

Now, as she considered her grandfather's arguments, Nell admitted something to herself: Commenting on the political scene wasn't enough. She wanted to be in on the action.

Finally she said, "Mac, I'm going to put my cards on the table. Adam is my husband, and I love him. You, on the other hand, have never even liked him."

"That isn't true."

"Then let's put it another way. Ever since Adam opened his own firm, you've had it in for him. If I run for this office, you and I will be spending a lot more time together. If that's going to work, you've got to promise me that you'll treat Adam the way you'd want to be treated if the positions were reversed."

"And if I embrace him to my bosom, then you'll run?"

When she left an hour later, Nell had given her word.

IT WAS the third time Jed Kaplan had passed the ground-floor architectural offices of Cauliff and Associates on Twenty-seventh Street, off Seventh Avenue. The window of the converted brownstone contained a display that arrested him: the model of a forty-story apartment-office-shopping complex dominated by a gold-domed tower. The starkly postmodern building with its white limestone façade was a striking contrast to the warmth of the brick tower, which radiated light as the dome slowly revolved.

Jed jammed his hands in the pockets of his jeans as he slouched forward, his face pressed almost against the window. To a casual observer there was nothing unusual about his appearance. He was of average height, thin, with short sandy hair.

His appearance was deceptive, however; under his faded sweatshirt Jed's body was hard and muscular. His complexion had coarsened from long exposure to sun and wind. And eye contact caused most people to experience an instinctively uneasy reaction.

Thirty-eight years old, Jed had spent most of his life as a loner and drifter. After five years in Australia he had returned home for one of his infrequent visits to his widowed mother only to learn that she had sold the small parcel of Manhattan property that had been in the family for four generations, a building that had housed a once thriving fur business, with rental apartments above the store. They had quarreled violently about it.

"What'd you expect me to do?" his mother had pleaded. "Building falling apart; taxes going up; tenants moving out. The fur business is going down the toilet. It isn't good politics to wear fur anymore."

"Pop intended for me to have that property," Jed had shouted. "You had no right to sell it!"

"Pop also wanted you to be a good son to me; he wanted you to settle down, to get married, have a decent job. But you didn't even come when I wrote that he was dying." She'd begun to weep. "Adam Cauliff paid me a fair price. For whatever time I have left, I can sleep at night without worrying about bills."

With increasing bitterness Jed observed the model of the complex. He sneered at the legend: A BEACON OF BEAUTY, SETTING THE TONE FOR THE MOST EXCITING RESIDENTIAL DISTRICT IN MANHATTAN.

The tower was going to be erected on the land his mother had sold to Adam Cauliff. That land was worth a fortune, he thought. And Cauliff had talked her into believing that you could never do anything to develop it, because it was next to that old wreck—the landmark Vandermeer mansion. Then the mansion had burned, and a big-shot real estate guy, Peter Lang, snapped up that property and, by putting it together with the Kaplans', created this prime development site.

Jed had heard that some homeless woman was squatting in the Vandermeer and lit a fire to keep warm. Why didn't she burn down the stinking house *before* Cauliff got his hands on my property? Jed raged. Anger, profound and bitter, rose in his throat. I'll get Cauliff, he vowed. I swear to God, I'll get him. If we still had owned that property after they stopped calling that old dump a landmark, we'd have gotten millions for it.

Abruptly he turned away from the window. He walked to Seventh Avenue, then headed south. At seven o'clock he was standing at the marina of the World Financial Center. With envious eyes he viewed the sleek yachts that bobbed up and down in the rising tide.

A new forty-foot cabin cruiser was the object of his attention. The name written across the stern was *Cornelia II*.

Cauliff's boat, Jed thought.

Since his return to New York, Jed had been learning everything he could about Adam Cauliff, and he had been at this spot many times with always the same thought in mind: What am I going to do about that jerk and his precious boat?

AFTER the final session of his architectural seminar Adam Cauliff had dinner with two of his colleagues, then checked out of the hotel and drove back to New York.

At dinner Ward Battle had confirmed the rumor that Walters and Arsdale, the architectural firm Adam had worked for until he opened his own company, was being investigated for bid rigging and for accepting bribes from contractors.

"From what I hear, that's only the tip of the iceberg, Adam. As a former employee, you'll probably be asked a lot of questions. Just thought you should know. Maybe MacDermott can make sure they don't put much on you."

Mac help out? Adam thought scornfully. Forget it. If he believed I was involved in any funny-money deals, he'd boil the pitch for them to throw on me.

"I don't have anything to worry about," he had told Battle. "I was just one of the little guys there."

Adam had originally planned to stay over in Philadelphia. Nell did not expect him home until tomorrow. When he exited the Lincoln Tunnel, he hesitated for a moment, then turned uptown. Ten minutes later he pulled into the garage in his apartment building.

Shortly after they met, Cornelius MacDermott had laughingly observed, "Adam, you're a prime example of the difference between appearance and reality. You're from a one-horse town in North Dakota, but you look and sound like a preppy from Yale. How do you manage it?"

"Maybe you think I should wear overalls and carry a rake?" he had said defensively.

"Don't be so touchy," Mac had snapped. "I was complimenting you."

Mac would have liked Nell to end up with a preppy from Yale, Adam thought.

It was nearly two o'clock when, with careful, quiet steps, he entered the apartment and turned on the small foyer light. He opened the oak armoire, reached for the Chivas Regal, and poured a generous amount into a glass. He sat on the living-room couch, slowly sipping the Scotch, a man who, to the casual observer, might have seemed to be totally at ease, resting after a long day.

And it was a fact that people did observe Adam. He appeared taller than his six feet. Rigorous exercise had kept his body trim and disciplined. Light hazel eyes and a mouth that curved easily into a smile were the dominant features in his lean face. Darts of gray sprinkled through his dark brown hair.

Finally he went to the guest room to change, then methodically laid out his clothes for the morning. He tiptoed into the bedroom and slipped into bed. Nell's even breathing told him that he had succeeded in not waking her.

Fatigue hit him almost immediately, and he felt his eyes closing.

Friday, June 9
Two

LISA Ryan was awake well before the alarm was set to go off at five a.m. Jimmy had had another restless night, tossing and muttering in his sleep. Three or four times she had reached over and put a soothing hand on his back, hoping to quiet him. Finally he had fallen into a heavy sleep, and now she'd have to shake him awake.

I've hardly slept, Lisa thought, and today's my long day at work.

A manicurist, she was booked straight through until five thirty.

Her life didn't used to be this exhausting. Everything had started to go wrong when Jimmy lost his job. Unfortunately, the boss had overheard him commenting to a co-worker that someone was on the take: The concrete they were pouring was not nearly the quality listed in the specifications. After that, everywhere he applied, he heard the same story: "Sorry, we don't need you."

The realization that it had been naïve and stupid ever to have made the comment brought about the beginning of change in him. Lisa was sure he had been on the verge of a nervous breakdown; then the call came that his application to Cauliff and Associates had been passed on to the Sam Krause Construction Company. Shortly thereafter Jimmy had been hired, but the emotional turnaround Lisa expected didn't come about. And Jimmy had become furious when she suggested that he go for help.

In the last months Lisa had begun to feel infinitely older than her thirty-three years. The man sleeping next to her no longer seemed to be the man who as her childhood sweetheart had joked that he'd climbed out of his playpen to ask her for their first date. One minute Jimmy would fly off the handle at her and the children, then the next he'd have tears in his eyes as he apologized.

He'd begun having two or three Scotches every evening—and he didn't handle them well. Jimmy was home every night now, having even lost interest in going to the occasional baseball game with his buddies. Lisa had tried to make him realize that they were getting caught up with the credit-card charges. It didn't seem to make a difference. In fact, nothing seemed to matter to him anymore.

They still lived in the small Cape Cod in Queens that had been planned as their starter home when they married thirteen years ago. But three children in six years had meant buying bunk beds rather than a larger home. Lisa used to joke about it, but she didn't anymore—she knew it got under Jimmy's skin.

As the alarm finally rang, she turned it off with a sigh. "Jimmy." She shook his shoulder. "Jimmy."

Finally she was able to rouse him. Listlessly he muttered,

"Thanks, honey," and disappeared into the bathroom. Lisa got out of bed and went to the window. It was going to be a beautiful day. She twisted her light brown hair into a knot, pinned it up, and reached for her robe.

Jimmy came down to the kitchen ten minutes later. "Thought I'd join you for a cup of coffee," Lisa said lightly.

Jimmy was a big man, with hair that once had been fiery red and was now a copper brown. Working outdoors had given him a ruddy complexion. "That would be nice, Lissy," he said. He stood at the table as he gulped the coffee. "Don't wait dinner. The big shots are having one of those five-o'clock meetings on Cauliff's fancy boat. Maybe he's going to fire me and wants to do it in style."

"Why would he fire you?" Lisa asked.

"I'm kidding. But maybe he'd be doing me a favor. How's the painted-nail business? Can you support all of us?"

Lisa went over to her husband and put her arms around his neck. "I think you're going to feel a lot better when you let me know what's eating at you."

"Keep thinking that." Jimmy Ryan's powerful arms pulled his wife close. "I love you, Lissy. Always remember that."

"I've never forgotten it."

He turned from her and moved to the door. As it closed behind him, Lisa thought she heard him whisper, "I'm sorry."

THAT morning Nell decided to make a special breakfast for Adam, then instantly became irritated at the thought that she was using food to try to cajole him into going along with a career choice she had every right to make for herself. That realization did not keep her from going ahead with her preparations, however.

As she got out of bed, she could hear Adam in the shower. Nell had awakened when he came into the apartment last night but had decided not to let him know. Yes, she knew they needed to talk, but two o'clock in the morning did not seem the time.

She would have to bring it up at breakfast this morning, though. Mac had phoned last night to remind her that they were expected at the birthday dinner he was having for his sister, Nell's great-aunt Gert, at the Four Seasons restaurant; Adam would never forgive her if he got the word from Mac about her decision to run.

Wouldn't it be nice if Adam would just understand how very much I want to try to win Mac's old congressional seat, or at least be a part of the excitement this election year? Nell thought as she took a carton of eggs from the refrigerator. Wouldn't it be terrific if I didn't have to keep walking a tightrope between the only two men in the world who are important to me? Wouldn't it be nice if Adam didn't view my desire to pursue a career in politics as a threat to our relationship?

He used to understand, Nell thought as she poured fresh-squeezed orange juice. He used to say that he was looking forward to having a good seat in the visitors gallery on Capitol Hill.

She tried not to be bothered by Adam's preoccupied air as he hurried into the kitchen, slid onto the bench at the breakfast bar, and reached for *The Wall Street Journal,* all with only a nod of acknowledgment.

"Thanks, Nell, but I'm honestly not hungry," he said when she offered him the omelet she had prepared. So much for the extra effort, she thought.

She sat across from him and considered what tack she should take. From the closed expression on his face she could tell this wasn't the right moment to begin any discussion. And that's just too bad, she thought, feeling her irritation begin to mount.

She reached for her own coffee and the *Times.* A lead article caught her eye. "Adam, have you seen this? The district attorney may press bid-rigging charges against Walters and Arsdale."

"I know that," he said matter-of-factly.

"You worked with them for nearly three years," she said, shocked. "Will you be questioned?"

"Probably." He smirked. "Tell Mac he has nothing to worry about. The family honor will remain unstained."

"Adam, that's not what I meant!"

"Come on, Nell, I can read you like a book. You're trying to find a way to tell me that the old man has talked you into running for office. When he opens his newspaper this morning, the first thing he'll do is call you and say that having my name associated with this might hurt your chances. I'm right, aren't I?"

"You're right about my wanting to run for office, but the possibility of your hurting my chances certainly never entered my mind," Nell said evenly. "I know you well enough to know that you're not dishonest."

"There are varying degrees of honesty in the construction business, Nell," Adam said. "Fortunately for you, I stick to the highest standards, which is one of the many reasons I left Walters and Arsdale. Do you think that will satisfy Mac the Icon?"

Nell stood up, her irritation flashing. "Adam, look, I can understand why you're upset, but don't take it out on me. I am going to go for Mac's seat, since Bob Gorman is giving it up, and I think it might be nice if you supported me."

Adam shook his head. "Nell, I've been honest with you. Since we've been married, I've seen that politics is an all-absorbing way to spend a life. It can be tough on a marriage."

"I have news for you, Adam. It's a lot worse for a marriage if one spouse tries to keep the other from doing something he or she wants. All along I've tried to help you in your career, so please help me in mine—or at least don't make it so hard for me."

"So that's that, I guess." He shoved his chair back and stood. "Don't worry about dinner tonight. We've got a meeting on the boat; afterward I'll get something downtown."

"Adam, it's Gert's seventy-fifth birthday. She'll be so disappointed if you're not there."

He faced her. "Forgive me, but I do not want to spend this evening with Mac. Not even for Gert—whom I like very much."

"Adam, please. Surely you can come after the meeting. It's okay if you're late. Just make an appearance."

"Make an appearance? Campaign language is starting already. Sorry, Nell." In quick strides he headed for the foyer.

"Then, damn it, maybe you should skip coming home at all."

Adam stopped and turned. "I hope you don't mean that."
They stared at each other in silence. Then he was gone.

SAM Krause's newest girlfriend was not happy when he called Friday morning to cancel their date that evening.

"We could meet at Harry's Bar when you finish," she said.

"Look, this is business," he said brusquely. "We've got a lot of stuff to go over. I'll call you Saturday."

He hung up without giving her a chance to say anything more. He was seated in his office at Third Avenue and Fortieth Street, a large, airy room with walls covered by artists' renderings of skyscrapers built by the Sam Krause Construction Company.

It was only ten o'clock, and his already edgy mood had been exacerbated by a call from the district attorney's office requesting a meeting with him.

He got up and walked to the window, where he stood staring sullenly at the street below. He watched a car skillfully weave through the choking traffic and then smiled grimly as the car became boxed in behind a truck blocking two lanes.

The smile vanished, though, as Sam realized that in a way he was like that car. He had sidestepped a number of obstacles to get to this point in his life, and now a major hurdle was threatening to block his path, threatening to block it completely. For the first time since he was a teenager, he found himself suddenly vulnerable for prosecution.

He was a fifty-year-old large-boned man of average height, with weathered skin and thinning hair. What made him attractive to women was his air of absolute self-confidence, along with the cynical intelligence reflected in his slate-gray eyes. Some people respected him. Many more were afraid of him. A few liked him. For all of them Sam felt amused contempt.

The phone rang, followed by a buzz on the intercom from his secretary. "Mr. Lang," she announced.

Sam grimaced. Lang Enterprises was the third factor in the Vandermeer Tower venture. His feelings about Peter Lang ranged from envy—over the fact that he was the product of family wealth—to grudging admiration of his seeming genius at optioning apparently worthless properties that turned out to be gold mines.

He crossed to his desk and picked up the receiver. "Yeah, Peter? Thought you'd be on the golf course."

Peter was in fact calling from his father's waterfront estate in Southampton, which he had been given when his parents decided to divide their time between Saint John in the Caribbean and Martha's Vineyard. "Just wanted to make sure the meeting is still on."

"It is." Sam replaced the receiver without saying good-bye.

NELL'S newspaper column, called All Around the Town, ran three times a week in the New York *Journal*. It contained a potpourri of comments on what was going on in the city, from the arts to politics, from celebrity events to human-interest features.

This column is another thing I'll have to give up when I run for office, Nell thought as she walked into the study.

Another thing? What am I thinking about? she asked herself. After Adam left that morning, she had gone through her usual routine with anger-fueled energy, tidying the kitchen, making the bed. A quick general check of the apartment revealed Adam's navy jacket and his briefcase on the bed in the guest room.

He was too busy slamming out of here this morning to remember them, Nell thought. He probably was stopping at a job site; he just had on that light zip-up jacket. Well, let him come back for them. I'm not playing errand girl today. She hung the jacket in the closet and carried the briefcase to the small bedroom that had become their study.

But an hour later, sitting at her desk, it was impossible to ignore the fact that she had done nothing to make this situation easier. Hadn't she as much as told Adam not to come home tonight?

Suppose he takes me up on that? she asked herself, then refused to consider the possibility. We may be having a serious problem, but it has nothing to do with the way we feel about each other.

He must be at the office by now, she decided. She reached for the phone, then quickly pulled back. No. I gave in to him two years ago when he asked me not to run for Mac's seat, and I've regretted it every day since. Besides, it's not fair: I'd never ask Adam to forgo any part of his career as an architect.

Nell resolutely began to go through the notes she had put together for the column this morning, but then, unable to concentrate, she put them down. Her thoughts went back to last night.

When Adam slipped into bed, he had fallen asleep almost immediately. Hearing his steady breathing, she had moved closer, and in his sleep he had thrown his arm around her and murmured her name.

Nell thought back to the first time they met, and her immediate impression of him as the most attractive man she had ever met. It was his smile—that slow, sweet smile.

Just then the phone rang. Adam, she thought as she grabbed the receiver.

It was her grandfather. "Nell, I just saw the paper! I hope to God Adam hasn't got anything to worry about with this investigation into Walters and Arsdale. He was there during the time they are looking into, so if there was any hanky-panky going on, he must have known. He needs to come clean with us; I don't want him hurting your chances of winning this election."

Nell took a deep breath. She loved her grandfather dearly, but there were times when he made her want to scream. "Mac, Adam left Walters and Arsdale precisely because he didn't like some of the things he saw going on there. And by the way, didn't I tell you yesterday to please lay off him?"

"Sorry."

"You don't sound sorry."

Mac ignored her comment. "See you tonight. And speaking of which, I called Gert to wish her a happy birthday, and I've got to tell you, the woman is nuts. She's spending the day at some damn channeling event. She asked me if she could bring along a couple of those mediums she hangs out with, but I told her to forget it."

"But Mac, it *is* her birthday," Nell protested.

"That may be, but at my age I don't want any of those nuts studying me to see if my aura is fading. I've got to go. See you tonight, Nell."

Nell replaced the receiver in its cradle and leaned back in her chair. She agreed with her grandfather that Gert was a true eccentric. But, she reminded herself, it was precisely because of Gert's belief in the paranormal that she understood what I meant when I said that I felt that Mom and Dad had been there with me, both on the day they died and when I was caught in the riptide in Hawaii. Gert understands because she gets those feelings too.

Of course, for Gert they are more than "feelings," Nell thought with a smile. She is actively involved in psychic research and has been for a long time. But she's made it to her seventy-fifth birthday, and the least Adam should do is put in an appearance tonight. Gert thinks the sun rises and sets on him, Nell reflected. His refusal will disappoint her terribly.

That final realization erased any thought Nell might have had of calling Adam to try to put things right between them.

DAN Minor had inherited his father's height and rangy shoulders, but not his face. The sharply sophisticated and handsome features of Preston Minor had been softened and warmed by their genetic blending with the gentle beauty of Kathryn Quinn. The mouth and jawline were more relaxed. And Quinn genes gave Dan the full head of somewhat unruly sandy hair.

A colleague had observed that even in khakis, sneakers, and a T-shirt, Dan Minor looked like a doctor. Dan had a way of greeting people with genuine interest in his expression—interest that was followed by a second searching glance, as if to make sure that everything was all right with them. Perhaps it was fated that he would grow up to be a doctor; certainly Dan had always known he wanted to be a pediatric surgeon. It was a choice based on very personal reasons.

Raised in Chevy Chase, Maryland, by his maternal grandparents, as a young boy, he had learned to treat his infrequent visits from his father with increasing lack of interest. Dan hadn't laid eyes on his mother since he was six, although a snapshot of her—smiling, hair windblown, her arms wrapped around him—was kept in a hidden compartment in his wallet. The photo, taken on his second birthday, was his only tangible remembrance of her.

Dan had graduated from Johns Hopkins and then done his residency at St. Gregory's Hospital in Manhattan, so when they asked him to come back to head up their new burn unit, he accepted. He had, by then, established a solid reputation at a Washington hospital as a surgeon, specializing in burn victims. By nature somewhat restless, and with the sobering knowledge that a new millennium had begun, he decided it was time for a change in his life. He was now thirty-six, and his elderly grandparents were moving to a retirement community in Florida. His father remarried about this time, but Dan skipped his father's fourth wedding, just as he had skipped his third.

The new assignment began on March 1. In February he bought a condo in the SoHo district of lower Manhattan. Dan enjoyed the farewell dinners his friends threw for him, including the ones with the three or four women he had dated over the years. One of his friends presented him with a handsome new wallet, and when he switched his license and credit cards and money to it, he hesitated, then deliberately removed the old picture. He knew it was time to put all it represented behind him. An hour later he changed his mind and retrieved it.

His first evening in Manhattan, Dan set out to look for a place to have dinner. One of the things he had liked best about the SoHo area was that it was alive with restaurants. He found one he wanted to try, bought a paper, and settled at a table near the window.

Over a drink he began to study the front page, but then began to watch the people passing in the street. With a conscious effort he focused again on the article he had been reading. One of his millennium resolutions had been to try to stop his random search for his mother. There were just too many places to look, and the chances of ever finding her were so very dim.

But one of the reasons he had moved to New York was his hope of finding her. It was the last place she was spotted.

Hours later, as he lay in bed listening to the traffic on the street below, Dan decided to give it one last shot. If by the end of June he had found nothing, he would give up.

Adjusting to his new position took up much of his time. Then on June 9 he was delayed with an emergency operation at the hospital and had to wait until the next day to make what he swore would be one of his final attempts to find his mother. This time his destination was the desolate South Bronx. Without any real expectations he began showing her picture, asking the usual questions.

And then it happened. A shabbily dressed woman who looked to be in her fifties, her face careworn, suddenly smiled. "I think you're looking for my pal Quinny," she said.

FIFTY-TWO-YEAR-OLD Winifred Johnson never entered the lobby of the Park Avenue apartment building without feeling intimidated. She had worked with Adam Cauliff for three years, first at Walters and Arsdale, and then she had left with him last fall, when he started his own company. He had relied on her from the beginning.

A thin woman, almost frail in appearance, Winifred typically dressed in conservative business suits. Quiet to the point that people often forgot she was even around, she absorbed everything, noticed everything, and remembered everything. She had worked for Robert Walters and Len Arsdale from the time she graduated from secretarial school, but neither man ever seemed to notice the fact that she had come to know everything there was to know about the construction business. Adam Cauliff, however, had picked up on it immediately. He appreciated her; he understood her true worth.

Nell never appreciated him. Adam didn't need a wife with a famous grandfather who made so many demands that she didn't have time for her husband. Sometimes Adam would say, "Winifred, Nell's with the old man again. I don't want to eat alone. Let's grab a bite."

He deserved better. Sometimes Adam would tell her about

being a kid on a North Dakota farm and going to the library to get books with pictures of beautiful buildings. Other times he would encourage her to talk. Adam enjoyed her "insider" stories about the building world, tales from her earlier days with Walters and Arsdale.

"You mean that sanctimonious old bird was on the take when those bids went out?" he'd exclaim. And then he'd promise never, ever to say a word to anyone. She also remembered the night he had said accusingly, "Winifred, you can't fool me. There's someone in your life." And she had told him, yes, even giving the name. That was when she really began to trust him. She'd even confided that she was taking care of herself.

The uniformed clerk at the desk put down the intercom telephone. "Mrs. Cauliff is expecting you, Ms. Johnson."

Adam had asked her to pick up his briefcase and his navy jacket. Being Adam, he had been apologetic about the request. "The notes for the meeting are in my briefcase," he'd explained, "and I'll need the jacket if I change my mind and meet Nell at the Four Seasons." Winifred could sense from his tone that he and Nell must have had a serious misunderstanding. It only bolstered her certainty that their marriage was heading for the rocks.

As she rode up in the elevator, she thought about the meeting scheduled for Adam's boat. There would be just five of them. In addition to herself, the three associates in the Vandermeer Tower venture—Adam, Sam Krause, and Peter Lang—would be attending. The fifth was Jimmy Ryan, one of Sam's site foremen. Winifred wasn't sure why he'd been invited except that Jimmy had been pretty moody lately. Maybe they wanted to get to the heart of the problem.

She knew the others would be concerned about the story that broke in today's papers, although she didn't feel any concern herself. The worst thing that ever happens, even if they get the goods on you, is you pay a fine, she mused. You reach into your back pocket, and the problem goes away.

The elevator opened onto the apartment foyer, where Nell was waiting. Winifred saw the cordial smile on Nell's face fade. "Is something wrong?" Winifred asked.

Dear God, Nell thought with sudden alarm, why is this happening? But as she looked at Winifred, she could almost hear the knowledge filter through her being: *Winifred's journey on this plane of existence is completed.*

ADAM reached the boat fifteen minutes before the others were due to arrive. Entering the cabin, he saw that the caterer had left a selection of cheeses and crackers on the sideboard. The liquor cabinet would have been stocked at the same time.

He had found that the casual atmosphere of the boat, combined with the social tone that drinks gave a meeting, served to loosen tongues—those of his associates as well as potential clients.

Throughout the day he had been tempted to phone Nell but then finally had decided against it. He hated to quarrel with her almost as much as he had begun to hate the sight of her grandfather. Nell simply refused to acknowledge the fact that Mac wanted her to run for his former seat for only one reason: He intended to make her his puppet. All that pious mouthing about retiring at eighty was a lot of baloney. The truth was that his opponent might have staged an upset. Mac didn't want to retire; he just didn't want to go out a loser.

Of course, he didn't want to go out, period. So now he'd get Nell to win the seat—and the power—back for him.

"Hello. It's me."

Adam hurried out on deck to give Winifred a hand as she stepped down to the boat, his briefcase and jacket under her arm.

Something was obviously distressing her, though. He could tell by the way she moved. "What's wrong, Winifred?"

"You can look right through me, can't you, Adam?" Clutching his hand, she tried to smile. "I have to ask you, and you have to be completely honest," she said earnestly. "Did I do something to make Nell angry at me?"

"What do you mean?"

"She wasn't at all like herself when I stopped by. She acted as though she couldn't wait to get me out."

"You shouldn't take that personally. Nell and I had a disagreement this morning," Adam said quietly. "I would guess that's what's on her mind."

Winifred had not released his hand. "If you want to talk about it, I'm here for you."

Adam pulled free from her grasp. "I know you are, Winifred. Thank you. Oh, look, here's Jimmy."

Jimmy Ryan was obviously ill at ease. His work boots left dusty imprints on the cabin carpet as he silently followed Adam's suggestion to fix himself a drink. Winifred watched as he poured himself a heavy Scotch. He stood awkwardly in the cabin.

Sam Krause arrived ten minutes later, fuming at the traffic and at the incompetence of his driver. With a curt nod at Jimmy he poured straight gin into a glass.

"Lang's late as usual, I see," he snapped.

"I spoke to him just before I left the office," Adam told him. "He was on his way, so he should be along any minute."

A half hour later the phone rang. Peter Lang's voice was clearly strained. "I've been in an accident," he said. "One of those damn trailer trucks. Lucky I wasn't killed. The cops want me to go to the hospital and get checked out. You can either call off the meeting or go ahead without me."

Five minutes later *Cornelia II* sailed out of the harbor. The breeze had stiffened, and clouds were beginning to pass over the sun.

"I DON'T feel good," eight-year-old Ben Tucker complained as he stood at the railing of the tour boat.

"The water's getting choppy," his father acknowledged, "but we'll be onshore soon. Pay attention to the view. You won't get back to see New York again for a long time."

Ben's glasses were smudged, and he pulled them off to clean them. He actually had liked going to the Statue of Liberty and Ellis Island, but now he felt as though he was going to barf. This tub smelled of diesel fuel.

Longingly he gazed at the private yachts in New York harbor. He wished he were on one of them. Someday, when he made money, that was the first thing he'd do—buy a cabin cruiser.

Ben's eyes lingered on the really keen yacht way over there: *Cornelia II*. He was so farsighted that with his glasses off he could read the letters.

Suddenly his eyes widened. "No-o-o-o . . ."

He didn't know that he had spoken aloud. As he had been watching it, *Cornelia II* had exploded, suddenly becoming an immense fireball, sending shiny bits of debris shooting high into the air before falling all over the waterway that led from the Atlantic Ocean.

Before merciful shock had blunted the vision of bodies being blown to bits, Ben registered an impression that settled immediately in his subconscious, where it would stay to become the source of relentless nightmares.

AND I even told him not to come home, Nell reflected as she agonized over the terrible day that was ending. Adam had replied, "I hope you don't mean that," and I didn't answer him. I thought about calling him later, but I was too proud. Why didn't I call? All day that awful feeling was hanging over me, an awareness that something was terribly terribly wrong.

Winifred—when I saw her, I sensed she was going to die!

It was like the feeling I had about my mother and father, when suddenly I knew that they were with me. They were gone by then, but they came and said good-bye. Adam, please say good-bye to me. Let me have a chance to tell you how sorry I am.

"Nell, is there anything I can do?"

She was vaguely aware that Mac was talking to her, vaguely aware that it was after midnight. Gert's birthday dinner had gone ahead as planned, none of them aware of what had happened. Nell had made the lame excuse that Adam couldn't be there because of an important meeting, but the disappointment on Gert's face had built up in her a new head of steam against him.

By the time Nell arrived home at ten o'clock, she had decided that she would have to work things out with Adam that night, assuming, of course, that he didn't accept her challenge to not come home. She would listen to his objections, see what compromises they could make. Being a good politician was all about being able to negotiate. Maybe the same qualities were necessary in a good wife.

When Nell walked into the lobby of her building, however, NYPD detective George Brennan was waiting for her there. Instantly Nell had known that something was wrong. Inside the apartment Detective Brennan gently told her about the accident and, with an apology, asked her some questions. Witnesses had seen her husband get on his boat, he told her, followed by at least three people. Did she know their names?

Too stunned for reality to sink in, Nell had told him that she understood it was to be an associates' meeting and that Adam's assistant was also going to be there. She told him the names of the associates. As he left, both Mac and Gert arrived.

"We heard the news on the radio," Gert said. "I'll stay with you tonight. You shouldn't be alone."

Nell shook her head. "Thank you, Aunt Gert. But I need to be alone tonight," she said.

As Nell walked Mac to the door, he said gruffly, "You're smart not to have Gert stay. She'd be going on all night in that channel-babble nonsense of hers." He put a gentle hand on Nell's arm. "I'm more sorry than I can express. After what happened to your mother and father, you certainly don't deserve to lose Adam this way."

I especially don't deserve to lose him after a quarrel, Nell thought, feeling a surge of resentment rise in her. Mac, you were the root of the problem, she told herself. Your demands on me—they do sometimes get to be too much. Adam was wrong about not wanting me to run for office, but he was right about that.

Gert appeared and took both Nell's hands. "I know there is little anyone can say that will offer any real consolation, but Nell, I want you to remember that you haven't really lost him. He's on a different plane now, but he's still your Adam."

"Come on, Gert," Mac said. "Nell doesn't need to listen to that kind of talk now. We'll talk in the morning."

They were gone. Nell walked back into the living room, aware that she was half listening for the sound of Adam's key in the lock. She moved about the apartment as though in a trance, arranging magazines on a side table, straightening pillows on the couch. When will it register, she wondered, that Adam is dead? Another pang of sorrow gripped her. Adam and I would have worked everything out. I just know we would have.

She needed him to be alive, needed him to open the door and come in and say, "Nell, let me say it first: I love you, and I'm sorry."

Adam's boat had blown up.

Adam named both his boats after me, Nell thought, but I hardly ever went out on either one with him. I've been so afraid of water ever since I was caught in that riptide in Hawaii. He begged me to come out with him. He promised he'd stay near shore.

Adam loved boats. In a way, what could have been a problem became a plus for us, Nell thought. So many weekends when Mac wanted me to go to political affairs with him, or when I needed to work on my column, Adam would go sailing or fishing. And then he'd come home, and I'd come home, and we'd be together.

We would have worked it out, she thought again.

Nell turned off the living-room lights and went into the bedroom. I wish I could feel something, she thought. I wish I could cry or grieve. Instead, I feel like all I can do is wait.

But wait for what? Wait for whom?

She undressed, taking care to hang up the green silk Escada pantsuit she had been wearing. It was new. When it was delivered, Adam had opened the box and examined it carefully. "That's gotta be great on you, Nell," he had said.

She had worn it tonight because in her heart she'd been hoping that he would feel as rotten about the quarrel as she did and would join them. I'd like to think he was planning to, she thought as she took a nightgown from the drawer. Automatically she washed her face, brushed her teeth, and got into bed.

She said her husband's name aloud, "Adam. Adam. I love you. Please come back!"

She waited. The faint hum of the air conditioner and the wail of a police siren were the only sounds she could make out.

"Adam, I'm sorry." Again Nell spoke quietly into the darkened room. "Please, somehow let me know that you can hear me. Mom and Daddy said good-bye to me. Adam, please let me sense your presence. Please give me the chance to tell you how sorry I am before I say good-bye to you."

For the rest of the night Nell waited, awake, staring into the darkness. As dawn broke, she was at last able to weep—for Adam, for all the years they would not spend together. And she was able to weep for herself, because once again she had to become used to living without someone she loved.

AT SEVEN thirty Lisa began to listen for Jimmy's car. She was looking forward to surprising him with the chicken-and-rice dinner that was his favorite meal.

She'd had the kids fed by six thirty, but she'd decided to wait to eat with Jimmy. She had set the dinette table for the two of them and even had wine chilling in the refrigerator, a special treat. Jimmy had looked so lost, so defeated, when he left the house this morning. She hadn't been able to get that image out of her head all day.

Was it possible that she'd heard him right, that he'd said, "I'm sorry," just as he was leaving? Sorry for what? she wondered.

Now the kids—Kyle, Kelly, and Charley—were at the kitchen table doing their homework. Kyle, the oldest, was twelve, and as usual needed no urging. Kelly was ten and a dreamer. "Kelly, you haven't written a word in five minutes," Lisa prodded. Charley, the seven-year-old, was copying his spelling words.

By eight thirty she was starting to worry. Where was Jimmy? Certainly not still on the boat. Overcast skies had turned into a storm.

Traffic was always terrible on Friday evenings, she told herself.

An hour later Lisa shooed the two younger children up to put on pajamas. Kyle went into the den to watch television.

Jimmy, where are you? Lisa agonized as the hands on the clock approached ten p.m. Something's wrong. Maybe you *did* get fired. Well, if so, you'll find something else.

At ten thirty the front doorbell rang. Sick with fear, Lisa rushed to open the door. Two men held up police badges for her to see. "Mrs. Ryan, may we come in?"

Without thinking, the question came to her lips. Her voice dull with pain, she said, "Jimmy committed suicide, didn't he?"

THIS is a terrible shock, Gert thought. Adam was so strong, so healthy. Suddenly she felt infinitely weary. In the quiet of her apartment she leaned back in her chair and closed her eyes. They welled with tears as Adam's face filled her mind.

He had a smile that would warm the hardest heart. The first time Nell had brought him to meet her, she had been radiant, so obviously in love. It was as though a light went on in Nell's soul when she met Adam. Gert felt a lump in her throat.

With a sigh she got up and went into the kitchen. She reached for the kettle and smiled to herself. Adam and I laughed together a lot, Gert thought. He wasn't like Cornelius, who gets so impatient with me. Adam even came here when our psychic group met. He was *interested.*

Well, she thought, if Nell has trouble accepting Adam's passing, I'm going to insist that she try to reach him through channeling. Adam will tell her that it was time for him to go, that she mustn't cling to grief, because he is here.

The kettle was whistling, and Gert turned it off quickly. Tonight the usually cheery sound of the steam had become a mournful wail. It was almost like a lost soul shrieking for surcease, she thought uneasily.

As A kid growing up in Bayside, Queens, Jack Sclafani had always wanted to be the cop when the neighborhood kids played cops and robbers.

Now, at age forty-two, living in Brooklyn Heights, Sclafani was a detective first-class on the district attorney's elite squad. He had worked with many fine men, but the one he liked best was his partner, George Brennan. So he came to full alert when he heard Brennan on the eleven-o'clock news, fielding reporters' questions about the cabin cruiser that had exploded in the harbor that evening.

Brennan was standing outside a modest house in Queens. "Mrs. Ryan has confirmed that her husband, an employee of the Sam Krause Construction Company, was planning to be at a meeting today on the *Cornelia II,*" he was saying. "A man of his description was seen boarding the boat before it sailed, so we are assuming that Mr. Ryan was one of the victims."

"How many were on the boat?" a voice asked off camera.

"We've learned that in addition to Mr. Ryan, four other people were expected to attend the meeting," Brennan replied.

"Isn't it unusual for a diesel-fueled boat to explode?"

"We're investigating the explosion."

"Wasn't Sam Krause about to be indicted for bid rigging?"

"No comment."

Sam Krause, Jack thought. You bet he was about to be indicted. So he was on that boat! Son of a gun! The guy was a blueprint for everything rotten in the construction business. There's a laundry list of people wanting to get rid of him. Krause knew too much. Diesel fuel doesn't cause explosions. I'll bet anything that if that boat was turned into confetti, somebody planted a bomb on it.

Wednesday, June 14
Three

"NELL, I can't tell you how sorry I am. I still can't believe any of this. It's just inconceivable."

Peter Lang was seated opposite Nell in the living room of her apartment. His face was bruised, and he looked genuinely shaken. For the first time Nell actually felt some empathy for this man. In the past she had always been put off by Peter's manner. "Cock of the walk," as Mac scornfully called it.

"I was so banged up that when I got home Friday night, I just turned off the phone and went to bed. The media called my parents, and it's damn lucky my father didn't have a heart attack. Mom couldn't stop crying when she found out I was okay."

"I can understand that," Nell said as she considered what her own reaction might have been. Suppose Adam had phoned and said that he hadn't been on the boat.

But there was nothing to suppose. The others wouldn't have gone out without him. Adam's boat, named after me, became his casket, she thought.

No, not his casket! Sunday they had found body parts that had been positively identified as Jimmy Ryan's. The odds of finding any more bodies, or parts, were almost negligible. Adam, Sam Krause, and Winifred must have been blown to bits or incinerated or swept by the strong tides past the Verrazano Bridge out into the Atlantic.

"There'll be a Mass for Adam tomorrow," she told Lang.

Lang was quiet for a moment, then said, "Nell, have the police confirmed that it was a bomb that destroyed the boat?"

"Not confirmed it officially, no."

But she knew that a bomb was suspected, and it was a thought that wouldn't let go. Why would anyone do that? Was it a random act of violence? She needed to know before she could find closure to this terrible thing.

Jimmy Ryan's wife needed an answer too. She had phoned Nell the day after the tragedy. "Mrs. Cauliff, I feel as though I know you," she said. "I've seen you on television, and I read your column. I don't know what they're telling you about my husband, but I don't want you to think he caused your husband's death.

"Jimmy did not do this. He was a victim, the same as your husband. Yes, he was depressed. But the police are insinuating Jimmy caused that explosion. Even if Jimmy was suicidal, he would never, ever have caused another human being's death."

Pictures of Jimmy Ryan's funeral had been in the papers. Lisa

Ryan, with her three children huddled beside her, was shown walking behind the casket that held the shattered remains of a husband and father. Nell shut her eyes.

"Nell, next week sometime I'd like to go over some business with you," Lang said softly. "There are a few decisions that have to be made, and I need your input. But there's time enough for that." He stood up. "Try to get some rest."

She was glad to close the door behind Peter Lang, ashamed of the resentment she felt that he had been spared.

"Adam," she said aloud. "Adam," she repeated quietly, as if he were listening.

Of course there was no answer.

I shared this home with Adam for three years, she thought. How will I adjust to being alone?

She had bought the apartment after she graduated from Georgetown, before entering Fordham Law, using money that had been held in trust until she was twenty-one. "Whatever little nest I carry you off to won't be in this league," Adam had joked when they began to talk of marriage. "Give me ten years, though, and I promise the picture will change."

"Why not spend those ten years here? I love this place."

She had cleared one bedroom closet for him and taken from Mac's brownstone the antique chest-on-chest that had belonged to her father. She went over to that dresser now and picked up the silver tray next to their wedding picture—the tray where Adam always put his keys and change when he undressed at night.

I hadn't realized how alone I'd always felt until we were married and he was here with me all the time, she thought. Thursday night he changed in the guest room. He didn't want to wake me up.

Suddenly it seemed fiercely important that she had missed that last night of watching him go through his familiar bedtime ritual.

ON WEDNESDAY afternoon Lisa's neighbor Brenda Curren and her daughter, Morgan, arrived to pick up Kyle, Kelly, and Charley and take them to a movie and dinner.

"Go get in the car with Morgan," Brenda ordered. "I want to talk to your mom." She waited a minute before saying, "Lisa, don't look so worried. You know they'll be fine with us. You need some time to yourself."

"Oh, I don't know," Lisa said dully. "All I see stretching out ahead of me is time. I wonder what I'm going to do with all those hours and days." She looked at her neighbor, saw the look of concern in her eyes. "But you're right, of course. I have to go through Jimmy's desk. I have to file for Social Security for the children. At least that will offer some income."

"You do have insurance, don't you, Lisa?"

"We have some," Lisa said. Enough to bury Jimmy, she thought, but that's about it. And we still owe fourteen thousand dollars on credit cards, at eighteen percent a month.

"Lisa, Jimmy always kept up this place so well. Ed asked me to tell you that if anything comes up that needs fixing, he'll do his best. Jimmy was a great guy, and we love you both. We'd do anything to help you out."

Lisa tried to smile. "I know you would. And you are helping me. Go ahead now and take my kids off my hands."

She walked Brenda to the door, then headed back down the narrow hallway to the kitchen. She looked at the stack of envelopes on the writing desk. The mortgage, gas, and phone bills were a week overdue. If Jimmy had come home, they would have sat together and paid them. My job now, Lisa thought. Something I get to do alone with all the time I have.

She wrote those checks and with a sinking heart pulled out the credit-card bills. She didn't dare to make more than a minimum payment on any of them this month. She caught sight of an envelope with columns of figures. How often had she seen Jimmy at this desk, adding up the bills, agonizing as they mounted?

And then he would go downstairs and sit at his workbench for a couple of hours, pretending to be fixing something, Lisa thought. He didn't want me to see how worried he was.

Why didn't he stop worrying once he went back to work? Lisa

wondered, asking herself once more the question that had plagued her over these last months. Almost without thinking, she crossed the room and opened the door to the basement. She walked down the stairs to the workroom and turned on the light. The kids and I almost never came in here, she thought. It was like a sanctuary for Jimmy. It hurt Lisa now to see that the broad table was painfully neat, the tools all in place. The sawhorses stood together in a corner, next to the file cabinet.

The file cabinet—Jimmy used it for records and papers he thought worth keeping. It was one other thing she'd have to examine carefully. Lisa opened the top drawer, glanced at the carefully labeled folders containing income tax statements.

Opening the second drawer, she saw neatly folded blueprints and specification sheets. They were his plans—plans for finishing the basement, plans for the built-in bunks in Kyle's room, for the screened-in porch. Under them, at the bottom, she saw a bulky box—no, two—sealed with brown wrapping paper and twine. She had to slip her fingers underneath to wrench them loose.

She placed the boxes on the table, then reached for a sharp-edged tool, slashed the twine, unwrapped the paper, and lifted the lid from the first box. In fascinated horror and disbelief she stared down at stacks of currency lying in neat rows.

An hour later, after a careful count, Lisa dazedly acknowledged that fifty thousand dollars had been hidden in this basement room by Jimmy Ryan, the beloved husband who had suddenly become a stranger.

IN THE two years since she had moved to New York from Florida, Bonnie Wilson, psychic and medium, had developed a solid clientele. Thirty years old, slender, with black hair, pale skin, and enviable features, Bonnie looked more like a model than a master of psychic phenomena, but, in fact, she was especially sought after by all those anxious to be in touch with a loved one who had passed on.

As she would explain to a newcomer, "Psychic ability can be

developed in all of us. However, even as a child, I had the ability to sense what is going on in other people's lives. As I studied, I found that when people came to consult me, the ones they loved, now on the higher plane, began to join us. My ability to communicate has become more and more precise. Some people find what I tell them disturbing, but most draw from it only the greatest comfort. God has given me this gift, and it is my obligation to share it."

Bonnie regularly attended the monthly New York Psychic Association meetings. Today, as she had expected, Gert MacDermott, a regular, was not present. In hushed tones the members discussed the terrible tragedy that had befallen her family.

"I'm going to visit her," Bonnie said. "I want to help."

EARLIER that day Jed Kaplan had set off on his favorite walk, starting at his mother's apartment at Fourteenth Street and First Avenue and ending up on the Hudson River at the North Cove marina. It was the fifth day in a row that Jed had made this journey, a walk that usually took him a little over an hour, and each time he enjoyed it more.

And now, just as he had on the previous days, Jed sat staring out over the Hudson, a slight smile on his lips. The thought that *Cornelia II* was no longer arrogantly bobbing in the water there sent a thrill through him. He savored the image of Adam Cauliff's body being blown to bits, starting with the startling, instantaneous recognition that must have registered in Cauliff's brain that he was indeed dying. It was an image Jed relived over and over in his mind.

He observed a cruise liner being piloted toward the Narrows and wondered where it was heading. Europe? he thought. South America? Hell, maybe he should try going to one of those places. Clearly it was time for him to push off. The old lady was driving him crazy, and he must be driving her crazy too.

When she had fixed him breakfast this morning, she said, "Jed, it's time for you to get on to something else. I'll give you money to make a fresh start somewhere."

Initially she had suggested giving him five thousand bucks. By the time he finished his breakfast, he had gotten her up to twenty-five thousand, plus she had let him see her will, which showed that she was leaving everything to him.

Jed went back to visualizing Adam Cauliff's death.

A witness to the explosion had been quoted in the *Post* as saying, "The boat wasn't moving. I figured they'd dropped anchor and were having a couple of drinks. Then all of a sudden *boom*. It was like an atomic bomb hit it."

Jed had cut out that account and kept it in his shirt pocket. His only regret was that he hadn't been there to see the explosion himself.

It was too bad about the other people who got killed, of course, but then they couldn't have been worth much. They were probably in on Cauliff's trick of talking senile widows into selling off property for a fraction of its worth. Well, at least there won't be a *Cornelia III*, he exulted.

"Excuse me, sir."

Startled out of his reverie, Jed sprang up, on the defensive. But instead of the homeless beggar he had expected to confront, he found himself staring into the knowing eyes of a grave-faced man.

The man held up his badge. "Detective George Brennan."

Too late Jed acknowledged to himself that hanging around the marina may well have been the stupidest mistake of his whole life.

DAN Minor's search for his mother finally promised to yield some results. The woman at the shelter who recognized the picture of her, and even called her Quinny, had provided him with the first ray of hope he'd had in a long, long time. And even a glimmer of hope was enough to energize him.

Today, in fact, he was so energized that once he was finished at the hospital for the afternoon, he quickly changed and raced off to Central Park to continue his search there.

It seemed as though he had been searching for his mother all his life. She had disappeared soon after the accident that almost killed him.

Occasionally, on his birthday, he would get an unsigned card that he knew was from her, the only confirmation he had that she was still alive. Then one day seven years ago he had been sitting in the family room with his grandmother when he had turned on the television and started surfing the channels, stopping with casual interest when he saw a documentary on homeless people in Manhattan.

One of the women interviewed was standing on a street corner on upper Broadway. When that woman spoke, his grandmother had jumped up.

The interviewer asked her name. "People call me Quinny."

"Oh, God, it's Kathryn!" his grandmother shrieked. "Dan, look, look! It's your mother!"

Did he actually remember that face? The face on the television screen was careworn, the eyes dulled; still, there were traces of the pretty girl she once had been. The dark hair was generously sprinkled now with gray, and it was unkempt. Still, to his eyes she was beautiful.

"Do you have a family, Quinny?" the interviewer had asked.

She had looked straight into the camera. "I had a wonderful little boy, once. He was better off without me, so I left."

The next day Dan's grandparents had hired a private investigator to try to track her down, but Quinny had vanished. She's in New York, Dan thought. I will find her. I will!

Lilly Brown, the woman at the shelter, had assured him, "Quinny will be back. She never stays away from New York long, and in the summer she sits in Central Park. It's her favorite place in the world, she says. I'll ask around for you."

For now I'll have to be content with that, Dan thought as he jogged the paths of the park. Summer is almost here.

WHEN Nell opened the door for Cornelius MacDermott, he reached out and put his arms around her.

"Nell," he said, "remember what the old Irish guys say to the bereaved at wakes? They say, 'I'm sorry for your trouble.' That means, 'Your trouble is my trouble. I share your grief.' You have to know how very very sorry I am about Adam. I'd do anything to keep you from having to go through the hurt I know you are experiencing right now."

Be fair to him, Nell told herself. He has loved me and cared for me as long as I can remember. Maybe he couldn't help being jealous of Adam. There were plenty of women who would have loved to marry Mac after Gram died. I was probably the reason he didn't get involved with any of them. "I know you would," she said. "I guess I just need some time to let everything sink in."

"Well, unfortunately, Nell, you don't have time," Mac said abruptly. "Come on. Let's sit down. We've got to talk."

Not knowing quite what to expect, she followed him into the living room. As soon as she was seated, he began. "Nell, I'm sorry to move on you like this. You haven't even had Adam's memorial Mass yet. But some things simply can't wait. This isn't just any election year. It's a presidential election year. Anything can happen, but our guy is ahead big time, and unless he does something really stupid, he's going to be the next President."

Nell looked at her grandfather's bright eyes. Nothing like a political campaign to get the old warhorse up and running, she thought.

"Nell, a couple more guys are about to throw their hats in the ring for my old seat. Tim Cross, for example."

"Tim Cross has been nothing but a wimp on the council," Nell snapped.

"That's my girl. You could have won that seat."

"Could have won? What are you talking about, Mac? I *am* going to go for it. I *have* to."

"You may not get the chance. Nell, Robert Walters and Len Arsdale came to see me this morning. A dozen building contractors have signed statements saying Walters and Arsdale paid them bribes in the millions of dollars to land the big jobs. Robert and Len are two fine men. I've known them all my life. They never pulled that stuff."

"What are you trying to tell me, Mac?"

"Nell, I'm telling you that Adam was probably on the take."

She looked at her grandfather. "No, Mac, I don't believe that. He wouldn't do it. It's also much too easy to lay blame on a dead man, not to mention convenient. Did anyone actually say they handed Adam the money?"

"Winifred was the go-between."

"Winifred! For heaven's sake, Mac, that woman didn't have the gumption of a sunflower. What makes you think she'd be capable of putting together a bribery scheme?"

"That's exactly it. While Robert and Len agree that Winifred knew the business and would have known how to do a scam, they also agree she'd never try to do something like that on her own."

"Mac," Nell protested, "listen to what you're saying. You're taking the word of your old buddies that they're pure as the driven snow and that my husband was a thief."

"Well, let me ask you this: Where did Adam get the money to buy that property on Twenty-eighth Street?"

"He got it from me."

Cornelius MacDermott stared at her. "Don't tell me you invaded your trust fund."

"It was mine to invade, wasn't it? I lent Adam the money to buy it and to open his own firm. If he'd actually been taking money, would he have needed to borrow from me?"

"If he didn't want to leave a paper trail. Nell, get this straight: If it comes out that he was involved in a bribery scandal, you can kiss your chance of being a Congresswoman good-bye."

"Mac, at the moment I'm much more interested in protecting Adam's memory than I am in worrying about my own political future." This isn't real, Nell thought, putting her hands over her face. In a few minutes I'll wake up from a bad dream, and Adam will be here, and none of this will have happened.

She stood suddenly and crossed to the window. Winifred, she thought. Quiet, timid Winifred. I saw her step off that elevator, and I knew she was going to die. Could I have prevented it?

From what Mac says, Walters and Arsdale are sure she was cheating. I can't believe Adam would have taken her with him into his company if he had thought she was dishonest. If there was bribery going on, Adam didn't know.

"Nell, you realize that this throws a whole new light on the explosion," Mac said. "It couldn't have been accidental, and almost certainly it was intended to make sure that someone on that boat wouldn't talk to the district attorney's office."

It's like the riptide, Nell thought. Wave after wave crashing into me, and I can't stay afloat. I'm getting drawn out to sea.

When Mac left, Nell went into the bedroom and opened the door of Adam's closet. The navy-blue jacket he had worn home from Philadelphia was on the hanger where she had hung it the next morning. I must have given Winifred his other one, she thought, just like this one except it had silver buttons. This was the one he wore the day before he died.

Nell took it off the hanger and slipped her arms through the sleeves. She had expected to feel comforted, almost as though Adam's arms were around her, but instead she had a chilling sense of alienation, following a sudden, startling remembrance of the angry outburst between them.

A premise, unbidden and unwelcome, was insinuating itself into her mind. Adam had been on edge for months. Was it possible that there really was something going on that she had not caught wind of?

She stood still, weighing what Mac had told her. Then she shook her head. No. No, I'll never believe that, she thought.

Thursday, June 15
Four

AFTER getting the call from his partner about the guy he had picked up at the marina and brought in for questioning, Jack Sclafani rushed to meet George Brennan.

"It's almost too easy," Brennan told him. "The way it's shaping up, this guy not only did it but then just sat around waiting for us to pick him up." He gave Jack a rundown on Jed Kaplan. "Thirty-eight, raised in Manhattan, always in trouble. His juvenile court record is sealed, but as an adult, he served on Riker's Island for beating up guys in bars. Apparently he gets really mean when he hits the booze or gets into drugs."

Brennan continued. "Father and grandfather were respected furriers, owned a loft building on Twenty-eighth Street. Kaplan got back here last month, after five years in Australia. From what the neighbors say, he went berserk when he heard his mother had sold the building to Adam Cauliff—at a fair enough price.

"What apparently has him nuts is that the lot more than tripled in value because the Vandermeer mansion next door, an old historical landmark, burned down last September. You can't be a historical landmark if you're a pile of ashes, so that property was sold to Peter Lang, the hotshot real estate entrepreneur. The guy who was supposed to be on the boat when it blew up, but who didn't make it to the meeting because of an accident."

Brennan reached for the coffee he had allowed to get cold. "Adam Cauliff was involved in a deal with Lang to build a fancy apartment-office-shopping complex on the combined parcels. He designed a tower to stand on the exact spot where the Kaplans used to hang their furs. So we've got motive and opportunity, but is that enough to arrest him? Absolutely not, but it's a good start."

"I'll bet he has a rap sheet in Australia too," Jack said. He paused. "What bothers me, though, is that if he did blow those people to kingdom come, I don't think he'd be stupid enough to hang around the marina."

IN THE hours shortly before dawn Ken and Regina Tucker were startled from their sleep by shrieks of terror. It was the second time since their ill-fated trip to New York City that their son, Ben, had experienced frightening nightmares.

They both sprang from bed and raced down the hall, pushed open the door to their son's room, flipped on the light, and rushed in. Ken grabbed the boy and held him tightly.

"It's all right, guy. It's all right," he said soothingly.

"Make the snake go away," Ben sobbed. "Make it go away."

"Ben, it was just a bad dream. We're here; you're safe."

"Tell us about it," Regina urged.

"We were floating on the river, and I was looking out over the railing. And the other boat . . ." Ben's voice trailed off.

"He's trembling all over," Regina whispered.

It took almost half an hour before Ben settled back into sleep. When they returned to their bedroom, Ken said quietly, "I think we'd better get Ben to a counselor. What a lousy break. You try to give your kid a memorable day, and he looks straight at a boat that explodes with four people on it. I wish we'd just stayed home."

AT THE memorial Mass for Adam that Thursday morning, Nell sat in the first pew of the church, her grandfather and great-aunt on either side of her. She felt detached, almost like an outsider observing the ceremony. As the ritual progressed, random thoughts washed through her mind.

She had sat here in this same pew twenty-two years ago at exactly the same kind of Mass—for her mother and father.

Adam had been an only child too. His father had died when he was in high school, his mother after he finished college.

Was that part of what drew her to him? she wondered. A shared sense of isolation?

She remembered that on their first date Adam had said, "I don't go back to North Dakota anymore. I don't have relatives there, and I feel a lot closer to the friends I made in college than I do to kids I grew up with."

Since Adam's death she hadn't heard from those college friends. She didn't think any of them were there at the Mass.

The church was packed with her friends, with Mac's friends, with the constituents who considered them family. Mac's hand was under her arm, urging her to stand. Monsignor Duncan was reading the Gospel. Lazarus, who came back from the dead.

Come back, Adam, please come back, she pleaded.

Monsignor talked about the senseless violence that had taken the lives of four innocent people. Then Mac stepped into the aisle and walked up the sanctuary steps to the lectern.

"Adam was my grandson by marriage," he began.

Mac is eulogizing Adam, Nell thought. He didn't tell me he was going to do that. Then she had the disturbing thought that perhaps no one else knew Adam well enough to volunteer. Adam, why isn't there someone here to speak for you? Why did someone hate you enough to kill you?

Mac returned to the pew. Next came the final blessing, then the closing music. The Mass was over.

As Nell walked from the church, a woman stopped her. "Could I talk to you?" she asked. "Please. It's very important."

"Of course." I know this woman, Nell thought. But from where?

The woman appeared to be about her own age. Her eyes were puffy, and lines of grief were etched in her face. It's Lisa Ryan, Nell thought, remembering the picture in the newspaper. She phoned me after the explosion.

"Mrs. Cauliff," Lisa began hurriedly, "I wonder if I can meet with you privately." She glanced around nervously. Suddenly her eyes widened, and a look of sheer panic came over her. "I'm sorry I bothered you," she said abruptly as she turned and rushed away.

She's terrified, Nell thought. But of what?

She looked back. Detective Brennan and another man coming out of the church were approaching her. Why, Nell wondered, would the sight of those two men terrify Jimmy Ryan's widow?

ON THURSDAY afternoon Bonnie Wilson phoned Gert MacDermott and asked to stop by for a brief visit.

"Bonnie, in all honesty, today isn't the best for me," Gert said. "The memorial Mass for Adam Cauliff was this morning, and afterward my brother arranged for people to go to the Plaza Athénée for lunch. I just got home."

"Gert, I feel I should come by. I can be there in twenty minutes, and I promise I won't stay more than half an hour."

Gert sighed as the phone clicked in her ear. I wish I'd learned to be a little more forceful, she thought. On the other hand, Cornelius is probably forceful enough for both of us.

It was good of him to speak so beautifully about Adam, she thought. Oh, poor Nell. If only she had shown some emotion. Instead she just sat there, as though in a daze. I wish she would let me stay with her for a little while. She's not accepting Adam's death.

WHEN Bonnie arrived, her intense gray eyes studied Gert's face. "Don't worry so much," she said calmly. "I think I can help your niece. I have a feeling you were just about to make yourself a cup of tea. Why don't we both have one?"

A few minutes later the two women sat across from each other at a small table in the kitchen.

"I remember my grandmother used to read tea leaves," Bonnie said. "I'm sure she had psychic powers she didn't understand. After she correctly predicted that a cousin would become very ill, my grandfather begged her to stop reading for people." Her long fingers wrapped around the cup.

Gert studied the younger woman with growing uneasiness. She knows something, she thought.

"Gert, you know what independent-voice phenomena are, don't you?" Bonnie asked suddenly.

"Yes, of course. From my understanding, it's very rare."

"Yes, it is. A new client came for a consultation yesterday. I was able to communicate with her mother on the other side. But then, just as her mother had to leave us, I felt that there was someone else who was trying to reach me."

Gert put down her cup.

"My client left, and I sat quietly for a little while, waiting. Then I heard it—a man's voice. But it was so soft that at first I couldn't understand what he was saying. I could feel his struggle to get through to me, and then I realized he was saying a name over and over: 'Nell. Nell. Nell.'"

"Was it . . ." Gert's voice trailed off.

Bonnie's eyes had widened. The dark gray irises had deepened to jet-black. She nodded. "I asked his name. His energy was almost gone, so he was barely able to communicate. But just before he left, he said, 'Adam. I am Adam.' "

WHEN the luncheon ended, Nell had walked home alone from the Plaza Athénée. She knew the ten-block walk back to her apartment would do her good, and she wanted the time to herself.

She had slipped away while Mac was holding court with the last of the luncheon guests, old friends who also happened to be movers and shakers in the party. Several of them had barely finished offering their condolences before they bluntly started talking politics with her.

Mike Powers, for example, had confided, "Nell, to say it straight, Bob Gorman hasn't accomplished diddly-squat. Good riddance to him. With you on the ticket we can win."

Can I win? Nell wondered as she walked up Madison Avenue. Will you still want me when Adam's former employers throw the blame for their own bid rigging and bribery on Adam and Winifred? Or was it possible that Adam and Winifred were dead because they knew too much about that bribery scandal?

And what was that scene at the church this morning? Why did Lisa Ryan panic when she saw the detective who was investigating the explosion? Was her husband responsible for it? Or could he have been the target? According to the newspapers, he had been out of work because he had complained about substandard material on a job. Was there something else he knew that made him dangerous?

As she walked, Nell became aware of the sun on her face. Finally lifting her head enough to look around, she realized that it was a picture-perfect June afternoon. Adam and I used to walk along Madison Avenue all the time, she thought sadly. They liked to look in the shop windows and to stop for coffee at one of the cafés.

She passed one of the smallest, with tiny wrought-iron tables and chairs on the sidewalk. As she watched, two women settled at a table, dropping their packages beside them. "Sidewalk cafés make me feel as though I'm in Paris," one of them said.

Adam and I spent our honeymoon in Paris, Nell thought.

Mac had been upset that she and Adam had known each other such a brief time before they were married. "Give it a year," he had counseled. "Who the hell is this guy, Nell? You hardly know him."

Mac, being Mac, had him checked out. "That college he attended is a cockamamy factory, Nell. Trust me, this guy is no Stanford White. And the places he's worked at are mom-and-pop operations, small-time builders."

But Mac, being Mac, was all bark and no bite where I was concerned—as always, Nell thought. He even accepted the small private wedding, once he accepted that I'd made up my mind.

She arrived at her building. Carlo, the doorman, wore an expression of concern as he opened the door for her. "Pretty rough day for you, Ms. MacDermott," he said.

"I'd say so, Carlo." Nell felt oddly comforted by his concern.

"Hope you can just take it easy for the rest of the day."

"That's exactly what I'm going to do."

"You know, I was thinking about that lady who worked for Mr. Cauliff," Carlo said.

"You mean Winifred Johnson?"

"Yeah. She was here last week, the day of the accident. She always seemed so nervous when she was here, so timid."

"That's right," Nell said.

"Last week, just when I was letting her out, her cell phone rang. I couldn't help but overhear. Her mother's in a nursing home?"

"Yes, she's in Old Woods Manor up in White Plains."

"I could tell the mother was complaining that she felt depressed," Carlo said. "I hope the old lady has someone to visit her now that Ms. Johnson is dead."

As Nell took the elevator up, she felt ashamed that it had not occurred to her all week to visit Winifred's mother, at least to offer sympathy and to see if there was anything she could do for her.

But there was a second reason to visit. Old Woods Manor was a very expensive facility. As she thought about it, Nell began to wonder how long Mrs. Johnson had been living at the manor and how Winifred had managed to pay for it.

Winifred might not be as much a mouse as everyone thought.

Now Nell wondered if the needs of an ailing mother might not have given Winifred the impetus she needed to cash in on her knowledge of under-the-table deal making. Maybe she did know something about the bribes Walters and Arsdale mentioned to Mac. And maybe *she* was the reason the boat had exploded—and Adam had been killed.

An hour later, showered and changed into a denim jacket and slacks, Nell took the elevator down to the garage level and got into her car.

PETER Lang had fully intended to attend the memorial Mass held for Adam Cauliff, but at the last minute he received a call from Curtis Little, an officer at Overland Bank, one of the potential investment partners in the Vandermeer Tower project. Little wanted him to give his associate, John Hilmer, an update on the status of the negotiations. They met in the boardroom of Peter's spacious offices on Forty-ninth Street and Avenue of the Americas.

"My father never stopped complaining when they changed the name of Sixth Avenue to Avenue of the Americas," Peter said to Hilmer as they took their places at the conference table. "These were his offices, and to the day he retired he told people he worked on Sixth Avenue. He was a very down-to-earth man."

Hilmer smiled slightly. It was his first meeting with the legendary Peter Lang, and there was nothing particularly "down-to-earth" about him. Even with the cuts and bruises from his accident, Lang exuded self-confidence and wore his expensive clothes with casual grace.

Lang pointed to a cloth-covered structure on the table. "In a moment you're going to see a model of an apartment-office complex designed by Ian Maxwell. As you may know, Maxwell just completed an award-winning fifty-five-story residential and business building on Lake Michigan. It's one of the most imaginative and beautiful structures constructed in Chicago in the last twenty years."

He paused, and the others saw an expression of pain come over his face. With an apologetic smile Lang reached for a pill and washed it down with a quick sip of water.

"I know I look as though I've been mugged, but my real problem is the cracked rib," he explained.

Curtis Little said dryly, "I'm sure under the circumstances you're happy to settle for the bruises and the cracked rib, Peter. I know I would be." He tapped his fingers on the tabletop. "Which brings us to the point of this meeting, Peter. Where do we stand with Adam Cauliff's estate?"

"Curt, you've been in on this from the start," Peter said, "but let me fill you in, John. As you know, the blocks between Twenty-third and Thirty-first streets on the West Side are ripe for renovation. I tried for some time to get the Vandermeer mansion removed from designated landmark status. We all agree that it is an outrage that vital Manhattan property is being held hostage because of sentimental attachments to useless, broken-down structures. I confess that I didn't actually think I'd ever be successful in having the board of estimate declassify it—that's why I never did go after the Kaplan property adjacent to it. I kept pressuring the board, though, and finally I succeeded. The irony, of course, is that the mansion burned down only hours after the board of estimate voted." He flashed a quick, sad smile.

"While I was working to free up the Vandermeer place, Adam Cauliff bought the Kaplan property. I offered him twice what he paid for it, but that wasn't what he wanted. He proposed instead that he be the architect of the complex we planned to build, and he wanted to involve Sam Krause in the construction."

Curtis Little stirred restlessly. "Peter, we are not prepared to provide funding for the Adam Cauliff proposal. It is imitative, pedantic, and a hodgepodge of architectural styles."

"I happen to agree," Lang said promptly. "Adam thought we'd do anything to get our hands on the Kaplan parcel. He was mistaken. Which is what brings me to Ian Maxwell's design."

Peter leaned forward and pulled the cloth, revealing a scale model with a postmodern art deco façade. "Ian was in town two weeks ago. I took him to the site. This is a tentative idea of how he believes he can erect the kind of tower complex we want without using the Kaplan property. I conveyed to Adam last week the fact that we had developed an alternative plan."

"Cauliff knew we weren't going along with his proposal?" Little asked.

"Yes, he did. He'd opened his own office on the expectation that we couldn't do without him, but he was wrong. I've told his wife— or widow, I should say—it's important that I see her on a business matter next week. I'll explain that we don't need her parcel, but that we'll pay fair market value for it."

"If she goes along . . ." Curtis Little began.

"If she goes along, Ian Maxwell will design our building with the tower to the side as we'd originally hoped to have it. Otherwise, the tower will be in the rear, which will work perfectly well."

"Would Cauliff have gone along with fair market value for the property?" John Hilmer asked.

Peter Lang smiled. "Of course he would have. Adam had an in-flated ego and an unrealistic opinion of his own potential, but he wasn't stupid. That's not to say that he was particularly happy that I offered to take the Kaplan site off his hands for a modest profit."

Curtis Little was studying the model. "Peter, you could put the tower at the back of the structure, but you'd lose most of the aes-thetic value of the building and a hell of a lot of rentable footage. I'm not at all sure we'd put money into it."

Peter Lang smiled. "Of course you wouldn't, but Adam Cauliff didn't know that. He was just a small-town guy playing in a league in which he didn't belong. Trust me. He would have sold."

John Hilmer studied Peter Lang across the table. A minor traffic accident had kept Lang from being killed in a fatal explosion, but not once had Lang expressed the slightest suggestion of regret that Adam Cauliff and three other people had lost their lives.

Lang is still furious that Adam Cauliff was shrewd enough to beat him to snapping up the Kaplan property, Hilmer thought. And now that he's dead, Lang's licking his chops because he's sure he'll get the property at his price. *Not* a nice guy, even in a hardball business.

Another thought hit him. Hilmer's son, a defensive tackle on his college football team, often came out of a game looking a lot worse than Peter Lang, who had tangled with a trailer truck.

CARRYING hot pastrami sandwiches and containers of steaming coffee, Jack Sclafani and George Brennan went to Jack's office after the memorial Mass. They ate quietly, deep in thought.

Then, in sync, they stuffed the aluminum foil, napkins, and uneaten garlic pickles into the plastic lunch bags and tossed them in the wastebasket. They looked at each other.

"What's your take on the widow Ryan?" Brennan asked.

"Scared. She ran like a rabbit caught in Farmer McGregor's cabbage patch when she saw us."

"What's she got to be afraid of?"

"I think we should pay her a visit," Sclafani said. "She may have proof her husband caused that explosion. Any report from Interpol on Kaplan?"

"He has a rap sheet in Australia as long as the Barrier Reef. Most of it is petty stuff, except one conviction. Get this: He was nabbed carrying explosives in the trunk of his car, stolen from a demolition company he worked for. They suspected he'd been paid to blow up something but were never able to prove it."

Sclafani stood up. "Search warrant?"

"You bet. I think the judge will go along with it."

"I still want to talk to Lisa Ryan," Jack Sclafani said. "Even if I saw Kaplan with a stick of dynamite in his hand, my hunch would still be that whatever is bugging her is the key to what happened on the boat that night."

OLD Woods Manor was off busy Route 287 in Westchester County, but when Nell turned up the long driveway that led to the facility, all traces of suburbia disappeared. The handsome stone edifice might have been the country residence of a wealthy landowner somewhere in England. She parked her car and went inside to the expensively furnished reception room.

An attractive woman escorted her to the second floor. She introduced herself as Georgina Matthews, a volunteer. "Mrs. Johnson's daughter's death has been such a blow to her. We're all trying to help, but I warn you, she's angry at the world."

Well, that makes two of us, Nell thought.

They walked down a tastefully carpeted hallway, passing several elderly people, all well cared for and exquisitely well groomed. Georgina Matthews tapped on a door, then opened it. "Mrs. Johnson's expecting you."

Rhoda Johnson was resting in a recliner, her eyes closed, her feet up. She appeared to be in her late seventies, a broad-shouldered woman with luxuriant salt-and-pepper hair. Nell was momentarily startled. Winifred had been painfully thin, her hair straight and fine. Obviously Rhoda Johnson had been fashioned from a different mold.

She opened her eyes and fixed her gaze on Nell. "They told me you were coming. I guess I should be grateful."

"Now Mrs. Johnson," Georgina Matthews cautioned.

Rhoda Johnson ignored her. "Winifred was doing just fine at Walters and Arsdale. They'd even given her enough of a raise so she could move me here. I hated the last nursing home. I told her over and over to stay put when your husband opened his firm, but she wouldn't listen. Well, was I right?"

"I'm very very sorry about Winifred," Nell said. "I know this is awful for you. I wanted to see if I could help."

"I'll leave you two to chat," Georgina Matthews murmured. She turned to Rhoda Johnson. "You be nice."

Nell waited until the door closed. "Mrs. Johnson, I understand how sad you must feel. I feel the same way myself. If you'd rather, I won't stay. I do understand."

"I guess it's not your fault." Mrs. Johnson's tone was only mildly belligerent. "But Winifred had a good job. Did she think of me when she took a chance and gave it up to work for your husband? No, she did not."

"Perhaps she had an insurance policy that might take care of your expenses here," Nell suggested.

"She never told me. Winifred could be pretty closemouthed."

"Did Winifred have a safe-deposit box?"

"What would she have to put in it?"

Nell smiled. "Then where did she keep her personal records?"

"In her desk in her apartment, I believe. A good apartment, still rent-controlled. I'd be there now if it weren't for the arthritis."

"Perhaps a neighbor would go through the desk."

"I don't want any neighbors going through my business." Rhoda Johnson looked at Nell intently. "Your grandfather is Cornelius MacDermott, one of the few honest politicians in the country. If I let you look for records, would he go with you?"

"If I asked him, he would. Yes."

Rhoda Johnson began to cry. "I'm going to miss Winifred," she said. "She didn't deserve to die. She just didn't have enough gumption—that was her problem, poor girl. Always trying to please people. Worked her fingers to the bone for that firm. At least they finally gave her the raise she deserved."

Maybe, Nell thought. And maybe not. "Can you think of anything else you'd like us to bring to you?"

"There are some framed pictures." Rhoda Johnson fumbled in the pocket of her sweater for a handkerchief. Watching her, Nell realized for the first time that Mrs. Johnson's fingers were almost deformed from arthritis.

"Oh, and would you try to find Winifred's swimming medals? A coach told me that if she'd stayed at it, she could have been another Esther Williams. But with my arthritis getting the best of me and her father out of the picture, I couldn't have her running all over the country, could I?"

AFTER Bonnie Wilson left, Gert agonized about how to tell Nell what she had just learned. How should she break the news to Nell that Adam was trying to contact her? She knew that Nell would resist. She refuses to understand that some people have genuine psychic gifts, Gert thought. Nell's frightened of the fact that she has psychic gifts herself. And it's no wonder, given how Cornelius made fun of her.

Gert's eyes filled with tears as she remembered how ten-year-old Nell had sobbed in her arms. "Aunt Gert, Mommy and Daddy *did so* say good-bye to me. You know how Daddy always ran his fingers through my hair? I was at recess, and he came to me and did that. And I felt Mommy kiss me. I started to cry. I knew they were gone. *I knew it.* But Grandpa says I imagined it."

But Cornelius couldn't explain the fact that Nell had that experience at precisely the same moment her parents' plane went off the radar screen, Gert thought. His answer was that I was filling Nell's head with nonsense.

I wouldn't dare let him know what Bonnie Wilson told me, Gert thought.

At eight o'clock that evening Gert called Nell. She tried not to sound nervous. "I'm just anxious to see how you are," she began. "Nell, there's something I have to tell you. . . ."

She rushed every word, anxious to get it out before either Nell hung up or she lost her courage and changed her mind about telling her grandniece about Bonnie's visit.

"Gert, I don't believe in all that stuff," Nell said softly. "You know that. I know that it means a lot to you, but it just doesn't work for me. So please don't bring it up again—especially not anything having to do with Adam."

Gert winced at the click as Nell broke the connection. What Gert did not know was that when Nell hung up the phone, she was trembling with fear and uncertainty.

Is it possible that Adam really is trying to reach me? Nell thought. I know that Mac hates for me to talk of it, but I do believe that the dead have a real presence in our lives. Why, then, should it be so improbable for Adam to try to reach me now?

RETURNING home to SoHo after his daily run in Central Park, Dan Minor showered, dressed in chinos, a sport shirt, and loafers and went to his bar refrigerator. He wasn't sure yet where he wanted to have dinner, but he did know a glass of Chardonnay with cheese and crackers was in order.

He settled on the couch in the sitting area of the spacious, high-ceilinged room. *Why do I feel so much more at home in a condo in Manhattan than I ever did in Washington?* he asked himself, although he knew the answer.

Some of Quinny's genes. His mother had been born in Manhattan. *How much of her do I actually remember, and how much of what I know comes from things I've heard about her?* Dan asked himself. *Why do I think that after all these years my mother and I could have any kind of relationship?*

But we could, he thought. *I know we could.* The private investigator they had sent to find her had been able to glean some information. "She's worked as an aide to old people," he told them, "and apparently she is very good at it. But when depression hits her, she starts drinking again and it's back to the streets."

The phone rang. Dan walked over and checked the caller ID. His eyebrows raised when he saw that the call was from Penny Maynard, the fashion designer on the fourth floor of his building. They had chatted a few times in the elevator. She was about his own age and sleekly attractive.

He picked up the phone.

"Dan," Penny said, "a couple of the other people in the building dropped by, and we all agreed it was time we got to know our resident pediatrician. So come on up and join us for pasta."

"I'd be delighted to come," Dan said.

Relaxed and cheered, he got back to his loft just in time to catch the ten-o'clock news. There was a brief segment covering the memorial Mass for the architect who had been killed in the boating accident in New York harbor.

Rosanna Scotto of Fox News was reporting. "The explosion that killed Adam Cauliff and three others continues to be under investigation. Former Congressman Cornelius MacDermott is escorting Cauliff's widow—his granddaughter, Nell—from the church.

Rumors are rampant that Nell MacDermott may run for the congressional seat her grandfather held for fifty years."

There was a close-up of Nell on the screen. Dan Minor's eyes widened. She looked very familiar. Wait a minute, he thought. I met her four or five years ago at a White House reception. We chatted for a few minutes and discovered we were both graduates of Georgetown. It's hard to believe that since that chance meeting she's been married, widowed, and now might be setting off on a political career of her own.

The camera lingered on Nell's face. The rigidly composed features and pain-filled eyes were a startling contrast to the sparkling young woman Dan remembered.

I'll write her a note, he thought. She probably won't remember me at all, but I'd like to do it. She looks so grief-stricken. Adam Cauliff must have been quite a guy, he decided.

Friday, June 16

Five

WINIFRED Johnson had lived in a building at Amsterdam Avenue and Eighty-first Street. At ten o'clock on Friday morning Nell met her grandfather in the lobby there. The marble floor was stained, the lighting dim.

"Nell, I think it's a big mistake coming here," Cornelius MacDermott said as the elevator lumbered up toward the fifth floor. "I don't know where the district attorney's investigation is going to lead, but if Winifred or . . ." He stopped.

"Don't *think* of suggesting that Adam was involved in bribery or bid rigging, Mac," Nell said fiercely.

"I'm not suggesting anything other than the fact that if the police decide to get a search warrant for these premises, it won't look good that you and I beat them to it."

"Mac, please." Nell tried to cover the catch in her voice. "I'm just trying to help. Mrs. Johnson is worried sick she'll have to leave Old Woods."

"Come on, Nell. We used to be honest with each other," Mac said as they stepped off the elevator. "You're not a Girl Scout. If there was bribery going on at Walters and Arsdale, you're hoping to find something that will tie Winifred to the problem and leave Adam as clean as the driven snow."

They walked down the dingy hallway. "Winifred's apartment is 5E." Nell reached into her shoulder bag for the keys Mrs. Johnson had given her and opened the door.

They stood for a moment in the foyer, getting their bearings. Already the place felt abandoned. A table to the left held a vase of wilting flowers. The living room was directly in front of them—a long, narrow, cheerless space with a threadbare carpet, an aging red velour sofa, an upright piano, and a library table. On the table were several framed pictures.

Nell walked to the table and studied the pictures. Most of them showed a young, eagerly smiling, waiflike Winifred in a bathing suit and receiving an award. "These have to be the pictures her mother wants," she told Mac. "I'll collect them on the way out."

Nell went back to the foyer and walked down the hall, her grandfather close behind her. She went on past a bedroom to the den, crowded with a couch, a television set, and a computer desk. She went over to the desk and opened the center drawer.

It was as though she had discovered another world. The drawer was stuffed with pieces of paper of every size and description, from sticky-backed notepads to architectural plans. On every one of them, in print, in handwriting, in large letters, Winifred had written four words: WINIFRED LOVES HARRY REYNOLDS.

THE manager of the salon at which Lisa Ryan worked had told her to take the whole week off. He'd said, "You need a little time to yourself so you can start the healing process."

The healing process, Lisa thought scornfully as she looked at the piles of clothing on the bed. Those must be the stupidest three words ever uttered. Someone had told her it would be therapeutic to keep busy, so here she was, cleaning out Jimmy's closet and drawers.

She glanced at the clock and was dismayed to see that the children would be home in twenty minutes. She didn't want them to see her sorting through their father's things.

The money—suddenly it flashed into her mind.

She had managed all day not to think about it. I don't know what to do, she thought. I don't know what to do.

The sudden sound of door chimes shattered the quiet. Lisa hurried downstairs to find a detective standing at her door.

Jack Sclafani felt a tug of genuine compassion. She looks as though she's been crying all day, he thought. "Detective Sclafani, Mrs. Ryan. I'd like to talk to you for a few minutes, if you don't mind."

Naked fear replaced the grief in her eyes. Finally she whispered, "Yes. Of course. Come in."

They sat across from each other in the small living room. Jack made a point of studying the large family portrait over the couch. "That was taken in happier times," he observed. "Jimmy looks every inch the proud husband and father."

The words achieved the desired effect. As tears welled in Lisa Ryan's eyes, she seemed to relax. "We had the world by the tail," she said quietly. "Oh, you know what I mean. We lived from payday to payday like most people, but we had dreams."

"Is it okay if I call you Lisa?"

"Yes, of course."

"Lisa, your first reaction when you heard Jimmy was dead was to ask if he had committed suicide. What was wrong in his life? I have a feeling it wasn't a problem between you two."

"No, it wasn't."

"Was he worried about his health?"

"Jimmy was never sick."

"If it's not a marital problem and if it's not health, then it's usually a money problem," Jack suggested.

Bingo, he thought as he saw Lisa Ryan's hands clench.

"It's easy to run up bills with a family." He sighed. "You put something on the credit card. You're sure you're going to pay it off, but then suddenly you need tires for the car or a new roof for the house. I'm married; I'm a father. It happens."

"We never ran up bills," Lisa said defensively. "At least not until Jimmy lost his job. Do you know why he lost it?" she burst out. "It was because he was honest and decent, and he was outraged that the contractor he was working for was putting lives in danger by using substandard concrete on the job. Well, for his conscientiousness he was blackballed," she said. "He was out of work almost two years until Adam Cauliff saw his résumé, and Sam Krause took him on."

Suddenly a possibility occurred to Lisa. Of course, she thought, that must be what happened. Jimmy had told her that Krause was known to cut corners. So in working for Krause, maybe he had been forced to go along with it or lose his job.

"It seems as though something was bothering Jimmy pretty badly even though he was working," Sclafani suggested. "Maybe there's something Jimmy would want us to know."

That's what happened, Lisa thought, barely hearing the detective's words. I'm sure of it. Jimmy saw something on a job that he knew was wrong. He was given his choice of being fired or being paid to look the other way. He felt he had no choice, but once he took money under the table, they had him.

"Jimmy was a good, honest man," she said.

Sclafani nodded at the portrait. "I can see that." This is it, he thought. She's going to talk about it.

"The other day, after the funeral . . ." Lisa began, but her words trailed off when she heard the sound of the kitchen door and the tramping of feet.

"Mom, we're home," Kelly called.

"I'm in here." Lisa sprang up, suddenly aghast that she had been about to tell a member of the police department that hidden downstairs was a packet of what could only be called "dirty money." The children were beside her, reaching up to kiss her. Lisa looked at

Sclafani. "Jimmy was mighty proud of these three," she said, her voice steady. "As I said, Jimmy Ryan was a good and decent man."

"SO WINIFRED had a boyfriend?"

"I'm shocked," Nell admitted to her grandfather. They were in a cab on the way home from Winifred's apartment. "I used to tease Adam by saying that she had a crush on him."

"She had a crush on him the way women had a crush on the Beatles or Elvis Presley. Adam buttered her up so she'd leave Walters and Arsdale and go with him," Cornelius MacDermott said.

"Mac!"

"Sorry," he said hastily. "What I mean is, Adam was a much younger man, married to a beautiful woman. Whatever Winifred was, she wasn't a dope. She was obviously involved with—or crazy about—some guy named Harry Reynolds."

"I wonder why he doesn't come forward?" Nell said. "I mean, it's as though Winifred just disappeared off the face of the earth. No one's contacted her mother except the building manager, who called about her plans for the apartment."

Nell had gathered the framed photographs on her lap. Cornelius MacDermott eyed the pile. "Want me to have Liz mail that stuff to the nursing home?"

"Okay," Nell agreed. "I'll call Mrs. Johnson and tell her it's on the way. And that we'll look in the office for Winifred's records."

The cab stopped in front of Nell's building. As Carlo opened the cab door for her, Mac's voice was hesitant. "Nell, you never filed a joint income tax return with Adam, did you?"

She was about to flare up at him when she saw the deeply worried look on his face.

"No, Mac. I filed separately," she said tightly. "But level with me. Is there anything you *know* that would suggest Adam wasn't on the up-and-up?"

"No," he said somewhat reluctantly. "Nothing."

"Then it's a combination of rumor and Walters and Arsdale's denial and that famous gut-level instinct of yours. Mac, I know you're trying to protect me, and I guess I should love you for it, but . . ."

"I don't feel very loved by you at the moment, Nell."

She managed a smile. "Truthfully, you're not; and then again, of course you are. Trust me, it's both." With an apologetic glance toward Carlo she stepped out of the cab. By the time she was in the elevator, she had made a decision.

She didn't begin to understand her own psychic abilities. She also didn't understand—or accept—the idea of a medium communicating with the dead. But if Bonnie Wilson claimed to be in touch with Adam, Nell knew she had to investigate that claim. If not for her sake, then for Adam's.

EACH day since the explosion of *Cornelia II* the search-and-recover coast guard team had continued the tedious process of searching for any remains of the boat and its passengers. On Friday afternoon, for the first time in four days, a find was made. In the area of the Verrazano Bridge a three-foot section of splintered wood bobbed through the water to shore. Pieces of a stained blue shirt with fragments of human bone were caught in the splinters.

Sam Krause's secretary had been asked to describe what he was wearing when he left the office. She was absolutely certain that it had been a long-sleeved blue sport shirt and khaki slacks.

George Brennan got the news of the find as he was leaving to meet Jack Sclafani at 405 East Fourteenth Street. In his pocket he had a warrant to search the Kaplan residence.

A distraught Ada Kaplan wept at the thought of what her neighbors were saying as her four-room apartment was searched inch by inch. Her son, Jed, sat at a table in the small dining area, an expression of contempt on his face.

He's not worried, Jack thought. If he did blow up that boat, he never had anything that could be evidence here.

They did have one small victory—the discovery of a bag of marijuana in a duffel bag in the closet. Enough to book for possession with intent to sell.

"Come on, you can tell that stuff is old," Jed protested.

Later, as they left Jed in the lockup, Brennan observed, "His mother'll put up the bond money, but at least the judge agreed to lift his passport." He didn't sound happy.

"He must have learned a lesson when he got caught in Australia with explosives in his car," Jack Sclafani said. "There was zilch in the apartment to tie him to that boat."

As they walked toward their cars, George Brennan received a call on his cell phone informing him that a woman's pocketbook had washed ashore in the same area near the Verrazano Bridge as the splintered wood. Inside the water-soaked wallet they'd found the credit cards and driver's license of Winifred Johnson.

"They say it was hardly even scorched," Brennan said when he had clicked off. "Crazy how that happens. It must have flown straight up, then landed in the water."

"Unless it wasn't on the boat when that bomb went off," Sclafani suggested after a thoughtful pause.

NELL spent the afternoon responding to the sympathy notes that had been piling up on her desk. When she was finished, it was nearly five o'clock. I've got to get out of here for a while, she thought. I haven't exercised all week.

She changed to shorts and a T-shirt, put a credit card and a ten-dollar bill in her pocket, jogged to Central Park, and began to run south. I used to run three or four times a week, she thought. How did I let myself stop doing it?

As she slowly eased herself into the old routine, enjoying the feeling of freedom that came with such open, unrestricted movement, Nell thought of the many cards of condolence she had received.

"We're so sorry about your tragedy . . ."

Why didn't I read one single letter saying what a terrific guy Adam was? Why do I feel so numb? Why can't I cry?

Nell picked up the pace, but she couldn't get the questions out of her mind.

Dan Minor looped around Central Park South and reentered the park, beginning the run northward. The late afternoon sun was warm, the breeze refreshing. The park was filled with joggers, Rollerbladers, and pedestrians.

Dan felt a stab of pain as he passed a bench occupied by an unkempt young woman wearing a threadbare dress, plastic bags overflowing at her feet. Is this the way Quinny has spent most of her life? he wondered.

Odd that it was easier to think of her as Quinny. Mom was someone else. Mom was a pretty dark-haired woman with loving arms, who used to call him Danny-boy.

As he ran, he had a fleeting impression of a tall woman with chestnut hair jogging past him. I know her, he thought. Dan stopped and turned. Of course. It was Nell MacDermott. He'd seen her on the ten-o'clock news last night.

Dan turned and jogged back toward Central Park South, following Nell MacDermott's chestnut hair.

As she approached Broadway, Nell slackened her pace. Now was the time to make up her mind.

She decided. If I am indeed going to see Bonnie Wilson and deal with her claims of being in touch with Adam, then I need to know a lot more about psychic phenomena than I do, she thought.

Dan followed Nell down to Fifty-seventh Street until she disappeared into the Coliseum bookstore. He stood on the sidewalk and stared at the window. Should he follow her in? Lifting the bottom of his long-sleeved sweatshirt, he mopped perspiration from his forehead. Maybe I should just write her a note, he thought.

But I'd really like to talk to her now.

Through the window he caught a glimpse of her between the racks of books. Then, with uneasy anticipation, he saw her walk to the checkout counter. She came out of the store, took two long strides to the corner, and raised her hand to signal a cab.

It's now or never, Dan thought. He took the plunge. "Nell."

She stopped. The tall sandy-haired jogger was vaguely familiar.

"Dan Minor. We met at the White House a few years back."

They both smiled. Dan added, "You were with your grandfather. I was Congressman Dade's guest."

I'm sure I know him, Nell thought as she studied his pleasant face. Then it came back to her. "Oh, yes, I remember. You're a pediatric surgeon. You went to Georgetown."

"That's right." Now what do I say? Dan asked himself. He watched as the spontaneous smile faded from Nell MacDermott's lips. "I just wanted to tell you how terribly sorry I am about your husband's death," he said quickly.

"Thank you."

"Lady, do you want this cab or not?" The taxi Nell had signaled had pulled over to the curb.

"Please." She put out her hand. "Thanks for stopping to say hello, Dan. It was good to see you again."

ON FRIDAY afternoon Ben Tucker was taken to the office of clinical child psychologist Dr. Megan Crowley.

He sat alone in the reception room while his mother went into another room to talk to the doctor. He knew that he was going to have to talk to her too, and he didn't want to, because she was sure to ask him about the dream. It was not something he wanted to talk about. He had it every single night now.

Mom and Dad tried to tell him that the dream wasn't real. They said that it was very hard for a kid to see a terrible explosion where people died.

They didn't get it. It wasn't the explosion. It was the *snake*.

The door opened, and his mother came out with another lady. "Hi, Ben," she said. "I'm Dr. Megan."

"Dr. Megan would like to talk with you, Benjy," his mother said.

He looked at the doctor. I'm not going to talk about the snake, he promised himself.

Dr. Megan surprised him, though. She asked him about school, and then she asked about sports. Then they talked about music class, and he told her that he hit a real clinker when he was playing the recorder today. They talked about a lot of things, but she never once asked him about the snake. She just said that she would see him again on Monday.

Saturday, June 17, to
Monday, June 19
Six

NELL had spent Friday evening reading the books she had purchased about psychic phenomena that afternoon after her run. By
Saturday afternoon she had gotten through all the sections of each
book that dealt with aspects she wanted to explore. What do I believe about all this? she kept asking herself.

She noted that in some books the author wrote about a person's
"aura." That last day, she thought, the day of the explosion, when I
saw Winifred, there seemed to be a kind of blackness around her.
That blackness, according to these books, is a symbol of death.

Nell had seen Bonnie Wilson on television. She had been positively startling in the way she talked to a woman about the circumstances of her husband's death.

The skeptics say that these people are just making lucky guesses,
based on information they have been clever enough to trick the subject into revealing. Well, I admit to being a skeptic, Nell thought,
but Bonnie Wilson could not have guessed everything she told that
woman. What about synchronicity? That's when you're thinking of
someone and a minute later that person calls you. It's as though one
person is sending a fax, and the other is receiving it. They're in sync.
Maybe the psychics who claim to be in touch with the dead are actually fax machines for the thoughts of the people who consult them.

Oh, Adam, why did I tell you not to come home that day? Nell
agonized. If I hadn't done that, would I be able to accept that
you're gone? But your death would still have left so many questions
unanswered. Who did this to you, Adam? And why?

Was the person who blew up your boat someone who wanted
you out of the way? Were you the target? Or was it Sam Krause?
Or Winifred? Jimmy Ryan's widow started to talk to me after the

Mass, but something made her run away. Could Jimmy have been the one who knew something dangerous?

For most of Saturday night Nell lay sleepless. I feel as though at any moment Adam might come in, she thought. Finally she dozed off, but she awoke again at six. Another beautiful June morning. She showered and dressed and went to the seven-o'clock Mass.

"May Adam's soul and the souls of the faithful departed rest in peace. . . ." Her prayer was the same as the week before, and would be the same for many Sundays to come.

On the way home from Mass she stopped to buy a bagel. It was still hot from the oven. I love New York on Sunday morning, she thought. On mornings such as this, it's like a small town just waking up.

This part of Manhattan had been Mac's electoral district, his streets. Will it be my district, my streets? she wondered.

Without Adam there would be no more agonizing about running for office.

She hated the realization that, for an instant, she felt a flicker of relief, knowing that at least that problem no longer existed.

PETER Lang spent the weekend at his home in Southampton, having turned down a half-dozen invitations. All his energy and thoughts were concentrated on his compelling need to have Nell MacDermott sell him the Kaplan land. With it he could finally be the force behind the creation of a masterpiece of architecture, a grand addition to the Manhattan skyline.

He had never put the Lang name on one of his buildings. He had waited, knowing that eventually he would find the perfect combination of location and design worthy of carrying his family's name.

When he approached Adam Cauliff with an offer, Cauliff had told him in so many words that he would see him in hell before he sold him the Kaplan parcel—thus the forced partnership.

Well, it looks like Adam will be showing up in hell before me, Peter thought with grim satisfaction.

Now he had to convince Cauliff's widow to sell him that property. She seemed financially well off. But he had one card up his sleeve, he mused as he walked down the flower-bordered path from his house to the ocean. One that was almost guaranteed to carry the day. Nell MacDermott was smart enough to know that he could do a lot to help her get elected and that it would be wise to get him on her side.

Peter Lang dropped the towel he was carrying, raced through the breaking surf, and threw himself into the Atlantic. The water was numbingly cold. As he swam with swift, expert strokes, he thought about his missed date with destiny and wondered if Adam Cauliff had still been alive when the water closed over him after the boat exploded.

BONNIE Wilson had told Gert to call her if Nell MacDermott wanted a consultation. She fully understood that even if Nell was anxious to see her, she still might hesitate. As a popular newspaper columnist, to be known to be consulting a psychic might bring her more publicity than she wanted. And there was talk of her running for Congress—the press was always looking for ways to discredit a candidate.

But on Sunday evening Bonnie received a call. "Nell would like to meet you," Gert said, her voice subdued.

"Something's wrong, Gert. I don't have to be a psychic to hear the stress in your voice."

"Oh, I'm afraid my brother is terribly upset with me. He took Nell and me to dinner tonight, and I let slip that you and I talked. Then he got all riled up and made the mistake of forbidding Nell to see you."

"Which of course means that she *is* going to see me."

"Maybe she would have anyhow," Gert said.

"Fine, Gert. Ask her to be here tomorrow at three."

THE salon was closed today; it was always closed on Mondays. In a way Lisa Ryan wished she were already back at work. By nine o'clock she had straightened up the house. There were still plenty of notes from friends and well-wishers to answer, but Lisa simply could not make herself get into them now.

She had to return the money. She knew with absolute certainty that Jimmy had been forced to accept it. And that Nell MacDermott might know something about whatever it was Jimmy was working on. After all, it was someone from Nell's husband's firm who had passed his application to Sam Krause Construction. What began as an apparent act of kindness had ended up with Jimmy dead. Somehow the money in that box was tied to it all.

Lisa's call to Nell was answered on the first ring.

Five minutes later Lisa Ryan was on her way to meet the other woman made a widow by the boat explosion, to ask her help in finding out what terrible thing at work had forced a good man to look the other way for fifty thousand dollars—and in finding a way to make it right.

GEORGE Brennan and Jack Sclafani were both present when Robert Walters, senior partner of Walters and Arsdale Design Associates, accompanied by the firm's chief counsel, arrived at the office of Assistant District Attorney Cal Thompson. Walters was there under a "Queen for a Day" agreement, which granted him limited immunity for anything he disclosed about bribery and bid rigging in the construction business.

His chief counsel had already issued a statement to the press: "Walters and Arsdale and its principals deny any wrongdoing and are confident they will not be charged with any criminal activity."

Behind the façade of casual indifference it was clear to both Brennan and Sclafani that Walters was nervous. Everything he did was just a little too perfect to be anything other than a well-rehearsed act.

I'd be nervous too, Brennan thought. The big guys in almost two dozen firms just like his already copped a plea, choosing the easy way out of this investigation. Most of them would end up with a slap on the wrist. So you pay a million bucks while your company is raking in half a billion. If the prosecutor really had the goods, a few big shots could actually go to jail for a couple of months. But when they come out—guess what? It starts all over again.

It's a simple racket, he thought. The powerhouse builders agree who's going to get the job. The lowest bid is still padded, but the architect accepts it—and gets a kickback in return. Then the next big project comes along, and bingo! The next powerhouse guy gives the low bid. Everything is rigged and, oh, so civilized.

"This is an industry in which legitimate sales commissions have been misconstrued—" Walters was saying.

His counsel interrupted. "My client meant to say . . ."

The questioning finally got around to what George Brennan and Jack Sclafani had come to hear. "Mr. Walters, was the late Adam Cauliff a member of your firm?"

Oh, he doesn't like that name, Sclafani thought as he watched Robert Walters flush with anger at the question.

"He was in our employ about two and a half years."

"In what capacity did Mr. Cauliff work?"

"He began as a staff architect. Later he was put in charge of mid-level reconstructions and renovations."

"What do you consider mid-level?"

"Projects that will bill less than one hundred million dollars."

"Was his work satisfactory?"

"I would say so."

"You say that Cauliff was with you for more than two years. Why did he leave you?"

"To open his own firm." Robert Walters smiled coldly. "Adam Cauliff was a very practical man. And he learned quickly. He was smart enough to purchase the parcel of land adjacent to the Vandermeer mansion, which was subsequently removed from landmark status."

"The mansion burned down, did it not?"

"Yes. After it had lost its landmark status. Peter Lang bought the property and had begun plans to erect a combined apartment-office building." Walters smiled grimly. "Adam Cauliff thought Lang would so desperately want the parcel that he would accept

Cauliff's design for the proposed building. It was not working out that way, however. Cauliff's design was pedestrian and imitative. The investors wouldn't touch it, and I understand that Lang told him so.

"Cauliff was in something of a bind. He would have had to sell the Kaplan parcel to Lang at whatever price he was offered. Otherwise, Lang might well have constructed a much less ambitious building, independent of Cauliff. Had that happened, the Kaplan parcel would have been so hemmed in as to be virtually useless. So you see, Cauliff was definitely in a tough spot."

The door to the office opened, and Joe Mayes, an assistant D.A., came in. From the expression on his face Brennan and Sclafani could see that something big had happened.

"Mr. Walters," Mayes asked abruptly, "did your firm renovate an office building on Lexington and Forty-seventh?"

"Yes. This morning we received notice that several bricks in the façade seemed loose. We're sending an inspection team to the site."

"I'm afraid the bricks are more than loose, Mr. Walters. The entire façade has collapsed onto the street. Three pedestrians were injured, one of them critically."

A FEW hours after Lisa Ryan's visit and shocking revelation Nell rang the doorbell at Bonnie Wilson's apartment on West End Avenue. Hearing the faint sound of approaching footsteps, she thought of making a dash for the elevator while there still was time.

What am I doing here? she asked herself. Mac was right. All this talk of mediums and messages is nothing more than hocus-pocus, and I'm an idiot to put myself in the position of being ridiculed if it ever comes out that I fell for this kind of thing.

The door opened.

"Nell, come in." Bonnie Wilson was rail thin. Her midnight-black hair was a startling contrast to her porcelain complexion. Her large gray eyes were fringed with heavy lashes.

She led Nell into a small study and gestured to a chair. "Please sit down. If, after we've chatted, you want to walk out, I won't be offended. Your aunt tells me you're very uncomfortable with the concept of contact with those who have passed on."

"Bonnie, I have to be very up front," Nell said stiffly. "I simply don't buy the concept of your being able to do something that sounds suspiciously like picking up a phone and contacting a dead person. Nor do I accept that someone on the 'other side,' in essence, contacts you."

Bonnie smiled. "I appreciate your honesty. Nevertheless I have been chosen to be a mediator between people who have passed over and their loved ones here. Usually someone comes to me who is grief-stricken and wants to be in touch with the person who has gone ahead.

"But sometimes it works a different way. For example, one day when I was helping a husband who had passed over give a message to his wife, I was contacted by a young person named Jackie who had died in an automobile accident. I didn't understand how I could help him. Then, a week later, I received a phone call from a woman I had never met." Bonnie Wilson's eyes darkened as she spoke. "Her son, Jackie, had died in an automobile accident."

"But there is much less coincidence in my being here now. To begin with, you know Gert," Nell protested. "The newspapers were filled with the story of the explosion on the boat." She stood up. "Bonnie, I'm afraid I've wasted too much of your time already. I should go."

"Adam asked for you, Nell. You haven't wasted my time if you'll just give me the chance to see if he wants to convey a message to you."

Reluctantly Nell sat down again.

Minutes passed. Bonnie's eyes were closed, her cheek resting on her hand. Then suddenly she tilted her head as though straining to hear someone or something. A long moment later she lowered her hand and opened her eyes.

"Adam is here," she said quietly.

In spite of her disbelief Nell felt a chill pass through her body. Be sensible, she told herself fiercely. "Can you see him?"

"In my mind's eye. He's looking at you with so much love, Nell. He's smiling at you. He's saying that of course you don't believe he's here. You're from Missouri."

Nell gasped. "I'm from Missouri" was an expression she had said jokingly whenever Adam tried to convince her that she could learn to enjoy boating.

"Adam wants to apologize. I'm getting from him that you quarreled the last time you were together."

I didn't tell anyone that we had quarreled, Nell thought. Not one single soul.

"Adam is telling me that there was something you wanted to do and that he was making it difficult for you. I see white roses over your head. They're a sign of his love for you."

Nell felt burning tears in her eyes. She did not believe her own words as she spoke. "Tell him I love him too. Tell him I'm so sorry we quarreled."

"He looks so pleased, Nell. But he is saying that he wants you to begin the new chapter in your life. Is there a situation that will take all your energy and time?"

The campaign, Nell thought.

Bonnie did not wait for her to reply. "Yes, I understand," she was murmuring. "He says, 'Tell Nell to give away all my clothes.' I see a room with racks and bins. . . ."

"I always take clothes to a church in our neighborhood," Nell said. "It has a room like the one you describe."

"Adam says that you should give them away in his name, to help him achieve higher spiritual fulfillment. And he says you must pray for him." Bonnie's eyes stared straight ahead, not seeming to see anything. "He is leaving us," she said.

"Stop him!" Nell cried. "Someone blew up his boat. Ask him if he knows who did that to him."

Bonnie waited. "I don't think he's going to tell us, Nell. He either doesn't know, or he has forgiven his assailant and does not want you to be unforgiving." She shook her head. "He's gone," she said. "No, wait. Does 'Peter' mean anything to you?"

Peter Lang, Nell thought. "Yes," she said quietly.

"Nell, blood is dripping around him. I can't be sure if that means this Peter was the assailant. I can be sure, though, that Adam is trying to warn you about him. He begs you to be careful."

ON MONDAY afternoon Dan Minor arrived home to find a message from Lilly Brown on the answering machine.

"Dr. Dan," she began, "I've been asking and asking around about Quinny, but nobody has seen her in months. That's just not right. There's a group she stays with sometimes on East Fourth Street, in the tenements there. They're wondering if maybe she's sick and got locked up somewhere. Sometimes when Quinny got big-time depressed, she wouldn't talk or eat for days."

Is that where I'll find her? Dan wondered, his heart sinking. Locked in a psychiatric ward—or worse? If Quinny had been in a protracted depression and not been forced into a shelter, anything might have happened to her.

I can't sit back any longer and wait for her to show up. I'll check out hospitals and walk around East Fourth Street myself. I became what I am for her sake, he thought. Please let me be able to tell her that, he prayed.

CORNELIUS MacDermott had a visit on Monday afternoon from Tom Shea, the party chairman for New York City. Shea needed to know one way or the other about Nell's decision on making a run for Bob Gorman's congressional seat.

"I don't have to tell you it's a presidential election year, Mac," he said. "A strong candidate for this seat is going to help get out the overall vote to put our guy in the White House. You're a legend in this district. Your presence at Nell's side will be a constant reminder to the voters of what you did for them."

"You ever hear the advice they give to the groom's mother before a wedding?" Mac snapped. "It's 'Wear beige and keep your mouth shut.' That's what I intend to do if Nell runs. She's smart, good-looking, knows what the job entails, and can do it better than anyone. Best of all, she cares about people. That's why she should run."

"Oh, come on, Mac," Tom Shea said good-naturedly. "People fell in love with Nell when they saw that picture of her as a ten-year-old, trying to dry your tears at her parents' memorial Mass. She grew up in the eye of the public. We can hold off the announcement till the dinner on the thirtieth, but we have to be sure that her husband's death won't make it too tough for her to campaign."

"Nothing is too tough for Nell," Mac said. "She's a pro."

When Shea left, Mac went to find Liz Hanley. "Liz, I blew up at Nell when I realized she was going to that psychic. Call her up and help me make peace. Tell her we'll have dinner."

"Blessed are the peacemakers," Liz said dryly.

"You've told me that before."

"That's because I've done this before. Where shall I tell her to meet you for dinner?"

"Neary's. Seven thirty."

IN THEIR Monday afternoon session Dr. Megan Crowley maneuvered the conversation around to the day Ben Tucker had observed the boat blow up in New York harbor. She would have preferred to wait, but Ben's nightmares were taking a toll on him.

She began by talking about Martha's Vineyard. "When I was little, I loved to go there," she said, "but boy, was that a long trip. Six hours in the car and then an hour on the ferry."

"Ferries stink," Ben said. "The one I was on made me want to barf. I don't ever want to go on one again."

"Oh, where did you go on one, Benjy?"

"My dad took me to see the Statue of Liberty." He paused. "That was the day the boat blew up."

Megan waited.

Ben's expression became reflective. "I was looking right at the boat. It was cool. I was wishing I was on it instead of on that stupid ferry." He frowned. "I don't want to talk about it."

"Ben, sometimes it helps to talk if something's bothering you. It's pretty awful to see a boat blow up."

"I could see the people," he whispered.

"If you would draw a picture of what you saw, I bet it would help you to get it out of your mind."

"I really like to draw a lot."

Megan had sheets of sketching paper and crayons waiting. Ben bent over the worktable, deep in concentration.

As Megan watched, she realized that he must have seen the accident in closer detail than even his father had realized. The sky in the drawing became filled with brightly colored debris, broken furniture and dishes.

Ben's face became pinched and tight as he drew in what was clearly a human hand.

He laid his crayon down. "I don't want to draw the snake."

NELL was at a corner table, sipping a glass of wine and nibbling on a breadstick when her grandfather arrived at Neary's.

Noting his surprised expression, she said airily, "Just thought I'd play your game, Mac. Arrange to meet at seven thirty. Arrive at seven fifteen. Then tell the other guy he's late so he'll be thrown off-balance."

"Too bad that's the only thing you've learned from me," Mac barked as he slid in next to her.

Nell kissed his cheek. Yes, they had their differences, but Mac was a rock, always there for her. She simply could not stay mad at him. "Hi, Grandpa," she said.

Their fingers interlocked. "Still my best girl, Nell?"

"Of course I am. The special tonight is sliced steak, your favorite. My favorite too."

Cornelius and Cornelia MacDermott smiled at each other. Inevitably they began to discuss the election. "It's never over till it's over, Nell," Mac said. "Every congressional district is important. People who feel strongly about one candidate will pull the lever down for everyone else on that same slate. You are a candidate who can make them do that."

"Do you really think so?" she asked.

"I know so. I haven't been doing this all my life for nothing. Let us put your name on that ballot, and you'll see."

"You know I will, Mac. Just let me have another couple of days to get my head together."

"You go to that psychic?"

"Yes, I did. Mac, she told me Adam was sorry he had opposed the 'new chapter' in my life. I'm sure that meant my going into politics. He wants me to go on with my life."

"If that's what you heard, it was pretty good advice."

"I'd say it wasn't much different from what Monsignor Duncan might have told me. The only difference," she added deliberately, "is that Bonnie Wilson hears it directly from Adam." Mac stared at her. "I know it sounds incredible," she said, "but when I was there, I believed it."

"Do you believe it now?"

"I believe the advice. But Mac, there was something else. Peter Lang's name came up. Again, I don't know what to think, but Adam is warning me about him."

"Nell, for God's sake! You're taking all this too seriously."

"I know. But Adam and Peter Lang were working to develop that property on Twenty-eighth Street."

"Look, Lang didn't get to where he is now without pulling a few fast ones, so chances are he's not lily-white. I'll get someone to nose around." Mac hesitated. "Nell, you must have heard about that façade that collapsed today on Lexington Avenue?"

"Yes. I caught it on the six-o'clock news."

"Right before I left the office tonight, I got a call from Bob Walters. Sam Krause did the work on that building, but Adam was the architect of record who designed the renovation. If corners were being cut, then arguably Adam was the one to have known about it. Several pedestrians were hurt in the collapse, and one may not make it." He paused. "Adam's name may come up in another criminal investigation."

Mac saw the glimmer of anger. "Nell," he said, his voice a plea, "I have to warn you. I don't want to see you hurt."

Nell flashed back to earlier in the day, when Bonnie Wilson was communicating with Adam: *He's looking at you with so much love. . . . He has forgiven his assailant.*

"Mac, I want to know every single thing they are saying about my husband, because even if it kills me, I'm going to get to the truth of all this. Somebody put a bomb on that boat and took Adam's life. I swear this to you: One way or another, I'm going to find out who it was."

Tuesday, June 20
Seven

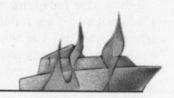

AS SHE opened the door to Peter Lang, Nell could not help wondering just how bad the traffic accident had been that kept him from attending the fatal meeting on Adam's boat. Less than a week had passed since she'd seen him, yet she could no longer detect even the trace of a bruise on his face.

Urbane. Handsome. A real estate visionary. Those words described Lang in the gossip and society columns.

Blood is dripping around him. . . . Adam is trying to warn you.

"I think about you a lot, Nell. How have you been?"

"I guess about as well as you would expect," she responded.

"You certainly look very well." Smiling, he took both her hands in his. "I feel odd saying that, but it is a fact."

"Nothing like keeping up appearances," Nell replied, freeing her hands and leading him into the living room.

"Oh, I suspect you're a very strong woman who takes pride in keeping up appearances." Lang paused. How much did she know? "Nell, Adam and I were in a business venture together. As you know, Adam had created the design for the tower complex we planned to build."

"Yes, he was very excited about the project," Nell said.

"We were delighted with his work. Adam was a creative and exciting architect. We will miss him terribly. Unfortunately, now that he isn't with us, I'm afraid we have to start all over. Another architect doubtless will have his own concept."

"I can understand that."

So Adam hadn't told her he was off the job, Lang thought. Surely there's no point telling her now. "As I'm sure you know, last August, Adam purchased a downtown building and lot from a Mrs. Kaplan. It adjoins a lot I have since purchased, and it was part of the equity he brought to the construction deal. The assessed value of that property as of last week was eight hundred thousand dollars, but I'm prepared to offer you three million dollars for it, a nice return on a ten-month investment."

"Why are you willing to pay so much money?" Nell asked.

"Because with it, we will have room to include a number of aesthetic additions, such as a curving driveway and more elaborate landscaping. I might add that when our tower complex goes up, it will have such a dominant presence that your property, assuming you retain it, may actually lose some of its present value."

"I'll think about it." Nell gave a slight smile.

Lang smiled in return. "Of course. Obviously you'll want to discuss this with your grandfather." He paused. "Nell, I may be out of line, but I'd like to think we're friends and that you can be up front with me. As you must be aware, there have been a lot of rumors around town, and I hope they're true, about your running for your grandfather's congressional seat."

Nell stood, indicating that their meeting was finished. "I never discuss rumors, Peter."

"Meaning that if you announce, you'll choose your own time to do it. Nell, I just want you to know that you have my wholehearted support in every way possible."

"Thank you." And you're about as subtle as a sledgehammer, she thought.

The door had barely closed behind Lang when the phone rang. It was Detective Jack Sclafani requesting that Nell agree to admit him and his partner to Adam's office to examine the contents of Winifred Johnson's desk and files.

"We can probably get a search warrant," Sclafani said, "but it would be easier to do it this way. And we can talk to you then too."

"I'll meet you there," Nell told him. Carefully she added, "I should tell you that at her mother's request I went to Winifred's apartment to look for insurance policies or other personal financial information. I found nothing."

THE detectives arrived on Twenty-seventh Street before Nell. Together they studied the architectural model in the office window.

"Pretty fancy," Sclafani observed. "You must get big bucks for dreaming up something as fancy as this."

"It looks better to us than it does to people who know architecture," Brennan replied. "According to Walters, they were turning it down."

Nell had gotten out of a taxi behind the two detectives just in time to hear Brennan's remark.

"What?" she demanded. "Did you say they were turning down Adam's design?"

Brennan spun around. "Mr. Walters was at the district attorney's office yesterday, Ms. MacDermott. That was what he told us."

Her expression hardened. "I wouldn't trust anything Mr. Walters said." With that, Nell walked to the door and rang the bell. "I don't have a key," she explained crisply.

She waited with her back to the two men, trying to calm herself. If what they said was true, why did Peter Lang lie to me less than an hour ago? she wondered. And why didn't Adam tell me about it? He should have told me.

The building superintendent appeared and opened the door.

Jack Sclafani could tell that George Brennan had the same reaction to Adam Cauliff's business quarters as he did: well-enough furnished but surprisingly small. Basically it consisted of a reception area and two offices.

"How many people did your husband employ?" he asked.

"He only had Winifred here with him. Today, so much of the work of an architect is done on computer that when you're starting out on your own, you don't need to take on a big overhead. Adam could farm out segments of the work."

Nell realized that she had spent much of the past two weeks trying to sound calm and self-controlled. What would these detectives think if they knew about Lisa Ryan's visit and challenge? *Find out where and why someone made my husband take fifty thousand dollars to keep his mouth shut, and help me find a way to make it right.* And what about the collapse of the building façade? Can they blame that in some way on Adam? She needed time to put the pieces together.

She realized suddenly that the two detectives were looking at her. "Sorry," she said. "Woolgathering, I guess. Being here is more difficult than I had thought."

She did not realize, of course, that the sympathy in their faces masked a sudden certainty that like Lisa Ryan, Nell MacDermott knew something that she was afraid to discuss.

Winifred's desk was locked, but George Brennan produced a ring of keys. "Her purse was recovered," he told Nell, "and these were inside. The purse was hardly scorched. That's the amazing thing."

"A lot of amazing things have happened in these last two weeks," Nell said. "Including the attempt of Walters and Arsdale to suggest that any irregularities in their company should be blamed on my husband. This morning Adam's accountant assured me there is nothing in his affairs that won't bear the closest scrutiny."

I hope so, George Brennan thought. "I don't want to keep you," he said to Nell. "Why don't we take a quick look."

It took only minutes to ascertain that there was nothing out of the ordinary to be found. "It's exactly the same as her desk at home except here we did at least find some insurance policies and the deed to Winifred's father's grave," Nell said.

The filing cabinet next to the desk held files, boxes of paper, heavy brown wrapping paper, and rolls of twine.

Jack Sclafani skimmed the files. "Run-of-the-mill correspondence," he said. He thumbed through Winifred's address book. "Do you mind if we borrow this?" he asked Nell.

"No, of course not. It probably should go to her mother anyway." Nell hesitated. "Look, I don't know whether this is relevant or not, but Winifred apparently was involved with a man named Harry Reynolds."

"How do you know that?" Brennan asked quickly.

"When I looked through the desk in her apartment, one drawer was stuffed with papers of every imaginable kind. On every one she'd written 'Winifred loves Harry Reynolds.' My impression when I saw it was that they'd been written by a fifteen-year-old girl with a terrible crush on someone."

"To me that sounds more like an obsession than a crush," Brennan observed. "Winifred Johnson was a quiet woman who lived with her mother until she went into a nursing home."

"That's right."

"Invariably that's the kind of woman who falls like a ton of bricks for the wrong guy." He raised an eyebrow. "We'll follow up on Harry Reynolds. Ms. MacDermott, we're going for a cup of coffee. How about joining us?"

Nell hesitated, then decided to accept. "Thank you, yes. I had a meeting with Peter Lang this morning I want to tell you about. My feeling is that he is both a liar and a manipulator, and he was definitely someone who stood to benefit from my husband's death."

CORNELIUS MacDermott had spent a sleepless night. On Tuesday he did not go to the office until nearly noon, and when he arrived there, Liz Hanley was startled to see that his normally ruddy complexion had faded to an unhealthy gray.

It was her concern for his health that convinced her she should go along with his plan to prove to Nell that celebrity psychic Bonnie Wilson was nothing but a charlatan.

"Call for an appointment," Mac told Liz. "Use your sister's name, just in case Gert ever mentioned you to this Wilson woman."

"If she has caller ID, she'll know perfectly well who I am."

"Good thinking. Your sister lives on Beekman Place, doesn't she? Pay her a visit and call from there."

When Liz got back to the office, she announced, "I'm seeing Bonnie Wilson at three o'clock tomorrow."

"Thanks, Liz. I knew I could count on you," Mac said somewhat sheepishly.

LISA Ryan went back to work at the salon on Tuesday. She arrived home at six to find her friend Brenda Curren in the kitchen. The enticing aroma of roasting chicken was in the air. The table had been set for six, and Brenda's husband, Ed, was working with Charley on his reading assignment.

"You're too good to be true," Lisa said quietly.

"We thought a little company might be welcome," Brenda said.

"It is." Lisa went into the bathroom and splashed water on her face. You haven't cried all day, she told herself. Don't start now.

Over dinner Ed Curren brought up the subject of Jimmy's workroom. "Lisa, I know Jimmy had some sophisticated tools. I think you should sell them right away. They'll lose their value very quickly." He began to carve the chicken. "If you'd like, I'll be glad to sort out everything that's down there."

"No!" Lisa said. Then when she saw the expressions on the faces of her friends and her children, she realized how vehemently she had refused a kind offer. "I'm sorry," she said. "I just don't feel up to dealing with it right now."

But when the Currens were gone and the children were asleep, she crept downstairs to the file drawer. It's like a time bomb, she thought, staring at the money. I have to get it out of here!

DAN Minor rearranged his Tuesday afternoon schedule in order to have time to go downtown to the Missing Persons Squad at One Police Plaza, the headquarters of the NYPD.

The detective he spoke to was sympathetic but realistic. "I'm awfully sorry, Dr. Minor, but you don't know if your mother was even in New York at the point you started looking for her. You're not even certain that she's 'missing.' Have you any idea how many people are reported missing in this city each year?"

Dan filled out a missing persons report, took a cab home, and changed into a light sweat suit and sneakers. His best chance, he decided, was to walk around the East Fourth Street area.

As he made his way rapidly across town, Nell MacDermott's face floated through his mind—a frequent occurrence since the day he had run into her in the park.

The thought of possibly seeing Nell again cheered Dan during the next two hours as he walked, block after block, in the area of East Fourth Street begging for information. He had fortified himself with a stack of his cards with his phone number, which he handed out to everyone he talked to. "Fifty bucks for anyone who can give me a lead to her," he promised.

Finally, at seven o'clock he gave up, took a cab uptown to Central Park, and began to jog. At Seventy-second Street he once again ran into Nell.

BY UNSPOKEN mutual consent Jack Sclafani and George Brennan waited until they were back in their offices before discussing what Nell had told them.

Jack settled at his desk and drummed his fingers on the arm of the chair. "She as much as said she thinks Lang may have had something to do with the explosion. Yet his story about the traffic accident seemed to check out."

"As I remember it, he claimed he was using a cellular phone and that the sun got in his eyes," Brennan said. "It could have been intentional. Anyway, she raised a lot of interesting questions." He pulled out a pad and began to jot down notes. "Here's one right off the top worth looking into: Exactly what kind of building did Lang really want to put up on that Vandermeer property, and how essential was the Kaplan parcel? That goes to motive."

"Add this one," Sclafani said. "When did Lang tell Cauliff that his design had been rejected?"

"Which leads to my next question, Jack. Why didn't Cauliff tell his wife that Lang had dumped him? That would be the normal thing to do, assuming they were a close couple."

"Talking about close—what do you think is going on with Winifred's boyfriend, Harry Reynolds?" Sclafani asked.

"I'll throw another suggestion on the table," Brennan said. "Let's dig around and see if we can't find a connection between Lang and our old friend Jed Kaplan."

Sclafani nodded. "Since we're making work for ourselves, I have one more name to add to the list."

"I can guess who it is: Adam Cauliff."

"Exactly. Kaplan hated him. Walters hated him. Lang rejected his design. He doesn't exactly come through as prince of the city. I wonder who else may have thought it would be a good idea if his boat didn't make it back to the marina."

"Okay. I'll make some background calls," Brennan said.

A couple of hours later Brennan poked his head into Sclafani's office. "Got some preliminary feedback from a guy I called in Bismarck, North Dakota. It seems Cauliff was about as popular with his former employer out there as ants are at a church picnic. This could be leading somewhere."

As THEY jogged together along the paths of Central Park, Nell realized that there was something very comforting about having Dan Minor running beside her. He seemed to exude an innate strength, a power that showed in the disciplined way he moved, in the firm grasp of his hand on her arm when she started to trip and he reached out to steady her.

They ran as far north as the reservoir, then circled back to the East Side at Seventy-second Street. Panting, Nell stopped. "This is where I get off."

Having serendipitously run into her again, Dan had no intention of letting her go until he had extracted her phone number. "I'll walk you home," he said promptly.

On the way he said casually, "I don't know about you, Nell, but

I'm getting hungry. Would you consider meeting me for dinner in about an hour or so?"

"Oh, I don't think—"

He interrupted her. "Do you have specific plans?"

"No."

"Don't forget, I'm a doctor. Even if you don't feel hungry, you have to eat."

After a few minutes of gentle persuasion they parted, having agreed to meet later at Il Tinello on West Fifty-sixth Street. "Better make that an hour and a half," Nell suggested. "Unless, of course, all the traffic lights turn green when they see you coming."

EARLIER that day, after she had returned home from Adam's office, Nell had spent several hours sorting and folding his clothing. Now the bed and the chairs in the guest room were covered with stacks of socks and ties, shorts and undershirts. She had moved all his suits and slacks and jackets into the closet there as well, and the maintenance men had taken his dresser down to the storage room.

Now, as she returned from the park and hurried into the bedroom, where she began to peel off her jogging shorts and T-shirt, Nell realized that the room seemed in some way to have a renewed sense of sanctuary.

I guess just looking at Adam's dresser and opening the closet and seeing his clothes made me think of how he died—so suddenly, she thought, without any chance to say good-bye. It also reminded me of those last angry moments before he stalked out of the house and out of my life forever.

After a quick shower she dressed in a periwinkle-blue silk pantsuit that she had bought last year and forgotten about. She remembered how much she had liked it. Best of all, it didn't have any link to Adam.

Dan Minor was waiting for her at the table when she arrived at Il Tinello. He sprang to his feet and smiled.

"All the traffic lights must have turned green," Nell said.

"Almost all of them. You look lovely, Nell. Thanks for joining me. I'm afraid I bullied you into saying yes."

"You didn't bully me. I'm glad you persuaded me to get out. I'm actually hungry."

Over a glass of wine they discovered the mutual friends they had in Washington. Over prosciutto and melon they talked about the presidential election and realized they would cancel out each other's vote. When their pasta arrived, Dan told her about his decision to move to New York.

"The hospital is becoming a major pediatric burn center, and since that's my area of specialization, it's a great opportunity."

He also told her about his search for his mother.

"You mean, she just dropped out of your life?" Nell asked. "Do you think she wants you to find her?"

"She had become an alcoholic and felt I'd be better off with my grandparents. She left because she blamed herself for an accident in which I was nearly killed. I want to show her how that accident proved, in fact, to be of enormous value to me."

He told about going to Missing Persons.

"Mac might be able to help," Nell said. "I know they'd search the records if he made a few calls. I'll talk to him, but you should drop by his office. I'll give you his card."

When the demitasse came, Dan said, "Nell, I've talked your ear off. Say you don't want to discuss it and we're off the subject, but I have to ask: How is it *really* going for you?"

"*Really* going for me?" Nell dropped the sliver of lemon peel into her espresso. "I don't know how to answer that. You see, when someone dies, but you don't have a body or a casket or a procession to the graveyard, it's almost like that person is still out there somewhere. I keep saying to myself, 'Adam is dead, Adam is dead,' but the words keep sounding meaningless."

"Did it feel that way when you lost your parents?"

"No. I knew they were gone. The difference is that they died in an accident. Adam did not—I'm sure of that. Think about it. Four people died on that boat. Someone needed to get rid of one of them, maybe all four of them. That person is still walking around, enjoying life, maybe having a late dinner right now, just as we are." She paused, looking at her hands. "I am going to find out who did this."

"You realize, Nell, that anyone who can so calculatingly take four lives is a very dangerous human being."

Across from him, Nell MacDermott's face contorted, her eyes widened and filled with panic.

"Nell, what is it?"

She shook her head. "No, it's all right," she said.

"It's not all right, Nell. What is it?"

For an instant she had felt just as she had when she was caught in the riptide. She had felt trapped and as though she were fighting for air. But this time, instead of trying to swim, she had been struggling to open a door. And instead of cold water, she had sensed burning heat—and an awareness that she was going to die.

Wednesday, June 21, and Thursday, June 22

Eight

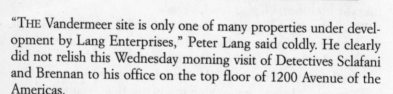

"THE Vandermeer site is only one of many properties under development by Lang Enterprises," Peter Lang said coldly. He clearly did not relish this Wednesday morning visit of Detectives Sclafani and Brennan to his office on the top floor of 1200 Avenue of the Americas.

"For example," he continued, "we own this building. I could drive through Manhattan and show you the other properties we own, as well as those we manage. But I have to ask, gentlemen, what is your point?"

Our point, buddy, Jack Sclafani thought, is that you're starting to look like the prime suspect in four murders, so don't get on your high horse with us.

"Mr. Lang, we appreciate how busy you are," George Brennan

said, "but I'm sure you understand our need to ask a few questions. You went to see Nell MacDermott yesterday, didn't you?"

Lang raised an eyebrow. "Yes, I did. What of it?"

"What was the purpose of your visit?"

"Purely business," Lang said, looking at his watch. "Gentlemen, you'll have to excuse me. I have a meeting."

"You're *having* a meeting, Mr. Lang," Brennan said. "When did you reject Adam Cauliff's design?"

"I would not say it was rejected. I would say that it needed considerable rethinking."

"That's not what you told his wife, is it?"

Peter Lang stood up. "I resent your tone and attitude."

"Mr. Lang, just one more question," Detective Sclafani said. "You made a peremptory bid for the Vandermeer property after the mansion was removed from landmark status, didn't you?"

"The city desperately wanted land I owned. I traded. The city got the better deal. Gentlemen, if you have further questions, you can call my lawyer." Lang switched on the intercom. "Mr. Brennan and Mr. Sclafani are ready to leave," he told his secretary. "Please show them to the elevator."

GERT MacDermott called Nell on Wednesday morning. "Are you going to be home?" she asked. "I made a crumb cake this morning, and I know it's one of your favorites."

"Was and is. Sure, Aunt Gert, come on over."

"Now, if you're too busy . . ."

"My column's almost finished. I'll have the kettle whistling."

"I'll be there by eleven."

At eleven the doorman phoned to say Ms. MacDermott was on the way up. Mac taught both Gert and me to be prompt, Nell thought. Adam, though, was always late.

She felt disloyal remembering that.

"You look better." Gert kissed her. She held a cake tin in her hands. "I tried to phone you last night, but you were out. Bonnie Wilson called to see how you were doing."

"That was nice of her." Nell took the cake from her great-aunt. "Come on. Let's have that tea."

As they sipped, Gert said, "Nell, anytime you're really down and want company, you know who to call."

Nell smiled. "You."

"That's right. And listen, I hope you've followed up on giving away Adam's clothing. Bonnie thinks it's important."

"I've started to pack his things. The superintendent is getting me some boxes. Saturday's still the day they accept donations, isn't it?"

"That's right." A small church on Eighty-fifth Street ran the thrift shop where Gert volunteered. "And on Saturday I'll be there. It's my day to check in whatever we get."

LIZ Hanley tapped on and opened the door of Cornelius Mac-Dermott's private office. "I'm on my way," she told him.

"Now, Liz, I feel a little guilty asking you to do this, but it is important."

"Mac, if that woman puts a hex on me, it's your fault."

"Come straight back here when you get finished with her."

"Or she gets finished with me."

BONNIE Wilson was a startlingly attractive woman and younger than Liz had anticipated. However, the atmosphere in the apartment was more in keeping with her expectations. The gloomy foyer made a startling contrast to the brightness of the June afternoon she had just left outside.

Meekly she followed Bonnie to a study on the side of the long hallway. "Why don't you sit on the couch?" Bonnie said. "That way I can hold your hands for a few moments."

Feeling increasingly nervous, Liz sat down and obeyed.

Bonnie closed her eyes. "You're wearing your wedding band, but I sense you've been a widow a long time."

How can she pick that up so quickly? Liz wondered.

"I see the number forty. You've been nostalgic the past few weeks because you would have celebrated your fortieth wedding anniversary. You were a June bride."

Dumbfounded, Liz could only nod.

"I hear the name Sean. Was there a Sean in your family? I don't think it's your husband. It's more like a brother." Bonnie raised her hand to the side of her head. "I feel the most intense pain here," she murmured. "I believe it means Sean was killed in an accident."

"Sean was seventeen," Liz said, her voice thick with emotion. "The car went out of control. His skull was fractured."

"He is on the other side, along with your husband and all your family who have passed over. He wants you to know they all send their love. Be comforted, knowing that is true."

Later, almost in a daze, Liz Hanley followed Bonnie back down the shadowy hallway. A table with a mirror over it held a silver dish with Bonnie's business cards. Liz reached to take one of them. Suddenly her blood went cold. She was looking into the mirror, but there was another face there, behind her own image. It was only an impression, gone almost before she caught it.

But on the ride back to the office in the cab, a shaken and troubled Liz acknowledged to herself that she was positive Adam Cauliff's face had materialized in that mirror.

She was equally positive that she would never, never, never even hint to anyone that she had seen that apparition.

BEN Tucker had nightmares again on both Monday and Tuesday nights, but they weren't as scary. Ever since he had drawn the picture of the boat exploding, and he and Dr. Megan had talked about how any kid would be upset seeing something that bad, he had begun to feel a little better.

He didn't even mind the fact that coming here today meant that he would be late for his Little League game—and when he walked into Dr. Megan's office, he told her so.

"Hey, you make me feel pretty good, Benjy," she said. "Do you feel like drawing today?"

This time it was easier, because the snake didn't seem so scary.

In fact, Ben realized that the "snake" didn't even really look like a snake. In these last dreams he had been able to see it more clearly.

He drew with quick, sure strokes. He was glad that Dr. Megan was off to the side, writing on some papers and not paying attention to him. It was a lot easier this way.

Sitting back, he looked closely at his creation. He thought it looked pretty good, although what he had drawn surprised him. He could see now that the "snake" wasn't a snake at all. That was just what it had looked like because everything had been so scary.

It wasn't a snake he saw sliding off the boat. It looked more like someone in a tight, shiny black suit and mask who was holding on to something that looked like a lady's pocketbook.

AT WORK on Wednesday afternoon Lisa Ryan received a phone call from Kelly's guidance counselor, Mrs. Evans. "She's grieving for her father," Mrs. Evans said. "She started to cry in class today."

Instantly heartsick, Lisa said, "But of the three, I thought she was doing the best. At home she seems fine."

"I tried to talk to her, but she wouldn't say much," Mrs. Evans said. "She is, however, very mature for a ten-year-old. I get the feeling she's trying to spare you, Mrs. Ryan."

It's not Kelly's job to spare me, Lisa thought despairingly. It's *my* job to spare *her.* I've been too wrapped up in myself—and too worried about that damn money. Well, I'm going to do something about that before another day goes by.

She fished around in her purse and found the number she wanted. She went to the pay phone. Then she told the manager to cancel her last two appointments. She hurried back to her station and smiled apologetically at her client. "I'm so sorry. I had a call from school. One of the kids was upset in class."

"That's a shame, but Lisa, can you please finish me up. I've got a million things to do myself."

AFTER he left the hospital on Wednesday afternoon, Dan Minor went to Cornelius MacDermott's office. When he had called for an appointment, he learned that Nell already had told her grandfather about him, so his call was expected.

MacDermott greeted him cordially. "You and Nell are both Georgetown graduates, I hear."

"Yes, although I was ahead of her by some years."

"How do you like living in New York?"

"Both my grandmothers were born here, and my mother lived here until she was about twelve, then moved to D.C. I've always felt that genetically I had one foot here and the other in Washington."

"So do I," MacDermott agreed. As they chatted, he realized that he very much liked Dr. Dan Minor. Another guy would have written off a mother who deserted him, especially one who was known to be a homeless drunk. This son, though, wanted to help her. *My kind of guy,* he thought.

"I'll see if I can't get some of these bureaucrats off their duffs and put on a real search," he said.

"If she's alive, I want to take care of her, but I know she may well be dead. If she is, and if she's buried in potter's field, I want to bring her to the family grave in Maryland. Either way, it would give great peace to my grandparents and me to know that she isn't still wandering the streets, sick and maybe delusional."

"Got any pictures of her?" Cornelius asked.

Dan opened his wallet and took out the picture he always carried. He handed it to Nell's grandfather.

As Cornelius studied the picture, he felt a lump in his throat. The look of love captured there between the pretty young woman and the young boy seemed to leap from the well-worn photo. Both of them were windblown, their faces pressed together, the boy's small arms wrapped tightly around the woman's neck.

"I also have a picture from the documentary film on the homeless that aired on PBS seven years ago. I had it aged digitally on the computer and adjusted to conform to the description her friend gave of how she looked last summer."

"We'll get duplicates and put posters around town," MacDermott promised. "And I'll get those guys to go through the files."

Dan stood. "I'm very grateful to you, Congressman."

MacDermott waved him to a seat. "My friends call me Mac. Look, it's five thirty, which means the cocktail flag is up. What's your choice?"

Liz Hanley walked into the office unannounced as the two men were companionably sipping very dry martinis. It was clear to both of them that she was upset.

MacDermott jumped up. "What happened to you, Liz?"

Liz sank into a chair. "I'll be fine. Mac, pour me a glass of wine. That'll help. It's just . . . Mac, Bonnie Wilson has changed my mind. I am convinced she's a genuine psychic—which means that if she warned Nell about Peter Lang, she's got to be taken seriously."

AFTER Gert left, Nell went back to her desk and reread her column for the Friday edition of the *Journal,* a piece about the long and frenzied campaigns that increasingly characterize presidential elections in the United States.

Her next—and, if all went according to plan, her final—column would be both a farewell and an announcement of her intention to view that campaign frenzy firsthand by becoming a candidate.

I made the decision two weeks ago, Nell thought, but only now does it seem as though all the confusion and doubt and self-questioning are over.

Had all the negativity come from Adam? she wondered. She got up from her desk and began to walk restlessly around the apartment, pausing at the bookshelves that flanked the fireplace in the living room. Adam had a habit of pulling out a book, glancing through it, then putting it back willy-nilly. Nell rearranged the shelves so that the books she especially enjoyed were all once more within easy reach of her comfortable club chair.

I was sitting in this chair, reading, when he phoned me that first time, she recalled. I'd gotten a little depressed after not hearing from him. We had met at a cocktail party and been attracted to each other. We had dinner, and he said he would call. But two weeks later I was still waiting.

I remember I'd just come back from Sue Leone's wedding in Georgetown. Most of the others in our crowd were married and swapping baby pictures. I was very ready to meet someone. Gert and I even joked about it. She said that I had developed an acute nesting instinct.

And then Adam phoned. He said his out-of-town business had taken longer than he'd expected. He had missed me but hadn't called, because he'd left my number in New York.

I was so ready to fall in love, and Adam was so appealing. We were married three months later. There was so much ahead. Life for us was just beginning.

As she sat in her favorite chair, Nell thought back to that heady, special time. It had all happened so fast. What had attracted her so totally to Adam? she wondered, sadly thinking of the man she had loved and then lost so abruptly. I know what it was: He was so absolutely charming. He made me feel special.

And of course there was more, Nell told herself, so say it straight. Adam was in some ways the antithesis of Mac. I know how Mac feels about me, she thought, but he would choke on the word "love." I was hungry for someone to tell me that I was loved.

But in other ways Adam and Mac were very similar, and I liked that too. He didn't have Mac's take-no-prisoners mentality, but he had the same moral stamina. Adam, like Mac, worked his way through college and graduate school.

"My mother wanted to pay my way," he had said, "but I told her she taught me to neither a borrower nor a lender be."

I admired that, Nell thought. I believed that Adam, like Mac, would give you the shirt off his back while at the same time harboring a horror of borrowing money himself.

All that changed later, though. Adam had no trouble asking me to invade my trust fund to lend him more than a million dollars. He asked Mac to help him get a better job. Then he left Walters and Arsdale to open his own firm, using the rest of the money he borrowed from me.

The last days had been so terrible. First she had lost her husband,

and then came all the suggestions that he wasn't the man she thought him to be. I don't want to believe he was in on that bid-rigging scheme, Nell told herself. He wouldn't have had to borrow money from me if he was getting paid off under the table.

But why didn't he tell me that his design had been rejected by Peter Lang? And why did he do such a turnaround when I began to talk seriously about wanting to run for Mac's seat? He blamed his anger on Mac. He said I would just end up being a puppet for my grandfather, that he would never let me be my own person. Well, now I have to wonder if I wasn't really just being manipulated by Adam.

What reason—other than his disdain for Mac—would he have to keep me away from the glare of the media?

An answer began to form in Nell's mind, one that chilled her to the bone.

Could there be some truth to the suggestion that he had been taking kickbacks? Was he in any way to blame for that defective renovation job on Lexington Avenue?

Anxious to put these questions out of her mind, Nell decided to tackle the chore she'd put off. The maintenance men had brought packing boxes for Adam's clothes. She went into the guest room and put the first box on the bed. The neat piles of underwear and socks disappeared into it.

Questions beget questions, Nell thought. As she packed, she allowed herself to face the one question that she had been most determinedly avoiding: Was I truly in love with Adam, or did I merely want to be in love with him?

If I hadn't rushed so quickly into marriage, would the initial attraction have worn off? Did I see in him what I wanted to see? The truth is, it wasn't a great marriage—at least, not for me. I resented having to give up my career goals for him. I wasn't sorry when Adam would take off for the weekend on his boat, fishing and cruising. I enjoyed the time alone, and it gave me time to spend with Mac.

Or could all my doubts be something else? Nell asked herself as she closed a box and picked up another one. Is it simply that I have grieved enough in my life and that now I am trying to find a reason not to grieve again?

I've read that people are often angry at the loved one who has died. Is that what's happening to me?

Nell placed chinos and jeans and short-sleeve shirts in boxes; ties and handkerchiefs and gloves were packed away. The bed was clear. She had no heart to start in on the closet. Nell looked at her watch. It was after six. Lisa Ryan had called earlier and had insisted on coming over again.

Lisa arrived with the elevator operator, who carried two heavy packages into Nell's apartment.

"Put them there," Lisa said, pointing to the round table under the window that overlooked Park Avenue.

The elevator operator glanced at Nell, who nodded.

When the door closed behind him, Lisa said defiantly, "Nell, I have nightmares that the cops will come in with a search warrant, find this cursed money, and arrest me right in front of my children. That's why you've got to keep it here until you can give it back to someone."

"Lisa, that is absolutely impossible," Nell told her. "I respected your confidence, but there's no way under the sun I can hold on to or send back money that was given to your husband because he went along with something illegal."

"How do I know your husband wasn't involved?" Lisa demanded. "There was something very strange in the way Jimmy got his job in the first place. Was Adam Cauliff in the habit of being a bleeding heart for a guy who was blackballed? Or did he get him a job because he thought poor Jimmy might just be desperate enough to be useful? That's what I want to know."

"I don't know the answer," Nell said slowly. "I do know that no matter who gets hurt, it's important to find out just how and why Jimmy was useful to someone."

Lisa's face drained of color. "Over my dead body will Jimmy's name come into this. I'll throw that damn money in the river first. I should have done that the minute I found it."

"Lisa, listen to me," Nell pleaded. "You've read about the building façade that collapsed on Lexington Avenue. Three people were injured, and one of them may die."

"My Jimmy never worked on Lexington Avenue!"

"I didn't say he did, but he worked for Sam Krause. If Krause did shoddy work on that building, then chances are he did the same on others. Maybe there's another job that Jimmy was on, in which corners were cut—another accident waiting to happen. From what you tell me, Jimmy was the kind of man who would want you to do whatever you could to avoid another tragedy."

Lisa's defiant anger faded, and she collapsed into deep, racking sobs. Nell put her arms around her. "Lisa," she said. "I know what you're going through. I don't have children to protect, but if knowledge of Adam's complicity in anything illegal comes out, it could cost me my political career. And having said that, I want your permission to talk to the detectives.

"I'll ask them to do whatever they can to keep Jimmy's name out of the investigation, but Lisa, if Jimmy knew too much, he may well have been the target in the explosion. And if someone is worried that Jimmy told you what he did to get that money, you might also be considered a threat. Had you considered that?"

"But he didn't tell me!"

Nell gently touched the other woman's arm. "You and I are the only ones who know that."

ON THURSDAY morning Jack Sclafani and George Brennan were once again at Fourteenth Street and First Avenue, visiting the apartment of Ada Kaplan.

"Is Jed home?" Sclafani asked.

"He's not up yet," Ada Kaplan said. "You're not going to search my house again, are you? I can't take any more."

"No, we're not going to search your house again, Mrs. Kaplan," Brennan said. "We want to talk to Jed, that's all."

"Maybe he'll talk to you. He hardly says a word to me." She looked at them appealingly. "What would he have to gain by hurting Adam Cauliff?" she asked. "Sure, he was mad, but if I hadn't sold Cauliff my building, I'd have sold it to that big-shot Realtor, Mr. Lang. I told Jed that."

"You spoke with Peter Lang?" Brennan asked.

"Sure I did. Right after that fire in the mansion, he came to see me. Had a check in his hand." Her voice sank to a whisper. "He offered me two million dollars."

"Was Lang upset when he learned you'd sold the property?"

"Oh, my, yes. I think if Mr. Cauliff had been there, he'd have strangled him with his bare hands."

"Are you talking about me, Mom?" All three people turned to see an unshaven Jed Kaplan standing in the doorway.

"No," Ada Kaplan said nervously. "I was just telling the gentlemen Peter Lang had been interested in my property."

Jed's expression became ugly. "*Our* property, Mom. Don't you forget it." He turned. "What do you two want?"

They got up. "Just the chance to make sure you're as charming as ever," Sclafani remarked. "We also don't want you to forget that until we say it's okay, you shouldn't plan any vacations. Don't be surprised if we drop in again."

"It's been a pleasure talking to you, Mrs. Kaplan," Brennan said.

On the way down in the elevator Sclafani spoke first. "You thinking the same thing I am?"

"Yeah. I'm thinking that Kaplan's nothing but a two-bit hood and that we're wasting our time on him."

They arrived back at headquarters to find an unexpected visitor. The receptionist explained, "His name is Kenneth Tucker. He wants to speak to whoever is handling the investigation into that boat explosion."

Sclafani shrugged. There's never a high-profile case that doesn't get its share of loonies with hot tips or crackpot theories, he thought.

Tucker, the typical young executive type, was escorted into the office. "I'll get right to the point," Tucker said. "My son and I were in New York harbor when that boat exploded. He's had nightmares ever since."

"How old is your son, Mr. Tucker?"

"Benjy is eight. We were returning from the Statue of Liberty. Truthfully, the whole episode was a blur to me, but Ben saw something that I believe may be significant."

Sclafani and Brennan exchanged glances. "Mr. Tucker, we spoke to a number of people who'd been on the ferry at the time, and they all agree that it was too far away for them to see distinctly."

Kenneth Tucker flushed. "My son is unusually farsighted. He wears glasses so that he can read, but he had taken them off. He kept saying that in his nightmares, when the boat blew up, a snake would leap off it and start coming at him. A child psychologist got him to draw what he had seen."

He handed them Ben's latest sketch. "He now believes he saw someone in a wet suit, and carrying a woman's pocketbook, dive off the boat at the moment it exploded. It may be a child's fantasy, but I felt you should at least see the sketch." He stood up. "Obviously the face mask prevented Ben from having even the faintest idea of what the person looked like. I hope you realize there's no point in questioning him. We want no media attention."

Brennan and Sclafani again exchanged glances.

"Mr. Tucker, we're very grateful," George Brennan said. "I can't be sure without more investigation, but your son's drawing could have significance. Ben's name will not be mentioned. I'm going to ask you not to reveal to anyone else what you've just told us. We're dealing with a multiple homicide, and whoever was responsible has to be considered extremely dangerous."

"Then we understand each other."

When the door closed behind Kenneth Tucker, Sclafani whistled. "The pocketbook was never leaked to the media, so there's no way the guy could have known that," he said. "That would explain why it was hardly singed. Whoever got off the boat was carrying it."

"And probably lost it in the water. If the kid was right, whoever jumped off barely got away in time."

Without knocking, Cal Thompson, the assistant district attorney, opened the door and poked his head in. "We've got ourselves another Queen for a Day. Sam Krause's top assistant came in with his lawyer. He admits they've been using substandard materials and consistently overbilling on jobs from Walters and Arsdale."

"Who at Walters and Arsdale was making the deal?"

"He assumed it was Walters and Arsdale themselves, but he can't swear to it. The contact was Winifred Johnson. They even had a name for her: Winnie the bag lady."

"She also seems to be one hell of a swimmer," Brennan said.

Thompson raised his eyebrows. "Unless I'm mistaken, her swimming days are over."

"Maybe yes. Maybe no," Sclafani replied.

ON THURSDAY morning Nell got up at dawn. Whatever sleep she had known during the night had been disturbed by bad dreams. More than once she also had awakened to feel her face wet with tears.

Were they for Adam? she wondered. In truth, she could not be sure. I'm not sure of anything, she admitted to herself that morning. But the room embraced her, filling her with the sensation of having come home.

And several times when Nell had awakened, Dan Minor's face floated across her mind. She found the image a reassuring sight, since he was a fellow traveler, another survivor of a broken childhood, another person on a quest for answers.

That same morning, over a cup of coffee, Nell decided to open the packages and count the money Lisa Ryan had thrust on her the night before. Lisa had said it was fifty thousand dollars. It might be wise to verify that figure, Nell thought.

The packages were heavy, and it was a struggle for her to haul them to the dining-room table. With meticulous care she opened the knots on the green-stranded twine, the brown wrapping paper.

Nell ignored a troubling sensation that settled into her subconscious she went ahead and opened the first box. She looked down at the neat stacks of bills.

There was no identification of any kind on the box. She poured herself more coffee and got out her calculator. As she counted and recounted each stack, she entered the figure. The first box contained twenty-eight thousand dollars in mostly fifty-dollar bills.

She opened the second one and began to count, noting that this one had well-worn smaller bills as well. No hundreds that might draw attention, she thought.

The total in the second box was exactly twenty-two thousand dollars. Not one cent less than the fifty thousand Jimmy must have been promised. But why didn't he spend any of it? she wondered. Was he so guilt-ridden that he couldn't bear to touch it?

As she began to fold the paper back around the first package, she suddenly realized what had been bothering her about these packages. She had seen this same heavy paper before, as well as the twine with the green thread running through it.

In Winifred's file drawer.

IN THE faint, early morning light Lisa Ryan got out of bed and put on her chenille robe. As she tied the belt, she was reminded that she had lost considerable weight since Jimmy's death.

One way to do it, she thought grimly.

There wasn't the slightest doubt in Lisa's mind that after Nell MacDermott talked to the detectives assigned to investigate the case, they would rush to talk to her again. Before they did, she wanted to try to figure out which sites Jimmy had been working on and when.

As she headed downstairs, Lisa looked in on the children. Kyle and Charley were fast asleep in their bunk beds. Kelly was in the glorified closet, as Jimmy had called it. Her slender body was curled in the fetal position. Strands of long, light blond hair covered her cheek.

Her journal was half hidden under the pillow. She wrote in it every night. They all had pledged never to read it, but Jimmy, made suspicious by Kyle and Charley, had made Kelly a strongbox that sat on her dresser. The box had two keys. One Kelly wore on a chain around her neck. The other Lisa kept in her dresser, in case the first one was lost.

Kelly had exacted a "cross my heart, hope to die" promise that Lisa would never use that key. But now Lisa knew she would break that promise. Kelly was the ultimate Daddy's girl. Lisa needed to know what Kelly, always observant and sensitive to moods, might have written about Jimmy at the time he plunged into depression.

NELL began to dial Detective Sclafani, but then abruptly broke the connection. Before she called him, she decided, she would go to Adam's office and get the twine and wrapping paper she had seen in Winifred's office.

She showered and dressed, putting on white chinos, a short-sleeve blouse, a lightweight blue denim jacket, and sandals. Then she left the apartment.

The cab turned left down Seventh Avenue as it headed south to Adam's office. A block before reaching it, they passed the fence around the ruined Vandermeer mansion.

The shabby, narrow building next to it was the one she now owned, Nell thought, the one Peter Lang wanted so badly. The one Adam had wanted so badly. "Let me off here," she said suddenly to the driver.

Getting out at the corner, she walked back and stood in front of her property. Most of the buildings in this area were old, but an apartment complex was going up across the street.

Her parcel was a narrow strip. Graffiti added to the deserted, shabby look of the dark stone building. All the tenants were gone.

What did Adam think he was going to do with this property? she wondered. How much money would he have needed to build something new in its place? Its only real value derived from its possibilities as an addition to the Vandermeer property, she realized.

So why was Adam so anxious to buy this parcel? At the time of the purchase the mansion still had landmark status.

Could Adam have had inside information that the landmark status was being removed?

It was another troubling possibility.

Nell turned and walked the block and a half to Adam's office. When she had left there on Tuesday, the superintendent had given her a spare key. She let herself in and went to Winifred's cubbyhole.

She opened the file drawer and took out the brown wrapping paper and twine. She had brought a shopping bag in which to carry them. Even without comparing the two side by side, she knew that the pattern of the twine was identical to the pattern of the twine around the boxes of money.

She had been in the office only a few minutes, but in that time she had become aware that the temperature was becoming increasingly warm. It's happening again, she thought, disorientation overtaking her. I have to get outside.

Nell slammed shut the file drawer, grabbed the shopping bag, and rushed back through the reception area to the outer door. She grabbed the doorknob and pulled, but nothing happened. The knob felt hot to the touch, and suddenly she was coughing. Frantically she kicked the door as she felt her hands begin to blister.

"Something wrong, Ms. Cauliff? That door sticking again?" The building superintendent was right there, shoving open the door with his shoulder. Nell stumbled past him to the steps outside.

It's happening again, she thought. It's a warning. The coughing began to subside, but she was gasping for air. She looked at her hands. The blisters she had felt did not exist.

STILL shaken by the bizarre experience in Adam's office, she returned to her apartment and dialed Jack Sclafani's number. He answered on the first ring.

"It's very important that I see you, and I have to ask you to come here, to my apartment," she told him.

"We'll be there in half an hour," he promised.

Next Nell went into the guest room and began to empty the closet. She removed the jackets and suits and slacks from the hangers. As she took the navy jacket from the closet, she held it in her hands. This is the one he intended to wear that last morning, she thought. Then he rushed out after we quarreled. The one I gave Winifred was the wrong jacket.

Nell started to fold the jacket to place it in the box, then hesitated. She remembered how a few days after his death, feeling bereft, she had put on this blazer, wanting to have some sense of his presence. Now I'm acting as if I can't wait to get rid of it, she thought.

There was a buzz from the intercom in the foyer. Nell hung the jacket over the back of a chair and hurried to let the detectives in.

Jack Sclafani and George Brennan sat with Nell in the dining room. They opened the boxes of cash and confirmed the count.

"You don't get fifty thousand dollars for looking the other way when the right concrete isn't used," Sclafani said. "Jimmy Ryan was on the take for something bigger than that."

"I thought as much," Nell said quietly. "And I think maybe I know who gave it to him." From a shopping bag she retrieved the ball of twine and the wrapping paper. "These came from Winifred Johnson's file drawer," she explained. "I noticed them when I was there with you."

Brennan held the twine used to wrap the packages of cash against a strand he unraveled from the ball. "The lab can verify it, but I'd swear that was cut from here."

Sclafani was comparing the paper. "I'd say this is a match too."

"I hope you understand that if Winifred Johnson passed on a bribe to Jimmy Ryan, it does not necessarily mean my husband was involved," Nell said with a conviction she did not feel.

Sclafani studied her. She doesn't know what to believe, he thought. She's playing straight with us, and we should be straight with her as well.

"Ms. MacDermott, this may be far-fetched, but we have a witness, an eight-year-old kid, who may have seen someone in a wet suit dive off your husband's boat before the explosion."

Nell stared at him. "Is that possible?"

"Ms. MacDermott, anything is possible. Is it probable? No. The currents are vicious. Maybe a strong swimmer could make it to shore."

"Then you believe this child did see someone?"

"The detail that hits home is that in the picture the kid drew, the diver is carrying a pocketbook. The truth is, we did find Winifred's purse, but we never released that detail to the press, so there is no way this kid could have known unless he really *did* see something— or is just very good at guessing. There are a few other facts we have that you may or may not be aware of." Sclafani paused; the next part would be difficult. "As you know, there are two people whose deaths we haven't been able to verify."

Nell sat in stunned silence, a look of confusion in her eyes.

"There's also another possibility," Brennan said. "Someone else—a fifth person—may have been on the boat, perhaps hiding in the engine room. We know from tests that's where the bomb was set."

"But even if that child was right," Nell said, "why would anyone want Winifred's pocketbook?"

"We're not sure. The only object in that purse that has value is a safe-deposit key that carries the number 332."

"Can't you just take it to the bank that issued it?" Nell asked.

"We don't know which bank issued it. The key has no other designation, and the task of going to every bank in the area is going to take time. But that's what we're doing, and we plan to keep looking until we find it."

She looked at him. "It was Winifred's pocketbook. And Winifred was a champion swimmer. Her apartment has photos of her winning gold medals. I realize that was a long time ago, but maybe she kept at it."

"We're already checking out that angle. We know she was a member of a health club and that she swam in the pool every day." He hesitated. "I'm sorry to ask you another question: Was your husband a good swimmer?"

Nell was stunned to realize that she didn't know the answer. That is one more thing I don't know about Adam, she thought. "I know Adam could swim, but as for how well, I'm not sure."

The two detectives stood up. "We'll be going to see Mrs. Ryan.

We'll do our best to keep her husband's name out of this part of the investigation, at least as far as the press is concerned."

"Can you just tell me this?" Nell stood and faced the men. "Do you have any hard evidence that my husband was involved in the bribery or the bid-rigging scandals?"

"No, we do not," Brennan replied promptly. "We do know that Winifred Johnson was the conduit for the transfer of a lot of money, perhaps millions of dollars. Based on the evidence you've given us here, it now appears that she was the one who prepared the money for Jimmy Ryan's payoff. The people who paid her have come forward, and they apparently had the impression it was all going to Walters and Arsdale themselves, but so far there's no proof. Winifred could have been working on her own or with the mysterious Harry Reynolds."

"What about Peter Lang?" Nell asked.

Sclafani shrugged. "Ms. MacDermott, this investigation remains wide-open."

In a way, what she had learned today was a comfort, Nell thought as she closed the door behind the detectives. In another way, though, it was unsettling. Sclafani was basically saying that no one had been cleared, including Adam.

She went back to the guest room. It took only fifteen minutes more to complete packing the suits and jackets in the boxes. She closed and marked them.

Then she noticed the navy jacket hanging on the chair and was hit with a sudden memory. Last summer she and Adam were out to dinner. The air-conditioning in the restaurant had been bone-chilling, and she'd been wearing a sleeveless dress. Adam had taken off this jacket and draped it over her.

But I told him that now he'd be cold; then he said that as long as I was warm, he'd be fine. He was the master of the small courtesies, of the tender phrase.

Nell sighed as she picked up the jacket. She would give it away. She put her hands in the pockets to be sure Adam had not left anything in them. There was a pristinely ironed handkerchief in the left-hand pocket. The right pocket was empty, the breast pocket too.

Nell folded the jacket, reopened the last box she had filled, and put it in. She had begun to close the top when she remembered that this jacket had several inside pockets as well.

Within the right inside pocket there was a small sac that buttoned for security. It was flat, but Nell thought she could feel something under her fingers. She opened the button and withdrew a tiny manila envelope.

From it she removed a safe-deposit key. It was stamped with the number 332.

AT THREE o'clock Lisa Ryan received a phone call at work that she had been dreading. She immediately phoned Brenda Curren, who promised to take her children after work. Somehow Lisa got through the rest of the afternoon.

When the two detectives arrived, she took them into the living room.

Lisa looked at Jack Sclafani and George Brennan. "I'll tell you everything I know," she said, "but I am pleading with you to keep Jimmy's name out of this investigation. Those boxes with the money were sealed. For all I know, someone asked him to hold them for them, and he never even knew what was in them."

"You don't believe that, Lisa," Sclafani said.

"I'm not sure what to believe. I *am* sure that if Jimmy knew sub-standard construction on a job might later cause a tragic accident, he would have come forward eventually. And I know also that since he is not here to speak for himself, it has to come out now."

"You told Ms. MacDermott that you found the sealed packages in your husband's file," Brennan said.

"Yes. The file cabinet in his workshop."

"You have no idea where they came from?"

"No. But I think I can pinpoint when he did something to be given them. It was this past September ninth."

"How can you be sure of that?"

"My daughter's diary." Lisa's voice faltered. "I swore to Kelly I'd never read it." She twisted her hands. "After reading the diary, I remembered that on Thursday, September ninth, Jimmy came home late. He was working at an apartment building renovation project on the Upper West Side, at about One Hundredth Street. Before he got home, I had a phone call from someone who asked to talk to Jimmy and said it was urgent, and I asked if I could take a message."

"Was it a man or a woman who called?"

"Man. He had a low, nervous voice. The message was, 'The job is canceled.' I was so afraid it meant Jimmy was out of work again. He got home around nine thirty, and I told him about the call. He was terribly upset."

"What do you mean by upset?"

"He turned ghostly pale and began sweating. But then he pulled himself together and said that the owner had demanded some changes that he'd already made and couldn't undo."

"Why do you remember this episode so clearly?"

"Only because of something Kelly wrote in her diary. At the time, I thought Jimmy was just terrified that something would make him lose the job. I remember that I went to bed and Jimmy said he wanted to have a beer and unwind, that he'd join me in a little while. Kelly wrote in her diary that she woke up and heard the television on. She went downstairs to say good night to him."

Lisa held up a piece of paper. "I copied this.

" 'I sat on Daddy's lap. He was so quiet. He was watching the news. Then, all of a sudden, he began to cry. I wanted to get Mommy, but he wouldn't let me. He said it was our secret that he felt sad. He had had a very bad day at work. He brought me up to bed and went into the bathroom. I could hear him throwing up, so I guess he just had a flu bug or something.' "

Deliberately Lisa tore up the paper. "I don't know much about law, but I do know that in a court this is not considered evidence. If you have any decency, you'll never refer to it publicly. But I would suggest that the job that was 'too late to cancel' is at the center of this whole payoff issue. I think the renovation Jimmy was working on then may need to be inspected."

The detectives left a few minutes later. Once they were in the car, Sclafani said, "You're thinking what I'm thinking?"

"You bet I am. We need to get a tape of all the September ninth late-night news broadcasts and see if there's anything reported on one of them that might be connected to Jimmy Ryan's big payoff."

"MS. NELL MacDermott, sir," Peter Lang's secretary said as she ushered Nell into his office.

Even his most sophisticated visitors usually commented on the superb view and his exquisitely furnished office. He had the feeling that Nell, however, was totally unaware of the view, the furnishings, the expensive art on the walls.

With a nod he indicated to his secretary that she should escort Nell to the chairs at the window that looked out toward the Hudson River.

"I have to talk to you," she said abruptly as she sat down.

"That's why you're here, isn't it?" he said, smiling.

Nell shook her head impatiently. "Peter, how well did you know my husband? And why did you lie to me the other day about your proposed use of the property Adam bought from the Kaplans?"

"Nell, let me put it this way. I met Adam a number of times while he was with Walters and Arsdale. My firm has been involved in construction projects with that firm for many years."

"Would you have called yourself his friend?"

"No. Frankly, I would not. I knew him—period."

Nell nodded. "What did you think of him as an architect? The way you spoke the other day, one might have thought that the world had lost a genius."

Dissembling was not the way to go with this woman. Lang smiled. "I don't think I went *that* far, did I? Quite frankly, it was just a courtesy to you to suggest that we would have used his design if he had lived. Since he obviously did not tell you that he was off the job, I saw no point in delivering that news after his death."

"You also lied when you said you only wanted the property I now own for landscaping," Nell said flatly.

Without responding, Lang went over to the wall and pushed a button. A hidden screen rolled down and was illuminated. In a panoramic view of Manhattan, buildings and projects, numbered and outlined in blue, dotted the landscape. A gold-lettered legend listed their names and locations.

"The ones marked in blue are Lang holdings, Nell. As I told the detectives, who all but accused me of setting the bomb that blew up Adam's boat, I would like to acquire the Kaplan property because we have a stunning design we'd like to go ahead with but that requires that extra bit of land."

Nell walked over to the illustration he indicated and studied it closely. Then she nodded.

"You're absolutely right," Lang said quietly as he retracted the screen. "I wasn't truthful with you, and for that I apologize. I would like to couple the Kaplan property with the Vandermeer land because my grandfather settled almost on that exact spot when he was an eighteen-year-old immigrant, just off the boat from Ireland. I would like to erect a magnificent tower of a building that would be a kind of monument to what three generations of Langs have accomplished."

He looked directly at her. "However, if I don't get the Kaplan land, I will move on."

"Why didn't you buy the Kaplan property yourself?"

"Because I had no use for it unless the landmark status was removed from the Vandermeer mansion."

"Then why do you think Adam bought it?"

"Either he had extraordinary foresight, or someone on the board of estimate spoke out of turn. And by the way, don't think that isn't being investigated."

She had one more question. "Do you know someone named Harry Reynolds?"

Lang looked puzzled. "I knew a *Henry* Reynolds at Yale. He taught medieval history. Why do you ask?"

Nell shrugged as she left the office. "It's not important."

Peter Lang, you do not get the Boy Scout award for sincerity,

Nell thought as she got on the elevator. You've got an almost maniacal ego. As far as that property goes, I believe you want it so much it hurts. But that isn't even the real reason I came here. I needed an answer, and I believe I have it.

She was the only passenger in the elevator. As it rushed down, she said aloud, "Peter Lang, you do not have blood on your hands."

DAN Minor both anticipated and dreaded checking his answering machine at the end of the day. For some reason the very act of aggressively searching for his mother was accompanied by the feeling that if her whereabouts were discovered, the news would not be good.

When he arrived home on Thursday, the message he found waiting was from Mac: "Give me a call, Dan. It's important." From the somber tone of Cornelius MacDermott's voice, Dan knew that the search for Quinny was over.

He was a surgeon whose fingers held the most delicate instruments, whose slightest miscalculation could cost a life. But those fingers trembled as Dr. Dan Minor dialed Cornelius MacDermott's office.

"I have your message, Mac."

"There's no easy way to say this, Dan. The picture you gave me matches the picture they took of a homeless woman who died last September. The vital statistics are right, and pinned to her bra she had the same picture you carry."

Dan swallowed. "What happened to her?"

Cornelius MacDermott hesitated. "The place where she was staying caught fire. She suffocated."

"Suffocated!" Dear God, Dan thought, anguished.

"Dan, I know how tough this is. I'll meet you in the Bellevue morgue tomorrow."

"Where is she now?"

"Buried. In potter's field. We can have her body exhumed."

"Thanks, Mac."

Dan replaced the receiver, took out his wallet, and sat down on the couch. From the wallet he took the photo he had carried with him ever since he was six years old.

Minutes, an hour went by as he sat straining for every memory of her, however vague.

Oh, Quinny, why did you have to die like that? he asked.

And why, Mother, did you blame yourself for what happened to me? *I* was the stupid little kid who caused the accident. But it turned out all right, actually better than all right. I wanted you to at least know that, he thought.

The doorbell rang. It rang again, this time persistently.

Reluctantly he got up, walked across the room, and opened the door. Nell MacDermott was standing there. "Mac told me," she said. "I'm so sorry, Dan."

Wordlessly he stepped aside and let her in. He closed the door, put his arms around her, and began to cry.

Friday, June 23
Nine

ON FRIDAY morning a messenger was sent to collect tape cassettes of the September 9 late-evening newscasts from New York City's six major television stations. Once gathered, they were delivered to the district attorney's office.

Detectives Sclafani and Brennan were waiting for the messenger, and when he arrived, they took the tapes to the tech room on the ninth floor of One Police Plaza and selected a VCR and television. Brennan pulled up chairs while Sclafani dropped the CBS tape into the player.

"Showtime," he told his partner. "Get out the popcorn."

The lead story was that fire had engulfed the Vandermeer mansion on Twenty-eighth Street and Seventh Avenue.

Dana Adams was broadcasting live at the scene. "The Vandermeer mansion, erected on one of the oldest original Dutch farms in the city and a landmark building empty for the past eight years, was engulfed in flames tonight. The fire, which was called in to the local fire station at seven thirty-four, spread rapidly through the building, at one point engulfing the entire roof. On reports that homeless people had occasionally been seen around the premises, firefighters risked their lives to search the structure. Tragically, in an upstairs bathroom they discovered the body of a homeless woman who apparently had died of smoke inhalation. She is believed also to have started the fire that consumed the building. Her name will not be released until it has been confirmed and the next of kin can be located and notified."

"The Vandermeer property!" Sclafani exclaimed. "Lang owns it."

"Yes, and Cauliff owned the property next to it."

"Which means they both stood to make a buck on that fire."

"Exactly."

Three hours later they had found no other story that in any way could conceivably concern Jimmy Ryan. They turned the tapes over to be copied for backup. "And run the six Vandermeer segments together," Sclafani directed the technician.

They went to Sclafani's office. "What have we got?" he asked.

"Coincidence, which we both know is a dirty word, and the opinion of a ten-year-old girl that Daddy got upset while watching that broadcast. Maybe after a couple of beers Daddy was just feeling down on his luck."

"Lisa Ryan said that his story was that the 'cancel the job' call related to work he'd taken care of."

"That's easy enough to check out, I guess." Brennan got up. "We've seen cases of homeless people accidentally setting fires in abandoned buildings," he said thoughtfully, "and other people losing their lives because of it."

"Take it from the other angle," Sclafani suggested. "When a homeless person is squatting in a building that burns down, it's easy to assume that's who caused the fire."

"Time to take a good look at exactly what happened in the

Vandermeer mansion. The Thirteenth Precinct would have the file."

"I'm going out with bag lady Winnie Johnson's key again," Sclafani said. "We need to find that bank."

"Unless it's too late."

"Unless it's too late," Sclafani agreed. "If an eight-year-old kid is right, someone got off that boat. My guess as of now is that he saw Winifred Johnson."

"You realize we're following up leads provided by a farsighted eight-year-old boy and a ten-year-old girl who keeps a diary." Brennan sighed. "Mother told me there'd be days like this."

ON FRIDAY morning Nell phoned the Old Woods Manor nursing home and inquired about Winifred Johnson's mother.

"She's really quite depressed," the nurse told her. "Winifred was a very dutiful daughter. She came up here every Saturday and some evenings during the week as well."

Winifred the faithful daughter. Winifred the swimmer. Winifred the bag lady. Winifred the lover of Harry Reynolds. Which one was she? Nell wondered. Was she all four? And was she now in South America or on one of those Caribbean islands that wouldn't send her back even if authorities located her?

"I'll come visit today," Nell promised.

She put the receiver down and went to the window. It was a gray, rainy morning, and when she had awakened, she had lain in bed for a long time. She had imagined Adam's face, painting it in scrupulous detail. On that last morning there had been no trace of the smile that had captivated her. He had been edgy and nervous, so anxious that he had walked off without his jacket or briefcase.

The jacket with safe-deposit key number 332 in it.

I should turn the key over to the detectives, Nell thought as she went into the bathroom and stepped in the shower. I know I should. But not until . . . She did not finish the thought.

A possibility, both grotesque and bizarre, had been forming in her mind—a possibility that by keeping the key she might be able to confirm or refute.

She had almost confided to Dan what she was planning and why it was necessary, but last night had not been the time for that. That was the time to let him talk out his own grief and pain. In halting, broken sentences he had told her about the accident that drove his mother away, about the long months in the hospital when he had kept praying that she would come to see him. About how his grandparents had helped him to heal.

I told him that I truly believe the people we love never really leave us, Nell thought as the water coursed over her. I told him about Mother and Daddy coming to say good-bye.

He asked if Adam had said good-bye in the same way. I shook my head. I didn't want to talk about Adam last night.

At ten o'clock she had gone into his kitchen and poked around. "You're obviously not one of those bachelors who's a gourmet cook," she had told him with a smile.

She found eggs and cheese and a tomato, and was able to put together an omelet and toast and coffee. It was almost midnight when Dan had gone downstairs with her and put her in a cab.

When she arrived home, there was a message on her answering machine: "Nell, I don't think I thanked you for coming tonight. It made me feel the way I would have felt as a kid if the hospital door had opened and the beautiful lady I loved was there. I know I have a hell of a nerve talking like this, and won't again for another six months, I promise. It's just that I'm so thankful that you've come into my life."

Nell had taken the tape out of the machine and put it in one of the dresser drawers.

She thought of the tape now as she dressed in light blue gabardine slacks and a blue-and-white man-tailored shirt. She was tempted to play it again, but she knew that the special, almost magical feeling it had given her would not be there today.

Nell had a feeling of dread about the day ahead of her. She had sensed it when she first opened her eyes. There was a catastrophe hovering in the air around her, in much the same way a tornado's spiraling black cloud hangs from the sky before touching ground.

She sensed all this but felt powerless to prevent it. She was *part* of it, an actor in an inevitable scene that had to be played out.

Through the years she had come to understand that what she was experiencing was precognition. *Precognition: the knowledge of a future event through extrasensory means.*

Nell tried to reason with herself. I thought it was precognition the other day when I experienced heat and burning and gasping for air. But when Dan's mother suffocated in that fire, that's what she must have been going through. Did I pick up vibrations from her?

Only time would tell.

AT NOON Dan Minor pushed open the door of the medical examiner's office on Thirtieth Street and First Avenue. Mac was waiting for him in the reception area.

He clasped Dan's hand. "I'm terribly sorry it turned out like this. Nell was shocked. I'm sure you'll hear from her."

"I already did. She came over last night." A hint of a smile touched Dan's lips. "After informing me I had almost nothing in the cupboard, she even cooked dinner for me."

"That sounds like Nell," Cornelius MacDermott said. He nodded to the door past the reception room. "A clerk back there has your mother's file ready for you to look at."

They had photographed Quinny. So thin, Dan thought—she must have been anemic. It was clearly the same face as the computer-aged picture, but in death a certain tranquillity had returned.

"The only distinguishing marks on her body were some scars on her palms," the clerk said. "The examining physician attributed them to burns."

There was a photograph of the snapshot he always carried. "Where is the picture now?" Dan asked.

"They're keeping that as evidence."

"Evidence! Evidence of what?"

"It's nothing to get upset about," Mac said soothingly. "She certainly didn't mean to burn that building down, but September ninth was unusually chilly. Quinny apparently threw some odds and ends in the fireplace, started a fire, and went up to the bathroom. The damper wasn't open, and in minutes the place was an inferno."

"My mother did not set that fire," Dan said positively. "And let me tell you why."

THE nurse tapped on the partially open door. "Company, Mrs. Johnson." Nell followed her in.

Rhoda Johnson was in the bedroom of her small suite, lying on the bed, propped on pillows, with an afghan thrown over her. As they entered, she opened her eyes.

"Nell MacDermott?" It was a question.

"Yes." Nell was shocked to see the visible difference in the woman since her last visit.

"I want you to do me a favor. Winifred used to pick up a coffee cake for me at the bakery in the mall a mile from here. Would you get me one today? I can't eat the food here. It's tasteless."

Oh, boy, Nell thought. "I'd be glad to, Mrs. Johnson."

"Have a nice visit," the nurse said cheerfully.

Nell pulled up a chair. "You're not feeling that great today, are you, Mrs. Johnson?" she asked.

"I'm all right. But people around here, they ignore me."

"I don't know about that. The nurse who was with me just now suggested I drive up today. And the lady last week . . ."

"They're okay. But the people who work in room service and clean up the place, they're not treating me the same since Winifred isn't around to slip them twenty-dollar bills."

"That was generous of her."

"Wouldn't you think they'd have a little sympathy?" Rhoda Johnson began to cry. "It's always been like this . . . people taking advantage. Forty-two years in that apartment, and the owner wants me out in two weeks. I have clothes in the closets; my mother's good china is there."

"Mrs. Johnson, let me just ask the nurse something," Nell said. "I'll be right back."

She was gone less than five minutes. "Good news," she reported.

"It's just as I expected. You're allowed to bring furniture here. Why don't we drive to your apartment next week, and you can select your favorite things. I'll have them delivered."

Rhoda Johnson looked suspicious. "Why are you doing this?"

"Because I'm sorry you've lost your daughter," Nell said.

"Maybe you think you owe me something. If she'd stayed with Walters and Arsdale, she'd be alive today!" Tears spilled from Rhoda Johnson's eyes. "I miss Winifred so much. She didn't always make it during the week, but Saturday was our day to visit, always. The last time I saw her was the evening before she died."

"That would be Thursday night, two weeks ago," Nell said. "Did you have a nice visit?"

"She was a bit upset. She said she wanted to stop at the bank, but she got there too late."

Instinct made Nell ask the next question. "Do you remember what time she got here that night?"

"It was a little after five. I remember because I was having my dinner when she came. I always eat at five."

Banks close by four o'clock, Nell thought. Winifred had plenty of time to get to one in Manhattan.

Rhoda Johnson wiped her eyes. "I shouldn't go on so. I know I'm not going to be here much longer. My heart's about as bad as it can get. I used to ask Winifred what she would do when something happened to me. You know what she said?"

Nell waited.

"She said she'd quit her job and be on the first plane to nowhere. That was her little joke, I guess." She sighed.

THE bakery was about a ten-minute drive. Nell bought the coffee cake, then stood for a moment on the sidewalk. She could see a large bank, off at a right angle to the mall. Why not? she thought. It's a good place to start.

She drove to the bank, parked, and went inside. A window at the far end had a metal sign: SAFE-DEPOSIT BOXES.

Nell walked over and opened her shoulder bag. She took out the small manila envelope, opened the clasp, and let the key slide out onto the countertop. The clerk smiled and handed her a signature card to sign.

"I'd like to speak to the manager," Nell said quietly.

Arlene Barron was a handsome African American in her early forties. "This key is tied to a criminal investigation," Nell explained. "I need to call the Manhattan district attorney."

Both Sclafani and Brennan were out, but she left a message. "I'm sure they'll be here with a search warrant," Nell told Barron. "Would it be violating security to tell me in whose name the box is registered?"

Barron hesitated. "I don't know if . . ."

"Is Harry Reynolds a cosignatory?"

"I really shouldn't divulge that information," Arlene Barron said as, almost imperceptibly, she nodded.

"I thought so. Please tell me one more thing. Has the box been opened since June ninth?"

"We don't keep those records."

"Then if by any chance someone tries to get into that box before the police get here, you've got to stall them. If the box hasn't been cleaned out already, it may contain crucial evidence in a multiple homicide."

WHEN Sclafani and Brennan arrived at the 13th Precinct station house, they found Mac and Dan Minor at the desk.

"Take a look at who's waiting," Brennan murmured to his partner. "Congressman MacDermott. Wonder what he's up to?"

"There's a great way to find out." Sclafani strode over to the desk with an expansive smile. "Sir, it's a pleasure to see you. I'm Detective Sclafani. Detective Brennan and I have been in constant touch with your granddaughter since the boating tragedy."

"Nell didn't mention you, but that shouldn't surprise me," Mac commented. He paused to shake hands with Sclafani. "I'm here on a totally separate matter. Dr. Minor here needs information concerning his mother's death."

Brennan had joined them. "I'm sorry, Doctor," he said to Dan. "Was it recent?"

Mac answered for Dan. "It was nine months ago. Dan's mother was a troubled woman. She suffocated in the fire at the Vandermeer mansion last September ninth."

The two detectives looked at each other. Ten minutes later the four men were seated at a long table in the private conference room. Captain John Murphy, the ranking officer on duty, had joined them. The case file and the box with Dan's mother's personal effects were on the table.

Captain Murphy extrapolated the significant information from the file. "The fire apparently traveled through a dumbwaiter shaft, spreading quickly to the roof. Despite the danger, four FDNY firemen connected by a tether explored the first two floors, which were almost fully engaged. The hook-and-ladder company sent in personnel to the third and fourth floors. They removed the body of an adult Caucasian female on the fourth floor. She had taken refuge in a bathtub and covered her face with a wet cloth. Despite intense efforts at CPR, she was declared dead at nine thirty p.m. Cause of death: suffocation due to smoke inhalation."

The captain glanced at Dan. "It may be some consolation to know that the fire never touched her."

"I appreciate that," Dan said, "but I need to know why she's being held responsible for setting it."

"It began in what had been the library. The window of that room blew out and some papers landed on the street, including a human-services or soup-kitchen card. That was why your mother was misidentified. The card belonged to another homeless woman who claimed that one of her shopping bags had been stolen."

"There was another homeless person in the building?"

"We have no reason to think so. There was certainly no other victim. We believe your mother must have been cooping in the Vandermeer mansion, started the fire accidentally—perhaps while trying to fix herself some dinner—and then went upstairs to use the only bathroom that still worked. She was trapped up there. The smoke was so dense she wouldn't have been able to find the staircase."

"Now let me tell you about my mother," Dan said. "She had a pathological fear of fire. There's no way she would have started one." He saw the looks of polite disbelief. "My father walked out when I was three years old. She went into a clinical depression that led to heavy, steady drinking. She controlled it during the day, but once I was in bed, she would drink herself into a stupor."

Dan's voice faltered. "I remember as a child waking up and tip-toeing downstairs, clutching my blanket. Invariably she'd be asleep on the couch, an empty bottle next to her. She loved a fire then and used to read to me on that couch near the fireplace before I went to bed. One night when I went down to check on her, she was passed out in front of the hearth. I shook the blanket out to cover her and part of it went into the fire. When I pulled it away, my pajamas caught on fire."

He stood up and took off his jacket. "I almost lost this arm," he said as he rolled up his shirtsleeve. "I spent a year in the hospital going through skin grafts and learning to use it again. The pain was awful. My mother was so guilt-ridden and afraid of facing possible charges of negligence that one day she left and never came back. She couldn't stand seeing what had happened to me.

"We had no idea where she was until seven years ago, when we saw her on a television documentary about the homeless. A private investigator we hired talked to people in shelters here who knew her. On one point they all said the same thing: She panicked at the sight of an open flame."

Dan's left arm was a solid mass of stretched, scarred flesh. "It's not a very pretty sight, but the kindness of those doctors and nurses is the reason I'm a pediatric surgeon today and in charge of a burn unit."

"You make a strong case, Doctor," Jack Sclafani said quietly. "It is entirely possible that Karen Renfrew, the woman who claimed her card had been stolen, actually started the fire. The mansion was very large. She might have been totally unaware that your mother was also in it."

Dan rolled down his sleeve. "I couldn't save my mother from

herself. But I can save her reputation, such as it is. I want her name removed as a suspect in setting that fire."

The phone rang. "I told them to hold calls," the captain muttered as he picked it up. He listened. "It's for you, Jack. Some kind of message."

When Sclafani hung up, he looked at Brennan. "Nell MacDermott left a message a little over an hour ago. She's found the bank. It's in Westchester, near the nursing home where Winifred Johnson's mother lives. She told them we'd be up with a search warrant."

He paused. "There's something else. Our guy in North Dakota just left a message. He's compiled a full report on Adam Cauliff, and he's faxing it now. Apparently he's come up with some very disturbing information."

Friday, June 23, midafternoon

Ten

RAIN began to fall as Nell drove back to the city—hard, driving rain that beat against the windshield. The brake lights of the cars ahead flashed red as the pace of the stream of traffic slowed almost to a standstill.

Nell's mind raced with the events of the morning, but she willed herself sternly to concentrate on her driving. It was only when she drove into the garage in her building and parked her car that she permitted herself to absorb the full impact of what she had learned.

Winifred had shared a safe-deposit box with Harry Reynolds.

Adam had a key to that box.

She hadn't figured out how to make sense of it, but there was a good chance Adam *was* Harry Reynolds.

"You okay, Ms. MacDermott?" Manuel, the elevator operator, looked at her solicitously.

"Thanks, just a bit shaky. The driving is rough out there."

It was nearly three o'clock when she opened the door of her apartment. Now she was almost frantic to be rid of Adam's possessions. He and Winifred must have had a secret relationship of some sort. It might have been strictly a dishonest business relationship. It might have been what he had made her think was a romantic relationship. No matter what the answer, she wanted no reminder of his presence in the apartment.

I fell in love with love . . .

I never will again! Nell vowed silently.

The blinking light on her answering machine indicated messages. The first was from her grandfather: "Nell, Dan and I were checking into his mother's death. We happened to meet Detectives Sclafani and Brennan. You left them a message, and now they seem to have some information about Adam. Unpleasant information, I'm afraid, faxed from Bismarck. They're coming to my office around five. Dan will be there. Please plan to join us."

Next was a message from Dan: "Nell, I'm worried about you. I'm carrying my cell phone. Please call (917) 555-1285." She was about to turn off the machine when his voice came again: "Nell, I'll say it again. I need you."

Nell smiled wistfully as she erased the messages. Let Aunt Gert be home, she prayed as she reached for the telephone.

Fortunately, Gert answered. "Nell, dear, I'm having one of those days I so enjoy. I'm putting photos of my psychic-group parties in an album. Do you know that Raoul Cumberland, who is so popular on that television show now, was at my house four years ago? And—"

"Aunt Gert, I hate to cut you off, but this is a crazy day for me," Nell said. "I have to ask you something. I'm bringing in five boxes of clothes tomorrow. That's a lot for you to be hanging and sorting. I'll be glad to stay and sort them with you."

"Oh, aren't you sweet? But that won't be necessary, dear. I have someone who's already volunteered to help. I promised I wouldn't tell anybody, though. She doesn't want to be involved in her clients' personal lives—"

"Aunt Gert, don't let on to Bonnie Wilson that I know. See you tomorrow."

Nell hung up and dialed Bonnie Wilson's number. On the fourth ring the answering machine clicked on.

"Bonnie, this is Nell MacDermott. I don't want to bother you," she said, "but do you think you could channel Adam to me again? It's urgent that I talk with him. I'll be at home, waiting for your call."

The phone rang nearly an hour later. It was Bonnie. "Nell, I just got your message. Of course, you can come over immediately. I'm not sure if I can contact Adam, but I'll do my very best."

JACK Sclafani and George Brennan brought sandwiches in from the delicatessen and dropped them off at the squad office. Before they could break for lunch, they had to phone the branch manager of the Westchester Exchange Bank. After that, they went before a judge to request a search warrant. Finally, they asked the D.A. to allow other members of their squad to open safe-deposit box 332. They didn't want to be away from the station if Karen Renfrew, the homeless woman whose soup-kitchen card had been found at the Vandermeer mansion, was located.

It was three o'clock before they got to eat. Sitting in Jack's office, they also began reading the report on Adam Cauliff that had come in from North Dakota.

"From a broken home. A juvenile record that was expunged, but look what it was for. Shoplifting. Petty theft. Questioned in the death of an uncle when he was seventeen. Mother inherited money. That was Cauliff's ticket to college," Sclafani observed. "How did our contact get this stuff?"

"Good police work. Keep reading."

"Chronic liar. Braggart. Believed to have advance knowledge of college exams. Faked letters of reference for first job, romanced owner's wife in second job. On another, suspected of selling contents of sealed bids to rival firms.

"The report ends with a psychiatrist's evaluation, and I quote," Sclafani read, " 'On the basis of the information I have been given,

I conclude that Adam Cauliff has a serious personality disorder and is probably a full-fledged sociopath. Like many such people, he may be very intelligent and have ample surface charm. His general behavior may be impeccable. But if events turn against him, then he will do anything necessary to secure his personal aims. Anything.' "

"Wow!" Brennan exclaimed. "How did a woman like Nell MacDermott get involved with a guy like this?"

The phone rang. Sclafani picked it up. "Good, we're on the way." He looked at Brennan. "They've found Karen Renfrew; she's at the Thirteenth Precinct. Let's go."

EVEN her oversize golf umbrella could not keep Nell dry for the few steps across the sidewalk from the cab to the door of Bonnie Wilson's building. Once inside the outer vestibule, she closed the umbrella and dried her face with a handkerchief. Then, taking a deep breath, she pushed the button to Bonnie's apartment.

"Come right up, Nell." As Bonnie was speaking, the buzzer unlocked the lobby door.

The elevator climbed to the fifth floor. As she stepped out into the hall, Nell saw Bonnie standing in her doorway. Behind her the apartment was dimly lit. Even so, Nell gasped, feeling a sudden catch in her throat. The faint light around Bonnie was beginning to darken.

"Nell, you look so worried. Come in," Bonnie urged.

Numbly Nell obeyed. Whatever happened in this place in the next little while was inevitable. She stepped inside, and Bonnie closed the door behind her. Nell heard the click of double locks, then the slide of the dead bolt.

"They're doing some work on the fire escape," Bonnie explained, her voice soft. "The superintendent has a key, and I don't want him barging in while you're here."

Nell began to follow Bonnie as she moved from the foyer. In the deathly quiet their footsteps resounded on the bare wood. As she passed the mirror, Nell paused and stared into it.

Bonnie stopped and turned. "What is it, Nell?"

They were standing side by side, their reflections gazing back at them. Don't you see? Nell wanted to shout. Your aura is almost completely black, just like Winifred's was. You're going to die.

Then, to her horror, as she watched, the darkness began to spread and encircle her as well.

ONCE again Dan called Nell's apartment, but there still was no answer. Maybe Mac has heard from her, he thought.

Cornelius MacDermott reported that while he had not talked to his granddaughter, he had heard from his sister. "It's not bad enough that she sent Nell to some loony psychic. Now she's had some kind of premonition that something bad is going to happen to Nell."

"What do you think she means, Mac?"

"It means that she has nothing better to do than to sit around and fret. Look at the way it's raining. Gert's arthritis is probably kicking up, and she's turning her own discomfort into some kind of psychic warning. It's like she's channeling the pain for all the rest of us to enjoy. I told her to come over here and listen to what those two detectives have to tell us about Adam. Gert thought he was tops because he danced around opening doors for her, but according to what Brennan told me, they've dug up a lot of dirt on that guy."

"Just one more thing, Mac. Is it like Nell to ignore messages? Do you think she's ill and maybe not picking up the phone?"

"Dan, don't *you* get started. I'll call over to her doorman and see if he's seen her either coming or going."

"I REPORTED my bag with my good things stolen hours before that fire," Karen Renfrew said angrily. She was with Captain Murphy and Detectives Sclafani and Brennan, seated in the 13th Precinct conference room.

"Who'd you report it to, Karen?" Sclafani asked.

"A cop who passed in a squad car. He said, 'Lady, haven't you

got enough junk in those carts without worrying if one bag fell off?'
But I tell you, it didn't fall off. It was stolen."

"Which probably means that whoever stole it was cooping in that
mansion," Murphy said. "And started the fire—"

"I can tell you just what that cop looked like. He was too fat, and
he was in the squad car with another cop called Arty."

"Karen," Sclafani said soothingly, "where were you staying when
your bag was stolen?"

"On One Hundredth Street. I had a nice doorway across from
where they were fixing up that old apartment building."

"What avenue crosses there, Karen?"

"Amsterdam Avenue. Why?"

"Yeah, what difference does that make?" Murphy asked.

"Maybe none. Or maybe a lot. We're following up on a guy who
was foreman on that job. According to his wife, he was extremely
upset because of a change-of-work order that had canceled a job
he was doing up there. We can't find any trace of any order, so we
figure maybe he was upset about something else. It just happens
that this all took place the same evening as the fire at the Vandermeer place, and we've been looking for some way to connect him to
both sites."

George Brennan looked at his partner. There was no need to
vocalize the rest of the connection they had just made. Jimmy Ryan
had been working across the street from where Karen Renfrew was
cooping. She was a wino. It wouldn't have been hard for him to
have lifted one of her bags and thrown it into the trunk of his car
while she was sleeping. It would be a good way of planting phony
proof that the mansion fire had been set by a squatter. The pieces
of this puzzle were finally falling into place. If this line of reasoning
panned out, Jimmy Ryan was guilty not only of arson that resulted
in murder but of stealing from a homeless woman.

"NELL, I can sense that you are very troubled."

The two women were seated at a table in the center of the room,
and Bonnie was holding Nell's hands.

Bonnie's hands are ice-cold, Nell thought.

"What is it you need to ask Adam?" Bonnie whispered.

Nell tried to withdraw her hands, but Bonnie gripped them even more tightly. She is frightened, Nell thought—and *desperate*. She doesn't know how much I know or suspect about Adam and the explosion.

"I need to ask Adam about Winifred." Nell tried to keep her voice calm. "I think she may still be alive."

"Why do you think that?"

"Because a little boy who was on a ferry from the Statue of Liberty saw the explosion. He saw someone dive off the boat, dressed in a wet suit. Winifred was a strong swimmer."

"The child might have been wrong," Bonnie said.

Nell glanced about. The room was filled with shadows. The only sound she could hear was the rain pelting the windows. "I don't think the child was wrong," she said firmly. "I think someone did escape. I think you know who it is."

A tremor ran through Bonnie's body, convulsing her hands. Nell was able to pull her own hands free.

"Bonnie, I've seen you on television. I believe you have genuine psychic powers. You have a rare gift, and I think you have been guilty of misusing it. I remember Gert told me years ago that a gift of psychic power must only be used for good. If it is abused, the one who possesses it will be severely punished."

Bonnie listened, her eyes fixed on Nell.

"You came to Gert, claiming that you had been contacted by Adam. I was distraught. I wanted so much to believe in you."

"Nell, I am sure that on the other side, Adam—"

"Bonnie, if you did channel to Adam, what you claim he said was untrue. I know now that he did not love me. A man who loves his wife does not have an affair with his assistant. He does not open a safe-deposit box with her under another name. That is precisely what Adam did."

"You're wrong, Nell. Adam did love you."

"No, I am not wrong. And I'm also not a fool. I know you are helping either Adam or Winifred by trying to get the key that was left in Adam's jacket. I hope it is Winifred and that Adam is dead. I cringe to think that for three years I might have been living and eating and sleeping with someone who could take three lives."

Nell reached into her pocket and took out the safe-deposit key. "Bonnie, I believe you know where Adam or Winifred is hiding. If you have assisted either of them in any way, you have become an accessory to multiple murder. Give this key to whichever one is still alive. Let him or her think it's safe to go to that bank in White Plains. It's your only chance for leniency."

"What do you mean, '*think* it's safe,' Nell?"

She had not heard the footsteps approaching from behind. She turned and looked up in shock and horror.

Adam was standing over her.

DAN Minor glanced at the window, hoping to see the rain let up. Unfortunately, it was still pouring against the glass, creating a virtual waterfall. His grandmother used to tell him that when it rained like this, the angels were weeping.

Where did Nell go? he kept asking himself.

He was in Mac's office with Mac and Gert and Liz. Nell's doorman had confirmed that she arrived home at about three o'clock and went back out shortly after four. She must have heard the message I left, he thought. Why didn't she call me back?

The elevator operator said she had seemed upset.

When Jack Sclafani and George Brennan arrived, they were introduced to Liz and Gert. Then Sclafani took over. "Let's start by talking about the homeless woman who reported the theft of her bag only hours before the mansion fire. We've been able to verify her story with the police officer she stopped that day. I don't think we'll ever have absolute proof, but we believe very strongly that Winifred Johnson paid Jimmy Ryan to set that fire and to make it look as if a homeless person had done it."

Dan interrupted. "That means my mother—"

"That means your mother has been cleared as a suspect."

"Do you think Winifred Johnson was doing this on her own?" Mac asked.

"We assume it was all done for Adam Cauliff."

"I don't understand," Gert said. "How did he stand to benefit?"

"It was because he had bought the Kaplan property next door. He was smart enough to know that it would increase enormously in value if the mansion was gone and the property no longer restricted by landmark status. He then would approach Peter Lang, who bought the property, and offer him a deal. He was also arrogant enough to think that he could force himself on the developer as architect for the project."

"According to Lisa Ryan, a man phoned Jimmy the night of the fire with instructions to cancel the job," Brennan explained. "Adam and Winifred may just have learned that the mansion had been removed from landmark status that same day. Thus there was no longer any need to set the fire."

"Well, it didn't do them much good," Liz commented. "Both of them were blown to bits on that boat."

"We don't think so," Brennan told them. Noting their astonished expressions, he said, "A witness claimed to see someone in a wet suit dive off the boat before the explosion."

"Thanks to some sleuthing by your granddaughter, Congressman," Sclafani said, "we have gained access to a safe-deposit box shared by a man and a woman who called themselves Harry and Rhoda Reynolds. Copies of doctored passports were faxed in to our offices. And while the man and the woman in the pictures are somewhat disguised, it is clear they are Winifred Johnson and Adam Cauliff."

"The box also contained nearly three hundred thousand dollars in cash and several million dollars' worth of bearer bonds and other securities," Detective Brennan added.

A long silence followed, broken finally by Gert, who asked, "How on earth could they accumulate that much money?"

"It's really not that hard with the projects Walters and Arsdale handle. They have billings of nearly eight hundred million on their books right now. Also, we think Winifred and Adam had been planning this for some time."

Looking at the distress on Mac's face, Sclafani said, "Congressman, you can go over this report at your leisure. I'm sorry. I know this will be a shock for Ms. MacDermott."

"Will she be joining us?" Brennan asked. "We'd like to thank her for all her help."

"We don't know where Nell is," Gert told him with distress and irritation, "and no one will listen to me, but I'm worried sick. Something isn't right. I could tell when I talked to her on the phone this afternoon that she was distracted."

Brennan and Sclafani looked at each other. "You have no idea where she is?" Sclafani asked.

"That bothers you," Mac snapped. "Why?"

"Ms. MacDermott found the other key to the safe-deposit box and was smart enough to investigate a bank near Winifred Johnson's mother's nursing home. If she has figured out where either Winifred or Adam is hiding and tries to contact them, she may be putting herself in grave danger."

"It has to be Winifred who swam away from the boat," Gert said, her voice trembling. "I mean, Bonnie Wilson channeled to Adam. He spoke to Nell from the other side."

"He *what?*" Sclafani asked.

"Gert, for God sake!" Mac exploded.

"Mac, I know you don't believe in this, but Nell did. She was even following Adam's advice that she give his clothes to the thrift shop. She's bringing them in tomorrow, and Bonnie Wilson even volunteered to help me unpack them. Bonnie's been so helpful through all this. The only thing is, I was surprised that she didn't tell me that she once met Adam at one of my parties. I found a picture of the two of them when I was making up my album."

Brennan jumped up. "I'll bet anything she was trying to get at that key. She's in on this in some way, whether with Adam or with Winifred."

"My Lord," Liz said. "I thought he actually had materialized."

They stared at her.

"What do you mean, Liz?" Mac asked.

"I saw Adam's face appear in the mirror in Bonnie Wilson's apartment. I thought she must have channeled him."

That's where Nell went, Dan thought. I'm sure of it.

Sick with dread he looked around, seeing the sudden fear he felt reflected in the faces of everyone in the room.

ADAM was standing over her.

Despite the dim light, Nell could make him out. It was Adam, but one side of his face was blistered and peeling, and both his right hand and foot were heavily bandaged. She could also see his eyes, which were filled with rage.

"You found the key and called the police," he said hoarsely. "After all my planning, after three years of putting up with that stupid, insipid woman, after nearly losing my life because you gave her the wrong jacket and I had to search for her damn pocketbook— after all that, plus the pain of these burns, I have nothing."

He raised his left hand. He was grasping something heavy in it. Nell tried to get up, but he shoved her back with his bandaged hand. She heard Bonnie scream. Then a stunning, smashing pain exploded in her head, and she was falling. . . .

FROM far away she heard moaning and sighing. Her hair and face were wet and sticky. Gradually she realized that she was the one making the sounds.

"My head hurts," she whispered. Then she remembered: Adam was alive. He was here. Someone was touching her.

"Tighter. Tie it tighter!" It was Adam's voice.

Bonnie was bending over her, weeping, in her hands a ball of heavy twine. She's tying up my legs, Nell thought.

"Her hands. Now do her hands." It was Adam's voice again— harsh and cruel.

She was on a bed, rolled onto her stomach. Bonnie was pulling her hands behind her, wrapping twine.

Nell tried to speak. Don't do this, Bonnie, she wanted to say. You only have a few minutes of life left. Your aura is completely dark now. Don't go with more blood on your hands.

Bonnie pressed her hand. She wrapped the twine more loosely. She wants to help me, Nell thought.

"Hurry up," Adam snapped.

Slowly Nell turned her head. She could see a pile of crumpled newspapers on the floor. Adam was holding a candle against them. The first curl of flame sprang up.

"See how you like it, Nell," Adam said. "I want you to feel the pain, just like I did. Because it was all your fault. Your fault that I didn't have the key. Looking like this, I couldn't even go to the bank and try to convince them to let me into the box. And all because of you and that stupid woman bringing me the wrong jacket."

"Adam, why . . ." Nell tried to speak.

"Why? Don't you understand anything?" His rage was tinged with disgust. "I was never good enough for you, never good enough to mix with your precious grandfather's cronies. Don't you realize that when you ran for office, it would be all over for me? There were things in my past that would have been embarrassing to a congressional candidate. Don't you understand what a feast the media would have had? I couldn't let that happen."

Adam knelt next to the bed, his face close to hers. "You forced my hand. You and that simpering Jimmy Ryan and Winifred with her wet, droopy eyes. Well, that's okay. It was time for a new start anyway." He stood up. "Good-bye, Nell."

"Adam, you can't kill her," Bonnie shrieked.

"Bonnie, you're either in this or you're not. It's your choice: You can stay, or you can walk out that door with me."

Just then the doorbell started to ring, its piercing sound reverberating through the apartment. Smoke was filling the room as the wall behind the papers caught fire, and from the outside hallway a voice shouted, "Police. Open up."

Adam looked at Nell. "Hear them, Nell? They're trying to help you. Well, you know what? They won't get in here in time." He shoved the dresser in front of the bedroom door. The flames were leaping at the curtains and the quilt on the bed. "Open the window," he shouted at Bonnie.

"They're working on the fire escape. We can't go out there, Adam. It's not safe," Bonnie sobbed.

Then he was pushing Bonnie out the window into the pouring rain. Nell saw the wild look on Adam's face as he took the time to close the window behind him, sealing her in that room.

She was alone—just her and the heat. The unbearable heat. The mattress was burning. With strength born of desperation Nell managed to slide off the bed, then to stand. Supporting herself against the dresser, she pulled her hands and feet free from the bonds that Bonnie had left loose. She shoved the dresser to one side.

The door was on fire. Nell tried to turn the handle. It was redhot. The blisters, the smoke—she had known this was going to happen. Blood was dripping in her eyes. She couldn't breathe.

Someone was hammering at the door to the apartment. She could hear them.

Too late, she thought as she slid to the floor and began to crawl. You're going to be too late.

A THIN trickle of smoke slid into the hallway. "The place is on fire," Sclafani yelled. As one, he and Brennan and Dan Minor kicked at the door. It refused to budge.

"I'll go to the roof," Brennan shouted.

Sclafani turned and raced down the stairs, Dan at his heels. They reached the lobby and ran out in the rain to the fire escape.

"Look!" Dan exclaimed.

Above them were two people, slipping and stumbling on the wet and treacherous steps.

INSIDE the burning bedroom the smoke was overwhelming. Nell could see nothing as she crawled across the floor, gasping for the last remaining hint of air. She had to find the window. Suddenly her head touched a solid object. The wall! She pulled herself to her knees and stretched up to grip the windowsill. All she felt was heated metal. A handle of the dresser. Dear God, she had gone around in a circle. She was at the door again.

I can't make it, she thought. I can't breathe.

She suddenly felt as if she were in the riptide again, pulled down into a swirling vortex. "Help me," she begged.

A voice came to her, only this time the voice that filled her head was not that of either of her parents—it was Dan, saying, *Nell, I need you.*

Turn around, she told herself. Picture the window. Stay near the bed, then go to your right. She crawled across the room.

I need you, Nell. I need you.

Choking and coughing, Nell plunged forward.

"POLICE! Stop!" Sclafani shouted. "Put your hands up."

Adam stopped. Bonnie tried to get past him. "Go back," he shouted, pushing her back up the stairs.

They made it past Bonnie's apartment on the fifth floor and reached the top landing. The roof was six feet over their heads. "It's useless, Adam!" Bonnie screamed.

Adam painfully pulled himself up onto the railing and reached up. His fingertips touched the edge of the roof. Beneath him he felt a lurch as the fire escape began to separate from the wall.

ON THE street below, Dan Minor could hear the sound of fire engines as they screamed their way down West End Avenue. He locked his fingers together, cupping Jack Sclafani's foot as the detective reached up and grasped the bottom rung of the fire escape. "Drop the ladder," Dan shouted.

Moments later he too was scrambling up the fire escape.

NELL hoisted herself up and stumbled as she reached the window. When she crashed against it, her shoulder broke the large single pane. Behind her she felt the rush of intense heat sucked outward. She thrust her body forward, then felt herself slide backward as the floor gave way beneath her feet. Her blistered hands grabbed the window frame. Shattered glass pierced her palms. Behind her was the roar of the fire. There were sirens below, and people yelling all around. Inside her head there was only calm. Is this what it's like to die? she wondered.

ADAM grasped the roof with his fingertips. With a superhuman effort he began to pull himself up. Then he felt Bonnie's arms around his legs. He tried to kick free but swayed and fell back to the landing.

Snarling, he picked Bonnie up and lifted her over his head. The fire escape gyrated beneath them.

"Let her go, or I'll shoot," Brennan shouted from the roof.

Sclafani raced up to the top landing of the fire escape. He was too late. Bonnie fell to the street below.

Adam vaulted back onto the railing. This time his fingers barely grasped the roof before they lost their grip. For a perilous moment his arms flailed the air.

Sclafani froze as he watched the man perform a deadly dance before he plunged down, falling without a sound until his body hit the pavement.

Just below Sclafani, Dan had reached the window that opened from Bonnie's bedroom. Seeing Nell at the edge of the inferno, grasping the window frame, he grabbed her wrists and held them in his own strong, sure fingers, until a moment later Jack Sclafani was beside him, helping him to pull her free.

"Come on!" Jack exclaimed. "This thing is going to go."

The fire escape was swaying wildly as they made their way down, half carrying, half dragging the now unconscious Nell. When they reached the extension ladder, a fireman yelled up, "Give her to me and jump!"

Dan lowered Nell into the fireman's outstretched arms. Then he and Jack Sclafani bolted over the railing and dashed out of the way as six floors of metal fire escape collapsed to the ground, covering the bodies of Adam Cauliff and Bonnie Wilson.

Election Day

A NEW President was being chosen who would lead the United States of America for the next four years. A new Senator would speak for the state of New York in the nation's most exclusive club. And at the end of the day the city of New York would know if the congressional district over which Cornelius MacDermott had presided for fifty years had chosen his granddaughter, Nell MacDermott, as its new representative.

Partially due to nostalgia but also with a nod toward superstition, Nell had located her campaign headquarters in the Roosevelt Hotel, the scene of all her grandfather's triumphs. As the polls closed, they sat together in a suite on the tenth floor, their attention focused on three televisions—one for each of the major networks.

Gert was with them, along with Liz Hanley and Lisa Ryan. Dan Minor had just called to say that he was on his way down from the hospital. Campaign aides wandered nervously in and out of the room. It had been a tough campaign.

Nell turned to her grandfather. "Win or lose, Mac, I'm glad you made me run."

"And why shouldn't you have run?" he responded. "The party committee agreed with me—the sins of the husband should not be visited on the wife. Although, being perfectly practical about it, if there had been a trial, the media circus would have made your campaign impossible. With Adam and the rest dead, though, it was yesterday's news."

Yesterday's news, Nell thought. Yesterday's news that Adam had betrayed her. Yesterday's news that he had made sure that anybody who could incriminate him died on that boat. Yesterday's news that she had been married to a monster. I lived with Adam for three years. Did I always sense that at the core of our relationship there was something terribly wrong? I guess I should have.

The investigator from Bismarck had uncovered more disquieting information about Adam. He'd used the pseudonym Harry Reynolds on one of his questionable deals in North Dakota. He must have told that to Winifred.

Nell looked across the room. Lisa Ryan caught her eye and gave her an encouraging thumbs-up. At the start of the summer Lisa had offered to help with the campaign. Nell had gladly taken her on, and Lisa had worked tirelessly, spending her evenings at headquarters, talking with voters on the phone, mailing out literature while her children spent the summer at the shore with Brenda Curren and her husband. Lisa had thought it better if they were out of the neighborhood until the talk about their father died down. It hadn't been too bad, though. Jimmy Ryan's name was in the police files, but he had received scant attention from the press.

"The children know their father made a terrible mistake," Lisa had said. "But they also know he was going to face up to it. His last words were, 'I'm sorry,' and now I know what he meant."

It had been decided that if Nell were elected, Lisa would work in her New York office. I hope that comes to pass, Nell thought, as she shifted her focus back to the array of television sets.

The phone rang. Lisa answered it, then came over to Nell. "It was Ada Kaplan. She's praying you win. She said you're a saint."

Nell had sold the Kaplan property back to Ada for exactly what Adam had paid her for it. Ada had then sold it to Peter Lang for three million dollars.

"Not a word to my son," she'd told Nell. "He gets what I promised him. The difference goes to the United Jewish Appeal."

"You're neck and neck, Nell," Mac said, fretting.

"Mac, since when do you fidget while watching returns?" Nell asked, laughing.

"Since you got in a race. Look, they're calling it a toss-up!"

It was nine thirty. Dan arrived, sat next to Nell, and put his arm around her. "Sorry to take so long," he said. "There were a couple of emergencies. How are things going? Shall I take your pulse?"

"Don't bother. I already know it's off the charts."

At ten thirty the pundits started declaring a shift in Nell's favor. "That's it! Keep it up," Mac muttered.

At eleven thirty Nell's opponent conceded. A cheer echoed thunderously in the auditorium below. The television monitor picked up the crowd in the Roosevelt's ballroom, singing a turn-of-the-century favorite "Wait 'Til the Sun Shines, Nellie."

> *Wait 'til the sun shines, Nellie,*
> *When the clouds go drifting by . . .*

They have drifted by, Nell thought.

> *We will be happy, Nellie . . .*
> *Sweethearts you and I . . .*

"You bet we will," Dan whispered.

> *Wait 'til the sun shines, Nellie,*
> *By and by.*

The song ended, and the crowd roared its approval. In the ballroom Nell's campaign manager grabbed the microphone. "The sun *is* shining!" he yelled. Then he began to chant, "We want Nell! We want Nell!"

Hundreds of voices joined him. "Come on, Congresswoman MacDermott," Mac said, urging her toward the door.

He took her arm and steered her while Dan and Liz and Gert all fell in step behind them.

"Now, Nell, the first thing I'd do if I were you . . ." Mac began.

MARY HIGGINS CLARK

© BERNHARD VIDAL

She was born in Manhattan, raised in the Bronx, and now has an apartment that offers spectacular views of Central Park. Clearly, Mary Higgins Clark, the reigning queen of romantic suspense, is no stranger to the power and magic of New York City, where the admirable and the unscrupulous rub shoulders every day. Always alert to plot possibilities, the author's antennae started to buzz during a publicity tour when she met a young woman who was a part-time psychic. Tantalizing what-ifs began to swirl in Clark's imagination and ultimately emerged as *Before I Say Good-Bye,* her twenty-second best seller. This novel also marks the author's entry into the brave new world of electronic publishing—a world Mary Higgins Clark is sure to conquer.

To learn more about Mary Higgins Clark and
Before I Say Good-Bye, visit the Select Editions website:

ReadersOnly.com
Password: *stay*

Julie and

Romeo

Jeanne Ray

Julie Roseman
never could have imagined
she would speak a kind word
to Romeo Cacciamani—let
alone fall in love with him.
These days her life is just
full of surprises.

Chapter One

THE first time I heard the name Cacciamani, I was five years old. My father said it, and then he spit. The spitting I had seen before. I watched my father spit out his toothpaste into the sink. I had seen him spit once while mowing the lawn, when he claimed to have taken in a mouthful of gnats. But this particular spitting, the spitting done in association with the word Cacciamani, was done directly onto the cement floor of the back room of Roseman's, our family's florist shop. That floor, like everything else in my father's world, was kept meticulously clean—nary a leaf hit that floor—and so, even as a child, I recognized the utter seriousness of his gesture.

"Pigs," my father said, referring not to himself for what he had done to his floor, but to the name that had led him to do it.

I wish I could remember the rest of this story, how the Cacciamanis had come up in the first place, but I was five. Fifty-five years later only the highlights of such memories remain.

People love to say that hate is a learned thing. Children mimic their parents; every contemptible piece of narrow-mindedness is handed down from generation to generation like so much fine family silver. I doubt it is as easy as this, as I know my own two daughters have picked up a few things in this world I will not take responsibility for, but then I think of my father and the small shimmery pool of his spit on the floor. I hated Cacciamani with all the passionate single-mindedness of a child, without even knowing what or who it was. I decided it was a fish. My father, who loved just about everything, was not a fan of fish, and so I assumed the conversation must have gone something like this:

> MY MOTHER: Howard, I got some nice fresh Cacciamani for dinner tonight.
> MY FATHER: Cacciamani! (Spit) Pigs!

For the next several years I imagined pale-fleshed, rubbery bottom feeders, the dreaded Cacciamani, snuffling around blindly in Boston Harbor. When exactly I made the transition from fish to family, from family to rival florists, I don't know. My path did not cross with Cacciamanis. We did not go to the same school. Their name was rarely spoken, and when it was, there was a great fanfare of unexplained wrath that I gladly participated in. We were a liberal family, aware of the recent persecution of our people and therefore unlikely to persecute others. As far as I knew, the only prejudice we had was against the Cacciamanis. And back then there were only three Cacciamanis for me to hate: a father, a mother, and a son. I remember seeing the mother at Haymarket several times on Saturdays. She was beautiful—tall and thin, with black hair and red lips. Still, I thought it was an evil sort of beauty. Then their son grew up, married, and had six children, many of whom married and had children of their own. The Cacciamani clan grew by leaps and bounds, and as far as I was concerned, the whole lot of them were worthless—a fact that was reinforced when Tony Cacciamani tried to marry my daughter Sandy when they were in high school.

So that was how I came to hate Cacciamanis. Now let me tell you how I stopped. It was five years ago when I came to hate my husband, Mort. Mort ran off with Lila, a thirty-eight-year-old bouquet-grasping bridesmaid he met at a wedding while delivering flowers. Apparently he met her at several weddings. She was practically a professional bridesmaid—many friends, few dates. There went Mort and Lila. After that I knew what it was to really hate someone for your own reasons, which is much more poignant than hating on someone else's behalf. I didn't know I had ceased to carry an axe for the Cacciamanis. I simply hadn't thought of them for years. And then one day, while attending a seminar at the downtown Boston Sheraton called "Making Your Small Business Thrive," I practically walked into a man with the nametag ROMEO CACCIAMANI. I steeled myself for the great wave of fury, but nothing, not even a twinge. What came instead was, Poor Romeo Cacciamani; his shop must be going bust, too, if he's at this thing.

He tilted his head. "Julie Roseman," he said, reading my tag.

And there he was, a nice-looking Italian guy sitting right at sixty. He was wearing pressed khaki pants and a white polo shirt. No gold chains. I was so surprised by my utter lack of hostility that I wanted to laugh. I wanted to shake his hand, and I would have, except I had a Styrofoam cup of hot coffee in one hand and several folders in the other. "Romeo Cacciamani," I said with wonder.

"It was something else, wasn't it? Roth?"

I nodded. "Roth," I said. "And Roth no more."

He raised his eyebrows in a not-unfriendly way, as if he should be shocked and wasn't. Something occurred to me then: Did Cacciamanis still hate Rosemans? I knew that Mort and Romeo had gotten into it over the years, but now Mort was gone and my parents were dead and my younger brother, Jake, scarcely a Roseman at all, was making twig furniture in Montana. That left me and my daughters, Sandy and Nora. "Are your parents . . ."

"My father's been gone eleven years now. My mother lives with me. Almost ninety. When is the last time I saw you?"

No sooner had he said it than he remembered the answer to his own question. I could see the edges of his ears turn red. "Fifteen years," I said, and left it at that. That was the last time we had seen each other, but that was not the last time I had seen him. Over the years I had seen Romeo plenty—as we drove past each other in our cars, as I turned my grocery cart into his aisle and then caught the mistake in time. For all I knew, he had been studiously avoiding me as well. We both lived in Somerville, a big enough place to avoid someone for years. We owned the only two florist shops in town, so it stood to reason that if one of us was providing the flowers for a wedding or funeral, the other one wouldn't be there.

"How's Sandy?" he said.

"She's good." I wasn't going to be asking about his Tony.

"Things turned out for her okay?"

I shrugged. "You have kids. You know how it is. Her marriage didn't work out. She's back home with me now. Two children." I felt awkward. I wanted to say everything was fantastic for her, say it not for myself, but for Sandy, who in her weaker moments still felt the loss of Tony Cacciamani.

Romeo scratched the top of his head, where all of his hair appeared to be intact. "That was a sad thing," he said. "A very sad thing. What my son was doing with a Roseman—"

"A Roth," I corrected. "Sandy was a Roth."

He smiled. "You're all Rosemans as far as I'm concerned. And your husband was the biggest Roseman of them all."

"My husband only looked like a Roseman. In the end he proved to be otherwise. He met somebody else." I don't know what possessed me to include this last bit of information, but once it was said, there was no taking it back.

Romeo nodded sadly. Maybe he thought he'd known what kind of guy Mort was all along, or maybe he felt sorry for me, but either way I knew it was time for our reunion to come to an end. "I need to get going," I said, struggling to get a look at my watch. "I want to get a seat for the advertising panel."

He let me go graciously, said something about it being nice to see me again. Had he always had such a nice face?

"Romeo?" I said. I don't think I had ever called him by his first name. It was always "Mr. Cacciamani," even though we were the same age. Besides I thought Romeo was a ridiculous name for an adult. "I read in the paper about your wife. I was sorry about that." It was so long ago—three years, four? I should have sent a card at least.

He nodded a little. "Thank you."

"I didn't know her, but she seemed like a lovely woman."

"Camille was a lovely woman," he said sadly; then he turned away.

AFTER the moderator announced that it was essential for every small-business owner to set aside ten percent of gross revenues for advertising, I stopped listening. A great idea, unless you plan to make payroll or have dinner every now and then. Instead my mind drifted back to what Romeo had said about Mort being the biggest Roseman of all. It hit the nail on the head, and I wondered how a Cacciamani could have so much insight into my life.

The whole time I was growing up, I worked in my parents' shop. Even as a little girl, I was in the back room filling up the water picks or wrapping corsages with florist tape. When I got older, my father moved me out front to work the cash register, and when I was in college, I came in early to do the arrangements for the day. I loved the shop when I was young: the cool dark world of the walk-in on a hot summer day, the bright yellow of an African daisy in February, the constant, dizzying perfume of the gardenias. But then I met Mort, and he started hanging around the store, so helpful, so polite. From our second date my mother was saying, "When is he going to marry you?" Like he'd been stringing me along for years and I was about to let my best chance get away. I was all of twenty-one, just minutes away from being yesterday's fresh pick. Six months later Mort asked my father if he could marry me. Me they told. "Julie, Julie!" my mother said when I walked into the store, and my father's eyes were beaming from all the tears, and Mort was just standing there, a grinning idiot, like I was going to be so proud of him. They'd sold me off, or at least that's what it felt like. My brother had bailed out on the business, and in Mort they had found a responsible son to assume the Roseman mantle. I was nothing but the conduit for the transaction. But this is my memory speaking. I'm sure I was happy at the time. I have a vague idea that I loved Mort then.

I made my own bouquet for the wedding: white tuberoses, white hydrangeas, white peonies. It was the most beautiful work I'd ever done. Then at the end of the reception I walked to the front of the banquet hall. All my single girlfriends were there—Gloria, my maid of honor, all the bridesmaids. I turned my back, and with all my might I threw my beautiful bouquet up over my head. The flowers sailed right out of my hands. It was nearly thirty-five years before I got them back again.

Mort didn't want me in the shop. This was rule number one when we got back from our honeymoon. My parents agreed. They could only afford one employee, and since Mort would be taking over sooner or later, what mattered was that he learn the business. I could work as a secretary, with the understanding that I would quit as soon as I got pregnant. Nobody put a gun to my head. That was just the way things went. Mort became the Roseman, and I became his wife.

My parents retired, safe in the knowledge that Mort was there, and they died before he got around to proving them wrong. For this I am grateful. At least he didn't cause my parents any pain. But for all their love and unquestioning trust, they did one very strange thing: They left me the shop. Just me. Mort cursed and raged for weeks. "What a slap!" he said. "A betrayal!"

I didn't understand what he was talking about. "It's ours," I said. "My name, your name, what difference does it make?"

Mort said it made a big difference, and he was after me to sign over the title. While I've done a lot of dumb things in my life, I'm pleased to report that this wasn't one of them. He groused. I stalled. He left. It turns out Lila had her eye on my parents' shop. Mort and Lila's Flowers. The very thought of it makes me weak.

A lot can change in thirty-five years. While I was driving car pools and taking Nora and Sandy to tap and ballet classes, the world of flowers was moving forward. I went into the shop from time to time, but I was surprised one day when I noticed that the cash register was a computer and no one had told me about it. Shipping, billing, trucking, taxes—the depth of my ignorance was bottomless. I had never noticed that we now sold fancy ribbon and vases. There was even a wire rack of greeting cards beside the door.

Mort didn't leave a manual when he and Lila packed off for Seattle. Nor did he leave much money. He just left.

What a beautiful story this would be if the wronged wife pulled it out of the fire and took the business straight to the *Fortune* 500. It didn't work out that way. I stayed in bed for a while, and when I got up, I found a lot of rotted flowers and unpaid bills. I couldn't sell the store. It had been my parents' entire life, and as little as I knew about flowers, I knew less about just about everything else. Five years later I was spending money I didn't have on a seminar that was telling me to put ten percent into advertising.

My hips were getting stiff in the folding chair, and my coffee was cold. Fortunately, I had taken a spot at the back of the auditorium, and I slipped out into the hallway. It was empty except for an orange bench on which sat one Romeo Cacciamani.

The first time I saw Romeo in the Sheraton, I was amazed to find I no longer hated him. The second time I saw him, I was considerably more amazed to find my heart jumped up as if there had been a tiny trampoline installed in my chest.

He glanced up at me and then looked down at his hands. "Oh," he said, his voice disappointed. "You've got coffee. I was going to ask you if you wanted a cup of coffee."

I looked at the white cup in my hand and dug it into the sand in a clean ashtray. "I'd like a cup of coffee," I said.

ROMEO Cacciamani held the door open for me, and I stepped outside into a beautiful late spring day. There were a million things that should have been going through my head: Why has he asked me for coffee? Does he want to talk about what happened with the kids? Is he going to tell me he hates me in the fine tradition of his family? But in truth, the only thing I was thinking was, Wouldn't Mort just die? Please, God, let Mort be in Boston on business. Let him be across the street watching us. Let Mort think that we are wildly in love and that I am planning on signing over every last petal I have to this man. Nothing would kill Mort faster.

At a Starbucks down the street we found a table among the full-time students and unemployed writers who believed that coffee shops were libraries.

"Two bucks for a cup of coffee," Romeo said, sinking into his chair. "Why didn't I think of that one?"

"Beanie Babies," I said. "I should have come up with those."

"We sell them at the store," he said. "I hate them. People call all day long, 'Do you have Spots? Do you have Gobbler?' We had to put in an extra line so the flower calls can come through."

Not only had I not thought of making Beanie Babies in time, I hadn't even thought of selling them. "So business must be good."

He glanced down at our mutual stack of small-business folders. "You know how it is." The thought seemed to depress us both, and for a while we just sipped our coffee in silence.

"I've thought over the years maybe I should write to you," Romeo said. "And then I saw you today, and I thought—"

But he stopped, and I was too curious to wait politely. "What would you write to me about?"

"Oh, the family stuff." He stopped and shook his head. "Sandy. I look back on all that, and I think I just didn't . . . I didn't handle that whole thing so well. All the yelling and Camille crying. I still think they were too young to get married. It may have been okay to bust up the wedding, but I don't think we should have busted *them* up. That was about us, not about them."

It had been a terrible night, freezing cold and pouring rain. Tony Cacciamani had actually brought a ladder to our house. Sandy was going to climb down the ladder, and they were going to get married, but it fell and there was Sandy, hanging off her second-story bedroom window, screaming. We said it was all a Cacciamani plot, that Tony was really trying to kill Sandy.

"That was a long time ago," I said. And it was, but it made me sad to even think about it.

He nodded. "A long time. I have one daughter. Plummy. I don't know if you know that. She's twenty now, at Boston College. Such a smart kid. I wonder where she came from. She's not like anybody else in the family. But when all that happened with Sandy and Tony,

Plummy was just a little girl. I didn't know anything about girls then."

I was remembering Sandy, sixteen years old, up on her bed crying and crying and Tony Cacciamani calling the house all the time and Mort hanging up on him. Mort told Sandy that Tony had never called her. I never thought about it anymore. It was a dark chapter in my parenting history. "I understand," I said. "We don't have to talk about this." Anyone who knows me knows that "We don't have to talk about this" is a very simplistic code for "Stop talking about this." Romeo did not know the code.

"What I mean to say is," Romeo went on, "now Plummy is a young lady, grown up. I think I have a better understanding now of how it must have looked from your side. When you have boys, you think that all the world's problems come from girls. Then you have a girl, and man, you start to take another look at all the boys out there. The world starts looking like a dangerous place."

That made me laugh. I tried to snap myself out of the past.

"Well, you protected your daughter," Romeo said. "That's what I would have said in that letter I didn't write to you."

"We didn't do such a great job ourselves. We weren't exactly models of civility. Mort said some awful things about Tony, about you. God, the screaming that went on." I tried to remember what I thought about Romeo Cacciamani when he and his wife had sat on our couch. Was he nice? Was he bright? Did I think he was a good-looking guy? Was it possible that he had simply become such a good-looking guy in the last fifteen years?

"Mort hated us. That was for sure. Mort Roseman's daughter sneaking off with a Cacciamani." He shook his head. "That's powerful stuff."

"Roth," I reminded him. "Mort Roth."

Romeo shrugged.

"I hated you, too," I said, and then was horrified by my own sudden inclination toward candidness.

But as far as Romeo was concerned, I hadn't confessed anything more serious than a dislike for decaf. "Cacciamanis and Rosemans," he said. "Very bad blood."

I saw this as my opportunity to get the answer to a question that had been bothering me for years, one that I could never ask my family because it was too obvious and I was too stupid. "Why do we hate each other?"

"I'm not sure." Romeo took a long drink of his coffee. "I could say it was because of what happened to Tony and Sandy, but I certainly hated all of you a long time before that. My parents hated your parents. Whew!" He shook his head. "Now that was hate. My mother crept into your parents' yard one night and poured salt on the roots of all your mother's roses."

"She killed the roses? Are you kidding me? My mother always said it was a Cacciamani curse." They had simply withered up, and after that she couldn't make a single thing grow there.

"It was Cacciamani table salt. Maybe the same thing. One time— I must have been in about the eighth grade—I had gone to a birthday party, and you were there. I didn't talk to you or anything. I knew better than that. But that night I told my father that I thought you were sort of cute, and he washed my mouth out with soap. Ever had your mouth washed out with soap?"

I shook my head. I tried to assume the least coquettish tone possible. "So you thought I was cute?"

"I was at that age. I was trying to hack my father off, even though I didn't know it would hack him off that much." He looked out the window. "But yeah, I thought you were cute then. Actually, I think you're cute now."

Let me establish something here: Things had not been so hot between me and Mort in the years before he left. Since Mort, nothing. I was not proud of this, but I had no idea what to do about it. I had no time to do anything about it, not between working around the clock and taking care of the house and helping Sandy out with her kids. I had some attributes left, and yes, there were times that people flirted with me. But a real compliment from a seemingly nice man, well, that hadn't happened for a very long time. It was like a faint song—sweet and far away.

"I don't remember you at a party," I said. "I wish I did."

He smiled. "I was very cool. I came and stood around the edges for a minute. Then I left. That was my style."

As much as I wanted to see where this might go, I couldn't get my mind off the salt. "So why did your mother kill our roses?"

"That part I could not tell you. I always thought you knew. The way they said the word Roseman around our house, you'd have thought there'd been a murder somewhere along the line."

"I don't think my parents killed any Cacciamanis."

"What about your grandparents?"

"Jews in Lithuania. They didn't get to Italy much. I hear the train service was bad. But your mother is still alive. Can't you ask her?"

"Salting the roses is what I *know* she did. The things I don't know, I wouldn't want to know. My mother is a tough lady. If she hasn't told me by now why she hated the Rosemans, she's never going to tell me."

"What about your kids?"

Romeo drummed his fingers on the top of the table. He had nice hands, thin and strong like maybe he played the piano. He still wore his wedding ring. "I'm afraid that one is my fault."

"Ah, don't worry about it. Mort and I didn't exactly talk you up to our girls over dinner."

"They hate us?"

Nora hated. Nora with her Lexus and her cell phone, her tax attorney husband, and blisteringly hot real estate career—Nora hated the Cacciamanis with a passion that would rival anyone's in the family. She was a daddy's girl. She would walk out of her best friend's wedding if the Cacciamanis had done the flowers. Sandy hated them, too, but for her own reasons—because she really did love Tony. She named her little boy Tony, which I thought was a very questionable move, but I never said a word. "They hate you."

"My boys get a grudge, and that's it—real Cacciamanis all of them. Plummy I'm not so sure about. She does her studies. She dances. She works in the shop. I don't think she's got time to hate anybody. So you don't seem to hate me, and I don't seem to hate you. What do you think happened to us?"

I explained how things changed for me after Mort. I told him that, if someone had asked me how I felt about the Cacciamanis this morning, I would have said something awful out of the sheer reflexive habit of it all, but that when I saw him, just another failing small-business owner like myself, it all seemed to be gone.

He was a good listener. "I understand," he said. "When Camille died, well, I changed my mind about a lot of things. I would have been happy to go on hating the Rosemans like always, but when I lost Camille, I lost all my energy for trivial things. I inherited her good sense when she died."

"That's quite a gift."

"Quite a gift," Romeo repeated slowly. "So really, it's not so different. We both lost the person we loved, and the hate just went with it."

"It's not the same. I didn't love Mort. Not like you loved Camille."

"Nobody loves the same way, but you loved Mort. You must have. Otherwise you wouldn't have stayed with the idiot for so many years."

I laughed, and Romeo laughed; then he put his hand over my wrist and patted it. It was nice, a friendly little touch.

When we stepped outside, the sun was still bright and the air was crisp and as sweet as hyacinth. Romeo Cacciamani bounced on his toes a couple of times. "The lecture on self-employed retirement accounts starts at three," he said.

"So, what good is that going to do me? I don't have any money for a retirement account. Besides, I'm never going to be able to retire."

"Me neither," Romeo said. "Too many kids."

"How many kids?"

"Six. The five boys and Plummy."

I whistled.

"So, I guess it's back to Somerville." He looked down the street as if he were expecting his ride to pull up. "You drive?"

"Are you crazy? Parking was a fortune. I took the bus."

He nodded, and again he scanned the street, looking as far away from me as possible. "Ever walk to Somerville?"

"From downtown?"

He nodded. "It isn't that bad. You walk that far every day just around the store. I do. Let's say we give it a try, and if it doesn't work, we split a cab back."

There was no sign of rain, and I had had the good sense to leave my folders on the table in Starbucks. Where had I come to in my life that walking from Boston to Somerville could seem like an act of wanton recklessness? "Sure," I said. "Hell, yes."

And so we started back, out of the shadow of the Prudential Center and off toward Massachusetts Ave. We made the very very long trip over the Mass. Ave. bridge, where the sky reflected pink light into the Charles River and the last of the day's sailboats skated across the water. Who knew that walking to Somerville could be such a beautiful thing to do?

It was a longer trip than we expected. Romeo suggested we stop in La Groceria and have a plate of spaghetti for dinner. They had a very nice bottle of not-so-expensive Chianti. What was funny was we didn't much talk about our families. We talked about movies and a television show we both liked. We talked about growing up in Boston and the trips we had taken. After dinner we walked for a long time without saying anything at all. It was pretty, the houses at dusk, all the warm orange light coming from the windows. It didn't bother me, not talking to Romeo. I never felt that we had run out of things to say; we were two people who knew each other well. Two people who had nothing but time.

As soon as I saw the silvery Lexus in the driveway, I knew I was in serious trouble. I was late. I had forgotten that it was Sandy's night for school and I was supposed to be watching the kids. She must have waited and waited and finally called her sister as a last possible resort for childcare. I sat down on the low brick wall around my little front yard, wanting to put off for a moment what I knew was coming. I loved Nora, but she did not tolerate forgetfulness nor suffer inconvenience gladly. I wanted just a minute to think about my happy evening. Romeo, thankfully, had veered off toward his own home five blocks ago. I would not have wanted him to see me hiding from my daughter in my yard.

I touched my fingers to my lips to make sure I wasn't wearing any bread crumbs, and then I went inside. Nora had every light in the house blazing. My grandchildren, Tony and Sarah, eight and four respectively, were both up. They were both crying.

"My God!" Nora said, coming toward me like a train. "I was just telling the children I was going to have to call the police. Mother, where have you been? I was absolutely sure you were d-e-a-d."

"You were dead!" Sarah wailed, and shimmied up into my arms. Tony banded himself around my waist.

My back is not the back it once was. I tried to steady myself beneath the weight. "I'm not dead. Shush. Look at me." Such a wealth of tears! "Do I look dead?"

Sarah shook her head, but the crying had taken on a life of its own and could not be stopped. I rubbed small circles on her back. "Tony," I said, looking down on his head. "Are you all right?"

Tony, never much of a talker, nodded into my waist, moving around an extra ten pounds I should lose. The whole thing broke my heart. There was so much passion in their fear. I looked at Nora, who spread her hands open as if to say, Look at all the suffering you've caused.

"I just forgot," I said. "I forgot it was Sandy's school night."

"So where were you?" Nora said.

I felt very bad, yes, very guilty, but I could see the irony of my situation. In high school Nora put us through hell, staying out until four in the morning, saying she was running down the street for a Coke and coming back six hours later on the back of some boy's motorcycle. This well-dressed real estate broker with the lizard shoes and the diamond earrings who folded her arms across her chest had been grounded by me, her mother, more times than I could count. "I went to the seminar. I ran into a friend. We had dinner and walked home."

"Walked home? From the Sheraton?"

Enough was enough. I put Sarah down and peeled Tony off me.

They tottered toward the sofa, drunk with their grief. "Nora, I'm sorry you had to come over here, and I thank you for your help with the children." I tried to put the mother-note of authority back into my voice, not that it had ever meant a thing to her, anyway.

"Alex and I were on our way out the door to dinner when Sandy called. She said you were only going to be a few minutes late. She didn't tell me she hadn't even heard from you."

"I'm sorry."

"We had reservations at Biba."

I didn't know what that was, but I apologized again.

The children had returned to their normal breathing patterns and fell into an exhausted stupor on the sofa. Nora put on her coat, which was cut like a trench coat but was made from a pale yellow silk that looked simply lovely on her. I never could get over the way Nora had turned out, so successful, so striking, so, frankly, rich. Never write off a kid who gives you bunches of trouble. I suppose that's the moral of the story. "You look so nice," I said.

"Well, we were going out." Nora shrugged and picked up her purse. Then she smiled at me. "It's okay. I forget things, too."

Slightly patronizing, but I'd take it.

"Who did you run into, anyway?"

I laughed at the thought of it, the whole happy absurdity. "You'd never guess. Never in a million years."

Nora returned my happy look. It was a little game. "Who?"

"Romeo Cacciamani. Can you believe that?"

I should have lied. Just because I had run into the enemy of all Rosemans and found nothing in my heart but peace did not mean that such peace would be shared by all members of my tribe.

Nora dropped her purse. "You *what?* You did *what?*"

Tony and Sarah, even in their diminished states, heard the shift in tone and raised their sleepy heads.

"Nora," I said quietly. "Go home. We can talk about this some other time."

"Tell me!" Nora said. Nora actually roared. She was capable of that.

I kept my voice very soft, but there was no undoing this. "I ran into Romeo Cacciamani at the conference. We got to talking. We had dinner."

"Cacciamani? You ate dinner with a Cacciamani?"

It was amazing. She sounded exactly like her grandfather when she said the word. I half expected her to spit.

"I asked myself, What was this huge feud all about, anyway?"

"You don't *know*? Why don't you ask Sandy? Sandy *knows*."

Now the children heard their mother's name, and all the crying started up again. "I mean before that. Nora, let it drop. He's a perfectly decent person."

"I'm not hearing this," Nora said. Then a thought of utter horror occurred to her. "Did you *walk home* with him?"

"No," I said. "Of course not."

"He let you walk all the way from downtown alone?"

"Stop this. Stop. Go home. I'm going to put the children to bed."

"Mother, swear that you will never see that man again."

"He lives in Somerville. I'll see him at the grocery store."

"You know what I mean."

"Good night, Nora."

"Swear it. I am absolutely not leaving until you swear it."

For a second a picture of that reality crossed my mind. "Sure," I said. "I swear it. Now go."

Nora blew out like a storm. Not a word to me or the children. So I swore; what did it mean? I hadn't seen Romeo in fifteen years, and it would probably be fifteen years before I saw him again. So what?

I put the children to bed, the last vestiges of any happiness from my evening stomped out like a bug beneath my heel. I was sixty and back to buttoning up flannel jammies. But they were sweet children, and even though I wished that Sandy's marriage had worked out and that they all lived happily in another house, most days I didn't mind having them there.

"You're not going anywhere, are you?" Tony said, his voice all trembly. He was such a little boy for eight.

"Down the hall and straight to bed is the only place I'm going."

I leaned over and kissed him hard on the forehead until he giggled and squirmed.

I kept my word to Tony and went straight to sleep. But I did have a dream that bears mention. Romeo Cacciamani was throwing pebbles at my window. I got up in the dark and opened the window to stick my head outside. In the dream my window opened easily, and there was no screen to contend with. I was wearing a very pretty white nightgown.

"What do you want, Romeo Cacciamani?" I said.

He was standing in the middle of the street in his khaki pants and windbreaker, looking up at my window. He looked so handsome in the moonlight. How had I always missed that? I wanted to put my hand on his cheek.

"I had to see you," he said. "I couldn't sleep. I knew I was never going to go to sleep again if I didn't get to see you." He smiled at me and waved. "Good night, Julie."

"Good night, Romeo."

And then I woke up. Here's the worrisome part: I was standing at the window. I've never been a sleepwalker, and I wondered if I could have fallen out. Then I remembered that the windows were all painted shut. I looked out onto the dark street. There was no one there, and I was a nut.

IN THE morning Sandy came into my room and closed the door behind her. It was six a.m., and the children weren't awake yet. She was wearing sweatpants and a Celtics T-shirt. She had her glasses on, and the springs of her hair had yet to be brushed down. "You went out on a date with Romeo Cacciamani?"

"Absolutely not," I said. I had been lying in bed staring at the ceiling, thinking about ordering carnations. "We ran into each other at this conference and had dinner. End of story."

Her lip began to quiver. "Why would you do that to me?"

I sat up, alarmed. "No, honey, this had nothing to do with you."

"Why else would you have dinner with him?"

"Sandy, I don't know. It was such a small thing. We ran into each

other. We started talking. We got hungry. We ate. That was it. I
promise you."

"You hate the Cacciamanis." She was wiping beneath her glasses
with the back of her hand. She was so sensitive, poor Sandy.

"I did hate them. You're right. But when I saw Romeo yesterday,
I just didn't hate him anymore."

"He's Romeo now?" She came over and slumped down on the
corner of my bed. She was too thin. Ever since her divorce, I could
see her shoulder blades sticking out behind her like wings. "If he
was around, if I had to hear his name, I really don't think I could
stand it."

"He isn't around. He isn't here."

"So you won't see him anymore?"

"I'm not seeing Mr. Cacciamani. I just ran into him."

Her face brightened a little. She wiped again beneath her glasses.
"So you aren't going to see him again?"

These girls, they did not give me an inch. What difference did it
make? It was an easy thing to promise. I wouldn't see him. "I won't."

Sandy crawled up to me on the bed. She was thirty-two years old,
but sometimes she reminded me of Sarah, who was very mature for
four. She put her arms around my neck and lay down beside me. "I
really love you, Mom."

I told her the truth without explaining how extremely complicated that truth felt to me at the moment. I told her I loved her, too.

Chapter Two

WHEN my girls were growing up, I believed them to be the beating
heart of the world, the very center of the universe. Unfortunately,
they knew I believed this, and so they came to believe it themselves.
As far as they were concerned, I was their mother, pure and simple, even after they were grown. They could not imagine that I

wouldn't do what they wanted me to do, as that was the nature of our relationship. And maybe they were right. We were talking about Cacciamanis, after all. I could hate Romeo again—I was sure of it, even though I had been thinking of him all morning in distinctly unhateful ways. Sixty years of hate versus one plate of spaghetti and a long walk? No contest.

SANDY had dropped out of college in the beginning of her junior year. She was bored with the work and happily in love with a fellow whose name was also Sandy. They married and became Sandy and Sandy Anderson, believing the novelty of a shared name would be enough to sustain their relationship. They were wrong. Now Sandy the husband lived in Maui, where he taught surfing, got stoned, and forgot to pay his child support, and Sandy the wife went to school three nights a week in hopes of becoming a nurse. During the day she helped me out at the flower shop, and I paid her a salary I could not afford in hopes of giving her a sense of independence. She was a good worker. She was charming to the customers and had a nice way with flowers. Her arrangements were pretty and cheerful. (Mort's flowers, on the other hand, had aspired to look as much like the FTD promos as possible. They appeared to be two-dimensional even as they were sitting in front of you.) Sandy was also very good about deliveries. She never dawdled, and she had a brilliant sense of direction, which she certainly did not inherit from me.

The day after my dinner with Romeo, Sandy and I went in early to get the morning's deliveries ready and then packed them into my car. We had always had a white Ford van with the name Roseman's painted on the side along with a big bouquet of roses. I loved that van. It made me feel successful. But when times started getting tight, the van was the first thing to go.

Sandy looked over the delivery sheet. "Well, at least everything is nice and close today. I shouldn't be gone long at all."

As she left, I told her to be careful. I always worried about her knocking on strange doors.

I took my time sweeping up and wiping down the glass door. I moved a bucket of star-gazer lilies out to the sidewalk. It was a cool day, and we needed to sell them soon if they were going to have any petals left on them.

The phone rang, some guy wanting to send an apology bouquet. "I've been bad," he told me.

"I understand." He said he wanted to spend seventy-five dollars, not including tax and delivery, so I figured he had been really bad. "What do you want to say on the card?"

The line was quiet for a while. "Don't know. What would you want to hear?"

"I don't know," I said. "You haven't done anything to me."

"But what do other guys say? I'm no good at this."

"The basics are usually safe: 'I love you.' 'I'm sorry.' "

"I like that. Write that down."

"And her name?"

"Catherine."

"Catherine with a C or a K?"

Again there was quiet. "No idea."

I sighed and wrote it out with a K. "If it's wrong, I'll tell her it was my fault."

"That's brilliant," the man said. "I only wish I could blame the rest of it on you, too." He gave me his credit-card number, and I wrote it down.

I pinned Katherine's order to the corkboard and then went into the cooler and started changing the water and clipping back the stems so that everybody would get a better chance at life. For all the years I'd been in the store, I'd never gotten tired of the flowers. I'd gotten tired of the bills and the credit-card companies and the bad checks, but the flowers themselves still amazed me. I was in the business of happiness. There were funerals, of course, hospital stays, but even then the role of the flowers was to cheer. Mostly it was about love. Flowers provide a means of expression for people who don't know what to say. Hand the person you love a bundle of flaming poppies, their twisted stems heading in every direction, their petals waving out like windblown flags. They look so promising, so much like life. She'll get the message.

We weren't open yet, but I had unlocked the door to put the lilies outside. I was in the back, working my knife across a bunch of rose stems, when I heard the bell chime. I wiped my wet hands on my jeans and went out to the front.

There between a display of potted chrysanthemums and a bucket of terribly expensive freesias stood Romeo Cacciamani.

"You've got a real nice store," he said. "I've never actually been in here before. My parents used to tell me the Rosemans sold voodoo stuff—dried bats, eye of newt. Do you have any eye of newt?"

What I thought: Why am I wearing this disgusting shirt of Mort's?

What I thought next: How long ago did Sandy leave?

What I said: "No newts."

He nodded. "You've never been in Romeo's, have you?"

Romeo's was the name of his store, named for him by his parents, a tribute to their one and only child. It was a romantic name, of course, a flower-giving sort of name. It also drove my parents insane because they came before us in the phone book.

"I've never darkened your door." I was so glad to see him you would have thought he was dropping off my lottery check. How could I be that glad?

He knelt down beside some sweet peas I had just gotten in and began to fluff them out a little. I was thankful he was focusing on the sweet peas, which were hard to come by, reasonably priced, and dazzling in their freshness. "I think you'd brighten the place up." He did not look in my direction, and it would have been reasonable to assume he was talking about the flowers.

"So maybe someday I'll see your store." What was he doing here, exactly? Out at the Mount Auburn cemetery my father was doing loops in his grave. Cacciamani hands on our stalks. Besides, if Sandy was to walk in the door, there would be a meltdown to rival anything in Chernobyl.

"Julie Roseman," he said to the flowers. The way he said my name caused my heart to stop for one beat. "I had a very nice time last night."

"I did, too," I said. "Until I got home."

Then he looked up at me. "You didn't tell them, did you?"

"I don't know what I was thinking. It was a huge mistake."

Romeo shook his head. "I told everybody I went to a movie by myself. I do that sometimes."

"I wish I'd thought of that. How many do you have at home?"

"Well, there's me, and there's my mom. Plummy's living at home because I am barely making tuition at B.C. Then Alan, he's my youngest son—he's thirty-two. He got laid off last year. He had a really good computer job and then nothing, so now he's home with his wife, Theresa, and their three kids. They've got a dog, too. Junior. Do you count the dog?"

"I do."

"Okay. So there's nine of us."

"You were smart not to tell them. But my God, dinner. You'd think we'd committed a crime." I looked at my watch. "Listen. I don't mean to rush you, but Sandy is going to be back here any minute, and I'm just not up for a repeat performance. I know that's terrible. Everyone should be over this dreaded curse by now, but they aren't, so . . ." I shrugged.

"So why did I come?"

"We might need to jump ahead to that point, yes." I could feel the sweat coming up under my arms, the sweat of fear—Sandy looking for a parking space; Sandy locking the car.

"I haven't done this in such a long time. I was nineteen when Camille and I got married. A guy gets out of practice."

And then, of course, I saw it. Maybe in another setting, another time I would have strung it out and enjoyed it, but now I was only in a hurry. "Would you like to have dinner with me?"

He smiled a smile so grateful, so relieved, that I wished I had asked him the minute he'd walked in the door. He nodded his head.

"Good. When?"

"Tomorrow."

Curse fate and baby-sitting. "Can't," I said. "Sandy has school tomorrow, and I've got the kids. Sandy, Sandy. You really need to get out of here."

"Tonight."

"Tonight. Would you mind going out the back?"

"Fine," he said. He started to stand up and then reached for my hand. He had been squatting with those flowers a long time. I pulled him to his feet. For a second I held his warm hand. I felt a small current zip up my arm and into my chest.

"I'll pick you up."

"No, no," he said with a certain panic in his voice. "Can't do that. What if we meet at the library?"

"My grandson likes to go to the library. He'd tell."

He closed his eyes. "Why can't I think?"

"The CVS in Porter Square," I said. "Seven o'clock."

And then I saw her, Sandy, through the window. "Out," I said, pointing to the back. "Go, go, go!" For a sixty-year-old man whose legs were stiff, he managed to fly when he needed to. And I, for the first time in thirty-nine years, had a date.

ALL day long I worked to keep my fingers free of the scissors' blades. I knew that I was bound to chop one off. I mixed up orders and forgot to hand out a single packet of Floralife food.

"What is it?" Sandy kept asking me. "Are you mad at me about this morning? Are you worried about Tony and Sarah?"

"I'm just tired," I said. "I didn't sleep well."

Finally she relented. It was time to pick up Sarah from preschool. We weren't busy, so I told her to take the rest of the day off. Once she was gone, I called my best friend, Gloria. Gloria had suffered mightily through her first marriage and had been rewarded in her second one. We had been friends since the seventh grade. She was my maid of honor and the person who drove me to my divorce hearing. Gloria and I go way back.

"Cacciamani!" she said. She was laughing so hard that she finally had to put the phone down and get herself a glass of water.

"I'm insane," I told her.

"You were insane for hating the guy all those years. You aren't insane for going out with him. I think he's nice. He's good-looking."

"You know him?"

"I don't *know* him, but I've bought flowers from him."

"What were you doing buying flowers at Romeo's? I thought you bought your flowers at Roseman's."

"I always buy them at Roseman's now, and I usually did before, but honey, I've got to tell you, Mort drove me crazy. The man could not stop talking. If I was in a hurry, it was just so much easier to go to Romeo's."

"You have a point there. So you don't think I'm awful? The girls are going to hate me."

"The girls will never know, if you have an ounce of discretion in you. You're an adult, after all. Besides, I never could figure out what in the hell this family feud was all about, anyway. Why did you all hate them so much?"

"That's the weird part. I don't know. And Romeo doesn't know why they hated us. Just a tradition, I guess."

"So the tradition is over. Where are you going?"

"We're meeting at the CVS in Porter Square."

"That pretty much leaves all of your options open. Do you know what he likes to do?"

"He likes to walk."

"So flat shoes. Put perfume behind your knees. Men love that."

"I don't think he'll be coming in contact with the backs of my knees."

"You're better off if you're prepared, emotionally speaking. You have to think through all of the scenarios."

But I couldn't think through any of them. Suddenly I was paralyzed with a kind of fear I hadn't known since Mort told me about Lila. "Listen, Gloria. Will you come over tonight and pick me up? Show everybody that we're going out to dinner and then drive away with me. The girls will get suspicious if I go out again tonight."

"You want me to drive you to the drugstore?"

"If you could," I said, ashamed of how pathetic I sounded.

"Sure, Julie," she said. "I'll be your alibi any day."

I closed the shop a half hour early and went home to go and sit in the tub. The house was miraculously empty, and the quiet gave me a false sense of peace. Maybe we would have a nice dinner and nobody would find out.

SANDY, Tony, and Sarah returned from McDonald's at six o'clock. At six fifteen Nora walked in. I would have bet money on it. Sandy was in the kitchen, encouraging the children to sit in chairs while eating some ice cream.

"I was just showing a house down the street," Nora said, perfectly cool. "I thought I'd drop in and say hello." Nora had on an emerald-green suit with an Hermès scarf tied loosely around her neck. My little Harley girl. She would have had a real future with the CIA.

"You look awfully nice," I said.

"You look nice yourself," Nora said. "Going out?"

"I am, actually. Gloria and I are going to dinner."

"In the middle of the week?"

"We eat during the week."

"Just wondering," Nora said. "Maybe I'll stick around for a minute. I haven't seen Gloria in ages. She's happy with Buzz, isn't she?"

"Things turned out very well for them."

Nora paced around a little, smoothing down her skirt, readjusting a lampshade. She didn't want to be there. She wanted to get home to Alex, but she still had to check up on me. I couldn't be too mad at her, considering that her worst suspicions of my character were exactly correct. "How are things going at the shop?" she asked.

"Not good. You know that."

"I don't see why you just don't give it up. Take the capital out and get yourself a condominium."

"I want to make this work."

"It's not *going* to work, Mother. The business falls off every year. Everything Daddy worked for is going to be for nothing."

"It was never your father's work. It was my father's work." I had made a solemn vow to myself never to talk Mort down to the girls, but where business was concerned, I failed. Mort had made the place thrive, but he never cared about flowers. I was in no mood to hear about how I was ruining his hard work.

"Call it whatever you want," Nora said. "What I'm worried about is you. It's the Cacciamanis. You know that's the reason the business is failing. They poison our name in the community every chance they get. The big weddings, the fund-raising dinners—that business is all going to Cacciamanis."

"We do plenty of weddings. In fact, I've even been thinking about starting a wedding-planner business on the side. I'm always helping girls find a caterer and pick out bridesmaids' dresses."

"I think they're anti-Semitic." Nora never listened to me.

"That's crazy. You can't call someone anti-Semitic just because they don't like you. Are we anti-Catholic?"

"Of course not. You just don't understand."

"Oh, please," I said. Then the doorbell rang, and I was awash with gratitude. I went into the kitchen and kissed Tony and Sarah good night. Sandy looked at me wistfully for a minute, and so I leaned over and kissed her, too.

Nora had let Gloria in, and they were standing in the living room laughing, the best of friends. "Time to go," I said.

"Maybe I could come," Nora said. "Alex has a meeting tonight, and I don't have any plans. It could be fun, just the girls."

Gloria took a deep breath and put her hand on Nora's shoulder. "Honey," she said, "forgive me, but I need your mom all to myself tonight."

"Is everything okay?"

Gloria shrugged and managed to look both hopeless and brave. "I've just got some things I need to talk to her about. She's such an angel to me, you know."

"Hi, Gloria," Sandy called from the kitchen.

"Hi, sweetheart. Kiss the kids for me. We're running." Then Gloria put one arm around my shoulder and manhandled me out the door before any further discussion could evolve. I got into her Plymouth, and she all but floored it getting off my street. "I thought you were just being a wimp wanting me to pick you up tonight, but that felt like a regular jailbreak."

Gloria pulled up in a red zone in front of the CVS. It was ten minutes until seven. "Do you need me to pick you up?"

I shook my head. "I'll get home fine."

"Or maybe you won't." She gave me a kiss. "Think positive."

I wondered what I could have been thinking of, asking a man to meet me in a store with fluorescent overhead lighting. Slowly, casually, I began to make my way up and down the aisles, trying not to look so incredibly suspicious that I would be arrested for shoplifting before he even got there. In the makeup aisle bottles of tan foundation claimed to make your skin young and dewy. There was a lipstick called French Kiss. Skin creams offered the miracles of youth, the overnight face-lift, and an age-recovery complex. The magazine aisle was not kinder. "How to Make Him Beg for More," "Great Sex at 20, 30, and 40." I stopped and picked that one up. What happened to great sex at fifty? And what about sixty? Were we finished? Unentitled? Too thrilled to be taking our grandchildren to swim practice to even think about sex?

By the time I had wandered over toward the pharmacy, I was ready to call it a night. Lubrication creams next to adult undergarments. A wall of condoms in every conceivable color and texture, all promising protection against sexually transmitted diseases. I had forgotten about those. The magazine was right. I was over, out of business. I was standing there staring at the boxes, reading the hideously depressing slogans—"For Feeling Like Love"—thinking that sex was for the young, when I felt a tap on my shoulder.

"Shopping?" Romeo said.

I wasn't wearing my glasses, and so my nose was approximately three inches away from a box of condoms. "I think this may be the single worst instant of my life," I said.

"Good," he said. "Then things can only go up from here." Romeo smiled at me. He took my hand and led me out of the contraceptive aisle, which was considerate because if left to my own devices, I would have tried to claw my way out through the floor.

"Do you eat sushi?" he asked.

"Raw fish?"

"Plummy got me into it. It's what college kids eat. If you don't want to do that, we can go someplace else."

"No," I said. "Given the circumstances, I would say raw fish is exactly what we should be eating. It's reckless food, don't you think?"

"I do."

As we left CVS and walked toward the car, Romeo kept holding my hand. It's a wonderful thing to have somebody hold your hand. The last time Mort held my hand was as we were walking back down the aisle after our wedding. After that I held hands with my daughters when they were little, crossing the street and walking through parking lots. I was glad to have Tony and Sarah to hold hands with again. I was gladder still to be holding hands with Romeo, especially since I knew he had picked mine up not because he was afraid I might dart out into traffic, but because he liked the way my hand felt inside his own.

A piece of dating advice for the out of practice: If you're nervous about a date, especially if it is a date with your sworn enemy, try shaking off that nervousness by doing something that you would feel even more nervous about, say, skydiving, armed robbery, or eating sushi. The restaurant, in Harvard Square, was pretty, very quiet, with paper walls and soft lighting. There was an ikabana arrangement at the hostess station that Romeo and I both admired. I let him order, because not even the most enlightened feminist knows how to order sushi if she's never eaten it before. The waitress brought us a bottle of sake. "Never pour your own," Romeo said, filling my glass. "It's bad luck. Plummy told me that." Then he handed me the bottle, and I filled his glass. "To the most beautiful florist in Somerville," he said.

"Don't sell yourself short." I touched my glass to his glass.

"No, really," he said. "It's you. It is absolutely you."

I felt drunk after two sips, and it had very little to do with the sake. Then a black lacquered tray arrived, covered in slabs of raw fish perched on top of tiny bricks of white rice. Suddenly the thought of having to eat my dinner seemed so much more frightening than having a date that I didn't feel nervous around Romeo at all. To celebrate, I popped a piece of salmon into my mouth. It wasn't bad. The eel I spit discreetly into my napkin, as I did the abalone, which was a little bit like biting into a human ear.

"I used to do that, too," Romeo said. "You get used to it." He stretched his arms across the table, and for a second he touched my hands. "I still can't believe I'm having dinner with you." Then he took his hands back again. "I have to tell you, you didn't bump into me by accident at that seminar."

"What?" I left one hand casually on the table just in case he wanted it.

"I was walking through, and I saw this woman, this beautiful woman. I only saw her for a second, but—I don't know—I felt like I knew her."

I wasn't loving this story.

"So I circled back around so I could see the nametag, only you didn't see me."

"Me?"

"Then I came back a third time. I practically walked right into you. We talked for a minute, and then you were gone." He snapped his fingers. "I completely lost my nerve. I thought, Well, that's it. I had every intention of leaving, but I found myself waiting for you out in the hall. Do you ever just have a feeling about something— you know you've got to do it no matter what?"

"Not until recently," I said. I picked up the bottle of sake and refilled Romeo's glass.

"I'd like it if we could get to know each other better," he said.

"As people, you know, not just as Rosemans and Cacciamanis."

"I think that's a fine plan," I said. "So, tell me about your children." Children were always a big part of the story.

Romeo smiled and leaned back in his chair. He liked his children, I could tell. "Oh, let's see. Camille and I started early. Joe, the oldest, he's forty. He owns a trucking company, and he's doing okay for himself. He's married and has three kids. Then there's Raymond. He's still single. He works with me in the shop. Nicky is in the air force, stationed over in Germany. He married a German girl about five years ago, and now they have two kids. Then there's Tony." He sighed. "He's thirty-three now. He works for the World Health Organization. He's in Ecuador giving out vaccinations."

"Did he ever get married?"

Romeo shook his head. "Nope. I have to tell you, I think I really screwed things up for Tony. He was in love with Sandy, and not just kid stuff. I don't think he ever got over all that."

I thought of poor Sandy at home with her kids and their Happy Meals, her nursing books, and her homework. She never got over it herself.

"Anyway, Alan I told you about. He and Theresa are home with their three. And then there's my Plummy. It was such a wonderful thing for Camille to have a girl. She's a real treat."

"And a real surprise, it sounds like."

"Five boys, we thought we were all through with that. We thought we had the whole rhythm thing down, and then Plummy. We named her Patience, because Camille said that's what it took to get a girl. The boys all called her Plummy. They'd say, 'Isn't she just plummy?' I think they picked it up from the Beatles. The boys were all crazy about her."

I liked the idea of all those children—all their friends, their boyfriends and girlfriends, and later their children. "It sounds nice."

"Camille made it nice. She was a wonderful mother. I think back on all the things she had to do. I didn't understand it until she was sick, until I had to start doing them myself. She took care of us."

We ate green tea ice cream for dessert and drank tea out of little cups. We talked about the flower business. We laid out every trade secret we had, both of us, and I learned more over dinner than I ever had from a seminar. I told him how I wanted to do a little wedding planning on the side. That was the thing I was really good at: big parties, organization. Romeo said he admired that; he was crummy at organization. Romeo had hired on too many members of his family, and, while he said his product was good, he had a tendency toward disorder. He once missed an entire wedding. He had it marked down for the next week. I, on the other hand, still didn't feel like I had a handle on what I was doing, and every month the revenues slipped. We were both going broke.

It wasn't exactly a lighthearted conversation we'd stumbled into, but still, I felt like singing when we left the restaurant. Romeo said he would drive me home or at least to the end of my street. When we got there, he pulled over and turned off the car. "No one ever told me Rosemans were such good company," Romeo said.

"When we're not selling the dried beaks of nightingales."

"When Camille died, I thought, That's it. I'd known her since eighth grade. We were each other's family. I thought, There's never going to be enough time to get to know somebody like that again."

"Sure," I said. From a distance I could see my house. All the lights were off. My own family safe asleep.

"But the thing is, I do know you. I've been hearing stories about the Rosemans since I was born. They weren't the right stories maybe. . . ." He stopped and drummed his thumbs against the steering wheel.

"I know what you mean," I said. "In the end a Roseman and a Cacciamani are all the same thing."

"All the same thing," he said. He had a way of repeating what I said, and I liked it; he was really listening. And then Romeo Cacciamani did something truly miraculous. He leaned over, and he kissed me. It was just on my lower lip at first, and then my upper lip. Little kisses, and after each one he'd pull away from me like it was over, but then he would come back for more. He put his hands on my face; then he kissed my eyelids, then my forehead, and then the part in my hair. I put my hands on the back of his neck and kissed his mouth, his neck. This was the part that no one had told me while they discussed the evils of the Cacciamanis. No one said they were such good kissers. I was dreaming, sinking, swimming in a warm dark river of kissing. I could smell the soap on his skin and the fabric softener in his undershirt. Oh, Romeo, this makes it all worthwhile, all those nights of working late and coming home alone, crying over the books and the roses that came in with brown spots, the worrying about Sandy and Nora and the children, the anger at Mort, the missing my parents. All of it was washed back by the sea of tender kissing, maybe not forever but for now.

I knew nothing about time, but after a while we decided it was late enough. "Can I walk you down?" he said.

"Better not." I leaned forward and kissed him again.

"We'll manage this, right? We'll find a way to do this."

"I have every intention of it," I said. I put my hand on his hand and then let myself out of the car. I had walked all the way from Boston to Somerville. Tonight I felt like I could walk past my house and keep heading west. I could walk to Cleveland, to Nebraska, over the Rockies until I got to Oregon, and even then I wouldn't stop if I didn't want to. I could go into the ocean; I could swim. I was that sure of myself tonight. I could go on forever.

I WENT up the stairs to my room in the dark. My lips were puffy, and I kept touching them with my fingers, my tongue. They still had the goods. After such a period of neglect, what a thrill to find they still had all their spring intact. I turned on the lamp beside my bed, sat down on the edge, and bounced a couple of times. If I had been twenty, I would have gone to bed with him. I would not have known how to get out of the car after kissing like that. But now I was more sensible. I was supposed to believe in getting to know a person. I was supposed to be grateful for what I got.

So why did I want to go running down the street to see if I could catch up to his car? Here alone in a room with a bed, I wanted to put my head through the wall, I was so eaten up by desire. I had not had sex in, let's be honest, more than five years. Five years plus the last four or five months when Mort was here and we didn't have any sex and I didn't much care because I didn't know he was going. And before that, how long had it been? My fifties had more or less been a sexual wasteland, good years that I could have been burning down the house night after night had there been someone who wanted me, someone I wanted. So maybe tonight I had a chance, and I decided what . . . to wait? Why? Because I wanted to get to know him better? Who did I know better than a Cacciamani? Because I didn't want him to think I was that kind of woman? I was that kind of woman! Just give me the chance. I fell facedown on the bed and bit at my pillow to keep from screaming.

There was the strangest noise outside. It sounded like hail, almost like little rocks hitting the side of the house. Then I realized it *was* little rocks hitting the side of the house. I looked out the window, but I couldn't see anything, so I went back and turned out the light. There on the sidewalk outside my house stood Romeo Cacciamani.

I put my shoulder onto the window frame and tugged at the handles with both hands. Damn Mort, who said he could paint the windows himself! He probably knew that someday Romeo would come here at night and I'd never be able to get the damn thing open. He'd painted me in! Helpless, trapped, I looked down at Romeo and saw he was motioning, saying something without making any noise.

Come down, he was saying.

I flew down the stairs, like Tony, three at a time. I was out that door and back into the night and into his arms before I even knew I'd left the bedroom, back into the universe of kissing. It had been what? Ten minutes? Fifteen? But I had felt the loss of him more than I can ever remember feeling anything.

"I can't believe you came back," I said. I kissed him again.

"I didn't know where to go," he said. Stop, kiss. "I just kept driving around."

"Come inside." Kiss.

"I can't come in. You know that."

The front door was wide open, and the house was dark. He was right. Not inside. "Your house?"

"No, no, no."

"A hotel. I have credit cards."

He stood back for a second. We were dizzy. "Really," he said. "You'd go to a hotel?"

"Isn't that why you came back?"

"I just had to see you again. I didn't want to get my hopes up." He kissed me, hard this time, the kind of kiss that makes it abundantly clear what the other person has on his mind. It was joy. "I know," he said. "My shop. There's a place in my shop."

I went and closed the front door quietly; then we took off in his car. We kissed at every stop sign. Why did car manufacturers think bucket seats were a good idea? I think it was all part of a conspiracy. When we were repressed, they gave us bench seats, but once we figured out how to use them, they stuck a gearshift right in the middle of everything. I put my hand inside his shirt and touched the hair on his chest. Five years and four months makes a woman forget herself, and I had forgotten everything.

I had driven past Romeo's shop before, but it goes without saying that I had never been in it. Inside, it was dark, and in the dim shadows that the streetlight threw in from the window, I could see it was mostly bare. All the flowers would be in the cooler. I couldn't tell if it was nice or not, but I imagined it was beautiful. He locked the door behind us. "I have a little place in the back," he said. "I sleep here sometimes when I have a really big job to get out. I like to work at night." He took my hand and squeezed it, but we were both suddenly shy, unsure of where to turn next.

"Show me around," I whispered. I didn't want to make a sound.

"With the lights off?" he whispered back.

"Why not? You know where everything is." I wanted it to be this way. I wanted to slow things down, just for a few minutes, just so I could revel in what it felt like to want someone so badly and know I was going to get him.

He held on to me. "The plants are over here—mums, azaleas, some little potted perennials, African violets."

"Do you sell a lot of azaleas?"

"They fly out."

"I always figured people bought those at nurseries."

He kissed me until my knees felt loose and I had to lean against him. Had I known that such kissing existed in the world, I would never have married Mort.

"And these, these are my pride. Wait, let me get the flashlight." He disappeared into the darkness and came back with a circle of light. He shone it across a table of orchids. "Look at them," he said. "Aren't they something else?"

And they were, like flowers from a lusher, more ingenious planet: big ones, white and heavy as saucers of cream, little amethyst ones, tiny yellow spiders the size of thumbnails. "I never had the nerve to try orchids," I whispered.

"They aren't so hard. You just have to understand what they need. I think they are the most beautiful flowers."

"Show me the cooler," I said.

"Really?"

I took his hand, kissed his fingers. Romeo Cacciamani, whose name I was never allowed to say at the dinner table, I kiss your hands.

He pulled open the big steel door, and we stepped inside. There was a dim automatic light. It was exactly like mine. There was just enough room for the two of us to stand. The flowers were up on shelves, everywhere, packed in tight: bundles of roses in plastic wrap, daisies and lilies, pink and yellow stock, larkspur, Japanese iris, buckets of ferns, jade, and galex. They pressed in against us. I loved the smells blending and mixing, becoming one another. Then, up on the top shelf, I saw a beautiful arrangement.

"What's that?"

Romeo looked up. "It's for a birthday tomorrow."

"Who did it?"

"I did it. Who do you think does the flowers around here?"

"You made that?" I said, softly.

"Sure."

"Oh, my God," I said. "You really are a better florist than I am. That's brilliant. I mean it." His arrangement seemed reckless and at the same time had perfect balance. I never would have thought to use the tiny lilies of the valley and the foxgloves in with those giant white peonies. And then there were white English roses, as big as the peonies. White tulips came up from everywhere, and all of it balanced like a carving in white-pink marble. It was like something that had simply occurred in nature and soon would grow and spread and take over the room. I had been looking at flowers for as long as I can remember, and I had never seen anything so perfect before. "I think you may be a genius."

"What a nice thing to say." And when he kissed me this time, we both knew we were ready. If there had been more time or more light, I might have thought about my weight, my underwear, but maybe not. In that moment I was so happy with Romeo, I felt happy with myself. Where else should two florists come together than in a walk-in cooler stuffed to the rafters with flowers? We took off our clothes and stood together naked and holding each other as much for warmth as for love.

"Julie, it's freezing. There's a bed in the back."

To all the magazines that only document sex up to forty, I say this: Have you ever walked naked with your lover through a florist's shop at midnight? No? Then don't tell me about sex.

The way was dark, and he held my hand, stopping to kiss me and touch me. The very hands that had arranged those flowers arranged me now. We were Adam and Eve, and this was a dark, flowered Eden. "In here," he said.

"Who's that?"

"Romeo?" I whispered. "Is that you?"

"Raymond?" said Romeo.

"Dad? Dad, is that you?"

Maybe a better woman would have stuck by her man, but I was flying naked through the store. The lights came on just as I leaped for the cooler door. I pulled it tight behind me and cursed the safety precautions that did not allow me to lock it from inside. Our clothes were all over the place, strung over dahlias, crushing down the baby's breath. I untangled mine and inserted myself as quickly as any human being has ever put on clothing. As for my passion, my heart's desire, forget about it. All I wanted now was to exit.

There was a knock on the door. Romeo was calling my name, wanting to know if I was all right.

"Sure," I said. "Absolutely."

I was pretty much put together when he came in wearing a ratty plaid bathrobe. "That's my son Raymond. He was working late. He fell asleep." Romeo dressed quickly. "We have to go out there now."

"I'd rather not," I said. "I'm fine in here."

"I have to take you home."

"I don't see how," I said, but I knew he was right. He took my hand, and together we came out of the cooler.

Raymond was standing there in his boxer shorts and T-shirt, his arms folded across his chest. He was bigger than his father, softer in the face and with less hair, but still a nice-enough-looking guy. He had a big grin on, like this was a very funny moment, until he saw who I was.

"Raymond," Romeo said. "This is Julie Roseman."

"I know. And she can get the hell out of this store."

"Raymond!" Romeo said. It was his parental voice. I had one myself. Even though the son was in his thirties, the tone had some effect on him.

"How could you bring . . . bring"—he was struggling to find a properly awful word. He did not succeed, thank God—"*her* here?"

"Mrs. Roseman and I are friends," Romeo said.

"How you could bring her into Mama's shop. What is Grandma going to say, you bringing a Roseman here to—"

"Raymond, stop it."

"I won't stop it," he said, his own voice raised now. "Not a Roseman. Not a Roseman in this store. Not a Roseman with my father."

I must confess this outburst had very little effect on me, except to increase my wonderment at what, exactly, had gone so wrong between us. Raymond was not so different from my own girls.

"I'll take you home, Julie."

"She can walk," Raymond said.

At that point Romeo went at him; I think to strike him, but Raymond held up his palms. "Forget it," he said, and turned to walk out of the room. But before he left, he did the most remarkable thing: He said my name, and then he spit.

 Chapter Three

"WE ARE cooked," I said on the drive home. We had both been quiet for a while, both of us stunned as if by a sharp blow.

"Raymond," Romeo said, shaking his head. "If it had been Joe, all hell would have broken loose. If it had been Nicky or Alan, even Tony, I might have believed it. But Raymond is so easygoing. Of all my boys, I would have guessed that he would be the one who wouldn't care."

"Do you think he's going to tell?" I asked glumly.

Romeo sighed. "I guess I better get back there and try and talk him out of it. Raymond I can deal with, but if they all get into this, it's going to be impossible." He pulled up in front of my house. Too much had happened for us to try to play it safe.

"Not to sound too much like a teenager, but do you think I'm going to see you again?" I asked.

"You're going to see me. I'm crazy about you, Julie Roseman."

I kissed him again. I knew I was crazy for him, too. I said good night, and for the second time that night I went upstairs to my room.

I would have thought I'd spend the night staring at the wall and wringing my hands, but I don't think I'd ever been that tired in my life. I barely struggled out of my clothes and fell into bed.

WHEN SANDY WOKE ME, IT was bright outside—not just light, but daytime. "I took the kids to school already. Are you feeling all right? Did you and Gloria tie one on last night?"

I really had to think about what she was talking about. I could barely open my eyes. Dear Sandy had brought me both a cup of coffee and an alibi. "Gloria is such a bad influence on me," I said.

"White wine?" Sandy asked.

"Manhattans," I whispered. "Then pinot noir with dinner."

"Grape and grain. You shouldn't ever do that. Red wine always does me in." Sandy patted my knee beneath the covers. "Well, I'll go on in and get things started at the shop. You come when you can." She smiled at me, her heart full of sympathy for my hangover. She closed the door quietly behind her.

I leaned over and called Gloria.

"Naked?" she said. "You met his son naked?" She was laughing to the point of blind hysteria. I thought about hanging up on her, but she was my only ally.

"Shut up," I said. "I have no sense of humor this morning."

"Okay," she said, sputtering. "I'm with you."

"I wasn't naked when I met him. I made it back to the cooler and put my clothes on."

"So you had sex before you met the son or after?"

"Neither. We never got there. Believe me, after I met the son, sex was no longer on the agenda. I don't know if it's ever going to be on the agenda after last night."

"Raymond's going to tell, you know. I'm afraid you're going to have some major repercussions from this."

"Poor Romeo," I said.

"I'm not talking about Romeo. I'm talking about you. Those people hate the Rosemans, Julie. You watch your back."

Gloria read detective stories. She liked to use phrases like "Watch your back." I told her I would.

I SHOULD have spent the day in bed with cucumber slices on my eyes, but I pulled my hair into a ponytail and headed to the shop.

Work was the only way to take my mind off my problems. I couldn't imagine how I would see Romeo again, but when the despair felt like it was going to strangle me, I would remember those kisses—in the car, in front of the house, by the orchids, in the cooler. Those kisses were my salvation.

As I parked the car, I saw Sandy through the shopwindow talking to a customer. Even from a distance I could tell Sandy was cowering. I headed in and heard a loud voice. I stepped up my pace. I thought at first that we were being robbed. I was ready to jump him. A fistfight would have been right up my alley this morning.

"Hey," I bellowed, slamming the door behind me. "What's going on here?"

Sandy slumped against the counter, tears streaming down her face. "How could you?" she said to me.

"How could I what?"

Then the man turned around. Who knew which Cacciamani he was. Probably the military son, flown in from Germany just to kill me. This one was bigger than Raymond. This one was huge, the seams of his T-shirt hardly holding the fabric together over so many muscles. Still, though, he had Romeo in his face, and I felt at once fear and a weird sort of fondness for him.

"So you're Mrs. Roseman?"

There was no sense splitting hairs on my title. I told him I was.

"I was just telling your daughter here what a tramp her mother was. I guess it runs in the family. She didn't catch my brother Tony, and you're not going to get your hands on my father or our business."

Sandy sank down into a little wicker chair behind the counter and gave herself over to her grief.

"Look, Mr. Cacciamani," I said. "I would like nothing better than to set things straight between our families, but this isn't the way we're going to do it. Now, I need to ask you to leave my store."

"No, *you* look. I don't want any of you coming near my family. I can make you very sorry, Mrs. Roseman. A few insults, the cold shoulder, a little bit of screaming now and then, that was fine for my grandparents, my parents. But you're dealing with a different generation of Cacciamani now, *capisce?*"

I opened the door. "Out."

He leaned back against the counter and folded his arms, which barely made it across his massive chest. "Not till I know you understand what I'm saying. I know you Rosemans aren't so quick."

Maybe I should have been afraid of him, but I just kept thinking, No way is Romeo's son going to slug me. This was all some ridiculous war, and it was up to me to not knuckle under to it. "Which son are you?"

He held up one finger to illustrate his rank. "Joe."

"Joe, you take your threats against me and my family and get out of my store, or so help me God, I'm calling the police."

"It's okay," he said. "Maybe you do know what I'm talking about." There were five pots of tiny daffodils on the counter, and he leaned over and pinched off all their heads and held them in his hand. While he was stripping my plants, he said to Sandy, "Tony was never going to marry you. He told me you weren't any good."

She didn't even seem to register it. She kept her head down.

"Think about it, Mrs. Roseman," Joe said as he walked through my store dropping a careful trail of daffodil heads.

I locked the door behind him. "What a gorilla!" I admit it, the flame of hatred for all things Cacciamani shot up in my chest. I did my best to turn it down. Joe didn't understand, just as, until very recently, I had not understood. He probably wasn't such a bad guy.

I walked back behind the counter and started rubbing Sandy's back. Poor Sandy, it was a much bigger blow for her than it ever could be for me. "Sandy, are you all right, honey?"

"Don't touch me."

I held my hand still. "Did something happen before I got here?"

She kept her head down. Her massive collection of tiny dark curls covered her face and shoulders. "He said you were chasing Mr. Cacciamani through his shop last night when his brother Raymond came in and made you stop. He said you were naked."

"Oh, boy."

Sandy flipped her head up. " 'Oh, we were drinking Manhattans last night,' " she said in a high-pitched voice. " 'Gloria and I drank a whole bottle of pinot noir.' Did you actually make it all up in advance, Mother?"

"No."

"All I asked you was to not go out with Mr. Cacciamani. I thought you would understand." She started to cry again. "Everything about Tony, that part of my life—that was really painful for me, and so I asked you please do not go out with him. It wasn't like I was asking so much. After all, you always hated his guts. You couldn't respect me that much? You had to just look me right in the face and lie to me? Poor, stupid Sandy, just tell her what she wants to hear."

I looked at the little daffodil plants, their healthy green stalks pointing energetically to nowhere. I could see it both ways, her way and mine. Mothers don't like to hurt their children, not even when all they're doing is trying to have a life of their own. "Sandy, I am just so sorry I hurt you, and you're right: I never should have lied to you. But if you could see it from my perspective . . ."

"I don't want to."

"Well, give it a try, anyway. When you were in high school, you loved Tony, and your dad and your grandparents and I all took it very personally. We thought you said you loved him just to make us angry. But I know now that wasn't true. You didn't care that he was a Cacciamani. He was just Tony, the boy you loved. We were wrong to tell you not to see Tony anymore. You've got to understand that where you were fifteen years ago is where I am right now. I'd like nothing better than to wake up tomorrow and find out Romeo had a different last name. But it's not going to work that way. I really like Romeo. You should understand that better than anybody. I don't understand about all this hate, but I'm ready for it to be over."

Sandy took a deep breath. "That's pretty much what I said to you when I was in high school. And you know what you said to me, Mother? You said, 'Get over it.' " Sandy straightened up her shoulders and looked me dead in the eye.

"Get over it," she said.

SANDY TOOK THE REST OF THE day off, which was to say she picked up her purse and walked out of the store, tears streaming, hair springing along behind her. How had I come to this in such a short time? Things were bad, and I could only guess that they'd get worse. I wondered if Romeo knew by now that Joe had come to see me. I couldn't call him for fear of who might pick up the phone, and no doubt he was feeling the same way about calling me. The simple thing to do would be to knuckle under and give him up. But I didn't want to. He was right; we had been enemies for so long that we had bonded together. All the passion of hate had become the passion of love. The ions that had bound us together from the start had simply reconfigured.

All day long I went through my responsibilities in the dullest way. I handled the flowers as if they were spatulas. Every arrangement I put together I tore apart again, remembering the perfect bouquet in Romeo's cooler. I left the little headless daffodils in their place, even though all my customers remarked on them. "These didn't do very well," they said sadly.

"No," I said, as if I hadn't noticed. "I guess not."

I kept waiting for the other Cacciamani boys to come harass me. I thought it would be like a fairy tale. Each one who came would be bigger than the last, their threats scarier, until finally some fire-breathing Cacciamani boy nine feet tall and covered in hair would break down the door to my shop. "Release my father!" he would shout, and his breath would singe off my eyebrows.

But even under such duress I'd say to the fire-breather, "Sorry. No can do."

And when I had stood up to the very worst of them, the spell would be broken. They would all be restored to regular guys, decent sons who would dance the lambada at our wedding. It would be explained to me then: We were all victims of some ancient curse having to do with a slight made to some witch two thousand years ago for which we could not possibly be responsible. The phone rang, and suddenly my heart was filled with hope.

"I'm waiting for you at your house," Nora said. Then she hung up.

So the path to broken curses was going to be a little more treacherous than I had imagined. I flipped over the CLOSED sign and went
to meet my fate.

I LOVED Nora; I know I have mentioned this before. But the sight
of that Lexus in my driveway struck greater fear into my heart than
the sight of Joe Cacciamani decapitating miniature daffodils ever
could.

"Alex and I have talked it over, and I've told Sandy that she and
the kids can come and live with us," Nora said. This before, Hello,
Mother. This before, Heard you had a rough day.

"Nora, ease up on me, will you?"

"No, Mother, I will not ease up on you. When you look me in the
eye and you swear something, I expect I can take you at your word.
What can we count on now, hum? Can you tell me that? What else
are you lying about?"

"Okay, you win. You were adopted." This conversation was taking place in the entry hall. My purse was in one hand; my keys were
in the other. "Where are the kids?"

"Sandy thought it would be better if they didn't see you just now."

"Why, because I'm such an evil influence? A sixty-year-old
woman goes on a date, and the children have to be evacuated from
the house?"

"This *date,* as you call it, isn't the issue, though you have a hell
of a definition of a date, from what I hear. The issue is—"

"Hang on to that thought for one second, sweetheart, your
mother needs a glass of wine." I dropped my keys into my purse,
dropped my purse onto the floor, and headed for the kitchen. Nora
followed close behind in her smart gray pantsuit. I wanted to tell
her I couldn't argue with her while I was wearing dirt-covered jeans.
It put me at a terrible disadvantage.

"The issue is trust," she continued. "The issue is *family.* The
Rosemans do not keep company with the Cacciamanis. That was
your guiding principle when we were growing up."

I took the wine out of the refrigerator and held it up to her. She shook her head, and so I poured for one. "I made a mistake," I said. "I'm sorry. No one knows what we did to them or what they did to us. What happened with your sister in high school could have happened to anybody. It's time to put that one behind us."

"I can't believe I'm hearing this."

"Believe it."

"So you're telling me you're going to see him again?"

I took a sip. For a minute there I really wanted to open up to her, tell her about the jam I was in. Why did we always tense our backs before we spoke to each other? "I don't know. I'd like to. I keep thinking this all might blow over and I could go out with Romeo. He's so nice, Nora. That's the thing you won't believe. He's the nicest man I've ever met." I had tried talking to her one way; now I was banking on compassion. Never bank on compassion where Nora is concerned.

"So that's your answer," she said. "I'm taking the kids."

"For what *reason?*"

"If you don't see it by now, I can't explain it to you."

"Well, are they coming back tonight?" For all the times I'd wished that Sandy would pull her life together and get a place of her own, suddenly the thought of them leaving seemed so awful to me. And maybe I was proving myself to be a lousy mother, but I was one hell of a good grandmother.

"Sure," Nora said, looking at her watch. "They'll be back in a few minutes."

"And then they're going to your house?"

"Not tonight," Nora said. "I have to show a new listing, and Alex has a meeting. In fact, I need to get going."

"So you're moving Sandy and the kids out because I'm an unfit influence, but at a time that is more convenient to you?"

Nora started to say something, but she thought it over for a second, raised her eyebrows, and nodded. "More or less."

"I won't hold my breath."

"Think about what I said, Mother." Nora was back in her yellow silk coat and sailing out the door.

I had about ten minutes to finish off my wine and stare vacantly at the wall in the kitchen, in which time I came up with the idea of painting everything pale yellow. Then Sandy and the kids came home. Whatever my girls had been plotting, at least they had the decency not to tell the children about it. Tony and Sarah came flying at me like I had just come home from the Peace Corps.

"We didn't see you last night, and then we didn't see you this morning," Tony said breathlessly. "We haven't seen you in ages."

"Ages," I said, kissing his head madly and then his sister's head as well. I looked over at Sandy, who was hanging back by the door. She had a guilty look for having sicced Nora on me. I think she realized the punishment did not fit the crime.

"I drew you a picture," Sarah said. "Because you were gone for such a long time." She extracted a drawing from her pink Cinderella backpack. It was a stick figure with her hair in a flip, and she was holding a giant bunch of flowers.

"It's divine," I said.

"It's you," Tony said.

After Sandy went to school, I shifted into total indulgence mode. I made popcorn balls with Karo syrup and played go fish with real enthusiasm. We watched the video of *Lady and the Tramp,* a movie that moved me almost to tears in my present circumstances. I identified with both Lady and Tramp. Since it was Friday, I extended bedtime by an hour. In short, we partied. Maybe I was trying to secure my place in their hearts, but I really think that had already been done. I wasn't going to risk my family, and I wasn't going to be bossed. The trick was finding the line between those two things.

IT WAS still dark when I felt a hand shaking my shoulder. I used to get up on my own.

"Grandma?"

I rolled over. "Tony, baby, what is it?"

"Somebody's stealing your roses."

The clock said five forty-five. "Are you having a bad dream?"

He shook his head. "It isn't a dream. It's a lady. There's a really old lady outside, and she's stealing the roses."

Tony's bedroom was downstairs and in front; his window was just above the roses. I was up and in my bathrobe in a heartbeat.

"Don't go down there," he cried. "She'll do something awful."

"Not a chance, baby. I know who it is. It's a friend of mine. She's going to borrow the roses. I just want to go down and say hello to her."

"It's too early."

"You're absolutely right. I thought she was coming later. You sleep in my bed, and I'll come up in just a minute, and we'll sleep in together."

Again I was running down the stairs, running through the door and into the yard. The grass was cold and wet. The old bat had attached my hose to my spigot and was watering the roses. It was too early for blooms, but they had their leaves already and some nice little buds. I could see it all there: a spade and two empty giant-sized boxes of kosher salt. She had to use kosher.

"Hey," I said. "Turn my hose off!"

She looked good for almost ninety, still tall and thin, with a bunch of steel-wool hair. She looked at me with utter contempt. "What are you doing up so early?" she said. "Rosemans are a lazy bunch. Everybody knows that."

I ripped the hose out of her hand and threw it back into the boxwoods, still running. I didn't care how old she was, I was going to take her out. "Get away from my flowers. Get away from my family." Since my yard, like all Somerville yards, was about the size of a half bath, I was very much in her face.

"No, *you* get away from *my* family, you tart." She poked her bony finger into a soft spot beneath my collarbone in a way that hurt quite a bit. She knew just where to aim. There was a blue Dodge idling in front of my house, and when the old bat poked me, out flew yet another Cacciamani boy, this one not quite as big as the other two, which ruined my theory of expanding sons.

"Hey, you," he said. "Get your hands off my grandmother!"

Old woman Cacciamani smiled and folded her arms, her rott-weiler boy bounding up on me.

"Do you have eyes?" I said. "Do you see who is poking who here?"

"Whom," the old woman said. "Who is poking whom." She turned to Wolf Boy. "It's appalling. They can't even speak."

"Please," I said. "Both of you stay exactly where you are. This time I am calling the police."

"Everybody in town knows you're a crummy florist," the old woman said. "You probably think salt is fertilizer."

"Shouldn't you be dead already?" I asked.

"Hey," Cacciamani Boy said, lunging again.

She raised up the skeleton of her hand, which was draped in a layer of parchment paper so thin it let through the first rays of morning light. "Alan," she said. "Wait for me in the car."

"I'm not leaving you alone with her. It isn't safe."

"Alan. The car."

What a short leash these men lived on. In miserable obedience he slunk back to the Dodge. He didn't get in, but leaned up against it.

"I've had it with you Rosemans," she hissed. "I'm an old woman, and I've lived to protect my family from the likes of you, your parents, and your whorish little girls. I will not leave this earth until I know that my people are safe from yours."

"For the remark about my daughters alone I should break your sorry neck."

"Come near my Romeo again, and you'll know all about broken necks."

I tried to control myself. This could be my big chance after all, my shot at the truth. "Since you have ruined my sleep, frightened my grandson, and killed my roses, will you at least do me the courtesy of explaining to me what the hell your problem is?"

"You are unfit to be in the same room with my son."

"Fascinating. I mean before that."

"Your daughter tried to trap my Tony into a life of misery."

"Well, Tony surely contributed to that one."

"If he was going to marry her, it's because she lied to him. She probably told him she was pregnant. She probably tricked him."

"Please," I said, breathing deeply. "Before I am forced as a mother to cut your heart out, I want you to think back before the business with Sandy and Tony. What went on between you and my parents? I know this didn't start in the previous generation, because your crowd and my crowd did not run together in the old country." My hands were shaking. Every fiber of my being wanted to throw her to the ground and jump up and down on her. I have never felt such seething hatred in my life.

"Why should I tell you?"

"Because this is madness! It's insanity."

She looked at me for a while. "I owe you nothing." She went to poke again, but I saw it coming this time, and I stepped aside, at which point she fell face forward into my lawn.

I backed toward my door, my hands raised as a clear sign that I had not touched her and would not touch her. Cacciamani Alan came running back and scooped the old pile of sticks up in his arms. I went inside and closed the door, utterly disinterested as to whether she was dead or alive.

I OPENED Sandy's door. She was asleep in a cloud of curls. "Get up right now," I said without much tenderness. "I need your help."

She sat up quickly. She was a mother. She slept in her sweats and was used to waking up in a hurry. "What is it?"

"The roses," I said. "We've got to move fast."

Nora would have rolled over and gone back to sleep, but Sandy knew by the tone of my voice that I wasn't kidding around. This was a higher priority than whatever argument we were having. I went to the linen closet and got a stack of sheets and towels. I went to the kitchen and got a box of lawn-and-leaf bags. I went to the garage and got two shovels. There wasn't much time.

"What is it?" Sandy said, scurrying behind me.

"That old Cacciamani bitch salted my roses!" When I threw open the front door, I half expected the paramedics to be there performing CPR on what was left of her, but all the Cacciamanis were gone, swept away in the blue Dodge. The only trace that they had been there at all were the two empty boxes of salt. She had taken the spade, so I guessed she wasn't terminal.

"She salted the roses?" Sandy stopped to stare at me in horror.

"Yeah." I stuck my shovel in and heard a crunch. Sandy grabbed the other one, and we were digging.

"That's what Sherman did after he burned down the South," Sandy said. "That's like the lowest thing one human being can do to another. He wanted to ruin all the farmland so the people who came back after the fire wouldn't be able to feed themselves."

"I think she was operating under a similar impulse." I spread a sheet over the lawn. "Put all the dirt here. We might have a chance, but it's going to be tough. She took the time to water it in."

"She *watered* the salt?" Now Sandy was really throwing her back into the digging. She wasn't hurt anymore. She wasn't scared. She was mad. She was my girl. "Only a total sociopath would stop to water the salt."

"That's not all," I told her. "It turns out she salted my mother's roses, too. Years ago. We didn't know it, of course. We just knew they died and nothing could ever be planted in that spot again." One good thing was the old woman wasn't strong enough to dig very deeply. There were still pockets of coarse kosher salt in the ground. You had to kind of admire her for doing it herself, for making Alan stay in the car while she marched up my walk like Sherman to repeat the crime.

"How did your mother find out who did it?"

"She never did. Romeo told me." I pulled up the plants and gently loosened the dirt from their roots, then wrapped them each in a towel. My Queen Elizabeth, my London Best, my Pink Lady.

"You think about this, Mother. You think about the kind of family who would do this."

I thought about it while I dug even deeper to get out any salt that might have trickled down. "I'm thinking about it, Sandy. I'm thinking about very little else."

We went to the garage and began lugging out fifty-pound bags of dirt and fertilizer. We loaded up the ground with the best dirt money could buy. Then I rinsed off the roses' roots in the street, and together Sandy and I planted them all back again. By the time it was over, we were mud-caked, exhausted, and proud. Sandy came to me and hugged me for a long time.

"She didn't win," I said.

"The grocery store is full of salt," Sandy said.

"Then I'll dig them up as many times as I have to."

"What are you going to do, Mother?" Sandy said.

"I don't know yet." We sat down together on the front porch.

"I've been thinking about what you said. I want to try and see it your way."

"I appreciate that."

Sandy looked down the street in both directions. "Did Mr. Cacciamani say anything about Tony?" she asked tentatively.

Maybe this would hurt her; maybe it wouldn't. All I was sure of was that I shouldn't lie to Sandy about anything. "He never got married. He's in Ecuador giving out vaccines." I reached over and took her filthy hand in mine. "Romeo said he was so sorry about what he had done to break you up. He said that Tony had really loved you, that he never got over you."

Sandy kept her head down for a minute, and I didn't know if this was going to start her crying again. "I know this is terrible of me," she said finally. "But I think that's the nicest thing that anyone has ever said."

SATURDAYS were always a juggling act. The store tended to be packed for the first half of the day and utterly dead after two o'clock. Usually we just brought Tony and Sarah with us. Tony liked to work in the back. The more tasks you gave him, the happier he was. While he was perfectly willing to sweep the floors and unpack boxes of ribbon, nothing gave him a sense of purpose like filling up water picks, which he accomplished to absolute perfection. What he wanted to do was strip the thorns off roses, but I was twelve before my father let me have a knife. Sarah, on the other hand, was an up-front girl. I believe that "May I help you?" was her first complete sentence. People were very charmed. That kid could have sold water to fish. When there were no customers around, she would check all the plants for dead leaves. She pinched them off gently, carefully, and stuck them into her pockets.

The four of us worked briskly. Sandy and I were both invigorated by our morning's triumph over the salt and our own tenuous reconnection. But even in the midst of all the good feelings I could not help noticing the man who was parked in an older black Ford across the street. He would sit there in his car reading; then from time to time he'd get out and stretch up on his toes. Then he'd feed a couple quarters into the meter and get back in his car for more reading. Then he drove away; then he came back. He was a heavy man in a black raincoat, with a full head of close-cropped silver hair. He looked Italian.

Sandy didn't see him. I know that because if she had, she would have called the police. I knew there was no point in doing that now. As much as I knew that man was there for me, I couldn't call and complain about someone who was parking.

At two o'clock, as usual, customers stopped coming in. Sandy rounded up the kids to go home. I would stay until five, cleaning up and working on the books. People like to know you're open until five on Saturday, even if they never come by.

"Okay," Sandy said. "We're off." She kissed my cheek in celebration of our good day together. I held on to her for a second. I didn't know what was coming, but I knew it might be bad.

"Go," I said, trying not to choke up. "Have a fantastic day."

I stood at the door and waved good-bye to them. Tony and Sarah loved to wave and be waved to. After they had gone, I just stood there at the door. He watched Sandy and the kids drive away, and then he tossed his magazine onto the seat beside him, got out of the car, and came across the street. I was sick with dread but wanted to appear brave. I held the door open for him.

"My," he said, "that's service."

He was dressed as a priest. I was sure he caused less suspicion that way. "What do you want?" I said straight out.

He looked at me a little puzzled. "Want? Oh yes, some flowers. I was thinking about getting something different for the altar. We're in a bit of a rut."

I sighed. All the work of my day fell on me all of a sudden. I felt old. "Just get to it," I said. "I'm really tired of you people. If you're going to shoot me, shoot me, whatever." There was not one chance in the world that he was a priest who had spent the entire day in his car trying to figure out what floral arrangement he wanted for his church.

Now the man looked very puzzled. "Shoot you?"

"Whatever your plan is—threaten me, scare me to death. Whatever it is you have to do, I just want to get it done, okay?"

"Do you know me?" the man in black asked.

"Sure. You're the guy who's been parked across the street off and on since nine o'clock this morning, waiting for my daughter and my grandchildren to leave so that you could have a private word with me. Am I right so far?"

"Oh, I am bad at this," he said, looking genuinely crestfallen. "It never occurred to me that you might notice."

"And this has to do with the Cacciamanis, correct?"

"How do you know all this? This is very impressive. Romeo was right: You really are something. Except for the shooting part. You're wrong about that. I have no intention of shooting you."

"Romeo?"

"I'm Father Alphonse," he said, sticking out his meaty hand. "You can call me Al."

"Father Al?"

"Just Al is fine. You're Jewish, right?"

I nodded. "Romeo sent you?"

"It isn't really part of my job description, but he's stuck. He's being watched by his family. You're being watched by your family. The idea is that no one suspects a priest, which is funny because you did. You really do break all the rules."

"I've been told that."

"Romeo and I go way back. From first grade at St. Catherine's. He was lining up for the priesthood himself, you know. Did he tell you that? Then he met Camille on a bus. He made the right choice. She was a great woman, Camille." He gave me a nervous look. "Meaning no disrespect to you."

"None taken."

"When God took Camille, Romeo never thought there was going to be anyone else for him. He thought his life was over. And he kept on thinking that until he met you."

"Me?"

"Romeo is crazy about you," the priest said.

Crazy about me? "Nobody else in his family is."

"Have they been giving you a bad time?"

"I wouldn't know where to start."

Al shook his head and clucked his tongue. "Romeo was afraid of that. He's very worried about you. There's a lot of bad blood between your families, a great deal of pain."

I looked at him. "Say, you wouldn't happen to know what's behind all this, would you? You're a priest. People tell you things."

"People do tell me things, but I'm not allowed to repeat them."

"Not even in emergencies?"

"Sorry." He took an envelope out of his coat pocket and handed it to me. "I can give you this, though."

The envelope said "Julie" on it. I wish I could say my heart leaped at the sight of Romeo's handwriting, but I had never seen his handwriting before.

"Go ahead," Al said, "read it. I'm supposed to wait for a reply." He turned his back and stared at the asters. He leaned over to sniff them. I opened the note.

Dear Julie,

I told you when I met you again that I had been wanting to write you a letter. Well, here it is. Sorry doesn't begin to express how terrible I feel about everything that has happened. If you are in half the trouble that I'm in, then you know what I'm talk-ing about. As much as I know the answer is to walk away from each other and forget about it, I just can't do that. Please meet me tomorrow morning in the CVS at nine o'clock. Tell Al I'll go to Mass tonight. Give me one day so that we can, at the very least, make things right between us, even if we can't make things right between our families.

Love,
Romeo

"Oh," I said, holding on to the paper.

"Good news, I hope," Al said.

"I don't know," I said. "I don't know what constitutes good news anymore."

"Well, you don't have to give me an answer now." He took out his wallet and gave me a business card. "You can call me. I have an answering machine. That's my private number."

I turned the card around and around in my fingers, trying to fig-ure it all out. "Listen," I said. "I know you've already been here all day, but could you stick around for ten minutes?"

"Sure," he said. "I've got ten minutes."

I put the letter and the card in the pocket of my smock. "Come in the back with me. I'll make you an arrangement. You said you wanted something new for the altar?"

"Oh, I was just making small talk. Romeo gives us our flowers."

"Well, this week the flowers at St. Catherine's are brought to you by Roseman's. That will be a first, Jewish flowers."

"Flowers are flowers," he said. "I'd never turn them down."

I got Al a stool, and he sat with me while I worked. The new flowers would come in on Monday morning, and so I used up everything I had. It took me a lot longer than ten minutes, but I gave him my masterpiece. The flowers were graceful, towering. It was not as good as Romeo's, but it was a deeply ambitious arrange-ment. It was all Al could do to work it into his car. He held my hand. He could not thank me enough.

"No," I said. "Thank you."

"Anything else?" Al asked me at the curb.

"Yes," I said. "Tell him yes."

I CLOSED up early. Why not? There were no more flowers. I called Gloria. "I need to shop," I said. "And I need advice."

"My two favorite things in the world. Buzz drove up the Cape this morning to fish. According to my calculations, he is absolutely stuck in traffic on Route 6 about now. I'll pick you up."

Over the years I had wondered many times why my marriage to Mort couldn't have been more like my friendship with Gloria. Not that I needed Mort to go shopping with me, but I wished I could have called him when I needed advice and he might be willing to drop everything. Mort would tell me to hold on, whatever it was could wait while he puttered through the tasks at hand. And even when I had his attention, it would wander. "Julie, look at that," he would say as I was pouring out my heart. "Do you see that water stain on the ceiling? How long has that been there?" Over the years I just stopped asking. If I had a little success that merited celebration, Gloria was the one I called. If it was a problem, a failure, a questionable lump that required someone sitting with me in the doctor's office for three hours, it was Gloria who was there. She had seen me through Nora's biker phase and Sandy's would-be childhood marriage. I had seen her through her daughter Kate's anorexia and her son Jeff's arrest after a one-night spree of stealing car radios. What Mort didn't understand was that I wanted someone to hash things out with, somebody who paid attention and remembered. That was Gloria. That was not my husband.

I told her about old woman Cacciamani on our way to Saks. I told her about Al the priest as we pulled into the lot. When we had parked, I showed her the letter.

"You were holding out on me," she said, digging through her purse for her glasses. I handed her mine. "This should have been first." She read it carefully. "This is good. And you said yes?"

"I said yes."

"I never would have thought otherwise."

We got out of the car and walked toward the store. I had no business spending money on anything, but after the last couple of days I'll admit I felt like I deserved a treat.

We swung through the doors, and immediately I felt comforted by the smell of perfume and face powder and new shoes. Gloria stopped at the Chanel counter, politely brushed off the salesgirl, and ran three different stripes of lipstick across the top of her hand. "Now, the first thing you want my advice on is your clothes. That's the easy part. The second thing you want my advice on is Sandy and Nora."

I picked up a tube called Splendor and drew a line across the inside of my wrist. "Precisely."

"I want to tell you to lie. Every instinct I have thinks that you should lie. But you won't, because you really can't. On the other hand, telling them is just going to be hell."

"Think Saigon in 1972."

"Right," she said. "That's your problem in a nutshell."

"And the answer?"

Gloria smiled at me sadly. "There isn't an answer, angel, because there isn't a question. You know you're going to tell them, you know it's going to be awful, and that's really all there is to it." Her eyes teared up a little bit.

I felt comforted by the depth of her sympathy. With Mort I was always trying to convince, to state and prove my case. Gloria only wanted to help me come to my own logical conclusions. "So I guess that's solved," I said heavily.

"Well, at least that leaves us the fun part. Don't forget you're going to spend the day with Romeo tomorrow."

"Given how this day started, it seems hard to believe."

Gloria discouraged me from buying the cotton sweater that came down almost to my knees. She encouraged me to buy a matching lace underwear set in a color called champagne. Then she steered me toward a phone in the women's lounge. "You need to call Nora now and tell her to come over."

"I can call her once I get home."

Gloria looked at me hard and handed me a quarter and a dime. "Tell her you're on your way and you want to meet her there."

I took the change and called my oldest daughter, who, to my complete surprise and disappointment, answered the phone. I requested the meeting.

"This is Cacciamani business, isn't it?"

"It is."

Nora sighed. "Sandy's already told me about salting the roses."

"Well, there's more."

"So much more you can't tell me over the phone?"

"It would be a lot easier if I could talk to you both together."

Nora sighed again. "All right. I'll be there in a half an hour."

I hung up the phone and looked at my watch. "She said a half an hour. We're going to have to really move it to be there on time."

"You have to stop being so afraid of her," Gloria said.

"Why?" I said. "She's scary."

Gloria drove me back to the flower shop so I could pick up my car. "You're going to have a wonderful time tomorrow," she said. "We'll look back on all of this and have one hell of a laugh. It will be years from now, but it will happen."

"I'm going to have to take your word on it."

She tapped the horn twice and waved as she drove away. I wished that she could have come home with me; but she didn't offer, because she knew it wasn't right and I knew it wasn't right and neither of us had to say it.

DREADED Lexus. Sandy and Nora were sitting in the kitchen.

"So here's the thing." I sat down across from them in the *Meet the Press* configuration these family meetings usually took on. "A priest came to see me at the shop today, a Father Al, and he brought me a letter from Romeo."

"After I left?" Sandy asked.

"Actually, yes. You had just gone."

"You're getting letters from Catholic priests now?" Nora said incredulously.

"He didn't write the letter. He only delivered it. And you might want to pace yourself, because there's more to come." I couldn't help but think about the night I had called both of the girls home to tell them Mort had left with Lila. Sandy was married then, and both girls brought their husbands. It was so humiliating to have to announce to them all that my marriage had failed and that their father preferred a much younger, much more attractive woman to me. Both girls cried. I thought that night was the hardest thing I was ever going to have to do. It turns out I was mistaken.

"He wants to see you," Sandy said.

Bless her for that. "Tomorrow morning."

Nora looked at her watch. "Well, seeing as how it's seven o'clock now, I don't think you're calling us over so we can discuss this."

"I wasn't planning on asking permission, if that's what you mean."

"The answer is no," Nora said, standing up. "We've been threatened and harassed. Property has been damaged." Nora took anything concerning property very seriously. "These aren't just people we don't like anymore. These are dangerous people. You just can't keep thinking that you're the only person in this world whose needs matter. You have to think about your family."

"I'll admit things have gotten out of hand, but I want to see Romeo again. I just don't want to lie to you."

Sandy was thinking about it, holding the past in one hand and the present in the other, making her silent assessments. I asked her where she stood.

"I think these are really really crazy people," she said quietly. "And I think you're making a mistake."

I could live with that.

"Don't call me," Nora said. "I have to detach myself from this." She picked up her purse and said good night.

"Does that mean 'Don't call me and let me know how it goes,' or does that mean 'Don't ever call me again'?"

"I'll let you know," Nora said, and then she was gone.

I had a real lump in my throat. It wasn't that I needed her approval or that she'd never come back. But we had been having the same old fight for so many years that it just made me sad beyond measure. She had been my baby. We had shared a body for a while. It seemed like ever since then I'd been missing her.

"So you aren't going to walk?" I said, turning around to Sandy.

"I'm not moving out. But I think this is a serious mistake. That's what you told me, and for that time in my life, you were right."

I was fairly stunned by her admission. I reached out and petted her hair. "I'm just so much older." I felt so much older.

"I know," she said without any unkindness. "That's why you should know better."

Chapter Four

I WAS up at six—up meaning out of bed. I had been awake since three. I conditioned my hair and blew it dry. I used some of Sandy's face scrub. I put on my champagne underwear. It was pretty. It would have been much prettier on the girl who sold it to me, but it would have been too big for her, and anyway, she wasn't here. I changed clothes three times. I thought that I had outgrown the ability to look into a full closet and think that there was nothing there. Finally I chose a pair of heavy linen pants and a dark blue boat neck sweater, an outfit that I thought made me look smart but unconcerned. I was growing less concerned by the minute. All of the things I should have been worried about were falling away: Nora's wrath, all the Cacciamani boys' threats, the old matriarch, who may or may not have died on my lawn yesterday. The hardest thing to put aside was Sandy, but I did that, too. I was happy. I was a woman getting dressed for a date with a man I knew I was crazy about. I put on the little amber drop earrings that I always got the most compliments on. I put on lipstick. I slipped on my most sensible walking shoes.

Sandy was in the kitchen with a cup of coffee, reading the paper. "You look so nice," she said. She looked mostly tired herself, like she might have been sitting there all night.

"I really appreciate that."

"Don't. I'd rather you didn't look nice. I thought about nailing your door shut, but then I figured the hammer might wake you up."

"I always was a light sleeper." I poured myself a cup of coffee.

"I just decided there comes a point in every woman's life when she has to accept the fact that her mother is all grown up and she should be allowed to make her own mistakes."

"Are we there already?" I sat down beside her. "It seems like only yesterday I was holding your head back and trying to pour liquid penicillin down your throat because you were half dying of something but you didn't like the taste of the medicine."

She smiled a little. "I don't remember that. I remember the scene, but in my version I'm pouring it down little Tony. Maybe that's why this whole thing is harder for Nora. She hasn't had kids of her own yet. She isn't used to being bent to somebody else's will. Kids make you good at not getting your own way anymore. I don't like what you're doing, but at least I understand that there's nothing I can do about it."

"Thanks, honey."

"Do you want me to drive you over there?"

I shook my head. "It's not far. I'm going to walk. It's nice outside." I stared at the clock. "It isn't time to go yet."

"Here," Sandy said, shoving half the Sunday paper toward me. "I'm going to make waffles for the kids."

I spread open the paper. I went through all of it while the kids watched cartoons. I read Sarah the funny papers. I washed the dishes. Then I alphabetized all the spices in the spice rack.

I looked at the clock again. "I could go now."

"If you want to be absurdly early."

"Where you going?" Sarah said.

"Grandma's got a play date," Sandy said. She looked at me with some fondness. "Get out of here."

I kissed them each good-bye. It was too early, but I couldn't control myself, and I started walking. I was thinking only about Romeo now, how much I used to hate him and how much I didn't hate him anymore. I was thinking about his hair, which was rough as a brush, half black and half gray. By the time I got to the end of Cedar and turned onto Elm, I was repeating his letter again and again in my mind. Love, Romeo. I was walking faster. It was eight thirty when I got there, and I had a light sweat on my forehead. I went into the store and went straight to the condom section, where lo and behold, a full half hour early, Romeo was waiting.

We stood there for a minute, grinning stupidly at our own good fortune.

"You met Al," he said.

"A great guy."

"He liked you. He said you thought he was going to shoot you."

"I'd had a bad couple of days."

"You are so beautiful."

"I was just thinking the same thing about you."

He reached out and took my hand. I stepped toward him, and then he kissed me. Very few people were in CVS at eight thirty on a Sunday morning. There in the condom aisle I wrapped my arms around his neck and he crossed his fine hands behind my back. That kiss was worth everything. Even if every rose had died, that kiss would have made it right. It was tender and passionate. We must have made a sight, two sixty-year-old people looking like they might just drop down and do it there in the birth-control aisle.

"Okay," he said. "Okay." He kissed my chin. "We've got a big day ahead of us." He took my hand again, and we went outside and got into his car. He held the door open for me. You would have thought we were in the South.

"So, where are we going?"

"Surprise," he said. "Are you hungry?"

The thought of food was impossible at the moment. I shook my head.

"Me neither." Romeo was a good driver. "So, you met my mother."

I looked out the window and watched Somerville shooting past me. "I didn't kill her, did I?"

"She's fine. Just a little scratched."

"She poked me once. Then the second time I dodged it. I swear to God, I never touched her."

"She poked you?"

"She did. See?" I pulled down the neck of my sweater to show him the round purple bruise and also the strap of the champagne bra for good measure.

He looked while driving. "The Cacciamani stigmata!" he said. "I've had that exact same bruise for probably fifty percent of my life. She has it perfected. It hurts like hell. None of us are ever smart enough to duck. We just stand there and take it."

"You've got a tough mother, if you don't mind my saying."

"I have a tough mother," he said with gravity. "She was a good mother in a lot of ways. She worked so hard for the business. She took good care of me and my dad. I think about what it must have been like for her, a pretty girl coming over from Italy all by herself, not speaking a word of English. But I'll tell you, she rules. When I married Camille, we bought the duplex underneath my parents' place—how's that for genius? I don't know how Camille stood it. My mother just took over everything she touched. It was like my kids had two mothers, one who was sweet to them and one who kicked their butts."

"She poked your kids?"

"She poked the kids. She poked my father. She even poked the mailman once for being late." He laughed a little. "Now she's poking you." He shook his head. "I really am sorry about that."

"If my daughter Nora had seen you, she would have done more than poke. How much trouble are your kids giving you?"

"I have to tell you, it's been a real surprise to me. I dropped the whole Cacciamani-Roseman thing so many years ago. I never would have imagined they'd keep the torches burning."

"So it's bad?"

"Very bad. Except for Plummy. She doesn't get it. She just shrugs the whole thing off and goes to school."

"Did you ever ask your mother, you know, what it's all about?" Not that I would blame him for a minute if he hadn't.

"She poked me and told me to mind my own business."

I stuck my elbow out the open window. I loved having somebody else drive. "I don't care," I said, leaning my head back. "Tomorrow, yes. Today, I am through with the whole thing."

Romeo reached over the gearshift and squeezed my hand.

As we took the expressway north to New Hampshire, we commented on the price of blossoming cherry boughs. We talked of the years we were broke and the years we were flush. We talked about how to raise a first-rate orchid. After crossing the New Hampshire state line, we drove on to Canobie Lake Park. I hadn't been to the park since the girls were in grade school.

Everything was different if you didn't bring the kids. I was always nervous in amusement parks—the revolting food, the creepy-looking carnies, the kids shooting off in every direction. But in the daylight, my two girls grown and my grandchildren safely at home, Canobie Lake Park seemed remarkably wholesome, if slightly tattered. The sawdust was clean. The ticket taker was a chubby woman about my age who was hardly menacing. The sky looked especially bright over the wooden spine of the roller coaster. The woman gave us each a bracelet to wear that would entitle us to go anywhere and do anything—absolute freedom.

"Does your family know you're here?" I asked Romeo.

Romeo shook his head. "I just snuck out. Sixty years old and I'm sneaking again. I haven't had any reason to sneak in a long time." He kissed me.

"I wonder what would have happened if we had met when we were young," I said, staring out at the beautiful day in front of me. "I mean, what if you had come up to me at that party in eighth grade? What would have happened if we had fallen in love in high school?"

"The same thing that happened to Tony and Sandy, only worse. Our parents would have killed us. Your father would have killed me, and my mother would have killed you."

"So, it was better that we didn't meet then."

"My family doesn't like you now, but at least they won't kill you."

I thought about mentioning Joe, who certainly seemed capable of killing me if he took a mind to, but why spoil the day? "Do you ride the rides?" I asked him.

Romeo stood behind me and put his arms around my waist. He bent over to put his chin on my shoulder. "I used to when I was a kid," he said softly into my ear. His voice made me shiver. "One of us would steal our parents' car, and we'd drive up here at night, jump over the fence. We'd buy one ticket for the roller coaster, and then we'd just refuse to get off. After the first couple of rides they'd quit trying to fight us, and they'd just leave us on all night."

"Bad kids," I said, feeling strangely breathless as his hand slid under the back of my sweater. "My father would have been right to keep me away from you."

"You want to try it?"

I'd never been on a roller coaster. They scared the living daylights out of me, but not as much as sushi. "Sure," I said. "Anything once."

THAT was how things started. It was the roller coaster and then the Scrambler, the Zipper. We took it all on. When we wanted to scream, we screamed. We held each other's hands and raised them over our heads. We went back to the roller coaster. The world spun in dazzling colors—yellow tents, black-haired children, dull grass, gold streamers. We stumbled to the Paratrooper. We did loop-the-loops and hung upside down suspended from our harnesses. We did not care. Gravity had no effect on us. I no longer knew when I was right side up or upside down. And it felt right. Now my body matched my life. I was reckless, disoriented, drunk with confusion and desire. As soon as the young man with the tattoo and the whiskey breath locked us in our cage, we were at each other like two mammals for as long as the price of admission allowed.

By noon I could no longer put together full sentences. "I think I need . . ." I no longer knew what it was I needed.

"Rest. I need to rest," Romeo said. He took my hand, and we stumbled to the far side of the park. "Do you play Fascination?"

"What is it?"

"All you need to know is that you sit down and nothing moves."

The Fascination Parlor was some combination of Skee-Ball, tic-tac-toe, and bingo. We cashed in bills for a handful of quarters and took two red vinyl stools at the end of long steel cages.

"This is where you win me cheesy stuffed animals that I keep in my bedroom," I said. "Nora always had a hundred of those things."

"I'm not going to win you anything," he said, feeding two quarters into the slot. "I've always been rotten at Fascination."

"Good."

He tossed a rubber ball up the rubber ramp and into the cage. Sure enough, it hit one wall and then the other and then came bouncing back to him.

"That's something," I said. "Do you bowl?"

"About like this, except the ball never rolls back to me." He threw another, which reached the same conclusion by following a completely different path.

"Are you doing this to be amusing?"

"Nope." He threw again, this time getting a spin on the ball. It dropped into a hole on the bottom and disappeared. "I'm not pretending to be bad so you'll feel sorry for me."

With every loss I found myself more profoundly attracted to him. He seemed so happy to lose. Mort would have stormed off four quarters ago, making it clear to everyone within earshot that the whole thing was rigged.

Romeo gave me the quarters. "Go to work," he said.

I picked up the rubber ball and sank it in the middle square.

"Hey," he said. "You're a ringer."

"I have good hand-eye coordination." I sank the next one in the upper left-hand hole. Maybe I had dumb luck. In all honesty the game just didn't seem that complicated. Ball three.

"Number seven!" the caller said. "Number seven wins the prize."

I had to check my seat to see if I was seven. When did I get to be so lucky? I told Romeo he had to pick the prize. After all, if he had won, he would have given it to me. He chose a stuffed cat with a small stuffed fish in its mouth. The fish had a huge smile on its face, as if it was thrilled to be devoured alive. "My granddaughter will like this," he said. "She has a thing for cats."

"Does she have a cat?"

Romeo shook his head. "One of my mother's rules—no cats." Should I worry about a man who lived with his mother? What difference did it make? I was never going to get anywhere near the old woman. Whatever relationship we had in the future would surely consist of long car drives and sneaking around. All around us people ate caramel apples and held hands. They screamed for their children and laughed outrageously at nothing. Romeo had one arm around my shoulder and one arm around the stuffed cat he called Tiger. This was a wonderful day, but it was as little like anything in my real life as I could possibly imagine. We went to a stand and bought clam fritters and Cokes.

"Hey," I said. "Not to spoil the mood or anything, but do you have any thoughts on, you know, this? Us? I keep going over it, and the only really logical thing to do is quit before we get started, but then, I think we've already started."

He kissed the top of my head. "Part of me says my family comes first," he said. "That's the primary law with the Cacciamanis, and I believe in it. I don't want to hurt my mother, and I especially don't want to hurt my children. The other part of me says to hell with that. I've been a good guy all these years, and I want to do what I want to do. Anyway, we're not hurting them. You're not a bad person. You're not going to tear my family apart."

"I don't think Nora is speaking to me. Sandy is speaking to me, but she's profoundly disappointed in my actions. I don't know how long I'm going to be able to hold up under that kind of pressure. I mean, you and I aren't going to run off and ditch our kids, never see our grandkids again."

"Maybe, over time, they'd get used to us together."

But neither one of us said anything to that. Every interaction I had with Cacciamanis, other than Romeo, only made things worse.

"Look," I said, pointing to a tent up ahead. "That's what we need, spiritual guidance." That's what the tent said: PSYCHIC READINGS AND SPIRITUAL GUIDANCE. PALMS, TAROT, CRYSTAL BALL.

"Oh, Al loves to give sermons on those things."

"I suppose he's against them."

"Al thinks you should take your spiritual guidance from God."

"Well, Al doesn't have children. We need extra help." All I wanted was a second opinion.

"I don't know," Romeo said, eyeing the tent like it was a center for some cult religion that snatched up teenage runaways and forced them into saffron robes.

"Hey, I rode the Zipper," I said. "I've made my leap of faith for the day. You need to make yours."

We walked over, and after a moment's indecision about how to proceed, I rapped on the wooden sign. A woman in her sixties who looked like every woman in my neighborhood stuck her head out from the flap. She had short salt-and-pepper hair, a light blue pullover, a little pink lipstick. She smiled at us and waved us in. It was cramped and dark inside. There were candles and a little electric fan. The fortune-teller was wearing jeans and gardening clogs. I was disappointed. I was hoping for something a little more exotic.

"You wanted Mata Hari," she said brightly. "I'm Ellen. I used to be Madame Zikestra, but the wig and the robes drove me insane."

"No, you're fine," I said. "I mean, I'm sure you're fine." Did she read minds or did everybody ask her the same question?

"I only do one at a time," she said pleasantly.

I shook my head. "This is a joint deal," I told her. "What we need to find out, we need to find out together."

"Okay," Ellen said. "But for the two of you it's twenty bucks."

I reached into my purse and put a twenty down on the table.

"There's only one chair," she said.

So Romeo and I split the chair, each hanging one leg off the side.

"All right. Let me see those hands."

We put our hands faceup on the table. Romeo had on his wedding ring, and Ellen tapped it. "You're not married," she said.

"Not to her," Romeo said.

"Not to anybody," Ellen said in a matter-of-fact tone. "Not to anybody alive, and we can't be married to the dead. That's the first thing I have to tell you."

Romeo looked more interested then.

She traced her nail lightly across my palms and then went to Romeo's, then back to mine. "Most days I sit in this tent and all these little girls come in. 'How many babies will I have?' 'Does he really love me?' 'Am I going to get a car for my birthday?' On and on and on. The things I see I could never tell them, anyway. They're only children, after all. They should have their happiness. For example, if you had come in here at fourteen," she said to Romeo, "you wouldn't have wanted to hear that you were going to fall in love with a very kind woman and that you'll have seven children together and one of those children will die when she is a little baby. I couldn't tell you that later on your wife was going to get breast cancer and die. To know all of that before would be unbearable." She shook her head in sympathy for it all. "If you had heard it and believed me, you would have thought it would be impossible to survive. But people survive terrible things. Now all those facts are history. Now I can tell you the truth. But if I had told you then, it would have been cruel."

Romeo closed his hands together like a book.

"Oh, come on. Don't do that," she said, and patted his hands. "Don't make me feel bad for talking. It's already happened. I didn't do it. It's good to see people who've had some life, people who want to know true things."

But I wasn't sure I did want to know. I wanted Madame Zikestra. I wanted twenty dollars' worth of reassurance that everything was going to be fine. "I think we should go," I said.

She ignored me. "Open your hands again," she said to Romeo. He did what she told him.

"There are so many funny things here, the two of you. I get the strongest sense of memory, like I've seen these two sets of hands before. Years ago two children came into my tent. I was still doing the whole magic fortune-teller thing then. They said they had to come in together. I set their hands up just this way, and I saw an amazing thing: The two of them had the same lines. Not the details, but in the big things they were twined together. I felt very sorry for them because I could see that they really were in love but that this love would separate them and whip them all across the world before they came together again. But I didn't tell them anything. I said what they wanted to hear—their parents would forgive them, there would be joy in their families, blah, blah, blah. It was true, but it was so far away. They never could have stood the pain if I had explained it to them."

Ellen had the careful, cheerful tone of someone who was giving you very complex directions to the expressway.

"And now I see the same two hands. You were right to say you had to come together. You were right to wait until now. If I had seen the two of you at fourteen, it would have been the same story, and I would have told you the same lie. But all the storms are clearing now, and the world is bringing you together again, as it should be. Just don't ever regret the past. It was all for a reason. You loved your wife," she said to Romeo, and then she turned to me. "And you, so you had to wait longer for love, but you had your girls, and so the waiting became another kind of love." Ellen looked so pleased to be telling us all of this.

I nodded. I felt physically ill. Maybe the rides were catching up with me. Mostly it was the awful notion of Sandy and Tony sitting in this tent fifteen years ago.

"So what do we do?" I said. "About the storm?"

"It's been a hell of a storm, but every storm in the world runs its course sooner or later. Two hands like these don't happen very often. Love each other madly. Do you understand what I'm saying?"

I suppose it was clear enough. At any rate, I would have agreed to anything if it meant getting out of there. Romeo picked up the stuffed cat. We said good-bye and stumbled out of the tent.

"I'm sorry," I said to Romeo. "I'm so sorry about that."

"Come on." He took my hand, and we began to walk at a brisk pace.

"Where are we going?"

"We're leaving."

I followed him to the car. I wanted to ask him about the baby he and Camille had lost. I wanted to ask him if he thought it was possible she was talking about our children, but I felt too awful about dragging him in there in the first place. I felt like I wanted to go to a dark place and sleep.

Five miles outside of Canobie Lake, we came to a little green-and-white motel called the Sylvan Park. Romeo pulled into the parking lot and told me to wait for a minute. I stared at the bushes, the cracked asphalt, and tried not to think about anything at all. He came back with a key. "Twenty-three," he said. He drove to the end of the row and parked the car. We went into the room and fell down on the bed without turning on the lights. I didn't think it was strange we had wound up here. I think it was the only place for us to go. He rolled over and held me close to him. "I found you," he whispered into my hair. "I found you." Romeo and I passed out together, tangled up, face to face, fully dressed.

Sleeping with someone is the ultimate intimacy, I think. Through sleeping we establish trust. When we woke up, we were already kissing. I let my shoes fall to the floor. I slipped out of my sweater and crumpled linen pants. Romeo took off his shirt and jeans. He touched the champagne underwear lightly with his fingers; he ran the palms of his hands over the cups of the bra, as if he had never seen anything so remarkable in his life. He was the one I was waiting for.

Sex stays with you, even in the years you never call it into service. When you call it up again, it's there, full of memory and response. Romeo's hands, Romeo's mouth, the lines of his naked legs, the warmth of his chest against my face—every corner of him brought me back to life. The sweet forgetfulness of where you leave off and the other person begins. We were the roller coaster now, the Scrambler, the Zipper. Love rolled us together and tossed us into the air. We were bigger than gravity. We stretched into it, closed our eyes, held on to each other, held tight. We slowed down and memorized each other's fingers. I held his earlobe between my lips. He traced my eyes with his tongue. We made love so deeply that I felt the very shape of my body changing. I whispered. He sang. Somewhere in it all, Romeo told me he loved me.

I returned the compliment.

IN SOMERVILLE, the houses were all dark, but my porch light was still on. We kissed good night.

"We never did come up with a plan," I said.

"We're the plan. The rest of it will just have to fall into place."

I got out of the car and waved. My bones felt soft. I felt like I could just slip underneath the door and float up to my bedroom. Instead I got out my keys and let myself inside. I flicked on the light in the hall.

There was someone sleeping on my sofa. The light seemed to wake him up, and Mort rolled over, stretched and smiled.

"Hey there, Julie," he said.

 Chapter Five

MORT liked that couch. One way or another he and that couch had logged in a lot of hours together over the years, and Mort did not look out of place there even though I hadn't seen him in five years.

"Ah, Mort," I said. What was there to say? Should I scream, yell? Certainly that would come, but at that moment my heart was too full of goodwill. Besides, I was more than a little relieved that it wasn't one of those hulking Cacciamani boys come to murder me for corrupting his father.

"You look good, Jules," Mort said. "A little rumpled, but good."

"And you've come to tell me this?" Why didn't this whole thing seem stranger to me? Even with the five-year lapse, I was still so used to talking to Mort.

Mort sat up and stretched as if trying to realign his entire body. He was the most unabashed stretcher I'd ever seen. Even after a nap on an airplane he would throw his arms over his head and roar. Then he would roll his shoulders, scratch his stomach, give his scalp several vigorous rubs with his fingertips.

Suddenly I had a terrible thought: What if something had happened with Lila? What if he was here because he wanted me back? "Mort, why are you here? You haven't come to tell me something horrible?"

He shook his head. "Nothing horrible, or at least nothing horrible in which you are not an active participant." He was starting to look righteous. He was waking up.

"Romeo?"

"Nora called me. She was sobbing on the phone. I have to fly all the way across country to try and straighten things out. Do you ever stop to think about what you're doing to the girls?"

As of today I was starting to think of myself as lucky, maybe for the first time in my life. All those years I had conversations with Mort in my head and thought of what I should have said. Now here was a chance to vent my spleen. "What *I'm* doing to the girls?"

"What you're doing," Mort said, not giving an inch.

"I'm a single, sixty-year-old woman getting on with her life. That's what I'm doing. I'm not married and neither is Romeo. We're not busting up any families, betraying any confidences. You want to talk about the girls? Let's talk about the girls, Mort. Let's talk about what the divorce did to them."

"You can't throw this off on my shoulders. This isn't about me."

"You're damn right it isn't about you. So get your sorry ass off my couch and get out of my house."

Mort got up off the couch. He looked good himself, I was sad to say. He was thinner. He was wearing nicer clothes. "We'll talk about this tomorrow when you're a little more rational. When you haven't been out half the night on a date." He managed to get a very nasty spin on the word "date."

I looked at my watch. "It isn't even midnight. And we have talked about this. We're not talking about this anymore."

Mort pointed at me, the veins bulging out on his temples where he had once had hair. "I'm not going to watch you throw my business and my family down the tubes over a stinking Cacciamani."

I opened the door. "Out." We had been here once before, this hallway, these words—only it was his sex life we were screaming about then.

"Grandma?" Tony called down from the top of the stairs.

"It's okay, baby. I'm home. I'm sorry we woke you up."

"Is Grandpa still here?"

"You've seen the kids?" I said to Mort.

"What do you think, I snuck in and got on the couch?"

"He's right here," I called up to Tony. "We were just talking."

Tony came padding down the stairs in his pajamas. "Hey, Grandpa."

"Hey, Killer," Mort said. Why would you call a child that?

"Are you going to spend the night?" Tony came over and looped himself in my arms.

"I'm going to spend the night at Aunt Nora's. I'll be back tomorrow when you get out of school."

"And Lila?" he said suspiciously.

"Lila's here?" I said.

"She's at Nora's."

"She played poker with me," Tony said. "She's not very good."

"Here?" I said. "She came here?"

"I wanted to see Sandy and the kids," Mort said. "What was I supposed to do, leave her in the car?"

"Yes, you were. Why are you bringing Lila out here, anyway?"

"She wanted to visit friends, and Nora sent us two plane tickets."

I put the heels of my hands over my eyes. "No more," I said, as quietly as possible so as not to frighten Tony. "Good night."

Mort finally said good night, and left.

"You and Grandpa don't get along," Tony said.

"Not particularly, but it's nothing that you should be worried about."

"I can't believe he likes Lila better than you," Tony said.

And on that bright note we went upstairs.

The night I had planned went something like this: I go up to my room, maybe light a candle. I take off my clothes and put on my nightgown, fluff up my pillows, and slide into bed. I don't go to sleep for a long time. I take my time to replay every second of happiness over in my mind. That's what I was going to do.

Instead I tuck Tony back into bed and then go into my room and try very hard not to slam the door. Just who in the hell did Mort think he was, showing up and telling me how I'm supposed to conduct my life? I tore off my clothes, including my champagne underwear, and threw them into a ball at the foot of the bed. My hands were shaking as I swallowed two Excedrin P.M. without water, got into a T-shirt, and sat down on the bed. Lila in my house? Playing poker with my grandchildren? And what about Nora? It was one thing to deal with her harping disapproval, but for her to call in the National Guard to prevent me from having my one shot at happiness—that was more than I could easily forgive. And why did it have to happen *tonight?* Why did they all have to come in and chop down the best day I've had in I don't know when? I shut my eyes and tried to think of Romeo, but all I could see was Mort's bald head, his face contorted in righteous indignation. I used to feel so terrible when he looked at me that way, and while I still felt terrible, it was a different kind of terrible entirely.

My problems were too big for Excedrin, and by five o'clock the next morning I was downstairs relining the kitchen cabinets. I'd had the new shelf paper for about a year, and I knew it was the only thing standing between me and a nervous breakdown. In the store I had thought it was incredibly cheerful—yellow with a pattern of tiny daisies—but now the daisies looked like little scurrying bugs.

"This is bad," Sandy said when she came downstairs at six. "I haven't seen you paper the shelves since you and Dad were splitting up."

"Well then, it's time. Does this look like bugs to you?"

Sandy peered at a shelf. "Sort of. So is this because you had a bad time with Mr. Cacciamani yesterday or because you know that Dad is in town?"

"Dad and Lila," I corrected. "And Nora bought the plane tickets."

"Not to be a turncoat or anything, but I didn't know about this until they were on the plane coming out here."

"I appreciate that." I started to cut another piece of paper.

"So are you going to see Dad?"

"I saw him last night."

"He came back?"

"He was on the couch when I got home."

Sandy got herself a cup of coffee. "He shouldn't have done that. He said good night. He left. I didn't want you to get ambushed. Did it go very badly?"

"Would you want to come home from a date in the middle of the night and find Sandy Anderson asleep on your couch?"

"I'd be so grateful to have a date, I doubt I would have cared." Sandy smiled at me. "I do get your point, though. How was your date, anyway?"

At the very thought of it I slumped down and threw aside the paper roll. "The date was great. Not that I can remember it very well now."

"Where did he take you?"

I eyed my younger daughter. "Honey, I don't mean to sound paranoid, but this is just between you and me, right?"

A cloud passed over Sandy's face, and a hurt look set in. "I was trying to show some interest. If you don't want to tell me, don't. I'm not Nora."

"Of course you're not Nora. I'm sorry. It's just that with—"

"I don't like this whole Cacciamani business. I think they're a bunch of thugs, but I'm trying to respect your choices. I should just stay out of it." Sandy walked out of the kitchen, and when I called her name, she did not come back.

Canobie Lake Park, I wanted to say. We went to Canobie Lake Park.

I cleaned up the paper scraps and put the plates back where they belonged. Then I got dressed and went to work. It was barely light outside, and I had already blown it at home. I liked to go in early on Mondays anyway so I could get all the new flowers unloaded and in their buckets before the customers came in.

I came in the back door, and as soon as I was inside the shop, I felt better. I ran my hand over the wooden workbenches my father had built, and looked at my stripper and scissors and clippers hung neatly up on the Peg-Board on the wall. It was more my home than my house was. It was the place that always calmed me down. The years I was married, I hardly ever came here, so I didn't associate the place so much with Mort. When I took it over again, it was like coming back to my family. I became a Roseman again. I understood, I guess, why my father thought I couldn't take care of the business, but I wished he could have seen me trying. I wished he could have known that I loved the store like it was family.

When I went to the front to wash the windows, I saw a box lying flat on the sidewalk, pressed against the door. It was a florist's box—of which I had a thousand—with a huge yellow bow. I wondered if it was some sort of weird return. I unlocked the door and brought the box inside. The sticker on the front said ROMEO'S. Written beneath it in handwriting I now recognized, it said "Keep Flat. This Side Up."

Flowers? No one had ever sent me flowers. "Like bringing coals to Newcastle," my father liked to say. My heart was beating like crazy. Romeo, Romeo. It felt too heavy to be flowers. I took the box to the bench, slipped off the ribbon, and pulled off the lid.

Vegetables.

Vegetables like flowers.

The tiniest leaves of spinach I had ever seen lined the whole bottom of the box like a cloud of florist's tissue. At the top there were two purple cabbages trimmed in white. Around them in a halo of red were twelve small tomatoes, then stalks of tender green asparagus sprouting leaves of six miniature Japanese eggplants. At the bottom there was a row of zucchini, then red new potatoes, then baby carrots, their fernlike tops still intact. The note was on a white florist's card that had HAPPY BIRTHDAY printed at the top with a line drawn through it.

Carissima Julie,
    Did you know you were a very hard person to buy a present for at six a.m. on a Monday?
    I love you,

                                                                Romeo

There was an arrow, and I turned the card to the back. "When is your birthday, anyway?"

I will admit it: I held the card to my heart. I dipped my face down to smell the asparagus. Could he have been at the front door as I was coming in the back? Had I missed him? Beautiful, beautiful vegetables. All was redeemed.

"Vegetables?" Gloria said over the phone.

"I know it sounds funny, but you should see them. It's art, I swear."

"Okay," she said, and I heard her take a sip of coffee. Gloria was nothing without coffee. "So was the underwear a hit?"

"Don't you want to hear about the day first?"

"I want to hear about the underwear first."

So I told her. I wanted to tell. Then I told her about the park. I told her about Mort.

"Mort? Excuse me?"

"I'm not kidding. He was there when I got home. Nora sent for him and Lila so that he could talk some sense into me."

"I take it all back—you should be scared of Nora."

"Right now I'm just angry. Look, Gloria. Would you do me another favor?"

"To aid the course of true love or thwart your ex-husband, anything."

"I'm going to owe you big after this. Go to Romeo's and tell him I got the vegetables. Tell him I'm crazy about the vegetables."

"What do you want me to say, exactly?"

"It doesn't matter," I said, knowing that Gloria and I were of the same mind on these matters. "Just go and talk about love."

SANDY was still sullen when she came to work at ten, but being that it was Monday, there was a lot to do and she had to get over it quickly. Actually, there wasn't as much to do as there should have been. Both of our flower shipments came up short, and since I had given everything left from the weekend to Father Al, there were no stragglers to back us up. There were no deliveries, so we stayed in the shop together, going over the plans for a big wedding.

Gloria swept in. "I saw him," she said. "I was just there."

"Saw who?" Sandy asked.

Gloria shot me a look, but I said, "Romeo. I asked Gloria to go over and thank him for a present."

"He sent you a present?" Sandy said suspiciously.

"Come on," I said. I took them both into the cooler and pulled the lid off the vegetable box. I dazzled them with my dinner.

"Wow," Sandy said, extending one tentative finger to an eggplant. "Are they real?"

"They are."

"They're stunning," Gloria said. "You were absolutely right. Now can we get out of the freezer? I know you are used to it, but I'm not."

We came out with the vegetable box.

"And you had to send Gloria over to thank him?" Sandy said. "You can't even go and see him?"

"Not exactly," I said. "You know how his family feels about me, and he knows how you and Nora feel about him. We're trying not to step on too many toes here." I wanted a few points for sensitivity.

Sandy picked up an asparagus stalk, twirled it gently in her fingers. "A guy who'd do something like this . . ."

"Is a wonderful guy," Gloria said. "Julie, you were right not to go over there. The place is crawling with Cacciamanis."

"What did he say?" Sandy asked, replacing the asparagus stalk carefully.

"Well, the first trick was getting him alone. I told the thug at the cash register that I wanted to discuss the flower arrangements for my husband's funeral and that I would rather speak to the owner in private. Did you know he has an office? Why don't you have an office?"

"You told him Buzz was dead?"

"I only told the first guy Buzz was dead. I told Romeo the truth when we were alone."

"So what did he *say?*" Sandy repeated.

Gloria looked at her. "He said he was crazy in love with your mother, okay?"

"That's enough for me," I said.

"He said he's thinking maybe you could go to dinner in Newton tomorrow night. He says he doesn't know anyone in Newton. I told him we know everyone in Newton."

"Tomorrow's my night with the kids," I said. "Maybe Wednesday."

"I can get a baby-sitter," Sandy said.

"Are you saying you're going to help me go on a date?"

Gloria and I were both staring at her.

"I'm saying those are very nice vegetables," Sandy said wistfully. "You don't see something like that every day. That's all. I'm going to go watch the front. You two talk." Sandy left us alone.

"That's a girl you can trust," Gloria said. "She's warming to this."

"It comes and goes. Tell me, what else did Romeo say?"

"Everything right. He said he couldn't stop thinking about you. He had a wonderful time at Canobie Lake, though to hear him tell it, you drove up there, played a couple rounds of Fascination, and came home."

"Did you tell him about Mort?"

Gloria shook her head. "I figured what's the point in making the poor guy crazy."

I heard the front doorbell and then Sandy's voice. "Hi, Dad."

There was a pause, some footsteps, and then Mort. "Would you look at this place? It's a dump. She's turned it into a dump."

"Speak of the devil," Gloria said. "Do you want me to stay?"

"I think you've done enough for one day."

"Mom?" Sandy called. "Could you come out here, please?"

Gloria went first, smiling. "Mort!" she said. "Imagine us both showing up at Roseman's."

Mort kissed her on the cheek. "You look good, Gloria." He said it in the same surprised and humbled tone he had used to tell me that I looked good. I wanted to kick him. "How's Buzz?"

"Just great. In fact, I'm off to see him right this minute. The next time you're coming to town, let me know first." Gloria gave Sandy a kiss and waved good-bye.

"So I guess she's in on this whole thing," Mort said, watching her walk away. "Your great conspirator. She must be loving this."

"Nobody is loving this," I said. With Gloria gone, I felt less confident.

Mort started pacing the shop from corner to corner. "I see you're killing the shop. Is that part of the romance? He talks you into tanking the business so he can be the only game in town?"

"Mort."

"Where are all the flowers? Can you tell me that? This is a flower shop. You're supposed to have flowers."

"There was some kind of trouble with the shipment, all right? It's just today. You want to tell me in all the years you worked here you never had a problem with delivery?"

"I had my problems, but I was always on the phone yelling at somebody. Who have you called this morning?"

I hadn't called anyone. The vegetables came and then Sandy and then Gloria. I didn't even think about it. "I'll run my store my way."

"Your store. That just galls me."

Sandy cleared her throat. "Mom, Dad, if you don't mind, I'm going to go now." Somehow she had made it all the way over to the door without our noticing.

"Ah, honey," Mort said. "Your mom and I are just talking."

"Talk all you want," Sandy said. "I just don't want to hear it."

She went through the door like a bullet. I watched her pack of curls bounce away in the sunlight. Sandy's hair went a long way toward giving her levity. No matter how hard she tried to storm away, she always bounced.

I went over and moved two pots of hydrangeas out of the late morning sun. "Sandy's right: We shouldn't be talking like this." I stopped and looked at Mort, my husband for more than half my lifetime. "Mort, just go, okay? We're only going to get into a horrible fight. You and Lila can have a nice vacation in Boston. See the kids, don't see me, tell Nora whatever you want to tell her. That isn't such a bad deal, is it?"

"So you'll stay away from the Cacciamani. Is that what you're telling me?"

I sank down into the little wicker chair. "How in the world could that be what I'm telling you?"

"Because that's what this is all about. Your father said that Rosemans and Cacciamanis had to keep away from each other. It was my job to make sure they did. That whole business with Sandy nearly broke your parents' hearts."

"I told you not to tell them."

"You don't understand, Jules. This Cacciamani bastard isn't just some guy I don't get along with. I've seen him operate for years—first with his old man and then with his pack of boys behind him. These aren't your average bad people. They're probably Mafia."

"Give me a break, Mort. What did the Cacciamanis ever do to you? Do you even have any idea what this whole feud is about?"

"What it's about?" Mort said. "What it's about? Julie, what rock have you been living under? It's about business. It's about them smearing our name all over town, saying we used old flowers for weddings. Saying we went to the cemetery and picked up our bouquets after funerals. They kept me out of Rotary. And it didn't start with Romeo. It goes back to his old man and that evil bag he was married to, may they rot in hell."

"Not so fast. She isn't dead yet."

"Is that possible?" Mort shrugged. "Then they're waiting for her. They're sharpening up the pitchforks. Those people undermined us in every way possible. They'd call our big accounts and say we had canceled, that they were going to be doing the flowers. And God forbid a Monday morning ever rolled by when I wasn't here to meet the shipment. Every rose in the bunch would have its head twisted off."

Okay. That one I believed. I had seen a Cacciamani behead a plant before. "So if this is true, some of it, any of it, how many of those same things did my dad do right back to them? And what did you do? Do you expect me to believe the Cacciamanis threw all the punches and the Rosemans stood there and took it?"

Mort looked like he couldn't possibly be hearing me right. "Of course I went after them. So did your folks. When we got hit, we hit back. That's called life, Julie."

"Life, fine, but then after a couple of generations, who throws the first punch? Are you reacting, or are you going out there to nail them?"

"What in the hell difference does it make? These are Cacciamanis we're talking about. All that matters is that we get them before they get us."

"But don't you see, Mort? It's a game. They played dirty. We played dirty. Everybody hates everybody. But if we decide to stop it, if both sides choose not to fight anymore, then the game is over. It's that simple."

"If you were playing with fair-minded people, which you're not. What I'm saying is that love blinds us." For a second he looked like he was as tired out by this whole thing as I was. "We don't always see the whole picture. That's why the people who are responsible for us have to step in and save us sometimes."

"But I don't need saving. When you ran off with Lila, I didn't believe she wanted what was best for you. But it was your life, and you were entitled to your own mistakes."

"I'm not going to let this drop, Julie."

"You're going to have to. Sooner or later you have to go home."

Mort sighed and looked around the shop. Without a moment's hesitation he picked up the best pot of purple cyclamen from a bunch of pots on a low platform and put it next to the cash register. "Got to get them up to eye level. You know that Lila and I have a shop now. Lila picked up on the business fast. She has a real good head for flowers."

"I'm glad to hear it."

Mort put his hands on his hips and surveyed the store, the lord of all he saw. "This is a great place. Do you know that? The space, the light. You couldn't find a place like this in Seattle. It could use some updating, but the feel of it . . . I always had a real connection here. From the first time you brought me in, I really believed that one day this was all going to be mine. I loved this shop."

"I know you did."

"Let me see the books, Julie. I know you're running the whole thing into the ground."

"It's my store now. Forget about it."

"I know it's your store, but I still have feelings for the place. Just give me a couple of hours. If the place was on fire, would you turn away my bucket of water?"

"Don't be stupid."

"No, *you* don't be stupid. I might be able to help you put out the fire. Why don't you try loving Roseman's more than you hate me."

It was only my vanity that stopped me. But the truth was that he was great with the books, and I was turning them into soup. He was right: We were going down. I did need help. "Okay," I said finally, waving him back toward the desk. "You know where everything is. Nothing has changed."

"Oh, Julie," he said sadly. "Everything's changed."

THE one good thing about having Mort look over the books was that it took his mind off Romeo. "Aargh!" he would yell while I was waiting on customers.

Some appeared frightened; others were simply confused. "He's trying to move the desk," I said calmly. "It's very heavy."

At one point Mort tore open the curtain that separated the front of the shop from the back. "What are you trying to do? Kill us?"

"Kill me," I said. "Not us. It's mine to lose."

"Well, congratulations on your newfound liberty, because you've lost it."

"How was I supposed to know what to do? For thirty-four years you never let me in the store, and then you up and run off to Seattle with Lila. There wasn't time to take a course in accounting. I had to get to work."

"That's why you pay people, Julie. They're called accountants."

"With what, Mort? You got the money, remember? That was the deal. The house is mortgaged up to the gutters. I've got a loan on the shop."

"You took a loan against Roseman's!"

I hadn't meant to tell him, but in the next thirty minutes or so he would have found out, anyway. I felt my eyes welling up with tears. I was overcome with shame and guilt. I had mortgaged my parents' store, borrowed against the very thing they had worked their whole lives to pay off. "I didn't know what else to do."

"You should have called me." Mort was seething.

"I wasn't going to call you. You know that."

Mort closed the curtain again and went back to work. I did a little watering and made a note to order Floralife. What would happen if I lost Roseman's? Who would I be without the flower shop? Nora didn't care a thing about flowers, but I wanted it to be there for Sandy if she wanted it. One day she could give it to Tony and Sarah. To think, out of sheer incompetence I could have frittered away the only legacy my family had—it absolutely killed me. I went into the back. "Just forget about it," I said to Mort. "You can't fix it. Go home to Lila. She must wonder where you are."

Mort didn't look up. He was punching on a calculator just as fast as his fingers would go. He had a pencil behind each ear. "Leave me alone. Get out there and sell some flowers."

I closed the curtain. I felt very weepy now. The way I saw it, I had lost or would eventually lose my marriage, my business, my daughters, and Romeo. Somewhere my parents were looking down on me and shaking their heads in despair.

Mort asked me to go out and get him a sandwich at one o'clock and said he'd watch the store. I bought myself a yogurt but then didn't even have the appetite for that. I stuck it into the cooler behind some daisies and resumed my worrying.

From two to five was usually when I worked on the books, but Mort was still back there, swearing and moaning under his breath. Today the bell rang at two thirty and in walked a very nervous-looking Romeo Cacciamani. He was wearing gray pants and a nice white shirt with rolled-up sleeves. He looked almost unbearably handsome.

"My God," I said, my voice automatically dropping to a whisper. "What are you doing here?"

"Your friend Gloria said this was when Sandy went to pick up her kids from school. Is this all right? Is Sandy here?"

I glanced behind me and moved quickly to the front of the store. I kissed him. I couldn't help it. "She isn't here, but you have to go. Really."

"I'm sorry. I know I shouldn't have come. I've been driving around the block for half an hour telling myself not to come. But I had to see you."

"I loved the vegetables."

"Did you? I just didn't know what to send. I wanted to buy you something big, like, say, California, but there wasn't time." He put his arms around me. "What about dinner tomorrow?"

"Sure," I said. "I can work something out, but you have to go now." I wanted him to stay and stay. I wanted to tell him everything that was happening.

"Is everything all right? You seem so upset."

"It's a stressful time," I said, and then, as if to prove my point, Mort came out from behind the curtain with three spiral ledgers. He dropped them.

"Cacciamani!" he yelled. "Get your lousy mitts off my wife."

Wife? I thought. Where was Lila?

"What's he doing here?" Romeo asked, his tone more curious than alarmed. He kept his mitts firmly on me.

"None of your damn business. Now get out before I set you on the curb in pieces."

Romeo seemed to smile a little in spite of himself. "I haven't heard that one in a long time."

"I swear, Cacciamani, get out of here now. You do not want to get into it with me."

"Of course I don't want to get into it with you. What in the hell is your problem, Mort?"

"My problem? My *problem?* You're my *problem,* buddy. You always have been. Except when I was here, you knew enough to stay away. Now I'm gone, and you're sniffing around my wife, ruining my business." Mort shook the few papers he was still holding in his hands. Somehow it seemed the two problems had become conflated in his mind. Now it was Romeo's fault that Roseman's was sinking, Romeo's fault that I wasn't sitting at home. The budget deficit—that was probably Romeo's fault as well.

Romeo scratched his head. "Your business? Your wife?"

"Well, they sure as hell aren't yours."

"Listen, Mort. Enough with the tough-guy talk. We never got along. So what? This isn't a turf war."

"It is a turf war, if that's your terminology. I want you off my turf."

Romeo took a small step away from me, toward Mort. "You don't live here anymore, unless I've gotten the story wrong."

"Let me tell you, Cacciamani, you've got everything wrong." Mort came out from behind the counter.

"Look," I said. "This is a ridiculous mistake. Mort is visiting, and Romeo is leaving. Let's just drop it."

"I'm not leaving," Romeo said. Mort was taller than Romeo, but Romeo was built like somebody who could throw an ox through a wall, or at least he could have twenty years ago.

Mort nodded, the veins coming up. "Well, good. That's really fine, because you're the one I've been wanting to talk to, anyway. You just saved me a trip."

"Mort," I said in a tone used to soothe nervous Doberman pinschers. "Settle down."

"Stay out of this, Julie. You," he said, pointing at Romeo, "need to stay away from my family. You stay away from Julie. You stay away from my girls. You stay away from my store."

"You can't tell him to stay away from me, Mort, or the store." It wasn't that I was completely against him at that moment. He had spent the day trying to rescue my books. He was tired and hugely frustrated, and I liked to think that had this meeting taken place at another time, it might have gone better.

Mort turned to me. "Are you on his side?"

"Please. Let's just all walk away from this."

"After everything he did to me?" Romeo asked, suddenly engaged. "Did to you? If he wants a fight, I'll give him a fight. I had put the past in the past." He turned to Mort. "But if you want to bring it up, I'm sure I can remember."

"A fight?" Mort said, his eyes bright as dimes. "You want to fight me?"

Who said these things? Fighting was only in the movies.

"If that's what you're looking for, come on."

No sooner were the words out of Romeo's mouth than Mort had the cyclamen in his hand and was hurling it straight at Romeo's head. Mort had been state-ranked in baseball when he was in college. They called him the Arm. The pot hit Romeo on the left temple and exploded into a fan of dirt, petals, stems, and terra-cotta shards. Romeo went down.

For all his fits of rage, I had never seen Mort strike another person. He didn't even spank the girls when they were little. I knelt beside Romeo. His head was bleeding spectacularly, and I was trying to brush the dirt out of his eyes. I loved him. It was one of those moments in life when you're sure.

"Mort, you stupid son of a bitch, you could have killed him!"

At the very mention of being killed, Romeo rose up from the ground and flew at my ex-husband like a creature with wings. He got his hands around Mort's throat and started beating his head into the counter. Mort somehow landed a hook on the exact spot where Romeo's head was already split open. Romeo, reflexively, brought up his knee.

It never occurred to me that intelligent grown men still fought, and yet there I was, watching it as if the whole thing were taking place underwater. I thought that fighting had rules. I was wrong. They were slugging, pulling. I think I saw Mort bite. They knocked over the card rack and smashed the African violets. "Stop it!" I screamed. "Stop it!"

With that simple command they fell apart, panting, bloody, and dislodged. They lay on my floor amid the dirt and the blossoms. In less than a minute they had both been ruined, the store had been ruined, I had been ruined. I went to Romeo, whose whole head was covered in blood. Both his forehead and his lip were bleeding now, and his left hand was turned at an unnatural angle. There was a bright red pool forming under his head.

But it was Mort who really concerned me. I think most of the blood on him was Romeo's, but there was a horrible swelling on the side of his head. I couldn't get him to respond to me. He lingered in a mumbling, half-conscious state and then slipped out of it. I put my head down on his chest and listened to his heart.

Romeo dragged himself into a sitting position, wincing at every inch. "Dear Mother of God," he said. "Tell me I didn't kill him."

"You didn't kill him," I said. "But I'm calling an ambulance."

Time happened in a dream. It seemed like the second the phone was in the cradle, the ambulance guys were rushing through the door. Because I had told them, when asked over the phone, that the cause of injury was a fight, they sent the police as well. Blue and red lights flashed brightly through the window of the store, and Ginger, the woman who runs the dress shop next door, came over to see if I'd been murdered.

"Do you know these men?" the young officer asked me as two paramedics started working on Mort and the third applied pressure to Romeo's head.

"Ex-husband," I said, pointing. "New boyfriend."

He nodded and closed his book.

"We've got a concussion here," one paramedic said of Mort.

"This one is losing a lot of blood," Romeo's paramedic said.

Romeo allowed himself to be hoisted onto a stretcher. They already had Mort's limp body tied onto a gurney, and side by side, like bunkmates at camp, they were slid into the ambulance. I got in between them for the short ride, just to make sure nobody woke up and tried to get things going again.

Inside the emergency room, they took Mort and Romeo off quickly. I called Sandy. "Listen carefully," I said. I told her to call Gloria to come and watch the kids. Then she should call Nora and come to the hospital. "Your father has been in a fight."

"The two of you were fighting?" Sandy said. "Fistfighting?"

"It was Romeo," I said. It didn't matter if she knew or Nora knew or any of them knew. It was over. No one could come back from something like this.

"How bad is it?" Sandy said, her voice tentative.

"Not bad like death. Not even bad like permanent injury. But bad," I said.

"How's Romeo?"

"Um, I'd guess about the same. I have to call his family."

I sat with the phone in my hand for several minutes before I pulled myself together and called the store.

"Romeo's," a voice said.

I asked to speak to Raymond. Despite our unpleasant first meeting, I remembered Romeo saying he was the most rational of his sons.

"You bet," the voice said, so cheerful, so helpful. It sounded like the place was packed. There was a pause, and I tried to keep from sobbing. A different yet very similar voice came on the line. "Raymond Cacciamani."

I cleared my throat. "Raymond, don't hang up the phone. There's been an accident, and your father's in the hospital. This is Julie Roseman." I thought it was best to put that fact at the end.

"Somerville Hospital?" he said as if he was taking an order for a delivery.

"Yes."

Raymond hung up the phone. Personally, I would have asked a couple of questions. For all he knew, Romeo was dead. I was planning on begging him to come alone. I was going to tell him it was only a cut and everything was fine. Too late for that. I didn't think there was any point in trying again.

I went to the nurses station and made inquiries.

"Are you a relative?" the nurse asked without looking up.

"Ex-wife to one and friend to the other—girlfriend."

"So not exactly family in either case. Nobody's ready to have company right now, anyway. Why don't you just wait another minute?"

So I slumped down into a yellow plastic chair and waited, waited for Nora and Sandy and the Cacciamanis. Waited to pay the price for a little happiness.

A BROKEN ex-husband, a battered new lover, two hysterical daughters, and a whole host of raging Cacciamanis—that was what I braced myself for. What I forgot, amazingly enough, was the one thing that would truly, deeply disturb me: Lila the wife. When she clicked through the electric doors in her high heels, Nora close behind, I felt the last bits of whatever inner glue I had holding me together give way. Lila Roth, both bridesmaid and bride. We had met before, or if not met, passed one another in the driveway while she was helping Mort move out and I was leaving so as not to watch.

Lila was a blonde. Maybe real, maybe not. She had a certain kind of thinness that smacked of self-obsession. She was wearing eye shadow; her nails were shell pink; she wore stockings with open-toed shoes; her teeth were bleached a toilet-bowl white. Need I go on? Not a single detail escaped me.

"Where is he? What have you done with him?"

What have I done with him? Like maybe I had put him in a storage closet? "Mort's going to be fine." I had no data with which to support this. "He's being seen by the doctors now."

"The doctors!" she said. "He's with doctors!"

"This is a hospital."

"Mother, what happened?" Nora said, looking a little less confident, as if perhaps even she understood her own culpability in the day's events.

"Your father showed up at the shop, and then Romeo showed up. I wasn't expecting either one of them. They got into a fistfight."

"So your boyfriend did this. You admit it!" Lila said.

"I admit it," I said.

"Nora, you're my witness." She turned to me. "I will sue you, so help me God."

But Nora was falling down on her witnessing duties. She was dialing her cell phone and pacing off across the lobby for privacy. "I don't know what you're going to sue me for exactly," I said. "I wasn't involved in the fight."

Lila was only stumped for a second. "It happened in your store. That means you're liable."

"Well, seeing as Mort threw the first flowerpot, I would say you were liable if I was the kind of person who sued other people, which I'm not."

"You bitch," Lila said. "I told Mort this was lunacy, flying across the country to try and straighten out your love life. But he had to help you. He had to be the good guy. This is how you thank him."

"This is how I thank him," I repeated. "Aren't you a little curious about how he's doing? Don't you want to talk to his doctors?"

Lila flashed her blinding incisors at me and then stomped off.

"I can't believe you let this happen," Nora said. "Alex is on his way over. If she talks about suing again, maybe he can shut her up."

I hit Nora once when she was fifteen. She came home drunk at four in the morning after I had spent the night on the phone with the police and local area morgues. She came in the front door and proceeded up to her bedroom without stopping to say hello. When I called out her name in a mixture of relief, joy, and fury, she told me to drop dead. I slapped her openhanded across the face, exactly the way every child psychologist will tell you you must never do. I replayed that scene over in my mind for years, trying to think how I could have handled it differently, properly, but to this day smacking her seemed like the only logical response to her actions. There in the hospital waiting room I put my hand on her shoulder. "If you want to see your father and his wife, you invite them out to see you. Buy them plane tickets, I don't care. But don't you ever, ever conspire against me with anyone again and expect me to forgive you because I am your mother. I am sick and tired of forgiving you, Nora."

Nora now wore the same look of utter incredulity that she had worn at fifteen, the imprint of my hand fresh on her cheek. "I was trying to *help* you," she said. "I called Daddy so he could talk sense into you. Clearly, Mr. Cacciamani is a dangerous man. Do you still think he's so wonderful after what he did to my father?"

"Nora," I said, trying very hard to keep my voice steady. "I think you should go and comfort your stepmother, because if I have to talk to you about this for one more minute, I'm going to say something we'll both feel bad about later."

Again with the open mouth, the disbelieving hurt. I was sure I was doing the wrong thing. I could not help it. Not every relationship works out. It hadn't worked out with Mort; it wasn't going to work out with Romeo. Was it possible I could ever come to such a point with a daughter to say, "Enough's enough" and "See you around"?

God forgive me for what I know to be a small-minded slur against Romeo's family, but when they came in the door, I couldn't help but think of *West Side Story,* the Jets walking down the streets of Hell's Kitchen snapping their fingers. There were so many of them, and they all looked so much alike. The wives all looked like sisters, and though I had met four of his sons before (counting Tony, who was still in Ecuador), I couldn't remember which was which. My only lucky break was that the old woman didn't appear to be in attendance. They came toward me in a mass, and just as I thought they were going to stomp me to death, the whole pack veered to the left to the nurses station. There was a flurry of inquiries, some raised voices, and then they disappeared through the swinging double door marked NO ADMITTANCE: HOSPITAL PERSONNEL ONLY. That was it.

Two minutes later Father Al came in looking flustered and concerned. "Al," I said, and waved him down.

I could see the confusion on his face. He was trying to place me as a parishioner, and then he remembered. "Julie, oh. Julie. Are you all right?" He patted my hand. It was such a relief to have someone pat my hand.

"I'm fine."

"What about Romeo? Raymond called me. He said there was an accident, and he said something about you."

I could imagine what the something was, but Al was a priest and wouldn't say. "He's going to be fine, I think. He got into a fight with my ex-husband."

"Mort? Mort's in town?"

"You know Mort?"

"I don't know him myself, no, but I've heard plenty about him."

"Well, they ran into each other."

"And Romeo's children"—he looked around nervously—"have they come in yet?"

"They're already in the back with him. I don't even know if they saw me."

"This is going to be bad," he said. "Romeo will be fine. He was such a scrapper when we were in school. I thought he had outgrown it."

"He probably had. He was provoked."

"We'll keep that between us." Al looked toward the doors. "I really should go in there."

"Will you let me know how he is? Tell him I'm out here? I know they'll never let me in to see him, but I don't want him to think I just walked away."

"He knows that."

I suddenly felt a great sob come up before there was time to properly suppress it. "I'm absolutely prepared to give him up. I don't mean to sound so melodramatic, but I can't keep causing him all this trouble with his family. I love Romeo. I only want what's best for him. You know that, don't you?"

Al took me in his arms and let me cry on his black shirt for a minute. Gloria would have done the same thing. I pulled myself upright and ran my hands beneath my eyes. "Go on," I said. "I'm fine."

Al nodded and smiled at me; then he went through the doors without even stopping to ask the nurse's permission.

What if Romeo thought I was gone? What if he didn't even know I was out in the lobby? All I wanted was to hold his hand, to tell him everything was going to be fine. I wanted the chance to tell him all sorts of comforting lies about how everything would turn out fine. But once Mort threw that pot of flowers, I lost all of my rights or I realized I'd never had any to begin with.

Sandy came in next. It was starting to feel like a terrible episode of *This Is Your Life*. If I stood there long enough, my third-grade teacher would come in. "I always thought that Julie Roseman was trouble," she'd say.

"Dad?" Sandy asked me.

"I don't know. Nora and Lila are back there with him now. I'm afraid I'm persona non grata on both sides. No one has come out to tell me anything."

Sandy, never a take-charge sort of girl, went up to the nurse and asked for the status of Mort Roth and Romeo Cacciamani.

"Are you a relative?" the nurse asked. She'd seen a lot of relatives.

Sandy told her yes. "Roth is my father, and Cacciamani is my uncle."

"They're related?"

"By marriage," Sandy said. "Not blood. They hate each other."

"Obviously," the nurse said. She thumbed through some papers and then nodded her head. "Hang on a second." She picked up the phone.

"You go in and see your dad," I said. "I can wait here."

"Then I'll wait with you for a minute. Dad's got Lila and Nora. That's a pretty full house."

I wanted to kiss her. I kissed her. "How are the kids?"

"Their life is a party. They couldn't believe Gloria was coming over. She's going to take them shopping."

"Okay," the nurse said, putting down the phone. She looked at me. "You're the ex-wife slash girlfriend, correct?"

"Correct."

"What the hell, it's nothing serious. Many bruises for both parties. Roth looks like a concussion and two broken ribs. They'll keep him overnight for observation, but he should be out of here with a splitting headache by morning. Cacciamani had eighteen stitches, a broken left wrist, and, coincidentally, two broken ribs. They'll let him go in about an hour."

Sandy and I took our places in the chairs. "What a day," I said. "What a horrible, horrible day."

"Do you want to tell me what happened?"

"Not particularly."

"I was just starting to like him a little, the idea of him at least."

"Romeo?"

Sandy nodded.

"That's really nice. I'm giving him up now. Nobody needs all of this. My love is going to kill him, and I couldn't stand that." I felt like I was going to start crying again. "Go see if your father's awake." Mort had ruined my life once again, but I still couldn't help feeling vaguely responsible for his pulverized state. If it wasn't for me, he wouldn't be bleeding now. Of course, if it wasn't for Mort, I wouldn't have been dating to begin with.

Sandy pushed out of her chair. "I'll be back in a minute."

"Take your time," I said. "I'm not going anywhere." I was so tired I thought about stretching out over the chairs and slipping off into a coma. I hoped they would notice me in a day or two and give me a room, hook me up to a nice glucose drip. I couldn't imagine going back to work, and I couldn't imagine going home. The hospital seemed like a fine place to set up camp.

There was a pretty, waiflike girl with long black hair and a dark purple scarf looped around her neck wandering through the waiting room. She would stop in front of people and ask them a question. They shook their heads, and she moved on to the next group. She looked like the gypsy princess in every film that had a gypsy princess—huge sad eyes and exceptional posture. She started to walk toward me. "Mrs. Roseman?" she asked.

I looked up at her and blinked in agreement.

"I'm Patience Cacciamani."

"Plummy?"

She nodded. She had tiny gold rings on all of her fingers, and one of her ears was pierced three times. On her this looked like a good idea.

"My dad wanted me to tell you he's okay. He made everybody else go out in the hall so he could talk to me alone. He wants to know if you're okay."

The fact that she was talking to me was so confusing that I could barely understand her words. "I'm okay."

She sat down in Sandy's chair. "You don't look so great, if you don't mind me saying."

"I don't mind at all."

"I had wanted to meet you, but it never occurred to me it would be like this."

"You wanted to meet me?"

"Sure," she said. "Dad's crazy about you."

"But what about your brothers?"

She waved her hand. "They're idiots. Not idiots, really. They're good guys one at a time, but when you put them together, they're like—I don't know—a bunch of moose or something."

This made me smile.

"They won't actually hurt you—I hope you know that—but they do seem to despise you. I don't mean to be rude, but I think we should be able to speak frankly."

Where this child came up with this much poise was beyond me. It made me want to go out and have a couple more holes put in my ear. "I agree. Absolutely. Tell me about your father."

She stared off into the waiting room trying to conjure him in her mind. "Stitches here," she said, and drew a line with her finger across her own temple. I could see the flowerpot landing there now. "And here." She touched her lip. "He broke his wrist, but only one little bone, and there are two cracked ribs." She pressed a hand into her ribs. "It must have been one hell of a fight."

"It was."

"How's the other guy, your ex?"

"I hear he has a concussion. They're keeping him overnight."

"That's good. I don't mean good that he's hurt, but this way all the boys will be able to say Dad won. Dad doesn't have to spend the night."

"That is good."

"My family has some wicked problem with your family. I think everybody needs to let go of their anger."

"That makes two of us."

"Well, you and Dad like each other. That's a positive start, don't you think?"

"I did think," I said. "But right now it's all a little confusing."

She nodded and gave me a sad smile like the statues of Mary that were everywhere in this town. She looked toward the double door and sighed. "I guess I should be getting back. They're going to be releasing him soon. We're supposed to pick him up around back. It was very nice meeting you."

"You, too. You'll tell your dad I hope he's okay?" Romeo, Romeo. All I wanted was to hold him in my arms.

"I'll tell him," she said. Plummy leaned toward me and brushed my cheek with the back of her hand. "You get some rest."

She wasn't two steps away from me when her extended family started pouring into the waiting room.

"Plummy!" the big one yelled. "You get away from her."

"Shut up, Joe," Plummy said without the slightest hint of inflection.

They came toward me in a clump.

"I thought I made things clear to you," Joe said, pointing a finger in my direction. His face was red, and he was breathing hard.

"Joe," Plummy said. "Do you want me to get Dad out here and have him see you talk to Mrs. Roseman this way?"

"Shut up," he said to his sister.

She walked up to him. She was taller than I had realized. She got her face very nearly in his face. "No, you shut up, Joseph." She kept her voice low. "People are staring at you. They're going to throw you out of the hospital. Leave Mrs. Roseman alone, okay. That's what Dad told me to say. Leave her alone, or I'm telling."

I wanted to be this girl. I had never in my life possessed one ounce of her confidence.

Joe gave me one more point. "You're ruined." He and his pack retreated.

Plummy looked at me and shrugged. "Forget him," she mouthed. Then she added in a bright voice, "Bye, Mrs. Roseman." She followed them out the door.

Chapter Six

IT WAS a very tentative time in my family. The things that had been said in the hospital were put aside. The next afternoon when Mort was released and went back to Nora's, there was an unspoken agreement that we would all play nice for his sake. Everyone moved slowly and with exaggerated politeness. I waited almost a week before visiting so as not to ruffle any feathers. "Would you like a cup of coffee, Julie?" Lila asked me.

"Oh, no, but thank you." I stood on the front steps of Nora's house balancing a macaroni-and-cheese casserole dish on my up-turned palms. Mort's all-time favorite. I was sure it would be swirling down the garbage disposal before I got my car started.

"Don't you want to come in, say hello to Mort?" It sounded like she was singing the invitation. *"Don't you want to come in-n-n-n-n, say hel-l-l-l-oooo?"*

Actually, I did want to see Mort. I'm not exactly sure why. Maybe it was because since the fight I'd felt like everything had changed, and I wondered if he felt it, too. "Let him get his rest," I said, the thing I knew Lila wanted to hear. "If he wants to call me later, I'll be glad to come back over. How is he doing?"

"Oh, the doctor says he's super. The swelling in his face has gone down a lot. Really, it's just his ribs that hurt. We should be going home soon."

"Mother?" Nora called out. "Is that you? Won't you come in?"

"I'm just dropping off a casserole. I need to get to work. Tell Mort I hope he feels better." Notice I said "Mort" and not "your father," so as to not make Lila feel excluded. I went down the steps, turned and waved. Nora and Lila stood at the door waving back. What a pretty pack of Stepford wives we made.

I hadn't talked to Romeo all week. I sent him a get-well card— who knows if he got it? He sent me a note saying that he would call as soon as the dust settled. But this was a Sahara sort of dust. It never settled, not even for a minute. Every day after that there was another note from him, saying that he loved me, saying that he missed me. I sat on my bed and read them and cried and cried. I was ruining his life, ripping up his family, and getting him punched, and that wasn't the thing to do when you loved someone as much as I loved Romeo. The right thing to do was to walk away. I understood how much I loved him then, when I knew I was going to walk away.

I didn't talk about Romeo, though I thought of nothing else. It would have conflicted with the Geneva Accord of Good Manners. At home Sandy was so nice to me you would have thought I had a terminal illness. She worked harder at the store, harder around the house. In the evenings she took Tony and Sarah over to see Mort, and all her reports were glowing. "He looks fantastic," she said. "You'd hardly know that anything had happened to him."

I imagined the same was true of Romeo. I imagined that everyone was getting back to normal, except for me.

Gloria was helping out all over the place—at home, at work. She had bought a couple of new outfits that she thought would look good in a florist shop, drawstring pants made out of natural hemp and loose linen jackets covered in a cabbage rose print. She looked more like a florist than I ever did. She had gone in with her spare set of keys the night of the fight and cleaned everything up. She swept all the evidence into plastic garbage bags and took them out to the Dumpster.

"You can't keep working for me like this," I said. "It's too much."

"I like it," she said. "I haven't had a job since Buzz and I got married." Buzz owned an insurance company.

"But nothing's wrong with me."

She put down a bucket of baby's breath. "Julie, you've got to call him. You've got to straighten this out."

"Nothing to straighten," I said. "Nothing at all."

"He loves you."

"I'm destroying his life. I won't do it anymore."

And so I continued to make my way through the fog. I spent so much time thinking about things I shouldn't have been thinking about that I completely failed to notice what was going on around me. It was Gloria who called the obvious to my attention a few days later.

"Julie?"

"Hum?"

"There aren't any flowers."

"Hum?"

"There aren't any flowers coming in."

"What?"

She put her hands on my shoulders and turned me around so that I had to look at her square in the face. "There are *no* flowers."

I sniffed the air. With a couple of good sniffs I could take a pretty accurate inventory. Gloria was right. We were down to a handful of carnations, some leatherleaf fern, one bucket of home-grown gladiolas.

"I kept thinking you'd notice. I kept thinking they'd show up."

I thought about Mort. *Get on the phone, yell at somebody.* I ran past Gloria and took my place at the desk. I called the first number, but there was no one to yell at. The receptionist put me on hold and left me there for fifteen minutes. When I called again, she sent me back to hold. When I called back a third time, she hung up on me. My second distributor at least did me the courtesy of telling me my account had been canceled before he hung up on me. I called people I used for special occasions and was told they no longer delivered to my neighborhood. I called people I had never used before and was told they were no longer taking on new accounts. Everywhere I went, I hit a wall.

"How bad is it?" Gloria said.

"Very bad."

"Very bad like an enormous screwup or very bad like a Caccia-mani?"

"The latter."

"You have to call him," Gloria said. "I'll call him. He wouldn't let this happen to you. He doesn't know about it."

"I'm sure you're right," I said. "But Romeo didn't do it, and he's not going to be able to undo it, either. Joe runs a trucking company. He's got roots in the business that spread all the way to Idaho." I tossed my pencil down onto the table. "I'm wrecked," I said. "Simple as that."

"No," Gloria said. She had tears in her eyes. She was taking this hard, as I would once I was able to grasp what had happened. "You have to fight."

"I can't keep on fighting. I've lost. This just polishes off what I started."

Gloria sat down on the floor and put her head between her knees. "I think I'm going to be sick."

"That makes two of us."

I put a sign in the window: ON VACATION.

I was going to tell Sandy what had happened when I got home, but she was on her way out the door to Nora's with the kids as I was coming in. "Dad and Lila are going home in the morning," she said. "I'm going to go over and say good-bye. Do you want to come? I know he'd like to see you."

Tomorrow was Sunday. I didn't have to tell her about the shop right now. "I don't think so, honey. It seems like it would be better if I sat this one out. You say good-bye to him for me, okay?" I kissed the kids. "Sandy, ask Nora to come by on her way home from the airport tomorrow. I'd like to talk to her."

"Another family conference?" Sandy asked suspiciously.

"Not exactly. I just think I'm a little out of touch."

After they left, I made myself a bag of microwave popcorn for dinner, washing it down with a bottle of wine. When that was over, I went to bed.

It was after ten o'clock when the phone rang, and for a brief instant I was hopeful. But it was Mort.

"Jules? Can you hear me?"

"Sure," I said. "Why are you whispering?"

"Sandy and the kids left a little while ago, and everybody is going to bed. I'm down in the kitchen. I told Lila I wanted a glass of milk."

"You hate milk."

"She doesn't know that. Listen, Julie. I was sorry I didn't get to see you to say good-bye. We never seem to do a good job at ending things."

"Yeah, well, I wanted to say I was sorry about your head. I think it was largely your fault, but I know that if it wasn't for me, it wouldn't have happened."

"I threw the pot at the guy."

I was stunned. What he said sounded almost like an admission of something, and that wasn't Mort's style.

"I've had a lot of time to think, even with my sore brain."

"So what do you think?"

"It's been nice, being back. I've liked seeing the girls, and Tony and Sarah. I just thought if things were more okay between us, then it would be easier for me to come back and see them. We don't have to be in some huge fight all the time, do we?"

I told him we did not.

"That's great, Jules. You're a real trouper. And the Cacciamani stuff—"

"Don't even go there."

"Really, I have to say it. I think the guy's a jerk, but I understand that it's your business. We're all entitled to throw away our own lives, right?"

Sandy must have been working on him in his reduced state. "Don't worry about it, Mort. Romeo and I are through. Nobody bounces back from a fight like that."

"I bounced back," Mort said.

"Well, you're tougher than the rest of us."

"About the store," he said, and I felt my heart freeze inside my chest. "I got a lot of work done before the fight, but you need to see an accountant. I'll pay for it. I know you don't want me to, but that store matters to me a lot. I don't want to see it go under just because you don't know what you're doing."

My eyes filled up with tears. Mort would hear the truth later from one of the girls. Let him have a good night's sleep. Let him get on that plane tomorrow for Seattle. "Okay," I said. I had forgotten to pull the shades down on the windows, and now I could see the moon setting off the tender spring leaves on the trees. It was a beautiful thing.

"I don't mean to say you haven't done a good job. You've kept the place afloat. And the flowers look great. It's just the books."

"I understand."

"I should go," he said. "They're going to find me down here. They've kept real tabs on me. You'd think I was an old man."

Then the tears were running down my cheeks. "Good night, Mort," I said.

"Good night, Jules."

WHEN I opened my eyes and looked at the clock, it was ten thirty in the morning and the room was flooded in light. I had not slept until ten thirty since I was in junior high school. I leaned over and checked my watch on the nightstand, thinking the clock must be wrong, but it wasn't. I got up, brushed my teeth, and got dressed. It was Sunday morning, and the kids were downstairs watching cartoons.

"We kept the volume down," Tony said. "You're sleeping."

I waved to them and wandered into the kitchen. Nora was there at the table with Sandy, and they were drinking coffee and talking.

"God, did I oversleep. I'm sorry." I got myself a cup of coffee and joined them. "You should have come up and gotten me."

Nora shook her head. She looked positively happy. Maybe she was just glad to have gotten rid of her houseguests. "I just walked in from the airport. Besides, you needed to get some rest."

"Did Lila and your dad get off okay?"

"Not a hitch. Dad even made a fuss about carrying his own suitcase," she said.

"Good," I said. "That's good."

"So now life gets back to normal," Nora said. She reached over and gave me an uncharacteristic squeeze on the wrist.

I looked at both my girls—smart, good-looking girls, girls whom I loved even as they drove me insane. I wanted to remember them in the last peaceful moment I was going to see for a while. "Not exactly."

Both of them set their coffee cups down. They clicked against the table at the exact same instant. "I knew it," Sandy said.

"It's Roseman's. There were a lot of problems to begin with."

"What happened?" Sandy said. The two words were like heavy stones thrown off the side of a building.

"All our flowers have been cut off. I've called every supplier I could think of. No one will deliver to us anymore."

"How is that possible?" Nora asked.

"Cacciamani," Sandy said. "They've ruined us. That's it, isn't it?"

"I don't know that," I said.

"You know what's happened." Sandy went and closed the door so Tony and Sarah wouldn't hear us. "You can figure this out."

"I can figure it out."

I wouldn't have expected this. Sandy was ready to toss the kitchen table through the window, but Nora was just sitting there staring into her coffee cup.

"We'll get around it," Sandy said. "I don't care if I have to drive to New Hampshire every morning and bring the flowers back myself. They are not going to close us down."

"I don't know," I said.

"I know!" Sandy said, and hit the table with her fist. "Damn it, Mother, snap out of it. You're going to have to fight them."

"We don't have to fight them," Nora said. "We already won."

Sandy stopped and looked at her sister.

"How did we win?" I said.

Nora didn't look smug. I'll give her that much. She just laid out the facts like she would on any other deal she had closed. She was a powerful businesswoman, my older daughter. I forgot that sometimes. "I bought the Cacciamanis' building. I did some research. It turns out they never owned the place. They had rented it all these years. They had a great deal. A classic old Somerville deal where the owner seemed to forget they were there and never raised the rent."

"You bought the building?" Sandy said, sitting down.

"I sent them the eviction notice yesterday. They have two weeks to get out. The way I see it, they probably don't have anything saved. There are too many kids for that. They'll never be able to find another place for what they were paying. They'll stumble. They'll fall. They'll never get up."

"Whew," Sandy said. "I hope you never get that mad at me."

"It's business," Nora said.

What surprised me was that I didn't feel angry at Nora. I had to be fair. If I could see the reasoning behind Joe Cacciamani's attempt to destroy me, then I had to be able to see the logic of Nora bringing down Romeo. This was where we had come to. This was who we were.

"Come on," I said. "Get the kids and get in the car."

"Where are we going?" Sandy said.

"The Cacciamanis'."

"I'm not going," Nora said calmly.

"We're all going," I said. "All of us together. This is the last absolute dictate I will issue as your mother, but you are going."

Nora sat there for a minute. I thought there was going to be a
fight. Instead she walked to the sink and rinsed out her cup. "All
right."

"Why do we have to go?" Tony said when I told the kids.

"Because there aren't any adults to stay home with you," Sandy
said.

"Who are these people again?"

"Friends of Grandma's," she said. "Sort of."

SOMERVILLE, like Rome, was a city built on seven hills. I lived in
Spring Hill. Romeo lived in Winter Hill. I had been to his house
once before, years ago during the whole Sandy and Tony affair.
There had been two meetings: one at our house, one at theirs. He
lived on Marshall Street. I remembered it clearly.

"What are you going to say?" Nora asked. She was driving, and
I was giving directions. Sandy and Tony and Sarah were in the back.

"I just want to tell them it's over: all the fighting, the undermin-
ing. The Roseman family is now officially out of the game."

"What about the building?" Nora said. "I've closed on it."

"Then you'll rent to them. I don't know. You'll figure it out. All
I know is that I want us to be a certain kind of people. I want us to
be decent people." I felt a sense of lightness in my chest. In Somerville the irises and peonies were blooming with mad abandon.
Everything felt so easy all of a sudden. We may not get our heart's
desire, but we could all be decent people.

Sandy was quiet in the back seat. She must have been to this
house before. She must have sneaked in a back door in the dark.
On Marshall Street I told Nora to slow down. I was looking at all
the houses. "It's up there on the left," Sandy said. "The one with
the balloons on the mailbox."

"Balloons!" Sarah said. Sarah was mad for balloons.

"Maybe they were expecting us," Nora said.

There was definitely something up at the Cacciamanis'. We had to drive all the way around the block before Nora found a parking space. "Couldn't we do this later?" she said as she opened her door. "When they aren't having a party?"

"We'll never come back. You're right: The timing isn't great. But I really think it's now or never." Even if we were interrupting something, we were doing so in the name of peace. They'd be happy to hear they hadn't lost their store.

"Never is not a bad option," Nora said.

"Do we have a present?" Tony asked.

"Sort of," Nora said, and opened up her door. "It's called real estate."

Sandy and Nora and I made slow time up the block. Tony and Sarah kept racing ahead and then coming back for us.

"Come on, come on," they yelled, most likely figuring that where there were balloons there was usually cake. I figured we had almost no shot at the cake.

The house was a double-decker with four units, meant to manage a large Catholic family. On one door there was a wreath of flowers, pink and white roses all the way around. It was so simple, so utterly charming, I knew it had to be Romeo's. My heart rose and sank a hundred times just going up the walk.

"I don't know about this," Sandy said quietly.

"Are we going in or what?" Tony said. He ran ahead and pushed the doorbell three times and then ran back and stood behind us. The way we froze to the sidewalk, you would have thought he had pulled the pin out of a grenade.

"Mother," Nora said. "If you're trying to teach me a lesson about taking responsibility for my actions, I have now learned it. Turn around with me and start running like hell."

I was about to agree when a tan young man I didn't recognize swung open the door. He was wearing a pink paper hat that had *90!* sticking out of the top. He had a beard and was wearing Birkenstocks, shorts, and a World Health Organization T-shirt. He looked at us for one second and then made what can only be described as a high-pitched sound of almost unbearable happiness. He ran to Sandy and picked her up by the waist. He swung her around and kissed her neck. He said her name over and over again.

"Do we know him?" Tony said.

"He was a friend of your mom's a long time ago," Nora told him.

Tony Cacciamani put my daughter down. "My God," he said. "How did you know I was back? I only got here two hours ago."

"I didn't know," Sandy said. "Are you okay?"

"I'm fine. I'm so good now. You look so beautiful. You're all grown up." He looked at the rest of us. "Hey, Mrs. Roth. Hey, Nora."

"Hi, Tony," I said. I didn't know that Tony knew Nora. It occurred to me that my older daughter must have helped my younger daughter plan her trysts.

"And who are you?" he said to Tony and Sarah. "Nora, are they yours?"

"Mine," Sandy said. There was, of course, some embarrassment in the introduction of her son, Tony, to Tony Cacciamani.

"Hello," Tony said, shaking their hands, his voice more serious now.

"Sandy's been divorced for three years," Nora said. "Let's just skip right ahead to that."

For once I was grateful for Nora's directness. Tony brightened right back up and invited us inside. "You came for my grandmother's birthday party? Man, things really have changed since I've been gone."

"It's Mrs. Cacciamani's birthday?" I said.

Tony nodded his pink hat and put his arm casually around Sandy's shoulder, as if it had never left that spot. "Ninety today."

The living room was packed with Italians in party clothes, laughing and drinking, every one of them wearing a pink paper hat with *90!* sticking out of the top. There were tables full of sandwiches and vegetable trays, a punch bowl the size of a large fishtank, a pink-and-white sheet cake that took up one whole card table. In the corner there was an accordion player grinding through "That's

Amore!" It was one hell of a party. No one seemed to notice we were there. I plowed into the room looking for Romeo, and everyone I passed smiled and tried to scoot over to give me enough room to get through.

"Have you seen Romeo?" I asked a little boy at the punch table.

"I think he's in the kitchen," he said, and pointed. "That way."

I thanked him and pressed on to the kitchen door.

Plummy and her father were struggling with a bag of ice that had frozen together. The *90!*s on their paper hats were touching. He didn't look happy. There were neat lines of stitches in his forehead and near his lip and a plaster cast on his wrist.

It was the moment I was most afraid of—that he would not be glad to see me. I wondered if it was the last time I would ever see him. "Romeo," I said.

But when Romeo looked up and saw me, his mouth fell open and for a second he seemed to be caught just between laughing and sobbing. He smiled at me like his son had smiled at Sandy. He said my name over and over. He came to me and hugged and kissed me. "My God! You're here!"

"I've got to straighten things out, with you, with your family." I wanted to be serious and brave. I wanted to melt into him forever.

"I'm going to take this out to the living room," Plummy said, scooping up the ice bag. She smiled at me on her way out. "Hi, Mrs. Roseman."

"I love that girl," I said to Romeo.

He kissed me gently, because of his lip. The kitchen door swung shut, swung open. Two young men I didn't know walked in. By the expressions on their faces you would have thought they had caught us dissecting the family dog.

"Julie," Romeo said with some hesitation. "These are my sons Alan and Nicky. Nicky came all the way from Germany for the party."

"Julie Roseman?" Nicky said. Alan went back through the door.

In half a minute they were all there. I could hear Nora's voice rise above the others' in the living room. Then we were all back in the living room, and everyone's voice seemed to go up. The accordion player stopped in the middle of his song.

"Rosemans!" I heard the old woman yell. "There are Rosemans in my house!" We were easy to spot. We were the ones without hats.

"I'm sorry. I'm sorry," I said. I turned to Romeo. "Listen. This is so important, or I would never have come. I know about the lease."

Romeo put his eyebrows down. "Let's do this later," he whispered.

"What about the lease?" Raymond said.

"Nora bought your building."

"*Your* Nora bought it?" Romeo said.

At the mention of her name, Nora squared her shoulders and came across the room. "I'm Nora Bernstein," she said. "I bought the building."

"*You* evicted us?" Romeo said.

"She evicted us?" Raymond said.

"I was going to tell you after the party," Romeo told his son. "I didn't know who bought it."

"Get them out of my house!" the old woman screamed. She was wearing a blue pantsuit and had a pink paper hat that was bigger than everyone else's. It said *I'M 90!* on the top. She was pretty far away from me, which gave me some peace of mind.

"Come on," Raymond said, and put a hand on Nora's arm. "Let's go." Nora stared at him until he took it away.

"I bought it because I was trying to protect my mother. You cut off all her flowers. She's ruined because of you." This was less than true, since Nora had bought the building before she knew about the flowers, but she should be allowed to keep her dignity.

"I cut off her flowers?" Romeo said. "What are you talking about?"

"We don't need to get into that," I said to Nora.

"Yes, we do. You said this is honesty time." She turned to the crowd and clapped her hands three times. "Listen, people. There's going to be a game: true confessions. I bought Romeo's flower shop and evicted him. He contacted every flower distributor in the area to cut off my mother's supply and ruin her business."

The crowd collectively inhaled at this piece of information.

"Wait a minute," Romeo said. "I never did that."

Joe lumbered forward from the crowd. His *90!* hat seemed barely bigger than a folded Kleenex on his head. "I did," he said. "She'll never get her hand on another flower as long as I live."

"You ruined her?" Romeo stepped toward his son.

"You blackballed her?"

"You were right, Mom," Nora said. "This is so much better."

I took Romeo's arm. "It went both ways. That's the whole point. We have to stop this right now."

"Come in the kitchen," Romeo said to me; then he raised his voice in the crowd. "Cacciamanis, Rosemans, in the kitchen. No cousins, no kids. Mother, in the kitchen."

"I'm not going in there with them," she said.

Nora went over and whispered something in her ear. The old woman looked furious but followed us in.

"How did you do that?" I whispered to Nora.

"I told her she wasn't allowed in the kitchen."

Tony and Sandy were already in there. I don't know how they managed that. They were sitting at the table holding hands and looked surprised to see us.

"That's the girl!" the old woman said. "Get her off of Tony."

Romeo held his hand up to his mother. "Hang on a minute. So Joe, you went behind my back to ruin Roseman's?"

"She had it coming."

"Out," he said.

"What?"

"Out of my house." Romeo stood, feet apart, his arms crossed.

The point was to figure out how to make peace between Cacciamanis and Rosemans. The last thing I wanted to do was separate Romeo from his firstborn. "No," I said. "You can't do that. We're going to fix this."

"Don't you tell my father 'No'," Joe said, pointing a finger at me.

"We just need to stop it," I said, my voice sounding a little frantic. "We need to make an agreement once and for all. If you and I can't see each other anymore, I can accept that, but I don't want to live like crazy people."

"We can't see each other?" Romeo said. He looked at me as if such a horrible outcome had never occurred to him before. I thought at that moment I would cry for loving him so much.

Plummy, who was wearing a little lavender sundress with a black cardigan sweater, clapped her hands together. She was clearly ready to make order out of chaos. "Okay," she said. "Once and for all we're going to get to the bottom of this, and then we're going back to the party. Now, somebody here knows this story." She bit her lip and looked around the room. "Grammy," she said finally. "What's the story?"

"The Rosemans are pigs," she said.

"Okay, that's a start. Now, why are the Rosemans pigs?"

That was the question. Why were Rosemans pigs? Why were the Cacciamanis slimy fish?

"Come on," Plummy said.

"It's my birthday," the old woman said. She reached up and touched her hat as if to drive her point home. Unlike many members of the party, she had had the good sense to put her elastic strap in the back.

"Happy Birthday," Plummy said. "Everybody wants to eat the cake and watch you open your presents, but that isn't going to happen until you fess up."

"I want to go now." She was trying to pass herself off as feeble, but it didn't wash.

"I'm really sorry," Plummy said. "But you can't go until you tell us what happened. We've all waited long enough." The clear fact was that Plummy Cacciamani ruled. She was a kind and modest dictator, but she was a dictator nonetheless.

"I don't know anything," she said. "Don't you believe these lying Rosemans."

"You don't know anything?" Plummy asked.

The old woman looked away from her. "Nothing about them. Who'd want to know about Rosemans?"

"What about the letters?" Plummy said, as if this was one possibility.

"What letters?"

Plummy looked like the very picture of innocence. She reached up and twisted one of the gold hoops in her ear. "The letters under your mattress, in the pink silk handkerchief. The ones that all start, 'My Darling . . .' "

The eldest Cacciamani turned with flames in her eyes. She raised a finger to poke, but Plummy gently pushed it down. Everyone shifted to make sure they had a very clear view of the action. "Why are you reading my letters?"

"I clean your room, Grammy. I flip your mattress every month. I never thought it mattered before, but now I think it does."

"They're none of your business."

"I know that," Plummy said calmly. "That's why I never mentioned them before. But now we have this problem."

The old woman took a deep breath and leaned against the refrigerator. She looked trapped. "I'll tell you later," she said.

Plummy went and put her arm around her grandmother. She kissed the old woman's cheek. "You tell me later, and I'll just have to get everybody together again so I can tell them what you said. Tell me now," she whispered kindly.

We were all waiting—five sons, three wives, my two girls, Plummy, me and Romeo. Mattresses? Letters? We leaned toward her, mesmerized. Plummy let her grammy twist in the wind.

"Come onto the porch," the old woman said weakly.

Plummy nodded her head and patted the old woman's hand. She led her grandmother past the rest of us and out onto the back porch. We waited.

"How's your head?" I asked Romeo. "Does it hurt anymore?"

"Nah. Just the ribs a little when I breathe. How about Mort?"

I told him that Mort had healed up and gone home this morning. Romeo smiled. "That guy has a hell of an arm."

We waited and waited. In the other room people had started laughing again. The accordion had started up again. They had forgotten about us. They were there for a party. Finally Raymond went and looked out the back window.

"Can you see anything?" Romeo asked.

"Grammy's in the chair, and Plummy's kind of leaning over her. It looks pretty intense. I can't see what they're saying."

"I don't know why we have to shake her down on her birthday," Alan said. His pretty Italian wife stood next to him, nodding.

"Because we're not going to do this again next week," Nora said. "It isn't that much fun."

"Wait!" Raymond pulled back from the window. "She's coming in."

Plummy came back alone.

"Where's Grammy?" Raymond said.

"She's sitting down outside for a minute. She wanted some air."

"So what's the story?" Nora said.

"The story is this." Plummy leaned against the counter. She spoke to Nora. "My grandmother and your grandfather had a love affair."

"My grandfather?" Nora pointed at her chest.

"The hell they did," Joe said.

Plummy held up her hand but didn't look at him. "Please," she said. "This was a very long time ago. The Rosemans had their shop in Somerville, and Grammy and Grampy had a shop in the North End. Grammy met Mr. Roseman buying vases, and they fell in love. I guess it was all pretty hot. Grammy wanted to be closer to Mr. Roseman, so she talked Grampy into moving their shop to Somerville. She told him it was a better place to raise children. Daddy was three years old then, and they called the place Romeo's. The way I understand it, Mr. Roseman strung Grammy along bigtime. He kept promising Grammy that he was going to run away with her, but every time she was ready to go, he would come up with some lame excuse, and they never did it. After a while Grammy got really angry, and I guess she started doing things to the Rosemans. She said it started out small at first—she'd bad-mouth their flowers to other people. She threw a rock through their window once. Then she hid a dead fish in their storeroom, a flounder.

That was when Mr. Roseman got mad at her, and he paid a kid to dump a box of fleas in their store. It was back and forth, one thing and then another. Grammy told Grampy that the Rosemans were trying to ruin them to get their customers, that the Rosemans were trying to force them out of the neighborhood, and that they had to fight back. Who knows what Mr. Roseman told Mrs. Roseman? No one actually got ruined until now."

"And they fell for it?" Nora asked her. "My grandmother and old man Cacciamani? They just picked up the feud and ran with it without any more information than that?"

"Well, all of us did, too. Our families hated each other, and we didn't even have the fleas to deal with."

"You expect me to believe that?" Raymond said.

"Go ask her. She's told it once now. I bet she'll tell it again. Or go and read the letters under the mattress. They're pretty steamy."

"But she hated Mr. Roseman," Nicky said. "She hated him more than any of them."

"That's the way it works sometimes," Plummy said thoughtfully. "Big love makes for big hate."

"I still hate him," old Mrs. Cacciamani said. She was standing at the door, suddenly looking older than ninety. Her pantsuit was wrinkled, her party hat tipped to one side. "And I'll hate every last one of them until I die."

My father? I thought. My father and the Wicked Witch of the West? The woman he hated above all other life-forms? I could still hear his voice clearly in my head. I could hear every terrible name he called her. Of all the possible explanations, I had to admit this one seemed the most implausible to me.

"Mama, are you sure about this?" Romeo asked.

"Of course I'm sure. What do you think, I don't know who I was in love with?" Then, with surprising vigor, she slammed through the kitchen door and back into her party. It swung open, shut, open, shut, behind her.

The rest of us stood there listening to the accordion music coming through the wall.

"Just to recap," Nora said. "What this means is that the birthday girl was in love with my grandfather, my mother is in love with your father, and my sister is in love with Tony here."

Sandy looked mortified.

"That's what it's looking like," Plummy said.

Nora continued. "So the basis of this tedious, never-ending fight is that three generations of Cacciamanis and Rosemans have been in love with each other."

The room took a moment to digest this piece of information. Then Nora started to laugh, and pretty soon Sandy was laughing, too. Then Plummy joined in. At that point none of the rest of us got the joke.

"Mr. Cacciamani," Nora said. "Keep your store. Think of me as your benevolent landlord. You," she said, pointing to Joe. "Turn the delivery service back on for my mother's flowers tomorrow. Now I want to get out of here. I'm taking my car." She looked at me and Sandy. "Something tells me you two will find rides home."

Epilogue

THE story ends with a wedding, right? These stories practically have to. This wedding was on the first of July. Some people said it was awfully quick, but once they heard the whole story, they had to agree it was, in fact, a long time coming. The roses were fantastic. We're talking garden roses. When we were done, it looked like we had gotten our hands on every rose in Massachusetts. Romeo and I did the whole thing together. That was how we got the idea of combining our stores in the first place. We worked together like a dream. I made the bride's bouquet. I had long been liberated from the idea of white. Every color I could find went into that bouquet. It was even better than the one I had made when I married Mort. The wedding was in my backyard. We had a justice of the peace so that no one would get their toes stepped on religionwise, but Father Al was there, and I saw him moving his lips. Nora was the maid of honor. She insisted on the title. She said she couldn't bear to be anybody's matron of honor. Joe was the best man. Little Tony and Sarah did the rings and the flowers. It was a small wedding, except that no Cacciamani wedding could ever really be considered small.

Tony and Sandy went to the Cape for their honeymoon. They're saving money to buy a house. For the time being, they are living with me.

Everyone was asking at the wedding when Romeo and I were going to get married. But for us it isn't such an issue. We'd never get all of his family and all of my family into one house, anyway. We're together, trust me on that. The rest of it will fall into place over time. We keep a little apartment that none of the kids know about. It isn't a whole lot bigger than the bed we dragged into it. We've got two cups there, a corkscrew, a couple of old comforters for when it's really cold, some towels. It doesn't take much to make a place feel like home. To anyone who ever thought that love and passion were for the young, I say, think again. I am speaking from personal experience here.

Romeo says we live together at work. Most couples work apart but live in one house. We're just doing it the other way around. Things have gotten busy, now that we're doing the wedding and party-planning service. It turns out we actually need all the various family members we've got on the payroll. We're always at the same store—one day his, one day mine. The next thing we knew, they were both ours. It's Romeo and Julie's now. Two locations to better serve you.

JEANNE RAY

The publication of Jeanne Ray's first novel is a story in itself. After years of wanting to write a book but being too busy with children and career, the sixty-one-year-old nurse finally wrote *Julie and Romeo*. Her daughter, novelist Ann Patchett, sent the book to her agent, who sent it around New York. The editors at Harmony Books instantly fell in love with *Julie and Romeo*. The sentiment proved contagious, and movie rights were quickly snapped up by Barbra Streisand. "I feel like I was wandering down the path of life," Ray says, "and suddenly now I'm on the ramp to the freeway."

Ray and her husband, Darrell, live in Nashville, Tennessee. They have two daughters and ten grandchildren.

To learn more about Jeanne Ray and
Julie and Romeo, visit the Select Editions website:

📖 ReadersOnly.com
Password: *stay*

DEMOLITION ANGEL

ROBERT CRAIS

His explosive of choice is Modex—
fast, sexy, elite, and very very deadly.
And it's so hard to come by that he
reserves it for a privileged few—the best
bomb-squad cops in the country.

PROLOGUE

Silver Lake, California—CHARLIE Riggio stared at the cardboard box sitting beside the Dumpster. It was a Green Giant box, with what appeared to be a crumpled brown paper bag sticking up through the top. The box was stamped GREEN BEANS. Neither Riggio nor the two uniformed officers with him approached closer than the corner of the strip mall there on Sunset Boulevard.

"How long has the box been there?"

One of the Adam car officers, a Filipino named Ruiz, checked his watch. "We got our dispatch about two hours ago. We been here since."

"Find anyone who saw how it got there?"

"Oh, no, dude. Nobody."

The other officer, a black guy named Mason, nodded. "Ruiz is the one saw it. He went over and looked in the bag, the crazy Flip."

"So tell me what you saw."

Ruiz described seeing the capped ends of two galvanized pipes taped together with silver duct tape.

Riggio considered that. They were standing in a strip mall parking lot on Sunset Boulevard in Silver Lake, an area that had seen increasing gang activity in recent months. Gangbangers would steal galvanized pipes from construction sites, then stuff them with bottle-rocket powder or match heads. Riggio didn't know if the Green Giant box held a bomb or not, but he had to approach it as if it did. That's the way it was with bomb calls.

Charlie Riggio walked back to his vehicle. The bomb squad drove dark blue Suburbans crammed with all the tools of the bomb technician's trade except for the robots. You wanted the robots, you had to call them out special, and he wasn't going to do that. The damned robot would just get bogged down in all the potholes around the box.

Riggio found his supervisor, Buck Daggett, instructing a uniformed sergeant to evacuate the area for a hundred yards in all directions. The fire department had already been called, and paramedics were on the way. Sunset Boulevard had been closed.

"Hey, Buck, I'm ready to take a look at that thing."

All Riggio would be doing on the first pass was lugging out a portable X-ray to see inside the bag. If the contents appeared to be a bomb, he and Daggett would either de-arm the device or explode it in place.

"I want you in the suit, Charles."

The armored suit weighed almost ninety pounds. Made of Kevlar plates and heavy Nomex batting, it covered every part of Riggio's body except his hands. A bomb tech needed the dexterity of unencumbered fingers.

When the suit was in place, Riggio took the Real Time X-ray unit and lumbered toward the package. A safety cable and hardwire dragged behind him, the hardwire connecting him to Daggett via a telex communicator. A separate wire linked the Real Time to a computer in the Suburban's cargo bay.

The box was unremarkable. The crumpled brown paper bag was open. Riggio peered into the bag without touching it. He saw the two pipes Ruiz had described. The pipe caps appeared to be about two and a half inches in diameter and taped together, but nothing else about them was visible.

Riggio placed the Real Time X-ray unit on the ground at the base of the box, aimed for a side view, then turned it on. It provided the same type of translucent shadow image that security personnel see on airline baggage units, reproducing the image on two screens: one for Riggio on top of the Real Time, and another on the computer back at the Suburban.

Riggio smiled. "We got one, Buck. We got us a bomb."

"I'm seeing it."

The two pipes were impenetrable shadows with what appeared to be a spool of wire or fuse triangled between them. There didn't appear to be a timer or an initiator, leading Riggio to believe that the bomb was a low-tech garage project made by a local gang-banger, and not particularly difficult to de-arm.

"This one's going to be a piece of cake, Buck."

"Don't get cocky. Just take the snaps."

Riggio shuffled around the box, aiming the Real Time over the different angles. He felt no fear, because he knew what he was dealing with now and trusted he could beat it. Riggio had approached over forty-eight suspicious packages in his six years with the bomb squad; only nine had been actual explosive devices. None of those had ever detonated in a manner that he did not control.

He circled the box, getting front and side angles, then pointed the Real Time straight down for a top view. That's when he saw a shadow that hadn't been visible in the side views.

A thin, hairlike shadow emerged from the side of one pipe and extended up through the spool. This wire wasn't attached to the others, which confused Riggio until a sudden thought occurred to him: Maybe the spool was there only to hide this other wire.

In that moment fear crackled through him. He called out to Buck Daggett, but the words did not form.

The bomb detonated at a rate of twenty-eight thousand feet per second, twenty-two times faster than a 9-mm bullet leaves the muzzle of a pistol. Heat flashed outward in a burst of white light hot enough to melt iron. The air pressure spiked from a normal fifteen pounds per square inch to twenty-two hundred pounds, shattering the iron pipes into jagged shrapnel that punched through Riggio's Kevlar suit like hyperfast bullets. The shock wave slammed into his body with an overpressure of three hundred thousand pounds, crushing his chest, rupturing his liver, spleen, and lungs, and separating his unprotected hands. Charlie Riggio was lifted fourteen feet into the air and thrown a distance of thirty-eight feet.

Even this close to the point of detonation Riggio might have survived if this had been, as he first suspected, a garage bomb cooked up by a gangbanger with makeshift materials.

It wasn't.

Bits of tarmac and steel fell around him like bloody rain long after Charlie Riggio was dead.

CHAPTER
1

"TELL me about the thumb. I know what you told me on the phone, but tell me everything now."

Starkey inhaled half an inch of cigarette, then flicked ash on the floor, not bothering with the ashtray. She did that every time she was annoyed with being here, which was always.

"I missed."

"You didn't miss."

Detective-2 Carol Starkey took another deep pull on the cigarette, then crushed it out. When she first started seeing this therapist, Dana Williams wouldn't let her smoke during a session. That was three years and two therapists ago. In the time Starkey was working her way through the second and third therapists, Dana had gone back to the smokes herself and now didn't mind.

Starkey shrugged.

"No, I guess I didn't miss. I'm just fed up, is all. It's been three years, and here I am back where I started."

"So tell me about the little girl's thumb."

Starkey fired up another cigarette, then settled back to recall the little girl's thumb. "It was Fourth of July. This idiot down in Venice decides to make his own fireworks and give them away to the neighbors. A little girl ends up losing the thumb and index finger on her right hand, so we get the call from the emergency room."

"Who is 'we'?"

"Me and my CCS partner that day, Beth Marzik."

"Okay."

"By the time we get down there, the family's gone home, so we go to the house. The father's crying, saying how they found the finger but not the thumb, and then he shows us these homemade firecrackers that are so big she's lucky she didn't lose the hand."

"He made them?"

"No. A guy in the neighborhood made them, but the father won't tell us. He says the man didn't mean any harm. I say, your daughter had been *maimed,* sir, other children are at *risk,* sir, but the guy won't cop. I ask the mother, but the guy says something in Spanish, and now she won't talk either."

"Why won't they tell you?"

"People suck."

The world according to Carol Starkey, Detective-2 with LAPD's Criminal Conspiracy Section. Dana made a note of that in a leatherbound notebook, an act that Starkey never liked. She thought of notes as evidence.

Starkey had more of the cigarette, then went on with it.

"These bombs are six inches long, right? We call 'em Mexican dynamite. So many of these things are going off it sounds like the academy pistol range, so Marzik and I start a door-to-door. But the neighbors are just like the father—no one's telling us anything, and I'm getting madder and madder. Marzik and I are walking back to the car when I look down and there's the thumb. I just looked down and there it was, this beautiful little thumb, so I scooped it up and brought it back to the family."

"On the phone you told me you tried to make the father eat it."

"I grabbed his collar and pushed it into his mouth. I did that."

Dana shifted in her chair. "It's easy to understand why the family filed a complaint."

Starkey finished the cigarette and crushed it out.

"The family didn't complain."

"Then why—"

"Marzik. She had a talk with my lieutenant, and Kelso threatened to send me to the bank for an evaluation."

LAPD maintained its Behavioral Sciences Unit in the Far East Bank building on Broadway, in Chinatown. Most officers lived in abject fear of being ordered to the bank, correctly believing that it ended any hope of career advancement.

"If I go to the bank, they'll never let me back on the bomb squad."

"And you keep asking to go back?"

"It's all I've wanted since I got out of the hospital."

Irritated now, Starkey stood and lit another cigarette. "The job is all I have left, dammit." She regretted the defensive edge in her voice and felt even more embarrassed when Dana again scribbled a note.

"So you told Lieutenant Kelso you would seek help on your own?"

"No, I kissed his ass to get out of it. I know I have a problem, Dana, but I'll get help in a way that doesn't ruin my career."

"Because of the thumb?"

Starkey stared at Dana Williams with the same flat eyes she would use on Internal Affairs. "Because I'm falling apart."

Dana sighed. "Carol, if you came back because you want me to fix you as if you were broken, I can't do that. Therapy isn't the same as setting a bone. It takes time. Consider what happened to you. Consider what you survived."

"I've considered it for three years."

"Are you still drinking?"

"I haven't had a drink in over a year."

"How's your sleep?"

"A couple of hours, then I'm wide-awake."

"Is it the dream?"

Starkey was wondering how to answer when the pager clipped to her waist vibrated. It was the number of Barry Kelso's cell phone, followed by 911, the code the detectives in the Criminal Conspiracy Section used when they wanted an immediate response.

"I've gotta get this, Dana. It's my lieutenant. I'll step outside."

Starkey took her purse out into the waiting room. She dug out her cell phone, then punched the speed dial to return Kelso's page. "It's me, Lieutenant. What's up?"

"The bomb squad had a call-out. I'm on my way there now. Carol, we lost Charlie Riggio. He was killed at the scene."

Starkey's fingers went cold. "Was it a bomb?"

"I don't know the details, but there was an explosion."

Her stomach clenched. Uncontrolled explosions were rare. A bomb squad officer dying on the job was even more rare. The last time it had happened was three years ago.

"Ah, Starkey, I could put someone else on this if you'd rather."

"I'm up in the rotation, Lieutenant. It's my case."

"All right. I wanted to offer."

Kelso gave her the location, then broke the connection.

Starkey saw herself in the waiting-room mirror, abruptly white beneath her tan. She put her phone away, then went back to tell Dana that she would have to end their session early.

"We've got a call-out, so I have to go."

"You didn't finish the story." Dana said. "Did you catch the man who made the firecrackers?"

"The little girl's mother took us to a garage two blocks away, where we found him with eight hundred pounds of smokeless gunpowder. Eight hundred pounds, and the whole place is reeking of gasoline because he's a gardener. If that place had gone up, it would've taken out the whole damned block."

"My Lord."

Starkey started for the door. She stopped with her hand on the knob because she remembered something she had intended to ask.

"This guy we arrested, he tells us he's been building fireworks his whole life. You know how we know it's true? He's only got three fingers on his left hand and two on his right. He's blown them off one by one."

Dana paled.

"I've arrested a dozen guys like that. We call them chronics. Why do they do that, Dana? What do you say about people like that who keep going back to the bombs?"

Now Dana took out a cigarette of her own and struck it. She blew out a fog of smoke and stared at Starkey before answering.

"I think they want to destroy themselves."

Starkey nodded. "I'll call to reschedule, Dana. Thanks."

Starkey went out to her car and slid behind the wheel. She opened her briefcase, took out a slim silver flask of gin, and took a long drink. When she put away the gin, she ate a Tagamet antacid. Then, doing her best to get a grip on herself, Carol Starkey drove across town to a place exactly like the one where she had died.

HELICOPTERS orbited over the crime scene in layers, like a cake. Starkey saw them just as the traffic locked down, half a mile from the incident site. She left her car in an Amoco station and walked the remaining eight blocks.

A dozen radio units were on the scene, along with two bomb squad Suburbans and a growing army of media people. Barry Kelso was standing near the forward Suburban with the bomb squad commander, Dick Leyton, and three bomb techs. Kelso was a short man with a droopy mustache, in a black-checked sport coat.

Riggio's body lay in a heap in the parking lot, midway between the forward Suburban and the Dumpster. An LAPD criminalist named John Chen was working the body.

Smoking at a crime scene was against LAPD policy, but Starkey fired up before crossing the parking lot to confront Charlie Riggio's body. She had known him from her days on the bomb squad, so she expected this to be hard. It was.

Riggio's helmet and chest protector had been stripped off by the paramedics who had worked to revive him. Shrapnel had cut through the suit, leaving bloody puckers across his chest and stomach. A single hole had been punched in his face, just beneath the left eye, and his hands were missing.

Starkey turned toward Chen so that she wouldn't have to see the body. "Hey, John. What do we have here?"

"Hey, Starkey. You got the lead on this one?"

"Yeah. Is Buck Daggett here?"

"They sent him to the hospital. He's okay, but he's pretty shook. Leyton wanted him checked."

"Okay. What did he say? You got anything I can use?"

Chen pointed out the Dumpster. "The device was over there. Buck says Riggio was over it with the Real Time when it went off."

Riggio lay almost thirty yards from the Dumpster.

"Did Daggett or the medics pull him over here?"

Anytime there was an explosion, bomb techs were trained to expect a secondary device. She figured that Daggett would have pulled Riggio away from the Dumpster for that reason.

"You'd have to ask Daggett. I think this is where he fell."

"We gotta be thirty yards from the detonation point."

"Buck said it was a helluva blast."

Chen took a plastic bag from his evidence kit, showing her a piece of blackened metal about the size of a postage stamp. "This is interesting. It's a piece of the pipe frag I found stuck in his suit."

Starkey looked close. A squiggly line had been etched into the metal. "What is that, an S?"

Chen shrugged. "Or some kind of symbol."

"John, do me a favor and swab some of the samples tonight, okay?"

Chen went sulky. "It's going to be really late when I finish here, Carol. I've got to work the Dumpster, and then I've got to log in whatever you guys find in the sweep. It's going to take me two or three hours."

They would search for pieces of the device everywhere within a hundred-yard radius, combing nearby rooftops, the faces of the apartment buildings and houses across the street, cars, the Dumpster, and the wall behind the Dumpster. They would search for anything that might help them reconstruct the bomb or give them a clue to its origins.

Residue from the explosive would be present on any fragments of the bomb they found, as well as in the blast crater and on Riggio's suit. Chen would identify the substance by cooking it through a gas chromatograph, a process that took six hours.

"Couldn't you swab a couple of samples first, just to start a chrom, then log everything after? An explosive with this kind of energy potential could really narrow down the field of guys I'm looking at, John. You could give me a head start here."

Chen said, "I'll try, but I can't guarantee anything."

"I gave up on guarantees a long time ago."

Buck Daggett's Suburban sat forty-eight paces from Riggio's body. Starkey counted as she walked.

Kelso and Leyton saw her coming and moved to meet her. Kelso's face was grim, Leyton's tense and professional.

Dick Leyton, the twelve-year commander of the bomb squad, had selected Carol Starkey for the squad, just as he'd selected Charlie Riggio and every other tech. He had sent her to the FBI's bomb school in Alabama and had been her boss for three years. When she had been in the hospital, he had come every day to visit her, fifty-four consecutive days, and when she had fought to stay on the job, he had lobbied in her behalf. There wasn't anyone on the job she respected as much or cared for as much.

Starkey said, "Dick, I want to walk the scene as soon as possible. How many of your people can we use?"

"Everyone not on duty is coming out. You've got us all."

Kelso was frowning. "You shouldn't be smoking here, Starkey."

"Sorry." She made no move to put the cigarette out.

Kelso ignored the obvious rebellion. "You'll be working with Marzik and Santos on this."

Starkey felt another Tagamet craving. "Does it have to be Marzik?"

"Yes, Starkey, it has to be Marzik. They're inbound now. And something else. Lieutenant Leyton says we might have a break here. Nine one one got a call on this."

She glanced at Leyton. "Do we have a wit?"

"An Adam car took the call, but Daggett told me they were responding to Emergency Services. If that's the case, then we should have a tape and an address."

That was a major break. "I'll get on it. Thanks."

Kelso glanced at an approaching LAPD media officer. "I think we'd better go make a statement, Dick."

"Be right there."

Kelso scurried over to intercept the media officer.

Leyton stayed with Starkey. When the other man was gone, Leyton considered her. "How you doing, Carol?"

"I'm fine, Lieutenant. Kicking ass and taking names, like always. I'd still like to come back to the squad."

Leyton nodded, although both of them knew that the LAPD personnel unit would never allow it. "You were always a tough girl. But you were lucky, too."

"Right, boss." She smiled at him, and Leyton smiled back. She sighed deep and long, then turned and looked back at Riggio's body, which the coroner's people were placing into a body bag.

The mall was a small strip of discount clothing shops, a used-book store, a dentist, and a Cuban restaurant, all of which had been evacuated before Riggio approached the bomb. Starkey forced herself toward the restaurant, moving on legs that were suddenly weak, as if she'd found herself on a tightrope and the only way off was that singular door. She felt nothing but her own hammering heart and knew that if she lost control of it now, and of herself, she would certainly fall to her death.

When Starkey stepped into the restaurant, she began to shake with a rage beyond all hope of control. She had to grip the counter to keep her feet. If Leyton or Kelso walked in now, her career would be finished. She ground out her cigarette, clawed open her purse for the silver flask, and felt the gin cut into her throat in the same moment she cursed her own weakness. She took a second long pull on the flask, and the shaking subsided.

Starkey fought down the memories and the fear, telling herself that everything would be all right. She would beat it. She would win. She was a tough girl. She put away the flask, sprayed her mouth with Binaca, then went back out to the crime scene.

Starkey found the two Adam car officers, who gave her the log time of their original dispatch call. She used her cell phone to call the day manager at Emergency Services and requested a tape of the 911 call as well as an address of origin. What most people didn't know was that all calls to 911 were automatically taped and recorded with the originating phone number and that phone number's address. It had to be this way because people in an emergency situation couldn't be expected to provide their location.

When Starkey was finished with Emergency Services, she walked over to the apartment buildings across the street, where Marzik and Santos were questioning the few residents who had been let back into the area.

Jorge Santos was a short man with a quizzical expression. His name was pronounced "whore-hey," which had earned him the dubious nickname of Hooker. Beth Marzik, the only other woman in CCS, was divorced with two kids who stayed with her mother when she was on the job.

Starkey said, "Good news. Leyton says the call-out was responding to a nine-one-one."

Marzik smirked. "This good citizen happen to leave a name?"

"I already put in a call to Emergency Services. They'll run the tapes and have something for us as soon as they can. Now I've gotta get the uniforms set up for the sweep and see about the door-to-door."

Marzik frowned. "Well, we're not going to get to most of these folks tonight. A lot of the people who were evacuated went to relatives or friends after the damned thing blew."

"You're getting a list of residents, right?"

"Yeah. But that'll take forever. I *used* to have a date tonight."

Santos's face grew longer than ever. "I'll do it, Carol."

Starkey gestured back toward the apartment buildings behind them. "Look, Beth, I'm not saying do everybody on the damned block. Just ask if they saw something. Ask if they're the one who called nine one one. If they say they didn't see anything, tell 'em to think about it and we'll get back to them in the next few days."

Marzik wasn't happy, but Starkey didn't give a damn.

She went back across the street to the Dumpster, leaving Marzik and Santos with the apartments. John Chen was examining the wall behind the Dumpster for bomb fragments. Out in the parking lot four of the bomb squad technicians were adjusting radial metal detectors that they would use when they walked the lawns out front of the surrounding apartment buildings. Pretty soon everyone would be standing around waiting for her to tell them what to do.

Starkey ignored all of them and went to the crater. It was about three feet across and one foot deep, the black tarmac scorched white by the heat. Starkey wanted to place her hand on the surface but didn't, because the explosive residue might be toxic.

She went back across the street to find Marzik. "Beth? I got another idea. Try to locate the people who own all these shops and see if anyone was threatened or owed money."

Marzik nodded, squinting at her. "Carol, what is that?"

"What is what?"

Marzik stepped closer and sniffed. "Is that Binaca?"

Starkey glared at Marzik, then went back across the street and spent the rest of the evening helping the search team look for pieces of the bomb.

IN THE *dream, she dies.*

She opens her eyes on the hard-packed trailer-park earth as the paramedics work over her. Above her the thin branches of winter gum trees overlap in a delicate lace still swaying from the pressure wave. A paramedic pushes on her chest, trying to restart her heart. Another inserts a long needle. Cold silver paddles press to her flesh, and her body lurches from the jolt of current.

Starkey finds the strength to say his name. "Sugar?"

Her head lolls, and she sees him. David "Sugar" Boudreaux, a Cajun long out of Louisiana but still with the soft French accent that she finds so sexy. Her sergeant-supervisor. Her secret lover.

"Sugar?" She reaches toward him, but he is too far away. Two hearts that beat as one should not be so far apart. The distance saddens her.

Two hearts that no longer beat. The paramedics working on Sugar step away. He is gone.

Her body jolts again, but it does no good and she is at peace with it. She closes her eyes and feels herself rise through the branches into the sky, and all she knows is relief.

STARKEY woke from the dream just after three that morning, knowing that sleep was beyond her. She had finished at the crime scene just before midnight but didn't get home until almost one. There she showered, ate scrambled eggs, then drank a tumbler of Bombay Sapphire gin to knock herself out. Yet here she was, wide-awake two hours later.

The bomb that took Sugar had been a package bomb delivered by a meth dealer to murder the family of an informant. It had been placed behind azalea bushes on the side of the informant's double-wide, which meant Sugar and Starkey couldn't use the robot to wheel in the de-armer. The bomb was made of a paint can packed with smokeless powder and roofing tacks. Whoever had made it wanted to make sure he got the informant's three children.

Because of the bushes, Starkey and Sugar both had to work the bomb, Starkey holding aside the brush so that Sugar could get close with the Real Time. When two patrol officers had called in the suspicious package, they had reported that it was ticking. It was such a cliché that Starkey and Sugar had burst out laughing, though they weren't laughing now, because the package had stopped ticking. The Real Time showed them that the timer had malfunctioned; the builder had used a hand-wound alarm clock as his timing device, but the minute hand had frozen at one minute before reaching the lead that would detonate the bomb.

Sugar made a joke of it. "Guess he forgot to wind the damned thing."

She was grinning at his joke when the earthquake struck, an event every bomb tech working in southern California feared. It was only 3.2 on the Richter scale, hardly noticeable to the average Angeleno, but the minute hand released and the bomb went off.

The old techs had always told Starkey that the suit would not save her from the frag, and they were right. Sugar saved her. He leaned in front of her just as the bomb went off, so his body caught most of the tacks. But the Real Time was blown out of his hands, and that's what got her. Two heavy, jagged pieces sliced through the suit, ripped along her right side, and dug a gaping furrow through her right breast. Sugar was knocked back into her, microseconds behind the Real Time. The impact stopped her heart.

For two minutes and forty seconds Carol Starkey was dead.

Two teams of emergency medical personnel rushed forward even as pieces of the trailer fell around them. The team that reached Starkey found her without a pulse, peeled away her suit, and injected epinephrine directly into her heart at the same time they administered CPR. They worked for almost three minutes and finally—heroically—restarted her heart.

Her heart had started again; Sugar Boudreaux's had not.

Starkey sat at her dinette table, smoking and thinking about the dream and Sugar. She had started drinking almost as soon as she got out of the hospital. Her shrink had said that her issue was survivor's guilt. Guilt that she had lived and Sugar had not.

Everything had changed after the accident. Starkey pulled away from people. She protected herself with sarcasm and the single-minded pursuit of her job until the job was all that she had.

Starkey finished her cigarette, then returned to her bedroom to shower. She pulled off her T-shirt and looked at herself with an absence of feeling. The right half of her abdomen from her breast to her hip was rilled and cratered from the sixteen bits of metal that had punched into her. Two long furrows roped along her side following her lower ribs.

The worst of it was her breast. A two-inch piece of the Real Time had impacted on her right breast just beneath the nipple, gouging out a furrow of tissue before exiting her back. Even after reconstruction her breast looked like a misshapen avocado.

She had not been with another man since Sugar had left her bed that morning they went to work.

Starkey showered, dressed for the day, then called her office and found two messages.

"It's me, Starkey. John Chen. I got a pretty good swab from the blast crater. I'll set it up in the cooker, but that means I won't be out of here until after three. We should have the chrom around nine. Gimme a call."

The Emergency Services manager had left the second message, saying that she'd duped the tape of the 911 call reporting the suspicious device. "I left the tape at the security desk, so you can pick it up anytime you want. The call was placed from a pay phone on Sunset Boulevard at one fourteen yesterday afternoon. I've got a street address here."

Starkey copied the information into a spiral casebook, then made a cup of instant coffee. She swallowed two Tagamet before letting herself out into the sultry early morning air.

It was not quite five. She decided to drive back to Silver Lake and walk the blast site again.

STARKEY parked in front of the Cuban restaurant next to a male/female team watching over the scene in a radio car. The mall's parking lot was otherwise deserted except for three civilian vehicles that she remembered from the night before.

Starkey got out and held up her badge. "Hey, guys, everything okay?"

The female officer nodded. "Yeah. We're good, Detective."

"I've got the case. I'm gonna be walking around."

Starkey crossed Sunset to look for the address that the Emergency Services manager had provided. She brought her Maglite but didn't turn it on. The area was bright from surrounding security lights.

A pay phone was hanging on the side of a Guatemalan market directly across from the mall, but when Starkey compared it to the address, they didn't match. From the Guatemalan market she could look across Sunset at the Dumpster. She figured out which way the numbers ran and followed them to find the pay phone. It was housed one block east in a glass booth on the side of a laundry, across the street from a flower shop.

Starkey copied the names of the laundry and flower shop into her notebook, then walked back to the first phone and checked to see if it worked. It did. She wondered why the person who called 911 hadn't done so from here. The Dumpster was in clear view, but wasn't from the other phone.

Starkey was walking back across Sunset when she saw a piece of bent metal in the street. It was about an inch long and twisted like a piece of bow-tie pasta. She had picked up nine similar pieces of metal the night before.

She brought it to her car, bagged it in one of the spare evidence bags she kept in the trunk, then decided to look over the civilian cars again.

Two of the cars had been pinged by bomb frag and had suffered substantial damage. The third was a '68 Impala with bad paint and a peeling vinyl top. Starkey looked beneath it, found nothing, then noticed a star-burst crack on the windshield. She flashed the Maglite inside and saw a round piece of metal on the dash—a disk with a single fine wire protruding. She fished it out, examined it with no idea what it might be, then dropped it into her pocket.

Starkey climbed back into her car without looking at the team in the radio car, then headed downtown to pick up the audiotape before reporting to her office.

JOHN Michael Fowles, a.k.a. Mr. Red, leaned back on the bench across from the school, enjoying the sun and wondering if he had made the FBI's ten most wanted list. Not an easy thing to do when they didn't know who you were, but he'd been leaving clues. He thought he might stop in a Kinko's and use one of their computers to check the FBI's Web page for the standings.

The sun made John smile. He raised his face to it, letting the warmth soak into him. After a while he got up and walked away to check the most wanted list. Last week he wasn't on it. This week he hoped to be.

CHAPTER
2

THE Criminal Conspiracy Section, where Starkey worked, is housed on the fifth floor of an office building on Spring Street, a few blocks from the LAPD's seat of power, Parker Center.

Starkey noticed Marzik watching her as soon as she walked in, and decided to see if Marzik wanted to make something of the Binaca. Starkey went over, stopping in Marzik's face. "Is there anything you need to say?"

Marzik met her gaze without looking away. "Like what?"

Starkey let it go. If Marzik confronted her about the drinking, she didn't know what she could do except lie. "Okay. I've got the nine-one-one tape. Is Hooker in?"

"Yeah. I saw him."

"Let's listen to the tape; then I want to get over to Glendale. Chen's gonna have the chrom, and I want to see how they're coming with the reconstruction."

"They just started. How far could they be?"

"Far enough to know some of the components, Beth. We get some manufacturers, we get the chrom, we can get going here."

"We got all these interviews to do."

Marzik made her tired. "You guys can start in with the interviews while I'm over there. Round up Jorge and come to my desk."

Starkey borrowed a cassette player from the section sergeant and brought it to her desk. Each CCS detective had a desk in a partitioned cubicle in the larger main room, meaning that there was no real privacy. Everyone spoke in whispers.

Marzik and Santos showed up a few minutes later with coffee, Santos saying, "Did you see Kelso? He asked to see you."

Starkey glanced at Marzik. "Well, Jorge, nice of someone to tell me. Look, let's listen to this before I see him."

Santos and Marzik pulled up chairs as Starkey turned on the

tape. It started with the Emergency Services operator and was followed by a male voice with a heavy Spanish accent.

> EMS: Nine one one. May I help you?
> CALLER: Eh . . . *se habla español?*
> EMS: I can transfer you to a Spanish speaker.
> CALLER: No, is okay. Lissen, you better sen' a man to look here.

Santos stopped the tape. "What's that behind him?"

Starkey said, "It sounds like a truck. He's calling from a pay phone just off Sunset, a block east of the mall."

Santos looked at her. "How do you know that?"

"EMS called back with the address. I walked the scene again this morning." Starkey restarted the tape.

> EMS: Look at what, sir?
> CALLER: Eh, I look in dis box. I tink dere's a bomb in dere.
> EMS: A bomb?
> CALLER: Dese pipes. I dunno. It made me scared. Is by the trash dere. The beeg can.
> EMS: Could I have your name, sir?
> CALLER: You better come see.

The man hung up. Starkey turned off the machine.

Marzik frowned. "Why wouldn't he leave his name?"

Santos shrugged. "Could be he's illegal."

Starkey scrounged for paper to write on and drew a rough street map showing the mall and the location of the phones.

"He looked in the bag. That means he's here at the mall. He says it scared him, seeing the pipes, so why not use the phone here outside the Guatemalan place? Why walk a block east?"

Santos frowned. "If I found something I thought was a bomb, I'd want to get as far away from it as possible."

Starkey nodded. That made sense. "We've got the time of the call. Maybe someone around there saw something and we can straighten this out."

Santos nodded. "Okay. You want to do that while we get the apartment houses?"

"One of you guys swing past, okay, Hook? I've gotta see Chen over in Glendale."

Starkey gave them the addresses, then went in to see Kelso. She walked in without knocking. "You wanted to see me?"

Kelso jerked away from his computer. He had stopped telling her not to barge in over a year ago. "Would you close the door, please, Carol; then come sit down."

Starkey closed the door, then marched back across his office and stood at his desk. She was right about Marzik. She didn't sit.

Kelso wasn't sure how to come at what he wanted to say. "I just want to make sure you're okay with this."

"With what, Barry?"

"You seemed a little, ah, strained last night. I just want to be sure you're okay with being the lead here."

"Are you replacing me?"

"No, Carol. But this case strikes close to home with you, and we've had these, ah, episodes recently."

Starkey felt the shakes coming on but fought them down. She was furious with Marzik and terrified that Kelso might replace her. "Did Marzik say that I was drinking?"

"Let's leave Marzik out of this."

"You saw me at the crime scene, Barry. Did I act drunk or unprofessional to you?"

"That's not what I'm asking. You've been wound a little tight, Carol. We both know that because we've talked about it. Last night you were confronted with a situation very similar to one that you yourself barely survived. Perhaps you were unnerved. Anyway, I left our conversation last night thinking that I smelled gin. Did I?"

Starkey met his eyes. "No, sir. You smelled Binaca. I ate Cuban for lunch, and I was blowing garlic all day. That's what you and Marzik smelled."

He showed his palms. "Let's leave Marzik out of this. Marzik didn't say anything to me."

Starkey knew he was lying. If Kelso had smelled gin on her breath, he would've said something at the scene.

Finally Kelso settled back, relieved that he'd said what he needed to say and had been the responsible commander. "This is your case, Carol. I just want you to know I'm here for you."

Starkey went back into the squad room looking for Marzik, but she and Santos had left. Starkey gathered her things, so angry at Marzik that her hands were shaking.

STARKEY drove like a bat out of hell over to Glendale PD, pulling into the parking lot at eight thirty. Chen had said he'd have the chromatograph by nine, but Starkey figured that he'd built a paper-work cushion into that estimate.

She sat in her car, using her cell phone to call Chen. "John, it's Starkey. I'm out here in the lot. I'm on my way in to see Leyton. You have the results?"

Chen said, "Give me two minutes, and I'll be down. You're gonna love this."

The LAPD bomb squad is based in a low-slung modern build-ing adjacent to the Glendale police substation and piggybacked with the Scientific Investigation Division. Starkey let herself into the bomb squad reception area and asked for Lieutenant Leyton. He'd stayed out with the others at the crime scene, walking the sweep like everyone else. Dark rings had set in around his eyes, making him look older than she'd ever seen him.

Starkey handed over the evidence bag. "I walked the scene again this morning and found this. You got someone on the reconstruc-tion yet?"

Leyton held up the Baggie to look. The bit of metal would have to be tested to see if it was actually part of the device. "Russ Daigle. He's sorting what we recovered last night."

Starkey said, "Chen's on his way down with the chrom. I was hoping to snatch whatever component manufacturers you have so I can get rolling with this."

"Sure. Let's see what Daigle has."

She followed Leyton down a long hall to the squad room. It didn't look like any other squad room in the department; it looked like a high school science lab, with black Formica workbenches.

Every surface in the squad room was covered with de-armed bombs or bomb facsimiles, from pipe bombs and dynamite bombs to canister bombs and large military ordnance.

Russ Daigle was perched on a stool at one of the workbenches, sorting pieces of metal. One of the squad's three sergeant-supervisors, he was a short, athletic man with a gray mustache. He was wearing latex gloves.

He glanced up when he heard them, nodding toward a computer at the end of his workbench. "We got the snapshots up. Wanna see?"

Starkey moved behind him to see the monitor. "You bet."

The digital snapshots that Riggio had taken were displayed on the screen. They showed the two pipes as impenetrable black shadows neatly taped together with a spool of wire fixed to the cleft between them. All four pipe ends were capped. Starkey studied the images, comparing them to the bits of jagged black metal that were spread on white butcher paper. One of the end caps was still intact, but the others were broken. Daigle had already separated the major parts of all four caps and had made good progress with the tubes, but it was clear that half of the pieces were still missing.

"What do we have here, Sarge? Looks like galvanized iron pipe, two-inch diameter."

Daigle picked up a piece of end cap that showed a letter V cast into the iron. "Yeah. See the V? Vanguard pipe company. Buy it anywhere in the country."

Starkey made note of it in her casebook. She would compile a list of components and characteristics and feed them through the National Law Enforcement Telecommunications System—NLETS—to the FBI's Bomb Data Center and the ATF's National Repository in Washington. The BDC and NR would search for signature matches with every bomb report in their systems.

Daigle ran his finger up under the edge of the cap, flaking off something brittle and white. "See that? Plumber's joint tape. We got us a neat boy, here. Very precise. Even taped the joints. What does that tell you?"

Starkey knew that Daigle had already drawn a conclusion and was testing her. "You're plumbing your sink, you maybe want to tape the joints, but you sure as hell don't need to tape a bomb."

Daigle grinned. "Right. No reason to tape it, so maybe he does it out of habit. Could be he's a plumber or a building contractor. And he was particular. You see the tape shadow here, how carefully he wrapped the tape? We got us a particular boy here."

Already Starkey was getting a picture of the builder. He might be a skilled tradesman or a machinist or a hobbyist who took pride in precision, like a model builder.

Daigle said, "Did Chen show you the five?"

"What five?"

Daigle placed a piece of the tube frag under a magnifying glass. It was the S that Chen had pulled from Riggio's armor.

Starkey said, "It looks like an S."

Leyton said, "We're not sure what it is, an S or a five."

Chen came in at that point. Like the others, he looked as if he hadn't slept much, but he was excited when he handed Starkey the chrom results. "The explosive was something called Modex Hybrid. He didn't buy it at the local hardware store."

They looked at him.

"The military uses it in artillery warheads and air-to-air missiles. We're talking about a burn rate of twenty-eight thousand feet per second."

Daigle grunted. The burn rate was a measure of how fast the explosive consumed itself and released energy. The more powerful the explosive, the faster the burn rate.

Leyton said, "If we're talking about a military explosive, that should narrow the field, Carol. We see who's missing some, then find out who had access."

Chen cleared his throat. "It won't be that simple. The chrom showed a lot of impurities, so I phoned the manufacturer. Modex comes in three forms: military grade, which is made under government contract; commercial grade, which is made for foreign export only—EPA won't let anyone use it here—and homegrown."

Daigle scowled. "What's that mean, homegrown?"

"The company rep thought a kitchen chemist might've cooked up this batch. It's not that hard to do if you've got the components and the right pressure equipment."

Starkey said, "Okay. If you can make the stuff by hand, I need the component list and the recipe."

"The rep's going to put it together and fax it. I asked him for manufacturers, too. As soon as I get 'em, they're yours."

A unique explosive was a plus for the investigation, but Starkey didn't like what it implied. "If this stuff is a military explosive or needs some kind of high-end lab work, it changes my picture of the builder. This is a serious bomb."

Daigle crossed his arms, not liking it either. "Starkey's right. But why build a device like this and just leave it by a Dumpster? There's gotta be more to it."

"We talked to every one of the shop owners, Sarge. Nobody says they were threatened."

Daigle frowned. "One of them is lying. You don't build a bomb this powerful just to play with yourself. Somebody screwed somebody, and this thing is payback."

Starkey studied the snaps. "I don't see a detonator. No batteries. No power source. How did it go off?"

Daigle tapped the picture on the screen. "I got a theory. One pipe holds the explosive, the other the detonator. Look here."

He picked up two of the larger pieces of pipe, holding them for her and Leyton to see. "See the white residue here?"

"Yeah. From when the explosive burned off."

"Right. Now look at this other piece. Clean. Makes me think he had the detonator in this pipe, along with a battery."

"You think it was hooked to a timer?"

Daigle looked dubious. "And the timer just happened to let go when Riggio was standing over it? I don't buy that. I'm thinking Riggio set off some kind of balance switch."

"Buck said Charlie never touched the package."

"Well, that's what Buck saw, but Charlie must've done something. Bombs don't just go off for no reason."

Starkey remembered the twisted disk she'd found, took it from the Baggie, and showed it to the others. "I found this at the crime scene this morning. It could be part of the initiator."

Daigle put it under a magnifying glass. "Looks like we got a circuit board in here."

Chen crowded in and peered at it. He pulled on a pair of Daigle's gloves, then selected a narrow screwdriver and pried open the disk like a clamshell. "I know what this is."

A single word was printed inside the disk, a word they all knew, and so out of place it seemed absurd: MATTEL.

Chen looked stricken. "It's a radio receiver like they put in those remote-control cars for kids. Charlie Riggio didn't set off this device. It was radio-controlled."

Starkey knew what Chen was saying. She said, "The lunatic who built this bomb was right there. He waited until Charlie was over the bomb, and then he set it off."

Chen took a deep breath. "Yes. He wanted to see someone die."

KELSO tasted his coffee, making a face as if he'd sipped Drano. "You really think the bastard triggered the device from the scene?"

Starkey showed him a fax she had received from the radio control's manufacturer. It listed the receiver's performance specs and operating requirements.

"These little radio receivers operate on such low voltage that they're only tested out to sixty yards. The guy I spoke with gives us a ballpark maximum distance between transmitter and receiver of about a hundred yards. That's a line-of-sight distance, Barry. That puts our guy in open view."

"Okay. So what's your idea?"

"Every TV station in town had a helicopter overhead, broadcasting the scene. They had cameras on the ground, too. Maybe one of those tapes caught this mutt at the scene."

Kelso nodded, pleased. "Good thinking, Starkey. One other thing. Talk to Sergeant Daggett. Get him to thinking about the people he might've seen in that parking lot."

When Kelso closed his door, Starkey went back to her cubicle with her stomach in knots. Daggett would be shaken because of what happened, second-guessing every decision he'd made, every action. Starkey knew he would be feeling these things, because she had felt them, too, and didn't want to revisit them.

She sat in her cubicle for twenty minutes, thinking about the flask in her purse and staring at Buck Daggett's address in her Rolodex. Finally she stalked down to her car.

Daggett lived in a cramped Mediterranean-style home in the San Gabriel Valley, just east of Monterey Park. Five minutes after she left the freeway, Starkey pulled into Daggett's drive and knocked on the door. His wife answered. She was twenty years younger than Buck and attractive, though today she seemed distracted.

Starkey showed her badge. "Carol Starkey, Mrs. Daggett. I used to work with Buck. I'm sorry, but I don't remember your name."

"Natalie."

"Natalie. Sure. Could I see Buck, please?"

Natalie Daggett led Starkey through the house to their backyard, where Buck was changing the oil in his Lawn Boy. As soon as Starkey stepped out into the yard, Natalie vanished back into the house.

"Hey, Buck." Just looking at him caused an ache in Starkey's chest.

Daggett scrambled to his feet. "I'm trying to keep busy. I'd hug you, but I'm all sweaty."

"Busy is good, Buck. That's okay."

"You want a soda or something?"

"I don't have much time. We're running short."

He nodded, disappointed, then opened a couple of lawn chairs that had been leaning against the house. "I heard you caught the case. You doing okay over there on CCS?"

"I'd rather be back on the bomb squad."

Daggett nodded without looking at her.

"Buck, anyone call you about the bomb? You hear about it?"

"No. Hear what about the bomb, Carol?"

"It was detonated by remote control."

He stared at her without expression for a time, then shook his head, desperation edging into his voice. "That can't be. We didn't see a radio device. We didn't see any kind of detonator. If we'd seen anything like that, I would've yanked Charlie out of there."

"You couldn't have seen it, Buck. The power pack and initiator were inside one of the pipes. The explosive was in the other. Something called Modex Hybrid."

He blinked hard to hold back the tears, but they came anyway. Starkey felt her own eyes fill; the two of them were a fine pair.

Buck cleared his throat. "Modex. That's military, right?"

"They use it in warheads. But we're thinking maybe this batch was homemade."

"You're sure about the remote?"

"We found the receiver. The person who set it off waited until Charlie was over the bomb. We think he was watching."

Buck shook his head as if all of this was too much to bear.

"Listen, Buck, I'm getting together the videos that the TV stations took. I'd like you to come in and take a look. Maybe you'll see someone in the crowd."

"I don't know, Carol. My head was on the bomb. I was worried about getting good snaps."

"It'll be another day or two before we get all the tapes. Think about it, okay? Try to recall anyone or anything that stood out."

"Sure. I got nothing else to do. Dick made me take three days."

"It's good for you, Buck."

Daggett grudged a wan smile. "You know what they're making me do? I gotta go to the bank."

Starkey didn't know what do say.

"They call it trauma counseling. I gotta tell some headshrinker what it feels like seeing my partner get blown to bits. What's there to say about something like this? What did you say?"

"Nothing, Buck. There's nothing to say. Just tell 'em that. There's nothing to say. Listen, I've got to go. Sorry."

"I understand." Daggett walked Starkey to the front door, where she said good-bye. Natalie Daggett was nowhere around.

Starkey was paged twice as she walked out to her car, first by Marzik and then by Hooker. She called Marzik first, using her cell phone as she sat in Daggett's drive.

Marzik's voice was excited. "I got something, Starkey. I'm down by that flower shop across from the phone? Nine one one gets the call from the phone at one fourteen, right? Well, the owner's kid is out front, getting ready to deliver some flowers, and he sees a guy on the phone. And listen to this. He said it was an Anglo guy."

"The caller was Latino."

"This kid is solid, Starkey. He's sitting in his truck listening to the Gipsy Kings while they load the flowers. He's there from one to one twenty. I know he was there during the call because they logged his departure time. He says it was a white guy."

Starkey's pulse quickened. She tried not to let herself get excited, but it was hard.

Marzik said, "Why would a white guy pretend to be Latino unless it was the guy who set the bomb? We could have an eye-wit to the bastard who set the bomb."

"I think this is a good thing, Beth, but let's not get ahead of ourselves. Your wit only thinks the guy he saw was Anglo. Maybe the guy was Anglo, but maybe he only looked Anglo to the kid. We'll just have to see."

"I know you're right, but the kid comes across solid."

"Is he there now, Beth?"

"Yes, but he's got more deliveries to make, and it's getting late."

"Okay. Keep him there. I'm coming down." Starkey broke the connection, then punched in Santos's number.

Santos spoke in a whisper. "Carol, an ATF agent is here. He flew in from Washington this morning. He's in with Kelso, and now Kelso wants to see you. I think they're going to take over our case."

"Wait a minute. Did the guy say he wanted the case?"

"I've got to go, Carol. Kelso just stuck his head out. He's looking at me."

"I'm coming in, Jorge. Marzik turned up something good."

STARKEY made it back to Spring Street in twenty-five minutes. Santos caught her eye from the coffee machine and nodded toward Kelso's door. It was closed.

Starkey set her jaw and stalked to the door, knocked hard three times, then opened it without waiting.

Kelso gestured wearily toward her as he spoke to the man seated across from his desk. "This is Detective Starkey. She comes in whenever she wants. Starkey, this is Special Agent Jack Pell from—"

"The ATF. I know. Is he taking over this case?"

Pell had pale skin and intense gray eyes. Starkey guessed him to be in his mid-thirties, but if he was older, it wouldn't have surprised her. She tried to read the eyes, but couldn't; they seemed guarded.

Pell turned to Kelso without acknowledging her. "I need a few more minutes with you, Lieutenant. Have her wait outside until we're ready."

Her. Like she wasn't standing there. "This is our case, Lieutenant. One of *our* people died."

"Wait outside, Detective. We'll call you."

Starkey waited outside his door, fuming. She was cursing Kelso when her pager buzzed on her hip. "Damn. Marzik."

Starkey phoned Marzik from her cubicle.

"Carol, I'm standing here with this kid, and he's got deliveries to make. Where in hell are you?"

Starkey kept her voice low. "Back at the office. The ATF is coming in."

"You're kidding. What's happening?"

"All I know is that an agent is in there with Kelso now. Look, I'll talk with the kid when I'm done here."

"It's almost five, Carol. He's got deliveries."

"Okay, Beth, we'll get him tomorrow morning."

"Us or the ATF?"

"I'm about to find out."

Kelso stuck his head out, looking for her. Starkey put down the phone, wishing she had used the time to eat more Tagamet.

When she reached Kelso, he whispered, "Just relax, Carol. He's here to help us."

Kelso closed the door behind them, and Starkey gave Pell her best scowl. Those gray eyes were the coldest eyes she'd ever seen.

Kelso returned to his desk. "Agent Pell flew in from D.C. this morning. The information you fed into the NLETS system raised some eyebrows back there."

Pell nodded. "I don't have an interest in taking over your investigation, Detective, but I think I can help you. We flagged some similarities between your bomb and some others we've seen."

"Like what?"

"The Modex is his explosive of choice: fast, sexy, and elite. He also likes to use this particular type of radio detonator, hiding it in one of the pipes so you can't see it with the X ray."

"Who are we talking about?"

"He uses the name Mr. Red. We don't know his true name."

"Mr. *Red?* Is this guy some kind of terrorist?"

"No, Detective, this mutt isn't a terrorist. Over the past two years we've had seven bombings that show Modex Hybrid and a radio-triggering device similar to the one used here. We believe that four of the bombings were done for criminal profit. He blows up something or someone probably because he's being paid to do it. This is how he makes his money, Starkey. He's a hit man with a bomb. But he also has a hobby."

"I'm dying to know."

"He hunts bomb technicians, Starkey. He baits them; then he murders them. He's killed three so far, if we count your man, all with identical devices. I think he sees it as a competition. He makes bombs; bomb techs like you de-arm them, so he tries to beat you."

Starkey felt a chill.

Pell clearly read it. "I know what happened to you. I looked you up before I flew out."

Starkey felt invaded, and the invasion angered her. "Who and what I am is none of your business except for this: I am the lead investigator on this case."

Pell shrugged. "You signed the NLETS request. I like to know who I'm dealing with."

Thinking about it now, Starkey had a recollection of reading an ATF flyer on an unknown subject who might have been identified as Mr. Red. It was the type of flyer that passed through their office on a routine basis but bore little relevance, as the subject was operating in other parts of the country.

"I would have remembered this, Pell—some nut murdering bomb technicians. No one here has heard of this puke."

Kelso shifted. "They've kept that part of Mr. Red's activities on a need-to-know basis."

"We don't want copycats, Starkey. We've kept all the details of his MO and bomb designs classified except the components that we list through NLETS."

"So you're saying that your guy is our guy on the strength of a components list?"

"I'm not saying anything yet, but the Modex and the radio receiver are persuasive. And you've found this letter."

Starkey was confused. "What letter?"

Kelso said, "The number five we found etched into the frag. Agent Pell thinks it might be the letter S."

"Why do you think it's a letter?"

Pell hesitated. "We've found etchings in Mr. Red's work before. I'll need to read your reports and compare your reconstruction with what we know. Then I'll make a determination whether or not your bomber is Mr. Red."

Starkey could see her case slipping away. "Pardon me if I make up my own mind. But if you get to see mine, then I want to see yours. I want to compare what you have with what we find."

Kelso showed his palms. "Now, Starkey, we don't need to be adversaries here."

Pell gathered together a stack of papers. "That's not a problem,

Detective. Lieutenant Kelso was kind enough to share your case reports; I'll be happy to give you copies of mine. They're at my hotel now, but I'll get them to you."

Pell rolled the reports that Kelso had given him into a tube, then stood. "Could you set me up with a place to read these reports, Lieutenant? I'd like to cover as much ground this evening as I can before Detective Starkey and I get down to business."

Starkey faced Kelso. "What does that mean?"

Kelso came around his desk to open the door. "Relax, Carol. We're all on the same side here."

As Pell walked past Starkey with the reports, he said, "I won't bite, Detective. You don't have to be afraid of me."

"I'm not afraid of anything."

"I wish I could say the same."

Kelso called Santos to take care of Pell, then came back into his office and closed the door. "You couldn't have been any less helpful, Carol."

"I'm not here to be helpful. I'm here to find whoever killed Riggio, and now I've got to worry about the ATF second-guessing what I do and stealing my case."

"Try to remember that it's a team effort, Detective. If our bomber and his bomber are one and the same, we might be damned lucky to have his help. I've already spoken to Assistant Chief Morgan about this. He wants us to extend' our full cooperation."

"Marzik found a wit who might've seen our guy make the nine-one-one call. He says that the caller was Anglo."

That stopped Kelso. "I thought the caller was Hispanic."

"So did I." Starkey didn't add anything more. She figured that even Kelso was smart enough to see the implication.

"Well, I guess you'd better see to it."

"I was going to go see about it, Lieutenant, but I had to come meet Mr. Pell instead. Now it has to keep until tomorrow. The witness had plans."

Kelso looked disappointed. "See about it tomorrow, then, and keep me informed. You're going to close this case, Starkey. I have every faith in that. Now go home and get a good night's sleep."

Starkey let herself out, hoping that she wouldn't see Pell. It was after six when she pulled out into the downtown traffic, but she didn't go home. She turned her car west toward a bar called Barrigan's in the Wilshire Division.

SPECIAL Agent Jack Pell sat in a small white room not much bigger than a coffin to study the reports. After reading them, he felt that LAPD's Scientific Investigation Division and bomb squad had done an excellent job of forensics and analysis, though he was disappointed that only a single letter—the S—had been recovered. Pell wasn't so certain about the medical examiner's office. An important step had not been noted in the autopsy protocol.

He brought the reports into the hall and found Santos. "Do you know if the medical examiner took a full X ray of Riggio's body?"

"If it's not in the protocol, they probably didn't do it."

Pell paged open the autopsy protocol and found the attending medical examiner's name. Lee Richards. Twenty minutes later, after telephoning Richards, Santos drove Pell over to the medical examiner's building.

Inside, Santos identified them to the security guard, then went to grab a cup of coffee. Richards appeared a few minutes later, Pell following him into a cold tile X-ray room, where they waited while two technicians wheeled in Riggio's body. The body was zipped into an opaque plastic bag. Pell and Richards stood silently as the technicians took the body from the bag and positioned it on the X-ray table. The great Y incision that Richards had made down the chest and abdomen during the autopsy was stitched closed, as were the wounds where the frags had done their worst damage.

Richards eyed the body. "The entry wounds were fairly obvious. We took area X rays wherever the entries appeared to be of a significant nature, and that's where we removed the fragments."

Pell said, "That's the problem. If you only look where you see an entry wound, you'll miss something. Where are his hands? Were they recovered?"

"Oh, yes. I examined them. I know I examined them." Richards peered at the bony stubs of the wrists, then squinted at the technicians. "Where are the hands?"

The technicians fished around in the body bag and came out with the hands.

Richards looked relieved. He said, "We'll look over the body with the scope first. We see anything, we'll mark it. That'll be faster than screwing around with the X ray, okay?"

Pell was given a pair of yellow goggles to wear; then he watched them wheel Riggio's body behind a chromatic fluoroscope. The fluoroscope looked like an opaque flat-screen television, but when Richards turned it on, it was suddenly transparent. As the body disappeared behind the screen, its flesh was no longer flesh but transparent lime Jell-O, the bones impenetrable green shadows.

At Richards's direction the techs pushed the body slowly past the screen, revealing three shadows below the knee—two in the left leg, one in the right—all smaller than a BB.

By the time they finished scanning the body, they had found eighteen metal fragments. As Richards removed them, the taller technician rinsed them and placed them in a glass tray.

Pell inspected each bit of metal, but he found no etches or markings. Finally the technician handed him the last of the fragments. It was the largest piece, and Pell wanted there to be something on it so badly that his heart was hammering, but there was nothing.

Richards peeled off his gloves to glance at his watch. It was a Mickey Mouse watch. "We'll send these fragments over to SID in the morning."

Pell said, "That'll be fine, thanks."

It wasn't fine, and Pell didn't like it. A cold rage of frustration threatened to spill out of him. He was already thinking that he was too late, that Mr. Red might have come and gone and be on to another city, when the taller technician mentioned the hands.

"Doc, you gonna scope the hands?"

Richards grunted like they might as well, then placed the hands under the scope. Two bright green shadows were wedged among the metacarpal bones in the left hand. "Damn. Looks like we missed a couple."

Richards removed the fragments. Pell inspected both pieces, turning them over without hope until he felt an adrenaline jolt surge through his body.

The larger piece had six tiny letters etched into its surface, and they stunned him. They weren't what he expected.

Behind him Richards said, "Find anything?"

"No, Doc." Pell palmed the shard with the letters and returned the remaining piece to the tray with the other fragments. The lab technician did not notice that he returned one piece and not two.

Pell thanked Richards for his time and walked back into the outer hall, where the security guard stared at him.

"You looking for Santos?"

"Yeah."

"He took his coffee out to the car."

Pell was halfway down the hall when crimson star bursts appeared in the air before him. He remembered a men's room off the hall and shoved his way through the door. The dizziness hit him as he reached the sink. Closing his eyes didn't stop him from seeing the shapes. They floated in the air on a field of black, rising and twisting in slow motion. He turned on the cold water, clawed a towel from the rack, wet it, and staggered into a stall.

He slumped onto the toilet and pressed the towel hard to his eyes, waiting. He had done this before, and was scared because the time between bouts was shrinking. He knew what that meant, and it scared him more than anything in his life had ever scared him.

He sat breathing through the wet towel. When the floating monsters that haunted him vanished, he took out the piece of metal he had stolen and read the letters there.

Pell hadn't told Kelso and Starkey everything about Mr. Red. He hadn't told them that Mr. Red didn't just kill random bomb techs; he killed only the very best. When Pell had learned of the S, he thought it was from Charles. It wasn't.

Pell read the fragment again: "t-a-r-k-e-y."

JOHN MICHAEL FOWLES SAT in the periodicals section of the Dade County Regional Main Library. He considered the people at the surrounding tables. Mostly old people, reading newspapers and magazines. A group of preschool kids here on some kind of kindergarten field trip. A soft-looking man behind the research desk, reading a Dean Koontz novel. All of them just going along with their lives, oblivious.

John swung around to face the library's Internet research computer and tapped in the address for the FBI's website: www.fbi.gov. When the home page came up, he clicked on the Ten Most Wanted Fugitives icon and watched the page load.

Ten small pictures appeared, each with a link to its own page. John hoped to find his picture there. It wasn't. A perfect example, John felt, of government inefficiency.

Disappointed, he went back to the home page and clicked on the Unknown Suspects icon. Nine pictures appeared, three of which were artists' sketches. One of the sketches showed a studious young man with a balding pate, a rim of brown hair, brown eyes, and dorky glasses. John had starved himself for two weeks before letting himself be seen that time, and the witnesses had certainly noticed: The sketch showed him to be gaunt and undernourished. It looked nothing like his true self, just as today he looked nothing like his true self.

He clicked on the sketch, which brought him to a page showing a brief though inaccurate description of him, along with a catalogue of the crimes he was suspected of committing. He was pleased to note that the feds considered him extremely dangerous and that he used "sophisticated explosive devices for criminal gain."

John felt that the FBI's refusal to include him in the ten most wanted list was both cheesy and disrespectful. He believed himself to be the most dangerous man walking free in open daylight and expected to be treated as such.

He guessed he would just have to up the stakes.

Beneath the table was a small device he had built for this library, specifically to be used as a message. It was simple, elegant, and like every device he built, bore his signature. The local authorities would know within hours that Mr. Red had come to call.

"Excuse me. Are you finished using that?"

An older woman with a body like a squash stood behind him. She was holding a spiral notebook.

"You want to use the computer?"

"Yes. If you're finished with it."

John flashed a big grin, then scooped up his backpack and held the chair for her. Just before he stood, he reached beneath the table and turned on the timer.

"Yes, ma'am, I am. You sit right here. This chair's so comfy it'll make your butt smile."

The older woman laughed.

John left her there and walked out into the sun.

C H A P T E R
3

STARKEY woke the next morning on the couch, her body clenched into a fist, her neck stiff. It was four twenty a.m. She had gotten two hours' sleep.

Starkey felt disquieted by the dreams. A different quality had been added. Pell. He chased her. She had run as hard as she could, but her movements were sluggish, while his were not. Starkey didn't like that. Her dreams had been a constant since her injury, but she was resentful of this addition. It was bad enough that he was invading her investigation; she didn't need him in her nightmares.

Starkey lit a cigarette, then got herself together for the day. Breakfast was two aspirin and a Tagamet.

Marzik had left word on her voice mail that they could meet the wit, a kid named Lester Ybarra, at the flower shop at nine. By five thirty Starkey was at her office putting on the coffee.

She brought a cup back to her desk, then searched through her reference books. Modex Hybrid was a trinary explosive used as a bursting charge in air-to-air missiles. Trinary meant that it was a mixture of three primary explosives. Starkey took out her case notebook and copied the components: RDX, TNT, ammonium picrate, powdered aluminum, wax, and calcium chloride. RDX, TNT, and ammonium picrate were high explosives. The powdered aluminum was used to enhance the power of the explosion. The wax and calcium chloride were used as stabilizers.

Starkey searched her books for information on the primary components. TNT and ammonium picrate were available to the civilian population. RDX was different. Like the Modex, it was manufactured for the military, but unlike the Modex, it was too complicated to produce without industrial refining equipment. This was the kind of break Starkey was hoping to find in her manuals. Someone could make Modex if they had the components, but they couldn't make the components. They would have to acquire the RDX, which meant that the RDX could be traced back to its source.

Starkey decided that this was a good angle to work. She brought her notes to the NLETS computer, then punched up a request form asking for matches with RDX. By the time she finished entering the request, a few of the other detectives had begun to drift in. She gathered her things and left.

STARKEY parked behind Marzik outside the flower shop. They met on the sidewalk just as a short, thin Latino teenager stepped out of the shop.

Marzik introduced Starkey to Lester Ybarra.

Starkey offered her hand. "Hi, Lester. I really appreciate your helping us out like this."

"'S no pro'lem."

Marzik said, "Lester saw someone using the phone across the street between one and one fifteen the day the bomb went off. Lester, can you describe that person to Detective Starkey?"

Starkey said, "Before we get to that, Lester, how about helping me set the scene, so I can picture it? Your van was where? About here where my car is?"

"Yeah."

Starkey was parked outside the florist's front door in a red NO PARKING zone about fifteen feet from the corner.

"You always load the van out here in the street?"

"We got three vans. The other two was using the alley, so I had to be out here. I was supposed to leave by twelve thirty, but we got this big order. A funeral set. Twelve sprays. My dad said I hadda wait, so I brought the van around front here. When I saw the guy, I was behind the wheel. My sisters hadda make the sprays. So I was just sitting there in case the cops come and I hadda move."

Starkey nodded. She had noticed that Lester would have an easy, unobstructed view of the pay phone hanging on the laundry across the street. "Okay, Lester, I know you described the guy for Detective Marzik, but would you describe him for me?"

Lester described an Anglo man of medium height and build, wearing a faded blue baseball cap, sunglasses, dark blue trousers, and a lighter blue work shirt. Starkey took notes. Lester had not heard the man's voice. He thought the guy had to be in his forties.

When Lester finished, Starkey said, "Did you see which way this guy came from when he went to the phone?"

Lester shrugged. "I didn't notice."

"How about when he left? You see where he went?"

"I wasn't paying attention, you know?"

"Okay, Lester. You sure this guy was Anglo?"

"I'm pretty sure. His hair was light brown, kinda sandy."

Marzik frowned. "You could tell that with the cap?"

Lester touched his own ears. "The part I could see down here, you know?"

That made sense to Starkey. "Okay. Do you recall any identifying characteristics? A scar, maybe? A tattoo on his arm?"

"He was wearing long sleeves."

"He was wearing a long-sleeved shirt?"

"Yeah. That's why I couldn't see his arms. I remember it was greasy and old, like he'd been working on a car or something."

Starkey put away her pad. "Okay, Lester, thanks. I want you to come in later this morning with Detective Marzik and work with a sketch artist, see if we can't build a picture of this guy, okay?"

"That sounds cool. But my dad's gonna raise hell."

"You go take care of your deliveries, and we'll square it with your father. Detective Marzik will buy you lunch."

Lester vanished into the flower shop, but Marzik and Starkey stayed on the sidewalk.

"Why'd you tell him that?" Marzik asked. "It's not going to do any good. The guy's wearing a cap, sunglasses, and a long-sleeved shirt on a day it's ninety-five degrees. If it's our guy, he's wearing a disguise."

Starkey felt the urge for more antacid. "Why do you always have to be so negative?"

"I'm not being negative. I'm stating what's obvious."

"Then try this for obvious: *If* he's our guy, and *if* he's wearing the same clothes when he set off the bomb, and *if* he's on the news tape, the hat and sunglasses and long-sleeved shirt should make him easier to spot."

"Whatever. I'll go talk to the kid's father."

Marzik stalked into the shop without another word.

Starkey shook out a cigarette, lit it, and went to her car. She felt her pager vibrate. It was Hooker.

Starkey called him on her cell phone. "Hook, it's me."

"Listen, we got the helicopter news tapes you wanted. You want me to set up the room for us to watch?"

"Set up the room, Jorge. Marzik's going to bring the flower kid in to work with an artist. I want him to look at the tapes, too, but only after he's done with the artist. I don't want him seeing the videos first, then describing someone he's seen just because he thinks they look suspicious."

"I'll get it set up."

"One more thing. What happened with Pell last night?"

"He didn't like something in the coroner's report. I took him over there."

Starkey felt her stomach knot. "What didn't he like?"

"The M.E. hadn't done a full body X ray, so Pell made him do it."

"Did he find anything?"

"More frag, but Pell said it didn't amount to much."

Starkey felt herself breathe easier. Maybe Pell would lose interest and go back to Washington. "Okay, arrange for the artist and lock down the room for the tapes. I'll be there in a few minutes."

She ended the call, then went back to Marzik. "Beth? We've got the videotape. Jorge's going to set up the artist for you. After that, how about you bring Lester back to watch the tapes? Maybe he'll pick out the hat man."

"Whatever."

Starkey got into her car and left Marzik waiting in the heat for Lester Ybarra.

HOOKER was sorting through the tapes in a cardboard box when Starkey reached CCS. First thing he said was, "The ATF guy called. I put it on your desk."

Without bothering to read the message from Pell, Starkey fingered through the cassettes. They were in two sizes—big three-quarter-inch master tapes and half-inch VHS dubs that could be played on home machines.

Santos saw her frowning. "It's hours, Carol. The running times are written on the outside, along with whether it's a close-up or wide-angle."

"What does that mean, close or wide?"

"Some of the helicopters carry two cameras. Both focus on the same thing, but one is zoomed in close and the other is pulled back for a wider field of view."

Starkey was already thinking that the close shots wouldn't give her what she wanted. She pulled out three of the wide-angle VHS cassettes and brought them to her desk.

Behind her Santos said, "I've got us set up in the TV room upstairs. We can go up as soon as I'm done."

Starkey took a cigarette from her purse and lit up.

"Carol! Do you want Kelso to send you home?"

She crushed the cigarette with her foot as she fanned the air. "Didn't even realize I was doing it. I'm worried about this ATF guy, is all. Did he say anything last night when he finished with the M.E.?"

"Nothing. All he said was that they found some more frag."

Hooker finished logging the tapes and put the box under his desk. Official LAPD filing. "I'm done. We'd better get started."

Starkey thought about watching Charlie Riggio being killed, and her hands grew damp. "Jorge, look, I've got calls to return. You start without me, okay?"

Hooker was disappointed. "I thought you wanted to see this. We've only got the room for a couple of hours."

"I'll watch them at home, Jorge. I've got these calls."

Her phone rang then. Starkey snatched it up like a life preserver. It was Pell. "Don't you return your calls?"

"I've been busy. We've got a wit who might have seen the man who placed the nine-one-one call."

"Let's meet somewhere. We need to discuss how we're going to handle the case."

"There is no 'we,' Pell. If my guy isn't your Mr. Red, then it doesn't matter to me. I still want to see what you have on the first seven bombings."

"I have the reports. I have something else, too. Let's get together and talk about it. This is important."

Starkey told him how to get to Barrigan's, then hung up.

Santos had been watching her. He came over with a handful of cassettes. "Are the feds taking the case?"

"I don't know. He didn't say."

Santos shrugged and gestured with the tapes. "I'm gonna go up. You sure you don't want to come?"

"I've got to meet Pell."

Starkey watched Santos walk away, embarrassed that she had not been able to look at them with him. She had been to the bomb site; she had seen Riggio's body. After that her fear of seeing the tapes seemed inexplicable, though she understood it. Starkey wouldn't be seeing only Riggio on the tape; she would see herself, and Sugar.

She told herself to stop thinking about it, gathered her things, and left to meet Pell.

BARRIGAN'S was a narrow Irish bar in Wilshire Division that had catered to police detectives since 1954. The walls were covered with four-leaf clovers, each bearing the name and date of an officer who'd killed a man in the line of duty.

When Starkey entered Barrigan's, the bar was lined with detectives. She found a bench between a couple of Sex Crimes D-2s, struck up a fresh cigarette, and ordered a double Sapphire.

She was taking her first sip when Pell appeared beside her and put a heavy manila envelope on the bar. "You always drink on the job?"

"It's none of your business what I do. But for the record, Special Agent, I'm off duty. I'm here as a favor to you."

Barrigan's didn't have stools; the bar was lined with little benches hooked to a brass rail that ran along the bottom of the bar, each wide enough for two people.

Pell slid onto the bench next to Starkey, uncomfortably close.

"Move away, Pell. You're too close."

He edged away. "Enough?"

"You're fine. I just don't like people too close."

Starkey immediately regretted saying it, feeling it revealed more of herself than she cared to share.

Pell tapped the manila envelope. "These are the reports. I've got something else here, too."

He unfolded a sheet of paper and put it on the bar. It was a newspaper article that he had printed off the Internet. "This happened a few days ago. Read it."

BOMB HOAX CLEARS LIBRARY
By Lauren Beth, Miami Herald
The Dade County Regional Main Library was evacuated yesterday when a loud siren began wailing, and librarians found what they believed to be a pipe bomb fixed to the underside of a table.

> After police evacuated the library, the Dade County Emergency Response Team recovered the device, which contained the siren, but no explosives. Police officials are calling the incident a hoax.

Starkey stopped reading. "What is this?"

"We recovered an intact device in Miami. It's a clone of the bomb that killed Charlie Riggio."

Starkey didn't like this news. If the bombs were clones, that would give Pell what he needed to jump the case. She pushed the article away. "If your Mr. Red is in Miami, why aren't you on a plane headed east?"

"Because he's here."

"It looks to me like he's in Miami."

Pell glanced at Starkey. "Could we move to a table?"

She led him to a remote corner table. "Okay, no one can hear you, Pell. We're free to be spies."

Pell's jaw flexed with irritation. "The Miami police didn't give the full story to the papers, Starkey. It wasn't a hoax; it was a message. An actual note. He's never done that before."

"What did he say?"

"He said, 'Would the deaths of these people put me in the top ten?' "

"What does that mean?"

"He wants to be on the FBI's ten most wanted list."

"You're kidding me."

"It's a symbol, Starkey. He's some underachieving nobody who resents being a loser. He's not on the list, because we don't know who he is; no one makes that list unless we have an I.D. We don't, so he's getting frustrated. He's taking chances he didn't take earlier, and that means he's destabilizing."

Starkey understood why Pell was on it. When a perp changed his pattern, it was always good for the case. Any change gave you a different view of the man. If you could get enough views, pretty soon you had a clear picture.

"You said he's here in Los Angeles. How do you know that?"

Pell stared at her. "I didn't tell you and Kelso everything. When Mr. Red goes hunting, he does not hunt randomly. He picks his targets, usually a tech who's been in the news. He wants to say he beats the best a bomb squad has to offer. It's the ego thing."

Charlie Riggio wasn't exactly the big dog of the LAPD bomb squad, but Starkey wasn't going to say that. "That what he told you in his little note?"

"We know because he etches the target's name on the bomb casing. The first two techs he killed, we found their names in the frag during the reconstruction."

Starkey didn't say anything. She drew a large 5 in the water rings on the table, then changed it to an S. She guessed it came from "Charles." "Why are you telling me this here in a bar and not in Kelso's office?"

Pell glanced away. He seemed nervous about something. "We try to keep that information on a need-to-know basis."

"Well, I'm honored, Pell. I sure as hell have a need to know, wouldn't you say?"

"Yes."

"Makes me wonder what else you might be holding back."

Pell glanced back sharply. "As the lead, you could make statements to the press to help advance Mr. Red's destabilization. These aren't just little machines that he's building. These bombs are who he is, and he's meticulous about them. We know he takes pride in them. In his head it could become a one-on-one game that keeps him in Los Angeles and gives us a better shot to nail him."

"Me versus him."

"Something like that. What do you say?"

Starkey didn't have to think about it. "I'm in."

Pell sighed deeply, as if he had been afraid that she wouldn't go along. "All right, Starkey. We believe that he builds the bombs locally. He'll go into an area, acquire the things he needs, and build the bomb there, so he doesn't have to transport anything, risking capture on the airlines. I put a list of the Modex components in with the reports. I want you to run a local check for people with access to RDX."

Starkey looked smug. "It's already happening, Pell. I punched it in today."

He nodded without expression, and Starkey went on. "Do we have a photograph of this guy? There must've been a security camera in the library."

"There aren't any security cameras in the downtown branch, but I'll have a sketch by tomorrow. The wits described a white male in his twenties with bright red hair. We also have two other sketches from previous incidents. But all three look different. He changes his appearance when he lets himself be seen."

Starkey shrugged. "Whatever. I want a copy of all three of your sketches when you have them. Also, I want to see the bomb."

"As soon as I get the report, you'll get the report."

"You didn't hear me. I want the bomb. In my hands. I'm a bomb technician, Pell. I want to break it down myself, compare it to the Silver Lake bomb, and learn something."

Pell nodded. "Okay, Starkey, that's a good idea. But I think you should arrange it."

Starkey frowned. "*Your* people have the damned thing. It would be easier for you to get it."

"The more I do, the more pressure I'll get from Washington to take over the case."

She nodded. "Okay, Pell, I'll do it myself."

Pell stood, then gave her a card. "This is the motel where I'm staying. My pager number is on the back."

Starkey put it away without looking at it. "Anything comes up, I'll give you a call."

"Mr. Red is dangerous, Starkey. A guy like this in town, you don't want to be too drunk to react."

"I've already been dead once, Pell. Believe me, there are worse things."

Pell left. Starkey watched him until he stepped out of the bar into a wedge of blinding light and was gone. She returned to the bar and ordered a refill. She was convinced that Pell knew more than he was saying.

IT WAS almost seven when Starkey left Barrigan's and drove home. Her head hurt from the gin. She was hungry, but there was nothing to eat in her house, and she didn't want to go out again. She put the tapes in her living room by the VCR, then found a box of raisins and ate them standing at the kitchen sink. When she was finished, she poured a glass of milk and sat at the kitchen table to read the reports.

The envelope contained seven ATF explosives profiles written at the ATF's National Laboratory Center in Rockville, Maryland. Each report contained an analysis of a device that was attributed to Mr. Red, but several paragraphs in each report had been deleted.

Every one of the devices had been built of twin pipes capped and sealed with plumber's tape, one pipe containing the radio receiver (all receivers identified as being from the WayKool line of remote-control toy cars) and AA batteries, one the Modex Hybrid explosive. None of the reports mentioned the etched names that Pell had described. She thought that the deleted material probably referenced that.

When she finished with the reports, she poured herself a stiff gin. Then, her stomach in knots, she went into the living room and loaded the first tape into the machine.

The image was a wide shot of the parking lot. The bomb squad Suburban was in place, the parking lot and the nearby streets cordoned off. Riggio, already in the suit, was at the rear of the Suburban, talking with Buck Daggett. Seeing Daggett pat Riggio's helmet, seeing Riggio turn and lumber toward the bomb chilled her.

The bomb was a tiny cardboard square at the base of the Dumpster. When Riggio started toward it, the frame shifted to reveal a small group of people standing between two apartment houses. Starkey focused on them, but they were too small and shadowed to tell if any wore long-sleeved shirts and baseball caps.

Riggio reached the bomb with the Real Time.

Starkey knew what was coming and tried to steel herself. She glanced away, feeling her heart pound.

When she looked at the screen again, Riggio was circling the box, examining it with the Real Time. He finished his circle, hesitated, then leaned over the box. In that moment the killer pressed the switch and the light hurled Charlie Riggio away like an imaginary man.

Starkey stopped the tape and closed her eyes, her fist clenched tight as if it was she who had clutched the switch and sent Charlie Riggio to hell.

She felt herself breathe. She felt her chest expand, her body fill with air. She gripped her glass with both hands and drank. She wiped at her eyes.

After a while she pressed the PLAY button and forced herself to watch the rest of the tape.

The pressure wave flashed across the tarmac, a ripple of dust and debris sucked up after it. The Dumpster rocked backwards into the wall. Smoke rose from the crater as Buck Daggett rushed forward to his partner and pulled off the helmet. An Emergency Services van screeched into the lot beside them, two paramedics rushing in to take over. Buck stood watching them.

Starkey was able to pick out knots of people at the edge of the hundred-yard perimeter who were hidden behind cars or buildings. She froze the image each time, looking for long-sleeved males in blue baseball caps, but the resolution was too poor to be of much use. She watched the other two tapes, drinking all the while and thinking that any of those shadowed faces might belong to the man or woman who had built and detonated the bomb.

Later that night she rewound the tapes, turned off her television, and fell into a deep sleep there on her couch.

SHE is kicked away from the trailer by a burst of white light.
The paramedics insert their long needle.
She reaches for Sugar's hand as his helmet is pulled free.
His head lolls toward her. It is Pell.

CHAPTER
4

THE next morning Starkey was at her desk when Kelso approached. "I got a call from Assistant Chief Morgan last night. He asked how you were doing as the lead, Carol. He's going to want a report."

Starkey's head throbbed. "I'll go see him whenever he wants."

"He won't just want to look at you, Carol; he'll want progress. He suggested that we could forestall the ATF taking over this case if we had something to show for our efforts. Think about it."

Kelso stalked away and disappeared into his office.

Starkey's head throbbed worse. She had gotten so drunk last night that she scared herself and had spent most of the morning worried that her drinking was finally out of hand.

Marzik passed out copies of the suspect likeness that had been created from Lester Ybarra's description.

Starkey kept her eyes averted, hoping that Marzik would not notice their redness. She was sure the gin was bleeding through her pores and tried not to blow in Marzik's face when she commented on the likeness. "It's a ghost."

Marzik nodded glumly, agreeing.

The portrait showed a white male approximately forty years of age with a rectangular face hidden by dark glasses and a baseball cap. His nose was undistinguished in shape and size, as were his lips, ears, and jaw. It worked out that way more times that not. If a wit saw no identifying characteristics, the portrait ended up looking like every other person on the street. The detectives called them ghosts because there was nothing to see.

"Listen, Beth, Pell has three other likenesses that he's going to deliver. We can show those to Lester. Maybe something will click."

Marzik nodded. "Lester didn't have time to look at the tapes yesterday, but I've got him set up to come in this afternoon. You see anything last night?"

"Not on the wide shots. Everything is so murky you can't really see. We need to have them enhanced. Hooker's working on it. Listen, I need to check the NLETS, okay? We'll talk later."

Marzik nodded and went back to her desk.

When Marzik wasn't looking, Starkey popped an Altoid, then checked the NLETS system. She had expected one or two hits on the RDX, but nothing like what she found.

The California State Sheriffs reported that Dallas Tennant, a thirty-two-year-old white male, was currently serving time in the California state correctional facility in Atascadero, a facility for prisoners receiving treatment for mental disorders. On three separate occasions two years ago Tennant had exploded devices made with RDX. Starkey smiled. RDX was rare; three devices meant that Tennant had had access to a lot of it. She printed off the computer report, noting that the case had been made by a bomb-and-arson sergeant-investigator named Warren Mueller out of the Central Valley office in Bakersfield. Back at her desk, she looked up the phone number, then called, asking for Warren Mueller.

When Mueller came on, Starkey identified herself as a Los Angeles police officer. "I'm calling about a perp you collared named Dallas Tennant. Reason I'm calling is I got a kicker saying that he set off three devices using RDX. That's a lot of RDX."

"Three we know of, yeah. Coulda been more. He was buying stolen cars from some kids up here, then driving 'em out into the desert to blow 'em up. Crazy fool just wanted to see 'em come apart."

"You know where he got the RDX?"

"He claimed that he bought a case of stolen antipersonnel mines from a guy he met at a bar. My guess is that he bought it off one of these meth-dealing bikers, but he never copped."

Starkey knew that the vast majority of bombings were the result of drug wars between rival methamphetamine dealers, many of whom were white bikers. Meth labs were chemical bombs waiting to happen. So when a meth dealer wanted to eliminate a rival, he often just blew apart his Airstream.

"So you could still have a guy up there with RDX to sell?"

323

"That's possible, but we didn't have a suspect at the time, and we don't have one now. All we had was Dallas, blowing up his damned cars. The guy's your classic no-life, loner bomb crank."

"Did he have any more RDX at the time of his arrest?"

"Never found any of his works. Said he made everything at home. He had this rathole apartment, but we didn't find so much as a firecracker."

Starkey considered that. Building bombs was a way of life for bomb cranks like Dallas Tennant. It was their passion, and they inevitably had a place where they built their bombs, in the same way that hobbyists had hobby rooms. Might be a closet or a garage, but they had a place to store their supplies and practice their craft. Such places were called shops.

"Seems like he would've had a shop."

"Well, my feeling is that he shared a shop with the guy sold him the RDX, and that guy packed up when Dallas was tagged, but like I say, that's just my feeling."

Starkey didn't think much of Mueller's theory. As Mueller had pointed out, bomb cranks were introverted loners. Sharing their toys didn't fit with the profile. Starkey suspected that if Tennant didn't cop to his shop, it was because he didn't want to lose his toys. He probably spent hours every day fantasizing about the bombs he would build when he was released.

Starkey closed her pad. "Okay, Sergeant, I think that about does it. I appreciate your time."

"Anytime. Could I ask you something, Starkey?"

In that moment she knew what was coming and felt her stomach knot.

"You the same Starkey got blown up?"

"Yeah. That was me. Listen, all I've got here is what the sheriffs put out on the kicker. Could you fax your casework on Tennant to give me a little more?"

"This about that thing happened down there in Silver Lake?"

"Yes, sir."

"Sure. I can get to it right away."

"Thanks." Starkey gave him the fax number and hung up before Mueller could say any more.

She went to fill her coffee cup. When she got back to the fax machine, Mueller's casework was waiting in the tray. Starkey read it back at her desk. Tennant had an arrest history of fire starting and explosives that went back to the age of eighteen and had twice received court-mandated psychiatric counseling.

Starkey read Mueller's interview notes several times before she caught something that reinforced her belief that Tennant still maintained his shop. She decided that she wanted to speak with him.

Starkey called Atascadero and spoke to the law-enforcement liaison officer. "You have an inmate named Dallas Tennant. I'm working a case here in Los Angeles that he might have information relating to. Would you see if he'd talk to me without counsel?"

"When would you want to see him, Detective?"

Starkey glanced at the clock on the wall. "Later today. Say about two this afternoon."

"All right. He's going to want to know what it's about."

"The availability of an explosive called RDX."

The liaison officer took her number and told her he'd call back as soon as possible.

After she hung up, Starkey thought about what to do. LAPD policy required detectives to always work in pairs, but Marzik had interviews and Hooker was going to see about the tape. Starkey found Pell's card in her purse and paged him.

STARKEY completed the evidence transfer request, which she faxed to the ATF office in Miami, then waited for Pell in the lobby. The drive from downtown L.A. to Atascadero was going to be just over three hours. She had thought that Pell would want to drive, because men always wanted to drive, but he didn't. Instead, he said, "I'll use the time to read Tennant's case file; then we can work out a game plan."

She gave him the six-page report, then maneuvered out of the city and up the coast along the Ventura Freeway.

Pell said, "This is good stuff, Starkey. We can use this. Searching for the RDX paid off."

"I wanted to mention that to you. I want to make sure we don't get off on the wrong foot here."

Pell looked at her. "What wrong foot?"

"I know you think you were advising me, but I don't need it. You come in, start telling me what to do, and expect me to hop to it. It doesn't work that way."

"It was just a suggestion. You did it anyway."

"Just don't expect that I'll get coffee for you."

Pell stared at her, then glanced back at the report. "You spoke with the arresting officer?"

"Yeah. Mueller."

"Can I ask you to tell me what he said, or is that too much like asking you for a mocha?"

"I just wanted to set the ground rules."

She recounted her conversation with Mueller. When she finished, Pell shook his head. "Mueller dropped the ball about Tennant not having a shop. According to this, Tennant was buying stolen cars to destroy them. He bought the cars from a guy named Robert Castillo. Three cars, three explosions. Castillo said that Tennant had asked him to steal a fourth car. Tennant wouldn't need another car if he didn't have more RDX to destroy it or knew how to get more."

Starkey's grip tightened on the wheel. "That's what I figured. You said you had a suspect likeness coming from Miami. Did you get it?"

"Yeah. That, and the first two we have." He slipped them from his jacket and unfolded them for her. "Can you see?"

"Yeah."

"There were enough people in the library to put together a pretty good composite. Our guy shows to be six feet, one eighty or so, but he's probably wearing lifts and padding. The wits from the earlier sightings made him at five ten, with bright red hair."

Starkey glanced at the three sheets as she drove. Pell was right. None of the three looked very much alike, and none of them looked like the man Lester Ybarra described. The Miami likeness was as

Pell described, the second likeness showed a balding professorial-looking man with glasses, and the third showed a much heavier man with woolly Rasta braids, sunglasses, and a beard.

She handed them back to Pell.

He put the sheets away. "What about your guy? He match any of these?"

Starkey told him to open her briefcase, which was on the back seat. When Pell had the sketch, he shook his head. "How old is this guy supposed to be?"

"Forty."

"So he might've made himself up to look older."

"Maybe. If we're talking about the same guy."

"Mr. Red is in his late twenties, early thirties. That's all we know for sure. That, and him being white. He lets himself be seen, Starkey. He changes his look to play with us."

After that they drove in silence for a while. Starkey happened to glance over and found Pell staring at her.

"What?"

"You said you had gotten videotapes from the Silver Lake event. Did you look at them yet?"

"Yeah. I looked at them last night."

"Anything?"

Starkey shrugged. "I've gotta have them enhanced."

"That must've been hard for you. Looking at what happened. It must've been hard. It would be for me."

Pell met her eyes, then went back to staring out the window. She thought he might be pitying her and felt herself flush with anger.

"Pell, one more thing. When we get there with Tennant, it's my show. I'm the lead."

Pell nodded. "I'm just along for the ride."

THE Atascadero Minimum Security Correctional Facility was a village of brown brick buildings set in the arid ranchland south of Paso Robles. There were no walls, no guard towers; just a ten-foot chain-link fence and a single front gate with two bored guards.

Starkey said, "They're going to make us check our guns. Be faster with the paperwork if we leave 'em in the car."

Pell slipped a Smith 10-mm autoloader under the seat.

Starkey badged the gate guards, who directed her to the reception area. They left the car in a small parking lot, then went inside to find the law-enforcement liaison officer, a man named Larry Olsen, waiting for them.

"Detective Starkey?"

"Carol Starkey. This is Special Agent Pell, with the ATF. Thanks for setting this up."

Olsen asked for identification and had them sign the log. He led them out the rear through double glass doors and along a walk toward another building.

Olsen said, "I should tell you that Tennant is currently being medicated. Xanax for anxiety and Anafranil to help regulate his obsessive-compulsive disorder. He was off the meds for a while, but we had a problem and had to resume the treatment."

Pell said, "What kind of problem?"

"He used cleaning products and iodine he stole from the infirmary to create an explosive. He lost his left thumb."

Dallas Tennant was an overweight man with pale skin and large eyes. He was sitting at a Formica table that had been pushed against the wall, but stood when Olsen showed them in. His left hand was bandaged, strangely narrow without its thumb.

Olsen introduced them, then explained that a guard would be outside the room to remove Tennant when they were finished. After that he left.

Starkey noticed a thick plastic photo album on the corner of the table. The cover was of a tropical island at sunset with script letters that read, "My Happy Memories."

When Starkey glanced up, Tennant was staring at her. He smiled shyly. "That's my scrapbook."

Starkey directed Tennant where to sit. She wanted to be across from him, and she wanted Pell at his side so that Tennant would have to look at one or the other, not both. Tennant slid his scrapbook across the table when he changed seats, to keep it near him.

"First off, Dallas, I want to tell you that we're not looking to bring charges against you. We're going to overlook any crimes you admit to, as long as they don't include crimes against persons."

Tennant nodded. "I never hurt anyone."

"Fine. Then let's get started."

"Can I show you something first? It might help you."

"Let's not get sidetracked, Dallas."

He turned his book for Starkey to see, ignoring her objection. "It's very important to me. I wasn't going to see you at first, but then I remembered your name."

He had marked a place in the book with a strip of toilet tissue. He opened to the marked page.

Starkey felt her skin grow cold. Yellowed and encased in plastic was an L.A. *Times* article about the trailer-park bombing that had killed Sugar and wounded her.

She took a moment to make sure her voice would not waver. "Are all the articles in this book bomb-related?"

Tennant flipped the pages for her to see, revealing devastated buildings, crumpled cars, and disrupted bodies. "I was hoping I could get you to autograph it."

Before she could respond, Pell reached over and closed the book. "Not today. Today you're going to tell us where you got the RDX."

"That's mine. You can't take that."

Starkey was inwardly livid with Pell for intruding, but she kept her manner calm. "I'm not going to sign your book, Dallas. Maybe if you tell us where you got the RDX and how we could get some, maybe then I might sign it. But not now."

"I want my book. Mr. Olsen will make you give it back."

Starkey eased the book away from Pell and slid it across the table. Tennant pulled it close again. "I bought some mines from a man I didn't know. Raytheons."

"How many mines?"

Tennant had told Mueller that he'd bought a case, which, Starkey knew because she had phoned Raytheon, contained six mines.

"A case. There were six in the case."

Pell said, "What was this man's name?"

"Clint Eastwood. I know, but that was how he identified himself."

Starkey took out a cigarette and lit up. "How could we find Clint?"

"I don't know. You're not supposed to smoke in here."

"Mr. Olsen gave me permission. How did you find Clint?"

"I met him in a bar. He had a case of antipersonnel mines, I bought it, and then he was gone. I didn't want mines; I bought them to scavenge the RDX."

Starkey believed Tennant; high-order explosives were almost always acquired from military gear. But she also believed that his source wasn't some nameless yahoo in a roadhouse. Bomb cranks like Tennant were low-self-esteem loners. Starkey knew that Tennant's obsession with explosives was a sublimated sexuality. He would be awkward with women, sexually inexperienced in the normal sense. He would avoid face-to-face confrontations of any kind. He would lurk in hobby shops and swap meets and would be far too afraid to connect in a biker bar.

Starkey decided to change her approach. She took out the photographs of the three cars and the interview pages from Mueller's case file. "All right, Dallas. I can buy that. Now tell me, how much RDX do you have left?"

Tennant hesitated. "I used it all. I don't have any left."

"I can look at these pictures, Dallas, and tell that you didn't use all the RDX. We can calculate things like that. Start with the damage, then work backwards to estimate the amount of the charge. It's called an energy comparison."

Tennant blinked his eyes blandly. "That's all I had."

"You bought the cars from a man named Robert Castillo. He said that you asked him for a fourth car. Why would you need a fourth car if you only had enough pop for three?"

Tennant shrugged. "I had some dynamite." He averted his eyes. "I'm sorry. There's nothing to say."

"Sure there is. Tell us where we can find your shop."

Starkey was certain that if they could find his shop, they would find evidence that would lead to his source of the RDX.

"I didn't have a shop. I kept everything in my car."

"Nothing was found in your car."

"That's because I'm a very neat person. They even offered to reduce my time, but I had nothing to trade. Don't you think I would have made a deal if I could? It's not fair they keep me here. I never hurt anybody."

Starkey tried to appear sympathetic. "I believe that, Dallas, but the thing is, this is why we're here. We've got someone out there who doesn't care about people the way you do. This person is trying to hurt people."

Tennant nodded. "You're here because of the officer who was killed. Officer Riggio."

"How do you know about Riggio?"

"We have television here, and the Internet. Officer Riggio was killed with RDX?"

"RDX was a component. The charge was something called Modex Hybrid."

Tennant laced his fingers. "Did Mr. Red set that bomb?"

Pell came out of his chair so suddenly that Starkey jumped. "How do you know about Mr. Red?"

Tennant glanced nervously from Starkey to Pell. "I don't really. People gossip. I don't even know that Mr. Red is real."

Pell reached over and gripped Tennant's wrist above his bandaged hand. "Who, Tennant? Who's talking about Mr. Red?"

Starkey was growing uncomfortable with Pell's manner. She didn't like it that he was touching Tennant, and she didn't like the intensity she saw in his eyes. "Pell."

"What do they say, Tennant?"

Tennant tried to twist away. "Nothing. He's a myth. He's someone who makes wonderful elegant explosions."

"He kills people, you sick mutt."

Starkey pushed out of her chair. "Leave go of him, Pell."

Pell's face was bright with anger. He didn't leave go. "He knows that Red uses Modex, Starkey. We've never released that information to the public. How does he know?"

Pell gripped Tennant's bandaged hand. Tennant gasped.

"Tell me, you sonofabitch. How do you know about Mr. Red?"

Starkey shoved Pell hard, trying to move him away, but couldn't. "Dammit, Pell, leave go! Step away from him."

Tennant made a whimpering sound. "They talk about him on Claudius. They talk about the bombs he builds."

"Who the hell is Claudius?"

"Damn you, Pell. Let go." Starkey shoved at Pell again, and this time he let go of Tennant.

Pell seemed in control again. He stared at Tennant. "Tell me about Claudius. Tell me how you know about Mr. Red."

Tennant cradled his hand. "It's an Internet site. There's a chat room. We talk about bombs and the different bombers. They say that Mr. Red lurks there, reading what they say about him."

Starkey turned to Tennant. "Have you had contact with Mr. Red?"

"No. I don't know. If he's there, he uses a different name. All I'm saying is what the others say."

A red flower blossomed on Tennant's bandage; his wound was seeping.

Starkey said, "You okay, Tennant? You want the doctor?"

Tennant shook his head and picked up his book with his good hand. "I want you to sign."

Starkey signed the book, and then she called the guard and got Pell out of there. Tennant seemed fine, but she wasn't sure what he might say once they were gone.

Pell moved like an automaton, stalking out ahead of her, stiff with tension.

When they reached the parking lot, Starkey followed him to his side of the car. "You crazy bastard, what was that all about? Do you *know* what kind of trouble we could be in?"

Pell glared at her darkly. "He gave us something, Starkey. This Claudius thing."

"I don't give a *damn* what he gave us! You touched a prisoner!

If he files a complaint, it's over for me. I don't know about the ATF, but let me tell you, Pell, LAPD will have my hide on the barn! That was wrong, what you did in there. Wrong."

Pell took a deep breath. "I'm sorry."

She walked away from him, shaking her head. She was so angry that she didn't trust herself to speak.

That's when Pell said, "Starkey."

She turned back just in time to see Pell stagger against the car, then collapse to one knee.

Starkey ran to him. "Pell, what's wrong?"

His eyes were clenched shut, and he was as pale as milk.

Starkey thought he was having a heart attack. "I'm going to get someone. You hang on, okay?"

Pell caught her arm, holding tight. "Wait. I'm okay, Starkey. It's a migraine, that's all."

"You look like hell. I'd better get someone. Please."

"Just give me a minute."

Starkey had the frantic thought that he was dying right here in the parking lot. "Pell?"

Finally his color returned. "Sorry. I didn't mean to hurt you."

He looked at her then. She was very close to him. His closeness embarrassed her, and she scooted away.

"I'm okay now." He stood, balancing himself against the car, then used the door for support as he climbed in. By the time Starkey got behind the wheel, he had more color.

"You really screwed up in there."

Pell reached across the seat and touched her thigh. His expression surprised her; his eyes were deepened with regret. "I'm sorry. If he files a complaint, I'll take the bullet."

Starkey stared at him a moment; then she started the car, her leg feeling the weight of his hand as if it were still there.

IT WAS after seven when Starkey let Pell off at the curb outside Spring Street. The summer sun was still high in the west. She struck a fresh cigarette, then turned into the traffic.

In the long silence coming back to L.A., Starkey had decided that Pell was dangerous to her case and to her chances of reclaiming her career. Trading her job for this Claudius thing seemed like a sour deal. The only way she could protect herself was to report Pell. Then, if Tennant squawked, Starkey would be clear. She would have acted by the book. She would be safe. But reporting Pell was not an acceptable option. Even thinking about it made her feel cheesy and low.

She couldn't get Pell out of her head.

Starkey didn't know anything about migraine headaches, but what had happened in the parking lot had scared her even more than Pell's losing control with Tennant. She was certain that Pell was hiding something. She had enough secrets of her own to know that people didn't hide strengths; they guarded their weaknesses. Now she feared Pell's. The bomb investigators that she had known were all detail people; they moved slowly and methodically. Pell didn't act like a bomb investigator. His manner was predatory and fast, his actions with Tennant extreme and violent.

She drove home, feeling as if she was in a weakened position and angry because of it.

CHAPTER
5

"TELL me about Pell."

"He's with the ATF. That's Alcohol, Tobacco and Firearms."

"I know."

"If you knew, why did you ask?"

"I meant I know what the acronym ATF stands for. You seem irritable today, Carol."

"How inconsiderate of me. I must have forgotten to take my daily dose of mellow."

Starkey was annoyed with herself for mentioning Pell to Dana. On the drive to Santa Monica she had mapped out what she wanted to talk about, which had not included Pell, yet Pell was the first

Body

thing out of her mouth. "I put myself at risk for this guy, and I don't even know him."

"Why did you do that?"

"Nobody likes a rat."

"But he violated the law. He laid hands on this prisoner, and now you are in jeopardy for not reporting him. You clearly don't approve of what he did, yet you are conflicted about what to do."

Starkey shook out a cigarette, lit up. "The dream changed."

"How so?"

"Pell was in the dream. They took off Sugar's helmet, and it was that bastard Pell."

Dana nodded. "You're attracted to him."

"Oh, for God's sake."

"Are you?"

"I don't know."

"A little while ago you told me that he scared you. Maybe this is the true reason why. Are you going to act on this attraction?"

"I don't know."

Dana glanced at her clock. "Our time is almost up. I'd like to leave you with something else to think about."

"Like I don't have enough?"

Dana smiled. "You once made a joke about working on the bomb squad because you enjoyed the risk. You told me that you never thought of bombs as dangerous, that a bomb was just a puzzle that you had to solve, all neat and contained and predictable. I think you feel safe with bombs, Carol. It's people who scare you. Do you think that's why you enjoyed the bomb squad so much?"

Starkey glanced at the clock. "You were right. Time's up."

AFTER leaving Dana, Starkey worked her way through the crosstown traffic to Spring Street. She was at her desk, dry-swallowing a Tagamet, when Pell called.

"I wanted to apologize again about yesterday. I hope that what happened hasn't created a problem for you."

"Tennant could still destroy my career, but so far I'm safe."

"Did you report me?"

"Not my style, babe. Forget it."

"Well, like I said, if it comes to that, I'll take the hits."

She felt herself flush with anger. "You can't take the hits, Pell. I'm screwed for not reporting you whether you take the hits or not. That's the way it works here."

"Okay. Listen, there's another reason I called. I've got someone who can help us with this Claudius thing."

"What do you mean?"

"If it's true what Tennant said, that Mr. Red goes there, I'm thinking we can use that. The ATF has a guy at Cal Tech who knows about this stuff. I've set it up, if you're game."

"You're damn right I am."

"Great. Can you pick me up?"

The card from Pell's hotel was on her desk. She looked at it and saw that he was staying in Culver City near LAX. A place called the Islander Palms.

"Why don't we just meet there? You're way out in the wrong direction."

"I'm having trouble with my rental car. If you don't want to pick me up, I'll take a cab."

"Take it easy, Pell. I'll see you in twenty minutes."

THE Islander Palms was a low-slung motel with neon palm trees, sea-green trim, and an ugly stucco exterior. Starkey was surprised that Pell was staying in such a dump.

Pell got in the car without waiting for her to shut the engine. He looked tired, with dark rings under his eyes.

"Is the ATF on a budget, Pell? LAPD would put me up in a better place than this."

"I'll call the director and tell him you said to shape up."

As they drove across the city to Cal Tech, Pell explained that they were meeting a man named Donald Bergen, who was a graduate student in physics. Bergen was one of several computer experts employed by the government to identify and monitor potential presidential assassins, militia cranks, pedophiles, terrorists, and others who used the Internet for illegal activity.

Twenty minutes later they left the car in visitors parking and entered the Cal Tech campus. It was pretty; earth-colored buildings nestled in the flats of Pasadena. They found the computer sciences building, then walked along a sterile hall to Bergen's office. He was short and muscular, like a bodybuilder.

Pell introduced Starkey, and Bergen let them in, locking the door after them. "You can call me Donnie. I'm all set up for you."

Bergen's office was cluttered with software manuals and computers. He told them to sit where two chairs had been set up in front of a slim laptop computer. Starkey was uncomfortable, sitting so close to Pell that their arms touched, but there wasn't room to move away. Bergen pulled up a swivel chair.

"Show us how to find Claudius," Pell said.

"It's already found. I was there this morning."

Bergen twisted around to point out a stack of bright blue Power Macs. "What you do is search for word combinations. I've got software that floats on forty service providers, searching for different combinations of words on message boards, newsgroups, and in chat rooms. I tasked the software with looking for the word Claudius, along with a few others, and this is what we found."

Bergen punched several computer keys, and a page appeared. "That's Claudius."

It was a face with a head of flames. The face was tortured, as if in great pain. Starkey thought it looked Roman. Along the left side was a navigation bar that showed different topics: HOW TO, THE PROS, MILITARY, GALLERY, LINKS, MOST WANTED, and several others.

Starkey said, "What are all these things?"

"Pages within pages. The gallery is gruesome pictures of blast victims. The how-to pages have articles about bomb construction and a message board where these cranks can talk about it with each other. Here, let's take a tour."

Bergen used a mouse to click them through a tour of hell. Starkey watched diagrams of improvised munitions flick past on the screen, saw articles on substituting common household products for their chemical counterparts in order to create explosives. The gallery contained endless photographs of people who had been mutilated or killed by explosive blasts.

Starkey had to look away. "This is disgusting."

"But legal. First Amendment, babe. And you'll note that no one is admitting to crimes or to buying and selling illegal items. They're just hobbyists. Ha."

Pell said, "We're looking for someone who calls himself Mr. Red. They talk about him here. He might even visit."

"There's a *ton* of stuff about Mr. Red. These freaks think he's a hero." Bergen opened the message boards and punched up a string of messages devoted to Mr. Red. He showed Starkey how she could move from message to message.

She opened a message at random and followed the thread.

SUBJECT: Re: Truth or Consequences
FROM: BOOMER
The Unabomber was lucky. His devices were simple, crude, and embarrassing. If you want elegance, look to Mr. Red.

SUBJECT: Re: Truth or Consequences
FROM: JYMBO4
What elegance, Boom? So he uses a schmantzy goo like Modex, and nobody knows who he is. The Unabomber wasn't identified for seventeen years. Red's only been around for two. Let's see if he's smart enough to stay uncaught.

Starkey glanced at Bergen. "That's what they do here—they leave messages back and forth like this?"

"Yeah, but these guys are lightweights. The real kooks go to the chat room. See, most anyone can get where we are now, but you can't just sign on to the chat room. You've got to be invited."

"How did you get invited?"

Bergen looked smug. "I broke in. But normal people need what's called a hot ticket. That's special software that someone has to send to you via e-mail. These guys want to talk about things they can be arrested for, so they want privacy. They know that guys like me are out there, but they think they're safe in the chat room."

Bergen hit more keys, after which a window opened, showing two names having a conversation in a chat room. "They're having a conversation just like we are, only they're typing it. These guys could be anywhere on the planet."

Pell sighed. "I can see Mr. Red here, Starkey. These people would appeal to his ego. He would come here, read all this crap about how great he is. We can reach him here."

Starkey looked past Pell to Bergen. "We can leave messages here if we have a screen name?"

"Sure. Post messages, come into the chat room—anything you want if I set you up for it. That's why we're here, right?"

Pell nodded. "That's what we want."

"No problemo. Let's get to it, and you can get on your way."

Bergen showed them how to use the laptop and set them up with an Internet address through an anonymous provider owned and operated by the government. Then he showed them how to get to Claudius once they had accessed the Internet. They talked over how to proceed and decided to do something that Bergen called trolling. They chose the name Hotload. Then, writing as Hotload, they posted three messages about Mr. Red on the message boards. Two affirmed Hotload's status as a fan and the other reported a rumor that Mr. Red had struck again in Los Angeles. The idea was to provoke a response and establish a presence on the boards.

When they finished, Pell told Bergen that he would be back in a few minutes, then walked Starkey out.

Starkey said, "Why do you have to go back?"

"ATF business. Don't worry about it."

"Oh, go to hell, Pell."

"This annoyance— Is it perpetual with you?"

Starkey frowned without answering. She shook out a cigarette and lit up.

Pell thought about all the smoking and drinking, wondering if she had always been this way or if this Starkey had been born that day in the trailer park.

She waved the cigarette. "I've got to get back. I'm supposed to go out with Marzik, looking for people who saw our guy."

"You take the computer. We can get together at your place later to see if anyone responded."

She glanced at him, then shrugged. "Sure. We can do it at my place. I'll wait in the car."

Pell went back to Bergen's office. When the door was closed, Pell took out an envelope containing twelve hundred dollars, then watched as Bergen counted it.

Bergen said, "This is the first time you guys have paid me in cash. Usually I file a voucher. You want a receipt?"

"What I want is a second computer."

"You want another one? Just like the one I gave you?"

"Yes. Set up so I can reach Claudius."

"What do you need a second one for?"

Pell stepped closer. "Can you fix me up with a second computer or not?"

"It's another twelve hundred."

"I'll come back later. Alone."

AFTER Starkey dropped Pell back at his motel, she and Marzik spent the afternoon interviewing potential witnesses. No one recalled seeing a man in a baseball cap and long-sleeved shirt making a call.

At the end of the day they swung past the flower shop to show Lester Ybarra the three likenesses that Starkey had gotten from Pell. Lester shook his head. "They look like different guys."

"They're the same guy wearing three disguises."

"Maybe the guy I saw was wearing a disguise, too, but he looked older than these guys."

Marzik asked to bum one of Starkey's Tagamets.

Starkey drove home that night determined to give herself a break from the gin. She tried to watch television, but her thoughts kept returning to Pell and his saying that he would take the bullets if Tennant filed charges. One man had already taken the hits for her. She would never allow another man to do that again.

AT TEN minutes after nine the next morning Buck Daggett called her at Spring Street. "Ah, Carol, I was wondering if you've had any breaks."

Starkey felt a wave of guilt. She knew what it was like to be in Buck's position, feeling that you were on the outside of something so devastating. "Not really, Buck. I'm sorry."

"I don't want to be a pest, but I heard they found some writing in the frag. What's that about?"

"We're not sure what we found. It's either a five or an S." Starkey wasn't sure how much she should tell him about Mr. Red, so she let it go at that.

Buck hesitated. "A five or an S? Is that part of a message?"

Starkey wanted to change the subject. "I don't know, Buck." Santos waved at her, pointing at the phone. A second line was blinking. "Listen, Buck, I got a call. If anything develops, I'll let you know."

"Okay, Carol. I'm not nagging or anything."

"I know. I'll see you later."

The second call was John Chen. "We got an evidence transfer here in your name from the ATF lab in Rockville."

"Is it bomb components from the Miami library?"

"Yeah."

Starkey glanced at her watch. "I'll be there in twenty minutes. I want to look at it."

She was on her way out when Kelso steamed across the squad room, carrying a coffee cup that read WORLD'S SEXIEST LOVER. "Starkey, Assistant Chief Morgan wants to have a meeting this afternoon. One o'clock in my office."

Starkey remembered Tennant and Atascadero and felt the ground fall away beneath her. "About what?"

"About Riggio, Detective. Dick Leyton will be here, too, and I hope to hell you have something to say."

Starkey felt her panic ease. She told Kelso about Claudius, explaining that Tennant had learned about Mr. Red there, and that she felt it was a possible source of information.

Kelso listened, somewhat mollified. "Well, that's something. At least it looks like we're doing something."

"We *are* doing something, Barry."

Even with nothing to drink, he made her head throb.

Starkey was still shaking when she reached Chen's lab.

Chen said, "They sent two devices, Starkey."

That surprised her. "All I expected was the library device."

"We got that, but we also got the frag from a detonation they had down there. The reports say they're the same design, only one was really a bomb and the other wasn't."

Pell had told her about a sweatshop bombing, which was described in one of the seven reports she had read.

Chen led her to a corner of the lab where two white boxes rested on the black lab table. Both boxes had been opened. He said, "Everything's bagged, tagged, and logged. You've gotta sign here; then the ATF says you're clear to do whatever you want, including destructive testing."

Destructive testing was sometimes necessary to separate components or obtain samples. Starkey signed four federal evidence forms where Chen indicated, then gave them back to him.

Chen left the lab. Alone at last, Starkey pulled on a pair of vinyl gloves, took a breath, and felt the tension melting away. This was the part of the job that she loved. When she touched the bomb, when she had its pieces in her hands, she was part of it. The bomb was a puzzle that she was able to see in ways that others couldn't.

The ATF had sent both devices along with their respective reports. Starkey put the reports aside to read after she had drawn her own conclusions.

Her primary interest was in the disassembled parts of the intact device recovered from the Miami library. She laid these plastic bags out on the bench, organizing them by components. One bag contained the siren that had sounded to draw attention, another the timer, another the siren's battery pack. The siren had been crushed and two of the three AA batteries ruptured when Dade County de-armed the device with its water cannon.

When the bomb components were laid out, Starkey opened the bags. The two galvanized pipe cylinders had been blown open but were otherwise intact. The duct tape that had joined the pipes had been scissored but was still in place. She assembled the pieces. Some would no longer fit together, but she had everything close enough.

As Starkey placed her gloved hands on the components, she felt the substance of them. These were the same pieces of metal and wire and tape that Mr. Red had touched. He had acquired the raw components, cut them, shaped them, and fitted them together. Starkey knew that a bomb was a reflection of the person who built it, as individual as his face or his fingerprints.

Mr. Red was proud of his work to the point of arrogance. He was meticulous, obsessive. His person would be neat, as would his home. He would be a coward. He would only let out his rage through the perfect devices he constructed. He would see the devices as the self he wished to be—powerful, unstoppable. He was a creature of habit because structure gave him comfort.

Starkey examined the wiring, noting that where the wires were joined, each had been connected with a bullet connector of a type available in any hobby store. The connector sleeves were red. The wires were red. Mr. Red wanted people to see him.

Starkey put the bullet connectors under a magnifying glass and used tweezers to remove the clips. She found that the wire was looped around the connectors three times in a counterclockwise direction. No bullet connectors from Riggio's bomb had been found, so she had nothing to compare them with. She shook her head at Mr. Red's preciseness. Every wire, three times, counterclockwise. The structure gave him comfort.

Starkey examined the threads cut into the pipe ends and the white plastic plumber's tape that had been peeled away. She hadn't removed the tape from Riggio's bomb, because she hadn't thought it necessary, but now she realized that this was a mistake. The plumber's tape was a completely unnecessary part of the bomb, and therefore potentially the most revealing. It occurred to Starkey that if Mr. Red liked to write messages, he might write them on the tape, which had started out as a clean white surface.

She examined the tape fragments that the ATF people had stripped, but found nothing. The tape, designed to be crushed to make the pipe joint airtight, had been shredded when it was removed. Even if something had been written there, she couldn't have found it.

Deciding to examine the tape from the remaining joints, Starkey used a special wrench with a rubber mouth to unscrew the end cap of the first pipe. The plumber's tape was cut deep into the threads. She brought the magnifying glass over and, using a needle as a probe, worked around the root of the threads until she found the end of the tape. She worked the tape for almost twenty minutes before she got it free. She found no writing. She removed the end cap on the other pipe, then went to work on the second tape. Ten minutes later Starkey was unpeeling the tape when she realized that both joints had been wrapped the same way. Mr. Red had pressed the tape onto the top of the pipe, then wrapped away from himself, winding the tape over and down and around before bringing it under the pipe and back up again. Clockwise. Just as he had wound the wire to the bullet clips the same way every time, he had wrapped the plumber's tape to the threads the same way every time.

Starkey suspected that Mr. Red had a reason for wrapping the tape clockwise around the pipe threads. It bothered her that she didn't see it. She pretended to hold the pipe and wrap it, pretended to screw on the end cap, and she saw Mr. Red's reason. He wrapped the tape clockwise so that when he screwed on the end cap—also clockwise—the tape would not unwind and bunch. If everything went clockwise, the cap would screw on more easily. It was a small thing, but Starkey was beginning to see how his mind worked, and that meant she could beat him.

Starkey decided to check the taping on the sweatshop bomb but found only a fragment of an end cap. There would be a sample of joint tape in the threads, but not enough to tell her the direction of the winding. She went downstairs to the bomb squad, looking for Russ Daigle. He was in the sergeants bay. He smiled when he saw her.

"Listen, Russ, we got an end cap off Riggio's bomb, right?"

Daigle nodded. "Yep. Got one intact and a piece of another. I showed you the joint tape, remember?"

"You mind if I unscrew the end cap of the one that's intact? I want to look at the tape."

"You can do whatever you want, but it's going to be hard."

He brought her out to his workbench, where the pieces of the Silver Lake bomb were locked in a cabinet. Once Chen had released them, they were Daigle's to use in the reconstruction.

"See here? The pipe is still mated to the cap, but they bulged from the pressure, so you can't unscrew them."

Starkey felt her hopes sag. The pipe had been distorted into the shape of an egg. There was no way to unscrew the cap. "Can I take it upstairs and play with it?"

Daigle shrugged. "Knock yourself out."

Starkey brought the pipe upstairs, fit it into a vise, then used a high-speed saw to cut it in half. She used a steel pick to pry the inner pipe halves away from the outer cap halves, then fitted the two inner pipe halves together again in the vise.

It took Starkey almost forty minutes to find the end of the tape. Later she realized that it took so long because she thought it would be wrapped overhand like the tape on the Miami device. It wasn't. The tape on this joint had been wrapped underhand.

Counterclockwise, not clockwise.

Starkey stepped away from the bench. She flipped through the report that had been sent from Rockville and saw that it had been written by a criminalist named Janice Brockwell. She found a phone, called the ATF's National Laboratory, and asked for Brockwell. When Janice Brockwell came on, Starkey identified herself and explained what she had found on the Miami hoax device.

"That's a pretty cool notion, Starkey. I don't think we paid attention to the tape."

"Could you do me a favor and check the other Mr. Red bombs? I want to know if they match."

"You say the tape is wound clockwise, right?"

"Yeah. I want to see if the others match."

"I don't know how many intact end caps we have. Tell you what, Starkey. Let me look into it, and I'll get back to you."

Starkey gave Brockwell her number, then returned the bomb components to their boxes and locked them beneath the lab bench.

STARKEY arrived back at Spring Street with ten minutes to spare. She found Marzik and Hooker in the squad room but decided that she didn't have time to tell them about the Miami bomb. They could hear it when she went over it for Kelso.

She said, "Is Morgan here yet?"

"In there with Kelso. Dick Leyton's in there, too."

"Why are you guys still out here?"

Marzik looked miffed. "Kelso asked us not to attend the meeting. He probably thinks his office will look smaller with too many bodies in there."

Starkey thought Marzik's guess was probably true.

Santos reported that he had spoken with the postproduction facility and had some good news. "Between all the tapes," he said, "we've got pretty much of a three-hundred-sixty-degree view of the area around the parking lot. If our caller is there, we should be able to see him."

"When can we have the tape?"

"Day after tomorrow. We're going to have to go see the tape on their machine for the best possible clarity."

"Okay. That's something." Starkey popped a Tagamet, steeled herself, then knocked on Kelso's door.

Kelso answered with his smarmiest smile. He introduced her to Assistant Chief of Police Christopher Morgan, an intense, slender man sporting a charcoal suit. He shook her hand, bypassing pleasantries by asking her to bring him up to date.

Starkey briefed Morgan on the Silver Lake bomb, how it had

been detonated, and how they knew that the builder had been on the scene within one hundred yards. She also briefed him on Mr. Red. It took her less than five minutes to describe everything that had been done, including their development of Claudius as a possible source of information about RDX and Mr. Red.

"So what's the line of your investigation?"

"The components. Modex Hybrid is an elite explosive, but it's not complicated to make if you have the components. TNT and ammonium picrate are easy to come by, but RDX is rare. The idea now is to use the RDX to backtrack to whoever built the bomb."

Morgan seemed to consider her. "What does that mean, whoever? I thought it was understood that Mr. Red built the bomb."

"We're working under the assumption that he did, but we also have to consider that someone else might have built it."

Kelso frowned. "What are you talking about, Starkey?"

Starkey described comparing the joint tape from the Miami device with the tape from the Silver Lake device. She explained that the bombs linked to Mr. Red were all designed and constructed in the same way. "The difference in the Silver Lake bomb is small, but people like Mr. Red are creatures of habit."

Dick Leyton appeared thoughtful. "Was the direction of the tape noted in the seven earlier bombs?"

"I called Rockville and asked about it. No one thought to check the direction of the wrapping before."

Morgan crossed his arms. "But you did?"

Starkey met his eyes. "You have to check everything, Chief. I'm not saying we have a copycat; the security around the Mr. Red investigation has been tight. All I'm saying is that I found this difference. That bears consideration."

Starkey wished she'd never brought it up. Morgan was frowning, and Kelso looked irritated.

Leyton was the only one in the room who seemed interested. "Carol, if this were the work of a copycat, how would that affect your investigation?"

"It expands. If you assume that the Silver Lake bomb wasn't

built by Mr. Red, you have to ask who did build it? Who knows enough about Mr. Red to duplicate his bombs? Then you start to wonder, why copycat Mr. Red?"

Morgan heard her out, his face an impenetrable mask. When she was done, he nodded. "Those are fine questions you raise, Detective Starkey. But considering what we know, your copycat theory seems like a long shot. Long shots are enormous time wasters. All the evidence seems to point to Mr. Red."

"The tape was just something that didn't fit, that's all." Her voice came out defensive and whiny.

"Well, as long as we don't get sidetracked chasing theories that don't pan out. Keep your investigation moving forward. Investigations are like sharks. If they stop moving forward, they sink."

Starkey nodded. "It will move forward, Chief. We're going to get Mr. Red."

Morgan and Leyton left. Starkey wanted to follow them, but Kelso stopped her.

He closed the door. "Carol, forget this copycat business. It sounds like nonsense."

"It was an observation, Barry. Did you want me to ignore it?"

"It made you sound like an amateur."

JOHN Michael Fowles bought the 1969 Chevelle SS 396 from a place called Dago Red's Used Cars in Metairie, Louisiana. Bought it because the damned thing was red. A red car from Dago Red's for Mr. Red. John Michael Fowles thought that was a riot.

He paid cash, using money he had made from a bombing for hire in Miami, then drove to a nearby mall, where he bought new clothes and a brand-new Apple iBook, also for cash.

John was curious to learn what the ATF had made of his little love letter in the Dade County Library. He had been moving steadily since then, working Claudius to locate a new source of RDX, but was now anxious to read the alerts that had been written about him in the ATF and FBI bulletins. He knew that his little stunt at the library would not place him on the ten most wanted list, but he expected that field offices around the country would be buzzing with alerts.

John carried his purchases out to the big 396, then drove back to the Blue Bayou Motel, where he had acquired a room for twenty-two dollars.

Once in his room, John plugged the new iBook into the phone line and dialed up AOL. Typically he would sign on to Claudius to read what the geeps posted about him, and sometimes he would even pretend to be someone else, dropping hints about Mr. Red and enjoying his mythic status. John ate that stuff up: John Michael Fowles, urban legend, rock god. Using the name and account number from a stolen Visa card, he joined AOL, signed on to the Internet, then typed in the URL address for a website he maintained under the name Kip Russell. The website, housed in a server in Rochester, Minnesota, was identified by a number only and had never been listed on any search engine. It was a storage facility for software.

John Michael Fowles traveled light. He moved often and usually carried no more than a bag of cash. He was without real property, bank accounts, and credit cards (except those he stole or bought for temporary use). Wherever he relocated, he acquired the things he needed, paid cash, then abandoned them when he moved. One of the things he often needed but never carried was software.

Before John built bombs, he wrote software. He hacked computer systems, networked with other hackers, and was as deeply into that world and its ways as he was into explosives. With the software that waited for him in Rochester, he could open doors into credit card companies and banks, telephone systems and the National Law Enforcement Telecommunications System, including the FBI's Bomb Data Center, the ATF's National Repository, and some branches of the Defense Department, which he often scanned for reports of munitions thefts.

When John had accessed his website, he downloaded an assault program named Oscar and a clone program named Peewee. The downloading took about ten minutes, after which John hand-dialed the phone number for a branch of Bank of America in Kalamazoo, Michigan, and used Oscar to hack into their system. Peewee piggy-backed on Oscar and, once in the B of A system, cloned itself into a free entity that existed only within the B of A branch in Kalamazoo. Peewee, from Kalamazoo, then dialed into the ATF's National Repository. As expected, Peewee was stopped at a gate that demanded a coded password. Peewee then imported Oscar to assault the gate. Start to finish, the process took two minutes and twelve seconds, whereupon John Michael Fowles, also known as Mr. Red, had access to everything within the government's database of information on bombs and bombers.

The most recent entry was from Los Angeles, which surprised John. It should have been from Miami.

Curious, John opened the file and learned that an LAPD bomb technician named Charles Riggio had died in a Silver Lake parking lot. The last lines hit him with all the impact of a nuclear device.

Analysis finds residue of the trinary explosive Modex Hybrid.
Initial evidence suggests that the perpetrator is the anonymous bomber known as "Mr. Red."

Modex Hybrid. For a crazy, insane moment he wondered if he had built the bomb and somehow forgotten it, laughed aloud at that, then grabbed the iBook and his bag of cash and ran out of the motel.

He barreled the big red SS 396 along the edge of Lake Pontchartrain, stopping on the side of the causeway long enough to throw the iBook into the water, then drove like hell all the way to the airport. He put the car in long-term parking, wiped down the interior and doors to remove his fingerprints, then paid cash for a one-way ticket to Los Angeles.

No one knew better than John Michael Fowles what it took to make Modex Hybrid or how to find those things within the bomb community. Somebody had stolen his work, which meant someone was trying to horn in on his glory.

John Michael Fowles was not going to tolerate that.

CHAPTER
6

JOHN Michael Fowles got off the plane with twenty-six thousand dollars, three driver's licenses, and four credit cards.

Just being in Los Angeles made him smile. He loved the dry sunny weather, the palm trees, the good-looking babes in their skimpy clothes, the cool people, the slick cars, the hunger for wealth, the movie stars. It was a great place for devastation.

First thing he did was rent a convertible, strip off his shirt, slip on his shades, and cruise up Sepulveda Boulevard, looking good. He was past his mad now; now was the time for cold calculation and furious vengeance. Mr. Red had arrived.

John dropped the redneck persona and went black. He loved white guys who acted black. He bought oversized clothes from a secondhand shop in Venice, a new iBook, and the other things he needed, then took a room at a small motel called the Flamingo Arms. He shaved his head, draped himself with faux gold chains, then signed on to the Internet. He searched for news stories on the Silver Lake bomb, finding three pieces. The first two articles contained pretty much the same thing: the LAPD bomb squad had rolled out to investigate a suspicious package, whereupon Officer Charles Riggio, thirty-four, was killed when the package exploded. The detective leading the investigation, a woman named Carol Starkey, was quoted as attributing the bomb, which she called "a crude, poorly made device," to "an infantile personality." He laughed when he read that.

John was intrigued by the third story, about Starkey herself. She had been a bomb tech until she had been caught in an explosion. The article said that she had actually died but had been revived at the scene. He was fascinated by that.

In the final paragraph Starkey vowed to find the person or persons responsible for Riggio's death.

John smiled. "Not if I find the bastard first."

He dumped the news stories and went to his website in Rochester, where he found the phone number of a man he knew as Clarence Jester, who lived in Venice. Jester owned a pawnshop but was also an arsonist. Now in his late fifties, he had once served twelve years of federal time for starting fires. John had found Jester an excellent source of information about those in the bomb community.

"Clarence. It's LeRoy Abramowicz, my man. I'm in L.A. Thought I might swing by and do a little business. That cool?"

"I guess."

Anxious to get going, but hungry, John scarfed a burger on the way, ambling into Clarence Jester's pawnshop a few minutes later. Jester was a small, nervous man with thinning hair.

"Hey, Clarence. Let's go for a walk."

Business was always done outside, and Jester closed the shop without a word. Outside, he eyed John carefully. "You look different."

"I went black. Everybody's doing it."

In addition to being an arsonist, Jester bought and sold explosives and extreme pornography. John knew that whoever duplicated his bomb would have had to mix their own Modex Hybrid, which meant they would have had to acquire RDX. "Clarence, I'm looking for a little RDX. You help me with that?"

"Nobody has RDX. I got some TNT and PETN, though."

"Gotta be RDX."

"I can't help you with that."

"That's you. There's gotta be someone. Hell, this is L.A. Just point the way, Clarence. I find what I'm looking for, I'll kick back a finder's fee to you."

"The RDX is ringing a bell."

"There you go."

"Just a few years ago there was a fellow up north who got busted for blowing up cars. He was using RDX. I can maybe put you in touch with him."

John began to feel jazzed. "A customer of yours?"

"He didn't get the RDX from me, I'll tell you that."

Clarence proceeded to tell him about a man named Dallas Tennant, who was now serving time. "You can talk to him on Claudius."

"In prison?"

"You wouldn't believe the stuff I did when I was in prison."

"Do you know Mr. Tennant's screen name?"

"Got it in my computer. Hey, you heard the big rumor we got out here? They're saying Mr. Red came to town, blew up some cop in Silver Lake."

WHEN the last of the inmates had left the library, Dallas Tennant gathered the magazines and books from the tables. Mr. Riley, the civilian employee who managed the library, turned out the light in his office and left, thanking Dallas for his good work.

Inmates at Atascadero had enormous freedom, but there was still oversight. Dallas could work late at the library but was required to stop by the infirmary for his nightly meds. If he didn't report there by nine p.m., the duty guard would set about finding him.

Dallas checked the time. A guard would be along in about twenty minutes to see if Dallas was where he was supposed to be. Dallas went into Riley's office, then recovered the software diskette that he kept hidden behind Riley's file cabinet.

Though Atascadero was a modern facility and was linked to the California prison system via the Internet, no computer that prisoners could access was supposed to have Internet software installed.

Dallas had acquired his own software, arranging for his attorney to pay his monthly service charges from his rental income. He loaded the software onto Riley's hard drive, connected the modem to the phone line, and signed on. When he was finished for the evening, he would uninstall.

In moments Dallas Tennant was home again. Claudius. It was the one place where Tennant felt comfortable. His only friends were there, other anonymous screen names with whom he shared posts in the public areas and often chatted in the secret chat room. Tennant posted under the name Boomer.

He was scanning a message board thread he had created about

Mr. Red's appearance in Los Angeles when a messaging window appeared on his screen: "Will you accept a message from Neo?"

Tennant did not know a Neo, but was curious. He clicked to accept, and the instant-messaging window opened.

> NEO: You don't know me, but I know you.
> BOOMER: Who are you?
> NEO: Someone who admires your use of RDX. I want to discuss it.

Tennant, like all habitués of Claudius, was careful never to post anything incriminating outside of the secure chat area.

> BOOMER: Good night.
> NEO: Wait! You want to meet me, Dallas. I am giving you an opportunity tonight that others only dream about.
> BOOMER: How do you know my name?
> NEO: I know many things.
> BOOMER: You think highly of yourself.
> NEO: *You* think highly of me, Dallas. You have written many posts about me. Come to the chat room. I'm there now.

This changed things. If Neo had a key to the chat room, then someone had vouched for him. He was as safe as safe could be in this uncertain world. Tennant used his own key and opened the chat-room window. It was empty except for Neo.

> BOOMER: Who are you?
> NEO: I am Mr. Red. You have something that I want, Dallas. Information.
> BOOMER: What do you have to trade?

As soon as Starkey walked through her door that night, she regretted agreeing to let Pell come to her home. There was nothing in the house to drink except gin, tonic, and tap water. You could write your name in the dust on top of the television. She grabbed a shower, then dressed in jeans and a black T-shirt.

Anxious to see if Claudius would yield anything useful, Starkey set up the laptop on her dining-room table. She had just turned it on when she heard Pell's car in her drive.

When she opened the door, Pell was carrying a pizza and a white bag. "I hope you didn't make dinner. I've got pizza and antipasto."

"I've got a duck baking."

"I guess I should've called."

"Pell, I'm joking. My usual dinner is a can of tuna fish and some tortilla chips. This will be great."

She brought the food into the kitchen, feeling embarrassed that there was nothing to drink. She wasn't even sure she had clean dishes. "You don't drink gin and tonic, do you?"

"Maybe some tonic without the gin. Where's the computer?"

"It's in the dining room. You want to eat first?"

"We can eat while we work."

Starkey filled two glasses with ice and tonic. She felt a fierce urge to add gin to her glass but resisted.

As she got out plates and silverware, she considered telling Pell what she had learned about the plumber's joint tape, but she decided against it. She would wait until she heard from Janice Brockwell. She didn't want Pell to dismiss her the way Kelso had.

They brought their antipasto and pizza into the dining room and put two chairs together, just like in Bergen's office. Then Starkey signed on to Claudius.

They had posted three messages, two expressing enthusiastic admiration for Mr. Red, one asking if the rumor that Mr. Red had struck again in Los Angeles was true. This last message had drawn several responses, most of which doubted Mr. Red's appearance. As Starkey was concentrating on the posts, Pell reached across her and took the mouse. "Hang on. I want to read the last one again."

In the moment when his hand covered hers, she drew away from him as if she'd received an electrical charge, then felt herself flush with embarrassment. She covered it by taking back the mouse and asking, "What did you see?"

"Read it."

SUBJECT: Re: Truth or Consequences
FROM: AM7TAL

My sources inform me that The Man recently laid waste in Florida. History tells us that he waits awhile between gigs. Anybody got some Modex for sale? Ha ha. Just kidding!

Starkey reread the message. "You think he's Mr. Red?"

"No. He's talking about buying Modex, but Mr. Red buys the components and mixes his own. Let's post back to this guy, saying we could probably help him out with some RDX."

"Throw bait on the water."

"Yes. For him, and anyone else reading this stuff."

Pell turned the keyboard and shifted in his seat. His right arm touched her left. Starkey didn't jerk away this time; she let the touch linger. She glanced at Pell, but he seemed lost in composing the message.

SUBJECT: Re: Truth or Consequences
FROM: HOTLOAD
I might be willing to share some RDX for the right price.

They posted the message, and Pell closed the laptop. "I don't want you to think I'm telling you what to do, but could I ask you to run another NLETS search on the RDX?"

"I did, and the only name that comes up is Tennant."

"We've already gotten what we're going to get from him."

"Maybe from Tennant, but not from Tennant's case."

"What does that mean?"

"I reread Mueller's case notes. It's clear that he didn't need to find Tennant's shop or recover additional explosives to make his case, so he let a lot of stuff slide. His notes indicate that he didn't spend much time with Tennant's landlady or Tennant's employer, so there still might be something to find."

"That's good thinking, Starkey. That could pay off."

Starkey realized that she was smiling at Pell and that he was smiling back.

The house was silent. With the computer off, Starkey was all the more aware that she and Pell were alone. She wondered if he felt that, too, and suddenly wished for other sounds: the television, the radio, a car on the street. But there was only the two of them, and she didn't know what to do with that.

She abruptly cleared the plates, taking them into the kitchen. "Thanks again for the pizza. Next time's on me."

When the plates were in the sink, she returned to the dining room but didn't go to her chair. She didn't offer more tonic, and hoped it was apparent that she wanted Pell to leave.

She wedged her hands in her pockets. "So I guess we'll check back tomorrow. I'll call you about it."

Pell finally stood. She walked him to the door. "I'll see you, Pell."

"Good night, Starkey."

As soon as he stepped through the door, she shut it. She felt stupid and confused. She was still feeling that way when she went to bed, where she stared at the ceiling in the darkness and wondered why she felt so lost.

IN HIS motel Pell was staring at the computer when the monsters floated up out of the keyboard like writhing worms swarmed by fireflies. He stumbled into the bathroom, wet some towels with cold water, then lay on the bed, the cool towels on his face. His head ached from a pain so great that it left him gasping, and fearful.

He wanted to call Starkey, and he cursed himself for that. Every time they were together, he saw a deeper side of her, a surprising side, and his guilt was growing because of it. He hadn't counted on liking her. He hadn't counted on her liking him. It ate at him. But there was nothing to be done for it.

After a time the pain passed and his vision cleared. He climbed off the bed and went back to the computer. He pushed the guilt he felt about Starkey to the side and opened the door into Claudius. Her name had been on the bomb. Mr. Red wanted her. He could work that. Pell used a different screen name, one that Starkey didn't know, and began to write about her.

THE NEXT MORNING STARKEY was the first detective in the office as usual. Hooker arrived at five after seven; Marzik drifted in about twenty minutes later.

Marzik was stowing her briefcase when she glanced over. "How'd the big meeting with Morgan go?"

"He told me to keep the case moving forward."

Marzik dropped into her seat. "I hear you floated some notion about Silver Lake being a copycat. I'm kinda curious when you were planning on telling me and Hooker about it."

Starkey explained about the Miami device and the difference she had found in the direction of the tape. "I wanted to talk it over with you guys today. I didn't get a chance yesterday."

"Well, whatever."

Ignoring Marzik, Starkey scooped up the phone and called Warren Mueller in Bakersfield. When he came on the line, she explained that she had reason to believe that Tennant had a shop and more RDX also.

Mueller's voice was stiff. "What reason? If he's got a shop, we couldn't find it."

"Tennant told us the same thing he told you, that he salvaged the RDX from a case of Raytheon antipersonnel mines. That's six mines."

"Yeah. That's what I remember."

"Okay. Now, I'm looking at the pictures of these three cars you sent, and most of the damage seems to be from fire. I ran an energy calc on the RDX, and it seems to me that if he had used a third of his load on each car, the damage would've been much greater than it was. That implies to me that Tennant had more RDX."

Mueller's tone was defensive. "We searched that rathole he was living in. We had his car stripped. We searched the old lady's house and her garage, and I even had the Feebs bring out a damned dog for the flower bed, so don't try to make out that I screwed up."

"I'm not trying to make out anything, Mueller. Only reason I called is that there aren't many notes here from your interviews with his landlady or employer."

"There was nothing to write. She didn't want to talk to us."

"What about Tennant's employer?"

"He said what they all say, how surprised he was. We're not stupid up here, Starkey. Just remember, Tennant is sitting in Atascadero because I made my case. When you make yours, call me again."

He hung up before she could answer. Starkey slammed down her phone and shuffled through the casework. Tennant's landlady had been an elderly woman named Estelle Reager. His employer had been a man named Bradley Ferman, owner of a hobby shop called Robbie's Hobbies. She called them both, learning that Robbie's Hobbies was out of business. Estelle Reager agreed to see her.

Starkey gathered her purse and stood. "Come on, Beth. We're going up to Bakersfield to talk to Tennant's landlady."

ESTELLE Reager lived in a prewar stucco home south of Bakersfield. Mrs. Reager, who bore the lined, leathery skin of a woman who had spent much of her life in the sun, answered the door wearing jeans, a checked shirt, and work gloves.

Starkey introduced herself and Marzik.

Mrs. Reager eyed them. "A couple of women, huh? I guess none of the lazy men down there wanted to drive up."

Marzik laughed. When Starkey saw the twinkle that came to Estelle Reager's eye, she knew they were home free.

Mrs. Reager showed them through the house and out the back door to a patio. The driveway ran along the side of the house to a garage, behind which sat a small, neat guesthouse.

Marzik went to the edge of the patio to look at the guesthouse. "Is that where Tennant lived?"

"Oh, yes. Dallas lived there for four years, and you couldn't ask for a better young man. He was always considerate and paid his rent on time."

"It looks empty. Is anyone living there now?"

"No. It's so hard to find quality people in this price range, you know. May I ask what you're hoping to find?"

Starkey explained her belief that Tennant still had a store of bomb components.

"Well, you won't find anything like that here. The police searched high and low. But if you want to look through his things, help yourself. They're all right there in the garage."

Marzik looked at the garage, then at Mrs. Reager. "These were things that were here when the police searched?"

"Oh, yes." Mrs. Reager said that Tennant had continued to pay rent on his guesthouse for the first year he was in prison, but that he had finally written to her, apologizing that he would have to stop and asking if she would store his things. There were only a few boxes.

Starkey asked the older woman to excuse them and walked with Marzik to the garage.

"We're okay if we go into the garage, because it's her property," Starkey said. "But if we go into his boxes and find anything, we could have a problem."

"You think we need a search warrant?"

"Of course we need a search warrant."

Starkey went back to the landlady. "Mrs. Reager, I want to be clear on something. These things in your garage, they are things that the police have already looked at?"

"Well, they were in the guesthouse when the police came. I would guess they looked."

"All right. Now, you said that Tennant asked you to store his things. Did you pack them?"

"That's right. He didn't have very much, just clothes and some of those adult movies, which I threw away."

Starkey decided that there was nothing to be gained by searching the boxes. Her real hope was in identifying people with whom Tennant might have stored his components well before the time of his arrest. "Did you know any of his friends or acquaintances?"

"No one ever came here, if that's what you're asking. Well, I take that back. One young man did come by a few times. They worked together at that hobby shop."

Marzik said, "Did Tennant have any family?"

"Only his mother. She died, though. Dallas was heartbroken."

Starkey wasn't thinking about the mother. Something about the boxes bothered her. "Tennant continued paying rent to you for a year, even after he was in prison?"

"That's right. He thought he might be released, and he didn't want me to rent the house to anyone else."

Starkey glanced over at Marzik, and Marzik nodded. They were both wondering why Tennant didn't want to give up his apartment even when he had no use for it. Finally it came to Starkey. "Mrs. Reager, here's a guy who worked at a hobby shop. He couldn't have made much money. How do you figure he could afford paying rent while he was in prison?"

"Well, I don't know. His mother died just the year before all that mess came up. Maybe he got a little money."

They thanked her for her cooperation and went back to their car. Starkey started the engine, letting the air conditioner blow.

Marzik said, "Well, that was a bust."

"I don't know. I'm having a thought here, Beth. When Tennant's mother died, he could have inherited property or used the money to rent another place. I'll bet Mueller didn't run a title search."

It would take a day or two to run the title check, but they could have a city prosecutor arrange it through the Bakersfield district attorney's office. If something was identified, Bakersfield would handle the warrant. Starkey felt better as they drove back to Los Angeles, believing that she had something that kept her investigation moving forward.

"AND you are?"

"Alexander Waverly, attorney. I phoned about Mr. Tennant."

The guard inspected the California State Bar card and the driver's license, then handed them back, making a note in his log. "Right. You're Dallas Tennant's new attorney."

"Yes, sir. I phoned to arrange the interview."

"Okay, please sign here. I'll have to inspect your briefcase, and then you come around here through the metal detector, okay?"

He signed the register, careful to use his own pen, careful not to touch the counter or anything else that might be lasered for a fingerprint. The guard inspected his briefcase; then he passed through the metal detector, smiling at another guard who waited on the other side. He followed this second guard to another building. He was aware that a security camera had recorded him. The videotape would be studied and his picture reproduced, but he had confidence in his disguise. They would never recognize his true self.

John Michael Fowles was delivered to a small interview room where Dallas Tennant was waiting. Tennant was seated at a table, his good hand resting on a thick scrapbook.

The guard said, "You've got him for thirty minutes, Mr. Waverly. You need anything, I'll be down the hall."

John waited until the door was closed, then set his briefcase on the table. He gave Tennant a big smile, spreading his hands. "Ta-*da!* Mr. Red, at your service."

Tennant slowly stood. "This is . . . an honor. An honor. There's no other way to describe it."

Tennant offered his hand, but John didn't take it. He found his personal hygiene lacking. When Tennant realized that John wasn't going to shake hands, he pushed the heavy book across the table. "I'd like to show you my scrapbook. You're in here, you know?"

John ignored the book. He slipped off his suit coat, folded it over the back of the chair, then unbuckled his belt. "We'll get to the book, but first tell me about the RDX."

Tennant said, "Did you bring it? What we talked about?"

"Mr. Red is a man of his word, Dallas. Remember that. I expect you to be a man of your word, too. You're not gonna get carried away and brag to anyone that Mr. Red came to see you, are you?"

"Oh, no, never. If I told, you wouldn't come see me again."

"That's right." John smiled, absolutely certain that Dallas Tennant couldn't go the week without telling someone of their encounter. John had planned for that.

"You know, the police were already here. They came about the RDX. I didn't tell them anything."

"Good."

"One of them was a woman. Her name was Carol Starkey. She brought an ATF agent named Pell or Tell, something like that."

"Jack Pell."

Tennant looked surprised. "You know him?"

"You might say that. But you just forget about them. We got our own little business here, you and me."

John dropped his trousers, pulled down his shorts, and untaped two plastic bags from his groin. One contained a thin gray paste, the other a fine yellow powder. He placed them on top of Tennant's book. "This oughta wake 'em up around here, you set it off."

Tennant massaged each bag. "What is it?"

"Right now, just a couple of chemicals. You mix 'em together with a little ammonia like I'm gonna tell ya, and you'll end up with ammonium picrate, a very dangerous explosive."

John figured that Tennant had heard of ammonium picrate but probably had no experience with it. He was counting on that.

"Isn't that what they call Explosive D?"

"Yeah. Powerful as hell. You ever work with D before?"

Dallas put the bags aside. "No. How do I detonate it?"

John smiled widely, pleased with Tennant's ignorance. "Now, you just tell me who has the RDX, Dallas; then I'll tell you how to mix these things. I'll give you the power of life and death, right there in those little bags."

Dallas Tennant stuffed both bags down the front of his pants, then told Mr. Red who had the RDX.

ONCE John was in his car and past the security gate, he pushed hard toward the freeway. He had made Tennant promise not to mix the components for at least two days, but he knew that a goof like Tennant would mix the damned stuff as soon as possible. John was counting on that, too, because he had lied about what the chemicals were and how they would react.

They weren't Explosive D, and they were anything but stable. It was the only way he had to make sure that Tennant kept his mouth shut.

CHAPTER
7

STARKEY woke at her usual early hour. She made a cup of instant coffee, then drove to Spring Street. She was organizing her casebook when her phone rang. "Detective Starkey."

"It's Warren Mueller, up here in Bakersfield. Your people had our city attorney run a property check on Tennant's mother, a woman named Dorthea Tennant."

"That's right."

"You scored, Starkey. I'm standing outside the place right now. The old lady died owning a duplex up here that's still in her name."

Starkey felt a tremendous rush of energy. Marzik walked in as Mueller was saying it. Starkey waved her over, cupping the mouthpiece to tell her the news. "It's Bakersfield. We got a hit, Beth. Tennant has property."

Marzik pumped her fist.

Starkey said, "Listen, Mueller, you need to have your bomb squad roll. There might be explosive materials on the site—"

Mueller cut her off. "We're two jumps ahead of you, Detective. You didn't just score on the property; you got his shop. Our bomb people are securing the location now."

"What do you have, Sergeant?"

"This place his mother owned is a little duplex house. One's empty, but the other has people living in it. There's a converted garage in back. Tennant kept it locked. That's where he kept the goods."

"You find the RDX?"

"Negative on the RDX, but we got some TNT."

"We're hoping that there might be evidence that links Tennant with his source for the RDX. This has a direct bearing on the Silver Lake investigation, Mueller. If you find anything that gives us a trail, I want it secured."

"Will do, but there's more. These people in the house said they had a prowler out back about a month ago."

"Wait. Someone went into the shop?"

"They didn't see him enter or leave the building. All they saw was some guy looking around. The old man who lives in the duplex called out, but the guy takes off over the fence. My wit says it looked like he was carrying something."

"You're thinking the RDX?"

"Well, if there *was* RDX inside, he could have taken it."

"You get a description?"

"White male between forty and fifty, five ten to six feet, one eighty, baseball cap, sunglasses."

"Sergeant, we have a similar suspect from Silver Lake. If we fax our likeness up there, would you run it past those people, see what they say?"

"You bet."

"Give me your fax."

Starkey passed the number along to Marzik, then got back to Mueller. "One more thing. Was there any sign of forced entry?"

"No. Tennant had the place padlocked. Nothing was forced. So if this guy went in there and took the RDX, he had a key."

Starkey said, "This is good work, Sergeant. This is going to help us down here."

Mueller laughed. "I guess me and you're just about the best two cops ever to strut the earth."

Starkey smiled as she hung up.

Marzik said, "Are we detectives or what?"

Starkey asked Hooker to see about getting them a look at the enhanced tape. She wanted to see it as quickly as possible because the similar description of the man in the baseball cap gave weight to their 911 caller as the bomber.

As Hooker set it up, Starkey filled in Kelso, then paged Jack Pell. She wanted to share the news with him, which surprised her. She left her own pager number as the return.

The postproduction facility was a block south of Melrose, in an area saturated with used-clothing stores. Starkey and Santos drove over together, and a thin young man named Miles Bennell met them in the lobby.

Bennell escorted them along a hall past editing bays and into a dark room with a console facing a bank of television monitors.

"How much tape do we have?" Starkey asked.

"Eighteen minutes."

Starkey was surprised. "Out of almost six hours we got just eighteen minutes?"

Bennell sat at the console and pushed one of the buttons. The center TV monitor flashed with color bars. "If the only people who were in the shot were the two bomb squad guys, we cut it. That was most of the tape. We only get to see bystanders when the cameras changed angles or the helicopters rotated out of position."

"Okay, so what are we going to see?"

"Short clips. Anytime an angle caught a view of the crowd or the people hiding behind buildings, we clipped them. That's what we enhanced. You're looking for a man in a baseball cap and sunglasses, right?"

Starkey put the likeness drawing on the console for Bennell to see. "That's right, wearing a long-sleeved shirt."

Bennell continued adjusting his console. "We've got a couple guys in caps. Let's see what they look like. I can go as fast or slow as you like. We can freeze frame."

He pressed a button and the tape started, revealing several people clumped behind the cordon tape by the Cuban restaurant.

Santos pointed at a figure. "Here. Man here in a cap."

Bennell froze the tape. Starkey counted eight people in this slice of the crowd. The man Santos pointed out was wearing a red or brown cap with the bill forward. Lester Ybarra had described a man in a blue cap, but Starkey knew that it was easy to misremember a color. Because of the angle it was impossible to see if the man was wearing sunglasses or a long-sleeved shirt.

Starkey said, "Let's advance it and see what happens. I want a look at this guy's arms if we have it."

Bennell twisted a large dial to advance the frame. Twelve seconds into the shot, the man in the hat turned to look at the man behind him and could be seen wearing a short-sleeved shirt.

They worked back and forth through the tape for almost an hour. Finally Starkey called a cigarette break and was standing in the parking lot, smoking, when her pager buzzed. She felt a jolt of excitement when she saw it was Pell.

She called him from her car and told him what Mueller had found in Tennant's shop. Then she said, "Pell, listen, you got the pizza last time. I'll do dinner tonight."

"What time you want me over there?"

"How about seven?"

When they ended the call, Starkey asked herself what in hell she was doing. She hadn't intended to get together with Pell.

She returned to the editing bay. Watching the eighteen minutes of enhanced tape took almost two hours. By the time they finished, Starkey was satisfied that they had a fairly complete picture of everyone within one hundred yards, the maximum range of the radio transmitter. But she was also disappointed because the man in the baseball cap was not to be found.

They finished on a shot that showed Riggio over the bomb in the instant before the detonation. Buck Daggett was by the Suburban.

Santos looked crestfallen. "I was sure he would be here."

"He is, Jorge. Somewhere. He has to be here somewhere."

Bennell seemed as disappointed as Santos. "He could be sitting on the sidewalk behind one of these cars, and we'd never see him."

Starkey knew that wasn't likely. The representative from the radio-control manufacturer had said that the transmitter had to "see" the receiver, which meant that it had to have a clear line of sight.

Starkey knew that Mr. Red had to be somewhere. The only question was, where?

JOHN Michael Fowles was perusing the stacks of the Beverly Hills Library. He knew where to find the remains of the RDX now and would soon recover it, though that would keep for a day or two.

Tennant had been helpful that way, the creepy doof. John hated the socially disgusting fingerless misfits like Dallas Tennant who inhabited his world. They gave serious explosives hobbyists a bad name.

After John had learned what he needed to know about the RDX, he had enjoyed hearing about Carol Starkey. He even looked in Tennant's book just to see the articles on Starkey. After he had finished with Tennant, John had driven back to Los Angeles and here to the library. He spent several hours reading old newspaper stories about Starkey, wondering if she was as good a bomb technician as the stories portrayed.

John was fascinated that Starkey had actually been killed by a bomb and had then returned from death. To have been so close to the blast, to have felt it press over her body like some insane kiss. He marveled at the experience. He thought that he and Carol Starkey might be soul mates.

When he left the library, John returned to his room at the Bel Air Hotel, a romantic bungalow renting for eight hundred dollars per night, thanks to his latest American Express card. He signed on to Claudius. The past few days he had noticed an increased number of posts about himself and about RDX. Several of the posters were even spreading the rumor that Mr. Red was behind Silver Lake. John didn't like that. Now that he knew Tennant had told Starkey and Pell about Claudius, he realized what was happening: Starkey thought that he had killed Riggio and was baiting him. She had fallen for the copycat's ploy. John was both annoyed and elated. He enjoyed the idea of Starkey trying to catch him.

He read through the new posts and found that they were no longer only about him. Many were about Starkey.

The last post intrigued him:

SUBJECT: Showdown

FROM: KIA

If anyone can take Red down, it's Starkey. I heard he already tried to get her, and missed. Ha. You only get one shot.

Good-bye, Mr. Red.

John wondered what Kia had heard that made him think Mr. Red had tried to kill Starkey. She was becoming the star, and he was becoming . . . the other guy.

He dialed on to his site in Minnesota. When he had the software he wanted, he hacked into the local telephone company and downloaded Carol Starkey's address.

JOHN Michael Fowles entered Carol Starkey's home through the bathroom window. He moved quickly through the house and found her laptop on the kitchen table. The computer was what he wanted. He booted it up and was surprised when only one icon appeared on the screen. It hit him then; Starkey didn't know a thing about computers. When Tennant told them about Claudius, Pell must have set her up through the feds.

It only took moments after that. John hooked his Zip drive to the laptop, installed the necessary software to copy her files, then uninstalled the software to remove all traces of what had happened. Later, at the hotel, he would open her files to confirm the screen name that she used on Claudius.

Now he was inside her house. When he had her screen name, he would get inside her mind.

ON HER way home Starkey stopped at a Ralphs market, where she picked up a roasted chicken, mashed potatoes, and some diet soda. When she was waiting in line, it occurred to her that Pell might not drink soda, so she picked up a quart of milk, a bottle of merlot, then added a loaf of French bread. She couldn't remember the last time she'd had a dinner guest.

The traffic moving out of downtown was brutal, and Starkey was late getting home. Pell was already there, parked in front of her house. He got out as she pulled into her drive and walked over to meet her. She got out with the bags, but when she saw the expression on his face, she wanted to reach for her Tagamet.

He looked as if he wasn't sure if he wanted to be here. "Help you with those?"

She gave him one of the two bags, telling him about Bakersfield as she let them into the house. When she told him that a man was seen at Tennant's shop who could have been the same man making the 911 call, Pell seemed interested, but when she described the suspect as a man in his forties, Pell shrugged. "It's not our guy. Mr. Red is younger."

"Maybe our guy isn't Mr. Red."

Pell's face darkened. "It's Mr. Red."

Starkey felt herself growing irritated at Pell's certainty. She thought again of telling him about the joint tape, but she still wanted to wait for Janice Brockwell. "Look, maybe we shouldn't talk about it. I think we've got something good here, and you're dumping on it."

"Then maybe we shouldn't talk about it."

They put the two bags on the counter near her sink. Starkey took a deep breath, then faced him. She decided that the only way to survive the evening was to get it out in the open. "Tonight is a date."

Pell looked uncomfortable. He searched her eyes, then stared at the bags. "I don't know about this, Carol."

Now she felt humiliated. "I've got to tell you, I feel really stupid right now, so if you think I'm as stupid as I'm thinking I am, I wish you would leave."

"I don't want to leave. Why don't we put these things away and have dinner?"

He worked for several minutes while she stood there. Finally Starkey pitched in, taking freshly washed plates and silverware from the dishwasher. Some date. Nobody was saying anything.

Starkey put the chicken and mashed potatoes to one side and took out a knife to cut the chicken, thinking she should have got a salad. She felt thoroughly dispirited, which Pell seemed to read.

He said, "Why don't I help? I'm a pretty good cook."

"I can't cook for anything."

"Well, since the chicken's already cooked, you probably can't mess it up too badly. All we have to do is put it on plates."

Starkey laughed. Her body shook with it, and she feared she

might cry, but she refused to let herself. Pell came to her, but she held up a hand, stopping him. She knew that doors were opening. Maybe because of what had happened to Riggio, but maybe just because it had been three years and she was ready. She thought, then, that it didn't matter why. It just was.

"I'm not very good at this, Pell. I'm trying to let myself feel something again, but it isn't easy."

Pell stepped closer and put his arms around her. She tensed, but he did nothing more than hold her. Slowly she relaxed, and when her arms went around him, he sighed. It was as if they were giving themselves over to each other. Part of her wanted it to grow into more, but she wasn't ready for that.

"I can't, Jack."

"Shh. This is good."

Later they brought the food into the dining room. She asked him about the ATF and the cases he worked on, but he often changed the subject or turned his answer into a question.

Later still, when the dishes were cleaned and put away, he stepped away from her, still awkward, and said, "I guess I should go. I hope we can do it again."

Starkey laughed. "You must be a glutton for punishment."

Pell stopped in the door and seemed to struggle with what he wanted to say. He had been struggling for all of their time together, and now she wondered why. "I like you, Starkey."

She felt herself smile. "Do you?"

"This isn't easy for me either. For a lot of reasons."

She took heart in that. "I like you, too, Pell. Thanks for coming by tonight. I'm sorry it got kinda weird."

Pell stepped through the door and was gone. Starkey listened as his car pulled away, thinking that maybe a little weirdness was good for people.

STARKEY finished straightening the kitchen, then checked her messages at work. Warren Mueller had called.

"Hey, Starkey, it's Warren Mueller. I ran that crappy picture you faxed past the old man at Tennant's place. He thought they kinda looked alike, white guy around forty, the hat and the glasses. I'm gonna have our artist work with him, see if we can't refine the picture. We get anything, I'll fax it down. You take care."

She hung up, thinking that their picture might be crappy, but everyone was seeing someone who looked more or less like the same guy and nothing like Mr. Red.

Starkey decided to check Claudius. She signed on and noted that several people had responded to their post about RDX, though no one offered to buy or sell it.

She was reading when a message window appeared on her screen: "Will you accept a message from Mr. Red?"

A tingle of fear rippled up her back as she opened the window.

> MR. RED: You've been looking for me.
> HOTLOAD: Who is this?
> MR. RED: Mr. Red.
> HOTLOAD: That isn't funny.
> MR. RED: No. It is dangerous.

Starkey went for her briefcase. She looked up Pell's hotel number and called him there. Getting no answer, she phoned his pager.

> MR. RED: Are you calling for help, Carol Starkey?

She stared at the words. She knew that it couldn't be Pell; he didn't have a computer. It must be Bergen. Bergen was the only other person besides Pell who knew about Hotload.

Starkey's phone rang—Pell calling back.

She said, "I think we've got a problem with Bergen. I'm on Claudius. This window just pops up, and whoever it is knows that I'm Hotload. He says that he's Mr. Red."

"It must be Bergen. I'll see about him tomorrow."

> MR. RED: Where are you, Carol Starkey?

When Starkey put down the phone, the message was hanging there, waiting. She made no move to respond.

MR. RED: Okay, you're not having any, so I will be gone. I will leave you with the World According to Mr. Red. I did not kill Charles Riggio. I know who did. My name is Vengeance.

JOHN Michael Fowles signed off Claudius and broke the cell phone connection through which he had signed on to the Internet. He was in his car, parked just up the block from Starkey's house, in the dense shadows of an elm tree heavy with summer leaves. He could see the lights in her windows. He watched.

DALLAS Tennant carried the ammonia in a paper cup, pretending it was coffee. He was walking very quickly because he was anxious to get to his cell and make the explosive. True, he had promised Mr. Red that he would wait for a few days, but Dallas would have mixed the Explosive D yesterday as soon as Mr. Red had gone if he had had the ammonia and a detonation system. He didn't, so this morning when Mr. Riley was gone for lunch, Dallas had signed on to the Internet and printed out pornographic pictures from websites in Thailand. He had traded the photographs for the ammonia and the match heads and cigarettes he would use as a detonator.

Dallas reached his cell, then huddled at the foot of his bed with the two plastic bags and the cup of ammonia. Mr. Red's instructions were simple: Pour the ammonia into the bag with the powder, mix it well until the powder was dissolved, then pour that mixture into the bag with the paste. This mixture would stiffen to a tacky paste, and the explosive would be active.

Dallas poured the ammonia into the first bag, zipped the top, and kneaded it to dissolve the powder. He planned to set it off in one of the metal garbage cans behind the commissary. Just thinking about the can coming apart made him aroused.

He opened the second bag, added the powder solution, then sealed the top. He kneaded the second bag, and the contents grew warm and turned bright purple.

Tennant was concerned. After he had downloaded the pornography, he had web-searched a couple of explosives sites and read about ammonium picrate. Both articles had described ammonium picrate as a white crystalline powder, not a purple paste.

Tennant stopped kneading. Two thoughts flashed in his mind. One, that Mr. Red couldn't have been wrong; this must be ammonium picrate. Two, that some explosives don't require a detonator. Dallas had read about substances that explode just by being mixed together. There was a word for reactions like that, but Dallas couldn't remember it.

He was still trying to recall that word when the purple substance detonated, separating his arms and rocking Atascadero so deeply that all the alarms and water sprinklers went off.

The word was hypergolic.

CHAPTER

8

STARKEY'S phone rang. It was Janice Brockwell, calling from the ATF lab in Rockville, Maryland. "Hi, Detective. In the seven bombing events that we attribute to Mr. Red, we have six usable end caps. I broke the six and determined that the joint tape was wrapped in a clockwise direction each time."

"They were all wrapped in the same direction?"

"Clockwise. That's right. We're going to include this as part of Mr. Red's signature in the National Repository."

Starkey's heart pounded. If Mr. Red wrapped the joint tape in the same direction every time, why had the Silver Lake bomb been wrapped in the opposite direction?

Brockwell said, "You did good, Detective Starkey. Thanks."

Starkey put down the phone. She was excited. The Silver Lake bomb *was* different.

If the bomb was different, you had to ask why? And the most obvious answer to that was also the most terrible. Because a different person had built it.

Starkey knew bombs; she knew bombers. She decided that Mr. Red would not change his profile, even to taunt the police. The very fact of his signature screamed that Mr. Red wanted the police to be absolutely certain with whom they were dealing.

The feds had multiple suspect descriptions, all of which said Red was a man in his late twenties. Yet Lester Ybarra had described a man in his forties, as had the old man in Tennant's duplex. If Mr. Red had not built the Silver Lake bomb, then someone else had, someone who had gone to great lengths to make it appear to be Mr. Red's work. Starkey finally said the word to herself: copycat.

Copycats were most common in serial killer and serial rapist crimes. Hearing frequent news coverage of such crimes could trigger the predisposed into thinking they could get away with a one-shot homicide, using the copycat crime to cover a motive that was far removed from an insane desire to kill or rape. The copycat almost always believed that the cover of the other crimes would mask his true intent, which was typically revenge, money, or the elimination of a rival. In almost all cases the copycat did not know the full details of the crimes, because those details had not been released.

Yet this copycat knew all the details of how Mr. Red constructed his bombs except for the one thing that had never appeared in the bomb analysis reports: the direction in which Mr. Red had wrapped the plumber's tape. The pool of suspects who knew the components of Mr. Red's bombs and how he put them together was small.

Bomb cops.

Starkey took out her cell phone. She caught Jack Pell at his motel. "Pell? I need to see you."

They agreed to meet at Barrigan's. Starkey wanted to see him with an urgency that surprised her, and it occurred to her that she might be falling in love with him.

Even at ten in the morning Barrigan's was loaded with cops. Starkey shoved through the door and, when she saw Pell sitting at the same table where they had sat before, felt a flush of warmth.

He flashed a smile, clearly pleased to see her.

"Jack, it's time for you to take the case."

"What are you talking about?"

"I'm talking about the ATF taking over the investigation into Charlie Riggio's murder. I cannot carry it forward, Jack. I now believe that what happened in Silver Lake involves the Los Angeles Police Department."

"You think one of your people is Mr. Red?"

"I don't think Mr. Red is behind this."

Pell took her hand. "Hold on. I spoke with some people about Bergen this morning. Bergen was with other clients last night at the time you called me. You had Mr. Red last night, Carol. We've got the bastard. We can use this to bring him in."

"That can't be. He knew my name. He knew that Hotload is Carol Starkey. How could Mr. Red know that?"

Pell answered slowly. "I don't know."

"He told me he didn't kill Riggio. He said he knew who did."

Pell stared at her. "Is that what this is about? He tells you he didn't kill Riggio, and you believe him?"

"He didn't build the Silver Lake bomb."

"Did he tell you that, too?"

She told him about the call from Janice Brockwell, and how the Silver Lake bomb differed from every other bomb that had been attributed to Mr. Red.

Pell's voice took on a note of impatience. "It's just tape."

"Wrong, Jack, it is forensic evidence, and it shows that this bomb is different in the one way that no one knew about, because it has never been in any of the bomb analysis reports. He cut Riggio's name in the bomb to make us think it was Mr. Red."

Pell stared at the bar. "It's Mr. Red. Trust me on this. Every investigation turns up contradictory evidence. You've grabbed onto a few small bits, and now you're trying to turn the whole investigation. It's Mr. Red. That's who we're going to catch. Mr. Red."

"You're not going to help me, are you?"

"I want to help you, but this is the wrong direction. It's Mr. Red. That's why I'm here, Starkey. Mr. Red."

The warm feelings that she had felt were gone.

It should have helped, she later thought, that he seemed to be in as much pain as she, but it didn't. She was alone with it. She told herself that was okay; she had been alone for three years.

"Pell, you're wrong."

She walked out and drove back to Spring Street.

STARKEY settled into her cubicle and opened the casebook. One of the pages contained a list of all police officers at the Silver Lake parking lot on the day Riggio died. She felt surreal looking at the list. These were friends and co-workers. Starkey removed the page from the binder, made a copy, then put it back in the book.

The drive north to Glendale happened in slow motion. Starkey wasn't a homicide investigator, but she knew the first rule of any homicide investigation: Look for a link between the victim and the killer. She would have to look to Charlie Riggio and hope that something in his life would lead to who killed him. She felt sick about Pell. She was sure that he felt something for her but no longer trusted her certainty.

Starkey pulled into the police parking lot but did not leave her car. She stared at the modern brick bomb squad building and hoped that she was wrong about what the plumber's tape meant.

"How're you holding up, kiddo?"

Starkey nearly jumped out of her skin. "You scared me."

"I saw you sitting out here and thought you saw me. If you're coming in, you can walk with me."

Dick Leyton was smiling his kindly smile, the tall, benevolent older brother. She got out and walked with him because she didn't know what else to do.

"Has Charlie's desk been cleared yet?"

"Buck came by and boxed it for the family. Charlie had two sisters. Did you know that?"

"No, I didn't."

Leyton and Starkey walked together into the squad room, where Russ Daigle pointed out the box of Riggio's things beneath his desk. Starkey carried the box into the suit room, where she could be alone. Buck Daggett had packed carefully. The street clothes that Riggio had probably worn to work on the day he died were neatly folded. A cell phone was wrapped in a black T-shirt to keep it safe. Starkey finished with the box in less than ten minutes. She was hoping for a desk calendar or daybook that might give her an insight into Riggio's life, but there wasn't anything like that.

She brought the box back out to the squad room and stowed it beneath Riggio's now empty desk.

STARKEY left Glendale without knowing where she would go or what she would do. Leyton had said that Riggio had two sisters. She decided to start there.

Every casebook included a page on the victim. Starkey looked up the page and saw that Riggio was the middle child between two sisters, Angela Wellow and Marie Riggio. Angela lived in Northridge, which wasn't far from Charlie's apartment in Canoga Park. Marie lived south of Los Angeles in Torrance.

Starkey phoned Angela Wellow, identified herself, and expressed her condolences.

Angela's voice was tired. "You worked with Charlie?"

Starkey explained that she had, but that now she was a bomb investigator with the Criminal Conspiracy Section. "Angela, I'm calling because you live so close to Charlie's. We think he had some files at home on two other cases. We need them back. Could you meet me at his apartment and let me see if I can find them?"

"Charlie had files?"

"Bomb reports on older cases. We need them."

A note of irritation crept into Angela's voice. "When do you have to do this?"

"I'm available now. The sooner the better from our end."

They agreed to meet in an hour.

It took Starkey almost that long to get to Northridge. Riggio's apartment building was three blocks south of the Cal State campus. Starkey left her car in a red zone, then went to the glass security doors where she and Angela had agreed to meet.

A thin young woman opened the door and looked out. She was carrying a little boy who couldn't have been more than four. "Are you Detective Starkey?"

"That's right."

Angela Wellow must have parked beneath the building and entered through the inside. Starkey followed her through a central courtyard and up a flight of stairs to a second-floor apartment. The little boy's name was Todd.

"I hope this won't take long. My older boy gets home from school at three."

"It shouldn't, Angela. I appreciate your help."

Riggio's apartment was nice, a two-bedroom loft with a high arched ceiling and an expensive big-screen television. The couch was lined with large boxes.

Angela put down her little boy, who ran to the television. "What do your files look like? Maybe I've seen them."

"They're three-ring binders. They're probably black." Starkey cringed at the lie.

Angela stared at the boxes. "These are his clothes, mostly, and things from the kitchen. Charlie didn't keep anything like an office. There's his bedroom upstairs."

"Do you mind if I look?"

"No, but I don't have very long." Angela picked up the little boy and showed Starkey up the stairs.

More boxes waited on the floor, some empty, others partially filled. A dresser stood against one wall, a jumble of pictures wedged into the mirror frame.

"Is this your sister?"

"That's Marie, yes. These here are our parents."

Todd upended a box and climbed inside. Angela sat on the bed, watching him.

Starkey used her body to block Angela's view as she went through the boxes. There was a heavy photo album that she wanted to look through, but nothing else of interest. Starkey finished with the boxes, then went through the dresser and the closet without finding anything helpful. "Well, maybe I was wrong about those reports. Maybe Charlie didn't bring them home after all."

Angela had been saying how she was in a hurry to get home, but now she lingered. "Detective, could I ask you something? Were you and Charlie girlfriend and boyfriend?"

"No. I didn't know Charlie had a girlfriend."

"He had a girlfriend, but he never brought her to meet us. My parents were always after him, you know, when are you going to get married, when do we get to meet this girl?"

"What did Charlie say?"

Angela seemed embarrassed. "Some of the things he said, I got the impression she was married. It happens, right? I think she was married to someone Charlie worked with."

Starkey said, "I'm sorry. I don't know anything about that."

She wondered if the photo album held pictures of a woman who was married to someone else.

Angela suddenly glanced at her watch and jumped up. "Now I really am late. I'm sorry, but I have to go."

"It's all right. I understand."

Starkey followed Angela down, but now her mind was racing for a way to get a view of Riggio's photo album.

Todd was tired and cranky, and by the time they reached the door, he was squirming in his mother's arms. When Starkey saw the time Angela was having with him, Starkey took the keys. "Here, I'll get the door. That boy's a handful."

"It's like trying to hold a fish."

Starkey held the door to let Angela through. She pretended to lock the door as she closed it, but unlocked it instead, then placed the keys in Angela's purse.

Angela saw Starkey to the glass doors. Starkey walked out to her car, climbed behind the wheel, but did not start the car. Her heart was hammering. What she was about to do was insane. Worse, it was illegal.

Five minutes later Angela appeared in a white Honda Accord, turned south, and drove away. Starkey crossed back to the apartment building just as a young man was wrestling a mountain bike through the glass door. Starkey held it for him.

She walked calmly to the second floor, let herself into Charlie Riggio's apartment, and went directly to the box with the photo album. She found the album but didn't dare look at it there. She also grabbed a pile of what looked like phone bills.

She took the bills and the book, this time locking the door behind herself, and hurried down to her car. She drove straight home.

It was near the end of the album that Starkey found a picture taken at last year's bomb squad Chili Cookoff. She found a second like it taken at the Christmas party, and then a third that had been taken at a CCS Fourth of July barbecue. Starkey peeled the pictures from the album, asking herself if they could really mean what she thought they meant.

The pictures were all the same, a man and a woman, arms around each other, smiling, a little too close. Charlie Riggio and Suzie Leyton. Dick Leyton's wife.

STARKEY poured a tall gin and tonic and drank most of it. Leyton being a suspect was too big to get her arms around. She decided to deal with it as if Leyton were just another part of the investigation. She went to her own collection of pictures and found a shot of Leyton she'd taken at an LAPD Summer Festival Youth Camp. She brought it to Kinko's, made several copies, then returned home and phoned Warren Mueller.

"I've got a favor to ask, Sergeant. I have a photograph that I want you to show the old man who lives in Tennant's duplex."

"Is it the guy in the hat?"

"It could be. Here's the thing. I don't want anyone else to see the picture. I don't want to tell you any more than that, and I am asking you not to ask."

"All this makes me wonder who's in your picture."

"It's someone who would be hurt badly by this if I'm wrong, and I might be wrong."

"This guy in your picture— He's LAPD, isn't he?"

Starkey couldn't bring herself to speak.

"Okay. Okay, I'll take care of it. You fax up your picture. I'll go wait by the machine. If you're expecting to use this I.D. in court, I'm gonna have to make up a six-pack."

The suspect picture was never shown to witnesses by itself; the courts ruled this to be leading. Detectives were required to show a spread of pictures, hoping that the witness would identify the right one.

"That's fine," Starkey said. "One more thing. If we get a confirmation from your wit, I'll want to see Tennant about this."

Mueller cleared his throat. "I guess you didn't hear. Tennant's dead. Blew his damned arms off and bled to death."

"He blew off his arms? His arms were separated?" The energy it took to do that was tremendous. "What did he use, Mueller? You can't make anything like that out of cleaning products."

"Guess we'll know in a day or two."

Starkey was slow to speak. "I'll fax that picture now. I owe you one, Sergeant. Thanks."

Starkey gave Mueller a minute, put the photocopy of Leyton through her fax, then headed over to her computer. She lit a cigarette, turned on the computer, and signed on to Claudius. The chat room was empty. She waited for almost two hours, and then Mr. Red contacted her.

Starkey opened the window and typed a question.

HOTLOAD: Who killed Riggio?

MR. RED: If I tell you, it will spoil the surprise.

HOTLOAD: I already know. I just want to see if our answers match.

MR. RED: If you knew, you would have made an arrest. You might suspect, but you don't know. I will tell you a secret, though. Just between you and me.

HOTLOAD: What?

She waited, but nothing came back. She realized that he wanted her to beg. His need to manipulate and control was textbook.

HOTLOAD: What's the big secret, Crimson Boy? I'm on a timer here.

MR. RED: It isn't about Riggio. It will scare you.

HOTLOAD: WHAT?????

MR. RED: Pell is not who he seems. He is using you, Carol Starkey. He has been playing us against each other.

The statement came from nowhere, striking her like a board.

HOTLOAD: What does that mean, Pell is not who he seems?

No answers came back. The window hung there, unchanging. Starkey's first impulse was to phone Pell, but she felt caught between them, Mr. Red on one side, Pell on the other.

During the days when Starkey served on the bomb squad, the ATF had maintained a liaison agent with LAPD named Regal Phillips. Starkey called Phillips, explained her doubts about Pell, and asked if he could look into the situation for her.

Phillips told her that it might take a day or two but that he would call back. Starkey thanked him, then hung up and doused the lights. She did not sleep. She didn't even get into bed. She stayed on the couch in the dimness, wondering how a man she now trusted so little could mean so much to her.

EARLIER that day, when Pell left Barrigan's, he sat in his car, trying to figure out what to do. The look of hurt on Starkey's face had left him feeling like a dog. He knew that she was right: He was so obsessed by Mr. Red that he couldn't see anything else, but he had the fragment with her name on it. He had wanted to reach across the table and tell her everything. He had wanted to open himself, because he had also been closed, and thought that she might be the only one who could understand. He had wanted to tell her of his growing feelings for her, but there was only Mr. Red.

STARKEY left her house just after dawn. She had had it with the emptiness of her life, the conflicting thoughts about Pell and Dick

Leyton. She told herself to get her head in the case, so she made her way across town to Spring Street.

She needed to determine Dick Leyton's whereabouts at the time of the blast and thought that his time of arrival might have been noted in the casebook, but all it said was that Leyton was present. Starkey decided to ask Buck Daggett. She left CCS before the other detectives arrived and made her way to Glendale.

Starkey found Buck and Russ Daigle in the shed, the brick building at the rear end of the parking lot, where the squad practiced with the de-armer and the robot. They were standing over the robot, drinking coffee. Both men smiled when they saw her.

"Buck? Could I see you for a moment?"

Buck joined her at the door, the two of them stepping outside. She told him that she had come about the enhanced tape. That was her excuse for the conversation.

"I'll look if you want, but I don't know if I can stomach seeing Charlie like that."

She wanted to turn the conversation to Leyton. "There's no rush. Maybe I should ask Dick if he saw anything."

Daggett nodded. "He was back there behind the cordon."

Starkey felt sick. She told herself to be professional. This is why she was a cop. "When did he get on scene?"

"I dunno, maybe twenty minutes before Charlie went out."

"I'll talk to him about it."

Starkey walked back across the parking lot, feeling dizzy. Nothing fit anymore. She stared at the bomb squad building. The box with Charlie Riggio's things was still beneath his now empty desk. She thought of Riggio's cell phone there. If he and Susan Leyton had been lovers, he would probably have called her often, and there would be the record of it in his phone bills.

She got in her car and drove home.

STARKEY opened Charlie Riggio's phone bills, and there it was, so obvious that it jumped out at her. She didn't know the Leytons' home number, but she didn't need to know it. Charlie had called the same number in the same 323 area code two or three times every day, going back for months.

Starkey put the bills aside, took out her own phone, and dialed.

A familiar woman's voice answered. "Hello?"

"Hello, Susan."

"I'm sorry. Who?"

"This is Carol Starkey. I'm calling for Susan Leyton."

"Oh, hi, Detective Starkey. You dialed the wrong number. This is Natalie Daggett."

CHAPTER

9

NATALIE Daggett said, "Are you still there? Hello?"

"I'm here, Natalie. Sorry. I was expecting someone else. Are you going to be home for the next hour or so?"

"Buck isn't home. He went back to work."

"I know. I'll be stopping by to see you."

"What do you want to see me about?"

"I'm working on a little surprise for Buck. Because of what happened to Charlie. Sort of a welcome back party."

"Is that why you were calling Susan?"

"That's right. I'll see you in a few minutes."

"Oh. Oh, okay."

Starkey closed her phone. Not Dick, but Buck Daggett. She had searched the tapes for the killer again and again, and he was right there in plain sight, waiting for his partner to get over the bomb.

Starkey made the long drive to Monterey Park in good time. She didn't hurry. She was confident that Natalie did not know that her husband had murdered her lover. Still, Starkey was relieved when she pulled into the Daggetts' drive and saw that Buck's Toyota 4Runner wasn't home. She rang the bell.

Natalie looked drawn when she answered the door. Starkey followed her into a small dining room, where they sat at a bare table.

"What kind of surprise did you have in mind?"

"Natalie, I'm not here about a party. I went through Charlie's things, and I need to ask you about these." Starkey took the phone bills from her purse and put them on the table. She could see the fear rise when she mentioned Charlie's name. "These are Charlie's cell phone bills. You see your number there? You see how many calls he made? Natalie, were you and Charlie having an affair?"

Natalie nodded as her nose turned red and tears bled from her eyes. "Since last year."

"Does Buck know?"

"Of course not. He would be so hurt."

Starkey took back the telephone bills. "I'm sorry I had to ask."

"Are you going to tell Buck?"

Starkey stared at the woman, then lied. "No, Natalie. You don't have to worry about that."

BUCK Daggett didn't like it that Starkey had been spending so much time in Glendale. Her asking so many questions about that bastard Riggio made him nervous.

Buck had been proud of himself that he'd built in the connection between Mr. Red and Starkey. He had wanted to keep the investigation as far from Riggio as possible, but just his luck the only piece of her name that had been found was the damned S, letting them think it was part of Charles. Still, he'd thought everything was going to be fine when everyone started chasing their tails about Mr. Red, but now it looked as if Starkey had tumbled to the truth anyway. Or at least suspected it.

Buck Daggett had been out in the shed with the robot when Natalie called. The stupid bim couldn't help telling him that Starkey was coming by because they were going to toss a surprise party for him. Ha. Buck had hung up and raced home to see for himself.

As Starkey drove away from his house, Buck crouched in his neighbor's yard, watching her. He didn't know how much she had on him yet, but he knew she suspected him, and that was enough. Buck decided to kill her.

STARKEY PHONED MUELLER from her car, trying to catch him at his office, but he was gone. She left word on his voice mail that the man in the photo was no longer a suspect and that she would be faxing up a new image.

She phoned Beth Marzik next. "Beth, I want you to get together a six-pack and meet me at the flower shop. Call Lester and make sure he's there. I want a mix of Anglos and Latins in their forties. Don't tell anyone, Beth. Just meet me at the shop."

Starkey hung up before Marzik could ask any questions. Time was now a factor. Natalie might tell Buck about her visit. She didn't fear that Buck would flee; her concern was that he would move to destroy evidence.

She drove fast, swinging past her house for a snapshot of Buck Daggett before turning toward Silver Lake. When she reached the flower shop, Marzik and Lester were on the sidewalk.

Marzik left Lester and walked over as Starkey got out of her car. She had the six-pack sheet in a manila envelope. "You want to tell me what's going on here?"

"Let me see the sheet."

The six-pack was like a page from a photo album with places for six photographs. Detective bureaus kept files of them based on age, race, and type. Starkey pulled out one of the six pictures, then fitted in the picture of Buck Daggett.

Marzik gripped Starkey's arm. "Tell me you're joking."

"I'm not joking, Beth."

Starkey brought the sheet to Lester and asked if any of the men pictured was the man that Lester saw using the telephone.

Lester pointed out Buck Daggett. "I think it's him."

Marzik walked away.

"Is she okay?"

"She's fine, Lester. Thanks."

Starkey joined Marzik and laid it out for her. Then she called Kelso, telling him that they were on their way in.

When they reached Spring Street, Kelso was waiting behind his desk. Santos was on the couch.

Kelso said, "What is it, Carol?"

"It isn't Mr. Red, Barry. It was never Mr. Red." Starkey took it one step at a time, never mentioning Buck Daggett until the end. She went through the difference in the bomb devices, then the similarities, explaining that the builder would need to find a source of RDX in order to mix the Modex Hybrid that Mr. Red favored.

"RDX is the hardest of the components to find, Barry. The only person in this area in recent history who's had any was Dallas Tennant. Beth and I found Tennant's shop. A man similar in description to the individual who made our nine-one-one report was seen there about a month ago. I believe he went there for Tennant's RDX. I don't know how this man learned of Tennant's shop. I don't know if he discovered it the way Beth and I did, through a property search, or if he made a deal of some kind with Tennant. We can't ask Tennant, because Tennant is now dead."

"What man?"

Starkey handed the six-pack to Kelso and pointed out Buck Daggett's picture. "Lester Ybarra identified that man."

Kelso shook his head and looked up. "He made a mistake."

Starkey put Riggio's phone bills on top of the six-pack. "These are Charlie Riggio's cell phone bills. Look at every phone number I've marked. That's Buck Daggett's home phone number. Riggio and Natalie Daggett were involved. Natalie confirmed this to me less than an hour ago. I believe that Buck found out and murdered Charlie because of it."

Kelso's jaw flexed. "This is terrible, a Los Angeles police officer involved in something like this. We'll have to notify Assistant Chief Morgan, also Dick Leyton. We're not going to roll over there and arrest one of his people without telling him what's happening."

Starkey found herself liking Barry Kelso. She wanted to say something. "Lieutenant, I'm sorry."

Kelso rubbed at his face. "Carol, you don't have anything to be sorry for. I want to tell you that this is good work, but it doesn't seem like the thing to say."

"Yes, sir. I understand."

BUCK STILL HAD ALMOST SEVEN pounds of Modex Hybrid, plus components left over from copycatting Mr. Red's bomb. He concocted an elaborate list of errands to get Natalie out of the house. As soon as she left, he headed for the garage, where he kept the Modex Hybrid in a cooler. He shut the overhead door so no one could see him from the street, then opened the side door that let onto his backyard and turned on a utility fan; Modex vapors were toxic.

The Modex was in a large nonreactive glass jar. It was dark gray in color and looked like window putty. Buck wore vinyl gloves as he laid out the components so as not to leave fingerprints, but also to avoid getting the Modex on his skin. The stuff could kill you just from handling it.

Buck didn't see the kid enter his garage, didn't see the hard thing that knocked him to his knees.

BUCK was never fully unconscious. He knew that something had hit him and that he was hit twice more after he went down. He saw the kid over him, but he couldn't raise his arms to protect himself. The kid handcuffed him to the workbench, then disappeared from view. Buck tried to speak, but his mouth didn't work. He grew frightened that he was paralyzed, and cried.

After a while the kid came back and shook him. "You awake? C'mon, I didn't hit you hard enough to kill you."

"I don't have any money."

"I don't want your money, dumbass. You should be so lucky, I only wanted your money."

"Then what do you want? You want the truck, take it."

"What I'm going to *take* is the rest of this Modex. What I *want* is to teach you a lesson."

Buck wasn't thinking at his best. This kid was white, but he was made up like some kind of black rapper. It surprised him that he would know about the Modex. "I don't understand."

The kid leaned close. "You stole my work, you bastard. You pretended to be me. Can you spell error in judgment?"

"I don't know what you're talking about."

"Maybe this will help you understand."

The kid went to the bench. When he came back, he had one of the pipes. Wires led into an open end; the other end had been capped. He waved it under Buck's nose to let him catch the sharp smell of the Modex. "*Now* do you know who I am?"

In that moment Buck knew. "Please don't kill me. Please. Take the Modex and go. I'm sorry I pretended I was you, but I had to kill that sonofabitch who was screwing my wife and—"

Mr. Red put a hand over Buck's mouth. "Listen."

Mr. Red sat cross-legged on the concrete in front of Buck, holding the bomb in his lap as if it were a playful kitten. "You listening?"

"Yes."

"I'm seriously pissed off you tried to make everyone think it was me who killed that guy, but here's your shot. You got one shot, and here it is. What does Carol Starkey know?"

JOHN walked out to the stolen car he'd left on the street. He had left Buck at his bench, very much alive but unconscious. John had splashed some water on Daggett and slapped his face to bring him around. When he saw that Buck was waking up, he left.

John climbed behind the wheel, started his car, and shook his head. It was a hot day on a crappy street in the middle of Shitsville, U.S.A. How could people live like this? He let his car creep down the street as he counted to a hundred. When he reached one hundred, he figured Buck was fully awake.

That's when he pressed the silver button.

MARZIK, Santos, and Starkey sat at their desks, alone with their thoughts. Starkey was about to head for the stairwell with a cigarette when Regal Phillips called. His voice was careful. "You got a problem on your hands, Carol."

"Ah, can I call you right back?"

"Okay. I'm right here."

Starkey hung up, told Santos and Marzik she was going for a smoke, and brought her purse.

When she was in the stairwell, she called Phillips on her cell phone. "What do you mean, that I have a problem?"

"Pell isn't an ATF agent. He used to be, but not anymore."

"That can't be right. Pell had bomb analysis reports from Rockville. He had a spook at Cal Tech doing work for us."

"Just listen. Pell was an ATF field agent working for the Violent Crime Task Force. Twenty months ago he was in a warehouse in Newark, New Jersey, trying to get the goods on some Chinese AKs coming up from Cuba. You read those reports he gave you? Think Newark."

"Mr. Red's first bomb."

"Pell was in that warehouse when it went off. The concussion caused something in his eyes called *commotio retinae*. You catch it in time, you can fix it with the laser. Pell's didn't show up until later, and then it was too late."

"What does that mean, too late?"

"He's going blind. So the ATF retired him. You got a rogue agent on your hands, Carol. He's hunting down the bastard who took his eyes. You call the field office and get them in on this before Pell hurts somebody."

Starkey leaned against the wall, feeling numb. "I'll take care of it, Regal. Thank you."

After she ended the call, Starkey finished her cigarette. She went back into the squad room just as Kelso's door opened.

He stepped out and cleared his throat. "Detectives, an explosion occurred at Buck's home. He was pronounced dead at the scene."

BY THE time they reached Daggett's home, the fire was out and the sheriff's bomb investigators were already walking the scene. Starkey wanted to walk with them, but the commander of the sheriff's bomb squad refused to clear her onto the site until the body had been removed. Only Kelso was allowed in the garage.

Starkey, Marzik, and Santos stood in a tight knot in the front yard, Santos talking to burn off the nervous energy. "Do you think he killed himself?"

"I don't know." Starkey's first thought had also been suicide, but that was something they might never know unless Daggett had left a note.

After a while Kelso came up the drive and joined them.

"How many bodies?"

"Just Buck. It looks like Natalie wasn't home. Her car is missing. The thinking now is that it *was* a suicide."

Marzik said, "Why?"

"He spray-painted something on the wall above his workbench. We can't be sure it's a suicide note, but it could be. It says, 'The truth hurts.' "

The coroner investigators wheeled a gurney bearing a blue plastic body bag to their van.

Kelso started back down the drive. "Come on. We can go back now. I want to warn you all that his body was badly dislocated."

Marzik stopped and waved them on. "I don't want to see all that blood. I'm going to stay out here."

The aluminum garage door had been pulled out of its frame by the fire department. Starkey could see that it had been down at the time of the detonation by the way the aluminum panels were bowed outward. The firemen would have wanted to raise it to get water on the flames, but couldn't; they had probably set grappling hooks to pull it away. Inside the garage the sheriff's bomb investigators were sifting and photographing the debris exactly as Starkey and her people had done in Silver Lake.

The spray-painted words were above Daggett's bench: "The truth hurts." They were red.

A half-moon shape like a jagged crown of splinters was blown out of Buck's workbench. Wooden shrapnel sprouted from the inner garage walls like porcupine quills. Much of the bench was charred from the fire, but not the area shattered by the blast.

Starkey turned to one of the investigators and said, "How do you call the scene?"

"Judging from the way he came apart, I'd say he was right on top of it, there at his bench. His lower extremities are fine except for the wood frag they caught. Most of the damage was in his chest and abdomen. He was damn near eviscerated, which suggests he had the device against his stomach when it went off. If it was a suicide, I guess he figured tucking it into his stomach was the way to go. If it was accidental, he was probably setting the leg wires into the detonator and he caught a spark. That would be my guess."

Starkey walked back out onto the drive to consider the scene. The garage door had been bowed, the side door blown out, but the structural damage was minor. She guessed the energy released was about as much as two hand grenades. Big enough, but not on the order of what killed Charlie Riggio.

The side door had been blown off its hinges by the pressure change, which meant the door had been closed. She could understand that Buck would want the garage door closed so his neighbors couldn't see what he was doing, but it didn't make sense that he would close the side door. He was working with either Modex or RDX, and both threw nasty fumes.

Starkey went back inside. "What about his hands?" she asked.

"They were intact. We noted some lacerations and tissue loss, but they were still on."

Starkey couldn't see it. If Buck had committed suicide, she thought that he would have been holding the bomb tight against his body to make sure he died quickly. His hands would have been gone. If he was seating a detonator in the charge and the explosive had set off accidentally, his hands would still be gone.

Kelso called out to her. "Starkey, come over here."

She had an uneasy feeling as she joined Kelso and the others in the yard. She kept thinking about the red paint and that Mr. Red claimed to know who had imitated him. How could Mr. Red know that? From Tennant?

Kelso introduced her to two sheriff's homicide detectives named Connelly and Gerald. Connelly was a large, serious man; Gerald had the empty eyes of a man who had been on the job too long.

Gerald said, "There's something you may be able to help us with. Did you see Sergeant Daggett earlier today?"

"Not today. I saw him yesterday."

Gerald touched the left side of his forehead. "Daggett has a lump here that shows edema and bruising. We're wondering when he got it."

"I don't know. There was nothing like that yesterday."

Starkey wasn't liking this. First Tennant blows up, now Daggett blows himself up. Mr. Red claims he knows the copycat, and how could he know except through Tennant?

She looked back at the garage. "It wasn't a very big charge."

Gerald made a grin like a nasty shark. "You didn't see the body. It blew that poor bastard to shreds."

Starkey forgot about Gerald and spoke to Kelso. "Barry, I got a description from the bomb investigator in there. Daggett shows the injuries because of his proximity, but I don't think it was much of a blast. I can't know for sure how much RDX Tennant had, but it was more than this."

Kelso squinted at her. "Are you saying that some explosive is missing?"

"I don't know."

Starkey walked back to the street to smoke. She kept thinking about Buck's hands. His hands should be gone. She found herself wondering what Tennant had used to blow himself up and how he had gotten it. It took enormous energy to blow a man's arms off. She didn't like the little questions that had no answers. She thought about Pell.

Marzik came up, shaking her head. "Was it bad?"

"We've both seen worse."

"It must have been pretty damned bad. You're crying."

Starkey crushed out her cigarette. "Beth, get a ride back with Kelso, okay? I'm taking the car."

ALL the small, odd things about Pell made sense now; the crummy motel, him needing her to run the NLETS search and the evidence transfer, the way he had lost it with Tennant.

Starkey parked outside the motel and used her cell phone to call him. When he didn't answer after ten rings, she hung up and went inside. She knew Pell's room number from calling him there, found the room, then searched the halls until she found a housekeeper.

"Hi, I'm Mrs. Pell, in one twelve. My husband has both keys. Could you let me in?"

The housekeeper, a young Latina, looked up the room on her clipboard. "Shoe. I let you in."

She keyed the lock, and Starkey entered the room.

A computer was sitting on a spindly desk against the wall. Identical to her computer. She searched the room. She did not know what she was looking for, but she went through the bathroom, the chest, the desk, and Pell's suitcase without finding anything. Then she walked to the closet and searched the clothes there. A plastic Ziploc bag was in the inner pocket of his leather jacket. A piece of frag. She unzipped the plastic, dropped the fragment into her palm, and saw the letters t-a-r-k-e-y.

It didn't matter that it was Buck Daggett who had etched her name to mislead them; Pell thought that Mr. Red had built the bomb. Sitting in Barrigan's, he had *known*. That night in her house, holding her, he had believed that she was the target. And he had hidden that from her.

"What are you doing here?" Pell stood in the door. He looked like a hundred-year-old man.

Starkey held up the bit of black metal. "You bastard."

Pell didn't move. "Carol, I'm sorry."

"What was I, Jack? Bait? All along you thought he was after me, and you didn't warn me?"

He shook his head, his silence making her even more angry.

"It wasn't Mr. Red! Buck Daggett killed Riggio."

"It's Mr. Red."

"Stop saying that. Riggio was having an affair with Buck's wife, so Buck killed him. An eyewitness in Bakersfield put Buck at Tennant's shop. That's where Buck got the materials to make the bomb. We were on our way to arrest Buck when he was killed in his own garage with those same materials."

"Is that why you came here, Starkey? To tell me that?"

"No. I know that you're not on active duty anymore, and I know why. I'm sorry about your eyes, Jack, but I'm going to tell Kelso about you. He's going to call the ATF field office. I wanted you to know it was coming."

Pell started toward her.

Starkey shook her head. "Don't. I have tried for so long to feel nothing, but I opened myself to you, and you used me. Three years, I finally let myself feel again, and it was a lie."

She looked at Pell and saw that tears had filled his eyes. All of this was so much harder than it should have been.

"Good-bye, Jack." Starkey put the fragment bearing her name on the desk, then walked out.

STARKEY signed on to Claudius as soon as she reached home. As she had expected, Mr. Red was waiting for her. She opened the message window.

> MR. RED: Hello, Carol Starkey. I have been waiting for you.
> HOTLOAD: Did you kill him?
> MR. RED: I have smoked much ass in my time. Be specific.
> HOTLOAD: You know who I mean. Daggett. DID YOU KILL HIM?
> MR. RED: Oooo. Now she's shouting. If I answer this question for you, you must answer a question for me. Do you agree?
> HOTLOAD: Yes.
> MR. RED: The truth hurts.

She knew that he had given his answer. He had written that on Buck Daggett's wall. "The truth hurts."

> HOTLOAD: Why? Why did you do this?
> MR. RED: He took my name in vain, C.S. You're smart enough to know that he murdered Riggio, aren't you?
> HOTLOAD: I know what he did.
> MR. RED: Do you know this? He was building a second bomb

when I found him. He was going to do to you exactly what he had done to Riggio.

HOTLOAD: You can't know that.

MR. RED: He gave his confession. Moments before I knocked him out, laid him across the device he had built, and set it off. But you've had your question. Now it's time for mine.

HOTLOAD: All right.

MR. RED: By now you must know that Pell is not who he claims. How does it feel to be used by a man you love?

HOTLOAD: I am going to arrest you.

MR. RED: I am laughing, Carol Starkey. My work here is done. I have enjoyed you. Good-bye.

Starkey knew that there would be no more messages that night. She turned off the computer, then went to her answering machine and played the messages that Pell had left. She played them over and over, listening to his voice. It hurt.

C H A P T E R

10

STARKEY drank for most of the night. At ten minutes after five the next morning she paged Warren Mueller. She was too drunk to give a damn about the time.

Her phone rang twelve minutes later, a groggy voice on the line. "Starkey? Do you know what time it is?"

"Listen, I know how Tennant got the explosives that he blew himself up with. Mr. Red. Red went in there to see him. There's two things you need to do, Warren. First, check the video record for whoever went in there to see Tennant in the past couple of days. And here's the other thing. Get hold of Tennant's scrapbook."

"What are you talking about?"

"Tennant had a scrapbook, Mueller. A collection of clippings about bomb incidents. Anyone who went to see him had to look at it. Get the book and have it printed. There's no way Red went to see him and didn't touch that book."

She gave Mueller the rest of the facts. After that she showered, dressed, and packed up the computer. She would need it when she explained to Kelso about Claudius.

Starkey timed her arrival at Spring Street so that Kelso would be in his office. She asked Marzik and Hooker to join her, knocked on Kelso's door, then pushed her way inside.

Starkey put the computer on his desk. "Barry, there's something I need to tell you, and I want Beth and Jorge to hear it, too. Buck didn't kill himself. Mr. Red killed him."

Kelso frowned at Starkey. "Maybe I'm confused. Weren't you the one who said that Mr. Red wasn't involved here?"

"Mr. Red did not kill Charlie Riggio. That was Buck. Buck copy-catted Red's MO to cover the murder, just like we proved. But Mr. Red didn't like someone pretending to be him. He came here to find that person. He did."

Hooker said, "Carol, how do you know that?"

"Mr. Red admitted it to me through Claudius. Mr. Red and I have been in personal contact for almost a week."

She told them about the entire avenue of the investigation that she had held secret and how, through Claudius, it had led to her contact with Mr. Red. Kelso stopped her only once, when she was telling them about Jack Pell.

"How long have you known that Pell is not a representative of the ATF?"

"Since yesterday, Barry. I'm sorry. I was wrong for playing it this way, and I apologize. But we still have a shot at Mr. Red. I'm sure Buck had more Modex, and I think Red took it. I can contact him again. We can work him, Barry. We can catch the sonofabitch."

Kelso nodded, but he was angry. "We look like fools."

Starkey took a breath. "You don't, Barry. I do."

"That's where you're wrong, Detective. I'm going to call Morgan. I want you to wait outside. Marzik, Hooker, you, too."

Outside, Starkey apologized to Hooker and Marzik.

Hooker nodded glumly, then went to his desk.

Marzik was livid and didn't try to hide it. "If you cost me a promotion, I'm going to kick your drunken ass."

Starkey didn't argue. She sat at her desk and waited.

Kelso's door remained closed for almost forty-five minutes. When it opened, Kelso said, "Starkey, inside."

She had never seen him as angry as he was right now.

He said, "You're suspended immediately. You will be brought up on professional-conduct charges, as well as charges of compromising this investigation. If any criminal charges arise, you will be prosecuted. I advise you to contact a lawyer today."

Starkey went numb. "I know I screwed up, but Mr. Red is still out there. He has more Modex. We can't just end it like this."

"The only thing at an end is you. You're done. The rest of us are going to continue doing our jobs."

Starkey blinked hard, trying to stop the tears. "Please, Barry. Let me stay and help you catch this guy. I can get to him."

Kelso took a deep breath. "You're dismissed."

Starkey moved for the computer. She needed it to get to Mr. Red. "That stays."

She left the computer on his desk and walked out.

STARKEY drove out into the city with no idea of what to do. She had expected that Kelso would punish her, but she never thought he would jerk her from the investigation.

She was lighting a cigarette when her pager buzzed. She recognized Mueller's number by the area code and called him.

"You're gonna be the FBI's cover girl."

"The book?"

"Oh, baby. We got eight out of ten digits, both thumbs. The bastard went in there posing as Tennant's attorney."

"Warren? Is there a surveillance tape?"

"Yeah. And listen to this. We got his I.D.—John Michael Fowles, age twenty-eight. No criminal record. Had his prints in the federal casket because he enlisted in the navy when he was eighteen but washed out as unsuitable. He used to start fires in the barracks."

"Warren, listen, I want you to call CCS down here and give them this information. I'm off the investigation."

"What are you talking about?"

"I screwed up. I'll tell you about it, but I just can't right now. Would you call them, please? They're going to need this."

"Listen, Starkey, whatever you did, they gotta be crazy. I just want you to know that. You're a top cop."

"Will you call them?"

"Yeah, sure, I'll do that. Now you just take care of yourself, okay?"

Starkey said good-bye and closed her phone. John Michael Fowles. She saw him building his next bomb with Buck Daggett's leftover Modex. She wanted to be on that computer with him. She wanted to finish the job she had started, but Kelso had cut her out of it.

There was a way. She opened her phone again and called Pell.

PELL was certain that his pursuit of Mr. Red was at its end. He had been found out, and he was done.

He decided not to run. His retinas would soon detach completely and irreparably—and that would be that. He thought he might wait a day or two, hoping that Starkey and the L.A. cops could bag Mr. Red, and then he would turn himself in.

He felt no loss at missing Mr. Red. That surprised him. For almost two years his private pursuit had been his consuming passion. The loss he felt was for Starkey. The regret he felt was for the pain he had caused her.

Pell checked into a different hotel, then drove aimlessly until he found himself at a diner in Santa Monica. He sat there at the counter, thinking that he would try to make peace with Starkey.

When his pager vibrated, he recognized her number and returned her call. "You calling to arrest me?"

"No. I'm calling to give you one last chance to catch this bastard."

STARKEY FOUND HIM AT A rathole diner, waiting in a booth.

Her heart felt heavy when she saw him, but she pushed that aside and told him what had happened. "Here's the deal, Pell. If we get this guy, we are not going to kill him, we are going to arrest him. This is no longer your personal vendetta. Agreed?"

"Yes."

"If we get this set up, we are going back to Kelso. I want to do this the right way. I want to make sure it works."

"You want to save your job."

"Yes, Pell, I want to save my job. They might fire me anyway, but I want to go out as the police officer I am."

Pell nodded. "What do you need me for?"

"Mr. Red waits for me. He's got this fixation. I can use that. But I need your computer to get back on Claudius. Kelso took mine."

Pell stared out the window. "I should have told you what I was doing. I'm sorry I didn't."

"Stop. I don't want to talk about it. You want to do this or not?"

He looked at her. "I want to do it."

"Then let's go." She started to slide out of the booth.

He took her arm, stopping her. "I fell in love with you, Carol."

"Don't you say that."

He shoved himself out of the booth. "The computer is in my car."

THEY went to her place.

They set up the computer at the dining-room table, and Starkey signed on as before. When the flaming head stared out at her, she entered the chat room.

Pell said, "What are you going to say?"

"This."

HOTLOAD: John Michael Fowles.

"Who's John Michael Fowles?"

"Mr. Red. Warren Mueller got his prints off Tennant's book."

Starkey didn't expect Fowles to be waiting for her, but he was there almost at once. She opened the message window.

MR. RED: Excellent, Detective Starkey. You rock.

HOTLOAD: Your praise makes me blush.

MR. RED: How did you learn my name?

HOTLOAD: Do you want the truth, or do you want me to tell you what you want to hear?

MR. RED: The truth is a commodity. What will you want in return?

HOTLOAD: You will have to answer a question of mine. Do you agree?

MR. RED: I will not tell you my whereabouts. All else is fair game.

HOTLOAD: Agreed. The answer is Tennant's book. When I learned that you had seen him, I knew he would have made you look at the book.

MR. RED: I looked at his book, to read the articles about you.

HOTLOAD: Now, my question. Would you have come to Los Angeles if we had not baited you?

MR. RED: I will answer your question in person. Give me your phone number.

HOTLOAD: You must be nuts. That is farther than I'm willing to go.

MR. RED: I've had more than a few fantasies about you going all the way, Carol Starkey.

HOTLOAD: You get graphic, John, I'm gonna sign off.

MR. RED: What's in it for you is . . . the truth.

Starkey hesitated. She knew that they would have only one shot to bring him in; if he figured out what she was trying to do, her chance would be gone and so would he.

Pell said, "Be weak. He's male. If you want him, need him. Let him take care of you."

HOTLOAD: I am afraid. You want to be in the Ten Most Wanted. I am afraid you will use me to get there.

MR. RED: There are things I want more than being on that list.

HOTLOAD: Like what?

MR. RED: I want to hear your voice, Carol Starkey.

HOTLOAD: I will not give you my phone number.

MR. RED: Let us do this: Sign on to Claudius at exactly three p.m. today. I will be here. I will give you a phone number. If my phone doesn't ring in fifteen seconds, I will leave, and you will never hear from me again. If you call, we will talk for exactly five minutes, and I will answer your question. I'd like a longer conversation, but we both know what you'll be doing.

HOTLOAD: Yes. I will be tracing the call.

MR. RED: Fair enough, but I will beat you at that. You won't catch me.

HOTLOAD: We'll see.

"You've got him, Starkey."

"Maybe." She had what she needed to go back to Kelso, but everything depended on Mr. Red.

JOHN Michael Fowles was parked less than two blocks up from Starkey's house. He waited until she and Pell left, then drove back to his hotel to work on the new bomb. He was building a different kind of bomb this time, one just for Carol Starkey.

STARKEY wanted to maneuver John Michael Fowles, a.k.a. Mr. Red, into revealing his location so that she could bag him. To do that, she needed phone traps in place in the event they spoke on a landline, and the cell companies standing by for a triangulation in the more likely event that his number linked to a cell phone. Once his position was fixed, she needed bodies to close the perimeter. She feared that he would have explosives on his person, which required a call-out from the bomb squad. All of this meant that she needed Kelso's help.

First she phoned Dick Leyton. "Dick, I need your help. I know I'm in trouble, but please listen. I was just on-line with Mr. Red. I have a relationship with him, and we can use that to bag this mutt."

"Dammit, Carol, you need to—"

Starkey interrupted him, pressing ahead to convince him. "At exactly three o'clock he's going to be on-line again. He's going to give me a phone number to call. I'll call it, Dick. I think I can arrange a face-to-face. This is Mr. Red. Do you think we should walk away from an opportunity like this? Take me to Barry, Dick. Please."

They spoke about it for another ten minutes. They both knew that he would have to convince Morgan before Kelso would go for it. Leyton finally said that he would do it, telling Starkey to meet him at Spring Street by two o'clock.

When she hung up, she looked at Pell. "If Morgan goes for it, I guess he'll alert the ATF and the Feebs. Maybe you shouldn't come."

"I didn't come this far to quit, Starkey."

"Well, let's go."

She brought him back to the diner for his car, and then they went their separate ways.

STARKEY put her car in the red zone outside Spring Street at five minutes before two and went up with the second computer. Leyton and Morgan were already present. Pell hadn't yet arrived.

Leyton said, "Carol, why don't we go into Barry's office?"

Starkey followed them into Kelso's office.

Leyton said, "Carol, I sketched out our discussion to Chief Morgan and to Lieutenant Kelso. They're onboard with this. The dispatch office is standing by with secure communication to the patrol division. SWAT has been alerted, and the bomb squad is, as always, ready to roll."

Starkey nodded. "All right. Where do you want to do this?"

Kelso said, "Here in my office. You need anything?"

"Just a phone line. I'll use my cell phone to make the voice call."

Kelso cleared his desk so that Starkey could set up the computer. She caught a glimpse of Pell out in the squad room. He was talking with two federal agents.

At ten minutes before three Starkey was waiting to sign on with an audience crowded around her. Leyton came up behind her and rubbed her shoulders. "We've still got a few minutes. Get a cup of coffee."

Starkey left for the squad room, glad for the break. Pell was there with the two suits, but he wasn't in handcuffs. She didn't go for coffee. She went over to Pell. "Are these people with the ATF?"

The shorter of the two introduced himself as Assistant Special Agent-in-Charge Wally Coombs and the taller as Special Agent Burton Armus, both of the Los Angeles field office.

"Is Mr. Pell under arrest?"

"Not at this time. We'd like to ask you a few questions about all this."

"Later. Now I need Mr. Pell's assistance in the other room."

Coombs shrugged. "Sure."

Pell followed her back to Kelso's office. "Thanks."

At two fifty-nine Starkey was again in front of the computer. She opened the door into Claudius, but when she accepted Mr. Red's message, it wasn't what any of them expected.

> MR. RED: Sorry, babe. Changed my mind. A conversation isn't going to be enough for me. I am a man of LARGE appetites, if you catch my drift.
>
> HOTLOAD: We had a deal. You said you would answer my question.
>
> MR. RED: I said I'd answer your question in person. I will still do that.
>
> HOTLOAD: You know I won't meet you. No way I'll do that.
>
> MR. RED: Then you will never know why Buck Daggett died. Meet me, Carol Starkey. I will not hurt you.
>
> HOTLOAD: Where?
>
> MR. RED: Echo Park. You know the big fountain.
>
> HOTLOAD: Yes.
>
> MR. RED: Park on the south side of the pond and walk toward the concession stand. Walk all the way to the concession stand, and only from that direction. I will be watching you. If you come alone, we will meet.

They set it up on the roll, coordinating SWAT and the bomb squad to meet in a parking lot six blocks east of Echo Park. Plainclothes spotters were posted on the streets surrounding the park, equipped with radios. The phone people wrapped a wire on Starkey there in Kelso's office.

Starkey was to drive to the park in her own car and do exactly as Fowles had instructed. If and when he approached her and identified himself, the area would be sealed. Snipers would be in position.

The drive to Echo Park took twelve minutes. Starkey parked on the south side like he said, and fought the urge to throw up. He was Mr. Red. There would be a surprise.

The plan was simple. Point him out, hit the ground, let everyone else do their jobs. The mike taped between her breasts would pick up her voice. If she said, "Hello, Mr. Red," they would hear.

Starkey locked her car and walked toward the concession stand. It was a weekday summer afternoon. The park was jammed with families, kids with balloons. There was a long line at the concession stand. When she reached it, she stopped. No one approached her, and no one even looked like they could be Mr. Red. He could be anywhere; he could be nowhere.

A short, squat Hispanic woman and her four small sons joined the line. The oldest stood close by his mother's side, but the other three ran in circles, chasing each other and screaming. The two smallest boys raced behind the concession stand, came out from around the other side, and skidded to a stop. They had found the bag. At first Starkey wasn't sure what they were doing. The two small boys looked in the bag. Their older brother joined them. A plain paper shopping bag that someone had left at the corner of the concession stand.

Starkey didn't shriek or rush forward. This was Mr. Red. He was watching, and he would have a remote. She had to get those kids away from there. She walked toward the bag. "We have a possible device. I say again, possible device."

When she was closer, she raised her voice, made it sharp and angry. "Hey! Get the hell away from that."

The boys knew she was talking to them, but stared at her without comprehension. Their mother said something in Spanish.

Starkey said, "Tell them to get away from that."

The mother was chattering in Spanish when Starkey reached the bag and saw the pipes. "Bomb!"

She grabbed two of the boys—she could only get two—and lunged backward, screaming, "Bomb, bomb, bomb! Police officer, clear the area! Move, move, move!"

The boys screamed. Starkey pushed and shoved, trying to get the people in the line to move, even as police units roared toward her across the park.

And nothing happened.

RUSS Daigle said, "There's no charge in the pipes."

Starkey had guessed that forty minutes ago. If Mr. Red had wanted to blow it, he would have blown it when she was standing there. Now she was sitting in the back of Daigle's Suburban, just as she used to sit when she was on the squad. Daigle had sent the robot forward with the de-armer to blow the pipes apart.

"There was a note." Daigle handed her a red three-by-five index card. Dick Leyton and Morgan had walked over with him.

The note said, "Check the list."

Leyton squeezed her arm. "He's on the ten most wanted list. As soon as the Feebs had his identity, they added him. I'm sorry, Carol. It was a really good try."

Any relationship she'd had with Mr. Red was history. He would've seen what they had tried to do. She might sign on to Claudius again, and he might be there, but any hope of baiting him into a trap was gone. He had what he wanted.

Kelso came over. "Listen, Carol, we're still going to have to deal with what happened, but maybe we can work out something to keep you on the job. You won't be able to stay with CCS, but we'll see."

Starkey smiled. "Thanks, Barry."

She caught Pell's eye. Pell spoke to the two ATF agents, then walked over. "How you doing?"

"Been better. You hear they put him on the list?"

"Yeah. Maybe he'll retire. The sonofabitch."

Starkey didn't know what to think about that. Would Mr. Red stay in Los Angeles? Would he continue to kill, or would he simply vanish?

She looked at the two ATF agents.

"What's going to happen with your friends?"

"They told me to get an attorney. What does that tell you?"

"That you're screwed."

"We need to talk, Carol. About us."

Starkey shoved off the back of the Suburban. "I don't want to talk. I just want to go somewhere and heal. Good-bye, Jack. If I can help you when they interview me, I will."

Starkey looked deeply into the two dimming eyes, then walked away so that he would not see how very much she wanted that time with him.

CHAPTER

11

STARKEY did not drive back to Spring Street. She took a turn through Rampart Division. She watched the citizens and enjoyed the play of traffic. She was done with the bombs. She could live without working the bombs or being a bomb investigator and get along just fine. Still, she was heartened by what Kelso had said.

She thought about the bombs and Kelso until she realized that she was doing it so she wouldn't think about Pell, and then she couldn't get him out of her head. She turned for home, feeling empty, but not so empty that she wanted to fill that lost place with gin. That was something, and, she guessed, maybe she had Pell to thank for it, though she was in no mood to do so.

Starkey was hoping that she would find Pell waiting in the drive, but she didn't. Just as well, she thought, but in that same moment her chest filled with an ache of loss that she hadn't known since

Sugar died. She forced the thought of it and what it meant away. She was better now. She had grown. She would spend the rest of her day trying to save her job or deciding how best to leave it and the memory of Jack Pell behind.

She let herself into her home. The message light was blinking by the front phone, but she did not see it. The first and only thing she saw was the device on her coffee table, an unexpected visual jolt of twin galvanized pipes duct-taped to a small black box. Stark and obvious, it screamed bomb in a way that flushed acid through Starkey's soul.

"CAN you hear me?" His voice was surprisingly mellow. "I can see your eyes moving, Carol Starkey."

She smelled the overripe odor of what she thought was gasoline.

"You smell that? That's charcoal starter fluid. If you don't wake up, I'm going to set your leg on fire."

She felt the wet on her leg. The sharp throb behind her right ear was a swelling spike that made her eyes water. When she opened them, she saw double.

"Are you okay, Carol Starkey? Can you see me?"

She looked toward his voice. He smiled when their eyes met. A black metal rod about eighteen inches long sprouted from his right hand. He'd found her asp in the closet.

He spread his hands, presenting himself. "I'm Mr. Red."

He looked younger than his twenty-eight years, but in no way the shabby misfit that most bombers were. He was a good-looking man with beautiful even teeth; he had all his fingers.

She was seated on the hearth, arms spread wide, handcuffed to the metal frame surrounding her fireplace. Her legs were straight out before her. Her hands were numb.

The device was no longer on the coffee table. Now it was sitting on the floor inches from her feet.

He came over and sat cross-legged on the floor, stroking the device, proud of it. "The last of Daggett's Modex Hybrid. And this one really is for you. Got your name on it and everything."

She looked at the bomb. The two pipes were the same, but the black box was different. A switch topped the box, with two fine wires leading to a battery pack. This bomb was different. This bomb was not radio-controlled.

She said, "Timer."

"Yeah. I gotta be somewhere else when this one goes off. Celebrating my ascension to the ten."

Without another word he reached to the box, pressed the side, and a green LED timer appeared, counting down from fifteen minutes.

He grinned. "Kinda hokey, but I couldn't resist. It's my gift to you, Carol Starkey. You're going to see the actual instant of your destruction. Just watch the seconds trickle down until that final second when you cease."

"Screw you."

He went to her couch and came back with a wide roll of duct tape. He tore off a strip, then squatted beside her. He grabbed her hair, forced her head back, and pressed the tape over her mouth. She tried to twist away, but he pressed the tape down hard, then put on a second piece.

The timer was down to thirteen minutes and forty-two seconds. Fowles touched her head. "Perfect. Save a place in hell for me, Carol Starkey."

He stood then and went to the door, but she did not see him. She watched the timer, the green LED numbers spinning down toward eternity.

COOMBS and Armus were gentlemen about it. They wanted Pell's gun and his badge, which he had left in his motel, and they wanted to talk to him. He asked if he could meet them at the field office, and they said fine.

He drove to his motel, got the I.D. and the big Smith 10, then checked out. He got back in his car and went after Starkey, having no idea what he would say or do, only knowing that he could not let her go this easily. Coombs and Armus could wait.

Pell parked in front of her house, relieved when he saw her car in the drive. When she didn't answer, he looked through the little panes of glass beside her door. He thought she was sitting at the fireplace, but then he saw the handcuffs and the device at her feet.

Pell slammed the door with his foot, and then he was in, going through the door, when something hit him from behind and he stumbled forward, seeing flashing bursts of light.

He clawed out his Smith as he was hit again. He could feel consciousness slipping away, but the Smith came out and the safety went off and he fired up into the shadow above him even as the light bled into darkness.

STARKEY saw Pell go down. She saw him reach out his gun, and then he was shooting, shooting up into Fowles, who flipped back and sideways, then crawled toward her couch.

Starkey raked her face against her shoulders, trying to work the tape free, even as she watched the timer. It was winding down so fast the numbers blurred. 6:48.47.46.

Fowles tried to rise but couldn't.

Finally one end of the tape came free and Starkey found her voice. She screamed, "Pell! Wake up! Get up and get the keys!"

Pell pushed himself onto his back.

"Pell, we've got six minutes. This thing is gonna explode! Come over here."

Pell pushed onto his side. "I can't see you. I can't see anymore. There's nothing left but light and shadows."

Starkey's blood drained. She knew what had happened. The fight had finished the work on his eyes.

"Can you see up close, Jack? Can you see your hand?"

Pell held his hand in front of his face. "I see a shadow, that's all. Who hit me? Was it him?"

"You shot him. He's on the couch."

"Is he dead?"

"I don't know, Jack, but forget him! We have six minutes, ten seconds, and I'm handcuffed to this fireplace. Get me loose and I can de-arm that bomb!"

"I can't see, Carol. I'm sorry."

Starkey saw him push himself up onto his hands and knees. He was facing away from her. Across the room Fowles tried to rise, failed, and whatever life was left seemed to drain from him.

"Jack, quick now, okay? Turn toward my voice."

Pell turned. 6:07.06.05.

"Straight ahead of you is twelve o'clock. Fowles is at eight o'clock, just across the room. Maybe fourteen feet. He's on a couch behind the coffee table, and I think he's dead. The keys might be in his pockets."

Pell crawled, one hand feeling ahead for the table.

"That's it, Jack. Almost at the table. He's behind it."

When Pell reached the table, he shoved it aside. He found the couch, then walked his hands up Fowles's legs to the pockets. Fowles's shirt was wet with blood. 4:29.28.27.

"They're not here! The keys are not in his pockets!"

She searched the room with her eyes, thinking maybe Fowles had tossed the keys. She didn't see them.

Fowles moaned once and shifted.

Pell said, "He's still alive!"

Starkey's eyes went back to the flashing timer and watched the seconds trickle away. 3:53.52.51.

"Forget Fowles! The door's at five o'clock. Get out of here."

"No. I'm not leaving you!"

"Romantic, Jack. Very romantic."

He crawled toward her, barely missing the device, then walked his hands up her legs. "Talk to me, Carol. You're handcuffed to what?"

"An iron fire grate. The frame is set into the bricks."

His hands slid across her body, found her right hand, and felt over the cuffs to the iron frame. He gripped the frame with both hands and pulled, his face going red. He swung around and wedged his feet against the wall and pulled even harder.

"It's solid, Jack. The bolts are set deep."

"A fireplace poker. Maybe I can pry it out. There's gotta be something I can use." Pell's voice was frantic.

"I don't have any of that, Pell! I'm a rotten homemaker! Now get out of here!"

He looked toward her face with eyes so gentle and open that she felt sure he could see. "Where's the door, Carol?"

She loved him for going, loved him for sparing her the final three minutes of guilt that she had caused his death, too. "Behind you, seven o'clock."

He touched her face and let his fingers linger. "I did you wrong, Carol. I'm sorry about that."

"I absolve you, Jack. Hell, I love you. Now please go."

He followed her leg down to the device, cradled it under his arm, and began navigating toward the door.

Starkey realized what he was doing and screamed in a rage. "No! Pell, don't you do that! Don't you kill yourself for me!"

He crawled for the door, carrying the device under his left arm. "You're doing me a favor, Starkey. I get to go out a hero. I get to die for the woman I love."

Starkey knew that he was going to carry the bomb outside and blow himself to hell and leave her in here to carry the weight of it just as she'd done with Sugar. And then, only then, her eyes filled, and the only possible way to save them both came to her.

"Pell, listen! We can de-arm the bomb. I know how to de-arm the damned bomb!"

He paused and looked at her. "How much time?"

"I can't see it. Bring it over here, and I'll tell you what to do."

"I can't see, Starkey."

"I can talk you through it! We've still got a little time, but we're losing it. Bring it over here."

Pell followed her directions until he was next to her.

"Put it on the floor. Next to me. Now rotate it. C'mon. I want to see the time."

He did as she said. 1:56.55.54.

"How long?"

"We're doing great, Pell. Now turn it over. Lemme look at the bottom."

"Tell me what you see, Carol. Describe it."

"We've got a black Radio Shack timer fastened on top of a translucent Tupperware food storage container. Looks like he melted holes in the lid to drop the leg wires."

"Battery pack?"

"Gotta be inside with everything else. The top isn't taped. It's just snapped on."

She watched Pell's fingers feel lightly around the edges of the lid. She knew that he would be thinking exactly what she was thinking: That Mr. Red could've built a contact connection into the lid that would automatically trigger the explosive if the lid were removed.

"Open it, Jack. Just pop up the corners. Slow."

Pell wet his lips and nodded. He was thinking it, too. Thinking that this could be it, but that if it were, neither of them would know.

Pell opened the lid. 1:51.50.49.

"Don't lift the lid away from the container. Lift it just enough to test the tension on the wires."

He did as she instructed. "I can feel the wires pull against whatever's inside."

"That's the explosive and the initiator. Lift the top until you feel the wire pull."

He did. 1:26.25.24.

"Now tilt the container toward me. I want to see inside."

A squat quart-size metal cylinder that looked like a paint can sat inside the Tupperware with the end plug of an electric detonator sticking up through the top. Red and white leg wires ran from the end plug to a shunt, from which another set of wires sprouted up through the lid to the timer, and off to the left to a couple of AA batteries that were taped to the side of the can. A purple wire ran directly from the batteries to the timer, bypassing the shunt, but connecting through a small red box that sprouted yet another wire that led back to the detonator. Starkey didn't like that part. Everything else was simple, and she'd seen it a hundred times before. But not the red box, not the white wire leading back to the detonator. She was scared.

"Tell me what to do, Carol."

"Lift the cylinder out, okay? Just lift it out and put it on the floor."

He did as she instructed. 1:01.00.

"How're we doing with the time?"

"All the time in the world, Pell. No sweat."

With the bomb sitting on the floor, she could see it more clearly, but she still did not know the purpose of the tiny red box. It might be a surge monitor, and that scared her. A surge monitor would sense if the batteries had been disconnected or the wiring cut, and bypass the shunt and the timer. If they cut the wires or pulled the timer, the shunt would automatically fire the detonator.

"What do I do, Carol? Don't lose it on me, babe."

"Okay, Pell, I think there's a surge monitor cut into the circuit. We try to disconnect anything, it'll detonate the bomb. The timer won't matter."

"So what do we do?"

"Take a big chance, buddy. Put your fingers on the timer, then find the wires that lead down through the lid. I want you to be on the bottom side of the lid, okay, so you're closest to the device."

He did it. "Okay."

"There are five wires coming through the lid. Take one. Any one."

He took the red wire.

"Okay, that's not the one we want, so separate it from the others and take another."

Purely by chance he took the purple.

"That's it, babe. That's the one. Now follow it and you'll come to a little box, the surge monitor."

"Okay, I'm there. Two wires lead out the other side."

"Right. Before we can de-arm the timer, we've got to de-arm this little box, and I don't know how to do that. All I can do is guess."

He nodded without saying anything.

"Real easy now, I want you to separate the surge monitor from the rest of the device and put it on the floor."

"What do you want me to do with it?"

"You're going to stomp on it. It could detonate, Jack. It could just let go."

He didn't bat an eye or tell her she was crazy. "It's going to go anyway, Carol."

When he had the surge monitor on the floor away from the other wires, he crabbed around into a squat to position his heel over the monitor. "Am I lined up over it?"

"Do it, Pell."

Pell brought his heel down hard.

When he lifted his foot, the plastic square was in pieces. And they were still alive.

Starkey stared at the broken pieces. A set of small keys were in the debris. The handcuff keys. That bastard had put the keys in the bomb. She glanced at the timer. 0:36.35.34.

Something inside her screamed for him to scoop up the keys, unhook her, and let them both run. But she knew he could never find the keys and unlock her in time.

"What do I do? Talk to me, Carol. Tell me what to do!"

"Find the batteries."

His fingers traced over the device until they found the batteries taped to the side of the paint can. "Got 'em."

"Feel the wires coming off the top?"

"Got it. Now what?"

"Take it off."

Pell didn't move. 0:18.17.16.

"Take it off, Pell. Just unsnap the thing. We have to break the circuit, and we don't have any other way to do it, so we're going to cut the batteries out of the loop and pray there won't be a back charge that fires the detonator."

He didn't say anything for a while. 0:10.09.08.

"I guess this is it, then. How much time?"

"Six seconds."

He tilted his head toward her. "Thanks, Starkey."

"You, too, Pell. Now pull off the damned cap."

He pulled.

The timer continued reeling down, and Starkey felt her eyes well. "I'm sorry, Jack."

She closed her eyes and tensed for something she would never feel. 0:02.01.

"Starkey? Are we okay, Starkey?"

She opened her eyes. The timer showed 00:00, but there was no explosion.

Pell said, "I think we're still alive."

JOHN Michael Fowles heard Starkey's voice, and Pell's. He realized that they were working to de-arm the bomb and, in that moment, wanted to laugh, but he was bleeding to death. He lifted his head just enough to see the bomb. They had done it. They had de-armed it. John laughed then, blowing red bubbles from his mouth. They thought they had saved themselves. They were wrong.

PELL was holding her. He had crawled to her when the moment had passed and put his arms around her. "Tell me how to get to the phone. I'll call nine one one."

"Get the keys first and unhook me. There were keys in the surge monitor. They probably go to the handcuffs."

Pell followed her directions to the keys, then back to her. When her hands were free, Starkey rubbed her wrists.

Beyond Jack, from the couch, Fowles made a sound like a wet gurgle, then rolled off the couch onto the floor.

Pell lurched around. "What was that?"

"It's Fowles. He fell off the couch."

Fowles reached a hand toward her dining room. His legs slowly worked as if he was trying to crawl away.

"I'll call for an ambulance. He's still alive."

Starkey rose, then helped Pell to his feet. Fowles inched past the coffee table, leaving a red trail.

Starkey said, "Just lay there, Fowles. I'm getting help."

She left Pell by the front door, then went back to Fowles just as he edged to the far end of the couch.

"Fowles?" Starkey came abreast of him as he reached behind the end of the couch, his back to her.

Fowles slowly teetered onto his back, once more facing her. What Starkey saw then made all of her training as a bomb technician come screaming back at her: *Secondary! Always clear the area for a secondary!*

Fowles was clutching a second device to his chest. He looked up at Starkey with a bloodstained smile. "The truth hurts."

Starkey pushed away from him, trapped in a nightmare moment with legs that refused to move. Then she rushed in a panicked, horrible lunge for Pell and the door as John Michael Fowles gazed up through the red lens of his own blood at a crimson world, then pressed the silver button that set him free.

AFTER

STARKEY stood in the open front door of the house they were renting, smoking. She couldn't wait to move back to her own house, though the repairs would take another month. Not one window or door was square after the blast because of the overpressure. Starkey had reached Pell in the doorway when the device detonated. The pressure wave washed over her, kicking her into Pell and both of them through the door. That's what saved them. Kicked out the door, off the porch, and into the yard. They had both been cut by glass and wood splinters, but it could have been worse.

Starkey finished the cigarette. She tried not to smoke in the house because it irritated his eyes. She had been twenty-three days without a drink. When she was done with that, maybe she would try to kick the smokes. Change wasn't just possible, it was necessary.

They weren't going to prosecute a blind man. The ATF had made a lot of noise about it at first, but Starkey and Pell had gotten Mr. Red, and that counted for a lot.

Starkey was still waiting to hear about herself. She had a good lawyer, and Assistant Chief Morgan's support, so she would do all right. She had the month off, and then the hearing. Morgan had told her that he would take care of it, and she trusted him. Barry Kelso called from time to time, asking after her. She found that she liked hearing from him. Beth Marzik had never called.

Pell said, "Come here. I want you to see this."

Jack had placed candles around the bedroom. He had them in little stubby candleholders, twinkling on the dresser and the chest and the two nightstands.

"They're beautiful, Jack. Thank you."

"Don't move." He followed her voice, edging around the bed to her.

Pell had been living with her since he left the hospital. Neither of them knew if his staying here would be permanent, but you never know.

Starkey pulled him close and kissed him. "Get in the bed, Jack."

He smiled and eased himself into the bed. She went around, pulling the shades. It was still light out, but with the shades down the candles cast them in a copper glow.

Starkey took off her clothes and moved into his arms. She allowed his hands to move over her body. His fingers brushed her old scars, and the new scars. He saw with his hands. "You're beautiful, Carol."

ROBERT CRAIS

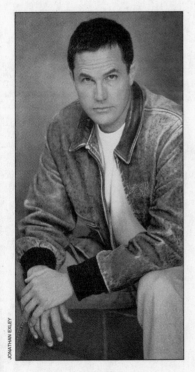

JONATHAN EXLEY

Robert Crais grew up in Baton Rouge, Louisiana, among a family where just about all the men worked either in the chemical refinery industry or as cops. He chose neither. Instead he struck out for Hollywood, where he built a successful career writing for television. Crais is best known for his work on *L.A. Law* and *Hill Street Blues,* but he feels his finest scripts were those he wrote for the first season of *Cagney & Lacey.*

After nine years of TV, Crais turned to crime novels, which, he says, are more fun than writing for the small screen: "Books are my own private amusement park, and I get to build whatever rides I want. If I want it to be all roller coasters, then I get to drive."

To read an exclusive interview with Robert Crais, visit the Select Editions website:

ReadersOnly.com
Password: *stay*

Winter Solstice

Rosamunde Pilcher

A quiet, safe place in the country, far from urban chaos. But is it far enough away to mend their broken lives?

Elfrida

BEFORE Elfrida Phipps left London for good and moved to the country, she made a trip to Battersea Dogs' Home and returned with a canine companion. It took a good—and heartrending—half hour of searching, but as soon as she saw him, sitting very close to the bars of his kennel and gazing up at her with dark and melting eyes, she knew that he was the one. She did not want a large animal, nor did she relish the idea of a yapping lapdog. This one was exactly the right size. Dog size.

He had a lot of soft hair—some of which fell over his eyes—ears that could prick or droop, and a triumphant plume of a tail. His coloring was irregularly patched brown and white. When asked his ancestry, the kennel maid said she thought there was Border collie there and a bit of bearded collie, as well as a few unidentified breeds. Elfrida didn't care. She liked the expression on his gentle face.

Her new companion traveled away with her, sitting in the passenger seat of her old Ford Fiesta and gazing from the window in a satisfied fashion, as though this were the life to which he was happy to become accustomed.

The next day she took him for a shampoo. He returned to her fluffy and fresh and smelling sweetly of lemonade. His response to all this sybaritic attention was a show of faithful, grateful, and loving devotion. He was a shy, even timid, dog, but brave as well. If the doorbell rang or he thought he spied an intruder, he barked his head off for a moment and then retreated to his basket.

It took some time to decide on a name for him, but in the end she christened him Horace.

ELFRIDA, with a basket in her hand and Horace clipped to his lead, closed the front door of her cottage and set off briskly into the October afternoon toward the post office and general store.

The village was Dibton in Hampshire, and here Elfrida had come to live eighteen months ago, leaving London forever and making a new life for herself. At first she had felt a bit solitary, but now she couldn't imagine living anywhere else. From time to time old acquaintances from her theater days came to stay with her, sleeping in the tiny back bedroom where she kept her sewing machine, earning a bit of pin money making elaborate and beautiful cushions for an interior-decorating firm in Sloane Street.

When these friends departed, they needed reassurance. "No regrets?" they would ask. "You're happy?"

"Of course I am. This is my geriatric bolt-hole, where I shall spend the twilight of my years."

So by now there was a comfortable familiarity about it all. She knew who lived in this house, in that cottage. People called her by her name. Some of the inhabitants were commuting families, the man of the house setting out early each morning to catch the fast train to London. Others had lived here all their lives in small stone houses that had belonged to their fathers, and their grandfathers before that. Still others were new altogether, employed by the electronics factory in the neighboring town. It was all very ordinary and undemanding. Just, in fact, what Elfrida needed.

Walking, she passed the pub, the Dibton Coachhouse. Farther on she passed the church, with its yew trees and lych-gate and a notice board fluttering with parish news. The street curved, and at the end of it she reached the village shop. She tied Horace outside.

Inside, the shop was bright with electricity, low-ceilinged, and very warm. An up-to-date arrangement of display shelving that had been installed some months ago made it difficult to know at first glance who was in the shop and who wasn't, and it was not until Elfrida rounded a corner that she saw the familiar back view, standing by the till and paying his due. Oscar Blundell.

Elfrida was past the age when her heart leaped for joy, but she was always pleased to see Oscar. He had been almost the first person she met when she came to live in Dibton. She had gone to church one Sunday morning, and after the service the vicar had stopped her outside the door, his hair on end in the fresh spring breeze and his white cassock blowing like clean washing on a line. He had spoken a few welcoming words and then was diverted. "And here's our organist, Oscar Blundell. Not our regular, you understand, but a splendid spare wheel in times of trouble."

And Elfrida turned and saw the gentle, amused face, the hooded eyes, the hair thickly white. He was as tall as Elfrida, which was unusual. She towered over most men, being five feet eleven and thin as a lath, but Oscar she met eye to eye and liked what she saw there. He wore a tweed suit and a pleasing tie, and when they shook hands, his grip had a good feel to it.

She said, "How clever. To play the organ, I mean. Is it your hobby?"

And he replied quite seriously, "No. My job. My life." And then smiled, which took all pomposity from his words. "My profession."

A day or two later Elfrida received a telephone call.

"Hello. Gloria Blundell here. You met my husband after church. The organist. Come and have dinner on Thursday. You know where we live—the Grange. Turreted red brick at the end of the village."

"How very kind. I'd love to."

"Splendid. See you Thursday, then. About seven thirty."

"Thank you so much." But the receiver at the other end of the line had already been replaced. Mrs. Blundell, it seemed, was not a lady with time to waste.

The Grange was the largest house in Dibton, approached by a drive through hugely pretentious gates. Somehow none of this exactly fitted in with Oscar Blundell, but it would be interesting to go. You never really got to know people properly until you had seen them within the ambience of their own home.

On Thursday morning Elfrida had her hair washed and the color given its monthly tweak. The shade was officially called Strawberry Blond, but sometimes it came out more orange than strawberry. This was one of the times, but Elfrida had more important things to worry about. Clothes were a bit of a problem. In the end she put on a flowered skirt that reached her ankles and a long cardigan-type garment in lime-green knit. The effect of hair, flowers, and cardigan was fairly dazzling, but looking bizarre was one of Elfrida's best ways of boosting her confidence.

She set out on foot, a ten-minute walk down the village, through the pretentious gates, and up the drive. For once she was dead on time. The front door was opened by a local lady in a flowered apron.

"Good evening. Mrs. Phipps, is it? Come along in. Mrs. Blundell won't be a moment, just went upstairs to fix her hair."

"Am I the first?"

"Yes, but others'll be here soon. The drawing room—"

But they were interrupted. "You're Elfrida Phipps." Looking up, Elfrida saw her hostess descending the wide staircase. She was a large lady, tall and well built, dressed in black silk trousers and a loose, embroidered Chinese jacket. She carried a tumbler half full of what looked like a whisky and soda.

"I got a bit delayed, and then there was a telephone call. Hello." She held out her hand. "Gloria Blundell. Good of you to come."

She had an open ruddy face, with very blue eyes, and hair that, like Elfrida's, had probably been tweaked, but to a more discreet shade of soft blond.

"Good of you to invite me."

"Come along in by the fire. Thank you, Mrs. Muswell."

Elfrida followed Gloria into a large room, much paneled in the style of the '30s and with a vast red brick fireplace, where burned a log fire. The room was furnished with hugely padded and patterned sofas and chairs. Curtains were plum velvet braided in gold, and the floor was scattered with thick, richly colored Persian rugs. All exuded an air of warmth and a cheerful masculine comfort.

"Have you lived here long?" Elfrida asked.

"Five years. The place was left to me by an old bachelor uncle. Always adored it. Used to come here as a child."

"Where did you live before?"

"Oh, London. I had a house in Elm Park Gardens." She had a restoring swallow from her glass, then set it down. "What would you like? Sherry? Gin and tonic? Oscar's church, St. Biddulph's, where he was organist, was only ten minutes away. I suppose we'd have stayed there forever, but the Grange came to me. As well, we have this child, Francesca. She's twelve now. It's better to bring a child up in the country. I don't know what Oscar's doing. He's meant to pour drinks. Sorry, did you say sherry or gin and tonic?"

Elfrida said gin and tonic and watched Gloria Blundell pour her one. She then generously replenished her own glass with Scotch.

"There. Now sit down, tell me about your little cottage."

"Well . . . it's little."

Gloria laughed. "Poulton's Row, isn't it? They were built as railway cottages. Are you frightfully cramped?"

"Not really. I haven't got much furniture, and Horace and I don't take up much room. Horace is my dog."

"Haven't been inside one of those houses since I was a child and used to visit the widow of some old station porter. I shall have to come and see. And what do you do?"

"Sorry?"

"Garden? Play golf? Good works?"

Elfrida hedged slightly. She knew a forceful woman when she met one. "I'm trying to get the garden straight."

"Do you ride?"

"I've never ridden a horse in my life."

"I used to ride when my sons were boys, but that's a long time ago. Francesca's got a pony, but she's not all that keen."

"You have sons as well?"

"Oh, yes. Grown up now and both married. Oscar's my second

husband, you see. Of course, we had known Oscar for years at St. Biddulph's. He played divinely at my husband's funeral. When we married, everybody was astonished. 'That old bachelor,' they said. 'Do you have any idea what you're taking on?' "

It was all marvelously intriguing. "Has Oscar always been a musician?" Elfrida asked.

"Always. He was educated at Westminster Abbey Choir School and then went on to teach music at Glastonbury College. He was also choirmaster and organist there for a number of years. And then he retired from teaching, got the post at St. Biddulph's. I think he'd have continued there until they carried him out feetfirst, but my uncle died, and fate decreed otherwise."

Elfrida felt a little sorry for Oscar. "Did he mind saying good-bye to London?"

"For Francesca's sake he put a brave face on it. And here he has his music room, and he does a little private coaching. Music is his life. He loves it when there's an emergency and he can play for morning service in the Dibton church. And of course, he's always sneaking over to have a little quiet practice on his own."

The door from the hall opened, and Gloria turned. "Oh, there you are, old boy. We were just talking about you."

ALL at once, and all together, the other guests arrived, filling the house with the sound of their voices, and the dinner party was on its way. It was a formal evening, lavish and traditional, with excellent food and a great deal of splendid wine. They ate smoked salmon and a crown of lamb, and there were three puddings and then a creamy Stilton. When the port was handed around, Elfrida was now on to glasses of water, which she poured for herself from a cut-glass jug. The other women enjoyed their port, Gloria perhaps most of all. But when Mrs. Muswell said that coffee was all ready in the drawing room, Gloria led the way across the hall with a steady step.

They gathered around the fire, but Elfrida, lifting her cup of coffee from the tray, saw through the uncurtained window that a first star hung in the heavens over the top of a distant budding beech.

There was a window seat, and she went to sit on it, cradling her cup and saucer in her hands and watching the stars.

Presently she was joined by Oscar. "Are you all right?" he asked.

"Of course. Such a lovely evening. And your daffodils will very soon be in bud."

"You like gardens? Would you like to take a little stroll and be shown around? It's still not dark."

She glanced at the others, in full flood of conversation.

"Yes, I would like that, but wouldn't it be rude?"

"Not at all." He took her cup back to the tray. He set it down and turned to Gloria. "Elfrida and I are going to have a stroll around the garden."

Gloria said, "It's cold. Make sure the poor girl's got a coat."

In the hall, Oscar lifted from a chair a thick leather coat lined in sheepskin. "It's Gloria's. You can borrow it," and he draped it gently over Elfrida's shoulders. Then they stepped outside into the chill and purity of the spring evening.

They walked. At the far end of the lawn was a spacious walled rose garden, the bushes pruned and richly composted. Clearly, when summer came, there would be something of a display.

"Is this all your work?" Elfrida asked.

"No. I plan, but I employ a laborer."

Side by side they strolled down the wide graveled pathway. He said, "I hope you didn't feel too distanced at dinner. I'm afraid we're something of a parochial lot."

"Not at all. I enjoyed every moment. I like to listen."

"Country life. It teems with intrigue."

"Do you miss London?"

"From time to time, enormously. Concerts and the opera. My church—St. Biddulph's."

"Are you a religious person?" Elfrida asked impulsively.

"I don't know. But I have spent the whole of my life steeped in sacred music, and I would find it uncomfortable to live in a world where I had no person to thank."

"For blessings, you mean?"

"Just so."

"I understand, but even so, I'm not a bit religious. I only went to church that Sunday because I was feeling isolated and I needed the company of other people. I didn't expect the lovely music."

"The organ is a new one."

They trod in silence for a moment. Then Elfrida said, "Do you count that as a blessing? The new organ, I mean."

He laughed. "Yes, of course I do."

"What else?"

He did not immediately reply. She thought of his wife, his lavish house, his music room, his friends. She thought it would be interesting to know how Oscar had come to marry Gloria. Had he, after years of bachelordom, meager salaries, and dusty academic rooms, seen looming in the future the emptiness of old age and taken the easy way out? The wealthy, forceful widow, the capable hostess, good friend. Or perhaps it was she who had done the stalking. Whatever, it seemed to work.

"I married late in life, and for some reason it never occurred to me that I should have a child of my own. When Francesca was born, I was amazed, not simply that she was *there,* but so beautiful. And familiar. As though I had known her always. A miracle. Now she is twelve, and I am still astounded by my good fortune."

"I would like to meet her."

"You shall. I think you'll be charmed by her. When Gloria inherited this house, I kicked against leaving London. But for Francesca I went with the tide. You, I believe, also fled London?"

"Yes. I'd lived there from the moment I left school. I was on the stage, you see. Much to my parents' disapproval. But I didn't mind about disapproval. I never have, really."

"An actress. I should have known."

"And a singer too. And a dancer. Revues and big American musicals. I was the one at the back of the chorus line because I was so dreadfully tall. And then years of fortnightly rep and then bit parts on television. Nothing very illustrious."

"Do you still work?"

"Heavens, no. I gave it up years ago. I married an actor, which was the most dreadful mistake for every sort of reason. And then I got married again. But that wasn't much use either."

"Was number two husband an actor as well?" Oscar's voice was amused, which was exactly the way Elfrida wanted it to be. She seldom talked about her husbands, and the only way to make disasters bearable was to laugh about them.

"Oh, no. He was in business. He had the conviction that if a man feeds and houses his wife and doles out a housekeeping allowance, then he has kept his share of the marital bargain."

"Well," said Oscar, "and why not? An old-established tradition, going back for centuries. Only then it was called slavery."

"How nice that you understand. Turning sixty was one of the best days of my life, because I got my old-age pension book and knew that I could walk down to the nearest post office and be given money, cash in hand, for doing nothing. I'd never in my life been given something for nothing. It was like a whole new world."

"Did you have children?"

"No. Never children."

"You still haven't explained why you moved to this particular village."

She said, "I haven't told anybody, but there was this man. So special, so loving, funny, and perfect. Another actor, but successful and famous this time, and I won't say his name. We lived together for three years in his house in Barnes, and then he got Parkinson's disease, and it took him two years to die. It was his house. I had to leave. I saw an advertisement for the cottage in Poulton's Row. I have very little money, but it wasn't too expensive. I brought my dear dog, Horace, with me for company, and I have my old-age pension, and I have a little job making cushions for a rather snob interior designer in London. I always liked to sew, and it's good to work with lovely, expensive materials." It all sounded very trivial. "I don't know why I'm telling you all this. It's not very interesting."

"I find it fascinating."

"I don't see why you should, but you're very kind." It was getting too dark to read his expression. "I think perhaps it's time we went back to the others."

"Of course."

"I love your garden. Sometime I must see it in the daylight."

That was Thursday. The following Sunday morning, rain drummed down against the windows of Elfrida's cottage. She intended to spend the morning warm, comfortable, and idle, reading.

But just after eleven she was interrupted by the ringing of the doorbell. Horace let out a couple of barks.

Astonished but not alarmed, Elfrida made her way to the front door, and there she found a small girl in jeans and sneakers and a dripping anorak. Her auburn hair was braided into plaits, and her face was freckled and rosy from the chill, damp outdoors.

"Mrs. Phipps?"

There were bands on her teeth, a mouthful of ironmongery.

"Yes."

"I'm Francesca Blundell. My mother said it's such an awful day, would you like to come for lunch?"

"But I've only just been to dinner—"

"She said you'd say that. She was going to phone, but I said I'd bicycle."

"You biked? I think you'd better come in before you drown."

"Oh, thank you." Briskly Francesca stepped indoors.

Elfrida closed the door. "This is Horace, my dog."

"He's sweet. Hello. Do you mind if I take off my anorak?"

"No. I think it would be a very good idea."

Francesca draped it over the newel-post of the steep and narrow staircase. She looked about her. "I always thought these were the dearest little houses, but I've never been inside one of them. That's why I biked. I think it's perfect. Where does that door go?"

"Into the kitchen. I'll show you." Elfrida led the way. Her kitchen was no larger than a boat's galley.

"Oh, I love it. What's upstairs?"

"A tiny bathroom, a bedroom for me, and a workroom, where I do my sewing. If I have a guest, they have to sleep there."

"I think it's exactly right. For one person and a dog. Like a doll's house. I'd better go now. Thank you for letting me see your house."

"A pleasure. Thank you for bringing that kind invitation."

"Mummy said a quarter to one."

"I'll be there, and thank you for coming."

"I'll come again," Francesca promised.

OSCAR, Gloria, and Francesca were Elfrida's first friends. Through them she met others. The Foubisters, who were old-established and held the annual summer church fete in the park of their rambling Georgian house; Commander Burton Jones, Royal Navy retired, a widower; the Dunns, he an immensely wealthy man.

All amiable enough, but Elfrida found none of them as interesting or stimulating as the Blundells. She spent Christmas with them and New Year's Eve, and when she threw her first party for her new friends, it was Oscar who volunteered to be her barman.

However, there were limits and reservations. There had to be if Elfrida was not to be absorbed by, and beholden to, the Blundells. She had left London to make a life of her own and knew that it would be only too easy for a single and fairly impoverished female to be swept along (and possibly drowned) in the churning wake of Gloria's social energy.

So from time to time Elfrida had learned to step back, to keep to herself. Every now and then she escaped from the confines of Dibton, packing Horace into the passenger seat of her old car and driving far out across country, where she and Horace could climb a sheep-grazed hill and she could relish her precious solitude. On such occasions it became possible to be analytical about her involvement with the Blundells.

First, she liked Oscar immensely—perhaps too much. She was well past the age of romantic love, but companionship was another matter. From their first meeting outside Dibton church she had been instantly taken with him.

Elfrida was neither sanctimonious nor a lady with enormously high moral standards; indeed, all the time she lived with him, her dear dead lover had been the husband of another woman. But Elfrida had never met his wife, and the marriage was already on the rocks by the time he and Elfrida found each other, and for this reason she had never been consumed by guilt. But there was a scenario Elfrida had witnessed more than once—that of the single lady, widowed, divorced, or otherwise bereft, being taken under the wing of a loyal girlfriend, only to scarper with the girlfriend's husband. A reprehensible situation and one of which she strongly disapproved.

In Elfrida's case it was not about to happen.

Second, Francesca, at twelve years old, was the daughter whom, if she had ever had a child, Elfrida would like to call her own. She was independent, open, and totally straightforward, yet possessed of a sense of the ridiculous that could reduce Elfrida to helpless laughter, and an imagination that was fed by the voracious reading of books. During school holidays Francesca frequently turned up at Poulton's Row to play with Horace or to ask endless questions about Elfrida's theatrical past, which she found fascinating.

Francesca's relationship with her father was unusually close. Their delight in each other's company went far beyond that of the normal parent and child. From behind the closed music-room door could be heard the two of them playing duets on his piano. Evenings he read aloud to her, the two of them curled up in his huge armchair.

As for Gloria, she was a man's woman, closer to her grown-up and married sons than to her lately conceived daughter. Elfrida had met these sons—Giles and Crawford Bellamy—and their pretty, well-dressed wives when they turned up at the Grange for a weekend. Elfrida got the impression that neither of the brothers approved of her, but as she didn't much like either of them, that was not bothering. Their mother doted on them, and it was patently clear that in her eyes neither son could do wrong.

Francesca, Elfrida decided, was not that important to Gloria, not as absorbing as her own hectic life-style, parties, friends. Important too was her position as social mentor. Only once had Elfrida fallen from grace. It was during a convivial evening at the Foubisters' home, a dinner party of great formality and style, with candles lit and silver gleaming and an aged butler waiting at table. After dinner, in the long drawing room, Oscar had moved to the grand piano to play and, after a Chopin étude, had suggested that Elfrida should sing.

She was much embarrassed. She had not sung for years, she protested. But old Sir Edwin Foubister added his persuasions.

At that moment Elfrida caught sight of Gloria's face, set in an expression of disapproval and dismay, and she knew that Gloria did not want her to sing. Did not want her to stand up with Oscar and entertain the little group. She did not like others to shine, to steal attention away from herself.

Elfrida had dined well and drunk delicious wine, and emboldened by this, a tiny flame of self-assertion flickered into life. She had never allowed herself to be bullied and was not about to start. So she smiled into Gloria's threatening frowns and then turned and let the smile rest upon her host. "If you want, I should like to very much."

"Splendid." Like a child, the old man clapped his hands.

And Elfrida crossed the floor to where Oscar waited for her.

"What will you sing?" he asked.

She told him. An old Rodgers and Hart number.

A chord or two for introduction. It had been a long time. She straightened her shoulders, filled her lungs. *"I took one look at you, / That's all I had to do."* Her voice had aged to thinness, but she could still hold, truly, the tune. *"And then my heart stood still."*

And she was all at once consumed by reasonless happiness and felt young again, standing by Oscar and, with him, filling the room with the music of their youth.

While everybody marveled and congratulated Elfrida on her performance, Gloria drank her brandy and scarcely spoke. When it was time to leave, Sir Edwin accompanied them out to where Gloria's highly powered car was parked. Elfrida got into the back, but it was Oscar who slipped in behind the driving wheel, and Gloria was forced to take the passenger seat of her own vehicle.

Heading home, Oscar asked his wife, "How did you enjoy your evening?"

Gloria replied shortly, "I have a headache," and fell silent.

Elfrida saw the sad truth. Gloria, hardheaded and with a stomach like a tin bucket, drank too much. She was never incapable, never hung over. But she drank too much. And Oscar knew it.

OSCAR. And now here he was, in Mrs. Jennings's shop on a gray, icy October afternoon, picking up his newspaper.

Mrs. Jennings looked up. "Afternoon, Mrs. Phipps."

With his hand full of change Oscar turned and saw her. "Elfrida, good afternoon. How are you?"

"Oh, surviving. A bit fed up with this weather."

As Mrs. Jennings priced the contents of Elfrida's basket, Oscar said, "I'll give you a ride home, if you like."

"I don't mind walking. I've got Horace with me."

"He's welcome to join us. Thank you, Mrs. Jennings. Good-bye."

"Cheerio, Mr. Blundell. Regards to the wife."

Outside, Elfrida untied Horace's lead, and the three of them made their way to Oscar's old car. She got into the passenger seat, and Horace jumped up and sat on the floor between her knees. As Oscar switched on the ignition, she said, "I never expect to meet anyone in the shop in the afternoons. Mornings are the social time. That's when you get all the chat."

"I know, but I forgot about the papers. Gloria's in London. I've got to meet her off the six-thirty train."

"Would you like to come back and have a cup of tea with me?"

"I wouldn't say no to a cup of tea."

They drove down the main street, then turned into Poulton's Row. At her gate he drew up, and they decanted themselves. Horace, freed of his lead, bounded ahead up the path, and Elfrida, lugging her basket, followed him. She opened the door.

"Don't you ever lock it?" Oscar asked from behind her.

"Not for a village shopping spree. Anyway, there's little to steal. Come along in." She went to the kitchen and dumped the basket on the table. Then she filled the kettle at the tap and set it on the stove.

Oscar looked about him. "You know, you have made this little place very charming."

Elfrida went to the doorway and stood leaning against the lintel. "It's a muddle, I know. I'm not very good at throwing things away. And there are one or two little bits and pieces I've been carrying about with me for years, dating back to the giddy days when I was on the stage. A silk shawl or the odd knickknack rendered theatrical lodgings a little more bearable."

"I particularly like your little Staffordshire dogs."

"They were always part of my luggage."

"And the little traveling clock."

"That traveled too."

"It appears well worn."

"Battered would be nearer the truth. I've had it for years. It was left to me by an elderly godfather. I . . . I have one thing which I think might be very valuable, and it's that little picture."

It hung to one side of the fireplace. Oscar put his spectacles on, the better to inspect the painting. "Where did you get this?"

"A present from an actor. We were both in a revival of *Hay Fever* at Chichester, and at the end of the run he said that he wanted me to have it. A leaving present. He'd picked it up in a junk shop, and I don't think paid all that much for it, but he was excited because he was sure that it was a David Wilkie."

"Sir David Wilkie?" Oscar frowned. "A valuable possession. So why did he give it to you?"

But Elfrida would not be drawn. "To thank me for mending his socks?"

Oscar returned his gaze to the painting. It took up little space, being only about eleven inches by eight, and depicted an elderly couple in eighteenth-century dress sitting at a table, on which lay a huge leather Bible. The background was somber, the man's clothes dark. But the woman wore a canary-yellow shawl and a red dress, and her white bonnet was frilled and ribboned.

"Is it insured?"

"It *is* my insurance. Against a rainy day. When I find myself on the streets with only a couple of plastic bags, then, and only then, will I think about selling it."

"A hedge against disaster." Oscar smiled.

From the kitchen Elfrida's kettle let out a startling toot, which meant that it was boiling. She went to retrieve it. Oscar followed and watched while she made the tea, which she set on the table.

They sat facing across the table, and she busied herself cutting some gingerbread. She said, "Oscar, I am going away."

"Forever?" he asked fearfully.

"Of course not forever."

His relief was evident. "Thank God. What a fright you gave me."

"Autumn always depresses me. A sort of limbo between summer and Christmas. And I'm going to have another birthday soon. Sixty-two. Even more depressing. So time for a change."

"Perfectly sensible. It will do you good. Where will you go?"

"To the very end of Cornwall. I have a cousin who lives there— Jeffrey Sutton. He's about three years younger than me. We've always been friends."

Oscar shook his head in some bewilderment. "I never knew that you had a cousin. Or any sort of relation."

"I am a bit denuded of family, but Jeffrey's a special person, and we've always kept in touch."

"Has he a wife?"

"Actually, he's had two. The first was a woman of such self-absorption as to beggar belief. He remained constant and enduring, but when his two daughters were grown, he walked out. When the very acrimonious divorce was over, he married a girl he'd known for years and almost at once started another little family. A boy and a girl. They live on a shoestring in Cornwall, keeping hens and doing bed-and-breakfast for summer visitors."

"What about his daughters? What happened to them?"

"I've rather lost touch. The eldest, Nicola, married some man and had a child. She was always complaining about the unfairness of life. She was always jealous of Carrie."

"Carrie being her sister."

"Precisely so. And a darling. Jeffrey's nice personality all over again. About ten years ago, when I had to have some female operation, she came to take care of me. She stayed for six weeks. We got on like a house on fire. She must be about thirty now."

"Did she marry?"

"I don't think so. Last time I heard, she was working in Austria for some big tour company, being a ski rep and making sure every tourist was in the right hotel. She always loved skiing." Elfrida poured his tea. "So you see, I do have a family, if not a particularly close one." She smiled. "How about you? Confession time."

"Well, I had a Scottish grandmother. How's that for starters?"

"Hoots toots."

"She had a great big house in Sutherland and a certain amount of land. I used to spend summer holidays with her. But she died when I was sixteen, and I never went back."

"What was her house called?"

"Corrydale. Enormously comfortable. Huge meals, and gum boots and fishing rods lying around the place. She was totally unpretentious and enormously talented."

"In what way?"

"I suppose a talent for living. And for music. I think I inherited my small talent from her. She set me on the road to my chosen career. There was always music at Corrydale."

"What else did you do there?"

"Go out in the evenings and pot rabbits. Fish for trout. Play golf. My grandmother was an avid golfer. If it was warm enough, I might bicycle to the beach and fling myself into the North Sea. Then my grandmother died. The war was on. My uncle Hector inherited and went to live there."

"Didn't he invite you for summer holidays?"

"Those days were over. I was sixteen. Into music."

"Does he still live there?"

"No. He's in London now. He's very old."

"And Corrydale?"

"He made it over to his son, Hughie McLennan. My cousin. A feckless fellow whose one idea was to live a grand life and do things in tremendous style. Hughie decided that life north of the border was not for him, so he sold up and scarpered off to Barbados. As far as I know, he's still there, leading the life of Riley. We used to put up with each other, but we were never friends."

"So everything's sold up and you'll never return?"

He leaned back in his chair. "Actually, I could go back. When my grandmother died, she left Hughie and me a house."

"Is it a big house?"

"Not particularly. It's in the middle of the little town. It used to be estate offices, but then it was converted to a dwelling house."

"How too exciting. I wish I had a house in Scotland."

"Half a house. I suppose one day Hughie will either offer to buy me out or suggest that I buy him out. But it's not something I worry about. Now, when are you off to Cornwall?"

"Next Thursday."

"For how long?"

"A month."

"We shall miss you," said Oscar, and she felt warmed.

WHEN the day came to return to Dibton, Elfrida could scarcely believe that she had been in Cornwall for a month, so swiftly had the weeks sped by. They tried to persuade her to stay, but it was time to pick up the thread of life again. To return to her own little nest.

Tomorrow perhaps she would telephone the Grange and speak to Gloria. And there would be cries of delight that she was back again and an instant summons to come and see them immediately.

But first, of course, before even reaching Poulton's Row, Elfrida knew that she must do some food shopping. So her first port of call must be Mrs. Jennings's mini supermarket.

The Dibton church clock stood at half past two as she drove into the main street of the village. Outside Mrs. Jennings's, she parked the car and went into the shop. She picked up a basket and moved up the aisles, taking what she needed from the shelves. Finally she presented herself at the counter. Mrs. Jennings looked up.

"Mrs. Phipps. Well, what a surprise. I haven't seen you for weeks. Have a good holiday, did you?"

"Wonderful. Just back. Haven't even been home yet, because I had to buy some provisions." She put the wire basket on the counter and reached for a *Daily Telegraph*. "I haven't read a newspaper for weeks. To be truthful, I didn't miss it."

Elfrida saw that Mrs. Jennings was staring at her, biting her lip and looking much troubled. "Is anything wrong, Mrs. Jennings?"

Mrs. Jennings said, "You haven't heard?"

Suddenly Elfrida's mouth was dry. "No."

"Mrs. Blundell—she's dead. A car smash at Pudstone roundabout. She was bringing the little girl home from a Guy Fawkes firework party. November the fourth, it was. A great lorry. She couldn't have seen it. It was a dreadful night. Pouring with rain."

Elfrida, stunned by shock, said, "And Francesca?"

"She died too. That great car, smashed and flattened to bits. The police said it was instant." Mrs. Jennings's voice shook a little. "You've gone white as a sheet, Mrs. Phipps. Would you like a cup of tea?"

"No. I'm all right." Which she was, because she was numb, quite calm and cool, shocked beyond horror. She said, "A funeral?"

"A couple of days ago. Here in the village."

So she had missed even that chance to mourn and comfort. She said, "And Oscar? Mr. Blundell?"

"Hardly seen him. At the funeral, of course, but not since then."

Elfrida thought of Francesca, laughing and teasing her father, playing duets with him on the piano, curled up in his big armchair and the two reading a book together. And then blotted the image from her mind. She said, "Is he at the Grange?"

"Far as I know. The vicar went to call, but he didn't even want to see the vicar. Mrs. Muswell goes up to the Grange each day, but she says he just stays in his music room. She leaves a tray for his supper on the kitchen table, but she says most times he doesn't touch it."

"Do you think he would see me?"

"I wouldn't know, Mrs. Phipps. Except that you and them were always friends."

"I should have been here."

"Not your fault, Mrs. Phipps. I'll put these things through the till, shall I? I feel I've spoiled your homecoming. I'm sorry."

"Thank you for telling me. I'm glad it was you and not anybody else."

She went out of the shop and got back into her car. Heavy-hearted, she started up the engine and moved on. She turned in to the Grange, rode up the drive, saw the elaborate face of the house and, outside the front door, a large limousine with a uniformed driver.

She parked a little way off, got out, and went up the steps. She did not ring the bell but opened the door and went inside.

She stood for a little, listening, hoping for comforting domestic sounds from the kitchen or a thread of music from upstairs. Nothing. The silence was suffocating, like a fog.

She crossed the hall, thick carpets blanketing her footfall, and went through to the drawing room. She saw that a man sat in the wing chair by the empty fireplace. Tweed trouser legs, polished brogues. Not much else was visible.

"Oscar," she said softly, moving forward to look down at him, and experienced the second stunning shock of that dreadful day. For here was Oscar, aged beyond belief, all at once an old man, bespectacled, wrinkled, and hunched in the padded chair, a gnarled hand clenched over the ivory handle of an ebony stick. Instinctively her hand went to her mouth to stop a scream.

He looked up at her and said, "My word," and instantly such relief flooded through her that she thought her legs were going to give way. Swiftly, before they did this, she sat with a thump on the padded leather seat of the club fender. He went on, "I never heard you coming in. Did you ring a bell? I'm a bit deaf, but I'd have heard the bell. I'd have come to the door."

He was not Oscar, aged beyond belief, just another person resembling him. Maybe twenty or so years older than Oscar. An old gentleman well into his eighties and speaking most courteously with a strong Scottish accent.

"No," she told him, "I didn't ring the bell. I just walked in."

"You'll forgive me not getting up. I'm a bit stiff and slow these days. Perhaps we should introduce ourselves. I am Hector McLennan. Oscar is my nephew."

Hector McLennan. Who had once owned Corrydale but now lived in London, and whose son Hughie lived in Barbados.

She said, "Oscar told me about you."

"And you, my dear?"

"Elfrida Phipps. I have a house in the village. I live on my own. Gloria and Oscar were endlessly kind to me. I'm sorry I was so rude when I first came in. I thought you were Oscar, and then of course I realized my mistake."

"Oscar aged by grief?"

"Yes, I suppose so. You see, I haven't seen Oscar yet. I've been in Cornwall for a month. I've only just heard about everything from Mrs. Jennings in the village shop. What happened?"

The old man shrugged. "Gloria drove her car onto the roundabout, right into the teeth of this great articulated lorry."

"You mean she never saw it?"

"It was very dark. It had started to rain."

"Mrs. Jennings said she'd been to a party with Francesca."

"That's so."

Elfrida bit her lip. After a little she said, "Sometimes at the end of a party she'd have a strong drink," and immediately wished she hadn't said such a thing.

But the old man was unfazed. "I know, my dear. We all knew. Sometimes she overdid it a wee bit. And then to drive home. Oscar knows this better than any of us. He is consumed with guilt because he didn't take Francesca to the firework party himself. I think it never occurred to him that it was anything more than a children's party. But I suppose there were other parents there, and it just went on. The rain started just before they set out. And then a momentary lapse of concentration, a confusion of lights, a heavy vehicle, a wet road . . ." He spread his hands in a gesture that said it all. "Finished. All over. Lives wiped out."

"I've even missed the funeral."

"I missed it too. I had a touch of flu. My doctor forbade it. This is my first visit, though of course I have been in touch over the telephone. It was while I was speaking to him that I became aware of his situation. So as soon as I could, I made the journey down from London to talk things through. I am aged, but I am still his uncle. No doubt you saw my car and driver at the door."

"Yes." Elfrida frowned. "You said 'his situation.' Does that have special meaning? Am I allowed to be told?"

"No secret, my dear. Gloria has left everything, including this house, to her sons. They intend selling."

"And where do they imagine Oscar's going to live?"

"They suggested some old folks' home—the Priory."

"You mean they're throwing him out? Into an old folks' home? Oscar? They must be mad."

"No, I don't think they're actually insane. Just avaricious and without heart."

"Then Oscar must buy another house."

Hector McLennan regarded Elfrida over the top of his spectacles. "Oscar is not a man of means. A pension, of course. And a little put by. But not enough to buy a decent house."

"Gloria's sons must know that." Another thought occurred to her. "And Gloria must have known too. Surely she could have left Oscar *something.* She was so generous."

"Maybe she intended to. In all likelihood it never occurred to her that she would die before Oscar. Or perhaps she simply never got around to making a new will. We shall never know."

"But he can't go and live in an old folks' home. He can come and live with me." But even as she said it, she knew that this was an impractical suggestion. There was scarcely space for one at Poulton's Row, let alone two. And where would she put his grand piano? "That's stupid. No, he can't."

"My notion is that he should move away. This house, this village, is too filled with poignant memory. That's why I drove down today. I put forward my suggestion, but he seems unable to make any sort of decision. Doesn't seem to care what happens."

"Where is he now?"

"He was called to the garden. Some problem with the green-house heating system."

"What was *your* suggestion?"

"That he goes back to Sutherland. Corrydale and the wee Estate House. Half of it belongs to him. My Hughie, who is the co-owner, lives in Barbados and is likely to stay there. It was let, but at the moment it's standing empty. I discovered this from our erstwhile factor, Major Billicliffe. He's retired now, but he still lives on the Corrydale estate. At the time of Hughie's big sale he bought his house. I gave him a telephone call, and we spoke at length. He says the place is in good condition. Furnished. No frills, but the essentials of day-to-day living should be there."

Elfrida thought this all over. Sutherland. She imagined it: peat bogs and sheep. Remote as the moon. She said, "It's a long way for Oscar to go all on his own."

"He's known at Corrydale and Creagan, the little town. He's family—his grandmother's grandson and my nephew. He will be remembered, even though he's not been back for fifty years."

"But is he up to such an uprooting? Such upheaval? Why not return to London and be near the church where he was organist?"

"A regression. And one haunted, I should think, by memories of his child. And saddest of all, he has abandoned his music. It's as though the best part of him has died."

They fell silent. This silence was disturbed by the slow tread of a person crossing the gravel in front of the house. Elfrida saw Oscar pass by the long window, and she got to her feet.

The front door opened and closed. They waited. A long pause. Then he was there, surveying the pair of them. His thick white hair fell across his forehead, and he put up a hand to push it aside. She had imagined him diminished, felled by tragedy. But heartbreak is a hidden thing, and Oscar was a private man.

"Elfrida. I saw your little car."

She went to meet him, and he took her hands in his own and leaned forward to kiss her cheek. His lips were icy against her skin. She looked into his eyes. "Dear Oscar, I'm home again."

"How long have you been here?"

"About fifteen minutes. I drove up from Cornwall this morning. I went into the shop, and Mrs. Jennings told me. I hadn't known. I haven't read a newspaper for a month. So I came straight here and walked in on your uncle."

"I see." He let go of her hands and turned to Hector, who sat in his chair and watched their reunion. "I am sorry I kept you waiting, Hector, but you have had Elfrida for company."

"And very pleasant it has been too. Now I must be on my way."

They all moved, at the old gentleman's pace, to the hall, through the front door, and down the steps.

"It was good of you to come, Hector, and I really appreciate it."

"Dear boy, give thought to my suggestion. It may seem a little drastic, but it would at least give you a breather. You mustn't stay here. Billicliffe's got the key of your house. Give him a ring." He turned to Elfrida. "Good-bye, my dear. I have much enjoyed meeting you. I hope one day we'll be able to renew our acquaintance."

"I hope so too."

The chauffeur held open the door. Oscar embraced the old man. "Thank you again for coming, Hector."

The car started up. They stood and watched Hector go, borne off at a dignified pace. It was cold and damp. Elfrida shivered.

Oscar said, "Come indoors."

"Are you sure you don't want me to leave as well?"

"No. I want you to stay with me."

"Would you like me to make us a cup of tea?"

"I think that would be an excellent idea."

"May I bring Horace indoors? He's been shut in the car all day."

"Of course."

She went across the gravel to where her little car was parked and set Horace free. Gratefully he leaped out. Then they all went back into the house.

Oscar led the way into the warm kitchen, where it was comforting. Elfrida found the kettle, filled it, and put it on the Aga to boil. She turned to face Oscar. "I wish I was articulate and brilliant at thinking of things to say. But I'm not, Oscar. I'm sorry. I just wish I'd known. I would have come back from Cornwall. I would at least have been at the funeral."

He sat now at the kitchen table, and as she spoke, he buried his face in his hands. For a dreadful moment she thought that he was weeping. She heard herself rabbiting on. "I had no inkling."

Slowly he drew his hands from his face, and she saw that he did not weep, but his eyes were filled with an anguish that was almost worse than tears.

He said, "I would have been in touch, but I had no idea where in Cornwall you were."

"That was because I had no idea that you might need to know." She took a deep breath. "Oscar, I do know about loss and bereavement. All the time that Jimbo was so ill, I knew it was terminal. But when he died, I found myself quite unprepared for the pain and the terrible emptiness. And I know, too, that what I went through then is simply one tiny fraction of what you are going through now. And there is nothing I can do to help, to ease you."

"You are here."

"I can listen. If you want to talk, I can listen."

"Not yet."

"I know. Too early. Too soon."

"The vicar called very soon after I had been told that both Gloria and Francesca were dead. He tried to comfort, and he mentioned God, and I found myself wondering if he had taken leave of his senses. You asked me once if I was religious, and I don't think I was able to answer your question. I only knew that my music and my choirs meant more to me than any churchly dogma. Thundering away on the organ, pulling out all the stops, hearing the boys' voices soar to the rafters. That was when I truly believed, when I knew a faith that I thought nothing could rock."

He fell silent. After a bit she said, "And now, Oscar?"

"It was all to do with God. And I cannot believe in a God who would take Francesca away from me. I sent the vicar home. He departed, I think, in some umbrage."

Elfrida was sympathetic. "Poor man."

"He will no doubt survive. The kettle's boiling."

It was a welcome interruption. Elfrida busied herself finding the mugs, the teapot and the tea; spooning tea; pouring the boiling water. She carried everything over to the table and sat facing Oscar, just as they had sat that day in her little house in Poulton's Row an eternity ago, before she went to Cornwall.

"You like builders' tea, don't you?"

"Yes. Strong and black."

She poured her own mug and left the pot to stew. She said, "Hector told me about your stepsons' selling the house."

"They think that I should book into the Priory, a Victorian mansion converted for the benefit of desiccated gentlefolk."

"You won't go there."

"I admit I would rather not."

"What do you want to do?"

"I would like to be left alone to lick my wounds, but I can't be left alone here, because Giles and Crawford want me out of the way so that they can put the house on the market."

"Brutes." She poured his tea, black as ink, and pushed the mug toward him. "Hector McLennan told me his suggestion."

"I had a suspicion that he might have."

"Is it such a bad idea?"

"Elfrida, it's mad. Sutherland is the other end of the country. And I haven't been there for fifty years. For all Hector's optimism I should not know a single soul."

Elfrida persisted. "Is it very isolated? Your house, I mean."

"No. It's in the middle of Creagan, the little town. It's just that I can't imagine what the hell I would do with myself."

"Well, you can't stay here, Oscar. And you go into the Priory over my dead body. So you must consider any available alternative. You could come and live with me at Poulton's Row, but as you know, there is scarcely space for me and Horace in that little cottage."

Oscar made no comment on this wild suggestion.

"Scotland," she mused. "It would at least be a fresh start."

"I am sixty-seven and at the moment in no shape to start anything. And although I can scarcely bear to speak to any person, I still dread being alone. Solitary. Living alone is the worst. Empty rooms. Even before I married Gloria, there were always colleagues, choristers—a whole world of lively company. My life was full."

"It can be again. Never the same, I know. But you have so much to give people. A generosity of spirit. We mustn't waste it."

He frowned. "You said 'we.' "

"A slip of the tongue. I meant *you*."

Oscar reached out for the teapot and poured himself a refill, then said, "Suppose I drove to Scotland, to Sutherland. If I made that journey, would you come with me?"

She stared into his face, wondering if she had heard right. "Come with you?"

"Why not? Is it such a bad idea to go together? Somehow we'll get there. We shall collect the key from Major Billicliffe, find my house, take possession, and spend the winter there."

"Christmas?"

"No Christmas. Not this year. Would that be so bad? It's so far north that the days will be short and the nights long and dark, and I probably won't be a very lively companion. But by spring perhaps I shall be stronger. Time will have passed. Here, as you so clearly stated, I have no future."

"And my house, Oscar? What should I do with it?"

"Let it. Or shut it up. It will be safe."

He meant it. He was asking her to go away with him. He needed her. She, Elfrida. Eccentric, disorganized, not beautiful any longer, even a little raffish. And sixty-two years old.

"Oscar, I'm not sure that I'm that good a bet."

"You underestimate yourself. Please come, Elfrida. Help me."

She had been impulsive all her life, made decisions without thought for the future, and regretted none of them, however dotty. Looking back, all she regretted were the opportunities missed, either because they had come along at the wrong time or because she had been too timid to grasp them.

She took a deep breath. "All right. I'll come."

"Dear girl."

"I'll come for you, Oscar, but I owe it to Gloria as well. You and Gloria and Francesca were my first friends when I came to Dibton. I feel ashamed. We've been talking, and this is the first time I've said their names to you." A lump had swelled in her throat, and it became difficult to talk. She was crying, but the tears, strangely, were something of a relief, warm and wet, rolling down her cheeks. "I . . . I've only been to Scotland once. To Glasgow, ages ago, with a touring company." Fumbling up her sleeve for a handkerchief, she found one and blew her nose. "And I couldn't understand a single word anyone said to me."

"There's a Glaswegian for you."

"It wasn't funny at the time."

"It's not funny now, but as always, you've made me smile."

"Like a sort of clown?"

"No, not a clown. Just a dear, funny friend."

Sam

AT SEVEN o'clock on the first dark Friday morning of December, Sam Howard wheeled his trolley of luggage out into the arrivals hall of Heathrow Airport. There was nobody to meet Sam. No wife, no driver. No welcome, however tame. He knew that outside the heated terminal building it would be very cold. It had been cold in New York, but a dry, crisp cold that stimulated.

His trolley was awkward, laden with two suitcases, a huge American golf bag, and his briefcase. He maneuvered it out into the wet cold to the queue for taxis. He had only to wait five minutes or so. The taxi driver was a morose man with a walrus mustache.

"Where to, guv?"

"Wandsworth, please. SW17. Fourteen Beauly Road."

" 'Op in."

The driver did not stir himself to help with the luggage, apparently having decided that Sam was young and fit enough to deal with it. Accordingly, Sam humped it aboard and climbed in. The taxi trundled forward, windshield wipers going full tilt.

Sam was grateful his first appointment was not until Monday at twelve thirty, when he had to present himself at Whites for lunch with Sir David Swinfield, chairman of Sturrock and Swinfield and Sam's ultimate boss. Until then his time was his own.

The taxi drew up at a red traffic light. Suddenly the driver spoke, flinging the question back over his shoulder. "Golf clubs. Been on 'oliday?"

"No," Sam told him.

"On business, then?"

"You could say. I've worked in New York for six years."

Rain streamed down. "Not much of a mornin' for comin' 'ome."

Green light. They moved forward again.

"No," Sam agreed. He did not add, *And I'm not coming home.* Because right now he did not have a home, which seemed to figure with the vagrant image. For the first time in his life—and he was now thirty-nine—he found himself without bricks and mortar to call his own. He was staying with his old friends Neil and Janey Philip, in their house on Beauly Road.

Bundled gloomily in his overcoat, cocooned in the back of the taxi, he thought of homes, remembering to the very beginning: Yorkshire and Radley Hill, where, an only child, he had been born and brought up. It was a place comfortable as an old tweed jacket, which he had thought would never change, but of course it did. During his last year at Newcastle University his mother died, and after that nothing was ever quite the same again.

The family business was a small woolen mill in a small Yorkshire town. Recession hit, and the mill came up against sophisticated competition from Europe. At the end Sturrock and Swinfield, the huge textile conglomerate based in London, moved in. Sam was given a job under the new umbrella, but his father, too old a dog to learn new tricks, took early retirement. Unable to fend off the stress of loneliness, boredom, and enforced inactivity, he died twelve months later of a massive heart attack.

Out of the blue came a summons from Sir David Swinfield, the chairman. Sam was told that he was being transferred to the United States, to New York.

He took to New York like a duck to water, relishing every aspect of the stimulating cosmopolitan melting pot that made up the city. Home there was a walk-up in Greenwich Village, but after he married Deborah, she persuaded him to move, and they ended up in a fancy duplex on East Seventieth Street.

Homes. East Seventieth Street had been the last, and that too had gone. Along with Deborah.

She had never been a moral coward. She told him face to face that she was leaving. She was tired of playing second fiddle to Sturrock and Swinfield and tired of being married to a workaholic. There was, of course, another man.

Slowly it was borne upon Sam that he had had enough of New York. He wanted England. He wanted to go home. He wanted misty skies and temperate green fields and warm beer.

And then one evening, at the nadir of his despair, the telephone rang in the apartment, and it was Sir David Swinfield from London. "I want you back in the U.K., Sam. I need you to be general manager of the McTaggart Mill in Scotland."

So on Monday at twenty-five past twelve, Sam presented himself to the porter at Whites and asked for Sir David Swinfield. Sir David was in the bar, he was told, and expecting a guest.

Carrie

CARRIE dreamed of Austria and Oberbeuren. In the dream the sky was a deep blue and the snow so dazzling that every frozen flake glittered like a jewel. She was skiing. An empty piste. Floating down through the white fields that spread to infinity on either side. She was alone. And then, far ahead, she saw another lone skier, a black silhouette hurtling away from her, down the slope. She knew that the skier was Andreas, and she called his name. *Andreas. Stop and let me be with you. Let us ski down together.* She topped a rise and saw that he had heard her call and was waiting, leaning on his sticks, watching for her.

He was smiling. White teeth in a deeply tanned face. Andreas. She reached his side and stopped, and only then saw that it was not Andreas at all, but another man, with a wolfish grin and eyes hard as gray pebbles. And the sky was not blue any longer but storm-dark, and she was afraid. . . .

The sense of fear awoke her, eyes flying open to the darkness. She saw a strip of uncurtained window, the streetlights beyond. Not Austria, not Oberbeuren, but London, the spare bedroom of her friends Sara and David Lumley. The dream receded. Andreas, who had never been truly hers, was gone. It was all over.

She reached for her watch on the bedside table. Six o'clock on a dark December morning. She closed her eyes and slept again.

At nine o'clock she awoke once more. By now David and Sara would already have set off for work. She had been there for a week and had accomplished little—done nothing about finding herself a new job. Carrie's only contact with her family had been to call her father in Cornwall and have a long and comforting conversation. "You will get in touch with your mother, won't you?" he had said. She knew that it could be postponed no longer.

Carrie did not look forward to seeing her mother or her sister, Nicola. She knew that they would have much to tell her, none of it good news. However, the sooner it was over with, the better.

She pulled on her dressing gown and went downstairs. She reached for the telephone and punched the number.

"Hello."

"Ma."

"Who's that?"

"Carrie."

"*Carrie?* Are you ringing up from Austria?"

"No. London. In Putney. Just across the river from you."

"How long have you been back?"

"About a week. But there's been a lot to do. Otherwise I'd have called before."

"A week? Is this a holiday?" Dodie's voice was querulous, as though in some way her daughter had pulled a fast one on her.

"No, not a holiday. I chucked my job in. Decided I'd done it for long enough."

"I always imagined you were there for good. We haven't seen you for years. What happened?"

"Nothing happened. Just a whim."

"Will you get another job?"

"Have to. Look, Ma, I thought I'd come and see you. How about lunch?"

"I can manage soup and pâté. Would that be all right?"

"Perfect. How's Nicola?"

"Oh, my dear girl, I think she's gone mad. I'll tell you all about it when you come." A pause, and then Dodie added—some bright idea having obviously just occurred to her—"Actually, all this might be rather fortuitous. You coming home, I mean. She'll be back for lunch, but perhaps you could get here a bit earlier, and we can have a private chat about it all."

Carrie began to wish she hadn't telephoned. She said, "And what about Lucy?"

"Lucy's here too. She's got a morning off school. She spends most of her time in her room. She won't disturb us."

"I'd like to see her."

"Oh, you will, you will. What time will you be here?"

"Eleven thirty?"

"I'll expect you."

After Dodie rang off, Carrie found herself laughing. Not from joy, but because her mother's chill and ambiguous welcome was exactly what she had both dreaded and expected.

It had always been thus. A lack of communication, an antipathy perhaps, that Carrie had learned to accept even before she entered her teens. Being with other families, seeing how they behaved with each other, had compounded her perception, and had it not been for the presence of her father, she could well have grown up with no knowledge of loving or of being loved.

Nicola had been the first child, and then five years later Carrie arrived. So different were the sisters, it seemed that each belonged solely to a single parent. As though Dodie had produced Nicola without cooperation from Jeffrey, and Jeffrey had fathered Carrie in some miraculous fashion entirely by himself.

He was her father, her friend, her ally. Jeffrey drove his daughters to school while their mother lay in bed, sipped China tea, and read novels. It was he who had first taken Carrie skiing at Val d'Isère when she was only ten. It was one of the best holidays of Carrie's life and the start of a passion that had never left her. Nicola had turned down the invitation, partly because she was hopelessly unathletic, but also because she liked being on her own with Dodie, so that the two of them could go shopping together and buy new dresses for Nicola to wear to all the Christmas parties that she had no intention of missing.

Clothes, boys, and parties were Nicola's passionate interests, and it surprised nobody when she became engaged at twenty-one to Miles Wesley, who held a respectable job with Hurst and Field-more, an old-established property agent.

CARRIE was the first person Jeffrey confided in that he was leaving Dodie. Carrie was nineteen and at Oxford, reading English and philosophy and relishing every moment of her new life. Her father looked less stressed than she had seen him look for a long time.

But sounds of resentment and recrimination were to echo for a long time. At the end of the day, though, most people had to agree that Dodie had done very well for herself. He contested nothing.

Dodie moved herself into a charming old-fashioned apartment in Fulham. "My little lonely nest," she told her friends, sounding both wistful and plucky, and everyone said she was marvelous, but in truth she was as content as she had ever been, with bridge parties, shopping, and holidays abroad.

Seven years after Dodie's divorce Nicola Wesley discovered that Miles was having it off with another woman, and she grabbed this opportunity to flounce out of a marriage that had become both predictable and boring. She flounced to her mother and her mother's spacious and pretty apartment. All of which might have been quite fun and companionable had not Nicola brought with her nine-year-old Lucy, and Dodie knew that her halcyon days were over.

CARRIE took a shower, washed her short hair, and dressed. Lately she had not bothered too much about how she looked, but this morning she knew that the time had come to take a bit of trouble.

So, slim camel-colored trousers, a cashmere sweater, polished boots. Gold earrings, gold chains around her neck. She checked her leather shoulder bag, went downstairs.

In the hall was a long mirror, and as she pulled on her coat, her reflection gazed back at her. She paused, regarding herself. Saw a tall, slender woman. Chestnut-brown hair shone with cleanliness; a lock like a bird's wing swept across her forehead. Her eyes, accentuated by shadow and mascara, were large and dark as coffee, and her face was still tanned from the reflected sunlight of the snow-fields. She looked all right. Confident. Not a person to be pitied.

She did up the buttons of the coat, a dark gray loden piped with forest green that had been bought a year ago in Vienna. Andreas had helped to choose the coat and then insisted on paying for it. *You will wear it forever,* he told her, *and you will always look a million dollars.*

They had walked through the streets, arm in arm, to Sacher's and there lunched in some style, and . . .

Don't think about it.

At Dodie's flat, she pressed the bell.

Dodie opened the door almost at once. "Carrie!"

She looked much as she always had—small and trim, with dark, neatly dressed hair flashed with a streak of white that was entirely natural and so enviable. She wore a little cardigan suit, the skirt fashionably short, and court shoes decorated with square gold buckles. A still pretty woman, with apparently everything going for her. Only her mouth gave her away, molded by the years into an expression of constant discontent. Carrie had always been told that the eyes are the mirror of the soul, but had long ago decided that a person's mouth is the true giveaway of character.

Carrie stepped through the door, and Dodie closed it carefully.

"Hello, Ma. How are you?" she asked, shedding her coat. "You're looking marvelous."

"Thank you, dear. You're looking well too. So brown."

They kissed formally, touching cheeks. Dodie turned and led the way into her sitting room. It was a pleasant room, with large windows facing south onto a balcony and, beyond, the view of the river. In the white marble fireplace there flickered a small mock-coal electric fire. Dodie settled herself beside this in her own chair.

"It was good of you to come so promptly. I wanted to tell you about everything, this ridiculous drama that's suddenly blown up."

"Nicola?" Carrie lowered herself into the chair on the other side of the white sheepskin hearth rug.

"She'll be back soon."

"Where's she gone?"

"Travel agent."

"Is she planning a trip?"

"I think she's gone mad. I said that, didn't I, over the telephone. She met this American at some party a few weeks ago, and they've been seeing each other ever since."

Carrie thought it sounded quite hopeful and not at all mad.

"What sort of American?" she asked cautiously.

"Oh, quite presentable. A businessman. Railways or steel or something. He's based in Cleveland, Ohio—wherever that is. He's called Randall Fischer. He's divorced. And now he's invited Nicola to go and spend Christmas with him at his place in Florida."

Carrie could not imagine what the drama was about. "So what is so dire?"

"Don't you see, Carrie? It's Lucy."

"You mean Lucy is not included in the invitation?"

"She most certainly has been included, but she refuses to go. She says she won't know anybody and that Randall only asked her because he feels he has to."

Carrie was sympathetic. "I see her point. What age is she? Four-teen? And I'll admit it's a bit embarrassing watching your own mother in the throes of a love affair."

"But what will she do?"

Now, thought Carrie, we're getting to the nub of the matter. "For Christmas, you mean? Stay with you, I suppose. Where else would she go?"

Dodie did not at once reply. Instead, she got to her feet and stood at the window, gazing down at the river. Carrie waited. Then her mother turned. "I can't deal with her on my own. I have a life to lead. I have plans made. The Freemans go every year to the Palace Hotel in Bournemouth. They've invited me to join them, and I'm not going to change my plans for a stubborn little girl."

No, Carrie thought, I don't suppose for a moment you'd even contemplate such a thing. She said, "What about her father? Miles. Can't she spend Christmas with him and his new wife?"

"Miles and his wife are going to St.-Moritz to ski for Christmas with a grown-up party. Miles said it was out of the question."

Carrie said, "In that case, you seem to have come to a deadlock."

All at once it seemed Dodie did not want to meet her daughter's eyes. "That's what I meant on the telephone. About your abrupt return from Austria coming at a fortuitous time."

"You mean *me. I* take Lucy off your hands."

"I didn't mean that. I thought maybe . . ." She hesitated. "Your father— He's Lucy's grandfather. Surely—"

"Look, Ma, I've spoken to Jeffrey."

"You call him Jeffrey now?"

"I've called him Jeffrey ever since the divorce. He's my father, I know, but he's also my friend. We talked about Christmas, but he's got his wife's brother and his wife and baby coming down. Not an inch for two more people."

Dodie let out a sigh and sat back in her chair. "I really can't go on like this. No cooperation from anybody."

"But Ma . . ." She did not finish. There came the sound of a key in the lock of the front door.

"Nicola's back," Dodie said.

When Nicola came into the room, Carrie got up and turned to face her sister. She said, "Hi."

"Carrie!" Nicola's jaw dropped. "I thought you were in Austria."

"I was," Carrie told her, "but I'm back now."

The sisters eyed each other. They had never been close, never been friends, never shared secrets. And it occurred to Carrie that Nicola, as she matured, was growing to look even more like their mother. The same height, the same neat figure, thick dark hair. The same small, mean-tempered mouth. Put them side by side, and they could easily have been mistaken for a pair of cross little twins.

Whenever she thought of Nicola, Carrie always had a mental picture of her wearing some little outfit. Now Nicola did not let her down, for there was the immaculately tailored trouser suit beneath a car coat of faux leopard. Her sack bag was of brown suede.

She gave Dodie a cold look. "I suppose Mother's been telling you about all the drama. Getting you on her side."

Dodie and Nicola were clearly, at this moment, on the worst of terms. Carrie decided that Lucy must have been having a hellish time between the pair of them.

Dodie looked hurt. "Nicola, that's not fair," she protested.

"No, but I bet it's true." Nicola settled herself with a thump in the middle of the sofa. "Anyway, it's too late now. I've booked my flight. I'm going on the eighteenth of December for two weeks."

Carrie said, "There seems to be a problem with Lucy."

"She was asked to Florida, but she refuses to come with me."

"Ma suggested that I look after her for Christmas, but I can't."

"Why not?"

"No house. No home."

Nicola chewed her thumbnail. "Anyway, I'm going. I'm going to Florida with Randall, and nobody's going to stop me."

Carrie, sympathetic in a way but thinking of Lucy, tried reasoning. "But Nicola—"

She got no further. Nicola rounded on her. "It's all very well for you."

Carrie wondered how many thousands of times in her life she had heard that familiar wail: *It's all very well for you.*

"You've never had a family. You don't know what it's like being tied day in, day out to a child. Term time and holidays. Keeping Lucy amused, dealing with problems at school. All on your own. As far as I can see, your life has been one long holiday. Nothing but skiing and having a good time. Not a care in the world."

Carrie, with some difficulty, kept her voice even. "My job was public relations officer for a prestigious travel firm, and each morning nine people reported in to my office. In high season I often worked seven days a week. So let's hear a little less about irresponsibility."

"It's not the same." Mulish, Nicola stuck to her grudge. "Not the same as bringing up a child."

Carrie gave up. "Look, this isn't getting us anywhere."

Nicola ignored her. "It's up to you, Mother. You'll have to forget about Bournemouth for the moment."

Dodie became incensed. "I shall do no such thing."

Carrie no longer could listen to this pointless sniping of the two of them. "Do stop," she told them sharply.

Rather surprisingly, they did.

"If you don't mind, I'd like to go and have a chat with Lucy, since she couldn't talk less sense than either her mother or her grandmother. Where's her room?"

"Next to the kitchen." Nicola jerked her head. "At the back."

Carrie went from the room and closed the door behind her.

Lucy

DODIE'S apartment had been designed with a small and undistinguished room for a housemaid or a hard-worked cook-general. Lucy Wesley, when she came to live with her grandmother after her parents' divorce, had been given this room and did not really care that it was both cramped and sunless, because it was her own. The walls were yellow, which imparted the illusion of sunlight, and the curtains were white voile. Lucy had her bed, piled with teddy bears;

a large table with drawers for doing her homework; and lots of shelves for her huge collection of books. Her computer sat on the table, along with a small television set, and when her school friends came to visit, they were always loud with envy and admiration, mostly because the space belonged to Lucy only and she didn't have to share it with some tiresome younger sister.

Lucy was an extremely tidy person. On the shelves her books stood in straight lines; her bed was smooth, her clothes folded. Once a week Mrs. Burgess, who came to clean for her grandmother, went through Lucy's room with Hoover and duster, but from time to time Lucy cleaned it again herself, polishing the mirror and the silver frame that held the photograph of her father.

She missed him dreadfully, not simply as a person but because—like a piece of furniture that had lost a leg—with his going, all sense of family had collapsed, fallen sideways, crooked and useless, and Lucy knew that it was unmendable and would never be the same again. From time to time she saw him, but his new wife was wary of involvement and clearly had no interest in children or step-daughters or anything except her absorbing job.

Lucy felt she could no longer confide in her father, because of divided loyalties on both their parts. Sometimes she felt that she would burst if she didn't find someone adult to talk to.

Now, at a quarter to twelve on a Friday morning, she had finished her homework and was writing in her diary. The diary was fat as a little Bible, leather-bound, with its own tiny lock and key. It had smooth thick paper that was a pleasure to write upon, and had been a present from Cornwall. "Happy Christmas, Lucy," was written upon the flyleaf. "From Grandfather."

Lucy had kept up the diary ever since she had received it. There were no dates, just lovely clean pages, which meant you wrote the date yourself and then the day's doings underneath. Sometimes there was little to record, but other days, if she had been to the cinema or to a concert, she could use up two or three pages. She got a lot of satisfaction writing, with her best pen, on the thick, creamy paper.

She wrote:

Mummy has gone to the travel agent this morning. She went right after breakfast. She and Gran are scarcely speaking to each other because of Christmas and Bournemouth and Florida. I wish they would understand how I would hate Florida. You can't swim all day in a pool, and I don't like Randall that much.

The diary was better than having nobody to confide in, but a person would be better. She thought about Carrie, Mummy's younger sister and a splendid aunt. Carrie would be perfect because she talked to you as though you were a grown-up and yet was always prepared to do exciting and innovative things. Once, they had gone down the river together in a boat all the way to Tower Bridge and had lunch on board.

Every now and then during the course of the morning Lucy had heard the telephone ring and Gran's low voice chatting away. And about an hour ago someone had rung the bell and come to visit. She had no idea who it could be, and did not particularly care. Later she heard the rattle of a latchkey in the front door and knew that her mother had come back from the travel agent.

After about five minutes she heard somebody approaching her door. Her mother, come to impart the latest news about plans to Florida. Lucy felt almost sick with apprehension. But then there was a soft knock, and she knew it wasn't Mummy, because Mummy just barged in.

Before she could bring herself to say "Come in," the door opened slowly and a head came around the edge of it.

"Am I interrupting?" Not her mother. Not Gran. But . . .

Carrie. Lucy found herself dumbfounded. She felt the warm blush of sheer pleasure creeping up into her cheeks.

Carrie said, "Surprise. Don't goggle. It's really me."

Slowly Lucy got to her feet. She said, "Goodness."

Carrie came into the room and closed the door behind her. She stooped and planted a kiss on Lucy's cheek. She looked about her. "What a pretty room. It used to be very gloomy."

"Gran did it up for me. She let me choose the colors."

"Perfect. All sunny." There was a small blue armchair by the bed, and Carrie sank into this. "Have you been working?"

"Yes. Homework." Lucy picked up her diary, stowed it away in a drawer, and then sat again, swiveling her typist's chair around so that she faced her aunt. "How long are you home for?"

"Indefinitely. Chucked the ski job in. I'm both homeless and unemployed, but it doesn't matter. How's everything with you?"

Lucy shrugged. "All right."

"There seems to be a certain crisis. You must be wondering what on earth is going to happen next."

This was in character, and Lucy was grateful. Carrie had always been completely direct. Suddenly Lucy felt much better and even strong enough to ask, "Mummy didn't buy two air tickets for Florida, did she?"

Carrie laughed. "Don't worry. She's going on her own. So that little battle you've won. It must have been something of a fight."

"Do you think I'm being stupid, not wanting to go with her?"

"No. I think you're absolutely right. You'd be like a sore thumb, a green gooseberry. Much better for Nicola to be on her own. But it does pose problems."

"You mean Christmas?"

"I mean you. What do you want to do? I bet nobody's even asked you that."

"Not really."

"I suggested you go to your father, but apparently he and his wife are off to the ski slopes. You haven't got cozy school friends with cozy mothers you'd want to go and be with?"

Lucy felt a bit abashed, because she hadn't. She had school friends but nobody special, nobody with a motherly mother.

Carrie's dark eyes were filled with kindness.

Lucy said, "I did think perhaps I could go to Cornwall. To Grandfather."

"Would you like that?"

"Yes, I think I would. The only thing is, I've never been—"

Carrie said, "I think it's a wonderful idea, and I think one day you should go. But not this Christmas, because I spoke to Jeffrey when I got back from Austria, on the telephone, and I know they've got a houseful. Their house isn't very big anyway."

Hope died. "Oh, well. It doesn't matter."

"But you should certainly go one day. In the spring perhaps. They'd love it, and you'd love all of them. So we'll have to come up with something else."

We was significant. "We?"

"Yes. Orphans of the storm together. What shall we do?"

"You mean for Christmas?"

"Of course for Christmas. Perhaps we should go away."

"But where?"

There seemed to be no answer to this. They gazed at each other, and then Carrie got to her feet. She said, "I've an idea. I just had it this moment. Have you ever heard of Elfrida Phipps?"

Lucy shook her head, wondering what was coming next.

"She's heaven. A cousin of Jeffrey's. Your gran could never stand her, because she was rather wild and an actress and had lots of boy-friends and husbands. But I always loved her, and when I was at Oxford, I started seeing her again, and we made terrific friends."

"How old is she?"

"Oh, ancient. Over sixty. But more fun than anyone you ever knew. Once, ages ago, she was ill after an operation, and I stayed with her until she was better, and we've always kept in touch. Now she's living in a little village in Hampshire. She says the house is weeny, but there'd be space for you and me. Would that be a good idea, do you think?"

"For two weeks? Would she mind?"

"I would bet my bottom dollar that she'll jump at it."

"How will we ask her?"

"I'll ring. I've got her number."

"Now?"

"No, not now. We don't want the others to know our plans until they're all cut and dried."

Carrie pushed back the cuff of her cashmere sweater and looked at her watch. "Heavens, it's nearly one o'clock. I'm starving, aren't you? Your gran said she'd give us soup and pâté, but I'm not sure if that's going to sustain me. Why don't I take all four of us out to lunch. Is there somewhere cheap and cheerful not too far away?"

"There's Rosetti's. It's a five-minute walk."

"Italian?"

"Spaghetti and stuff."

"My favorite food. What do you say? Shall we go and round up our mothers and tell them they're in for a treat?"

Lucy felt as though suddenly she had walked from a dark and cold corner into a blaze of warm sunshine. All part of being relieved, shed of worry, and having Carrie back again, a benevolent presence who was making everything all right.

By THE time Carrie reached the Lumleys' little terrace house, the overcast midwinter afternoon was already sinking into dusk. She went into the kitchen, made a mug of tea, and settled down by the telephone with her address book.

Carrie punched in Elfrida's number and waited. There was no reply, and clearly Elfrida had never got around to investing in an answering machine. After two more tries later in the evening, Carrie began to be a little concerned. It was, after all, a long time since they had been in touch. But she knew that if anything had happened to Elfrida, Jeffrey would have let her know.

Jeffrey. She would ring her father. Jeffrey would surely know the whereabouts of his cousin.

He did.

Oscar

IN MIDWINTER it was an alien land. Monotone beneath a sky scoured white by the wind. The hills, sweeping down to the coast, were already topped by an icing of snow, and the snow merged with the clouds, so that the summits of the hills were lost to view, veiled.

It was alien because Oscar did not remember the landscape thus.

Always, as a boy, he had come in the summer to visit his grand-mother at Corrydale, and in summer, so far north, the afternoons had stretched on until ten or eleven o'clock at night, and at bedtime the shadows of trees fell across golden sun-washed lawns.

He walked with Horace. He had left the house after lunch, setting out with a stout stick to help him on his way and insulated against the cold by a fleece-lined jacket and a tweed hat, pulled low over his brow. His boots were sturdy, and once he had traversed the streets of the little town and climbed the hill to the gate above the golf links, he was able to step out at some speed.

Horace bounded cheerfully ahead, and they followed a footpath high above the links, winding between thickets of gorse. After a mile or so this path led over a stile and along the track of a disused railway. The sea lay to his right, beyond the links and the dunes. He stopped to listen and heard the breakers on the beach and the cry of gulls. He saw, to his mild surprise, that there were a few hardy golfers out, brightly dressed figures striding down the fairways, hauling their clubs on trolleys behind them.

The old railway track petered out into a thicket of broom, and rounding this stretch, Oscar saw that they had reached the end of the links, the turn of the course, and the ninth tee. It was then that he heard the voices. Below him a group of four men were making their way to the tee. Oscar was instantly wary, fearing that one of them might be Major Billicliffe and that he would be spied and forced into introductions and convivial chat. His fears were, thankfully, ill-founded. Billicliffe was not one of the group.

MAJOR Billicliffe was the main reason that Oscar had kept a low profile ever since their arrival in Creagan. From time to time, urged by Elfrida, he had nipped across the road to the supermarket, and his daily outing was a trip to the newsagent to pick up *The Times* and *The Telegraph.* On these occasions he kept an eye open just in case Billicliffe should be bearing down upon him, loud with greeting and invitations to his terrible house.

Elfrida thought Oscar was being feeble. "He's harmless, Oscar, just a stupid old man. You must be firm if you meet him. Polite but firm."

"He is a terrifying bore."

"You can't cower indoors for the rest of your life. It's ridiculous."

"I am cowering indoors because the weather is inclement, to say the least of it."

"Rubbish. You spent the whole of Saturday raking leaves in the garden in the pouring rain."

"Billicliffe can't get into my garden."

"He could see you over the wall. He's tall enough."

"Don't even suggest it."

This walk with Horace was Oscar's first real foray into the countryside, and he had started out because all of a sudden he was restless and knew a physical need to stretch his legs. Even the prospect of encountering Major Billicliffe did not put him off.

It was all very unfortunate. Because Billicliffe, retired factor of Corrydale, was the man who had had custody of the key of the Estate House, and calling upon him to take possession of this key had been their first priority.

The occasion had not been propitious. At the end of a long winter drive from Hampshire, which had taken two days, both Oscar and Elfrida were exhausted. As they crossed the border into Scotland, the rain had turned to sleet and then snow.

Darkness fell early, and the final miles were achieved in nighttime conditions. As well, Oscar became confused by new road systems that had been built since his boyhood visits.

But somehow in the darkness they found the main gates to Corrydale and a rutted lane that led to a small stone house with a single curtained window lit from within. At once the quiet was ripped apart by deep-throated barking and furious, eerie howls.

But then the barking stopped. The door of the cottage was opened. A lanky, gangling figure stood there.

"That you? Blundell? Been waiting . . ."

The sentence was not finished, simply left hanging in the air.

Oscar and Elfrida got out of the car. "I'm sorry," Oscar apologized. "Difficult, driving in the dark. It's all unfamiliar. We've come for the key, and then—" He had been going to say, "We'll be on our way," but Major Billicliffe overrode him.

"Of course. Hector rang me. Got it here. Come along in. Just going to have a sniffer. You'll join me."

"Well—"

"Splendid. Come in out of the cold."

He stood aside, holding the door open in a hospitable manner, and after a moment's hesitation Oscar capitulated.

"Thank you," he said weakly, and put out a hand to steer Elfrida in front of him. "This is my friend Elfrida Phipps. She came to share the driving with me."

"Splendid. Splendid. Charmed to meet you, ma'am." He took Elfrida's hand, and for a moment Oscar thought he might be about to press a kiss upon it, so courtly was his manner.

Elfrida said, "Hello."

They followed him into a small, low-ceilinged sitting room, where a tiny fire in a tiled grate did little to warm the air. All seemed to be in a state of sad confusion. Sagging leather chairs, a carpet covered in dog's hairs, ashtrays brimming with pipe ash.

At the back of the room was another door, behind which the enraged dog had been shut away. Whines and heavy breathing emanated from beyond, and every now and then they heard a thump as the imprisoned brute flung his weight against the door.

Elfrida, naturally enough, began to look a bit nervous. "What kind of dog is it?" she asked.

"Labrador," Major Billicliffe told her. "Dear old bitch. Wouldn't hurt a fly. Now, what can I get you?"

He made his way across the room to where stood an old trolley on wheels, laden with bottles and with one or two smeary glasses.

Oscar longed for a cup of tea but knew that that would take much longer to prepare. "A Scotch would be splendid. Very small."

"And the lady?"

Elfrida, as well, was clearly longing for a hot cup of tea, but she said bravely, "A sherry?"

"Got some somewhere." He held up the bottle.

Pouring drinks, he talked. Oscar and Elfrida stood by the miserable fire and did not interrupt. " 'Fraid the housekeeping's a bit hit-and-miss these days. Wife died couple of years ago. Miss her like hell, but what can one do?" To look at, Major Billicliffe was something of an old wreck, knock-kneed as a horse on its way to the knacker's yard, with thin, stockinged legs that ended in a pair of enormous black unpolished brogues. His head was bald, sparsely covered with a few strands of gray hair, and his eyes were rheumy. His mustache was tobacco-stained. It was hard to imagine him as a dapper upright officer in any regiment of the British army.

"About time we had a bit of new blood about the place. Funny we've never met before, you and I, but then, it's years . . ." He came shambling over to deliver their drinks and returned to the trolley to deal with his own thirst, which seemed to require an enormously dark whisky in a small tumbler.

"Sit down. Make yourselves comfortable."

"We mustn't be too long."

"Won't take you five minutes to get to Creagan." Without much alternative Oscar and Elfrida perched on a sofa, side by side. Major Billicliffe lowered his tremendous height into the only armchair.

"I'm retired now, of course. Good of Hector to let me buy this cottage, but it was standing empty anyway. And Hughie couldn't care less. Buggered off to Barbados and sold the place up. Hotel. You probably saw the sign. All plate glass and bathrooms. And the bar prices are daylight robbery. Never go near the place. Take my pleasures in the golf club. Do you play golf? You should join. Put your name up if you like. Short walk from the Estate House."

Oscar nodded and, feeling desperate, said, "The key to the Estate House. If you could let me have it, we'll get out of your way."

"Ah, yes. Got it somewhere." Major Billicliffe heaved himself to his feet and crossed the room to an old open rolltop desk. He rooted around, feeling into pigeonholes. At last, "Eureka!" he exclaimed, and held up a large old-fashioned key tied to a crumpled label.

Oscar and Elfrida finished their drinks and rose to their feet.

Oscar took the key. "Thank you. I am so sorry we disturbed you."

"Didn't disturb me at all. Splendid to have a bit of company. And perhaps I'll pop in at the Estate House. See how you're settling in."

Elfrida smiled. She said, "Of course. But don't come quite right away. Oscar's not been very well, and we'll need a little time."

"Of course, of course. But we'll certainly see each other around."

NOW, in the middle of his walk, Oscar paused to watch the golfers until the last player whacked his ball into what appeared to be orbit. Then Oscar and the dog continued on their way.

He was beginning to feel a bit weary. In the far distance he could see, silhouetted against the gray clouds, the random rooftops and the church spire of the town. It seemed a very long way off, but he spied a small wooden shelter provided for the convenience of golfers. He decided to sit for a moment to get his breath.

He thought about the golfers, companionably playing their game deep into the dusk of a dying afternoon, and knew an envy that was almost resentment. They were together. Friends. Talking, joking, competing. They would have a drink in the clubhouse, part, return to their families. Ordinary men.

He wondered if he would ever be ordinary again.

He had always despised self-pity, and now, sitting huddled in the small wooden shelter, he fought it like a lion, striving to be positive, to count present blessings. First was the Estate House—the fact that he owned a bit of it and that it stood empty, a timely sanctuary to which he had fled. Second was Elfrida. Her companionship had saved his reason, and in her own uncomplicated way she had got him through the blackest times, comforting simply by accepting his limitations. When he fell silent, she left him alone. When he felt compelled to talk, Elfrida listened.

And third was the knowledge that even if he did not stay forever in this remote northern community, there was no need, or even the possibility, of returning to the house that had been Gloria's, a space haunted by memories of Francesca and filled only with a cold and numbing silence.

I must go on, he told himself. "I must go on." This time he said the words aloud, and Horace, who had been lying down, sat up and looked hopeful. Oscar got to his feet.

By the time he reached the clubhouse, it was dark, and Oscar was very tired. He saw the blaze of lights shining out from wide windows, behind which figures could be seen, relaxed as though in a friendly pub. In the car park, on the tailgate of a well-worn estate car, a man was perched in the act of changing his studded golf shoes for a pair of brogues. The man tied the last lace and got to his feet.

Oscar came alongside. "How did you get along?"

"We gave up on the fifteenth. Chickened out. Too dark and too cold." The man came forward. Oscar saw a ruddy face, a head of thick graying hair, and a pair of piercingly blue eyes. "Forgive me, but you're Oscar Blundell."

Oscar found himself disconcerted by being identified. He said, "Yes," and it sounded like an admission.

"I knew you'd come back to Creagan." (What else did he know?) "I've only been here for twenty years, so I never met your grandmother, Mrs. McLennan. But I did have the pleasure of a good friendship with Hector. Just for a short while, before he handed Corrydale over to Hughie and went south to live. I'm Peter Kennedy, by the way." He stuck out a hand, which Oscar took in his own gloved one. "Welcome to Creagan."

"Thank you."

"I'm just going in for a cup of tea. Would you care to join me?"

Oscar was silenced, hesitating. He thought of the solace of a restoring and hot cup of tea. On the other hand, in that brightly lit and convivial clubhouse, he would perhaps be introduced, have to talk to strangers, answer questions.

But there was something so warm and genuine about his new friend, so disarming and sincere, that he could not bring himself to refuse the invitation outright. "Yes, I would like to join you. Thank you very much."

"I'm delighted."

They incarcerated Horace in the back of Peter Kennedy's car. He gazed at them reproachfully through the rear window as they walked together into the clubhouse. In the foyer, lined with cabinets containing silver trophies and shields, portraits of former captains glowered down at them. To the right, glassed doors fed into the main room, furnished with tables and comfortable chairs, with a small bar in the corner. As they entered, one or two people looked up, but nobody took much notice of them except an elderly waitress. She wore a black skirt and a white blouse, and her white hair was waved. Spying them, she was at once all smiles.

"Mr. Kennedy, I didn't think we'd be seeing you this evening."

"Hello, Jessie. Are we too late for a cup of tea?"

"Never too late." Her eyes turned to Oscar.

"Jessie, this is Mr. Oscar Blundell. He's come to stay at the Estate House."

"Oh, my, that's who you are. I'd heard you'd moved in, but I haven't seen you around. Are you a golfer too?"

Oscar removed his hat. "I'm sorry, no."

"We'll have to rectify that. Now, Mr. Kennedy, where do you want to sit?"

But before there was time to tell her, an interruption occurred. From across the long room there came a shout, a deep voice ringing out like a clarion, startling everyone. "Peter! Come have a word. I haven't seen you for a week."

Peter Kennedy swung around, and Oscar, following his gaze, saw in the far corner a heavily built and aged man sitting in a wheelchair, waving a knotted stick.

"Would you mind, Oscar, if I left you for a moment? It's old Charlie Beith, and I must go and pay my respects."

"Of course."

Jessie took charge. "Come and sit down and get comfortable. Would you like a scone? And do you prefer Indian or China tea?"

Oscar said, "I'm sorry, but who is Peter Kennedy? I've just met him in the car park. He knew my uncle, but I don't know—"

"You mean you don't know what he does or who he is? He's our minister. The minister of the church."

The minister. The man whose job it was to comfort. Peter Kennedy's spontaneous friendliness had seemed genuine, but this new knowledge rendered it depressingly suspect. Did he already know why Oscar had returned to Creagan? Had Hector, with only the best of intentions, been in touch with Peter Kennedy? Explained the situation? Suggested perhaps a pastoral visit? Comforting chats, counseling, a gentle urging back to a church in which Oscar no longer believed?

Jessie said, "Are you all right?"

He looked into her concerned and motherly face and realized that his own was suffused with heat. A heat kindled by an inner turmoil that was frighteningly akin to panic. He knew that he could not stay there, or he would suffocate.

With a huge effort he made himself speak. "I am sorry. I've just remembered"—his voice sounded unreal, like a voice from another room—"I must get home. A telephone call." Backing off, he apologized again. "I'm sorry. Please explain to Mr. Kennedy."

He turned away from her and carefully, slowly, made for the door. He stepped out into the bitter air. The cold wind was an assault, and he stopped to steady himself, to let the icy air fill his lungs. He pulled on his old tweed hat. He was all right. He was surviving. All he had to do was get himself home. To be safe. Alone with Elfrida. He went down the steps and crossed over to the car park and retrieved Horace from Peter Kennedy's car. Then he was on his way, walking at a tremendous pace. Escaping.

❊ Elfrida

IN DIBTON the Women's Institute was great on mystery tours. These usually took place on a Saturday afternoon and entailed the ladies' being piled into a bus and whirled off to some unknown destination, quite often a stately home. Being spirited away so abruptly by circumstances outside her control—to the north of Scotland, to Creagan and the Estate House—was, Elfrida decided, the mystery tour of all time. From the moment she and Oscar had departed from Dibton, she had no idea of what lay in store for her, and there never came an appropriate moment to ask. So precipitant had been their departure, so swift the packing process, and so brief the time for good-byes that details of their destination lost all importance. They just had to get away.

Elfrida handed the key of Poulton's Row over to her neighbor, with as few explanations as possible, and asked her to keep an eye on her Ford Fiesta, on the pavement outside the cottage. Then Oscar had to get in touch with Hector McClellan and put him in the picture, while Elfrida telephoned her cousin Jeffrey in Cornwall and tried to explain to him the circumstances of what she was about to do.

Without any clear idea of what sort of clothes she would need, she packed a suitcase with an assortment of garments (warm) and shoes (stout). Then an ancient, squashy zipped bag for her most precious things—the possessions that had always traveled everywhere with her: the silk shawl, wrapped around the little painting by Sir David Wilkie; the Staffordshire dogs; her clock; her current piece of tapestry; a few photographs in silver frames; and half a dozen books. Oscar's luggage was a leather holdall, a bulging briefcase, and his fishing gear.

"Do you intend to go fishing, Oscar?"

"No idea. But I can't travel to Scotland without my rod. It would be almost sacrilegious."

There was space for all this in the back of Oscar's Volvo and still room for Horace, his blanket, biscuits, and water bowl.

The encounter with Major Billicliffe had been the final hurdle. With that accomplished and the key safely in Oscar's pocket, the last few miles were easy, almost carefree. The dark road ran downhill toward the sea, between dense stands of conifer. Elfrida opened her window and smelled pine and a sturdy whiff of salty air. Then the trees fell away, and ahead could be seen a straight and silvery line that was the sea. Far away, across the water, a lighthouse blinked—a pinprick in the darkness. Then ahead the glow of streetlights, and houses with windows lit behind drawn curtains. A street of stone houses, like a terrace. She saw the church looming, the lit clock like a round lantern, high in its tower. The hands stood at seven o'clock. Now larger, handsome houses, set back behind tall stone walls. Creagan. Another turning, another street.

Oscar drew up at the pavement's edge and turned off the engine. He laid his hand over Elfrida's. He said, "Dear girl, we're there."

The Estate House. So Elfrida saw it for the first time, by the light of streetlamps. Square and solid, set back from the road behind a wrought-iron railing and a forecourt of sea pebbles. The face of the house was a child's drawing, with a door and five windows. Above these, set in the slope of the slated roof, two dormers jutted. They got out of the car, and Elfrida set Horace free. He leaped down into the road and began to sniff for unfamiliar smells.

Oscar unlatched the gate and went up the path. Elfrida and Horace followed him. With the key he opened the door, and it swung inward. He found a light switch and turned it on.

They entered, and Elfrida instantly felt the warmth and smelled the cleanliness of a place newly scrubbed and polished. Ahead a staircase rose to a half landing and an uncurtained stair window. On either side, doors stood closed, but at the end of the hall a third door was open, and Oscar went through this and turned on another light.

Elfrida closed the front door, sealing away the chill of the winter evening. She followed Oscar into a kitchen, where stood an old-fashioned painted dresser and a wooden table. Beneath the window was a clay sink and at its side a capacious gas cooker, dating back perhaps forty years or more.

Oscar said, "Hardly all-singing, all-dancing." He sounded a bit apologetic.

"It's fine," Elfrida assured him, and meant it.

"Elfrida, are you about to cry?"

"I might be."

"Why?"

"Relief."

THAT had all happened three weeks ago. It was December now, a Friday, and five o'clock on a dark midwinter afternoon. Oscar, who had set out after lunch with Horace at his heels, his first real expedition into the country, had still not returned.

Elfrida made a mug of tea and took it upstairs to the sitting room. They called it the sitting room, but indeed it was a drawing room, formal and spacious, with a huge bay window looking out over the street and the church. Hours could be wasted simply sitting on the window seat and watching the world go by. Cars and delivery vans coming and going. Shoppers pausing on the pavement to chat. Strings of chattering children, walking to and from school.

The room was furnished, as was all the house, with the bare minimum of furniture: a thick Turkish carpet, a sofa and two chairs, a table against the wall, a glass-fronted bookcase, in which a few old books leaned against each other. No pictures, no ornaments.

Unpacking, she had put her modest stamp upon the place. The David Wilkie now hung opposite the fireplace, above the heavy oak table, which Oscar used as a desk. The Staffordshire dogs and her clock occupied the empty marble mantelpiece. Her half-done tapestry lay across the seat of a chair. Earlier on she had lit the fire. Now she went to the window to sit and watch for Oscar. But no sooner had she settled herself, with her mug between her hands, than the telephone rang. It had scarcely rung since they had taken up residence. She went to answer the call.

"Hello."

"Elfrida, it's Carrie. Carrie Sutton."

"Carrie! Where are you?"

"In London. How are you?"

"All right."

"Jeffrey told me you were in Scotland. Gave me your number. Elfrida, I've got to ask you a favor—a huge favor."

"Ask away."

"It's about Christmas."

IT WAS, necessarily, a very long telephone call. Finally they were finished. Elfrida went downstairs, where in the hall Oscar was shedding himself of jacket and hat. "You've been ages."

"We went for miles. The other end of the links and back. I'd forgotten it was so far." He put up a hand and ran it over his hair.

He looked, she thought, exhausted. She said, "A cup of tea?"

"I think I'm ready for something stronger."

"A Scotch. Go upstairs. There's a fire. I'll bring it to you."

In the kitchen, she poured his drink and made herself another mug of tea. She went upstairs with the mug in one hand and the tumbler in the other. She found Oscar standing at the mantelpiece, gazing down into the fire.

He turned his head and smiled gratefully. "How good you are." He took the drink and lowered himself into one of the armchairs.

Elfrida went to draw the curtains, shutting away the night. "I was sitting in the window, watching for you."

"I was delayed. Outside the golf club I met a man. We talked. He asked me into the club for a cup of tea. He is called Peter Kennedy, and he is the minister."

Elfrida waited. Finally, "So, Oscar?"

"It occurred to me that perhaps Hector had forewarned him. I had thought him simply a friendly chap, but I am afraid he was being kind. I want to be left alone. I walked away. Came home."

"Oh, Oscar."

"I know. Rude and mannerless."

"I'm sure he'll understand."

"I hope so. I liked his face." He took a deep breath that sounded like a terrible sigh. He said, "I hate myself."

"Oh, my dear, never do that."

She sat facing him in a little wide-lapped Victorian chair. She said, "Perhaps this isn't an opportune moment, but I have to ask you something. I have had a telephone call. Jeffrey's daughter Carrie Sutton. She has returned from Austria. She wants to come and spend Christmas with us."

"But we are not having Christmas."

"I told her. A lamb chop for lunch and no tinsel. She understands. She says she's not interested in Christmas either."

"Then let her come."

Elfrida hesitated. "There is a complication."

"A man?"

"No. Jeffrey's grandchild. Carrie's niece, Lucy. If Carrie comes, then Lucy must come too."

There was a very long silence. Oscar's eyes turned from Elfrida's face and gazed into the fire. "How old is the child?"

"Fourteen."

"Why does she have to come?"

Elfrida shrugged. "Some sort of selfish muddle that is always happening in my family." Elfrida bit her lip. "I can ring Carrie and tell her no. A little girl around the place would be more than painful for you. I shan't think any the less of you if you say no."

"It can make no difference. It can change nothing. You want them here, I think. Then tell them to come."

"You are a dear, kind, brave man," she said.

"There's space for them?"

"The attics are empty," Elfrida said. "Perhaps we could buy a bed, and Lucy shall sleep up there."

"We'll need to buy more than a bed."

"Not very much more."

"It's what you want. That's all that matters. Tell them they're welcome." He drank a bit of his whisky, seemingly deep in thought. Then he said, "Telephone Carrie now. If they take the train or come by airplane, we can send a taxi to meet them at Inverness. If they're driving, warn her about the snow."

Elfrida was filled with gratitude for his generosity of spirit. To have him sitting there mulling over such mundane details made her feel a great deal better. "I'll ring her right away." She pulled herself to her feet. "Thank you, Oscar."

NOW, Saturday morning, and Elfrida was the first downstairs. She had dressed in thick corduroy trousers and two sweaters and was glad of these when she opened the back door to let Horace out. During the night there had been a deep frost, and all was iced and sparkling, and her footsteps left marks on the crunchy grass of the little lawn. In the east, over the sea, the glow of dawn was a streak of pink. It was, she decided, going to be a fine day.

She was sitting at the table, drinking coffee, when Oscar came downstairs to join her, and at once Elfrida noticed his appearance. Normally he wore a thick shirt under a warm pullover. Very informal. But this morning he had put on one of his better shirts, a tie, a waistcoat, and his good tweed jacket.

She poured his coffee. "You're looking very smart."

He picked up his plate of bacon and eggs from the hot plate. "Thank you. I made an effort because I am going calling."

Elfrida was genuinely surprised. "Who are you going to call on?"

He sat down. "Rose Miller. A very old friend."

"You've never mentioned her. Should I be jealous?"

"I don't think so. She must be eighty-five. She was my grandmother's parlormaid. She lives on the Corrydale estate in a small cottage. I am going to go and pay my respects."

"Oh, dear Oscar, I'm absolutely delighted. But I don't entirely understand your change of heart."

"It was yesterday. Meeting the minister. If Peter Kennedy knows about me, then so will many other people. By now Rose Miller is bound to have heard I've come back. And she will be intensely hurt if I don't get in touch with her. So I have decided to go."

Suddenly she felt more cheerful than she had for a long time. Things slowly were looking up. Oscar was going calling, and next week Carrie and Lucy would be here. She decided that perhaps yesterday had been the turning point, although she had not recognized it as such.

"Maybe while you're at Corrydale you should look in on Major Billicliffe. He's probably dreadfully lonely. You could just drop in casually to pass the time of day. Perhaps ask him along for a drink or something when Carrie and Lucy are here."

Cunningly Oscar steered the discussion off at a tangent. "When are they coming?"

"They're flying to Inverness on Friday morning, and I've asked the taximan to go and get them."

AFTER OSCAR DEPARTED, Elfrida had nearly finished a little cursory housework when the doorbell rang. Horace, as usual, filled the house with panic-stricken barking.

"Oh, Horace, be quiet!" She went down the hall to open the heavy door, swinging it wide to an unknown female figure.

Her visitor was perhaps in her late thirties, tall and slender and marvelously unconventional in her appearance. She had very dark, almost raven-black, hair, cut in a fringe and hanging loose and straight to her shoulders. She wore a battered Barbour over a long red woolen skirt and what looked like Doc Marten boots. A tartan muffler was wound about her neck, framing a face beautifully boned and innocent of makeup. Her cheeks were tanned, rosy this morning with cold, and her eyes deep-set and dark as black coffee. She carried a little rural basket containing eggs.

She smiled. "Hello. You're Elfrida Phipps? I hope I'm not disturbing you, but I'm Tabitha Kennedy. Peter Kennedy's wife."

"Oh." Elfrida made much effort not to appear too astonished. She had never seen any person in her life less likely to be a minister's wife. "How really nice to meet you." She stepped back indoors, holding open the door. "Do come in."

But Tabitha Kennedy hesitated. "Not if you're busy. I just brought you some eggs from my hens."

"I'm not busy, and fresh eggs are a real treat. Come on, I'll give you a cup of coffee."

Tabitha stepped through the door, and Elfrida closed it behind her. "I'll put the kettle on. Oscar's gone to Corrydale to call on someone called Rose Miller."

"Goodness, there'll be a reunion. Rose always adored Oscar. Never stops talking about him." Tabitha followed Elfrida into the kitchen, put the basket of eggs on the table. "I'm glad Oscar's not here. One of the reasons I've come is to apologize, and now I shan't have to."

"Apologize? For what?"

"Peter sent me. He's afraid he was rather crass and pushy yesterday afternoon. He hopes so much that he didn't upset Oscar."

"I think Oscar feels he's the one to apologize. It was rude, just running away like that, but he panicked and fled. He was filled with remorse. He knew he'd behaved dreadfully badly."

"Hector wrote and told us about Oscar's wife and child dying in that appalling car accident. It takes a long while to move out of something like that and get back into life again."

"It's called grieving."

"I know. It can't have been easy for you."

"As a matter of fact, it's been hellish."

Elfrida heard herself come out with this and was amazed that the impulsive words had been spoken, because the moments of hellishness she had never acknowledged, nor admitted, even to herself. "I think frustration is the worst, because there is not a mortal thing one can do to help. And then impatience. And then guilt for feeling impatient. More than once I've had to bite my tongue. And another thing is, I'm quite a sociable animal. I like making friends and getting to know people, but because of Oscar, I've had to keep a low profile. I've probably created a very snooty impression."

"I'm sure not."

"Today I have a feeling that the hellish time might just about be behind us. Perhaps going to see Rose Miller is a step forward."

"If Peter came to see Oscar, would that be a good idea? They could put things right between them."

"I think it's a marvelous idea, but tell him to telephone first."

"I'll do that."

The coffee was made, the jug set on the tray. Elfrida picked it up. "Let's go upstairs. It's more comfortable."

She led the way, and Tabitha followed. "I'm always impressed by this beautiful staircase. It gives such a grand feel to your entrance." She paused on the half landing to gaze out at the garden. This, still frosted and bleak with midwinter, climbed the slope of the hill in a series of terraced lawns, with a path and small flights of steps running up its center. "I'd forgotten how much land there is."

"Oscar gardens, but so far he's just swept up a few leaves."

Elfrida, laden with the tray, went on upstairs. Low sun streamed through the open sitting-room door. "Shall we sit by the window?"

"Let's. The sun is so gorgeous." Tabitha unwound her muffler, took off her Barbour, and settled herself on the window seat.

"Have you lived here long?" Elfrida asked.

"About twenty years. Both our children were born in the Manse."

"How old are they?"

"Rory's eighteen. Just left school. He's got a place at Durham University, but he's not taking it up till next year. And Clodagh's twelve and, for some reason, mad on horses."

Elfrida looked at Tabitha, sitting there in her black polo-neck sweater and with her young girl's hair, and was filled with curiosity. "Do you like being a minister's wife?"

"I adore being married to Peter. And I'm not totally a minister's wife, because I teach art at the school. I can't wait for you to meet Peter. I'd ask you up to the Manse, but perhaps we'd better wait until he and Oscar have sorted themselves out."

"I can't think of anything I'd like more."

Tabitha had finished her coffee and now looked at her watch. "I must fly. Peter's got an early meeting in Buckly this afternoon, and I must feed him soup before he goes."

When Tabitha had gone, Elfrida inspected the contents of the fridge. She heard the front door open and shut and knew that Oscar had returned. She went out into the hall to meet him.

"You're back. How was Rose Miller?"

"In splendid form." He took off his hat and hung it on the newel-post at the foot of the banister. "We had a great crack and a glass of elderberry wine."

She led him back into the kitchen. He took off his thick jacket and pulled out a chair and sat down. Elfrida eyed him. For a man who had just returned from sipping elderberry wine with an old admirer, he looked tired and preoccupied.

"Are you all right, Oscar?"

"Yes, I'm fine. I did what you told me, Elfrida. I went to see Major Billicliffe."

"Oh, good man."

"No, not good. I don't feel good at all."

"Why not? What happened?"

He told her. On his way home, as he passed Billicliffe's house, he had heard the dog howling. The sound was as arresting as a cry for help, and Oscar had been instantly rendered alert with concern.

Listening, Elfrida was aghast, already dreading the end of the story. "What did you do?"

"Went to ring the bell, but nothing happened except the dog stopped howling and started barking. I tried the door, and it was open. So I went in and called out. But no answer. The dog had been shut in the back. I tried the other ground-floor room. The chaos there was worse than the sitting room. Drip-dry shirts hanging over the backs of chairs, papers and boxes piled on a table. I went up the staircase and opened the door at the top and peered in. And there was the old boy in bed."

"He wasn't dead?"

"For a moment I thought he was. And then he stirred."

"Thank heavens for that."

He had not been dead, but he looked ghastly and was clearly very unwell. However, realizing that he had a visitor, he had tried to rally himself, pulled himself up on his pillows, put on a brave face. Yesterday, he explained, his cleaning lady had turned up and been so concerned by his appearance that she had telephoned the Creagan G.P., Dr. Sinclair. Dr. Sinclair drove immediately to Corrydale, where, after a fairly thorough examination, he told Major Billicliffe that he thought it best if he went over to the hospital in Inverness for tests in order to get to the root of his troubles.

"When does he have to go to Inverness?"

"Monday. Dr. Sinclair's booked him in."

"And how will he get there?"

Oscar realized that the old man, the old soldier, was very frightened by the prospect of hospitals, tests, illness, pain, and a possible operation. So he had suggested to Major Billicliffe that he, Oscar, should drive him to the hospital and see him safely installed.

At the offer Major Billicliffe had become quite emotional. "But why?" he had asked, fumbling for a grubby handkerchief to wipe away the weak tears of an invalid. "Why should you bother about a stupid old buffer like me?"

"Because I should like to. Because you are part of Corrydale. Because of my grandmother and Hector." Major Billicliffe looked unconvinced. Oscar finished, "Because you are my friend."

Elfrida was much touched. "You are sweet. He won't be nearly so afraid if you are there. What about the dog?"

"I went downstairs and let her loose in the garden. She was not fierce at all, just a dear old Labrador needing a bit of attention. Her name, incidentally, is Brandy."

"Interesting."

"I took her to Rose Miller and filled Rose in with all that had occurred. She was very distressed. By the time I left, she was already girding herself up to go and do a bit of tidying up and cooking for him. At eighty-five years old, there's nothing she loves so much as a challenge. She kept saying, 'He's mad on the whisky, but he's a dear, good chentleman and too proud to ask for help.' "

"And what about the poor dog?"

"Rose is going to arrange for her nephew, Charlie Miller, to look after the dog."

"Oh, Oscar, what a morning you've had."

"But I'm glad I went." He smiled. "How about you?"

"Tabitha Kennedy came to see me. I've so much to tell you."

"Then tell me over lunch. Let's treat ourselves at the pub. We'll have a sandwich, and I'll stand you a gin and tonic, and we'll drink to . . ." He hesitated. "Us?"

"Oh, Oscar." Elfrida came around the table, put her arms about him, and hugged. It was being a good day.

Oscar

AFTER a late breakfast on Sunday morning Oscar, bundled up as usual against the cold, walked down the street to the newsagent's to pick up the Sunday papers. The little town was empty and quiet. It was a brilliant day, cloudless and with no breath of wind.

Returning, he met Elfrida and Horace setting out for a good long walk along the beach. She said, "Come with us," but he declined her invitation, because he wished to settle down with the Arts section and catch up with all that was happening in London.

He went indoors and up the stairs to their magnificent sitting room. Elfrida had laid the fire, so he lit it and settled down in considerable comfort to read.

The church bells disturbed him. The tower clock told him that it was half past ten. He dropped the paper and went over to the window seat and perched there, half turned, looking down onto the street. He found it fascinating on Sunday mornings how the empty town slowly but steadily began filling up.

The church was coming to life, and presently he heard, as though from very far away, the tones of the organ: "Sheep May Safely Graze." Muffled by stone-thick walls, but recognizable to Oscar's professional ear as a good instrument and competently played.

At first Oscar had found having the church so close as a neighbor a little disconcerting. A constant reminder, nudging at his shoulder, of all he had lost. Sitting now, he watched groups of people converging. He knew that he only had to cross the road and he would be swept up into the stream and, like a swimmer caught in a current, sucked through those imposing doors and into the soaring nave.

He left the window and went back to the fire and his newspaper. But when the congregation began to sing their first hymn, he lowered the paper and listened, staring into the flames.

> *"Hark, a thrilling voice is sounding,*
> *Christ is nigh, it seems to say.*
> *Cast away the dreams of darkness*
> *O ye children of the day."*

A good old classic Advent hymn. He remembered rehearsing the choir at the school where he had taught, imploring them to sing as though they truly believed the message of hope.

He thought, I must get in touch with Peter Kennedy.

THE NEXT NIGHT, OSCAR LAY awake for a long time, thinking about Godfrey Billicliffe. At last he knew his Christian name, learned in the course of helping the ward sister fill in countless forms before leaving the sick old man to her tender mercies.

The Monday undertaking had not been as demanding as he had feared. The drive to Inverness had gone smoothly, and old Billicliffe, encouraged by caring attention, had talked much about his life.

It was when they were speeding down the motorway across the Black Isle, and Inverness was in view across the water, that Major Billicliffe said, "Been thinking, Oscar."

"What have you been thinking about?"

"What's going to happen. . . . Turning my toes up."

"You're not going to turn your toes up," Oscar assured him.

"Never know. Have to be prepared for all contingencies. Learned that in the army. Prepare for the worst and hope for the best." A long pause. "Wondered . . . if you'd agree to be my executor. Good to know . . . Capable hands . . ."

"I'm not so sure my hands are capable."

"Rubbish. Hector McLennan's nephew . . . Friends all dead . . . Thought you might . . . Appreciate it . . ."

His unfinished sentences Oscar found maddening. He said as calmly as he could, "If it would set your mind at rest, I'd be happy to be your executor. But—"

"Splendid. Tell my lawyer. Nice feller. Keen fisherman. I must tell him you're my executor. Suppose I can ring up from the hospital?"

"Has he got a name?"

Major Billicliffe gave a snort, which perhaps was meant to be laughter at Oscar's quirky question. " 'Course he's got a name. Murdo MacKenzie. Firm's MacKenzie and Stout. Inverness."

"Of course."

He did not speak again until they had reached their destination.

The hospital was the Royal Western, and once he arrived, matters were taken out of Oscar's hands. The ward sister was ready and waiting for admission, with her clipboard and her forms. All went smoothly until she came to "Next of kin."

"Next of kin, Major Billicliffe?"

Suddenly he looked bewildered. "Sorry?"

"Next of kin. You know, wife, children, brothers or sisters."

He shook his head. "I have none. I have no one."

"Oh, come along, there has to be someone."

Oscar could not bear it. "Me," he said firmly. "I am Major Billi-cliffe's next of kin. Oscar Blundell. You can write it down. The Estate House, Creagan." He gave her the telephone number.

Finally all was written, recorded, and signed. And it was time for Oscar to leave. He said good-bye.

"You'll come again?"

"Of course. Provided we don't get snowed in."

"Thank you for bringing me. Obliged . . ."

"Not at all."

And Oscar walked away from the old man.

HE COULD have done no more. Later, when there was news of the invalid, he and Elfrida would set out on the long drive once more to visit Godfrey Billicliffe. Elfrida, if anybody, would cheer him up. She would probably take him grapes.

A clout of wind struck the house. Oscar turned into the pillows and closed his eyes and all at once found himself thinking about Francesca. This often happened in the dark hours of a restless night, and he dreaded the inevitable aftermath—a torment of rekindled, anguished loss. He slid his hand beneath his pillow to fumble for his handkerchief, knowing that he would probably weep. But instead of weeping, he became aware of a sort of quiet, as though he were more at ease with himself than he had felt for weeks. Francesca. He saw her running across the sunlit lawns of the Grange, toward him. And the image stayed, poignant but especially sweet.

Holding it close, he slept.

THE next morning dawned a day of dismal weather. Elfrida had bought herself a notebook and over lunch made lists for an after-noon of shopping with Tabitha Kennedy in Buckly.

"I've got to think of everything," she told Oscar. "There isn't time for forgetting. Carrie and Lucy will be here on Friday."

Oscar watched with amusement. He had never seen Elfrida so organized. When she and Tabitha had departed, he was alone. Aware of his procrastination, he thought, Peter might be at home today.

He went to the telephone, looked up the number, and punched the digits. He heard the ringing tone, the response.

"Creagan Manse." The warm, familiar voice. "Peter Kennedy."

AT HALF past five Oscar, bundled up and hatted, set off on the stepped lane that led up the hill. He remembered the location of the Manse from sixty years ago, when he was sometimes brought for tea by his grandmother. He pressed the bell.

The door was flung wide, and Peter Kennedy stood there, warm with welcome. He wore a thick polo-neck sweater and a pair of worn corduroys and looked comfortingly unchurchly. "Oscar! Come away in."

Oscar went into the hall and saw the Turkish carpet, the oak hall stand, the antique cist on which stood a neat stack of parish magazines. On the bottom stair stood a pair of football boots.

"Take your coat off. We've got the place to ourselves. I've a fire on in my study. Come along in." Peter led the way into his study, a bow-windowed front room with a huge littered desk and two ancient leather armchairs, walls with shelves of books, a marvelous smell of peat smoldering in the fire basket.

Oscar said, "A peat fire. I'd forgotten about peat. I must try and get hold of some, just for that smell."

"I'm very fortunate. One of my parishioners has his own peat patch, and he keeps me supplied. Now make yourself comfortable. Would you like a cup of coffee?"

Oscar did not immediately reply.

"A glass of Laphraoig? I keep it, but only for special occasions."

Malt whisky. Laphraoig. Irresistible. "I think I'd like that more than anything."

"I thought you might, so I am prepared."

And Oscar saw on the desk a small tray neatly set with the bottle of Laphraoig, two small tumblers, and a jug of water. So much for the coffee. He was touched.

"The girls aren't back from Buckly yet?" Peter asked.

"No." Oscar lowered himself into one of the chairs.

Peter handed him his drink and then settled down in the other chair, facing his visitor. He raised his glass. *"Slàinte."*

"Good health."

The Laphraoig was like nectar. Clean, delicious.

Peter said, "Buckly's a depressing town at the moment. Most of the people are unemployed. The woolen mill went to the wall."

Oscar frowned. "Not McTaggarts? What happened?"

Peter told him. "The old man died; the sons weren't interested. The workforce got a bit of financial help and took it over themselves. They were doing all right, and then we had a spell of dreadful weather, the river burst its banks, and the place was flooded. Everything lost, destroyed. There's some word of a takeover. One of those big textile conglomerates. Sturrock and Swinfield. From London. But so far nothing seems to have happened."

"What a tragedy." Oscar frowned. "I can't think why I haven't heard of this, but just now I don't read the newspapers properly, and I haven't talked to many people. That's why I'm here. To apologize to you. I should have come before."

"Please, don't feel bad. I realized that I had taken you unawares, and I should have waited for a more suitable occasion to make myself known to you. I hope you weren't too upset."

"I don't know what came over me. It was ridiculous."

"Please, think no more of it. Another time you must join me there for tea or for a drink. The best would be if you felt like joining the club. It's such a splendid course, it would be sad to live here and not experience at least one round."

Oscar took another sip of the Laphraoig. "Godfrey Billicliffe also invited me to join the golf club."

"I understand that you drove him to hospital yesterday."

"How did you know that?"

Peter Kennedy smiled. "Dr. Sinclair rang me to put me in the picture. It was very good of you."

"Did you know he was ill?"

"No. I don't think anybody knew. How did you guess?"

"I went to see Rose Miller. On the way home I heard Billicliffe's dog howling, so I called in."

"I have to go to Inverness on Friday for a meeting. I'll pop into the hospital and pay a visit. See how he's getting on."

"I said I would stand as his next of kin. So I imagine that if there is any news, then I shall be informed."

"Keep me in touch. Now, how is your uncle Hector?"

"Growing older. Living in London. He came down to see me after . . . the funeral and suggested I come back here."

"I know, Oscar. He wrote me a long letter. I wanted to come right away to talk with you. But my instinct told me that for the time being you needed to be on your own. I hope you didn't get the impression that I was either uncaring or inattentive."

"No. I didn't think that."

"Sometimes . . . just to talk to a stranger, a person disassociated, is very often easier."

"It's difficult to know where to start. It all seems to go a long way back. I never thought I should be married. I had my work as a schoolmaster, teaching piano and training the choir. For company other masters and their wives. I was very happy. And then I grew older, and the headmaster retired, and I decided that the time had come for a change. As well, I had been offered the post as organist and choirmaster at St. Biddulph's in London. The music at St. Biddulph's had always been renowned for its excellence. I moved to London.

"I met the Bellamys soon after my arrival at St. Biddulph's. From the first they were enormously hospitable and kind to me. When George Bellamy became ill, I used to go to their house to keep him company, play backgammon with him. When he died, I arranged the music for his considerably important funeral.

"After the funeral Gloria continued to invite me to various small social affairs. Sometimes we went to the cinema together or spent a day at Kew. I thought little of it but much enjoyed her company. And then one day, in a quite matter-of-fact fashion, she said that she thought it would be a good idea if we married. It all sounds, I know, a little cold-blooded, but the truth is that I was extremely fond of her and she, I think, of me.

"She was a wonderful wife, still a comparatively young woman and brimming with physical vitality. When she told me she was pregnant, I was incredulous. I had never in all my life imagined that I would become a father. And when Francesca was born—that tiny child—I was filled with a wonder which I don't suppose I shall ever experience again. It was as though a miracle had occurred. And she never stopped being a miracle.

"Sometimes, as she grew older and was running about and talking nineteen to the dozen and generally making the usual din that all children make, I would watch her and still find it unbelievable that she was actually mine, that I had helped to create this beguiling, beautiful, miniature human being.

"Then Gloria was left this house in Hampshire, and we moved from London. I missed St. Biddulph's, but from time to time I played the organ for morning service in the village church."

Here Oscar paused to take another sip of the Laphraoig.

Peter spoke. "Have you known Elfrida for always?"

"No. We didn't meet until she came to live in our village. She was alone, and Gloria took Elfrida under her wing. She was amusing, full of life, and we all enjoyed her company. When Hector suggested I leave Hampshire and return to Creagan, I knew I couldn't do it on my own. I dreaded being alone. So I asked Elfrida to come with me. It is a measure of her generous heart that she agreed.

"When I first met Elfrida, I remember she asked me if I was religious. I told her that it is hard not to believe when you have been steeped in the liturgies and traditions of the Anglican Church for most of your life, and I felt I needed some being to thank. Because I was fortunate. I was content. The marriage was working well, and because of Francesca, I could have no regrets.

"Then a split second, and Gloria and Francesca were both dead. If a God was there—and I had never been totally certain that He was—I didn't want to have any part of Him.

"I should have been with them. I should have been behind the wheel of the car. If only. 'If only' is my nightmare."

" 'If only' is like hindsight," Peter said. "A useless exercise. As for God, I hope that no one has sought to try and comfort you by saying that God must have needed Francesca more than you. I would find it impossible to worship a God who deliberately stole my child from me. Such a God would be a moral monster."

Oscar was astounded. "Is that what you really believe?"

Peter nodded. "It is what I truly believe. Thirty years in the ministry has taught me that the one thing we should never say when a young person dies is 'It is the will of God.' We simply don't know enough to say that. I am in fact convinced that when Francesca died in that terrible accident, God's was the first heart to break."

"I want to move on, to go on living, to be able to accept, to be able to give again. I don't like taking all the time."

"Oh, Oscar. It will be all right. For a while what you are probably going to need most is not people who will quote the Bible to you, but close friends who will continue to hold your hand and lend you a listening ear when you want to speak about Francesca."

Oscar thought about Elfrida, and Peter paused, as though to give him time to argue this conception. But Oscar did not say anything.

"Life is sweet," Peter went on. "Beyond the pain, life continues to be sweet. The basics are still there. Beauty, food, and friendship, reservoirs of love and understanding. Later you are going to need others who will encourage you to make new beginnings. They will help you move on, to cherish happy memories and confront the painful ones with more than bitterness and anger."

Oscar remembered the dark night and the image of Francesca and how, for the first time, the memory did not reduce him to the painful tears of loss but filled his being with a peaceful comfort. Perhaps that had been the start of his recovery. Perhaps this conversation, this interview—whatever one called it—was the continuance.

He did not know. He only knew that he felt better, stronger, not so useless. Perhaps, after all, he hadn't done so badly.

He said, "Thank you."

"Oh, my friend, I wish I could give you so much more."

"No. Don't wish that. You have given me enough."

Lucy

Lucy had flown only twice in her life. Both times she had found it tremendously exciting, but today she made an effort to be consciously casual about the whole business to give the impression that she was a seasoned, experienced traveler.

Her clothes helped. Her mother, perhaps to assuage unadmitted stirrings of guilt, had taken Lucy to the Gap and bought her daughter a number of delectable things. So she was wearing the new, warm jeans, lined in red brushed cotton. Her boots were pale suede with thick rubber soles, and her jacket was scarlet, quilted and padded. As well, Nicola had bought her two polo-neck sweaters, a black miniskirt, and two pairs of thick black tights. Last night she had washed her hair and this morning brushed it back into a long ponytail, secured with a cotton scrunchy. She felt sleek and neat. A credit to Carrie.

Carrie looked elegant in long boots, her loden coat, and a black fur hat. Lucy was very aware of heads turning to watch as Carrie walked by, pushing their trolley with the luggage. The only thing was, poor Carrie had a bit of a cold. She said she would be fine once she started breathing the clean, cold Scottish air.

In the plane, Lucy had a window seat, and she sat with her forehead pressed against the little window, staring down at land spread like a greenish gray quilt, patterned with slow-moving cloud shadows.

When the plane began to lose height, the terrain slowly took shape, and she saw snow on the tops of mountains. Then the blue gleam of the sea, boats, and a bridge over a wide firth.

They landed, huge tires thumping on tarmac. "We are going to be met," Carrie told her, "by a taxi from Creagan."

It was a spectacular drive. The road led through farmlands and over bridges, and on the high ground the tires of the taxi scrunched over snow. It followed the shores of a tidal sea loch and ran through small villages with stone cottages and sturdy no-nonsense churches.

In Creagan, Alec, the taxi driver, drew up at the pavement's edge before the Estate House. There came the sound of barking, and the next moment the front door of the house was flung open and down the path came Elfrida Phipps and her dog.

"Carrie! Oh, my darling girl." She flung her arms around Carrie. "You're here. I've been so looking forward . . . so excited . . ."

Lucy, standing aside, watched. Elfrida was very tall and thin, and she had a lot of wild hair the color of marmalade. She wore tartan trousers and a huge thick gray sweater. Her eyelids were blue, and she wore a lot of lipstick. Lucy could understand why Gran didn't approve. Kissing, she had left lipstick on Carrie's cheek.

Carrie said, "Elfrida, you look wonderful. Scotland clearly agrees with you."

"Darling, it's bliss. Bitterly cold, but bliss."

"You have to meet Lucy."

"But of course." She laughed. "Isn't this ridiculous, Lucy? We're relations, and we've never set eyes on each other. But your grandfather was my most favorite cousin, and we used to have wonderful wild times together." She put her hands on Lucy's shoulders. "Let me look at you. Yes, pretty as paint. This is my dog, Horace, who, I am pleased to say, has stopped barking. He's been looking forward to meeting you because he hopes you'll take him on long walks on the beach. Come along, everybody, and meet Oscar."

They all streamed up the path and into the house in single file, Elfrida leading the way, then the dog, then Carrie, Lucy, and, finally, the taxi driver, laden with luggage. They went up a wide staircase. Lucy liked the feeling of the house and the faint suggestion of something delicious cooking in the kitchen.

They had reached the first-floor landing. The pleasing staircase rose on to the upper floor.

Elfrida raised her voice to call, "Oscar! Here they are!" And then, in her ordinary voice again, "He's in the sitting room. You two go and say hello, and I'll show Alec where to put the suitcases. Carrie's in here, Alec, and then Lucy's upstairs."

Carrie took Lucy's hand in her own, which was comforting, and they went into a beautiful sitting room, filled with light.

Oscar was waiting for them, standing with his back to the fireplace. He was as tall as Elfrida, but not as thin as she, and he had a fine head of silvery hair and a quiet and kindly face, not rugged but strangely unlined. His eyes were hooded, and drooped at the corners. He wore a checked shirt and a blue Shetland sweater.

Carrie said, "Oscar, how do you do. I'm Carrie Sutton."

"My dear." He came forward, and Lucy thought he must find himself a little astonished to be welcoming a guest as sensationally glamorous as Carrie. But pleased as well. "How good to see you. Have you had a peaceful journey?" They shook hands.

"Perfect," Carrie told him. "No problems."

"Elfrida's been mad with excitement all morning."

"It's so good of you to have us." Carrie looked about her. "And what a marvelous house you have."

"I own only half. I am part owner."

"That doesn't make it any less special." She let go of Lucy's hand and put an arm around her shoulder. "This is Lucy Wesley."

Lucy swallowed her nervousness. She said, "How do you do." He looked down at her, and she willed herself to meet his eyes. For what seemed a long time he said nothing. She knew that he must be thinking of his own daughter, twelve years old and now dead. And then he smiled at her and took her hand, and his clasp was warm and friendly, and after that she wasn't nervous any longer.

"So you are Lucy?"

"Yes."

"And you are going to have to sleep in the attic."

Carrie laughed. "Oscar, you don't make it sound very tempting."

"Don't worry, Lucy. Elfrida has made it entrancing for you. "Now"—he let go of Lucy's hand—"it's half past twelve. Why don't you both go and find your rooms and get settled, and then we'll have lunch. Elfrida has spent much of the morning concocting something heartening to eat after your long journey."

Lucy's spirits rose. The worst—the initial encounters—were over. Oscar was kind. And Elfrida had said she was as pretty as paint.

THEY had lunch in the kitchen. After that Carrie and Elfrida had coffee, but Oscar did not want any. Instead, he looked at his watch and said, "If Horace and I do not set out for a walk now, then we won't be home before darkness falls." He looked at Lucy. "Would you like to come with us?"

"For a walk?"

"We could go on the beach, and then you will know the way."

She felt very gratified to be invited. "Yes, I'd love to."

"Perhaps, Oscar," said Elfrida, "you could wheel her round the town first and show her where the shops are. It won't take more than five minutes."

"If that's what she'd like. Have you got a warm coat, Lucy?"

"I've got my new jacket."

"And a warm hat. The sea wind can freeze your ears off."

"Yes, I've got that too. Shall I clear the table?" Lucy asked.

Elfrida laughed. "How well brought up you are. Of course not. Carrie and I will do that when we've finished our coffee. Off you go with Oscar before it gets too cold."

Five minutes later they set off together—the elderly man, the girl, and the dog. Horace wore his lead, and Lucy held its other end in her gloved hand. Down the street, all around the church wall. The gift shop, the chemist, the bookstore, the butcher, the newsagent.

"This is where I come to pick up the morning papers. If I want to be lazy and lie in my bed, then you can do it for me," Oscar said.

The petrol pumps, a shop displaying knitted sweaters, the supermarket. Lucy paused to look through a wrought-iron gate to where a side door of the church stood open. She longed to go inside. She could see an inner, closed door. "Is the church open?" she asked. "Can we go in now? Just for a moment. Churches are so nice when they're empty. Like empty streets. You can see their shape."

He took a deep breath, and for an instant she thought he was going to refuse. But he let it all out in what sounded like a deep sigh. "All right," he said.

They tied the end of Horace's lead to the handle of the outer door and left him there. He did not look pleased.

Inside, their footsteps rang on the flagged floor and echoed up into the roof. Sunlight poured through the stained-glass windows, and the arched ceiling soared upward, the plaster between the curved beams painted the blue of a summer sky.

Lucy wandered off to investigate. She read the words on old memorial slabs, people from another age who had been true servants of God and regular worshippers. By the time she had inspected everything—from the ornate font to the kneelers, each handsomely upholstered in handstitched needlepoint—Oscar had tired of standing and was settled comfortably in the front pew.

Lucy felt a bit guilty and went to sit beside him. "I'm sorry for being so long."

"I am pleased that you are interested in such things."

"Carrie told me that you were an organist and taught music."

"That's true. I was choirmaster as well. Do you listen to music?"

Lucy shrugged. "Only pop and such." She thought about this. "Except sometimes at school we get taken to concerts. We went to an open-air concert in Regents Park this summer. At the end they played the 'Music for the Royal Fireworks,' and there was a fireworks display at the same time. I really loved that."

"An experience."

"Yes. It was lovely." She sank her chin into her new jacket and gazed up at the tall stained-glass window that faced them—Mary with the baby Jesus. She said, "I wouldn't want a birthday in the middle of winter. I wouldn't want to be born on Christmas Day."

"Why not?"

"Well, for one thing, you'd probably only get one present. And for another, it's usually rather dark and gloomy weather."

"When is your birthday?"

"July. Much better. Only thing is, I'm usually at school."

Oscar said, "Actually, I don't think Christ was born in winter-time. I think he was probably born in the spring."

"Really? Why do you say that?"

"Well, the shepherds were guarding their flocks, which probably meant that it was lambing time. They were watching out for wolves, in case they came and ate the babies."

"Then why don't we have Christmas in the spring?"

"I think the early Christians were a cunning lot. They simply adapted what was left to them by the pagan inhabitants of the countries which they converted. There had always been the celebration of the winter solstice, the shortest day of the year. I suppose to cheer themselves up, those pre-Christians had a party, lit fires, caroused, burned candles, baked cakes." Oscar smiled.

"So the early Christians just used the same party?"

"Something like that."

"But added other bits as well."

"Their belief in the Son of God."

"I see." Considered, it seemed a very practical arrangement.

Lucy was silent for a moment. Then she said, "Do you like Christmas?"

"Parts of it," Oscar told her, sounding cautious.

"I don't really like it much. There's such a buildup, and then it's sort of . . . disappointing."

"Which proves that we should never expect too much." High above them the church clock struck half past two. Oscar said, "Perhaps we have lingered long enough. Come along. We have to get as far as the beach, and before very long it will be dark."

Carrie

OSCAR, Lucy, and Horace were gone, off for their walk, and Carrie and Elfrida were left alone, still sitting at the kitchen table with their coffee. They smiled at each other. Two women of different generations, but old friends who had not been together alone for too long and who now relished their peaceful privacy.

Carrie said, "What a perfectly sweet man."

Elfrida, she thought, for all her sixty-two years, looked as vital and energetic as a young girl.

"Isn't he?" Elfrida said with satisfaction.

"I'm so pleased they've made friends. Lucy was apprehensive. I hope it's not going to be too much for you, having us here."

"It's brilliant. Just what we need."

"It doesn't have to be an all-singing, all-dancing Christmas. Lucy and I both have a low expectation of the festive season."

"Us too. Though once he knew you were coming, Oscar did order a Christmas tree."

"Lucy will love that. She can decorate it."

"How is your mother?"

"Just the same." No more needed to be said.

"And Nicola?"

"Ditto. Unlike wine, they do not improve with age."

"And your father?"

"Haven't seen him. But we spoke on the telephone."

"I had such a wonderful month with them all in Cornwall, in October. And then I got home to hear this terrible thing that had happened to Oscar. It was like moving out of one world and into another. Life can change with such shocking abruptness."

"I know." Carrie thought about Andreas and then didn't think about him. She said again, "I know."

A silence fell. Carrie knew what was coming next.

"And you, Carrie?"

She finished her coffee and set down the cup. "I'm fine."

"I don't think you are. For one thing, you look tired. And thin."

"Look who's talking. Admit, Elfrida, we'd neither of us have ever won a prize for the most voluptuous."

"Why did you suddenly come back from Austria?"

Carrie shrugged. "Oh, reasons. Sometime I'll tell you."

"You're not ill?"

"No. I'm fighting a cold and I am a bit tired, but I am not ill."

"I feel you're unhappy. I wish I could help."

"You are helping. By having us here."

Elfrida ran a hand through her unruly fiery hair. "I will say no more. Now"—her manner changed; she became cheerful, in charge once more—"what would you like to do this afternoon? Perhaps a nap. I'll find a hot-water bottle."

Bed and a hot-water bottle. Carrie could not remember how long it was since some other person had cherished her, had said, *You look tired.* And, *How about a little rest?* She had spent too many years being strong, looking after others and their problems. Canceled reservations, faulty ski tows, unsuitable bedrooms, the lack of snow or too much of it, lost passports, money . . . And then returning to London to be faced with family problems.

She was tired of being the sturdy pillar against which everybody leaned. Upstairs before lunch she had seen the enormous double bed, downy and soft, with its white cover. She had longed right then and there to climb beneath the blankets and sleep.

Perhaps a nap. She was filled with grateful love for Elfrida. She said, "I don't think there's anything I'd like more."

They went upstairs. "Lucy's in the attic. You've seen your room, and there are two bathrooms. And this"—she opened another door—"is the second spare bedroom. I could have put her in here, but it's small and a bit dreary. The attic seemed to me a much more attractive space for her, and I had all the fun of putting it together."

Carrie peered into the small and undistinguished room, almost totally taken up with another enormous bed. It was clearly unoccupied, and for the first time she began to feel a bit uncomfortable, suspecting what was going to happen next.

"Elfrida?"

Elfrida took no notice. She opened the final door with a flourish that had a touch of defiance about it. "And this," she said, "is us."

It was a spacious and important room, the master bedroom of the original house, with tall windows facing out over the light of the dying afternoon. In it stood a looming Victorian wardrobe, a pretty Victorian dressing table, and a chest of drawers. And an enormously high and wide bed. Over this was spread Elfrida's scarlet silk shawl, the embroidery faded, the fringe beginning to fray, but still marvelously opulent and recognizable from the old days.

And other possessions. A man's ivory brushes on the chest of drawers, dark blue pajamas folded on a pillow.

There fell a small silence. Then Elfrida said, "You're not shocked?"

"Elfrida, I'm me. I'm not Dodie. You don't have to explain to me." Carrie put her arms around Elfrida and hugged. "It's all so sweet. Needing each other and finding each other."

"Oscar still has a long way to go. Some days he's been so depressed that he scarcely speaks. But I've learned to leave him alone. He has to deal with his grief in his own way."

"It can't have been easy."

"Oh, darling Carrie, nothing is. And now I shall find you a hot-water bottle, and you shall go to sleep."

Oscar

OSCAR was having a bonfire. After breakfast he had decided to clear out the potting shed and burn all the rubbish. He got his fire started, and soon it was blazing nicely. The thick smoke rose and billowed and made everything smell of autumn. So intent was he on this labor that he did not hear the gate behind him open and shut.

"Oscar."

Startled, Oscar swung around to face Peter Kennedy, dressed for golf in his red jacket and long-peaked baseball cap.

"Heavens, I never heard you."

"I didn't mean to sneak up on you. I saw the smoke and guessed I'd find you here. I wanted to tell you that I was in Inverness yesterday and I saw Godfrey Billicliffe at the hospital."

"That was good of you. How is he?"

Peter shook his head. "Not good news, I'm afraid. He's very ill. He has cancer."

Cancer. Oscar said, "Oh, God. How long has he got?"

"A little time. He's dying. But he's comfortable and quite peaceful, rather enjoying the attention and the nurses taking care of him."

"I must go and see him."

"No. He asked me to tell you no. He's doped and frail and already has the look of a man on his way out of this world. But he asked me to send you his regards and to say how grateful he was for your kindness."

"I didn't do anything."

"You did. And you were there when he most needed a friend. He really is quite peaceful. Perfectly lucid. I think, accepting."

Oscar sighed. "I'm down as his next of kin."

"They'll let you know. Or myself. We'll keep in touch."

"Thank you for telling me."

"I knew that you would want to know." Peter paused. "There's something else. It occurred to me that you might be missing your music." He felt in the pocket of his red golf jacket and produced a small brass key. "The church is always open, but the organ locked. I have discussed it with Alistair Heggie, our organist, and he is happy for you to use it anytime you feel so inclined." Before Oscar could protest, Peter had taken his wrist and pressed the key into his outstretched palm, closing his fingers about it.

Oscar said, "Oh, no."

"You might not even want to. But I like to think that you can if the impulse takes you."

"You are too kind."

"Just put it somewhere safe." Peter grinned. "It's our only spare." He turned as if to go and then turned back again. "I very nearly forgot another reason I came. Tabitha says would you all like to come up to the Manse for a drink and a mince pie on Tuesday evening at six. Everybody's welcome. Don't dress up. Our children will probably be around."

"Tuesday." Oscar, still holding the key, made a mental note to tell Elfrida. "Tuesday at six. I think we'd like that very much."

"Splendid." Peter went through the gate and latched it behind him. "We'll see you then."

"Have a good round. And thank you for coming."

Lucy

ON MONDAY morning, when Lucy descended from her private aerie in the attic, she saw that Carrie's bedroom door was closed. Downstairs she found only Oscar and Elfrida in the midst of breakfast.

As she appeared through the door, Oscar laid down his coffee cup and smiled. "Lucy, how are you this morning?"

"I'm fine, but where's Carrie?"

"Carrie's not well." Elfrida got up from the table to collect sausages from the hot plate for Lucy. "I don't think she's got flu, but she isn't throwing this horrible cold off. Two sausages or three?"

"Three, please, if there's enough. Is she still in bed?"

"Yes. I looked in to see her, and she said she'd coughed all night. I took her a cup of tea, but she doesn't want anything to eat. I'm going to ring Dr. Sinclair and ask if he'll have a look at her."

Lucy sat down to her sausages. "She must be all right for Christmas. Can I go and see her?"

"I shouldn't until we know what's wrong. It might be frightfully contagious, and then you'd come out in spots. Or sores."

Lucy ate her sausages, which were delicious. "It's really disappointing, because we'd planned a long walk on the beach this morning with Horace. Will *you* come, Oscar?"

"I can't this morning. I'm going to get my hair cut, and then I'm going to pick up the meat from the butcher."

"Oh, I see." It was hard not to sound downcast.

He smiled. "You can go on your own. Take Horace. He will guard you. You can be a lone explorer."

Lucy brightened. "Can I?"

"Of course," Elfrida said.

Lucy mulled over this new prospect of freedom and was rather taken with the idea of setting out with the dog all by herself. The day that Oscar had taken her to the beach, she had seen youngsters climbing rocks, riding bicycles, and not an adult in view.

With Horace on his lead Lucy set off across the square and then turned up the road that led to the golf club. The right-of-way led across the links, and when she reached a shallow summit, she saw the whole horizon, cold and still as steel, and a great arc of sky, gray with low cloud. It was half tide, and small waves washed up onto the shining wet sand. Far away she could see the lighthouse.

Lucy unclipped Horace's lead, and he ran ahead of her. In the shelter of the dunes the sand was deep and soft and difficult for walking, so she went out onto the wet, hard sand and, looking back, saw her own footsteps, with Horace's footpads circling them. She was alone. Not another soul, not another dog.

She rather liked knowing that nobody knew *exactly* where she was and that if she met somebody, they wouldn't know *who* she was. So she belonged to nobody but herself.

The beach ended at an outcrop of rocks. Lucy paused to get her bearings. Hillocky dunes separated the beach from the golf links, and as she hesitated, trying to decide which way to go next, she heard the sound of a motor and saw, above the rocks, a tractor trundling toward her over a rise. Clearly there had to be a sort of road. She decided she would walk home that way and with some difficulty hauled her way up a sandy cliff. Horace bounded ahead of her and out of sight. Reaching the summit, she saw the track.

Horace was already down there, waiting for her but not looking her way. He had, it was obvious, sensed strangers. He stood, ears pricked, with his plumy tail up like a flag, watching. Lucy looked and saw, coming up the slope from the direction of the town, another dog walker, striding out in purposeful manner. She was dressed in boots, thick trousers, and a sheepskin coat and wore a tam-o'-shanter slanted at a cocky angle over cropped gray hair. Her dog, running free, spied Horace and stopped dead. The two animals eyed each other for a long moment, and Lucy was all at once petrified with dread because the other dog was a rottweiler.

Horace began to bark. The rottweiler slowly moved forward, his shining body tense, muscles flexed. A snarling sound came from deep in his throat, and his dark lips rolled back from his teeth. Horace gave another bark, and with that, the rottweiler pounced.

Lucy screamed. Horace screamed as well—a dog scream that sounded like a howl for help. He was being flattened, bitten, and bruised, and however he struggled, he could not escape.

The dog's owner had a chain leash in her hand, but it was obvious that she was too wary to start manhandling her pet while he was in this frame of mind. Instead, she produced a pea whistle, which she blew sharply, and proceeded to shout orders. "Brutus! Brutus! Down, boy! Down! To heel!"

The rottweiler took absolutely no notice whatsoever.

"Get hold of him," Lucy wailed, hysterical with horror. Horace, Elfrida's darling dog, was about to be murdered. "Stop him!"

She had forgotten about the approaching tractor. Now, like the cavalry in some old western, it trundled into view in the nick of time. The door was flung open. The driver jumped down and, sprinting the last few yards and without showing the slightest fear or hesitation, went straight into action, landing his heavy boot into the muscled backside of the rottweiler. "Get off, you bloody brute!" The startled rottweiler abandoned Horace and turned to attack this new enemy, but the young man grabbed his studded collar and with some strength hauled him away from his prey.

Lucy, in a thousand years, could never have imagined any person being so levelheaded, strong, and brave.

"What the bloody hell do you think you're doing?" he demanded of the dog's owner, grabbing the chain leash from her hand and somehow clipping it to the collar of the snarling, struggling beast. He then dragged the animal toward her, and she took the leather loop in both her hands.

"Don't you swear at me," she said.

"Why didn't you keep the dog on its chain?"

"He was attacked." She became belligerent.

"He was no such thing. I saw it all. If you lived here, you'd know better than to walk a savage dog on a public footpath."

"I do *not* live here," said the woman, as though this were something to be proud of. "I'm staying with my sister in her caravan."

"Well, go back to her caravan and shut your dog up."

"Don't speak to me in that tone of voice."

"I'll speak to you any way I like. I work for the golf club. If I see that dog running free again, I'll report you to the police."

"And I shall complain of impudence—"

But at this point Brutus took charge. He had spied two innocent golfers striding down the fairway and, with his blood up and a desperate need to sink his teeth into some other throat, set off on the hunt. His owner, willy-nilly, went too, trailed in his wake, her short trousered legs going like pistons.

Lucy by now was sitting on the grass with Horace in her arms, his head pressed against the front of her jacket. The young man came to kneel beside her. She saw that he was very young, his face windburned, his eyes blue. He had short yellow hair that looked dyed, and there was a gold ring in his left ear.

He said, "Are you all right?"

And Lucy burst into tears. "Yes, but Horace—"

"Here." Gently he examined poor Horace, stroked the long hair off his face, making comforting noises as he did so. "I think he'll be all right. Just superficial cuts and bruises."

"He only barked," Lucy sobbed. "He always barks. He's so stupid. I thought he was going to be dead."

"Lucky he isn't."

"He's not even my dog. He's Elfrida's. We just came for a walk."

"Where from?"

"Creagan."

"I'll take you back in the tractor. I can take you as far as the clubhouse. Can you walk from there?"

"Yes, I think so."

He led the way back to the tractor. Lucy clambered up into the cab. There was only one seat, but she perched herself on the very edge of this, and Horace was placed at her feet, where he sat and leaned heavily against her knee. Then the young man jumped up beside her, slammed the door shut, and put the tractor in gear.

Lucy had stopped crying. "I feel so guilty. I should have looked after Horace better."

"Not a thing you could do."

Lucy smiled and said, "Thank you so much for helping."

"You're staying at the Estate House, aren't you? With Oscar Blundell?"

"Do you know him?"

"No, but my father does. Peter Kennedy, the minister. I'm Rory Kennedy."

"I'm Lucy Wesley."

"Didn't I see you in church yesterday?" he asked.

"Yes, but I didn't see you. I suppose because there were so many people. Do you work on the golf course?"

"Yes, for the time being. This is the start of my gap year. I finished highers in July, and next year I go to Durham University."

"I'm rather dreading my gap year."

"How old are you?"

"Fourteen."

"You've time enough to make plans. My mother told me I have to lend you my old TV. Do you want it?"

"It would be kind of you, but I'm managing without one."

"I'll look it out." For a bit they thumped along in silence. Then he said, "I believe you're all coming up to the Manse for a drink tomorrow evening. There's a hooley in the school hall at seven o'clock. My sister, Clodagh, and I are going. Do you want to come with us?"

"What's a hooley?"

"A dance."

Lucy was at once filled with anxiety. She had been to parties but never a dance. She said, "I don't know."

"Why not? It's just the schoolkids, practicing reels for the Hogmanay parties. Good fun."

Reels. "I don't know how to do reels. I don't know the steps."

"So it's high time you learned." He turned his head to smile down at her in a friendly and encouraging manner, and rather to her own surprise she found herself saying, "All right. Yes. Thank you. Do . . . do I have to dress up?"

"Heaven forbid. Jeans and trainers."

As they had been talking, it had been growing threateningly dark. Now the first large white flakes of snow drifted from the leaden sky. Rory said, "I wondered when that would start. You could see the snow clouds coming down from the north. The weather forecast this morning said we're in for some heavy falls."

"Is it going to be a white Christmas? I've never had a white Christmas."

"Good for sledging. Hard work for the snowplows."

By now they were grinding up the slope that led to the clubhouse. Rory turned the tractor into the car park, killed the engine, opened the door, and climbed down. "Will you be all right now?"

Snow settled on his hair and shoulders. Lucy clambered down behind him, and he lifted Horace down. Horace gave himself a shake and even wagged his plumy tail. Lucy took the lead from her pocket, and Rory clipped it onto Horace's collar.

"That's it, then." He grinned down at her. "You get home now."

"Thank you so much."

She walked down the hill into the falling snow. Bravely Horace limped along beside her. She turned back to wave.

It had been a momentous outing. A long walk, a dogfight, a tractor ride, a snowstorm, and an invitation to a dance. She could scarcely wait to get home and tell Oscar and Elfrida all about it.

IT WAS an enormous relief to Elfrida when she heard the front door open and Lucy's voice calling out. Ever since the snow started, she had been blaming herself for letting the child go off on her own. When she heard Lucy in the hall, she rushed out to meet her. Lucy and Horace stood on the doormat, both encrusted in snow and with a terrible story to tell.

It was told in the warm kitchen while Lucy shed her coat and hat and pulled off her boots. "This horrible dog, a rottweiler, went for Horace, and then there was a tractor . . . Rory Kennedy . . . And he was frightfully brave . . . and brought us back to the golf club in his tractor. Elfrida, I am sorry, but I couldn't stop it. And poor Horace has got bites and bruises. It was so frightening."

She was clearly much upset by the whole incident but, in an extraordinary way, excited as well, having come through the entire adventure and bringing Horace home alive. Her cheeks were pink and her eyes bright. She was a sweet child, of course, but serious-minded, and docility did not suit a fourteen-year-old. This metamorphosis was hopeful, and Elfrida knew that by sending Lucy off on her own, she had done exactly the right thing.

As for Horace, he sat on the floor and looked sorry for himself.

"What happened, Horace?" Elfrida asked him. "Were you attacked by a savage hound?" She turned to Lucy. "But darling, your jeans are soaked. You should go and get some dry clothes on."

"All right." Lucy started to go but turned back. "Elfrida."

"What is it, duck?"

"Rory Kennedy's terribly nice. And he's got dyed hair."

"Dyed hair?" Elfrida put on an expression of horror. "What would your grandmother say?"

Lucy told her, in Dodie's voice, " 'Dis-gusting'!" And she grinned and was gone, and Elfrida heard her running, two at a time, up all the stairs to her attic bedroom.

Sam

THEY stood at the bar of the Duke's Arms in Buckly, an austere little pub that had made no concessions to either the tourist trade or trendy decor. The walls were pitch-pine tongue-and-groove, the lighting bleak, and all smelled of old beer and whisky.

Fergus Skinner said, "What'll it be?"

"A half of lager, please," Sam replied.

"Will you not take a dram?"

"I'm driving."

Fergus had brought Sam here, crossing the snowy road from the church hall after the meeting with the millworkers. It was, he told Sam, his customary haunt, a place where a man could sit and enjoy a peaceful dram without some person engaging him in conversation.

"That is a pity," he said now, and ordered a large Bells for himself. "I'm walking." But if this was meant to be funny, there was not a gleam of humor in his eye.

He was a tall man in his early forties, but looking older, with the dark hair and pale skin of a true Highlander. His features were strong—deep-set eyes, a beak of a nose, a long lantern jaw—and his expression somber.

Fergus Skinner had been foreman at the mill in the old days, and when the McTaggart family broke up, it was he who had rallied the workforce and organized the management buyout. Almost unanimously he had been voted in as manager of the new enterprise, and the demise of the business, destroyed by the flood, had been harder on him than anyone else.

But he remained undefeated. When Sam rang him from London from the offices of Sturrock and Swinfield, asking him to set up some sort of a meeting with the workforce, Fergus Skinner had done his stuff. Because of this, the meeting had been well attended, so much so that latecomers found standing room only.

Now the two men carried their drinks to a wobbly table by the tiny fireplace, where a peat fire smoldered. Fergus raised his glass. "Your good health."

"And the future." The lager, un-iced, tasted warm.

"The future."

It had been a good meeting, held in the Buckly Church Hall because the mill was still in a state of desolation and disrepair. Sam and Fergus had sat upon the raised platform. Sam had seen not only men but women as well and here and there a child too small to be left alone at home.

To begin with, the atmosphere had been cautious. Sam had started by introducing himself as the new general manager of McTaggarts, who would be taking overall charge of the reconstruction of the ruined mill and the restart of the business. The response to this was silence, and he knew they probably regarded him as simply a moneyman, sent from London by Sturrock and Swinfield. So he told them a bit about his background. A Yorkshire boy, born and bred to the woolen industry, and a family mill very like McTaggarts of Buckly. How they too had been faced with financial difficulties and been rescued by Sturrock and Swinfield, which was why he, Sam, was there today.

The atmosphere relaxed. People settled down in their chairs.

Sam went through the feasibility study and restructuring. A business built on traditions and goodwill but moving forward. So new products. New markets. New machinery. He asked for questions.

Hands were held up. "Will that mean retraining?"

He told them yes. Other questions came thick and fast. "Would there be redundancies?"

He said yes, to begin with. But once the new mill was up and going, there would come expansion and so, new job creation.

A woman asked if there would be work for her, a hand finisher, or would it all be done with this new sophisticated machinery. Sam told her that with the luxury goods they intended to manufacture, there would always be work for hand finishers.

The most vital question was, How soon would they get back to work?

At the soonest, nine months. There was a great deal to be done. Plans were already drawn up and on display at the back of the hall.

The outward appearance of the old mill would remain the same. Inside, it would be gutted and totally rebuilt. There would be a shop to attract tourists, and the architect had made provision for a small tea shop. Both shops would offer increased employment.

And who would get the building contracts?

Sam explained that all local builders, plumbers, electricians, and joiners would be approached for estimates.

Finally it all became something of a general discussion, which was exactly the way Sam wanted it to be. By the end he felt that he had won some trust and, hopefully, cooperation.

Fergus stooped to place another lump of peat onto the dying fire. "Where are you staying?"

"In Inverness, in a hotel." Sam glanced up at the round clock on the wall, standing at half past five. "I should be off. It's a long drive."

"But you have a good car. A Land Rover Discovery."

"I bought it in London when I knew I would be living here."

They went outside, and it was snowing again. Fergus said, "I think, before you set off for Inverness, you should telephone the AA. Get a check on conditions. The Black Isle can be a hazard on such a night as this."

"Maybe. I'll see how I go."

"It has been a pleasure to meet you."

"The pleasure's mine, Fergus."

They said good-bye, shaking hands. Sam climbed up into the big car, reached into his coat pocket for the ignition key, and brought out two keys: the one for his car and the big old-fashioned key to Hughie McLennan's Estate House, attached to its label with a knot of string. He had met Hughie by chance in London. "You need a house," he had said. "I have one for sale in Creagan, near Buckly. No harm done going to cast your eye over the place."

Surely, while he was so close to Creagan, it would be worthwhile to see how it looked. No need to go inside. Just decide if it would be worth returning to inspect with an eye to buying.

He felt adventurous. He started the engine and headed for Creagan. He crossed a long bridge over a firth, and a couple of miles after that, his headlights touched the luminous road sign: TOURIST ROUTE CREAGAN. 2 MILES. He took the turning, and the single-track road wound alongside the shores of the sea loch. He came into the town by way of a tree-lined road and in the light of streetlamps saw the church and the square and the old walled graveyard. He drove very slowly around the church, trying to get his bearings, wondering which was the house Hughie McLennan had described. He decided to ask directions from a couple walking toward him.

"Excuse me. I'm looking for the Estate House."

"You're there." The man, amused, grinned. "You're here." He jerked his head, indicating the house behind him.

"Oh, I see. Thank you."

"You're welcome." They set off on their way.

Sam sat in his car and stared at the house. It could not possibly be Hughie's house. Hughie had said his house was empty, untenanted. And this house had windows that, behind carefully drawn curtains, were filled with light.

Sam told himself that he should simply drive on. But he did not like mysteries and knew that this one would niggle at him. He took the house key and climbed down from the Discovery and walked up to the front door. There was a bell, and he pressed it.

He waited for a bit. All at once an outside light came on, and the door was opened.

He was not quite sure who or what he had expected. An elderly pinafored lady? Or a man in bedroom slippers? What he didn't expect was a tall dark girl in jeans and a pullover. A sensationally good-looking girl who would have turned heads on Fifth Avenue.

Carrie

THAT morning the doctor, as he had promised, had popped into the Estate House to check on Carrie. When he had gone, Elfrida came upstairs and put her head around the door. "What did he say?"

"I'm all right, but I have to stay here for another day. I'm sorry."

"Don't be so silly. Do you want a hot-water bottle?"

"No. Warm as toast."

The day progressed, and through her window Carrie watched the weather and was glad she did not have to be out in it. It was all rather cozy. She remembered as a child being ill, and in bed, and the awareness of others getting on with the business of day-to-day life without herself having to participate in any sort of way. The luxuries of self-indulgence, idleness, and total irresponsibility were all things that Carrie had long forgotten.

OSCAR, Elfrida, and Lucy departed at a quarter to six for the little party at the Manse. Carrie heard the back door slam behind them. She got out of bed and ran a wonderful scalding bath, soaked for ages, then put on jeans and her thickest sweater, did her hair, splashed on some scent, and at once felt a great deal better. I am recovered, she told her reflection in the mirror.

She went downstairs to check on Horace. "Do you want to come upstairs by the fire?" she asked him, but Horace did not. He closed his eyes and went back to sleep again, warm in his basket.

She went to the sitting room, where the fire was blazing, and settled down with Oscar's morning newspaper. She was in the middle of a feature article about a well-known, if elderly, actress when the fearsome ring of the front-door bell drilled through the house.

Carrie said, "Damn." Perhaps it was some person whose car had broken down and now wanted to borrow a telephone. In exasperation she tossed the paper down and ran downstairs, turning on light switches as she went. She flung the big door open to the snow and the cold and the solitary man who stood there, with the beam of the outside light streaming down upon him. He had dark, very short hair and wore a thick navy-blue overcoat, the collar turned up around his ears. His hair, his coat, his ears were all liberally sprinkled in snowflakes.

She glanced over his shoulder and saw the large and prestigious vehicle parked in the road. She said, "Yes?"

"I'm sorry. Is this Hughie McLennan's Estate House?"

Carrie frowned. "No. Oscar Blundell's Estate House."

It was his turn to hesitate. And then he held up in his gloved hand a key with a label knotted to it with string. On the label was written ESTATE HOUSE. He said, "Perhaps I have made a mistake."

There must be, of course, explanations. "I think," Carrie said, "you'd better come in."

But he hesitated. "Are you sure?"

"Of course. Come on."

He went past her into the house, and she closed the door.

He looked embarrassed. "I hope I didn't disturb you."

"Not at all. Take your coat off. We'll hang it here."

He had put the key back into his pocket and now shucked off his overcoat. She saw that he was conventionally, even formally, dressed, in a dark gray flannel suit and a tie.

"Perhaps," he said, "I should introduce myself. Sam Howard."

"Carrie Sutton." They did not shake hands. "Come up to the sitting room. There's a fire on there."

She led the way up the stairs and into the huge sitting room. Entering, he observed, as newcomers invariably did, "What an amazing room."

"It's unexpected, isn't it?" She went to pick up the abandoned newspaper. "And lovely during the daytime, because it's always full of light." She laid the paper on the table. "Would . . . would you like a drink or something?"

"You're kind. I'd love to, but I'm driving to Inverness."

"Inverness! In this weather?"

"I'll be okay."

Carrie doubted this, but it was no business of hers. She said, "Then why don't we both sit down, and you can tell me why you have the key to Oscar's house."

His expression was rueful. "To be honest, I'm not quite sure." But he came and settled himself in Oscar's chair and at once looked quite relaxed and at home. She thought that he had an interesting face, neither handsome nor homely. Unremarkable but interesting. His eyes, deeply set, were unusual. "But I am sure we can clear up the confusion. Tell me, did Mr. Blundell once live in Hampshire?"

"Yes, he did."

"And does he have an elderly uncle living in London? And a cousin called Hughie McLennan?"

"I'm afraid you're asking the wrong person. I'm just a guest, and Oscar and Elfrida have gone out for drinks. They won't be back till about eight o'clock." She glanced at the little clock on the mantelpiece. "It's nearly seven now. If you wanted to wait—"

"No, I can't wait. I must be on my way."

"But I still don't know why you have a key to this house."

"I was given it by Hughie. He wants to put the property on the market. Put it up for sale."

Carrie stared at him. "For sale? But it's Oscar's house."

"I think they are joint owners."

"I know they're joint owners. Oscar told me. But even so, Hughie McLennan—whoever he is—has no right to put a house up for sale when he doesn't even own it."

"Yes," he agreed with her. "It does seem a bit suspect."

"Why would you want to look at it? Do you want to buy it?"

He said cautiously, "I might. I have a new job, in Buckly. Getting McTaggarts, the woolen mill, back on its feet again. I shall be based here, and I'll need somewhere to live."

"Where's Buckly?"

"About twelve miles south. I've just come from there." He was on his feet. "But right now I think I should make tracks."

"And *I* think it's important that you see Oscar. It's only fair to him that he should know what is happening."

Carrie went to the big bay window and drew back the heavy curtain. Outside, Sam's Discovery, parked at the pavement's edge, was already blanketed in snow. She thought of the long miles to Inverness. She said, "I don't think you should go. Come and look."

He joined her, and together they gazed out at the clearly deteriorating conditions. Carrie felt a bit sorry for him. "It really is bad."

"Yeah. Fergus Skinner, the manager at the mill, said I should phone the AA and get a report."

"I'll find the number for you." She went out onto the landing and came back with the phone book and looked up the emergency number. "Here it is."

He took his mobile phone from his pocket. He got through almost at once and inquired about road conditions, the A9 to Inverness. Then a long silence as he listened. Then, "Okay. Thank you. Good-bye."

They looked at each other. He said, "You were quite right. The road is impassable. I had no idea it would be so bad."

"I'm sorry."

"I . . . I'd better be off. Get out of your way."

"Where will you be off to?"

"There'll be some guesthouse, hotel. I'll check in there."

"You'll find nothing at this time of year. You'll have to stay here."

"Here? But I'm a stranger. I can't just come and—"

"Of course you can. Anyway, there doesn't seem to be an alternative. There's an empty bedroom, I know." Carrie smiled. "What do they say? Any port in a storm."

"But . . . Mr. Blundell—"

"I expect he will be delighted to have another guest. And most interested in what you have to tell him. And his companion, Elfrida, will be pleased, I'm sure. There's nothing she likes better than impromptu house parties. There is dinner in the oven and plenty of hot bathwater. What more could any man want? A toothbrush?"

"I have one in the car. And my electric razor. But if it's all right, I should make another call."

"Feel free." (He obviously needed to ring home, explain to his wife what had happened.) "You don't want anybody worrying."

He used his mobile once more and was speaking to the receptionist at some hotel in Inverness. "Just to let you know, I'm stuck in Creagan in a snowstorm. Just keep the room. Thanks."

"Is that all?" Carrie asked. "No more calls?"

He slipped his mobile back into his jacket pocket. "Nope."

"Right. Well, in that case, why don't you have that drink?"

"That would be very kind. Scotch? On the rocks?"

"Fine. I shan't be a moment."

She ran downstairs and in the scullery found a tray, on which she loaded the whisky bottle, the ice bucket, two glasses, and an opened bottle of wine. She carried the tray upstairs and found her visitor gazing intently at Elfrida's little picture. He had put on a pair of horn-rimmed spectacles, which made him look rather scholarly. When Carrie appeared, he took these off. "What a fine little painting."

"Yes. It belongs to Elfrida. It's a David Wilkie. She says it's her insurance policy against the day when she runs out of money."

"It's a treasure. Here, let me have that." He took the tray while Carrie made space on the table, shunting aside a few papers.

She said, "I'll let you do your own drink."

"How about you?"

"The wine."

She went back to her chair by the fire and watched him, liking the neat movements of his hands. Intrigued, in an objective sort of way, because his appearance at the Estate House, his reason for being there, and his reason for staying on (bad weather) all seemed like a sort of contrivance. The plot of a play perhaps. The start of a film that could turn out to be disturbing, even terrifying.

He handed her her glass and then sat again where he had sat before. He said, "Good health."

"And to you too."

"You're visiting?"

"I live in London. I have a young niece. I brought her with me. We're staying for Christmas and the New Year."

"Has she gone to the drinks party too?"

"Yes, and then on to some sort of reel party. Do you know this part of the world well?"

"No. I don't know it at all. I come from Yorkshire. Then I was based in London for a bit and then New York for six years."

"What is your job?"

"I'm basically a wool broker. I work for Sturrock and Swinfield. They bought out my father's woolen mill, and I've been with them ever since."

"Working up here is going to be a bit of a culture change, isn't it?"

"Yes," he agreed with her. "A bit."

"What did you say the mill was called?"

"McTaggarts of Buckly."

"Is it a going concern?"

He said, "No," and then explained the chain of events that had brought it down. And what he was expected to take on—gutting and rebuilding the mill and getting the business up and going.

"Why don't you just bulldoze the mill and start afresh?" Carrie asked.

"Because it's a beautiful old building. Over a hundred and fifty years old. It would be vandalism to destroy it."

"And *you* have to have someplace to live?"

"Yes." He smiled. "But I can't sort that one out until I've spoken to your host. You said you live in London?"

Carrie didn't really want to talk about herself. "I've been in Austria for three years, in Oberbeuren, working for a travel firm called Oversees. But I've been offered a job in their London head office."

"Are you going to take it?"

"Yes. Why not?"

"You'll miss Austria and the mountains."

"Yes." For a moment neither of them spoke, and the silence was fraught with unsaid words. Then she said, "Your glass is empty. Would you like another drink?"

Elfrida

OSCAR and Elfrida, arm in arm and making their way with tremendous caution, walked home. In the hall, they shed wet coats, snow-encrusted boots, and sodden hats. Then they went upstairs. In the sitting room they came upon a peaceful and companionable scene. The fire blazing, the two most comfortable chairs drawn up to its warmth. And in them, looking as though they had known each other forever, Carrie and a complete stranger. Possibilities flashed through Elfrida's mind. An acquaintance of Carrie's come in search of her. A longtime admirer, staunchly constant . . .

Carrie saw them and at once rose to her feet. "Elfrida, you're back. We didn't hear you. Did you have a good party?"

"Yes, it was splendid. But you're not meant to be out of bed."

"I got bored."

By now the unknown man was also on his feet, waiting to be introduced. Elfrida's first impression of this stranger was one of businesslike formality, in his beautifully cut dark gray suit, his neat tie, and his closely barbered head of hair. His tanned complexion accentuated his light hazel eyes. And despite her sixty-two years, she knew a frisson of physical attraction that dimmed in no way her affection for Oscar. It was just a sort of recognition, an ardent memory of how things once had been for her.

"Elfrida, this is Sam Howard. . . . Elfrida Phipps. And my host, Oscar Blundell."

"How do you do." They all shook hands.

Sam Howard said, "I'm really sorry about this intrusion."

"Why is it an intrusion?"

"Because I'm in your house . . . unasked."

Carrie laughed. "I gave Sam a drink, Oscar. Do you want one?"

"Badly."

"I'll get some more glasses. What about you, Elfrida? I'm having a glass of wine."

"I'll join you." Elfrida felt tired. She sat on the sofa. "I've been standing for two hours, eating sandwiches and mince pies and chatting with people."

"How about Lucy?"

"She disappeared with the Kennedy children to some other room and hasn't been seen since. They'd gone to the reeling by the time we left. Just the way it should be."

"That's good. I'll get those glasses. And soda for Oscar."

She left them. Oscar by now had sat himself down in his own armchair, and they were left with the strange man. Elfrida, smiling in her most friendly fashion, said, "Now tell us exactly who you are and why you're here. You must be an old friend of Carrie's."

"Actually, I'm not."

He pulled a chair up to sit near Elfrida and began to explain.

Oscar picked it up at once. "Peter Kennedy told me about McTaggarts' being taken over, but I didn't realize that things were already moving."

"They aren't exactly moving yet, but we're on our way."

"That's splendid news. Have you been in this business for long?"

"All my life, really. My father owned a small mill in Yorkshire."

"Does this mean you're going to be living up here?"

Carrie reappeared with a second tray, bearing glasses and soda. Sam sprang to his feet and went to relieve her of this. He poured whisky and soda for Oscar, wine for Elfrida, and topped up Carrie's glass.

"What about you?" Elfrida asked him, but he said he was all right and returned to his chair at her side.

Carrie said, "How far have you got?" She curled up in her chair.

Sam Howard took over again. "This is all rather personal and very complicated. Just say that before I came up here, I was staying in London with old friends—Janey and Neil Philip. One evening an old acquaintance of Janey's parents came for dinner. He was called Hughie McLennan."

He paused, giving time for this to sink in. Then Oscar spoke. "You wouldn't be talking about my cousin Hughie? But Hughie's in Barbados."

"No. He was back in London. To see friends and deal with various business matters, I guess."

"What an extraordinary coincidence."

"We talked for a bit. And then he learned that I was coming up here to Buckly, and he asked me where I was going to live. I said that I'd have to find somewhere, and from his pocket he produced the key to this house. He said he owned half of it and his cousin the other half, but that he wanted to sell."

Oscar said, "Why the hell didn't he get in touch with me? His father— Hector knew where I was."

"I think he hadn't seen his father."

"Well, what a turnup for the books." Oscar took an enormous slug of his whisky. "Why did he suddenly decide to sell this place? We've boxed along for so many years, sharing the trickle of rent, I never imagined he'd want to put it on the market. And certainly not without discussing it with me."

"My guess is that he needs a bit of ready cash."

"Not surprised. Alimony for three ex-wives must cost a bomb. You knew I shared the ownership?"

"Yes. He told me. I said nothing could possibly be arranged until you, his cousin, had been consulted."

"So why are you here?"

"He had the key with him. He said, as I was coming north, why not have a look at the house. He told me it was empty. With that, he simply took the key out of his pocket and handed it over to me."

"Did he mention a sum?"

Sam said, "A hundred and fifty thousand."

"Split down the middle, seventy-five thousand?"

"That's right."

"Suppose I wanted more?"

"It's negotiable. I'm simply quoting your cousin."

"I see." Oscar finished his drink.

Sam said, "I really have to apologize to you both. And I'll give you Hughie's key, and we'll forget the entire business. It's just that I had to tell how it all came about so that you understand."

Elfrida, who had managed to keep silent, now felt that the time had come to get her word in. "You've made everything extremely clear, Mr. Howard. Are you staying in Buckly?"

"No. At a hotel in Inverness. This afternoon was my first meeting with the workforce. I started back to Inverness and then had this idea that I'd make the diversion to Creagan and come and case the joint, as it were. The house was so obviously lived in that my curiosity was aroused, so I got out of the car and rang the bell. I was never much good at mysteries."

"I see." Elfrida decided it was all very exciting. She could picture it. The handsome stranger, the ring of the doorbell, and . . . Carrie, going to open the door and let him in.

She said, "Carrie, I hope you have asked Sam to stay for dinner."

Carrie began to laugh. A glance passed between her and Sam that Elfrida decided was almost conspiratorial, as though they had an amusing secret to share. What had they been up to?

Carrie took pity on her. "Elfrida, all the roads to Inverness are blocked with snow, so we have another guest for the night. Do you mind?"

Elfrida said, "I can't think of anything I would like more." And it was almost impossible to keep the pleasure out of her voice.

IT WAS nearly midnight. Elfrida lay in bed, and beside her Oscar read his book: *Love in the Time of Cholera.* She thought back over the many events of the evening, most of them unexpected. She, Oscar, Sam, and Carrie had finally sat down to their supper in the kitchen at nine o'clock. They were on to coffee when Lucy and Rory Kennedy returned from their dancing.

Carrie put out an arm and drew Lucy close. "You had fun?"

Lucy kissed her. "It was the best."

While Oscar and Sam sat over their coffee, Carrie and Elfrida went upstairs to make up the last spare bed for Sam. They found sheets and pillowcases and a bath towel and an extra blanket.

"What more," asked Elfrida, "could any man need?"

"He's got a toothbrush. He told me. And a razor."

"Jimmy-jams?"

"He probably sleeps in the buff anyway."

"And how do you know?"

"Instinct, Elfrida. Feminine instinct."

They both laughed. Carrie said, "You're a saint. I had to ask him to stay, but the best was knowing you wouldn't mind."

"I've always loved a full house. This is a house for parties and people. Oscar and I have been rattling around in it for too long. Now it's full." She said this in tones of greatest satisfaction. "Stretched to its limits. A family house. Just the way it should be."

A FAMILY house. Elfrida lay in bed and felt the house around her like a shield, a refuge. She said, "Oscar, if Hughie wants to sell his half of this house, couldn't you buy him out?"

"Seventy-five thousand. If I sold everything I owned, I might scrape up twenty."

"You could get a mortgage."

"Not for that amount. Not at my age. And I've always had a horror of mortgages. I've never had much, but I've never been in debt."

"If I had seventy-five thousand, would that help?"

"If you had seventy-five thousand, it wouldn't be to bail me out."

"I love this house so much. It is so strong, so unpretentious, so adaptable. Can't you feel it, like a heartbeat, keeping us all going, sheltering, taking care of us all? You can't lose it."

"I think I am not as fanciful as you."

She lay, silent, carefully framing in her mind what she was going to say. "Oscar, listen to me. If I sold my little picture, my David Wilkie, how much do you think that would fetch?"

"That is your treasure, your insurance, not mine."

"If it is worth what I think it is, then we should sell it. Why keep a little picture if you can buy security? I can't bear to think of this darling place going to other people."

Oscar reached for her hand. "You are the dearest person."

"We'll talk about it," she told him, "in the morning."

 Lucy

IT IS *half past eight in the morning, and I am writing in my diary. I should have written in it last night, but I was so tired.*

It was fabulous.

We walked up to the Kennedys' house. When we got there, other people were there as well. We were all introduced. Then Rory and I left all the grown-ups in the sitting room and went into the kitchen, and there were three other boys there—friends of Rory's from school—and his sister, Clodagh, who is twelve and very skinny and sharp, with bright blue eyes and fair pigtails.

We all sat around and drank Coke, and Clodagh was very flirty. We had an enormous macaroni and cheese, and salads, and then a very rich chocolate cake and ice cream. When that was finished, we all walked down the hill to the school gym.

There were lots and lots of children of all ages, from about seven to grown up. The headmaster is called Mr. McIntosh, but they all call him Waterproof behind his back, but I bet he knows about this. He was quite young and very nice. There was a proper band. An accordionist, a drummer, and a fiddler. There was a terrible din, and everybody was larking around, and then Mr. McIntosh told everybody to be quiet in quite a soft voice, and they were. He said it was time to get started and we were going to do a Strip the Willow because it wasn't too difficult for little ones and learners (me).

Rory said he would do it with me. It wasn't a very difficult dance, just spinning round and round with your partner or some other person in the line and then coming all the way back again.

By the end we were all hot and breathless, but there was lemonade, and then we started again. We did a reel called Hamilton House, then the Dashing White Sergeant. I didn't dance with Rory all the time, but lots of other people came and asked me. Some boys wore their kilts, with rugby shirts or old tweed waistcoats.

The time absolutely flew, and it was so strange because however breathless and hot you felt, as soon as the music struck up again, you simply didn't want to stay off the floor.

It all ended at about ten o'clock. Rory walked back to Oscar's house with me. A strange man was there, called Sam Howard, and he is going to live up here and run some old woolen mill in Buckly. Very nice-looking and just about the right age for Carrie.

Rory says he is coming today with a television set for my room. Not that I need one, because so many things are happening here all the time. The best is knowing that things are going to go on happening. I've never felt like this in London.

Elfrida

ELFRIDA was, as usual, the first downstairs in the morning. It had stopped snowing. She could see the garden, all form and shape obliterated. Bushes and trees drooped beneath the weight of the snow, and shrubs, pillowed, had lost all identity. It was very still and quiet.

Horace, it seemed, was beginning to recover. He clambered out of his basket and came to greet her, plumy tail waving. She stroked and patted him, and they held a small conversation, and then she opened the back door and he stepped out. But he quickly came indoors again and returned to his basket.

Elfrida dealt with breakfast—laid the table, made coffee, fried bacon. She was drinking her first cup of coffee when Sam Howard appeared, still in his sharply cut and formal suit because, of course, he had nothing else to wear.

She said, "I shall lend you a sweater."

She went upstairs, raided Oscar's chest of drawers, and unearthed a blue Shetland jersey with a polo neck. Back in the kitchen, she found Sam in his shirtsleeves. She tossed the sweater to him, and he pulled it on, his head emerging from the collar like the head of a swimmer rising from the deep.

"That's much better," she told him. "Now you can relax."

Elfrida put bread into the toaster and then filled his coffee cup. They sat at the table together, and it felt companionable.

"I feel so bad about last night," Sam said.

Elfrida said, "Why? It was no trouble. All we did was feed you and make up a bed."

"I didn't actually mean that, although it was very kind of you. I meant barging in, clutching the key of your house, and saying I'd come to buy it. I lay awake last night hoping I didn't offend Oscar or upset him."

"Oscar's not that sort of a man. For a moment he was a bit cross, but with Hughie, not with you."

"I"—Sam reached for his coffee cup—"I . . . suppose Oscar wouldn't think of buying Hughie out?"

"We talked about it last night, but Oscar and I haven't known each other for all that long. I am not as yet permanently a part of his life, so it is difficult for me even to make suggestions."

"But wouldn't it be sensible for him to buy Hughie out?"

"Yes, sensible, but not financially possible."

Sam's presence was so strong and sympathetic that Elfrida went on, confiding in him, as she felt she could confide in no other person. "Last night I said, 'Oscar, I have my little picture.' "

"You are talking about your David Wilkie?"

"Exactly. It was given to me years ago. I've never had it valued, because I've never insured it."

"Would you sell it?"

"For Oscar I would do anything. It's given me pleasure for many years, but surely to be able to own such a lovely house as this is of more importance."

"I agree," said Sam. "You've no idea how much it's worth?"

"Not really. And this is scarcely the time and the place to start getting it appraised. I wouldn't know where to start."

Sam said, "Janey Philip—she's married to my oldest friend. Janey used to work for Boothby's, the fine-art dealers. I could ring her. I'm sure she'd have some bright suggestions."

"It's a bit close to Christmas to start trying to sell pictures."

"We don't have to do it right away."

"And the snow. It precludes everything. Are you still snowed in with us, Sam? I hope so. But you obviously want to get home."

"At this moment I haven't got one. My wife and I separated."

"Oh, Sam, I'm sorry. So what will you do for Christmas?"

"I'll stay in Inverness and then get back to Buckly and start getting the show on the road. I'm giving celebrations a miss this year."

"You must spend Christmas with us. I couldn't bear you to be sitting in a hotel lounge in Inverness. Oscar and I didn't mean to have Christmas either. We thought we'd go pagan and celebrate the winter solstice with a lamb chop. But then Carrie and Lucy asked themselves, and Oscar ordered a Christmas tree and bought some decorations. And I'm just now thinking about food. I'm useless at this sort of thing. But we could gather a bit of holly and go and shoot a turkey or whatever one does. And anyway, it's the people who count, isn't it? The friends you spend Christmas with? Don't go. It would be such fun for all of us to be together."

Sam said, "You're the most hospitable, generous person I think I've ever met. But I tell you what I'll do. I'll ring the AA and see what's happening on the roads. If they're clear, then I'll go back to Inverness. I really have a hell of a lot of work to do. If they're still impassable, then I'll accept, with much gratitude, your invitation."

"Oh, good. I'll pray for blizzards. Do my snow dance."

"What will Oscar say?"

"He'll say 'Splendid' and go and read his newspaper."

CARRIE was the next to appear. "Where is everyone? I thought I heard voices."

"You did. It was Sam, but he's gone to his room to telephone."

"There's still the most dreadful lot of snow." Carrie poured coffee and put another bit of bread in the toaster. Then she sat down and saw that Elfrida had started a shopping list. "What's this?"

"I've been procrastinating, and now we've only got four days. I've been trying to start in on Christmas."

"Why don't you let me take over? I'm a professional organizer. Where can I go and do a mammoth shop?"

"There's a PriceRite supermarket at Kingsferry—if the road's been cleared. When Sam's spoken to the AA, we'll know."

"Is Sam going back to Inverness?"

"Depends. If he's marooned, then I've asked him to stay. Over the festive season, as they say."

Carrie's face showed no expression. She simply said, "In that case, we'll be five in the house." She drew the list toward her, picked up the pencil, and started in. "Now, are we going to have a Christmas dinner?"

"Yes. But we'll never get a turkey into that little oven."

"Then we'll have chickens. Two chickens." Carrie wrote furiously: "Chickens, brussels sprouts, potatoes, frozen peas, carrots, masses of fruit, butter, French bread, cranberry sauce, cinnamon sticks."

"And the wine?" she asked.

"Oscar will want to deal with the wine."

"And smoked salmon, nuts, and Christmas cake. Should we have cold ham? Terribly useful for Boxing Day and sandwiches."

"Brilliant. And a big pot of soup. I'll make it." For once, Elfrida felt competent and efficient. Soup was her specialty—chicken stock and any handy vegetable. "And perhaps buy crisps and dips in case we decide to have a party."

"A party? Who would we ask?"

"Well . . . the Kennedy family. And the doctor and his wife. And the nice bookshop man and his wife. They were at the Manse yesterday, and he and Oscar got on like a house on fire."

Oscar, on cue, came through the door. "With whom did I get on like a house on fire?"

"The bookshop man. Oscar, we are going to have a little party, so we shall ask him and his wife."

"When shall we have a little party?"

This had not been decided. Then Carrie said, "Saturday. Saturday night is party night. The day before Christmas Eve."

Oscar said, "I shall have to buy some drink."

"If the bridge is open, Carrie's going to PriceRite in Kingsferry to do all the shopping. Perhaps you could go with her."

"Yes, perhaps I could."

Then Lucy appeared, and Elfrida left Carrie to feed her and Oscar. Elfrida was feeling happier, now that plans had been made. She went into the sitting room, where the detritus of the previous evening stood about. She tidied up a bit, and was brushing the hearth when, from behind her, she heard Sam speak. "Elfrida, I'm afraid you've got me for Christmas."

"Wonderful." She made no attempt to keep the satisfaction out of her voice and then thought it might be tactful to be a bit sorry for him. "Poor Sam. You're stuck."

"The roads are passable until the Cromarty Bridge, but Inverness is totally snowed up. No traffic in or out."

"Carrie and Oscar are planning a shopping expedition to PriceRite. That's across our bridge. Do you think they'll make it?"

"They'll make it that far, no problem."

"Have you telephoned your hotel?"

"Yes, and my chairman, David Swinfield. And I've spoken to Janey. There's a Boothby's representative for this part of the world—Sir James Erskine-Earle. He lives at Kingsferry House."

"Heavens." Elfrida was much impressed. "How grand."

"An appraisal doesn't mean you have to sell. And, whatever, you really should insure it. Shall I give him a ring?"

"Yes, do that. See what he says."

He left her, and Elfrida stayed where she was, gazing across the room to where her little treasure hung. The old couple sitting at the table with their family Bible—he so somberly attired, she proud in her red dress and yellow silk shawl. Their faces wise and kind, emanating a certain dignity, a repose. They had seen her through a number of desolate days. She was very fond of them.

But they were not as important as Oscar.

Five minutes later Sam was back, looking pleased with himself. "All fixed. He is coming over to Creagan this afternoon for some committee or other. He's going to drop in about four o'clock and cast his eye over your painting. He sounded rather interested."

Elfrida felt nervous. "It's rather exciting. Shall I tell Oscar?"

"I would. You don't want to start feeling underhanded."

"No. You're quite right. Thank you, Sam, for your trouble."

"The least I can do. Now, you said Carrie and Oscar were going over to Kingsferry to shop. Instead, why don't I take her, and then I can help cart everything home?"

Elfrida thought this a marvelous idea and for more reasons than one. "How kind you are. Oscar loathes shopping."

"I have ulterior motives." (Better and better.) "Because I must buy clothes. I can't go round looking like a tailor's dummy for the next five days."

Elfrida said brightly, "Of course," but felt let down because she had hoped his ulterior motive was getting Carrie to himself.

"And I should like to buy some wine for Oscar. Perhaps I should have a word with him before I go."

"That's a good idea. About wine Oscar has strong opinions."

"And rightly so."

Outside, in the brightening morning, the seagulls clamored, perched on the ridge of the high roof. Elfrida said, "In one way I should like you to have this house. It has such dignity and solidity, just right for the important head of a company." She looked at him sitting there in Oscar's blue sweater, and it already felt as though he had been with them all forever. "It is very satisfactory having young and competent people around us again. Oscar and I have both been dreading Christmas. Under the circumstances, I felt it could be nothing but a sad and bitter time. But now, with you and Lucy and Carrie with us, it can't be as emotive as we had feared. Whatever, there's nothing we can do to stop it happening, so we might as well make it fun. Perhaps it will be like one of those parties one longs not to have to go to, and then it turns out to be one of the most memorable and the best. Do you know what I mean?"

Sam said he knew exactly what she meant.

Lucy

HALF past ten in the morning, and everyone was occupied.

Sam and Carrie had departed in Sam's impressive Discovery for Kingsferry and PriceRite, armed with a list that went on forever. Elfrida had taken Horace for a small walk. Oscar was by the fire in the sitting room, much relieved he didn't have to go shopping.

So Lucy made her own plans. This morning she would buy Christmas presents. Having her holiday money made things much easier because she wouldn't have to penny-pinch.

Elfrida, Oscar, Carrie. Now she added Sam and Rory and perhaps Clodagh too. Otherwise it might look a bit odd.

She put on her jacket and boots and went downstairs. Christmas all at once was becoming real. They were going to have Christmas dinner in the evening. That meant Lucy could wear her new black miniskirt. Going down the long hall thinking about this, she paused and then, on an impulse, opened the door of the disused dining room. It was dark and gloomy and in need of a good dust and polish, but in her imagination she saw it lit by firelight and candles, the table groaning with delicious foods.

An idea took shape, but there wasn't time right now to think it through, so she let herself out of doors and started off down the pavement to do the rounds of the modest shops.

In the jersey shop she unearthed a very long red cashmere scarf, which she knew would look quite perfect wound around Carrie's elegant neck. In the bookshop she bought wrapping paper with holly, and some glittery string. She chose a book for Oscar filled with full-page color photographs of old Scottish country houses, castles, and gardens. For Sam she got an ordnance survey map of Creagan and the surrounding district, which included Buckly.

The chemist was next. For Clodagh little hair ornaments that she could clip to the end of her pigtails. For Rory a big bottle of Badedas. Her father had always used Badedas in his bath.

Elfrida was the most difficult. What could one give to Elfrida that would begin to pay back for all the laughs and the spontaneous affection that she had given Lucy?

Then, struck by an idea, she went into Arthur Snead Fruits and Vegetables. There she ordered, for delivery Saturday, six stargazer lilies. They would open slowly, spreading out into pale pink petals, and fill the whole house with their heady fragrance.

She set off for home. Once back, she would go to her bedroom and settle down to wrapping all her presents. However, as she pushed the front door open, she heard voices from the kitchen and, investigating, found Elfrida there, stirring a pot, and Rory Kennedy. On the kitchen table stood a television set.

Rory said, "Hi." He was wearing a fleecy jacket and rubber boots.

"Hello. I . . . I thought you'd be working."

"Not much to do on the golf course in weather like this. So I borrowed Dad's car and brought the set down for you."

Lucy looked at it. "I thought it would be old. It doesn't look old."

"It's color. Just that I got myself a bigger one."

Elfrida said, "Lucy, you'd better show Rory where it's to go."

"It's four flights of stairs," Lucy told Rory.

He grinned. "I think I could just about manage."

She led the way. At the top she went into her room, and Rory followed her and placed the television set on the table. He looked appreciatively about him. "Hey, this is a cool room. And lots of space."

They found a suitable power socket, and Rory plugged in the set and switched it on. Sitting cross-legged on the floor, he fiddled with the internal aerial until the picture became quite clear. *Superman* was on. "Do you want me to leave it on?" Rory asked.

"No. I know how to work it now." Lucy settled herself on the floor beside him. "It's really kind of you to let me borrow it."

"No problem." He switched it off, then looked about him. "At home, in London, do you have a room like this?"

"No. It's not nearly so big, but it's pretty."

"What's it like living in a city?"

"It's all right."

"Must be great, all those museums and exhibitions and concerts and plays. I've only been once. My dad took me when he had to attend some conference."

"It's different if you live there all the time."

"Suppose so." After a bit he asked, "Are you homesick?"

She looked at him in astonishment. "Homesick?"

"You know . . . missing your mother, your things. Clodagh won't even go away for a night. Bawls like a baby."

"No." Lucy heard her own voice, all at once surprisingly sharp and strong. "No, I'm not homesick. I'm not even thinking about going back to London. I've put it out of my mind."

"But—"

"You don't understand. It's not like here. It's not like this house, like your house, full of people and friends your own age coming and going. It's my grandmother's flat, and she doesn't want my friends around the place. She gets headaches, she says."

She stopped, giving Rory an opportunity to comment on this flood of confidence, but he said nothing. Lucy went on.

"It's so different here. You can do anything. You can go to the beach or exploring or out at night, and nobody stops you. And here they all treat me as though I were a person, not a child. I'm fourteen now, and sometimes I feel I've done nothing except go to school. It wouldn't be so bad if I had a brother or a sister. Specially a brother, because just being with women all the time can be dreadfully lowering. They talk about such unimportant things, like clothes or restaurants or other people."

"Where do you go to school?"

"It's called Stanbrook. Quite near where we live. I really like it, but it's all girls, and sometimes I think it would be really fun to go to a comprehensive. You'd meet so many different people."

Rory said, "How about your father?"

"Mummy doesn't like me seeing him. And anyway, he's got a new wife, and she doesn't want me around much either. I've got a grand-father, called Jeffrey Sutton. He's Carrie's father. But he lives in Cornwall with a new young wife and two little children."

"Can't you go and stay there?"

"Yes, I could, but Gran's bitter about him and unforgiving, and his name is scarcely ever mentioned. One day I'll really be brave and say I want to go and stay. But I suppose I'll have to wait until I'm a bit older to do that."

"You don't have to wait. You have to do it now."

"I think," said Lucy sadly, "I haven't the nerve." It occurred to her that he was very good at listening and was clearly sympathetic. Lucy found herself filled with grateful affection. She said, "I'm sorry. I didn't mean to say all this."

He was watching her. She met his eyes and smiled. He said, "Do you want to come sledging this afternoon? I'll ring up some of the others. We'll go to the golf course—there are some really good slopes." He glanced at his watch. "It's nearly twelve. How about you come back home with me now, and we'll get my ma to give us some food, and then we'll get hold of the others?"

Lucy said, "I haven't got a sledge."

"We've got three or four in the garage. You can borrow one."

"But won't your mother—"

"No, she won't mind. There'll be enough food. There always is." He pulled himself to his feet, then hauled Lucy up. "Stop being so worried," he told her. "Stop putting difficulties in your own way."

"Is that what I'm doing?"

"Not anymore."

Elfrida

THE Kingsferry shopping expedition had been highly successful. Not only had Sam and Carrie brought back with them cardboard boxes stuffed with food, vegetables, cereals, fruits, and Christmas goodies, but also wine, beer, mixers, Coke, and six bottles of Grouse whisky. Moreover, Sam had kitted himself out with a

wardrobe of country clothes: corduroy trousers, warm shirts, a thick
ribbed sweater, Timberland boots, and a Barbour jacket.

After lunch he and Oscar set off to walk to the golf club, where
Sam had made an appointment to talk about becoming a member.
Elfrida watched them go and thought it was good for Oscar to have
a bit of masculine company.

So she and Carrie were left to prepare for the arrival at four
o'clock of Sir James Erskine-Earle.

"Shall I make some scones?" Carrie asked.

Elfrida was impressed. "Can you?"

"Of course."

On the table in the sitting room Elfrida laid out five plates and
small knives, cups and saucers, and the butter dish and jam jar. She
looked across the room at her little picture, which perhaps after today would be gone forever.

"If I may not have time to say good-bye," she told it, "I will now.
It's been lovely having you."

Oscar and Sam returned from the golf club in good heart. They
had been introduced to the captain and a few other members,
admired portraits and trophies, and then walked home.

When he came, on the dot of four o'clock, Sir James Erskine-
Earle was something of a surprise. The doorbell shrilled, and
Elfrida ran down to let him in. She was a little taken aback to be
faced by a man so young. He removed his tweed cap, and she saw
his mousy hair, cut like a schoolboy's.

"Mrs. Phipps?"

"Yes, Sir James. Please come in." She led him upstairs. "It is so
good of you to come at such short notice."

"Not at all." He had a charming voice and an ingenuous smile. "I
always enjoy such occasions when I am asked to cast my eye over
something special."

She led him into the sitting room and introduced him to the others. "Oscar Blundell. And Carrie, my niece. And Sam Howard, who
is coming to run the old woolen mill in Buckly."

"We spoke on the phone, I think. How splendid to meet you."

Sir James moved, inevitably, over to the window, as newcomers always did. Across the street twinkling Christmas lights shone like jewels against the old stone face of the church. "What an outlook." He turned back to face them all. "But I mustn't waste your time rubbernecking. Where is this picture you want me to see?"

"It's . . ." Elfrida cleared her throat. "It's here."

"May I take it down?"

"But of course."

He gently lifted it down. "What a lovely thing. Sir David Wilkie. A portrait of his parents. Painted about 1835."

"I didn't know it was his parents."

A silence fell. Sir James Erskine-Earle took his time. He put on a pair of rimless spectacles, turned the painting over, and closely inspected the back.

Finally he laid the picture carefully down. "How did you come by it, Mrs. Phipps?"

"It was a present. A long time ago—thirty years. From a friend."

"And do you know where he bought it?"

"I think in a junk shop. In Chichester."

"Yes." He nodded. "That figures."

"I've . . . I've always believed—been led to believe—that it's an original. But I've never had it appraised nor insured."

He looked at her and smiled that engaging, youthful smile. He took his spectacles off and said, "I am really sorry, but it's a copy."

Nobody could think of anything to say.

"It is a most charming and beautifully executed work, but it isn't the original."

Oscar found his voice. "How can you know?"

"The original passed through Boothby's about a year ago. It was larger than your little painting, Mrs. Phipps, which leads me to believe that this copy was never intended as a forgery but more as a work of respect and admiration. A student, perhaps, wishing to emulate the master's style."

Finally Elfrida made herself ask the dreaded question. "What is it worth, Sir James?"

"Please. Jamie," he said. "A thousand? Maybe more, maybe less. It would depend on the market."

A copy, and worth only a thousand. Elfrida's insurance against an impoverished and lonely future. A thousand. In a funny way, for herself she didn't particularly mind. There was no point in selling it, and so she could go on enjoying it for the rest of her life. But all her plans for buying Hughie out and ensuring Oscar's security were reduced to dust.

For a dreadful moment she thought she might burst into tears. In some despair she turned to Carrie, and Carrie's dark, beautiful eyes were upon her, warm with sympathy and understanding. Elfrida opened her mouth to say something, but there were no words, and Carrie came to her rescue.

"I think," said Carrie, "that I shall go downstairs and boil a kettle, and we'll all have a restoring cup of tea."

And then Sam spoke for the first time since he had been introduced to Jamie Erskine-Earle. "I'll come lend you a hand."

Elfrida knew it didn't take two people to boil a kettle, but she was grateful to Sam for removing himself from a difficult situation.

When the others had gone, Jamie Erskine-Earle said again, "I am so sorry."

Elfrida knew impatience—with herself and with him. "Oh, for goodness' sake, it's not your fault."

Carefully, precisely, Jamie rehung the little picture. He said, "At least it will continue to give you joy."

Oscar said, "I am relieved that she has no reason to let it go."

Elfrida went to the fire, in need of something to do that might assuage her disappointment, took a log from the basket, and hurled it onto the flames. She stood watching it catch flame.

And then, behind her, Jamie spoke again. "I'm sorry, but who is the owner of that interesting little clock?"

Elfrida turned to frown at him in puzzlement. "The clock?"

Oscar told him, "It is Elfrida's."

"It caught my eye. So unusual. May I look?"

Elfrida nodded. Jamie Erskine-Earle put his spectacles on again, took the little clock down from the mantelpiece, and examined it. He said, "A traveling chronometer. Marvelous. How did you come by this little treasure?"

"Do you mean treasure as sentimental or treasure as in trove?"

He answered politely, "I'm not sure."

She told him, "It was left to me by an elderly godfather. An old seafaring man. You can see, one dial is for hours, one for minutes, and one for seconds. I have to wind it every day. I suppose I could get it fitted with a battery, but it seems—"

"Heaven forbid. It's far too rare."

"Rare? Surely it's just an old-fashioned seagoing clock."

"Practical, but handsome too."

She looked at it in his hands, and all at once the clock took on a new luster. The outside leather was still rich and dark, and the lid, which folded across like the cover of a book, was lined with a bruised pad of velvet the color of coral. Around the circular face, which contained the dials, the leather was decorated with a wreath of miniature golden leaves. The key, the hinges, the tiny locks were brass.

She said, "I don't know how old it is. Perhaps you can tell me."

"Alas, I am not a clock expert. But," he added, "I have a colleague who is. If you will let me, I can show it to him."

"Why?"

"Because I think it is special."

"It wouldn't be worth seventy-five thousand pounds, would it?"

Jamie Erskine-Earle said, "I really don't know. Mrs. Phipps, would you . . . would you let me take it away with me? I can send my colleague a photograph of the clock. I shall, of course, give you a receipt for it and will keep it under lock and key."

"Of course."

"If I could have a box or something to wrap it in."

Oscar unearthed a sheet of bubble wrap that he had salvaged from a parcel of new books. "Will this do?"

"Perfect."

Oscar wrapped the clock, and Jamie Erskine-Earle sat at Oscar's desk and wrote out his receipt.

Sam

SAM opened his eyes to darkness and bitter cold. It was the cold that had woken him, and he realized that his eiderdown quilt had slipped off the bed. He heaved himself over, reached down for the quilt, and dragged it back into place. Waiting for warmth, he looked at his watch. Half past seven in the morning.

His room, by now familiar, lay about him, the corners deep in shadow. He wondered why it all rendered him such satisfaction. It had all felt, from that very first embarrassing evening, a bit like coming home. A little like being on board a ship, isolated from the rest of the world but intensely involved with the other passengers. The house, like that ship, contained them all, and did so with a grace, as though content to have the spacious rooms filled once more—fires lit, voices calling, footsteps on the stairs.

A good house, and Sam wanted it. That was the problem. Its location was perfect. As well, it would be a house with a future. His future. Owning it, Sam would never have to leave. He would soon be forty. He didn't want to go on moving—buying and selling, starting anew. He wanted to stay. Here.

But half of it belonged to Oscar Blundell. He liked Oscar enormously, and this made nothing easier. And yet he couldn't get rid of the feeling that here, in this solid Victorian town house, he was destined to settle and spend the rest of his days.

He remembered, for no particular reason, a recent afternoon in London when he had walked down Kings Road, clogged with shoppers and traffic, and told himself there was no person in the world who would expect a Christmas present from him. But now he must, sometime, get busy so that on Christmas morning he would have packages to hand out. Four of them: Oscar, Elfrida, Lucy, Carrie.

Carrie.

Having lost Deborah, returning to London and his new job, the last thing on his mind had been the possibility of another woman coming into his life. But Carrie had been waiting for him, the last link on that extraordinary chain of coincidences. It was Carrie who had opened the door of the Estate House to him.

Carrie, with her smooth cap of chestnut hair, her dark and expressive eyes, her slenderness, her long neck. Her slanting eyebrows, the fascinating mole at one end of her mouth. Her voice, deep-toned, with an underlying suggestion of laughter, so that he could never be sure when she teased or when she was serious. She was totally without artifice. If she had nothing to say, she said nothing. If she spoke or aired an opinion, it was deliberate, considered, intelligent. Over meals she was attentive but often silent. Her relationship with Elfrida and Lucy was, however, deeply affectionate and caring.

He found it impossible to guess what Carrie thought of him. She was totally at ease, in charge of the situation but at the same time reserved to the point of withdrawal. When they had driven to Kingsferry to do the huge supermarket shopping, he had thought that he could break through this barrier, but every time the conversation veered around to Carrie and her private life, she had turned the conversation in a totally different direction.

He found himself wondering if she had once been married, but knew that he could never pluck up the nerve to ask such a question. Sometime, somewhere along the line something had gone wrong. And Carrie was not about to confide in Sam.

The less she gave away, the more he longed to know. He wondered if this obsession was the beginning of falling in love with her. Otherwise, why should it matter so much? And what was the point of falling in love with a woman deeply committed to her career and her ill-assorted family, who would never jettison the lot and come to live in the north of Scotland with Sam Howard?

All this quite apart from the fact that he was still married to Deborah.

SAM dressed, then went quietly out of his room and downstairs. From the kitchen flooded mouthwatering smells of bacon and coffee. There he found only Carrie, reading *The Times*. She looked up and said, "Good morning."

That first evening he had been knocked sideways by the unexpected glamour of the girl who had opened the door for him. She had, he later learned, been struck down by a bout of flu and because of it had looked pale, frail. But he had still thought her sensational. But now the flu was a thing of the past, and this morning she wore a red cashmere sweater, and the bright color rendered her vital, radiant, and more attractive than ever. In his present mood of well-being he knew a physical urge to sweep her up into his arms, breaking down imagined barriers and starting to talk.

She laid the newspaper down and got to her feet. "There's bacon." A plate sat on the warmer, covered by another plate. She set it down on the table and removed the top plate. He saw not only bacon but eggs, a sausage, and a fried tomato.

He looked at the feast in some amazement. "Who cooked this?"

"I did. I'll make fresh coffee."

He felt much touched. "You are sweet." He sat and buttered a slice of toast. "Where is everybody?"

"Around and about. We have to fetch the Christmas tree this morning. Oscar wondered if you would do that in your car."

"We? Are you coming with me? Where—"

"Corrydale Estate. Oscar's drawn a map. I shall have to come to be your navigator. Besides, I want to see Corrydale. Oscar says the grounds and the garden used to be amazing, but of course it's different now because it's a hotel."

Sam was filled with a silent satisfaction. He could think of no better way of spending this fine morning than driving Carrie to Corrydale, collecting the Christmas tree, and having a nose around the place. But he only said, "Right," because he didn't want Carrie to sense his pleasure and then start backing off.

OSCAR'S little map proved to be a meticulous plan of all that lay within the Corrydale boundary wall—a small maze of roads, woodland, and a long shoreline. Each estate worker's house had been drawn and named: Billicliffe's house, Rose Miller's house, the gamekeeper's house, Home Farm. The last was the gardener's house. A little way off, along a winding driveway and standing in some grandeur all on its own, he had drawn Corrydale House. It reminded Sam of the endpapers of a Pooh Bear book.

The boundary wall appeared on the left-hand side of the road, and they saw the notice: CORRYDALE COUNTRY HOTEL.

Sam turned in through the gates, and the formal drive led downhill between an avenue of huge oak trees. They moved on slowly, past Major Billicliffe's stone house, Rose Miller's cottage, the farmhouse and a field of sheep, the gamekeeper's cottage, and finally reached the gardener's house. Sam drew up, and they climbed out of the car. As they did so, a young man appeared. He wore a deerstalker.

"Charlie Miller?"

"Yes, that is me. You'll be Sam Howard." Leaning against an aged Ferguson tractor was a cut tree. "Oscar phoned. He said six foot would be tall enough, so I picked this one out. It's a good shape, and no broken branches."

"Looks fine to me."

"Two pounds a foot. Twelve pounds. And a stand. Two fifty. That's fourteen fifty you owe me." He was obviously not a man to beat about the bush.

Sam dug out his wallet.

Carrie now spoke. "Charlie, we've never been to Corrydale before, and we wanted to look around, see the house. But if it's private or we're not allowed . . ."

"Go anywhere you please. The hotel is closed anyway. While you're walking, I'll net the tree and load it."

"Thank you."

"No trouble. Have a good walk now."

THEY set off, footsteps scrunching on frozen ruts, the air sweet as chilled wine, the thin sunshine warming their backs and causing flurries of melted snow to drift down from the trees.

Carrie said, "There must once have been a lot of money. This is a huge establishment. Oscar doesn't seem to have *anything*."

"No, I don't think he does have much."

"Why didn't Oscar inherit? He would have made a lovely laird. It seems unfair."

"Hughie was the son of the eldest son. Primogeniture."

"Oscar deserves better. He and Elfrida. They deserve someplace to live together that they can call their own. I would like to be rich so that I could take care of them both."

"Will they stay together, do you think?" Sam asked.

"Probably. Neither of them has anybody else." For a bit Carrie said nothing more. Then she said abruptly, "I would like to see your mill."

Sam had never imagined her being interested. "Would you?"

"You told me it was a beautiful building. Shall we go one day?"

"If you want."

"I like seeing buildings and houses stripped down. Empty places, bare walls. I like imagining how they were, what they could become. You must feel excited about it all, getting it going again."

"Yes. It's a daunting prospect, but difficulties can be stimulating. And in Buckly I have a good man, Fergus Skinner, on my side."

"It's still a long stride from working in New York."

"I'm thirty-nine now. Been there, done that. You see, I was born and bred into the woolen trade, and I secretly believe that there is nothing so good-looking, so comfortable, so exactly right as a familiar, well-tailored tweed jacket. It'll stand up to anything the elements choose to hurl at it and by evening be perfectly acceptable at anybody's dinner table. I love the smell and the feel of tweed. I love the sound of well-tuned cogwheels, the clack of looms, the monstrous pistons of the carding machines. And I like the people who work them. So I am in my own world."

"I think you're fortunate. Coming to live up here in this enormous, clean, unsullied place." She went on walking.

Ahead could be seen the wall of a formal garden. The path led to a wrought-iron gate flanked by gateposts bearing stone armorial lions. There they paused for their first sighting of Corrydale House, a Victorian mansion, gabled and turreted, built of red stone, some of which was smothered in Virginia creeper.

"Nice," said Carrie after a bit. "What good times Oscar must have had."

Sam said, "Would you like to live here?"

"Do you mean in this house? In this place?"

"No. I just mean here in Creagan. In Sutherland."

"I have a job in London. I have to earn my living."

"Supposing you didn't? Would you be content? Could you bury yourself in such an environment?"

"I don't know. To leave London, I'd need to be free. No commitments. No responsibilities."

"Aren't you free?"

"There's Lucy." She unlatched the gate and opened it, and beyond was a wide path. "Lucy is the main reason for taking this London job. Somebody has to winkle her out of that dull, enclosed, totally female life she's forced to lead."

"She seems to be quite a well-adjusted child. Happy, even."

"That's because she *is* happy here, with Elfrida and Oscar and people coming and going. And of course, Rory Kennedy. Going back to London is going to be a real letdown."

Sam found himself resenting this maiden-aunt attitude. Carrie was too young, too beautiful to start structuring her life simply for the sake of one small niece.

"So what will you do with Lucy?" he asked.

"Oh, I don't know. Just be around, on the end of the telephone. *There.* Perhaps at Easter I'll take her away again—to Cornwall to stay with her grandfather, or maybe we could go skiing."

"Will you go back to Oberbeuren?"

"No." She had said the word almost before he had finished asking the question. "Not Oberbeuren. Somewhere else."

"You could go to the States—Colorado or Vermont. Sounds a long way to travel, but it would certainly be cheaper."

Carrie strolled beside him. "Have you skied in Vermont?"

"Yes. A number of times. We used to drive up for weekends."

"We," Carrie repeated. "You and your wife, you mean?"

So this was it. The nub around which they had both been circling, the moment of truth, the point of no return. He said, "Yes, with my wife. We're separated."

"Elfrida told me that. Children?"

"No. She didn't want babies. Not so soon. Someday, perhaps, she'd promise me. Anyway, last summer she met this guy. She told me she was leaving me to be with him."

"Are you still in love with her?"

"Oh, Carrie . . ."

"If you've been married to a person, they're part of you. You can never be free. You belong to them."

She spoke with such bitterness that Sam all at once knew that he only had to push a bit further and the closed door that had stood between them would finally, creakily, open.

He turned to her. "Carrie . . ."

But she strode on, and he had to catch up to her and take her by the arm and jerk her around to face him. He saw that her dark eyes were shining with tears. "Carrie, tell me."

"Why?" She was angry, blinking the tears away. "It's not worth talking about. And you wouldn't understand."

"I could try, and I think I would understand. I've been through bad times myself, trying to come to terms with a total rejection."

"I wasn't rejected," Carrie shouted at him, and all at once she was in floods of tears. Furious with herself, she pushed at him, trying to escape from his grip, but he held her shoulders and would not let go. "I wasn't rejected. I was loved. We were in love, and all we wanted was to be together. But the odds were too great—too many demands, responsibilities, traditions: his job, his family, his wife, his children, his religion, his money. I was simply his mistress. I didn't stand a chance. And finally, when Andreas walked away from me, I went to bits. So now you know, Sam, and perhaps you can accept the fact that I'm really not very interested in married men."

He opened his mouth to protest, but at that moment, with a wrench of her body, she slid out of his hold and set off at a run, stumbling in the snow. He went after her and caught her once more. "Oh, Carrie," and this time she did not fight him.

He took her into his arms, and she leaned against him, her shoulders heaving, weeping into his Barbour. Holding her, having her in his arms, was something he had been wanting to do all day. She felt slender, weightless, and he told himself that he could feel the beating of her heart through all their combined layers of winter clothing.

"Oh, Carrie." It was shameful to feel so elated when she suffered from such desolation and wretchedness. Trying to comfort her, he said, "It will be all right."

"It won't be all right."

So cold, so adamant was her voice that he was suddenly wise, realizing that it was hopeless to continue mouthing pointless platitudes. Standing there with his arms about her, Sam found himself confused and disoriented. Carrie was beautiful, intelligent, and desirable but also complicated. To truly understand her was going to take much patience and a lot of time.

He accepted this. He said again, "It will be all right."

"You don't know."

He had the good sense not to argue. After a bit her furious weeping calmed down. She made motions as though to pull herself together. Gently Sam put her away from him and watched as she wiped at tearstained cheeks with her padded glove.

He said, "I'm sorry."

"What for?"

"Because this wasn't what I had planned. I didn't mean to upset you so. This was simply an outing to pick up a Christmas tree and go for a walk. No ulterior motives. It just went wrong."

"Not your fault. Let's forget it, pretend it never happened. Walk on, the way we'd planned."

"We did talk. To talk is always good. I thought we never would."

"Is talking so good? I'm not so sure."

"Clears the air. Makes things easier to understand."

"I don't know that I want to be understood. Just left alone. Perhaps right now I'm better off not belonging to any person."

Sam said, Don't be too sure about that. But he did not say it aloud.

Lucy

THIS *morning Carrie and Sam went and got the Christmas tree. And I spring-cleaned the dining room. It was dusty.*

I explored and found four silver candlesticks, dreadfully tarnished but very handsome after I cleaned them. Then I went out and bought some candles (tall and cream, a bit like church candles).

I didn't want anybody to know about it so that it would be a surprise, but just before lunch Carrie and Sam got back with the Christmas tree, and there was a great discussion as to where we should put it. So then I had to admit about the dining room, and they all trooped downstairs to inspect what I had been doing. It was lovely because everybody was thrilled, and it all smelled polishy, and Elfrida said she had no idea the dining room could ever look so festive. And of course, that was exactly the right place for the tree. So Sam went out and brought it in. I love the smell of trees coming indoors.

In the afternoon we tied the decorations on the tree, and Sam fixed the lights and the star on the top branch. And Elfrida produced a whole roll of lovely tartan ribbon, so we made lovely bows and put them all over the tree, and with the tinsel and the lights turned on, it is the prettiest I think I've ever seen.

Tomorrow we have to get started on the party. I shall wear my new black miniskirt and my black tights and my new white sweater.

Oscar

"OSCAR, I am about to leave you on your own."

Oscar, settled by the fire, looked up from the newspaper. "Forever?"

"No. For about half an hour. I'm going up to the Manse to borrow some extra glasses for our party."

Elfrida had not been gone for ten minutes when the telephone rang. Heaving himself out of his chair, Oscar went to answer it. "Estate House."

"I wonder, is Mr. Blundell there?" A female voice, very Scottish.

"Speaking."

"Oh, Mr. Blundell, this is Sister Thomson from the Royal Western in Inverness. I'm afraid it's sad news. Major Billicliffe died early this morning. I have your name as his next of kin."

Old Billicliffe. Dead. Oscar found himself struggling to think of something to say. All he could come up with was, "I see."

"It was all very peaceful. He had a quiet end."

"Thank you very much for letting me know."

"There are personal possessions you'll want to collect. And any other arrangements . . ." Sister tactfully did not finish her sentence.

But Oscar knew exactly what she was driving at. He said, "Of course. Thank you. I'll be in touch."

All at once he needed to sit down. Billicliffe was dead, and Oscar was not only his next of kin but his executor. He pondered for a bit as to what he should do next. The lawyer. Oscar had made a note of the lawyer's name: Murdo MacKenzie, MacKenzie and Stout, Inverness. He looked up the firm in the telephone book, then punched the number.

He thought, There will have to be a funeral. A church. People will have to be told. I must tell Peter Kennedy. And an announcement in the newspaper—just a few lines.

"MacKenzie and Stout."

"Oh, good morning. Could I speak to Mr. MacKenzie?"

"Who shall I say is calling?"

"Oscar Blundell, from Creagan."

"Hold on a moment, please."

Murdo MacKenzie came on the line almost at once. "Mr. Blundell, good morning. What can I do for you?"

"Good morning. I'm sorry to bother you, but I've just heard . . . from the hospital . . . that Major Billicliffe died this morning."

"Oh, that's sad news. I am sorry." (He really sounded sorry too.)

"Major Billicliffe asked me to be his executor."

"He told me you had agreed to take the duty on."

"That's why I'm calling. I suppose there will have to be a funeral, but where and when and how? He has friends in Creagan, who will certainly want to be there. An undertaker will have to be approached, of course, and the bank notified and the registrar—"

Murdo MacKenzie smoothly intervened. "Mr. Blundell, why don't you leave all this to me? Major Billicliffe wished to be cremated, so that precludes many headaches. There's an excellent undertaker in Inverness I know well."

"That's enormously kind of you. And all the other details— probate and the bank and such. Freezing his account—"

"We'll deal with those details."

"And his personal possessions . . ." Oscar thought of Billicliffe's battered leather suitcase. He felt a ridiculous lump grow in his throat. "They will have to be collected from the hospital."

"I'll telephone and have a word with the ward sister."

"I really can't thank you enough. You've taken a great weight off my shoulders."

"I know that Major Billicliffe did not want you to be inconvenienced. If any problems should arise, I'll give you a ring."

"It is more than good of you. Now, I'll waste no more of—"

"Mr. Blundell, don't ring off. I shall be writing to you, but as we're talking now, perhaps I should put you in the picture."

Oscar frowned. "Sorry, I don't understand."

"Once he was settled in hospital, Major Billicliffe wanted to see me. I called in early last Monday morning. He was very frail but perfectly lucid. He wished to do a new will. It was written that day, and he was able to sign it. You are his sole beneficiary, Mr. Blundell. He wants you to have his house at Corrydale and his dog. He had, as well, a few savings, which, once all bills have been settled, should come to about two thousand five hundred pounds."

Oscar could not think of a single thing to say.

"Major Billicliffe was anxious that you should know how much he appreciated your kindness to him."

Oscar said, "I wasn't kind."

The lawyer ignored this. "I don't know if you know the house?"

"I knew it in the old days, when it was the forester's cottage."

"I did the conveyancing when Major Billicliffe bought it from the estate. It is quite a modest establishment, but I would say with distinct possibilities. I'll put it all in a letter to you, and then you can decide what you do next."

"Thank you so very much."

"A pleasure, Mr. Blundell. Good-bye. Have a good Christmas."

Slowly Oscar replaced the receiver. He thought for a long time about the little house on the Corrydale Estate. Years ago, when the head forester and his homely wife had lived there, it had been a hive of activity, with four children underfoot, three dogs, and strings of washing flapping on the line. But always a vociferous welcome for a small boy, and a hot plate of scones dripping in butter.

Now it belonged to him.

The front door opened. "Oscar!" Elfrida had returned. "Can you come and help me?"

He went out to greet her.

"I've got two huge boxes in the back of the car."

"We'll bring them in later. I have something to tell you."

Her eyes went wide. "Oscar, you're looking quite flushed and excited. What has been going on?"

They sat at the kitchen table. "If I tell you, quite slowly because it's rather complicated, will you listen and not ask questions until I've got to the end? Otherwise I shall become confused."

"I'll try."

"Right. The first is that Major Billicliffe died this morning. I had a phone call from the hospital."

Elfrida put her hand over her mouth. "Oh, Oscar. To be all alone and dying . . ."

"He was in a ward with kindly nurses and people around him all the time. Not nearly so alone as he's been since his wife died."

"I suppose so." Elfrida thought about this.

He told her about telephoning the lawyer, Murdo MacKenzie, and having all responsibility removed from his shoulders. "But Elfrida, that's not the end. Billicliffe wrote a new will. He has left me his house, his dog, and two thousand five hundred pounds."

"He's left you his house? How terribly touching." Elfrida was silent for a moment, and then, astonishingly, she said, "Why don't you go and live there?"

Oscar stared at her in disbelief. "Live there? On my own?"

"No, stupid. I'll come with you."

"But you thought the house was horrible."

"There's no such thing as a place that cannot be improved. It was dog hairs and brimming ashtrays that made it so disgusting."

"But I have a house. I have this house."

"Only half. You could sell your half, and then you'd have seventy-five thousand pounds, and you could spend that on Major Billicliffe's house and live happily ever after."

"You mean . . . sell out here?"

"Oh, Oscar, don't sound so horrified. Sam Howard wants it, and Hughie McLennan is obviously agog to get rid of his half. When Sam and Carrie and Lucy have gone, we're going to be alone again, rattling around like a pair of peas in a drum. I think of here as a family house. It should have young people and children."

"Sam hasn't got any children."

"No, but he's bound to get married again."

He said, "Not Carrie. You mustn't matchmake."

"It's impossible not to. They're so perfect together."

"They're not perfect at all. He never stops being amiable, and Carrie is remote and prickly as a gorse bush. All that's happened is that they have been flung together by circumstances."

"Maybe so." Elfrida sighed. "But discounting Carrie, this is the right establishment for Sam, the manager of the resuscitated woolen mill, an important member of the community."

"Elfrida, if I did sell the Estate House, I couldn't be mad enough to sink that money into Major Billicliffe's cottage and leave myself with nothing put by."

"We don't know how much we'd have to spend. Supposing I sell my house in Hampshire, and we use that money for—"

"No. It's about all you own, and you must not sell it. Rent it out if you can, but you must never sell."

"Oh, well." She became resigned, and Oscar felt a brute. "It was a good idea while it lasted, but I suppose you're right." Then she perked up again. "Whatever, we must inspect it from attic to cellar. What shall we do with the dog?"

"I can bribe Charlie Miller to keep the dog."

Upstairs on the landing the telephone began to ring. Elfrida pulled herself to her feet and went upstairs. "Hello."

OSCAR sat on, patiently waiting for Elfrida to return to him, mulling over her wild ideas and wishing he could go along with them.

When she finally came down the stairs, he had never seen her eyes so bright. "Oscar"—she put her arms around him—"something simply utterly wonderful has happened to me." She sat once more facing him across the kitchen table. "That was Jamie Erskine-Earle, about my little clock. You know he said he was going to show a photograph to a colleague. Well, the colleague telephoned this morning, and he said the clock was a very rare timepiece. French, made by one J. F. Houriet, about 1830. Just imagine, Oscar, all these years I've owned it and never had the faintest suspicion. So I plucked up my courage and said, 'Is it valuable?' And he said, 'Yes.' And I asked what it was worth, and he said at auction . . . possibly . . . seventy to eighty thousand pounds."

"I am left without words."

"With that money we can really transform Billicliffe Villa into the most desirable of residences. Build a conservatory, a—"

"Elfrida, that money—if you sell the clock—belongs to you."

"Oscar, it belongs to us. And we'll end our days in a charming little cottage. We shall have Rose Miller for a neighbor, and a four-star country hotel in the garden. Who could ask for more?"

"But dear girl, we must be sensible."

"I hate being sensible! I want to go out and dance in the street. Shout our good news from the rooftops."

Oscar considered this as though it were a perfectly viable suggestion. Then he said, "Not until I've had a chance to get Sam on his own and explain the situation. He must know we are thinking about selling up here, because I am certain that he will want first refusal."

"Yes, you're right. I can't wait to go and look at it. But we can't go tomorrow, because of getting ready for the party."

"Sunday?"

"Christmas Eve."

"As good a day as any."

"All right. We'll go on Sunday morning. We'll all go. Sam and Carrie and Lucy as well. I'm sure Sam will be wonderfully practical. He'll talk about things like soffits and rap walls and be knowledgeable about rising damp. We could take a winter picnic. I shall make a pot of soup. Oscar, have we got a key?"

"Rose Miller will have one or know some person who has. I have to ring her anyway to let her know that the old boy has died. And I must call Peter Kennedy."

Carrie

THEY drove to Buckly to view the woolen mill, which was to be Sam Howard's future: McTaggarts of Buckly.

The mill stood on the outskirts of the small town. The main building was both impressive and good-looking. Built of local stone, its façade was long and pleasingly symmetrical. A central pediment was topped by a clock tower. The sloping roof was slate, pierced by skylights, and here and there the stonework was softened by ivy.

Sam drew up in front of the big door, and they stepped down into the snow. "What do you think?" he asked.

"I think it's very handsome."

"I told you. No question of bulldozing and starting anew."

He fitted a key into the brass lock, turned it, and pushed the door open. Carrie went past him and into a square high-ceilinged reception hallway. And devastation. The high-tide mark of the floodwater reached to nearly five feet.

A door at the back of the hallway led into a stone-floored space big as a warehouse and glass-roofed for light. It was empty, echoing, and piercingly cold. Involuntarily Carrie shivered.

Sam saw this and was remorseful. "Carrie, I'm sorry. Have you had enough?"

"No. I want you to show it all to me and tell me what you're going to do. It's mind-boggling, like being given charge of a totally impossible task."

"Yes, but with the resources of a huge conglomerate behind me. That makes a hell of a difference."

"Even so. They chose you to take on the job. I wonder why."

Sam grinned and all at once looked not simply boyish but, at the same time, bursting with eager confidence. He knew what he was talking about. He was on his home ground. He said, "I suppose because basically I'm a Yorkshire boy. And where there's muck, there's brass. Now come before you freeze, and I'll show you the rest."

BY THE time the tour was finished and they stepped once more into the outdoors, Carrie was chilled to the bone. Sam looked at his watch. "It's half past eleven. Would you like a heartening drink?"

"Hot coffee would do the trick."

So they drove into Buckly, and Sam drew up outside the Duke's Arms. Carrie eyed it without much enthusiasm.

Inside, a coal fire glowed and flickered in the old-fashioned hearth. There seemed to be only two other customers, both of them silent, male, and very old.

"Come on," Sam said. "Sit here, close to the fire." He pulled a chair away from a table. "Would you try a Whisky Mac? It's the most warming drink in the world."

It sounded more tempting than coffee. "All right."

Sam went over to the bar, and he and the barman fell into conversation, their voices low.

Carrie pulled off her fur hat, laid it on the chair beside her, and watched them. She thought that this morning she had seen for the first time the other side of Sam, the man who had walked in out of the snow. Sam, back in his own world, was no longer the amiable houseguest of the last few days, but a man in charge.

He returned to her, bearing their drinks. "Sorry. Conversation."

"What were you talking about?"

"The weather. There's a thaw on the way, and the road to Inverness is open again."

"Does that mean you're going to disappear instantly?"

"No." He shook his head. "I've been asked for Christmas, so I'm staying. Anyway, I've nowhere else to go. But on Boxing Day I must come down to earth with a bang and leave. I have to be in London next week. David Swinfield's set up a meeting."

"Lucy and I go on the third. We're on the morning flight." She bit her lip, thinking about this. "I'm not looking forward to it. I think Lucy is going to be desolate going back to that dull flat and a mother who won't be particularly delighted to see her."

"I shall buy her a splendid Christmas present."

Carrie was amused. "Have you still not done your shopping?"

"I shall go to Kingsferry tomorrow morning and get the lot."

He fell silent. The silence lay between them and felt comfortable. "I decided the other morning that life at the Estate House is a bit like being on a cruise with just a few other passengers. I have a feeling I could happily jog along in low gear for weeks, achieving nothing."

"I suppose it's all been a bit of a waste of time for you."

He frowned. "Never a waste of time. Never think that."

Carrie looked up and into Sam's face. Never a waste of time. . . . And an extraordinary thing happened, because all at once it was as though she had never truly seen him before, and now she knew that her recognition of him was too late, because he would go away, it would be all over, and she would probably never see him again.

Suddenly she felt dangerously emotional and quite unsure of herself. Yesterday at Corrydale, after her outburst of words and her angry weeping, Sam had taken her in his arms and held her until the tears ceased. And she had felt no warmth for him, no physical reaction to his closeness, only a grudging gratitude for his comfort, and shame for herself for behaving like a fool.

But now . . . the beginning of recovery perhaps. The melting of the coldness that had been her only armor. To love. To be loved again. . . .

"Carrie, can we talk?"

"What about?"

"You and me. Us. It seems to me that we've met each other at a bad time. Neither of us is free. You've taken on the moral responsibility for Lucy, and I'm still married to Deborah."

He watched for her reaction to all this, and his expression was both anxious and very serious. Carrie's response was clearly of great importance to him.

"What are you telling me, Sam?"

"Just that perhaps we should give ourselves a bit of time. I shall be living and working here in Buckly. You'll be in London. Hundreds of miles apart. But I shall be flying up and down to London for meetings. I thought perhaps . . . we could see each other again—go to a concert, out to dinner. Start over. Afresh. As though none of this time had ever happened."

Start over. Afresh. The two of them. Carrie said, "I wouldn't want this time not to have happened."

"I'm glad. It's been extraordinary, like days stolen from another life, another world. How shall I find you in London, Carrie?"

"Oversees. It's in the phone book. I'll cook you dinner."

"No promises. No commitments."

"No promises."

"So we leave it like that?"

"We leave it like that."

Sam said, "Good." And as though he were sealing their agreement, he covered her hand with his own. The two old men sat on, unaware that as they whiled away the last of the morning, the whole world had changed.

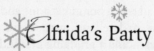

❄ *E*lfrida's Party

BY HALF past five Saturday evening the Estate House stood ready, dressed overall for Elfrida's party. The front door wore a wreath of holly, and once through the door, guests would see the dining-room Christmas tree revealed in all its glory—lit up and standing knee-deep in packages. At the far end of the hall the staircase rose, entangled with holly and ivy and sparkling with white fairy lights.

Now everyone had disappeared to shave, bathe, change, and generally doll themselves up for the evening ahead.

Oscar was the first to emerge. He closed the bedroom door behind him and stood alone for a moment to savor the Christmas transformation of his house, prepared and ready for an influx of guests. So much, he thought wryly, for the bleak winter solstice, which was all he had promised Elfrida. And he decided that the Estate House—normally so minimal and austere but now dressed and adorned to the nines—was a bit like a straitlaced elderly but much loved aunt who had put on her best finery and precious jewels for some special occasion and ended up looking not bad at all.

Oscar too had made an effort, and wore a favorite old smoking jacket and his best silk shirt. Elfrida, whom he had left at her mirror, had told him that he looked toothsome.

As he had dressed, Oscar had not allowed himself to think back to his last Christmas at the Grange. But now, in a moment of solitude, he did. He thought of Francesca, running down the great staircase, wearing a black velvet dress and with her hair flying loose. She had always seemed to be running, as though time were so precious that there was not a moment of it to be wasted.

Only a short while ago this memory would have shattered him with grief. But now Oscar simply felt grateful, because Francesca would always be part of his life, part of his being. And because, after all that had happened, he had somehow survived. And more, because he now found himself surrounded and sustained by friends.

The sitting room looked warm and welcoming and unnaturally neat and tidy. Elfrida had filled jugs with holly and white chrysanthemums, but the best was the huge vase of fragrant stargazer lilies that little Lucy had given Elfrida for Christmas. Elfrida had nearly burst into tears, so touched and delighted had she been.

ELFRIDA, with the final eyelash tweaked into place, gazed at her reflection in the long mirror of the wardrobe. She had put on black silk trousers and a filmy little black blouse, over which she wore a loose green silk coat. Dangling earrings and long strings of beads were the same jade green as the coat, and her eyelids were blue, her mouth scarlet, and her hair a freshly twinked blaze of flame.

She went to join the others. They all looked wonderfully sophisticated and glamorous. Lucy had somehow put her hair up and looked all at once about seventeen. Carrie, ravishingly beautiful, had a glow to her skin and a shine in her dark eyes that Elfrida had not seen for years. She had put on a sleeveless black dress, simple as a T-shirt, but with a skirt that flowed softly from her slender hips to her ankles.

Seeing her, Elfrida could not imagine how any man could stop himself from falling in love with her. Elfrida wanted above all else for Carrie to be happy again, but Oscar was right. This was too early for matchmaking. One just had to be content that Sam and Carrie seemed, at last, to have made friends.

They were all talking, but Oscar, standing by the fireplace, saw Elfrida as she came through the door. Their eyes met, and for an instant it was as though it were just the two of them, alone in the brilliantly lit room. He came across to take her hand.

"You look quite wonderful," he told her.

"I thought I looked a bit like a battered old actress, which of course I am. But a happy one." She kissed his cheek cautiously, so as not to leave a smudge of lipstick. "And you, Oscar?" They understood each other very well. "All right?"

He nodded. Downstairs the doorbell rang.

Elfrida's party at last was on its way.

A QUARTER past eight, and it was all over. Only the Kennedys lingered, and that was because they had been late arriving, coming to the Estate House from the party at the old people's home. Sam had built up the fire, and all had collapsed into chairs.

Elfrida said, "I can't believe it's gone so quickly."

"That's the sign of a good party," said Peter, and added, "Time flies when you're enjoying yourself." He shifted slightly in his chair and looked at his watch. "Tabitha, my love, we should be on our way."

"Oh, don't go," Elfrida begged. "Unless you have to. This is the best bit of a party. Talking it all over with the last of the friends. Stay, and we'll have kitchen supper. We'll finish up all the scraps, and we've got some soup."

"Are you sure?" Tabitha was clearly tempted.

"Of course you must stay."

Here Carrie took over. "In that case, I shall be in charge."

As Carrie went out of the room, the telephone began to ring. It had only rung once when she picked up the receiver. "Hello."

"Who's that?" The female voice was clear as a bell, but there was a tiny hiccup of hesitation on the line.

"It's Carrie."

"Carrie. It's Nicola. From Florida."

"For heaven's sake, how are you?"

"I'm great. Fine. What are you doing?"

"Just had a party. We're all sitting around recovering."

"Is Lucy there?"

"Yes. She's been having the time of her life. I'll get her."

Carrie laid the receiver down on the table and returned to the sitting room. "Lucy, your mother's on the telephone."

Lucy's head jerked around. "Mummy?"

"Yes. From Florida. Go quickly because it costs a bomb."

Lucy looked at Rory and then went out to the phone.

Carrie went downstairs. In the scullery, she found an enormous pot filled with Elfrida's soup. She put the pot on top of the cooker to heat through slowly and then went upstairs. The landing stood empty. The receiver was back on the telephone. No sign of Lucy. Carrie hesitated for a moment, all at once experiencing a pang of unexplained disquiet. And then, just as before, the telephone rang.

Carrie picked up the receiver. "Hello?"

"Is that the Estate House? I want to speak to Carrie."

Carrie's heart sank. "Yes," she said. "Hello, Ma."

"It's you. Thank heavens. Has Nicola been on to you?"

"Yes. She rang from Florida. But she wanted to talk to Lucy."

"Did she tell you?"

"Tell me what?"

"Oh, my dear, she's married. To Randall Fischer. This morning."

"She rang you before she rang Lucy?"

"Yes. She wanted to make arrangements for Lucy."

Here we go again, thought Carrie.

"She's talking about a honeymoon, not flying back to London until the end of the month. And she expects me to be in London so that I can get Lucy back to school. But I've planned to stay here, in Bournemouth, until the end of January."

"Is she going to spend the rest of her life in America?"

"I suppose so. If you marry an American, I suppose that's what you have to do."

"What about Lucy?"

"Lucy will just have to do what she's told. The problem is, who is going to look after her until her mother gets home?"

Carrie did not answer this question. She simply stood there, aware of a great wave of fury directed at her mother and her sister. She knew that if she made any remark, it would be wrong, precipitating a slanging match that would solve nothing.

"Carrie?"

"Ma, I think it would be better if I rang you back."

"Have you spoken to Lucy?"

"No, not yet. This is the first I've heard of the happy news."

"You've got my number? Here in Bournemouth?"

"Yes, I've got it. I'll call you. Tomorrow maybe."

"Don't leave it too long. I'm worried sick. Oh, and darling . . . you will have a lovely Christmas, won't you?"

"Lovely," Carrie told her.

She put the receiver down and stood for a moment, giving herself time to gather her wits. Nicola was now Mrs. Randall Fischer, and there was so much emotional debris littered around, waiting to be picked up, that Carrie felt she scarcely knew where to start.

Lucy was the first. She had been given the joyous news over the telephone by her mother, put down the receiver, and disappeared.

Carrie took a deep breath and climbed the stairs to Lucy's attic. The bedroom door was firmly closed. Carrie knocked. No reply. Gently she opened the door. All was darkness. She reached for the light and switched it on. "Lucy?"

A sulky hump under the blue-and-white duvet did not move or answer. Carrie crossed over to the bed and sat on the edge of it.

"Go away. I don't want to talk."

"Darling, I know. Gran rang from Bournemouth. She told me."

"I don't care if she told you. It doesn't make any difference. Everything's spoiled now. Everything. It always is. They always do."

"Oh, Lucy." Carrie laid her hand on the duvet, but Lucy jerked her shoulder and spurned the comfort of touch.

"I wish you'd go away and leave me alone."

Her voice was filled with tears. She was angry and resentful, and Carrie understood but still felt loath to leave her.

"To be truthful, I think your mother shouldn't have sprung this on you over the telephone, expecting you to be delighted. But I suppose we have to try to see her point of view."

All at once Lucy flung the duvet aside and turned up her face to Carrie's. It was ugly with anger and misery, and Carrie realized with despair that the anger was directed not simply against her mother but Carrie too . . . because they were adults, and there was not a single adult who could be trusted.

"Of course you take her side," Lucy shouted at Carrie. "She's your sister. Well, I hate her. I hate her because of all this and because I've never mattered. I matter even less now. And I won't go and live in America. And I hate Randall Fischer, and I don't want to talk about it. I just want to be left alone." She flung herself away from Carrie, pulled the duvet over her head, and buried her face in an already sodden pillow.

Carrie tried again. "The Kennedys are all staying for supper."

"I don't want supper. I want you to go away."

Carrie, knowing that it was hopeless to persist, went out of the room and down the stairs. She had no idea of what to do next.

When Carrie appeared in the sitting room, Elfrida said, "Darling, what's been going on? Two telephone calls."

Carrie said, "I don't know where to start." Sam reached for a chair and drew it forward, next to Elfrida. Carrie sat down with a grateful thump and felt Elfrida take her hand.

"Darling Carrie, tell us."

So she did, everyone listening attentively and with growing concern. Finally Carrie ended. "So the crisis is immediate and also long-term. Immediate, because there is nobody in London to take care of Lucy and get her to school—except, of course, dogsbody me. But the long-term problem is Lucy's future. She doesn't like Randall, and to be truthful, I don't think she's all that fond of her mother."

"She doesn't *have* to go and live in America," Elfrida ventured hopefully. "How about going to her school as a boarder?"

"It's a day school, Elfrida. And there are still holidays."

"Your mother?"

"Ma would never cope on her own. Wouldn't even try."

"Perhaps Lucy's father—"

"This is all ridiculous." A new voice broke in. Rory Kennedy had got to his feet, his blue eyes blazing with indignation. "It's ridiculous. You're all talking in circles, taking it for granted that Lucy will go back to London just as though nothing had happened. But she can't go. She has no proper home, and she's never felt loved. What has made her really happy has been staying here with Elfrida and Oscar. In Creagan. She told me she'd never been so happy as she is here. So don't send her back. Keep her here. She can stay with Elfrida and Oscar. Mum and Dad will be around, and Clodagh, and she's made friends with our friends. Then she can go to day school in Creagan. I think if you let her go back to London without any sort of plan for the future, it would be criminal. Unhappy teenagers do terrible, stupid things. Lucy belongs to you all far more than she belongs with her mother."

He stopped, red-cheeked from the passion of his feeling. For a moment an astounded silence filled the room. "Sorry," he said. "I didn't mean to speak out of turn."

Silence again. Then Peter Kennedy got to his feet to stand beside his son. "You didn't speak out of turn," he told him, laying a hand on the boy's shoulder. "You are right. Well said, Rory."

LUCY lay and stared at the sloping ceiling of her bedroom, exhausted by weeping and beginning to feel remorseful about the way she had behaved to Carrie. Listening to her mother burbling on, lyrical with excitement and as insensitive to others' feelings as she had always been, had all at once become too much, and Lucy, unable to listen to one more word, had simply put the receiver back on the telephone.

A tap on the door. The door opened. "Lucy?"

It was Oscar. He said, "How are you feeling?" as though he were a kindly doctor and she had been ill for a long time.

She said, "Awful. I don't know what will happen. That's the worst. I don't know what I'm going to do."

"I don't think you have to do anything. I think others have to do it for you."

"Who?"

"Now just listen. Downstairs we've all been having a little chat, and we've come up with an idea. Supposing after the New Year you don't go back to London with Carrie. You stay here with Elfrida, and *I* shall go back to London with Carrie and go and see your grandmother in Bournemouth."

Lucy was alarmed. "What are you going to say to her?"

"I am going to suggest that until your mother's new life is sorted out somewhat, you should remain in Creagan with Elfrida and myself. Just for the time being."

"But what about school? I have to go back to school."

"How about taking a term off from your school in London and going to school in Creagan instead?"

Lucy felt she had to get her facts straight. "You mean I wouldn't go back to London after the New Year? Just stay on here?"

"If you want to. Yours must be the decision."

"Gran doesn't approve of Elfrida," she told Oscar bluntly.

Oscar laughed. "So I believe. But she will, I am sure, approve of me. I shall present myself as a schoolmaster and a church organist, with an impeccable background and an unsullied reputation. Will she be able to resist that?"

Lucy said with a quirk of humor, "Not if it means getting shed of me."

"And your mother?"

"She won't care either. She never did care much. She'll care even less now that she's got Randall."

"Carrie's going to telephone them both tomorrow. She can outline our plans. You'll stay on with Elfrida and me in Creagan. Go to the local school. Get your GCSEs. After that maybe a coeducational boarding school where you could take your A levels."

"That's what Rory said when we talked about things. A coeducational boarding school."

"He's a wise lad. He is your champion. It was he who stirred us all to action."

"But Oscar, would you want me? Really want me?"

"More than anything. We love you. Perhaps I am being selfish. I need a young person about the place."

Lucy said, "When I first came here—when Carrie and I flew up from London—I was terribly nervous, because she had told me about your daughter. I was afraid that I would remind you of her . . . make you dreadfully sad again."

"You remind me of Francesca, but it didn't make me sad."

"What did she look like?"

"Long hair and freckles. She was two years younger than you."

"What did Francesca like doing?"

"Everything. She had a little pony and an old bicycle and a bedroom full of books."

"What was she really good at?"

"Living."

Their eyes met, and they gazed at each other, both silenced by the enormity of what Oscar had just said. It was as though he had spoken without thought, and the word hung between them. To her horror Lucy saw Oscar's eyes fill with tears, his mouth tremble. Then in an abrupt movement he covered his eyes with his hand.

She had never before seen a grown-up weep. She stared at him, wondering what she could do to comfort him. After a bit, to her huge relief, he took his hand from his face and reached into his breast pocket for his handkerchief. Then he blew his nose, made an effort to smile at her, reassuring. He said, "Sorry."

"It doesn't matter, Oscar. I don't mind. Really, I understand."

"Yes, I think you do. Death is part of living. I have to remember that, but from time to time the truth eludes me."

"Living is important, isn't it? And remembering?"

"More important than anything else." He stowed his handkerchief away. "That first day, the day you arrived, you and I sat in the church and talked about Christmas and the winter solstice. It was then that I remembered Francesca for the first time without total desolation. I remembered having exactly the same conversation with her a year or so ago, trying to explain about the Christmas star and the scientists' theory of time. And she listened but was not convinced. She didn't want to be convinced. She liked the story just as it was. Because the snow and the carols and the darkness and the presents were all part of a time when life took flight and the whole world soared to the stars."

Lucy said, "That's how this Christmas is going to be."

"Do you want to come downstairs now and have some supper?"

"I have to comb my hair and wash my face."

He went to the door. "Don't be too long, my duck."

❄ Christmas Eve

IN THIS fickle northern climate one woke each morning without any idea of what the elements were about to reveal, but today had dawned astonishingly pure and gentle, like a day stolen from spring. A low sun streamed down from a cloudless sky, even managing to engender a faint warmth. Birds sang from leafless trees.

Oscar and Elfrida were standing in the open gateway of Oscar's new property. They walked up the driveway, and Oscar put the key in the lock. The door swung inward, and Elfrida followed him, fingers crossed, into the little sitting room.

It felt very cold and a bit dank, but not nearly as bad as Elfrida had remembered and feared. The window at the back of the room let in a flood of sunshine, and Rose Miller had scoured, cleaned, and polished. In the fireplace were laid paper and sticks, ready for kindling.

Oscar said, "First things first," and knelt to set a match to the paper. At the back of the room stood a door. Elfrida went to open this and found herself in a mean and chill little kitchen. It had a clay sink, a tiny refrigerator, a gas cooker, and a small table spread with an oilcloth. A half-glassed door led out onto a bit of paving.

She went back to Oscar, who was piling coal onto flames. He pulled himself to his feet, dusting his hands on his corduroys. "Come. Let us go and explore."

They went into Major Billicliffe's dining room, then up very steep stairs that led to the upper floor. They inspected the two bedrooms. In Major Billicliffe's bedroom the bed was covered with a fresh cotton counterpane, and rag rugs had been laundered.

The second bedroom was smaller, and the bathroom was spartan, but the view from its window was of the sloping fields and the dazzling blue water and the distant hills. And Elfrida thought that for a house that was not exactly bursting with happy memories, it had a good feel to it. It had been neglected but was not without hope. It simply needed, like any human being, a bit of laughter and some tender loving care, and it would leap into life again.

From behind her Oscar spoke. "I am going to go out of doors."

She went back into the smaller bedroom for a quick reassessment, because this would have to be for Lucy. There would be space to put a desk for homework if they replaced the enormous double bed with a single divan.

Just then she heard the sound of Sam's Discovery drawing to a stop. The back door opened, and Lucy tumbled out. "Elfrida!"

She sounded joyous. Elfrida ran down the narrow stairway, to fling open the front door and hold wide her arms. Lucy bolted into them. "Elfrida, isn't this the sweetest house? Is this the sitting room? And look, you've already lit a fire! Where's Oscar?"

"Out in the garden."

With no hanging about, Lucy went galloping down the garden and calling Oscar's name. Then Carrie appeared, with a huge basket slung over her arm. She was joined by Rory and by Sam, hefting a heavy grocery box close to his chest.

"Is this all picnic?" Elfrida asked in some amazement.

"A feast," Sam replied.

FOR the Christmas Eve picnic at Corrydale, Carrie and Sam had done a splendid job. They had brought hot soup laced with sherry and drunk from mugs, fresh rolls filled with thick slices of ham and English mustard, a bacon-and-egg quiche, chicken drumsticks, tomato salad, crisp green apples, and chunks of cheddar cheese. Finally, a flask of fresh hot coffee.

Elfrida, sitting on a cushion with her back against the wall, turned her face up to the sun and closed her eyes. "That was the best picnic ever. Thank you, Carrie."

Rory and Lucy had disappeared indoors to inspect the little house. Now they appeared again.

"It's so nice, Oscar," Lucy told him.

"Where are you two off to now?" Oscar asked.

"We thought we'd take Horace for a walk down to the water and the beach."

Oscar tipped back the last of his coffee. "I shall come with you. After that feast I need exercise. Who's coming with us?"

"I shall," said Carrie.

"I shan't," said Elfrida firmly.

"I shall stay with Elfrida," said Sam. "I would like to do a building inspection."

SHOWING Sam Howard around Major Billicliffe's house was quite different from looking at it with Oscar. Sam tapped walls, turned taps, inspected window frames and power points.

Finally they were finished. "What do you think, Sam?" Elfrida asked nervously.

"It has great possibilities. And the location is out of this world. . . . Hang on. I just have to fetch something from the car."

When Sam returned, he brought with him a yellow scratch pad and a ballpoint pen. They sat together on the sofa. "Now," said Sam, "do you intend living in the place just as it is, or do you want to change a few things?"

"It depends," said Elfrida, "on how much it would cost."

"Supposing"—he began to draw a plan on the scratch pad—"supposing to begin with, you demolished the existing kitchen and bathroom. My suggestion would be that you make the dining room into a kitchen and maybe build a small dining area out to the south. There's a chimney, so you could install an Aga or a Raeburn for continual steady heat."

"Bathroom?"

"A new one"—he sketched it—"over the dining room."

Elfrida gazed at his suggestions, all drawn out for her on the yellow scratch pad. "Would it cost more than eighty thousand pounds?"

He laughed, his face creasing up with amusement. "No, Elfrida. I don't think it would cost as much as that." He looked at her. "Have you got eighty thousand?"

"No. But I hope to have. Jamie Erskine-Earle is going to sell my little clock for me. We never told you, but apparently it is very rare."

"Eighty thousand?"

"That's what he said. Top price, eighty-five."

"In that case, you have no problems. Go for it, Elfrida."

"How long will it take?"

"I suppose six months. I don't know."

"We'll have to stay in the Estate House until it's ready for us to move in."

"Of course."

"But you, Sam? You want the Estate House."

"I can wait. I'm not about to throw you out onto the streets."

A brilliant idea occurred to Elfrida. "You can live with us at the Estate House. You and Lucy and Oscar and me. You've already got a room there. You might just as well stay."

Again Sam laughed. "Oscar may not like the idea."

"Oh, Oscar will love to have you, and so shall I. It will be a new job for me—letting out lodgings. Oh, please say yes. I feel as though you were always meant to come and live there."

"Thank you," said Sam. "In that case, I accept, subject, of course, to Oscar's approval."

The sun was beginning to dip down out of the sky by the time the walkers returned. Oscar and Carrie were first.

"How was it?" Elfrida asked.

"Perfect," Carrie told her. "All the birds—ducks and cormorants and gulls . . . How did you and Sam get on?"

"Sam is brilliant. He's practically drawn the plans. You must come and look, Oscar."

It was half an hour before Rory and Lucy finally joined them, by which time Oscar had seen and listened to all Sam's ideas, been persuaded, and given his consent. Carrie approved as well. "You know, Sam, you actually are very clever."

Now the light was fading, and it was time to go back to Creagan. "Are we going to Midnight Service, Elfrida?" Carrie asked.

"I think so. Oscar doesn't want to come, but I'll go."

"Me too. And Lucy and Sam are coming as well."

Having packed up the remains of the picnic, the first party took their leave in Sam's car. Elfrida, Oscar, and Horace went out of doors to see the others off, then went back inside.

Elfrida said, "I don't want to leave. I don't want today to end."

"Then we'll stay for a little."

He sank tiredly down on the sofa. Elfrida put the last bit of wood on the fire and then sat beside him. She said, "We will live here, won't we, Oscar?"

"If you want."

"I do. But do you?"

"Yes. I admit I did have reservations, but now that I have seen it again and Sam has come up with all these ideas and possibilities, I think it is exactly what we should do."

The shadows lengthened. Elfrida sighed. "We should go."

But Oscar said, "Wait, I want to talk." He laid his hand upon her own.

"I'm listening," she told him.

"This is a new step we're going to take. Together. A real commitment. Don't you think perhaps the time has come for us to be man and wife? It's a formality, I know, because we could scarcely be more married than we already are. But it would put a seal on our union—an affirmation of our trust in the future."

Elfrida's eyes were filling with tears. "Oh, Oscar." She drew her hand away and began to search for her handkerchief. "You don't need to do this. I will stay with you happily for the rest of my life, but I don't want you to feel you have to marry me."

"I don't feel that. All things being equal, I should happily settle for carrying on the way things are. But we have Lucy now to consider."

"What difference does she make to how we live our lives?"

"Oh, my dearest Elfrida, just think. So far the people of Creagan have accepted us with great kindness, even forbearance. No questions. Not a single soul has cast a stone, not even a tiny pebble. But for Lucy it is different. She is going to the local school. Children are not always very kind. Rumors can be started, and even in this day and age, parents can be mean-spirited. I wouldn't want any of that sort of thing to rub off on Lucy."

"So for her sake we should be married."

"Put baldly, yes."

"But Gloria . . ."

"Gloria, of all women, would understand."

"You're sure?"

"Yes, I am sure. Because one thing is truly certain, and that is that you have helped me to start again, and it is you who have made a dark and painful time not only bearable and possible but even joyful as well. I told you a long time ago that you could always make me laugh. As well, you have made me love you. Now I cannot imagine an existence without you. Please marry me. If I wasn't feeling so bloody stiff, I'd get down on one knee."

"I'd hate you to do that." Elfrida, having at last found her handkerchief, now blew her nose. "But I'd like to marry you very very much. Thank you for asking me."

"So. We are betrothed. Shall we break the news or keep it to ourselves?"

"Let's keep it to ourselves. Just for the time being."

Oscar laughed and kissed her, and they might have sat on in the gloaming for the rest of the evening, but the last of the logs had burned out. It was time to leave. Oscar locked his front door and took her arm, and with Horace at their heels they walked in the deep blue evening light, down the pebbled path.

Lucy

Christmas Eve

So much has happened. The worst was Mummy ringing yesterday to say that she has married Randall Fischer. All I could think about was having to go and live in America or else have to live with Gran in London on my own. I had horrible hysterics and was beastly to Carrie, but that's all over now. Anyway, now it is all sorted out, and I'm going to stay here in Creagan with Elfrida and Oscar for the time being and go to day school in Creagan.

Carrie rang Gran and told her about our plans, and she went along with them. Later she rang Mummy in Florida and persuaded her too. And then I had a chat with Mummy and managed not to sound too delighted, in case she took offense and changed her mind.

So then Rory appeared, and we got a picnic together, and Sam drove us over to Corrydale. Oscar's little house is too sweet, tucked away on the estate with a few other little houses in view, great big trees, and a long view of the water and over hills.

I can't believe that I could be so miserable and despairing one day and so utterly happy the next.

The next time I write in my diary, Christmas will be over.

IT WAS TEN PAST ELEVEN WHEN the telephone rang. Elfrida, Carrie, Sam, and Lucy had just finished up a game of cards and were getting ready for the Midnight Service.

Oscar said, "Who's ringing us at this hour?" He went out of the room. Elfrida heard him say, "Estate House."

And then silence as the caller spoke, and then a murmured reply. The next moment he was back.

Elfrida was curious. "Who was it?"

"Nothing much. A mistake. I'm going to take Horace for a walk."

Elfrida stared at him in some astonishment.

"I just feel in the need of some fresh air. I may not be back by the time you set off for church. Have a good time." He left.

Elfrida's expression was puzzled. "Funny," she said to Sam. "You'd have thought he'd had enough exercise today to last him for a week." She went around the room puffing up cushions. "We shouldn't be too long making our way, I think. There's bound to be a huge congregation, and we want to be able to get a seat."

A few minutes later Lucy ran downstairs from her attic. "All ready, Elfrida, but Carrie's still getting ready."

"Well, you and I will go, Lucy, and bag a pew for the four of us. Sam, will you wait for Carrie and come over with her?"

"Of course."

Sam heard them slam the front door. He stood on the landing and waited for Carrie. He felt no impatience. He had waited during his life for countless women to appear. So now, in the house that would one day belong to him, he waited for Carrie.

"Oh, Sam." She came out of her room. "I couldn't find my silk scarf." She wore her loden coat. The errant scarf, all pinks and blues, was softly wound around her slender throat. He had never seen her more beautiful. "Have the others already gone?"

He said, "Yes," and put his hands on her shoulders, drew her close, and kissed her. Something he had been longing to do ever since that first night, when she had opened the door to him and found him standing on the doorstep in the falling snow. When at last they drew apart, he saw that she was smiling, and her dark eyes had never seemed so lustrous.

He said, "Happy Christmas."

"Happy Christmas, Sam. Time to go."

ELFRIDA and Lucy crossed the street. The square, lamplit, was already busy with people converging on the church. Voices called out, country people greeting each other, falling in step as they made their way.

"Elfrida!"

They stopped and saw Tabitha, Rory, and Clodagh behind them.

"Hello! I thought we were early, but it seems we're not. I've never seen so many people."

"I know." Tabitha wore a tartan coat and a red muffler. "People come for miles. . . . The only thing is, we've had a bit of a setback. Alistair Heggie, the organist, has got flu, so we won't have any proper music. We're going to use taped music."

"Oh, that is disappointing. Poor Peter."

They took the path that led to the wide flight of stone steps and the double doors of the church. Tonight these had been flung open. Light from inside streamed out onto the cobbles, and Elfrida could hear the taped music from within—a choir singing carols. It sounded a bit mechanical and tinny.

> "God rest ye merry, gentlemen;
> Let nothing you dismay.
> For Jesus Christ our—"

Silence. Either the tape player had broken down or some person had inadvertently switched it off.

"Oh, no," said Rory. "Don't say the tape player's got flu."

And then it started—a great surge of sound from the organ. Huge chords and waves of music filled the church, overflowed out through the open doors, resounded up and out into the night.

Elfrida stopped dead. She looked at Tabitha, and Tabitha's eyes were wide and innocent. For a long moment neither of them spoke.

Then Elfrida said, "Did Peter ring Oscar about a quarter past eleven?"

Tabitha shrugged. "No idea. Come on, kids, see if we can find somewhere to sit." She turned and ran up the steps, with her two children and Lucy at her heels.

After a moment Elfrida followed. The church was already nearly filled, the congregation shuffling into their places. The music thundered all about her, filling the huge void of the soaring arched ceiling, echoing down the long nave. She began to walk down the center aisle. Walking into the music was like stepping into a pounding sea of sound.

A hand touched her arm. She stopped. "Elfrida. Here." It was Lucy. "We're keeping seats for you and Sam and Carrie."

She took no notice, did not move.

The Christmas tree, lavishly decorated and twinkling with lights, stood in the middle of the transept, between the pulpit and the lectern. Beyond this, against the north wall of the church, the organ pipes soared. The organist's seat was enclosed by an oaken stall, so that he was not visible to the seated assembly. But Elfrida was standing, and she was tall. An overhead spotlight shone down upon him, and she could clearly see his head, his profile, and the thick white hair, rendered unruly by the unselfconscious exuberance of his own performance.

Beethoven: "Ode to Joy."

And Oscar Blundell, playing his heart out. Reconciled. Returned. Back where he belonged.

ROSAMUNDE PILCHER

© JERRY BAUER

Rosamunde Pilcher set *Winter Solstice* in Scotland, she says, because the book's "dark themes" are well suited to northern winters, when days are short "and life inclines to become claustrophobic." She knows her setting well—the Estate House, where so much of the action takes place, is modeled on her own holiday home there.

Like her heroine Elfrida, Pilcher loves dogs and has two long-haired dachshunds. Writing aside, she collects china, and is, she says, a devoted but "not a manic" gardener.

The prolific author of nearly two dozen novels, Pilcher has no plans to write another "just yet." Her many fans can only hope she doesn't keep them waiting for too long.

To learn more about Rosamunde Pilcher and *Winter Solstice,* visit the Select Editions website:

ReadersOnly.com

Password: *stay*

The volumes in this series are issued
every two to three months. The typical
volume contains four outstanding books
in condensed form. None of the selections in any
volume has appeared in *Reader's Digest* itself.
Any reader may receive this service by writing
The Reader's Digest Association, Inc.,
Pleasantville, N.Y. 10570
or by calling 1-800-234-9000.

Visit our website at
www.ReadersOnly.com

Some of the titles in this volume are also
available in a large-print format. For information about
Select Editions Large Type call 1-800-877-5293.

ACKNOWLEDGMENTS

Pages 6–7, 8: illustrations by Steve Johnson/Lou Fancher
Pages 148–149, 150: illustrations by Coco Masuda
Pages 270–271, 272: illustrations by Chris Kihlstrom
Pages 420–421, 422: illustrations by Sergio Martinez

The original editions of the books in this volume are published and copyrighted as follows:
Before I Say Good-Bye, published at $26.00 by Simon & Schuster, Inc.
© 2000 by Mary Higgins Clark
Julie and Romeo, published at $21.00 by Harmony Books,
a member of the Crown Publishing Group
© 2000 by Rosedog, LLC
Demolition Angel, published at $24.95 by Doubleday,
a division of Random House, Inc.
© 2000 by Robert Crais
Winter Solstice, published at $27.95 by Thomas Dunne Books,
an imprint of St. Martin's Press
© 2000 by Rosamunde Pilcher